THE
OXFORD BOOK OF
ENGLISH SHORT STORIES

To Uncle Boo —
   on his 80th birthday
with much love from a
branch of the Leaning
connection —
         Jennifer & Ruthie

THE
OXFORD BOOK OF
ENGLISH SHORT STORIES

Edited by

A. S. Byatt

OXFORD

UNIVERSITY PRESS

Great Clarendon Street, Oxford OX2 6DP

Oxford University Press is a department of the University of Oxford.
It furthers the University's objective of excellence in research, scholarship,
and education by publishing worldwide in

Oxford New York

Athens Auckland Bangkok Bogotá Buenos Aires Calcutta
Cape Town Chennai Dar es Salaam Delhi Florence Hong Kong Istanbul
Karachi Kuala Lumpur Madrid Melbourne Mexico City Mumbai
Nairobi Paris São Paulo Singapore Taipei Tokyo Toronto Warsaw
with associated companies in Berlin Ibadan

Oxford is a registered trade mark of Oxford University Press
in the UK and in certain other countries

In the compilation and introductory
material © A. S. Byatt 1998

First published 1998

First published as an Oxford Paperback 1999

British Library Cataloguing in Publication Data

Data available

Library of Congress Cataloging in Publication Data
The Oxford book of English short stories / edited by A. S. Byatt.
1. Short stories, English.   2. England—Social life and customs—Fiction.
I. Byatt, A. S. (Antonia Susan), 1936–
PR1309.S5088   1998
823'.0108—dc21   97-44998
ISBN 0-19-288111-6

3 5 7 9 10 8 6 4

Printed on acid-free paper
in Hong Kong

For

HARRIET HARVEY-WOOD

A discriminating and sympathetic Scot.

ACKNOWLEDGEMENTS

Many friends and colleagues have made suggestions for stories, and discussed Englishness with me. I should like to thank four in particular: Jenny Uglow, for general encouragement; Gillian Beer, for her discussion of Kipling's *Wireless*; D. J. Taylor, who introduced me to the stories of Mary Mann, and Peter Kemp, who recommended Malachi Whitaker. I should also like to thank Gill Marsden for all her work on the text.

We gratefully acknowledge permission to reprint the following stories:

J. G. Ballard: 'Dream Cargoes' reprinted from the collection *War Fever* (Flamingo/HarperCollins, London, 1990, and Farrar, Straus & Giroux, New York, 1991), Copyright © 1990 by J. G. Ballard, All rights reserved, by permission of the author c/o Margaret Hanbury, 27 Walcot Square London SE11 4UB.

H. E. Bates: 'The Waterfall' reprinted from *Country Tales* (Penguin, 1992), by permission of Laurence Pollinger Limited and the Estate of H. E. Bates.

Leonora Carrington: 'My Flannel Knickers' reprinted from *The Seventh Horse* (Virago, 1989), by permission of Little Brown, London and Librairie Flammarion.

Angela Carter: 'The Kiss' reprinted from *Saints and Sinners* by Angela Carter, Copyright © 1985, 1986 by the Estate of Angela Carter, by permission of the Estate of Angela Carter c/o Rogers, Coleridge & White Ltd, 20 Powis Mews, London W11 1JN and Viking Penguin, a division of Penguin Books USA Inc.

G. K. Chesterton: 'The Tremendous Adventures of Major Brown' reprinted from *The Club of Queer Trades* (Penguin, 1984) by permission of A. P. Watt Ltd on behalf of the Royal Literary Fund.

A. E. Coppard: 'Some Talk of Alexander' reprinted from *Ninepenny Flute* (Albatross, 1937), by permission of David Higham Associates.

Penelope Fitzgerald: 'At Hiruharama' reprinted from *New Writing* edited by Bradbury & Cooke (Minerva, 1992), and extract from *The Knox Brothers* (Macmillan, 1977), both by permission of the author.

John Fuller: 'Telephone' and 'My Story' both reprinted from *The Worm and the Star* (Chatto & Windus, 1993), by permission of Random House UK Ltd and The Peters Fraser & Dunlop Group Ltd.

Graham Greene: 'The Destructors' reprinted from *Twenty-One Stories* (Penguin, 1982), by permission of David Higham Associates.

Thomas Hardy: 'A Mere Interlude' reprinted from *Collected Short Stories* (Papermac, 1989), by permission of Macmillan.

Philip Hensher: 'Dead Languages' reprinted from *New Writing* (Vintage, 1997), Copyright © Philip Hensher 1997, by permission of The Wylie Agency.

Aldous Huxley: 'Nuns at Luncheon' reprinted from *Collected Short Stories* (Elephant Paperbacks, 1992), by permission of the Aldous Huxley Literary Estate, c/o The Reece Halsey Agency.

M. R. James: 'Two Doctors' reprinted from *Ghost Stories* (Penguin, 1994), by permission of Hodder.

Rudyard Kipling: 'Wireless' reprinted from *Mrs Bathurst and Other Stories* (OUP, 1991), by permission of A. P. Watt Ltd on behalf of The National Trust.

D. H. Lawrence: 'The Man Who Loved Islands' reprinted from *Love Among the Haystacks and Other Stories* (Penguin, 1960), by permission of Laurence Pollinger Limited and the Estate of Frieda Lawrence Ravagli; also reprinted from *Complete Short Stories of D. H. Lawrence*, Copyright 1922 by Thomas Selzer, Inc, renewal copyright 1950 by Frieda Lawrence, by permission of Viking Penguin, a division of Penguin Books USA, Inc.

Rosamund Lehmann: 'A Dream of Winter' reprinted from *The Gypsy's Baby* (Virago, 1982), by permission of the Society of Authors as the Literary Representative of the Estate of Rosamund Lehmann.

Ian McEwan: 'Solid Geometry', Copyright © Ian McEwan 1975, reprinted from *First Love, Last Rites* (Jonathan Cape), by permission of the author c/o Rogers, Coleridge & White Ltd, 20 Powis Mews, London W11 1JN and Random House UK Ltd.

Charlotte Mew: 'A White Night' reprinted from *Collected Poems and Prose* (Carcanet, 1981), by permission of Carcanet Press Limited.

Arthur Morrison: 'Behind the Shade' reprinted from *Tales of Mean Street* (Methuen), by permission of A. P. Watt Ltd on behalf of the Special Trustees of Westminster and Rochampton Hospitals and the NSPCC.

V. S. Pritchett: 'On the Edge of the Cliff' reprinted from *Complete Short Stories* (Hogarth Press, 1993), by permission of The Peters Fraser & Dunlop Group Ltd.

Alan Sillitoe: 'Enoch's Two Letters' reprinted from *Men, Women and Children* (Grafton, 1986), Copyright © 1986, by permission of Sheil Land Associates Ltd.

Elizabeth Taylor: 'The Blush', Copyright © Elizabeth Taylor 1958, reprinted from *The Blush* (Virago, 1986), by permission of the Estate of the Late Elizabeth Taylor, A. M. Heath and Co. Ltd, and Little Brown, London.

Rose Tremain: 'The Beauty of the Dawn Shift', Copyright © Rose Tremain 1996, reprinted from *New Writing* edited by Hope & Porter (Vintage, 1996), by permission of Sheil Land Associates Ltd.

Sylvia Townsend Warner: 'A Widow's Quilt' reprinted from *Selected Stories* (Chatto & Windus), by permission of Random House UK Ltd on behalf of the Estate of Sylvia Townsend Warner.

Evelyn Waugh: 'An Englishman's Home' reprinted from *Work Suspended and Other Stories* (Penguin, 1982), by permission of The Peters Fraser & Dunlop Group Ltd.

H. G. Wells: 'Under the Knife' reprinted from *Complete Short Stories* (A & C Black, 1987), by permission of A. P. Watt Ltd on behalf of The Literary Trustees of the Estate of H. G. Wells.

Malachi Whitaker: 'Landlord of the Crystal Fountain' reprinted from *The Crystal Fountain and Other Stories*, by permission of Carcanet Press Ltd.

T. H. White: 'The Troll' reprinted from *Blackwater 2*, edited by A Manguel (Lester and Orpen Dennys, 1990), by permission of David Higham Associates.

P. G. Wodehouse: 'The Reverend Wooing of Archibald' reprinted from *Mr Mulliner Omnibus* (Hutchinson, 1972), by permission of Random House UK Ltd and A. P. Watt Ltd on behalf of The Trustees of the Wodehouse Estate.

Virginia Woolf: 'Solid Objects' reprinted from *A Haunted House* (Penguin, 1973), by permission of the Society of Authors as the Literary Representative of the Estate of Virginia Woolf and Harcourt Brace & Company.

Every effort has been made to trace and contact copyright holders prior to publication. If notified the publisher will be pleased to rectify any errors or omissions at the earliest opportunity.

CONTENTS

INTRODUCTION

A. S. Byatt

There are many collections of English short stories. There are also collections of Irish short stories, Canadian short stories, Scottish short stories, West Indian short stories, and so on, collections which explore both
national subject-matters and national styles. In practice, collections of
English short stories will always be found to contain writers who also
appear in their national settings—James Joyce, Katherine Mansfield,
Elizabeth Bowen, Stephen Crane, Joseph Conrad, Henry James,
Muriel Spark, and Robert Louis Stevenson, for instance. This is partly
because of a linguistic confusion between 'short stories in English' and
'English short stories', but it goes deeper. There is a reluctance to think
about Englishness. The English are what other English-speakers define
themselves *against*. They are seen as imperialist, insular, nostalgic for
merrie England, class-ridden, complacent. There is even a hinted feeling that to think about Englishness might lead to racism or xenophobia.
It is not quite nice to think about being English. When I was asked to
put together an Oxford Book of English Short Stories, I hesitated. It
meant looking very narrowly for writers with pure English national
credentials, or there was no point. And I was afraid that the great
short story writers were indeed from elsewhere. Do we have anything
to compare with Maupassant and Chekhov, Shen Tsung-Wen and
Calvino, Borges and Kafka? Or, to keep to our own language, with
Patrick White, Samuel Beckett, R. K. Narayan, Raymond Carver, and
the great Alice Munro? I feared being marooned amongst buffers and
buffoons, bucolics, butties, and Blimps.

I decided to be stringent about the Englishness of the writers, and
beyond that to read as widely as possible with no preconceptions of
what I was looking for. I was very carefully *not* looking for stories that
would give images of England, or of the Empire; I very carefully tried
to have no preconceptions of any 'English' styles or subject-matter. The
pleasure was in discovery. I had a distant deadline, with time to reflect
and explore. I canvassed all my friends and acquaintances for names of
English writers—it was surprising how often they came up with Irish,
or Scottish, or Welsh. I also had no settled idea of the ideal short story.
My only criterion was that those I selected should be works of art, that
both the writing and the story should be startling and satisfying, and if

possible make the hairs on the neck prickle with excitement, aesthetic or narrative. Originally the publisher had thought that the collection could range more widely chronologically, could include tales from the seventeenth and eighteenth centuries. I even argued for folk-tales, and Canterbury Tales. But in the event I came to agree with H. E. Bates, who said, in his useful *The Modern Short Story* (1941), that the short story came into being with the great nineteenth-century experts in Russia and France, and flourished because of the market for it at the end of the nineteenth century and in the first half of the twentieth. I have included some Victorian short fiction, but nothing earlier. I have still had to leave out far too much splendid writing. I didn't want to include anything simply exemplary from earlier that was not gripping or beautiful now.

I found, reading in bulk, that I was developing a dislike for both the 'well-made tale' and the fleeting 'impression'. Manuals on how to write short stories, and much criticism, stress unity of form, stress that only one thing should happen, that an episode or incident should be developed, or an emotion caught, with no space for digression, or change of direction or tone. Much of the competent, and more than competent, work that was done during the days of Kipling and Wells, in the first generation, and the subsequent generation (Coppard, Bates, Pritchett), who wrote when there were regular outlets for them to earn a living by turning stories, has an ultimate stiffness—it is diligent, it is wrought, it is atmospheric, but it can be mildly admired and taken or left. Many of the stories in this collection break all the rules of unity of tone and narrative. They appear to be one kind of story and mutate into another. They make unexpected twists and then twist again. They pack together comedy and tragedy, farce and delicacy, elegance and the grotesque. The workmanlike English story is bland, and the great English story is remarkable for its lack of blandness. The workmanlike English story is even-toned and neatly constructed. The great English story is shocking—even the sparest and driest—and hard to categorize.

My original list of essential stories was much longer than the Table of Contents of this volume. Those who have been reluctantly omitted include Charles Lamb, Elizabeth Gaskell, Arnold Bennett, Vernon Lee, Walter de la Mare, Somerset Maugham, E. M. Forster, and Angus Wilson. In some of these cases it was because the writer's genius was in fact for the *long* story—Elizabeth Gaskell needs space to create emotion, and so do Bennett and Lee. In the case of Bennett I became wedded to *The Death of Simon Fuge*, a masterpiece of the mixed tones, precise observation, social shifts, and narrative surprises I was coming to see as English, but fifty-five pages long. None of his shorter stories managed not to seem contrived beside it, so in the end I left him out altogether. I felt much the same about Vernon Lee's *A Wicked Voice*, a piece of bravura supernatural mischief related to both Firbank and Hawthorne, set in Italy, rich and strange. None of her shorter tales stood up to it. Doris Lessing's shorter stories are ferocious and brilliant, but I had got wedded to *The Eye of God in Paradise* and had no space left when I saw it was too long. De la Mare's *All Hallows* was in the same predicament. I wanted Forster's *Story of a Panic* but in the end left it out, partly because it is already heavily anthologized, and partly because it does not entirely avoid the besetting English vices of archness and whimsy. Somerset Maugham and Angus Wilson were both, at the highest level, a little too mechanical. You could see round what they were doing, the effect they were trying to produce.

There are all sorts of threads of connection and contrast running through the final thirty-seven stories. There are examples of English social realism, from Mary Mann's grim little Norfolk tale of rural poverty, through Arthur Morrison's glimpse behind the shades in his mean streets, and Malachi Whitaker's pre-war Yorkshire, to the wartime Englands of Rosamund Lehmann's cold country house and Grahame Greene's blitzed London, and beyond that to Sillitoe's working-class Nottingham. There are English ghost stories, tales of the supernatural, from Dickens and M. R. James, through Kipling, H. G. Wells, and T. H. White. There is a surprisingly powerful line of English surreal fantasy, starting with William Gilbert (the father of the Gilbert and Sullivan Gilbert), moving through Ronald Firbank and (in a way) Virginia Woolf to Leonora Carrington and the science fantasy of J. G. Ballard and Ian McEwan. There are stories of sensibility, precisely delineated, from Hardy's reluctant bride to the shocked heroine of Elizabeth Taylor's *The Blush*, from H. E. Bates's brilliant fusion of class, sex, death, and landscape, to D. H. Lawrence's slow pacing of a consciousness paring down its world and detaching itself from it. There are rollicking stories of insensibility, Saki and Waugh, Wodehouse and Firbank, with an English range from high irony to pure orchestrated farce. There is menace—in Charlotte Mew and in Sylvia Townsend Warner as well as in M. R. James. There is science, often in alliance with fantasy— Kipling and wireless, Wells and anaesthetic, Ballard and organophosphates. There are Angela Carter's and John Fuller's oriental fables.

I made no attempt to select stories about England as a place, or about abroad as an environment, but here we have a surprising mixture of settings—Penelope Fitzgerald in early colonial New Zealand, Aldous Huxley in Italy and Germany, T. H. White in Scandinavia, Charlotte Mew in deep Spain, Trollope in Antwerp, Carter in Uzbekistan, and Sylvia Townsend Warner contemplating American quilts.

I have arranged the stories in chronological order—of their author's birth, rather than of publication. The first is therefore William Gilbert's *The Sacristan of St Botolph*, which introduces many of what I have come to think of as 'English' characteristics, including both the persistent temptation to whimsy, and a kind of extravagance of what Henry James called 'solidity of specification'—solidity, in this case, of the daemonic pig, with a bell round its neck, brought by an imp to attach itself to the sacristan who makes the foolish declaration that he would like to be subjected to the same temptations as Saint Anthony, and is induced to become a hermit in a shed on Kennington Common. The pig's presence—the irritating noise of its bell, its diet and sleeping habits and feelings—is rendered with an excess of information that is a delight, and prefigures the bravura rendering, by P. G. Wodehouse, of Archie Mulliner's imitation of a hen laying an egg. The sacristan, too, shows a resourcefulness in retaliation that is both unexpected and detailed, reminding me of that great English classic, Beatrix Potter's *The Tale of Mr Tod*. No matter that the end is not fully achieved; the whole is unforgettable.

Dickens's *The Haunted House* is not usually anthologized, partly because it was written as the framing introduction to a series of tales, each intended to take place in one room of the haunted house. This is a very artificial construction, and the story as it stands also has the slight *longueur* of introducing the characters who will play central parts in the ensuing tales. But I like it for the way in which Dickens's energy and imagination, the power of his writing, and his capacity to invest anything he does with crackling pace and presence make a whole from a series of initially disconnected themes and events. There is the farcical word-play about spiritualism, a kind of moody parody of an Ann Radcliffe Gothic, a patch of purely Dickensian comedy of humours about the domestic staff and their disasters, a sentimental retreat into the childhood of the narrator–author, a jokey appeal to the playful imaginary world of a compulsive reader of the Arabian Nights, a completely satisfying moment of pure tragedy, and a revelation of a ghost that takes

Dickensian farce towards the subtleties of Henry James. You would think it was impossible to string so many tones and topics together while keeping up the pace, let alone welding them into a new kind of story, with its unity conferred by the revelation of the ghost in the mirror. Yet he does it, and if it is hack-work, it is the hack-work of genius.

Anthony Trollope's *Relics of General Chassé* comes very early in his Collected Shorter Fiction, yet nothing later, or more serious, pleased me quite so much as this absurd and genial comedy that shades into the surreal. Again it depends for its success on solidity of specification. If the eminent clergyman were less solid, or the enemy trousers into which, in a fit of playfulness, he attempts to insert his amplitude, less specifically tight, the story would lose its point. The drama depends on the thinginess of things. And, like many good English tales, it develops the comedy far beyond the climax the reader may expect. The actions of the respectable British ladies with regard to the trousers, the reactions of the narrator and the trousers' owner, the idea of there being such a good-natured tale at all about something so unrespectable, are all *too much*, which is the secret of their success. And the matter is complicated. The actions of the impulsive cleric are absurd, but he himself is not: he is both likeable and oddly and weirdly dignified. He is a person, not a type, though he is in a farce. This also I think of as English.

Next comes Hardy's *A Mere Interlude*, one of the masterpieces of the English short story. The author of *Life's Little Ironies* understood the way in which human lives, taken individually, do not follow probable patterns, and are not easily contained by the categories of tragedy and comedy. In his novels, his coincidences may feel like the manipulation of the brooding author rather than simply chance circumstances, but here the distant narrator neutrally unfolds a tale in which the emotions are unexpected and yet steadily consequent from line to line, as are the events. The characters and their social situation are complex and believable—the teacher who decides flatly to marry a widower because she doesn't like teaching, the chance meeting with an old lover, the precise degree of his sentimentality and real affection, the marriage, the drowning, the matter-of-fact behaviour of the woman, the series of twists at the end, each changing the previous one, which had seemed to be a climax, a stopping-off point. It proceeds evenly, and contains a mystery.

With Mary Mann a quite different kind of voice is heard. Mann was the wife of a Norfolk farmer, who recorded village life in the 1890s. *Little Brother* is plain, and brief, and clear and terrible, though the narrator's tone is not simple. She is recording, not judging, but her telling is spiky with morals and the inadequacy of morals. If it has anything in common with its predecessors, it is again the dwelling on the concrete, the clothes, the mud, the body of the dead child, whose solidity is the certain thing about it. Mann's naturalism is followed by M. R. James's matter-of-fact supernaturalism, with its horrors contained and emphasized by its conventional frame of papery witness and distant precise records of the indescribable. James's ghost stories too depend on the evocation of the concrete—in this case the sheets and blankets on a bed, behaving as sheets and blankets cannot behave. Arthur Morrison's *Tales of Mean Streets* is a classic of English social realism, and Morrison tells this grisly tale with sober restraint and a certain dry wit. The 'shade', 'a cone of waxen grapes and apples under a glass cover' takes on a glittering symbolic meaning (which is never pointed out or at), partly because of its solidity again, and partly because of the resonance of the word 'shade' itself, its connections to darkness, death, and ghosts.

The stories by Kipling and Wells are both about the rearrangement of the modern consciousness by modern science—in Kipling's case the new world opened up by radio waves, and in Wells's the advances of surgery under anaesthetic, combined with an imaginative vision of the universe as revealed by modern astronomers. All Wells's stories are in some sense secular religious stories, looking for a place for wonder and a way of looking at what it is to be human. He was aware that human nature and consciousness themselves were changing, and he found ways of writing about the relations of body and mind (and in many of his tales society too) which turned the changes into immediate experience for the reader. The Kipling story is, in my opinion, another masterpiece. It creates, in concrete detail and solidity, a place, several people, an obsessively interesting moment of scientific advance, a comedy of manners, and poetry, as the disembodied voice of Keats speaks through the medium of the radio waves and/or the drugged chemist. This English short story draws unaffectedly and powerfully on the richness of earlier English literary writing—as do many of the others. And Kipling is not content only to quote Keats—he gives a bravura and convincing fictive account of the poet's mind working out the language of the poems, its strengths, its rhythms. And, beyond that, the matter-of-fact tragedy of the dying consumptive reaches back to that earlier death, and out to the human condition, radio waves or no radio waves. The tone is complex, shifting, various, and the story is a perfect whole, with all its parts working together. H. E. Bates hated Kipling, described his style as 'tinsel and brass', and wrote that 'no single syllable of his has ever given [me] a moment's pleasure'. He was more enthusiastic about Wells, describing him as 'a scientific inventor inoculated with a dream bacillus' and 'the teller of fairy tales talking in the language of scientific power'. Bates's own generation, bred, as he significantly claims, on Constance Garnett's translations of the great Russians, Chekhov and Tolstoy, was in revolt against the 'masculine' generation of the Yellow Book. He was sure that Kipling would be forgotten, despised for jingoism and class bias. He did not look for, and did not see, ironies, or ambiguities under Kipling's tone. Time changes writers and readers—after my reading, I felt that Kipling, with Hardy, and Graham Greene, was one of the true English masters of the form. It was hard to choose which Kipling to include—I have left out wartime stories, Indian tales, and ghost stories, not because they are not great, but because there was not space.

Charlotte Mew's *A White Night* is a further example of an English capacity to create pure horror from solid description. Its central mystery, the ritual live burial of a young woman at dead of night, is unforgettable precisely because of the awkward, conventional Edwardian narrator, worried about his friends locked by accident overnight in a Spanish church. The story stands between M. R. James's economy and the surreal ferocity of T. H. White; it is related to the de la Mare for whom I could not find space, but has a starkness in its very woodenness which removes it altogether from fluttering whimsy. It is followed by a completely opposed, but equally characteristic, English voice, Saki's sharp, remorseless tale of unredeemable human ferocity, *The Toys of Peace*. Saki also wrote tales as chilling as Mew's, and I hesitated over *Sredni Vastar*, and *The Interlopers*, with its sinister wolves. Saki writes a level, insouciant narration of great and small disasters in a way that is related to the voices of Wodehouse, Waugh, and Firbank. It is the English dandy voice, at its best devastating, at less than its best silly or trivial. I found that Saki's tales should not be read in bulk, for their idiosyncratic shockingness is diminished by proximity to other idiosyncratic shocks of rather the same kind, and his talent begins to look like a limited series of tricks. I have included *The Toys of Peace* because it is not much anthologized, and because I was bowled over by it when I read it, at my grandmother's, as a small child, and spent days puzzling out its wickedness. And because I like the civilization of children who *know* about

Louis XIV and put their knowledge to such satisfactory use. And because it is about the poetic imagination, shape-shifting, lawlessly and at will.

G. K. Chesterton's *Tremendous Adventures of Major Brown*, like Dickens's *Haunted House*, is a framing story for a series, *The Club of Queer Trades*. I like it because of its believable and unusual description of an Indian Army retired Major, because it is a pleasing example of English whimsy when it does work, combined with English religious mysticism in a very odd way, and full of concrete details that glitter, like the unexpected invention of the yellow pansies. It is a silly story with depth, a metaphysical tale and a shaggy dog story, and English in its gentleness. It looks back to William Gilbert, and forward to Leonora Carrington.

A. E. Coppard was one of the great exponents and practitioners of the short story form in the generation after the robust nineties. Bates says he was a model for his younger contemporaries because the short story was his chosen form; he was not a novelist writing occasionally. In this, and in other ways, he is comparable to V. S. Pritchett. Bates claimed that Coppard 'attempted to bring to the short story some of the fancy, delicacy, shape and coloured conceit of the Elizabethan lyric'. Doris Lessing identified him as part of 'a steadily flowing stream in English writing that is quiet, low in key'. He wrote about the countryside, in sketches reminiscent of Turgenev; he told wry little tales of rural dourness and enduring landscape. The story I have chosen, *Some Talk of Alexander*, is not 'typical' Coppard, as *Dusky Ruth* or *A Field of Mustard* would have been. It is a compressed mixture of an almost Wodehousian farce with a Lawrentian (or Wellsian) vision of the nature and savagery of the physical world. The hero is an English *petit bourgeois* whose disappointment in love is comic, and whose attempts to communicate his suicidal intentions are farcically thwarted by bridge-playing priorities. So, in a practical English way, he folds his clothes and swims out to sea. And in an equally English way, in the dark night and the water, he has a vision of what it is to be alive, of the fierceness and power of things. And discovers that he has crossed the estuary, and can begin again, naked. Upon which petty English social priorities again intrude. It is a good example of the English fondness for the little man and the importance of his life, though what made me choose it was the way the writing rises to meet the waves and the darkness.

P. G. Wodehouse's voice is unique. He writes about Englishmen confined by a very narrow class boundary and mostly within very limited intelligences, men whose vocabularies, at first glance, consist of a stereotyped set of aimless adjectives and jolly noises. And yet his range of stylistic games and surprises is immense. He can use Shakespeare without affectation, overtly and covertly in all sorts of ways; he can make extraordinary effects as he does in this story when he prefaces Archie Mulliner's imitation of a hen laying an egg with an ecstatic quotation from 'Come into the garden, Maud'. He is as much an original genius as Lewis Carroll or Edward Lear, and, like theirs, his genius is intimately involved in the range and depth of the possibilities of the English language. His pastiche of a Baconian encrypting in this story is masterly, as are his figures of speech: 'it was often said of Archibald that, had his brain been constructed of silk, he would have been hard put to it to find sufficient material to make a canary a pair of cami-knickers'. His comedy harks back to Dickens and Trollope and is a tough and innocent relation of Firbank and Waugh.

Both Woolf's *Solid Objects* and Lawrence's *The Man who Loved Islands* are cool, glittering studies of extreme and strange states of mind, one brief and concentrated, one long and constructed in loose rhythms of feeling. High modernism in English writing seems to be related both to a questioning of perception and to a desire to do away with the centre of self, or of social self—the central characters of both these tales cast off lives as businessmen for some increasingly pure, intense, and aesthetic experience. Both seem to me excellent examples of poetic prose, beyond the prose of sensibility. Both are tempered by an ironic narrative voice. Lawrence was one of the greatest describers of weather, as Woolf was one of the greatest describers of small objects, and both are at their best here. Lawrence's weather is weather of the body and weather of the soul; in this story he works by telling, by describing, not by preaching. It would have been good to be able to include one of his shorter stories about miners or farmers as well; no one was quite like Lawrence for conveying the essentials of someone in a physical description. But *The Man who Loved Islands* is late, supremely ambitious Lawrence, written in Lawrence's unique voice.

Firbank is frivolous, brittle, delicious, and decadent, an English sensibility at the other extreme from Arthur Morrison or Mary Mann. *A Tragedy in Green* is youthful showing-off. I like the idea of the magic annihilation of the Foreign Office, and the charmingly wicked heroine. Sylvia Townsend Warner's heroine is also performing a wicked magic, in a minor key, precisely and ornamentally stitching a pattern of death as Firbank's Lady Georgia constructs 'a gold and peacock-green cloud, like an Eastern prayer carpet advancing leisurely towards St James's Park'. Both stories depend for their effect, yet again, on the thinginess of things, the green parasol and the bulk of the Foreign Office itself in Firbank, the templates and materials, the hexagons and silks, of the quilt in Sylvia Townsend Warner.

Aldous Huxley's *Nuns at Luncheon* was one of the stories whose discovery pleased me most. The narrative voice, constructed by the dialogue between the worldly-wise narrator and his even more imperturbably sophisticated friend, is both unfeeling and naughty. But it is complicated in its own analysis of its own aesthetic greed, its own pleasure in the delectable *frissons* of shock in the tale of the nun's tragic undoing. The tale is both grotesque, farcical, and, under the frivolity, uneasily disturbing and sad. It speaks with many voices, tempting the reader into malice and lurching briefly into seriousness, always perfectly in control. And it turns on solid objects, most particularly on false teeth. It is the teeth that make the story implacably comic, and yet it is also the teeth that provide the unpalatable pathos. Very English.

Malachi Whitaker was known as the Bradford Chekhov, and was published by John Middleton Murry in *The Adelphi*, where she had first read D. H. Lawrence. Both Chekhov and Lawrence play a part in the tough, elegant, surprising forms of her tales. She was a true artist, one of the generation that flowered with Bates and Coppard, and quite as good as they are. To her too the story was a natural and central form, not an occasional one. She writes both about rural Yorkshire and about urban Yorkshire, is interested in hardship but also in comedy and endurance. I chose *Landlord of the Crystal Fountain* from many excellent possibilities, partly because the title delighted me. It is like *The Rainbow* in its evocation of a biblical and mythical reality in the solid existence of pubs and moorland. And its heroine, a canny, lower-middle-class schoolmistress on a journey, makes an interesting comparison with the similar heroine of Hardy's *A Mere Interlude*. Like Bates's story, *Landlord of the Crystal Fountain* negotiates the minutiae of the English class-consciousness in a subtle and unexpected way. I like stories in which energy overcomes inhibitions.

V. S. Pritchett is an acknowledged master of the short story. He had a sure sense of what sort of human pattern, how much and how little, could be contained in its space. He was good at symptomatic *things*, and equally good at whole atmospheres. I chose *On the Edge of the Cliff*, a relatively late story (1980), for the (English) way in which it makes the exploration of a part of the landscape, past and present, inextricably part of an exploration of the whole lives of the characters. But I chose it really for the relationship of an image and an observation. The image is that of an old man (with a young mistress watching) standing naked, ready to dive into the sea. 'He was standing there, his body furred with grey hair, his belly wrinkled, his thighs shrunk. Up went his bony arms.' The observation is casual and colloquial, and in the story placed like a line of a poem.

'What are you thinking about?' she asked without opening her eyes.

He was going to say 'At my age one is always thinking about death,' but he said 'You.'

Rosamund Lehmann's *A Dream of Winter* is both lyrical and precise, an evocation of a particular time and place, a cold country house in a wartime winter, the urgency of the feeling of entrapment and suppressed energy quite naturally embodied in the summer bees in the winter chimney. There is savagery in the lyricism, too. The note is not single, though the effect is unified. Evelyn Waugh's *An Englishman's Home* pleases me because it is a splendidly heartless exploration of the English rural pieties, and English snobbism, by a satirist who certainly shared the pieties he was mocking.

The virtues of Graham Greene's stories are those of his novels—spareness, tension, a vision of evil—but the art is that of a great short story writer. *The Destructors* is a masterpiece. Its world, the world of gangs of boys in a blitzed landscape, is completely real, physically and socially, and at the same time a microcosm, both of wartime England and of human nature. 'Man secretes evil as bees secrete honey' William Golding remarked after *Lord of the Flies*, his own study of what groups of boys, good and evil, could do together. Greene's study of the machinery of the gang is economical and convincing; his picture of the bombed house, with its Wren spiral staircase, is solid enough, and his plot is ingenious and terrible. What makes this tale English is again the mixed, ambivalent tone. It would take an English writer to end with the helpless laughter of the lorry driver at the destruction which the reader too cannot help admiring and laughing at—thus sharing in the wickedness.

H. E. Bates was prolific, a 'natural' with an ear and an eye for a telling detail, with a real literary passion as a reader, and an equally powerful passion for the earth, and particularly for its flora. It is a pity that Bates is so well known for the steaming farmyard farce of the Larkin family, for he was a considerable artist, with as many excellent stories to his credit as Pritchett, Coppard, or Elizabeth Taylor. His generation was adept at diffusing the human emotion into the landscape, English or foreign—into flowers, water, fields, already threatened and vanishing. It was hard to choose one story among so many good ones. Some of the most dramatic had also a fatal facility. I settled on *The Waterfall* because it is one of the best stories I have read about the English class system in all its shifting complexity. The dead vicar's impoverished sister encounters the vulgar rich tradesman. He offers warmth, and flowers, and the warmth is both physical and emotional. Her reservations and her response to his energy are most beautifully and mysteriously presented. The waterfall is both purely symbolic—a trickle to be undammed—and intricately wound into the narrative fabric of the tale. And again there is the twist, the third character, the engineer who brings laughter and a new relationship, or is possibly the third party to the existing one, who removes constraint. We experience Bates's people, and the pressures on them from themselves and others and the world of time and matter, as we experience our own lives, uncertain how to define what is happening, with a mixture of precise observation and deep and obscure emotion.

T. H. White's *The Troll* has that quality Hazlitt called 'gusto'. When I had my early idea of including English fairy-tales and folk-tales I was thinking of Jack and the Beanstalk, and the giant's classic cry 'Fee Fi Fo Fum | I smell the blood of an Englishman'. Here is a literary version of that, told by a narrator who heard it from his father, who encounters a Troll in a Lapland hotel on a fishing holiday. The narrator remarks, before embarking on a description of the Troll, seen through a keyhole,

I suppose the best way to tell the story is simply to narrate it, without an effort to carry belief. The thing did not require belief. It was not a feeling of horror in one's bones, or a misty outline, or anything that needed to be given actuality by an act of faith. It was as solid as a wardrobe. You don't have to believe in wardrobes. They are there, with corners.

The following description of the creature and the lady it is eating is a glittering *tour de force* of solidity. I have read no better description of hallucinatory bodily terror, and the narrator's father's outwitting of the beast, the small man escaping by the skin of his teeth, gives the reader a thrill of bodily relief. It is more blatant, and worse than, M. R. James because it is part of no convention of the supernatural. It is related to the sacristan's pig, but also to Charlotte Mew's buried nun, and, at a distance, to Mary Mann's real baby.

Elizabeth Taylor's *The Blush* is my classic example of the satisfying well-made short story. Taylor makes an atmosphere out of minor details, creates characters out of single traits, and engineers a narrative shock in an apparently desultory and innocent set of observations. Penelope Fitzgerald's *At Hiruharama*, which follows it, was first published in 1992, whereas *The Blush* appeared in 1958. Penelope Fitzgerald has been taken for an English woman of sensibility, writing about small concerns with wit, but she is much more than that. She makes metaphysical fables out of surprising observations, and while Taylor's kitchen, and her cleaning-lady's varicose veins, are in a sense part of some *normal* observation of English life, Fitzgerald sees everything as distinctive, individual, and important. Nothing in this tale is expected, neither the setting, nor the hero's problems with reading, nor the pigeons, nor the birth, nor the conversations, nor the averted disaster. Penelope Fitzgerald's sentences have a cool clarity that is part of a very modern English prose—related to the sharpness of Muriel Spark's Scottish wit, or V. S. Naipaul's polished mandarin elegance, but less edged, milder, more mysterious. The centre of Taylor's story, like Bates's, is the heroine's emotions, which are finally and flamboyantly expressed in the Blush itself. The centre of Fitzgerald's story, though the characters are admirable, irritating, and delightful, is the watching eye of the writer, the narrative unfolding, the mystery of societies and things. Outside this story are worlds on worlds of other settings and other sets of beliefs and behaviours, equally interesting, equally strange.

Fitzgerald gives reality a surreal edge. Leonora Carrington is a true surrealist, both as a painter and as a tale-teller, using the frames both of dream and of folk-tale, inventing imagined worlds and unprecedented preoccupations. Angela Carter learned from her, but Carter was always concerned with social and psychological pointers and meanings. Carrington is the thing itself, and the flannel knickers and the traffic island are part of both European surrealism and English grotesque.

Alan Sillitoe's *The Loneliness of the Long-Distance Runner* is a classic English long story. He writes in the tradition of Morrison, more drily than Coppard and Bates, and can be compared to Whitaker as a recorder of local, provincial worlds. I like *Enoch's Two Letters* because of the bravado of its exploitation of coincidence as a narrative device—*Enoch's*

Two Letters is directly descended from Hardy's interest in life's little ironies. And I like the solidity and stolidity with which he follows up his shocks.

J. G. Ballard's *Dream Cargoes* is science fantasy, at one level, and myth at another. It calls up *The Tempest*—the chemical waste ship, the *Prospero*, is wrecked on a tropical island—and beyond that, the rich, vanishing garden of *Paradise Lost*. It is part of contemporary international science fiction, and yet both the ideas and the writing look back to Wells and Kipling, and further back to Milton and Shakespeare. John Fuller's two brief tales, completely different from each other, are taken from *The Worm and the Star*, an extraordinary work of art made up of sixty-three similar fables, asking philosophical questions about the nature of things, and human questions about political and social relations, and artistic questions about the nature of, and need for, narration itself. These two cannot give an adequate idea of the richness and riddling clarity of the whole, but they can be a sample of a new, and elegant, English use of the form. Angela Carter claimed that she wrote fairy-tales because her most powerful reading experiences came from them, and not from the emotions of social realism. Her feminist reworking of Grimm and Perrault is widely read and studied, as are her American tales. I have chosen *The Kiss* because it has all her qualities of brilliance, exoticism, sensuality, violence, and detached irony in a space as small as John Fuller's. You never forget Carter's colours. And the *invention* in this tale, the exemplary things, eggs and vodka, could not be bettered.

Carter's prose glitters. Tremain's has a cool flow recognizable as hers, and it is above all for the rhythm of the writing that I have chosen *The Beauty of the Dawn Shift*, though I am also astonished and delighted by the ease and completeness with which she has imagined the life of a post-1989 East German. Tremain's imagination (like that of many other younger English writers) reaches out in a new way into unknown places and experiences—not out of exoticism, but out of curiosity. The dreamy precise prose gives the hero's journey a fabulous quality, yet it is simultaneously sensuously solid.

Ian McEwan's *Solid Geometry* is a *tour de force* of the specific and the marvellous: it is full of strange information that goes back to Wells (and beyond him to Burton's *Anatomy of Melancholy* and English interest in curiosities). It combines precise social observation (the decay of the marriage, the ecological clichés) with post-modern fictive self-consciousness—the characters see themselves as 'in a fiction seminar'.

Solid Geometry's title hints at the quality of thinginess I have been describing as English. Its matter-of-fact shocking climax exemplifies it. Philip Hensher's *Dead Languages* was first published in *New Writing 6*, which I co-edited. I found it more moving than I could quite account for, until I heard him read it. He prefaced his reading by saying that he had set out to parody a kind of writing that is everywhere now, and that he had found that after all his story was serious and was saying something. I don't know how he would characterize this style. It has an unspecific clarity, an economy of reticence and hinting, a sense of displacement. It is related to the restrained elegance of V. S. Naipaul's *The Enigma of Arrival* and Kazuo Ishiguro's lucid, international style. Both these writers use the English language perfectly, and with full knowledge of what has been written in it, to do something detached from Englishness, looking *at* Englishness. I wanted to end my collection with *Dead Languages* because Hensher's story is not only about the dead languages his unspecific colonial student had to learn from his nameless Mister. It is about the death of many kinds of English, the vanishing of Englishness, like the vanishing of McEwan's too too solid Maisie through the geometrical hoop of her arms. It has an ear for how the non-English see and hear the English. Hensher is a stylist; his rhythms are assured and precise. In his other fiction he tells inventive new stories in inventive new ways. This tale is not an elegy; it is an observation. But its coolness, its recording of the absence of much that I have left out, seemed a good place to end.

The subjects of these stories vary from the sublime to the ridiculous, from the momentous to the trivial, from the grim to the farcical. There is English empiricism, English pragmatism, English starkness, English humour, English satire, English dandyism, English horror, and English whimsy. There are characteristic mixed modes which seem to go back further than Austen and Defoe to Chaucer and Shakespeare. Wodehouse understands Sir Andrew Aguecheek, and Dickens understood how Shakespeare put the Porter into the murderous sequence in *Macbeth*. The language is as various as the subject-matter. The tradition of plain prose runs through Mann and Morrison, M. R. James, Whitaker, and Sillitoe. Richness and strangeness—combined with toughness—appear in Ballard, T. H. White, Carter, Firbank, Carrington. There is a nuanced prose of feeling in Pritchett, Townsend Warner, Lehmann, and Bates. There is rhythmic poetic prose in Lawrence, Woolf, and

Tremain. There is spareness in Hensher and Fuller. There is wit in Huxley, Saki, and Waugh. Many of the best stories shift from one of these modes to another. There is whimsy and innocence (Trollope, Chesterton, Wodehouse) and there is ferocity and savagery (Greene, Mew).

In the end, I found by chance a narrative definition of Englishness that I would like to end with. It comes from Penelope Fitzgerald's composite biography of the Knox brothers, her father and uncles. It concerns a boy at an English public school, Rugby, and a teacher known, in an English way, as the Bodger.

One midday a boy threw a squash ball which exactly struck the hands of the great clock that set the time for the whole school and stopped it. Masters and boys, drawing their watches out of their pockets as they hurried across the yard, to compare the false with the true, were thrown into utter confusion. It turned out that the boy, who confessed at once, had been practising the shot for two years. The Bodger called this 'un-English'. Eddie did not agree. The patient, self-contained, self-imposed pursuit of an entirely personal solution seemed to him most characteristically English.

This definition of Englishness fits with the eccentric differences and excellences of the English stories collected here. It is only partial, but that is its charm. The English are hard to sum up.

WILLIAM GILBERT

The Sacristan of St Botolph

MASTER WALTER DE COURCEY, although an indefatigable man of
business, was extremely punctual in his religious observances, and he
made a point, both in winter and summer, of attending early mass in his
parish church, St Botolph's, Bishopsgate. His departure for Windsor
was very sudden, in fact hardly any one out of his own house was aware
that he had left London. The officiating priest at the church was therefore much surprised at his non-appearance two days running; and as
Master Walter did not appear on the third, nor in fact for a week, he
began to fear he might be indisposed, and one morning, as soon as mass
was over, he directed the sacristan to call at the merchant's house and
enquire after his health. The sacristan was a certain Geoffrey Cole, a
very tall thin man with a low forehead, deep sunk eyes, harsh features,
and very large hands and feet. Although something of a miser, intensely
selfish, and most uncharitable, both in the matter of giving alms, and in
his feelings towards his neighbours, he was extremely punctilious in all
the external forms and ceremonies of the Church, and he flattered himself he was not only very religious, but even a model of piety. The more
he studied the subject, the more certain of his blissful state he became,
till at last he believed himself to be so good that the saints alone were his
equals. He would frequently draw comparisons between his life and
some of the inferior saints, and he generally concluded he could compare with them most advantageously. On the morning when he was
directed to call on Master Walter this train of thought especially occupied his mind, and by the time he had arrived at the house he was certain that in the whole city of London there was not another individual
so good as himself.

The person who received him was an old woman half imbecile from
age, who had formerly been Master Walter's nurse, and with her the sacristan had frequently conversed on matters of what he called religion.
When he had received from her an explanation of the merchant's

absence from church, the pair commenced talking on subjects connected with Church affairs, which consisted in fact of the sacristan's explaining to her what a good and pious man he was, and her complimenting him thereon. Before he left the house the nurse asked him if he would like to see the mirror, as she would have much pleasure in showing it to him. He accepted the offer at once, at the same time saying that vanities of the kind had but few attractions for him.

The nurse led the way to the chamber, and when they had arrived there, in spite of his mock ascetic manner, there was no difficulty in perceiving he admired the mirror greatly. Fearing, however, the real state of his mind might be detected by the old woman, he began to speak of it in terms of great disparagement, not indeed finding fault with its form and beauty, but dwelling on the absurdity of mortals setting their minds on such trifles, and neglecting subjects of far greater importance which concerned the welfare of their souls.

'But everybody cannot be so good as you are, Master Geoffrey,' said the old woman; 'and you ought to have a little feeling for those who are not.'

'I do not see that,' said the sacristan, taking the compliment without the slightest hesitation. 'I condemn all trifles of the kind. What would the blessed St Anthony have said to a vanity of this sort?'

'Ah!' said the old woman; 'but it would not be possible in the present day to find so good a man as he was.'

'It would be very difficult, I admit,' said the sacristan; 'but I am not sure it would be impossible. Do not think for a moment that I would attempt to compare myself with him; but I thought, while reflecting on his life as I came here this morning, that I should very much like to be subjected to the same temptations, to see if I could not resist them.'

'You surely do not mean that?' said the nurse; 'why, they were dreadful.'

'Indeed, I do,' said the sacristan, looking at himself in the mirror, 'I should like immensely to be subjected to them for a month, and then I could form an idea whether I was as good as I ought to be.'

'Well,' said the nurse, leaving the room with him, 'I trust you will never be subjected to anything of the kind.' After a little conversation of the same description the sacristan left the house.

After he had delivered his message to the priest and the functions of the day were over, he sought his own home in the rural district of Little Moorfields. He lived in a room on the top floor of a house occupied by a man and his wife who were employed at a merchant's house in the City. As the merchant and his family were absent, Geoffrey's landlord and his wife were requested to sleep at the house of business, and thus he had for the time the whole abode to himself.

His room, which was comfortably furnished, was the very picture of neatness and cleanliness, for he was very particular in his domestic arrangements; and his landlady, during her temporary absence at the house of business, called every day to put his room in order, and place his supper on the table.

Arrived at home he requested a neighbour's wife to light his lamp and fire for him, and that being done she left him. He then bolted the street door, went up to his own room, and after having a very comfortable and abundant meal went to bed, having, however, left ample food on the table for his breakfast the next morning. He was generally a very sound sleeper, and his slumbers that night formed no exception to the general rule; but, somehow or other, as morning advanced they were by no means so profound. He grew very restless, with a sense of oppression, and occasionally he heard a sound like the tinkling of a bell, which continued till daybreak, when the annoyance became intolerable. At last, when it was fully day, he aroused himself and sat up in his bed. What was his surprise and terror when he saw, stretched across the foot of it, outside the clothes, a large fat pig with a bell fastened round its neck with a leathern strap. His first attempt was to push the brute from the bed, but the only effect produced was that it placed itself in a still more comfortable position directly on his legs, and then went to sleep again. Enraged and in great pain, he immediately began to pommel the pig with his fist on the neck and head, but without other result than a few surly grunts. His passion increased to such an extent that he struck it still harder blows, when suddenly his attention was arrested by a loud peal of laughter, and he saw, sitting on his stool by the fireplace, an imp so intensely ugly that he was almost frightened to look at it. Somewhat recovering himself, he said, 'Who are you, and what are you doing here?'

'No matter who I am,' said the imp; 'but as to what I am doing, I am simply laughing at your ungrateful and absurd behaviour.'

'In what way,' said the sacristan, 'is my behaviour absurd?'

'In attacking in that violent manner your friend and pig.'

'My pig?' said the sacristan; 'I have no pig. It is none of mine.'

'O you ungrateful man,' said the imp. 'Did you not yesterday say you wished you could meet with some temptations similar to those tradition tells us annoyed St Anthony? And now, when you have a pig, and a very handsome one too, for your protection and society, the first thing you do is to pommel it as if you would kill it.'

'I did not know it was a pig of that description,' said the sacristan, with much solemnity of tone, 'or I should have treated it with the respect it deserves.'

'Well, then, do so now,' said the imp. 'To all appearance it will give you ample opportunity for a trial of patience.'

'But I cannot remain here all day,' said the sacristan, 'I must go to my duties; I shall be scolded as it is for being late.'

Then scratching the pig lovingly on the poll, he addressed it with much sweetness of tone and manner: 'If it is not asking you too great a favour, would you oblige me by getting off my bed? I am really very sorry to trouble you, but you are rather heavy, and I suffer from corns.'

But the pig took no further notice of these blandishments than closing its eyes more fast than ever, and falling into a sounder sleep.

'What am I to do?' said the poor sacristan, in a despairing tone.

'Exercise your patience,' said the imp. 'He is affording you capital practice.'

The sacristan was now silent, and for some time the imp said nothing, contenting himself with a quiet chuckle. Presently, however, he said to the sacristan,

'Come, I will assist you if I can. What do you want me to do?'

'To get this accurs— I mean blessed pig off my bed if you can.'

'I can do it easily enough,' said the imp; 'but you mortals are so ungrateful, it is ten to one you will be angry with me if I do.'

'On the contrary,' said Geoffrey, 'I shall be most grateful to you, I promise you on my word of honour. That is to say,' he continued, 'if it do not put the dear creature to much pain.'

'I promise you that it shall, on the contrary, be much pleased.'

'Pray proceed then.'

The imp immediately leaped off the stool, and going to the table took from it the food the sacristan had set aside for his breakfast, and placing it on the ground called out, 'Pig, pig.'

The pig lazily opened its eyes and looked on the ground. No sooner, however, did it see the food than its sleepy fit left it, and it jumped from the bed and commenced a furious attack on the sacristan's breakfast.

Master Geoffrey, in spite of his promise, was now dreadfully angry.

He leaped on the floor, and rushing to the pig attempted in vain to push it away from the food, the imp laughing lustily the while.

'Upon my word,' he said, 'I never saw in my life a man worse adapted for an anchorite than you are. Why, you ought to be delighted to see your pig enjoy itself so heartily.'

Master Geoffrey immediately left the pig and cast a very proper look of intense hatred at the imp, who seemed more delighted with it than ever.

'Did I not tell you,' he said, 'that you would be ungrateful to me for my kindness?'

The sacristan made no reply, but commenced dressing himself. He went on systematically with his toilet, casting occasionally an envious glance at the pig, but by the time he was fully dressed he had contrived to regain his equanimity. He now put on his cap as if to leave the house, and then, going to the pig, he patted it on the back and scratched its head, saying at the time,

'There's a good pig, go on with your breakfast, and when you have finished we will take a pretty pleasant walk together down to St Botolph's, and there I will leave you in the streets till my duties are over, and then we will walk back together comfortably in the evening.'

Here the imp set up a furious laugh, and stamped on the floor with pleasure.

'Bravo! admirable!' he said, 'upon my word you are a nice fellow. You know the Lord Mayor has lately published an order that all pigs found in the streets of the City shall have their throats cut, and their flesh given to the poor. Upon my word you are a very clever fellow, and I begin to like you immensely. I could not have done anything better myself.'

Master Geoffrey contented himself with casting another look of intense hatred at the imp, but he said nothing.

After a few minutes' silence the imp said to him,

'Now I know you want to ask me a question and are too proud to do it. You would enquire what you must do with the pig during the day?'

'I acknowledge it,' said the sacristan. 'What can I do with it?—of course I cannot take it to the church with me.'

'Leave it at home, then, I should if I were you, rather than be bothered with it all day.'

'Well, I should like to do that, but if my landlady should come and find it here she would very likely drive it away. Perhaps,' he said, after a moment's reflection, 'that would be the better way after all.'

'Not at all,' said the imp, 'it would be sure to find its way back again at night, so that would be of no use. I see you want to get rid of it.'

'Your base suspicions annoy me.'

'Indeed. Now let me advise you. Go round to the house your land-lady lives at, and tell her that you do not want your room arranged either today or tomorrow. She will be pleased to hear it, as I know she is suf-fering very severely from an attack of rheumatism. So you see you can leave the pig in your room without the slightest danger of its being found out by anyone. Now you had better go. Do not forget to bring the pig's supper back with you, or it will again be under the unpleasant necessity of eating that which you had reserved for yourself. Now goodbye.'

The sacristan then left the house, and after having called on his land-lady and assured her that there would be no occasion for her to arrange his room for him either that day or the next,—a piece of news which gave her great satisfaction, as the weather was cold and her rheumatism worse,—he continued his way to the church, where he had great diffi-culty in making his peace with the priest for being so late. When the duties of the day were over, he first went to an eating-house and ate a most hearty supper, determining that the pig should not deprive him of that meal. He then bought sufficient for his breakfast the next morning, and afterwards some vegetables for the pig. This last investment, we are obliged to acknowledge with great sorrow, caused him much annoy-ance. He had a violent objection to spend money on anybody but him-self, and although he wished to act up to the part of an anchorite as closely as he could, he never had heard of one spending money on a dumb animal, and he almost considered it to be a work of supereroga-tion to waste the money he had done on the pig. However, it was done, and there was no help for it. He sincerely repented his fault, and he could not say more; he would be more cautious another time.

When he arrived at home and had procured a light from a neighbour, he entered his room and found in it the pig and the imp. He showed little delight at the sight of either. The pig, on the contrary, received him with every mark of satisfaction, that is to say, as soon as it perceived the vegetables under the sacristan's arm.

The sacristan took no notice of the imp, but threw the vegetables down on the floor, setting aside, however, enough for the pig's breakfast the next morning, and it was soon occupied with its supper. The sac-ristan watched it thoughtfully as it fed, not a word being spoken the while either by the imp or himself. When the pig was fully satisfied, the sacristan swept up the remains, and opening the casement threw them into the street. He then closed it quickly as the weather was cold, intending to enjoy, if possible, a comfortable night's rest, when to his intense horror, he found the pig had leaped upon the bed and had stretched itself full length upon it from head to foot, so that it would have been difficult for the sacristan to have placed himself beside the pig even if he had been so inclined.

The sacristan could hardly contain his rage, indeed for a moment it partially broke out, but a roar of laughter from the imp induced him to restrain himself. With great difficulty he put something like an amiable smile on his countenance, and then addressed the pig with much genuine persuasion in his tone and manner.

'Come off the bed, there's a good pig,' he said, 'and I will make you up another on the floor, where you will be much more comfortable than you are there. Come now, there's a good pig.' But the only answer he got was a grunt.

'What in the name of Fortune,' said the imp, 'do you want the pig to get off the bed for?'

'Why to sleep there myself, of course,' said the sacristan.

'Upon my word, you are a pretty anchorite. You slept like a top all last night to my certain knowledge, and you want to go to bed tonight!'

'What am I expected to do then?' said the sacristan.

'Pass the night in meditation on the floor, of course; who ever heard of an anchorite sleeping two nights running? You will now find how invaluable is your pig. It will sleep soundly enough while you meditate, but the moment you fall asleep it will ring its bell. I see you do not like that arrangement, and I begin to suspect you are no better than a sham after all.'

'I will prove to you I am,' said the sacristan; 'that is to say if I am to have the pleasure of your company here all night.'

'That you will not have,' said the imp, 'but you will see me in the morning,' and he immediately vanished.

To say the truth, the sacristan passed a most uncomfortable night. Whenever he attempted to sleep, the pig rang its bell until the unfortunate man was fully awake, and then went to sleep himself. Several times in the course of the night did he beg the pig to keep quiet, and once he endeavoured to explain to it that he always meditated best with his eyes shut, but the pig would hear of no compromise, and continued faithfully to do its duty till morning. When day broke the imp made his appearance, and as before seated himself on the stool.

'What sort of a night have you passed?' said the imp.

'A very unpleasant—I mean a very happy one, indeed.'

'I do not believe you,' said the imp. 'I suspect after all you are not the man to resist temptation.'

'There you are certainly wrong,' said the sacristan. 'No man,' he continued, casting a most vindictive glance at the pig, 'was ever more cruelly tempted than I have been tonight, and yet I successfully resisted it. But after all I candidly admit that, all things considered, it will be exceedingly difficult for me to carry out my wish at present, much as it would disappoint me to relinquish it. You must perceive yourself that in a small room like this, I have no convenience or accommodation for a temptation of the kind.'

'O you coward!' said the imp. 'What, going to give in already? No accommodation indeed! Why, I should like to know how the anchorites of old managed?'

'They had the desert handy, where they had plenty of room.'

'Why do you not go there then?'

'How absurdly you talk!' said the sacristan peevishly. 'Why, the desert is so far off it would take me a life-time to get there.'

'Try Kennington Common, then,' said the imp. 'There will be room enough for you there, and I observed the other day at the farthest part a half-ruined shed that would serve you and your pig admirably for shelter.'

'If I went there,' said the sacristan, 'would it be necessary for me to take the pig with me?'

'Of course; its duty is to keep you from relapsing; and besides that, it would not stay behind though you wished it.'

The sacristan reflected for some minutes. To say the truth, the proposition of the imp did not altogether displease him. Near that part of Kennington Common resided a buxom widow very well to do in the world, who was rather fond of hearing the sacristan converse on serious subjects. He calculated that if bad weather came on, or if his provisions did not hold out, or if he were cold or dull, he could go to her house and instruct her.

'I think,' said he at last to the imp, 'your idea an excellent one, and I will carry it out. As soon as my duties for the day are over, I will go to the Common and remain there a week at least, that is to say, if the priest will give me leave of absence for so long a time, of which I have little doubt. I will go immediately and ask him.'

So saying he left the house, after giving the pig its breakfast.

In the evening the sacristan returned to the house with a large bundle of warm clothing, some boiled bacon and ham, and bread enough to last him for several days, which he placed on the table, and a very small quantity of food for the pig, which he threw on the ground, and on which the pig began to feed ravenously. The sacristan then seated himself on the bed to recover his breath, for he was greatly fatigued with the exercise he had taken.

'What may those things be for?' said the imp, pointing to the bundle on the table.

'It is warm clothing,' said the sacristan, 'for the nights are cold.'

'That is hardly *en règle*,' said the imp; 'you ought to take nothing more with you than you have on. The ancient anchorites never had even a change of linen.'

'You forget,' said the sacristan, 'they lived in warmer climates, where it was not required; here, where it is colder, it would be allowed. I have well studied that question, and I know I am right.'

'And that other parcel, what may that contain?'

'Boiled bacon and ham, and bread.'

'That is not orthodox.'

'Why not?'

'If you are going to live the life of an anchorite, you must live upon herbs and roots, and drink nothing but water; and, by-the-bye, if I am not mistaken, I see something in your bundle the form of which is remarkably like that of a leathern bottle of wine.'

'I have received a dispensation from the priest to eat meat for the next fortnight, and the wine is to be taken occasionally on account of my weak state of health.'

'You hypocrite!' said the imp; 'you have imposed on the worthy priest. You know there is nothing the matter with you.'

'I scorn your imputation,' said the sacristan with much virtuous indignation in his tone; 'I have practised no imposition on the holy man whatever. I went to a leech and told him I felt in a very weak state of health, and I gave him a crown to give me a certificate that a course of animal food with wine was necessary for me, and this certificate I took to the priest, who, on the faith of it, gave me the dispensation. If there is any sin in the matter it is the doctor's, not mine—I took good care of that.'

'Upon my word,' said the imp, 'I begin to respect you. You are evidently a man after my own heart.'

'I consider your hatred,' said the sacristan, 'a far greater compliment than your love.'

The sacristan now made preparations for his journey, and left the house with the pig.

'*Bon voyage*,' said the imp; but he received no answer.

The sacristan and the pig made their way without much difficulty through the City, and even crossed the crowded thoroughfare of London Bridge without anything occurring particularly worthy of remark. When they arrived at the Borough Market things did not go on so well. The pig had had but a very scanty supper, and the quantity of vegetables he found strewed about in the market offered an amount of temptation he could not resist. The market at the time was crowded, and the pig, in its eagerness to obtain food, ran in the way of the merchants and purchasers, and in return got many and sundry hard kicks, which appeared not to agree with its constitution.

It is well known that even the best pigs, when hungry, have but little of the moral quality of integrity about them, and the one whose history we are recording formed no exception to the rule. Not content with picking up the refuse vegetables which lay strewn about, it had the imprudence to walk off with a fine cauliflower from a trader's basket. This was perceived, however, and the hue and cry was immediately raised. The cauliflower was taken from it, and a perfect shower of kicks was rained on its sides. Some enquired to whom the pig belonged, and one asked the sacristan if it was his. We are sorry to be obliged to say that he replied in the negative, and still more sorry to admit that while his pig was being assaulted in this cruel manner, he looked on without the slightest expression of indignation or compassion on his face, and at last turned on his heel and continued his road, letting his pig disengage itself from the crowd as best it could.

He had hardly arrived at Newington when the pig joined him, grunting in a most lamentable manner. As last the pair reached Kennington Common, and the sacristan made directly for the shed mentioned by the imp. He found it without any difficulty, and without allowing the pig time to make a choice, he appropriated the driest and warmest corner to himself. The pig offered no opposition, for the treatment it had received appeared to have taken every particle of courage out of it, and it threw itself down in an opposite corner, and was soon fast asleep. The sacristan now undid his wallet, and, after having made a hearty supper, he put on some warm clothing and went to sleep, having first hung his wallet and provisions under the roof so as to be out of the reach of the pig.

Next morning he found the imp in the shed, but the pig had sauntered out for the moment into a neighbouring turnip-field.

'So you arrived here safely?' said the imp to the sacristan, who was occupied with his breakfast. 'I followed you under the form of a dog the whole of the way, and I must say your conduct was most cowardly and disgraceful. You looked on with perfect indifference when the pig was being so horribly maltreated in the market.'

'That is not true,' said the sacristan; 'I assure you that I felt bitterly for the poor animal. I felt as much pain from every kick it received as if it had been inflicted on my own person; but I said to myself, Here is a trial for me, and it is my duty to support it meekly and with patience. And I flatter myself I did so admirably. When the kicks were being showered so cruelly on its sides I not only made no opposition, but, wishing to see how far my own self-denial would go, I said, Kick on.'

'And, pray, why did you deny being its master?'

'That I might not appear proud. Pride is a sin I despise.'

'Capital! Now, what do you intend to do this morning?—meditate, I suppose?'

'No,' said the sacristan with a sigh; 'I would willingly do so, but unfortunately I am unable. I have occasion to go into the City.'

'Nonsense, you know you have got leave of absence for a fortnight, and there is no occasion whatever for you to go there.'

'You are in error,' said the sacristan mildly, 'for go I must.'

'Might I ask on what errand?'

'To get some wine.'

'How preposterous!' said the imp; 'you brought enough with you to last a moderate man for three days at least.'

'Not under the circumstances in which I was placed,' said the sacristan. 'You forget how cold it was.'

'What, in the name of Fortune, has that to do with it? Do you think the anchorites of old drank wine in that manner?'

'Possibly not, very possibly not; but their case was very different. They did not suffer from cold, for they lived in a warm climate. I do not, and I am justified in taking as much wine while living in this open shed as shall raise the temperature of my body to an equality with that of theirs in the African desert; and that cannot be done under a bottle a day. Now I have only one leathern bottle in my possession, and therefore you yourself must perceive that I am obliged, though sorely against my inclination, to go to London every day.'

'That is very sad indeed,' said the imp; 'but do you not think the anchorites, had they been placed in your position, would have attempted to abstain from wine? Judging from what I have heard of them, I think they would.'

'I do not agree with you. Judging from my own conscientious feelings on the subject, I am decidedly of the opinion they would not; nor will I try it, lest I might fall into a grievous and sinful error.'

'And what may that be?'

'In thinking that so sinful a mortal as I am could surpass the sanctity of those venerable men. I am not sure that even making the attempt would not be a mortal sin, and I shall not try it.'

'Just as you please,' said the imp. 'When do you start?'

'Immediately. Now, my faithful companion,' he continued, addressing the pig, who had just returned from the turnip-field, where, judging from the rotundity of its person, it had made an excellent breakfast, 'let us start off for London at once, that we may have plenty of time to see the sights; that is to say, after I have called on a friend of mine who lives in St Nicholas in the Shambles.'

But the pig took no notice of the invitation, and stolidly prepared a bed for itself in the corner of the shed. Doubtless a vivid reminiscence of the Borough Market,—through which it would have to pass,—was still fresh in its memory.

It was nearly dark when the sacristan returned to the shed that evening. He appeared in perfect good humour with himself and all the world; and if his cheeks were not rosy his nose was certainly slightly so. Altogether he presented the appearance of a person who had drunk a trifle more than was absolutely necessary for him, without being at all intoxicated. He hung up a bottle of wine under the roof, with some ham and some bread, and then, seating himself in his corner, he attempted to meditate, but did not succeed. He felt that evening especially the want of society, for even the pig lay fast asleep beside him, after a hearty supper in the turnip-field. He would have felt more comfortable if the imp had been there, although expressly sent to tempt him. The feeling of *ennui* grew on him till he found it almost unsupportable, and at last he determined, although it was rather late in the day for a person connected with the church to call upon a lone woman, to pay the widow a visit, and talk with her on moral subjects. The resolution was no sooner formed than he rose from his seat to put it in practice, and putting his cap on his head in a jaunty manner, he left the house.

To his sore annoyance, however, the pig, which had been as still as a dormouse while he was in the shed, showed unusual signs of liveliness when he quitted it. It rose up, and, following him, gambolled round in front of him, impeding his walk, and grunting and ringing its bell in a most absurd manner. This enraged him excessively, for although he had nothing to be ashamed of in visiting the widow, still, when a man calls on the woman of his choice, he does not wish it to be trumpeted forth to all the world, in such a very ridiculous manner. He attempted to drive the pig back again without the slightest effect, and we are sorry to add made use of such language on the occasion as any well-disposed sacristan would be shocked to repeat. At the same time it is but just to state that, when he found he could not get the pig to forgo its intention by any possible entreaties and threats, he honestly begged its pardon, and allowed it to accompany him.

When they arrived at the widow's door the pig placed itself close against it, so as to be able to enter at the same time with its master. This annoyed the sacristan exceedingly; of course he could not allow the pig to enter, yet how to keep it out he did not know. The widow, who was rather of a timorous disposition, called out before opening the door,

'Who's there?'

The sacristan immediately answered that it was he, and that there was a pig outside which seemed desirous to enter. Was it hers?

'No,' she said; 'pray drive it away.'

'I have tried to do so,' said the sacristan, 'but I have not succeeded.'

'Wait a moment, I will see what I can do;' and a minute afterwards the widow opened the door. Armed with a besom, she dealt the pig a tremendous blow on the snout.

Now it is well known that a pig, which may be as bold as a lion on all other occasions, will not face a housewife with a besom. So the sacristan's pig started back, and howled terribly, while its master, profiting by its retreat, entered the house.

The sacristan found a warm, blazing fire in the widow's little sitting-room, and the table was spread out for her solitary supper. The place had a look of comfort about it which directly went to his heart, and he regretted that so amiable a person should have no one always at hand to talk to her on serious subjects, and advise her in the management of her affairs. She appeared much pleased to see him, the more so as that evening she had been reflecting on her solitary lot. She immediately placed another platter on the table, and produced some wine, which she kept by her to use medicinally, as occasion required. The sacristan was touched by her kindness. In return he talked to her very comfortably, showing her the folly of setting one's heart on sublunary things, and doing full justice to her provisions the while. He would have been perfectly happy had it not been for the incessant ringing of the pig's bell outside the house. The widow, in the course of conversation, asked him what he was doing in that out-of-the-way part of the world. He told her he had requested leave of absence from his priest, and that during it he was determined to pass the time in meditation amid the solitude of the Common. She admired his resolution, and said that at any time when he might feel dull, she would be happy to see him; for which he thanked her, with evident gratitude, and said he would willingly profit by her offer.

In this cozy manner the conversation continued for some time, till at last the widow asked where he intended passing the night. The sacristan was on the point of telling her about the shed, when he remembered she might call upon him there, and discover that he was the owner of the pig, which still kept up his annoyance by incessantly ringing its bell; so he checked himself, and said that it would be on any part of the Common where he could find a dry spot.

'But, my good soul,' said the widow, 'you will catch your death of cold there, for you are evidently far from strong. I will tell you what I will do. I will make up a little bed for you in the back room.'

Before the sacristan could explain how gratefully he accepted her offer, both he and the widow were startled by what at first they considered an unearthly noise, but afterwards found to be the pig howling tremendously, and furiously ringing its bell at the same time.

'Somebody must surely be killing that pig,' said the widow.

'Poor pig!' said the sacristan, with great resignation in his tone; 'it is very sad, but we should remember it is the lot of its race, and we ought to smother our feelings.'

The widow now left the room to prepare the bed, and in a few minutes again entered, saying that all was ready.

Terrible as had been the cries of the pig before, they were *sotto voce* compared with those it now uttered. They might with ease have been heard as far as Newington; and to add to the discomfort, the sacristan could easily perceive that they were gathering a crowd about the house. What to do he knew not. He was perfectly aware the pig would not cease its annoyance so long as he remained in the house, and he had not the heart to leave, he was so comfortable in it. He endeavoured to support the infliction for nearly an hour longer, when, fearing that the widow would feel irritated if the pig continued its cries, and as he particularly wished to stand well in her good graces, he told her that happy as he was it was hardly becoming an anchorite to indulge in so much luxury, and that with much genuine sorrow he must leave her. She attempted to dissuade him, but in vain; and, with a profusion of thanks for her kindness, he left the house.

He found in the road not only the pig, which was now silent, but a great crowd as well. He pushed through them and was soon lost to their sight in the darkness. He had hardly proceeded a hundred yards when the pig joined him. The sight of the poor animal put him into a great passion, and as a reward for its ill-timed services, he bestowed on its ribs a dozen hearty kicks, resolving in his mind that if he were acting wrongly he would repent of it afterwards.

When he arrived at the shed he went to his corner, and first took down his bottle of wine, which he placed by his side. He passed a large portion of the night in meditation, principally on the good qualities of the widow, with occasional thoughts on the pig. From time to time he put the bottle to his lips and took a hearty draught to keep the warmth of his person up to the same temperature as it would have reached in an African desert.

When day broke he found the imp in the shed, accompanied by two others, more hideous than himself.

'You passed a very respectable night for an anchorite,' said one.

'In what was I at fault?'

'Your treatment of your friend the pig was infamous. You know you do not love him.'

'I admit it,' said the sacristan. 'As an anchorite it is my duty to detach myself from earthly affections, and the pig is a mundane animal.'

'So is the widow,' said the imp.

'But the widow has a soul,' said the sacristan, 'and it is my duty to talk seriously to her.'

'And a pretty face, and money as well,' said the imp.

'You may attempt to disturb my meditations by talking of the widow and her attractions as much as you please,' said the sacristan, 'but you will not annoy me.'

'Of that I am perfectly persuaded,' said the imp; 'but we will talk of something else. How do you intend occupying yourself today?'

'I have to go to the City for some more wine.'

'Very like an anchorite, indeed,' said the imp; reversing the empty bottle, from which but one drop fell.

'If you can prove to me that the anchorites of old would not have done the same during a cold night on Kennington Common, I will leave it off; till then I shall continue it.'

So saying, he put on his cap and left the shed, the pig making no attempt to follow him.

The sacristan continued this method of life for two or three days longer. During the time he made several attempts to call on the widow, but each time the pig kept so close to his heels that he was obliged to desist. One calm moonlight night he thought he would take a walk. He strolled in the direction of Camberwell, the pig following him. Presently he saw two female figures a little in advance, and he hastened to overtake them. When he had reached them he found they were dressed like ladies, but so muffled up in coifs and cloaks that it was impossible for him to see whether they were young or old, handsome or ugly. He entered into conversation with them, and they answered him very courteously. He walked by their side, talking of the beauty of the night and other congenial subjects. They continued walking on, conversing very discreetly, the pig from time to time ringing its bell, not in an angry manner, but simply as if in doubt on some subject passing in its mind. They proceeded with their walk till it got very late, and the heavens became covered with thick clouds, which totally obscured the moon from their sight.

At last, when it was at least ten o'clock, the sacristan was on the point of stopping to wish his fair companions good night, as it was time for him to return, when they heard before them the sounds of a violin most exquisitely played, but they could not see the performer. They continued their road onwards, listening to the music (by-the-bye it was the same air the devil played to Tartini in his sleep some hundred years afterwards). A spell seemed to be on them, for they could not stop, but followed the invisible musician. The pig now began to be very uneasy, and rang its bell in an angry manner; the sacristan, however, paid no attention to it, but walked onwards.

In this manner they marched for at least two hours, when at last the sacristan found himself on the borders of Blackheath. One of his lady companions then said to him, 'We are going to a very pleasant party tonight a little way farther on. I wish you would accompany us; I am sure you would be well received, and you would have an opportunity of immensely improving the minds of the company.'

In spite of the anger of the pig the sacristan consented, and presently they found themselves in the midst of a circle brilliantly lit up. On one side was a raised orchestra for some musicians, all of whom were of the most extraordinary shapes with instruments as strange. Their music, however, was of the most delightful description, so much so as to dispel all fear on the part of the sacristan, and inspire him with a wish to dance. Presently the whole circle was filled with dancers, all of the most fantastic, and many even of the most horrible shapes; still he felt no fear, but stood aside wishing to join them. At last his two lady companions, who had been standing beside him, threw off their wrappers, and appeared in costumes so disgracefully *décolleté*, that the author declines to describe them. The ladies seized the sacristan each by a hand and drew him gently into the middle of the circle, and then commenced dancing. The orchestra at the time played more brilliantly than ever, while the poor pig ran round and round outside the circle, uttering the most discordant sounds and ringing its bell furiously. The sacristan now danced with all his might, his grotesque figure flying about in all directions, while he performed the most eccentric steps. He became more and more excited with the scene, and danced with still greater vigour. But in a moment the whole vanished, and he found himself in pitchy darkness in the midst of the heath, and in a pouring shower of rain. He listened for a moment for the bell of his pig, but it was no longer heard. The spell under which he had been labouring for some days past was broken, and he found he had been making a great fool of himself. With much difficulty he discovered the high road to London, and arrived at his lodgings about daybreak. The next morning he commenced a new life. He became, not superciliously pious, but a good charitable man, doing his duty in the church, giving alms of all he had to the poor, and contented with being thought no better than his neighbours.

CHARLES DICKENS

The Haunted House

THE MORTALS IN THE HOUSE

UNDER none of the accredited ghostly circumstances, and environed by none of the conventional ghostly surroundings, did I first make acquaintance with the house which is the subject of this Christmas piece. I saw it in the daylight, with the sun upon it. There was no wind, no rain, no lightning, no thunder, no awful or unwonted circumstance, of any kind, to heighten its effect. More than that: I had come to it direct from a railway station: it was not more than a mile distant from the railway station; and, as I stood outside the house, looking back upon the way I had come, I could see the goods train running smoothly along the embankment in the valley. I will not say that everything was utterly commonplace, because I doubt if anything can be that, except to utterly commonplace people—and there my vanity steps in; but, I will take it on myself to say that anybody might see the house as I saw it, any fine autumn morning.

The manner of my lighting on it was this.

I was travelling towards London out of the North, intending to stop by the way, to look at the house. My health required a temporary residence in the country; and a friend of mine who knew that, and who had happened to drive past the house, had written to me to suggest it as a likely place. I had got into the train at midnight, and had fallen asleep, and had woke up and had sat looking out of window at the brilliant Northern Lights in the sky, and had fallen asleep again, and had woke up again to find the night gone, with the usual discontented conviction on me that I hadn't been to sleep at all;—upon which question, in the first imbecility of that condition, I am ashamed to believe that I would have done wager by battle with the man who sat opposite me. That opposite man had had, through the night—as that opposite man always has—several legs too many, and all of them too long. In addition to this unreasonable conduct (which was only to be expected of him), he had had a pencil and a pocket-book, and had been per-petually listening and taking notes. It had appeared to me that these aggravating notes related to the jolts and bumps of the carriage, and I should have resigned myself to his taking them, under a general sup-position that he was in the civil-engineering way of life, if he had not sat staring straight over my head whenever he listened. He was a goggly-eyed gentleman of a perplexed aspect, and his demeanour became unbearable.

It was a cold, dead morning (the sun not being up yet), and when I had out-watched the paling light of the fires of the iron country, and the curtain of heavy smoke that hung at once between me and the stars and between me and the day, I turned to my fellow-traveller and said:

'I *beg* your pardon, Sir, but do you observe anything particular in me?' For, really, he appeared to be taking down, either my travelling-cap or my hair, with a minuteness that was a liberty.

The goggle-eyed gentleman withdrew his eyes from behind me, as if the back of the carriage were a hundred miles off, and said, with a lofty look of compassion for my insignificance:

'In you, Sir?—B.'

'B, Sir?' said I, growing warm.

'I have nothing to do with you, Sir,' returned the gentleman; 'pray let me listen—O.'

He enunciated this vowel after a pause, and noted it down.

At first I was alarmed, for an Express lunatic and no communication with the guard, is a serious position. The thought came to my relief that the gentleman might be what is popularly called a Rapper: one of a sect for (some of) whom I have the highest respect, but whom I don't believe in. I was going to ask him the question, when he took the bread out of my mouth.

'You will excuse me,' said the gentleman contemptuously, 'if I am too much in advance of common humanity to trouble myself at all about it. I have passed the night—as indeed I pass the whole of my time now—in spiritual intercourse.'

'O!' said I, something snappishly.

'The conferences of the night began,' continued the gentleman, turning several leaves of his note-book, 'with this message: "Evil com-munications corrupt good manners." '

'Sound,' said I; 'but, absolutely new?'

'New from spirits,' returned the gentleman.

I could only repeat my rather snappish 'O!' and ask if I might be favoured with the last communication.

'A bird in the hand,' said the gentleman, reading his last entry with great solemnity, 'is worth two in the Bosh.'

'Truly I am of the same opinion,' said I; 'but shouldn't it be Bush?'

'It came to me, Bosh,' returned the gentleman.

The gentleman then informed me that the spirit of Socrates had delivered this special revelation in the course of the night, 'My friend, I hope you are pretty well. There are two in this railway carriage. How do you do? There are seventeen thousand four hundred and seventy-nine spirits here, but you cannot see them. Pythagoras is here. He is not at liberty to mention it, but hopes you like travelling.' Galileo likewise had dropped in, with this scientific intelligence. 'I am glad to see you, *amico. Come sta?* Water will freeze when it is cold enough. *Addio!*' In the course of the night, also, the following phenomena had occurred. Bishop Butler had insisted on spelling his name, 'Bubler', for which offence against orthography and good manners he had been dismissed as out of temper. John Milton (suspected of wilful mystification) had repudiated the authorship of Paradise Lost, and had introduced, as joint authors of that poem, two Unknown gentlemen, respectively named Grungers and Scadgingtone. And Prince Arthur, nephew of King John of England, had described himself as tolerably comfortable in the seventh circle, where he was learning to paint on velvet, under the direction of Mrs Trimmer and Mary Queen of Scots.

If this should meet the eye of the gentleman who favoured me with these disclosures, I trust he will excuse my confessing that the sight of the rising sun, and the contemplation of the magnificent Order of the vast Universe, made me impatient of them. In a word, I was so impatient of them, that I was mightily glad to get out at the next station, and to exchange these clouds and vapours for the free air of Heaven.

By that time it was a beautiful morning. As I walked away among such leaves as had already fallen from the golden, brown, and russet trees; and as I looked around me on the wonders of Creation, and thought of the steady, unchanging, and harmonious laws by which they are sustained; the gentleman's spiritual intercourse seemed to me as poor a piece of journey-work as ever this world saw. In which heathen state of mind, I came within view of the house, and stopped to examine it attentively.

It was a solitary house, standing in a sadly neglected garden: a pretty even square of some two acres. It was a house of about the time of

George the Second; as stiff, as cold, as formal, and in as bad taste, as could possibly be desired by the most loyal admirer of the whole quartet of Georges. It was uninhabited, but had, within a year or two, been cheaply repaired to render it habitable; I say cheaply, because the work had been done in a surface manner, and was already decaying as to the paint and plaster, though the colours were fresh. A lop-sided board drooped over the garden wall, announcing that it was 'to let on very reasonable terms, well furnished'. It was much too closely and heavily shadowed by trees, and, in particular, there were six tall poplars before the front windows, which were excessively melancholy, and the site of which had been extremely ill chosen.

It was easy to see that it was an avoided house—a house that was shunned by the village, to which my eye was guided by a church spire some half a mile off—a house that nobody would take. And the natural inference was, that it had the reputation of being a haunted house.

No period within the four-and-twenty hours of day and night is so solemn to me, as the early morning. In the summertime, I often rise very early, and repair to my room to do a day's work before breakfast, and I am always on those occasions deeply impressed by the stillness and solitude around me. Besides that there is something awful in the being surrounded by familiar faces asleep—in the knowledge that those who are dearest to us and to whom we are dearest, are profoundly unconscious of us, in an impassive state, anticipative of that mysterious condition to which we are all tending—the stopped life, the broken threads of yesterday, the deserted seat, the closed book, the unfinished but abandoned occupation, all are images of Death. The tranquillity of the hour is the tranquillity of Death. The colour and the chill have the same association. Even a certain air that familiar household objects take upon them when they first emerge from the shadows of the night into the morning, of being newer, and as they used to be long ago, has its counterpart in the subsidence of the worn face of maturity or age, in death, into the old youthful look. Moreover, I once saw the apparition of my father, at this hour. He was alive and well, and nothing ever came of it, but I saw him in the daylight, sitting with his back towards me, on a seat that stood beside my bed. His head was resting on his hand, and whether he was slumbering or grieving, I could not discern. Amazed to see him there, I sat up, moved my position, leaned out of bed, and watched him. As he did not move then, I became alarmed and laid my hand upon his shoulder, as I thought—and there was no such thing.

For all these reasons, and for others less easily and briefly statable, I find the early morning to be my most ghostly time. Any house would be more or less haunted, to me, in the early morning; and a haunted house could scarcely address me to greater advantage than then.

I walked on into the village, with the desertion of this house upon my mind, and I found the landlord of the little inn, sanding his doorstep. I bespoke breakfast, and broached the subject of the house.

'Is it haunted?' I asked.

The landlord looked at me, shook his head, and answered, 'I say nothing.'

'Then it is haunted?'

'Well!' cried the landlord, in a outburst of frankness that had the appearances of desperation—'I wouldn't sleep in it.'

'Why not?'

'If I wanted to have all the bells in a house ring, with nobody to ring 'em; and all the doors in a house bang, with nobody to bang 'em; and all sorts of feet treading about, with no feet there; why, then,' said the landlord, 'I'd sleep in that house.'

'Is anything seen there?'

The landlord looked at me again, and then, with his former appearance of desperation, called down his stable-yard for 'Ikey!'

The call produced a high-shouldered young fellow, with a round red face, a short crop of sandy hair, a very broad humorous mouth, a turned-up nose, and a great sleeved waistcoat of purple bars, with mother-of-pearl buttons, that seemed to be growing upon him, and to be in a fair way—if it were not pruned—of covering his head and overrunning his boots.

'This gentleman wants to know,' said the landlord, 'if anything's seen at the Poplars.'

' 'Ooded woman with a howl,' said Ikey, in a state of great freshness.

'Do you mean a cry?'

'I mean a bird, Sir.'

'A hooded woman with an owl. Dear me! Did you ever see her?'

'I seen the howl.'

'Never the woman?'

'Not so plain as the howl, but they always keeps together.'

'Has anybody ever seen the woman as plainly as the owl?'

'Lord bless you, Sir! Lots.'

'Who?'

'Lord bless you, Sir! Lots.'

'The general-dealer opposite, for instance, who is opening his shop?'

'Perkins? Bless you, Perkins wouldn't go a-nigh the place. No!' observed the young man, with considerable feeling; 'he an't over wise, an't Perkins, but he an't such a fool as *that*.'

(Here, the landlord murmured his confidence in Perkins's knowing better.)

'Who is—or who was—the hooded woman with the owl? Do you know?'

'Well!' said Ikey, holding up his cap with one hand while he scratched his head with the other, 'they say, in general, that she was murdered, and the howl he 'ooted the while.'

This very concise summary of the facts was all I could learn, except that a young man, as hearty and likely a young man as ever I see, had been took with fits and held down in 'em, after seeing the hooded woman. Also, that a personage, dimly described as 'a hold chap, a sort of one-eyed tramp, answering to the name of Joby, unless you challenged him as Greenwood, and then he said, "Why not? and even if so, mind your own business"', had encountered the hooded woman, a matter of five or six times: But, I was not materially assisted by these witnesses: inasmuch as the first was in California, and the last was, as Ikey said (and he was confirmed by the landlord), Anywheres.

Now, although I regard with a hushed and solemn fear, the mysteries, between which and this state of existence is interposed the barrier of the great trial and change that fall on all the things that live; and although I have not the audacity to pretend that I know anything of them; I can no more reconcile the more banging of doors, ringing of bells, creaking of boards, and such-like insignificances, with the majestic beauty and pervading analogy of all the Divine rules that I am permitted to understand, than I had been able, a little while before, to yoke the spiritual intercourse of my fellow-traveller to the chariot of the rising sun. Moreover, I had lived in two haunted houses—both abroad. In one of these, an old Italian palace, which bore the reputation of being twice abandoned on that account, I lived eight months, most tranquilly and pleasantly: notwithstanding that the house had a score of mysterious bedrooms, which were never used, and possessed, in one large room in which I sat reading, times out of number at all hours, and next to which I slept, a haunted chamber of the first pretensions. I gently hinted these considerations to the landlord. And as to this particular house having a bad name, I reasoned with him, Why, how many things had bad names undeservedly, and how easy it was to give bad names, and did he not think that if he and I were persistently to whisper in the village that any weird-looking old drunken tinker of the neighbourhood had sold himself to the Devil, he would come in time to be suspected, of that commercial venture! All this wise talk was perfectly ineffective with the landlord, I am bound to confess, and was as dead a failure as ever I made in my life.

To cut this part of the story short, I was piqued about the haunted house, and was already half resolved to take it. So, after breakfast, I got the keys from Perkins's brother-in-law (a whip and harness maker, who keeps the Post Office, and is under submission to a most rigorous wife of the Doubly Seceding Little Emmanuel persuasion), and went up to the house, attended by my landlord and by Ikey.

Within, I found it, as I had expected, transcendently dismal. The slowly changing shadows waved on it from the heavy trees, were doleful in the last degree; the house was ill-placed, ill-built, ill-planned, and ill-fitted. It was damp, it was not free from dry rot, there was a flavour of rats in it, and it was the gloomy victim of that indescribable decay which settles on all the work of man's hands whenever it is not turned to man's account. The kitchens and offices were too large, and too remote from each other. Above stairs and below, waste tracts of passage intervened between patches of fertility represented by rooms; and there was a mouldy old well with a green growth upon it, hiding like a murderous trap, near the bottom of the back stairs, under the double row of bells. One of these bells was labelled, on a black ground in faded white letters, MASTER B. This, they told me, was the bell that rang the most.

'Who was Master B.?' I asked. 'Is it known what he did while the owl hooted?'

'Rang the bell,' said Ikey.

I was rather struck by the prompt dexterity with which this young man pitched his fur cap at the bell, and rang it himself. It was a loud, unpleasant bell, and made a very disagreeable sound. The other bells were inscribed according to the names of the rooms to which their wires were conducted: as 'Picture Room', 'Double Room', 'Clock Room', and the like. Following Master B.'s bell to its source, I found that young gentleman to have had but indifferent third-class accommodation in a triangular cabin under the cock-loft, with a corner fireplace which Master B. must have been exceedingly small if he were ever able to warm himself at, and a corner chimneypiece like a pyramidal staircase to the ceiling for Tom Thumb. The papering of one side of the room had dropped down bodily, with fragments of plaster adhering to it, and almost blocked up the door. It appeared that Master B., in his spiritual condition, always made a point of pulling the paper down. Neither the landlord nor Ikey could suggest why he made such a fool of himself.

Except that the house had an immensely large rambling loft at top, I made no other discoveries. It was moderately well furnished, but sparely. Some of the furniture—say, a third—was as old as the house; the rest was of various periods within the last half-century. I was referred to a corn-chandler in the market-place of the country town to treat for the house. I went that day, and I took it for six months.

It was just the middle of October when I moved in with my maiden sister (I venture to call her eight-and-thirty, she is so very handsome, sensible, and engaging). We took with us, a deaf stable-man, my bloodhound Turk, two women servants, and a young person called an Odd Girl. I have reason to record of the attendant last enumerated, who was one of the Saint Lawrence's Union Female Orphans, that she was a fatal mistake and a disastrous engagement.

The year was dying early, the leaves were falling fast, it was a raw cold day when we took possession, and the gloom of the house was most depressing. The cook (an amiable woman, but of a weak turn of intellect) burst into tears on beholding the kitchen, and requested that her silver watch might be delivered over to her sister (2 Tuppintock's Gardens, Liggs's Walk, Clapham Rise), in the event of anything happening to her from the damp. Streaker, the housemaid, feigned cheerfulness, but was the greater martyr. The Odd Girl, who had never been in the country, alone was pleased and made arrangements for sowing an acorn in the garden outside the scullery window, and rearing an oak.

We went, before dark, through all the natural—as opposed to supernatural—miseries incidental to our state. Dispiriting reports ascended (like the smoke) from the basement in no rolling-pin, there was no salamander (which failed to surprise me, for I don't know what it is), there was nothing in the house, what there was, was broken, the last people must have lived like pigs, what could the meaning of the landlord be? Through these distresses, the Odd Girl was cheerful and exemplary. But within four hours after dark we had got into a supernatural groove, and the Odd Girl had seen 'Eyes', and was in hysterics.

My sister and I had agreed to keep the haunting strictly to ourselves, and my impression was, and still is, that I had not left Ikey, when he helped to unload the cart, alone with the woman, or any one of them, for one minute. Nevertheless, as I say, the Odd Girl had 'seen Eyes' (no other explanation could ever be drawn from her), before nine, and by ten o'clock had had as much vinegar applied to her as would pickle a handsome salmon.

I leave a discerning public to judge of my feelings, when, under these untoward circumstances, at about half-past ten o'clock Master B.'s bell began to ring in a most infuriated manner, and Turk howled until the house resounded with his lamentations!

I hope I may never again be in a state of mind so unchristian as the mental frame in which I lived for some weeks, respecting the memory of Master B. Whether his bell was rung by rats, or mice, or bats, or wind, or what other accidental vibration or sometimes by one cause, sometimes another, and sometimes by collusion, I don't know; but, certain it is, that it did ring two nights out of three, until I conceived the happy idea of twisting Master B.'s neck—in other words, breaking his bell short off—and silencing that young gentleman, as to my experience and belief, for ever.

But, by that time, the Odd Girl had developed such improving powers of catalepsy, that she had become a shining example of that very inconvenient disorder. She would stiffen, like a Guy Fawkes endowed with unreason, on the most irrelevant occasions. I would address the servants in a lucid manner, pointing out to them that I had painted Master B.'s room and balked the paper, and taken Master B.'s bell away and balked the ringing, and if they could suppose that that confounded boy had lived and died, to clothe himself with no better behaviour than would most unquestionably have brought him and the sharpest particles of a birch-broom into close acquaintance in the present imperfect state of existence, could they also suppose a mere poor human being, such as I was, capable by those contemptible means of counteracting and limiting the powers of the disembodied spirits of the dead, or of any spirits?—I say I would become emphatic and cogent, not to say rather complacent, in such an address, when it would all go for nothing by reason of the Odd Girl's suddenly stiffening from the toes upward, and glaring among us like a parochial petrifaction.

Streaker, the housemaid, too, had an attribute of a most discomfiting nature. I am unable to say whether she was of an unusually lymphatic temperament, or what else was the matter with her, but this young woman became a mere Distillery for the production of the largest and most transparent tears I ever met with. Combined with these character-istics, was a peculiar tenacity of hold in those specimens, so that they didn't fall, but hung upon her face and nose. In this condition, and mildly and deplorably shaking her head, her silence would throw me more heavily than the Admirable Crichton could have done in a verbal disputation for a purse of money. Cook, likewise, always covered me with confusion as with a garment, by neatly winding up the session with the protest that the Ouse was wearing her out, and by meekly repeating her last wishes regarding her silver watch.

As to our nightly life, the contagion of suspicion and fear was among us, and there is no such contagion under the sky. Hooded woman? According to the accounts, we were in a perfect Convent of hooded women. Noises? With that contagion downstairs, I myself have sat in the dismal parlour, listening, until I have heard so many and such strange noises, that they would have chilled my blood if I had not warmed it by dashing out to make discoveries. Try this in bed, in the dead of the night; try this at your own comfortable fireside, in the life of the night. You can fill any house with noises, if you will, until you have a noise for every nerve in your nervous system.

I repeat; the contagion of suspicion and fear was among us, and there is no such contagion under the sky. The women (their noses in a chronic state of excoriation from smelling-salts) were always primed and loaded for a swoon, and ready to go off with hair-triggers. The two elder detached the Odd Girl on all expeditions that were considered doubly hazardous, and she always established the reputation of such adventures by coming back cataleptic. If Cook or Streaker went over-head after dark, we knew we should presently hear a bump on the ceil-ing; and this took place so constantly, that it was as if a fighting man were engaged to go about the house, administering a touch of his art which I believe is called The Auctioneer, to every domestic he met with.

It was in vain to do anything. It was in vain to be frightened, for the moment in one's own person, by a real owl, and then to show the owl. It was in vain to discover, by striking an accidental discord on the piano, that Turk always howled at particular notes and combinations. It was in vain to be a Rhadamanthus with the bells, and if an unfortunate bell rang without leave, to have it down inexorably and silence it. It was in vain to fire up chimneys, let torches down the well, charge furiously into suspected rooms and recesses. We changed servants, and it was no better. The new set ran away, and a third set came, and it was no better. At last, our comfortable housekeeping got to be so disorganized and wretched, that I one night dejectedly said to my sister: 'Patty, I begin to despair of our getting people to go on with us here, and I think we must give this up.'

My sister, who is a woman of immense spirit, replied, 'No, John, don't give it up. Don't be beaten, John. There is another way.'

'And what is that?' said I.

'John,' returned my sister, 'if we are not to be driven out of this house, and that for no reason whatever, that is apparent to you or me, we must help ourselves and take the house wholly and solely into our own hands.'

'But, the servants,' said I.

'Have no servants,' said my sister, boldly.

Like most people in my grade of life, I had never thought of the possibility of going on without those faithful obstructions. The notion was so new to me when suggested, that I looked very doubtful.

'We know they come here to be frightened and infect one another, and we know they are frightened and do infect one another,' said my sister.

'With the exception of Bottles,' I observed, in a meditative tone.

(The deaf stable-man. I kept him in my service, and still keep him, as a phenomenon of moroseness not to be matched in England.)

'To be sure, John,' assented by sister; 'except Bottles. And what does that go to prove? Bottles talks to nobody, and hears nobody unless he is absolutely roared at, and what alarm has Bottles ever given, or taken? None.'

This was perfectly true; the individual in question having retired, every night at ten o'clock, to his bed over the coach-house, with no other company than a pitchfork and a pail of water. That the pail of water would have been over me, and the pitchfork through me, if I had put myself without announcement in Bottles's way after that minute, I had deposited in my own mind as a fact worth remembering. Neither had Bottles ever taken the least notice of any of our many uproars. An imperturbable and speechless man, he had sat at his supper, with Streaker present in a swoon, and the Odd Girl marble, and had only put another potato in his cheek, or profited by the general misery to help himself to beefsteak pie.

'And so,' continued my sister, 'I exempt Bottles. And considering, John, that the house is too large, and perhaps too lonely, to be kept well in hand by Bottles, you, and me, I propose that we cast about among our friends for a certain selected number of the most reliable and willing— form a Society here for three months—wait upon ourselves and one another—live cheerfully and socially—and see what happens.'

I was so charmed with my sister, that I embraced her on the spot, and went into her plan with the greatest ardour.

We were then in the third week of November; but, we took our measures so vigorously, and were so well seconded by the friends in whom we confided, that there was still a week of the month unexpired, when our party all came down together merrily, and mustered in the haunted house.

I will mention, in this place, two small changes that I made while my sister and I were yet alone. It occurring to me as not improbable that Turk howled in the house of night, partly because he wanted to get out of it, I stationed him in his kennel outside, but unchained; and I seriously warned the village that any man who came in his way must not expect to leave him without a rip in his own throat. I then casually asked Ikey if he were a judge of a gun? On his saying, 'Yes, Sir, I knows a good gun when I sees her,' I begged the favour of his stepping up to the house and looking at mine.

'*She's* a true one, Sir,' said Ikey, after inspecting a double-barrelled rifle that I bought in New York a few years ago. 'No mistake about *her*, Sir.'

'Ikey,' said I, 'don't mention it; I have seen something in this house.'

'No, Sir?' he whispered, greedily opening his eyes. ' 'Ooded lady, Sir?'

'Don't be frightened,' said I. 'It was a figure rather like you.'

'Lord, Sir?'

'Ikey!' said I, shaking hands with him warmly: I may say affectionately; 'if there is any truth in these ghost-stories, the greatest service I can do you, is, to fire at that figure. And I promise you, by Heaven and earth, I will do it with this gun if I see it again!'

The young man thanked me, and took his leave with some little precipitation, after declining a glass of liquor. I imparted my secret to him, because I had never quite forgotten his throwing his cap at the bell; because I had, on another occasion, noticed something very like a fur cap, lying not far from the bell, one night when it had burst out ringing;

and because I had remarked that we were at our ghostliest whenever he came up in the evening to comfort the servants. Let me do Ikey no injustice. He was afraid of the house, and believed in its being haunted; and yet he would play false on the haunting side, so surely as he got an opportunity. The Odd Girl's case was exactly similar. She went about the house in a state of real terror, and yet lied monstrously and wilfully, and invented many of the alarms she spread, and made many of the sounds we heard. I had had my eye on the two, and I know it. It is not necessary for me, here to account for this preposterous state of mind; I content myself with remarking that it is familiarly known to every intelligent man who has had fair medical, legal, or other watchful experience; that it is as well established and as common a state of mind as any with which observers are acquainted; and that it is one of the first elements, above all others, rationally to be suspected in, and strictly looked for, and separated from, any question of this kind.

To return to our party. The first thing we did when we were all assembled, was, to draw lots for bedrooms. That done, and every bedroom, and indeed, the whole house, having been minutely examined by the whole body, we allotted the various household duties, as if we had been on a gipsy party, or a yachting party, or a hunting party, or were shipwrecked. I then recounted the floating rumours concerning the hooded lady, the owl, and Master B.: with others, still more filmy, which had floated about during our occupation, relative to some ridiculous old ghost of the female gender who went up and down, carrying the ghost of a round table; and also to an impalpable Jackass, whom nobody was ever able to catch. Some of these ideas I really believe our people below had communicated to one another in some diseased way, without conveying them in words. We then gravely called one another to witness, that we were not there to be deceived, or to deceive—which we considered pretty much the same thing—and that, with a serious sense of responsibility, we would be strictly true to one another, and would strictly follow out the truth. The understanding was established, that any one who heard unusual noises in the night, and who wished to trace them, should knock at my door; lastly, that on Twelfth Night, the last night of holy Christmas, all our individual experiences since that then present hour of our coming together in the haunted house, should be brought to light for the good of all; and that we would hold our peace on the subject till then, unless on some remarkable provocation to break silence.

We were, in number and in character, as follows:

First—to get my sister and myself out of the way—there were we two. In the drawing of lots, my sister drew her own room, and I drew Master B.'s. Next, there was our first cousin John Herschel, so called after the great astronomer: than whom I suppose a better man at a telescope does not breathe. With him, was his wife: a charming creature to whom he had been married in the previous spring. I thought him (under the circumstances) rather imprudent to bring her, because there is no knowing what even a false alarm may do at such a time; but I suppose he knew his own business best, and I must say that if she had been *my* wife, I never could have left her endearing and bright face behind. They drew the Clock Room. Alfred Starling, an uncommonly agreeable young fellow of eight-and-twenty for whom I have the greatest liking, was in the Double Room; mine, usually, and designated by that name from having a dressing-room within it, with two large and cumbersome windows, which no wedges I was ever able to make, would keep from shaking, in any weather, wind or no wind. Alfred is a young fellow who pretends to be 'fast' (another word for loose, as I understand the term), but who is much too good and sensible for that nonsense, and who would have distinguished himself before now, if his father had not unfortunately left him a small independence of two hundred a year, on the strength of which his only occupation in life has been to spend six. I am in hopes, however, that this Banker may break, or that he may enter into some speculation guaranteed to pay twenty per cent.; for, I am convinced that if he could only be ruined, his fortune is made. Belinda Bates, bosom friend of my sister, and a most intellectual, amiable, and delightful girl, got the Picture Room. She has a fine genius for poetry, combined with real business earnestness, and 'goes in'—to use an expression of Alfred's—for Woman's mission, Woman's rights, Woman's wrongs, and everything that is woman's with a capital W, or is not and ought to be, or is and ought not to be. 'Most praiseworthy, my dear, and Heaven prosper yet!' I whispered to her on the first night of my taking leave of her at the Picture-Room door, 'but don't overdo it. And in respect of the great necessity there is, my darling, for more employments being within the reach of Woman than our civilization has as yet assigned to her, don't fly at the unfortunate men, even those men who are at first sight in your way, as if they were the natural oppressors of your sex; for, trust me, Belinda, they do sometimes spend their wages among wives and daughters, sisters, mothers, aunts, and grandmothers; and the play is, really, not *all* Wolf and Red Riding-Hood, but has other parts in it.' However, I digress.

Belinda, as I have mentioned, occupied the Picture Room. We had but three chambers: the Corner Room, the Cupboard Room, and the Garden Room. My old friend, Jack Governor, 'slung his hammock', as he called it, in the Corner Room. I have always regarded Jack as the finest-looking sailor that ever sailed. He is gray now, but as handsome as he was a quarter of a century ago—nay, handsomer. A portly, cheery, well-built figure of a broad-shouldered man, with a frank smile, as brilliant dark eye, and a rich dark eyebrow. I remember those under darker hair, and they look all the better for their silver setting. He has been wherever his Union namesake flies, has Jack, and I have met old shipmates of his, away in the Mediterranean and on the other side of the Atlantic, who have beamed and brightened at the casual mention of this name, and have cried, 'You know Jack Governor? Then you know a prince of men!' That he is! And so unmistakably a naval officer, that if you were to meet him coming out of an Esquimaux snow-hut in seal's skins, you would be vaguely persuaded he was in full naval uniform.

Jack once had that bright clear eye of his on my sister; but, it fell out that he married another lady and took her to South America, where she died. This was a dozen years ago or more. He brought down with him to our haunted house a little cask of salt beef; for, he is always convinced that all salt beef not of his own pickling, is mere carrion, and invariably, when he goes to London, packs a piece in his portmanteau. He had also volunteered to bring with him one 'Nat Beaver', an old comrade of his, captain of a merchantman. Mr Beaver, with a thick-set wooden face and figure, and apparently as hard as a block all over, proved to be an intelligent man, with a world of watery experiences in him, and great practical knowledge. At times, there was a curious nervousness about him, apparently the lingering result of some old illness; but, it seldom lasted many minutes. He got the Cupboard Room, and lay there next to Mr Undery, my friend and solicitor: who came down, in an amateur capacity, 'to go through with it', as he said, and who plays whist better than the whole Law List, from the red cover at the beginning to the red cover at the end.

I never was happier in my life, and I believe it was the universal feeling among us. Jack Governor, always a man of wonderful resources, was Chief Cook, and made some of the best dishes I ever ate, including unapproachable curries. My sister was pastrycook and confectioner.

Starling and I were Cook's Mate, turn and turn about, and on special occasions the chief cook 'pressed' Mr Beaver. We had a great deal of out-door sport and exercise, but nothing was neglected within, and there was no ill-humour or misunderstanding among us, and our evenings were so delightful that we had at least one good reason for being reluctant to go to bed.

We had a few night alarms in the beginning. On the first night, I was knocked up by Jack with a most wonderful ship's lantern in his hand, like the gills of some monster of the deep, who informed me that he 'was going aloft to the main truck', to have the weathercock down. It was a stormy night, and I remonstrated; but Jack called my attention to its making a sound like a cry of despair, and said somebody would be 'hailing a ghost' presently, if it wasn't done. So, up to the top of the house, where I could hardly stand for the wind, we went, accompanied by Mr Beaver; and there Jack, lantern and all, with Mr Beaver after him, swarmed up to the top of a cupola, some two dozen feet above the chimneys, and stood upon nothing particular, coolly knocking the weathercock off, until they both got into such good spirits with the wind and the height, that I thought they would never come down. Another night, they turned out again, and had a chimney-cowl off. Another night, they cut a sobbing and gulping water-pipe away. Another night, they found out something else. On several occasions, they both, in the coolest manner, simultaneously dropped out of their respective bedroom windows, hand over hand by their counterpanes, to 'overhaul' something mysterious in the garden.

The engagement among us was faithfully kept, and nobody revealed anything. All we knew was, if any one's room were haunted, no one looked the worse for it.

THE GHOST IN MASTER B.'S ROOM

When I established myself in the triangular garret which had gained so distinguished a reputation, my thoughts naturally turned to Master B. My speculations about him were uneasy and manifold. Whether his Christian name was Benjamin, Bissextile (from his having been born in Leap Year), Bartholomew, or Bill. Whether the initial letter belonged to his family name, and that was Baxter, Black, Brown, Barker, Buggins, Baker, or Bird. Whether he was a foundling, and had been baptized B. Whether he was a lion-hearted boy, and B. was short for Briton, or for Bull. Whether he could possibly have been kith and kin to an illustrious lady who brightened my own childhood, and had come of the blood of the brilliant Mother Bunch?

With these profitless meditations I tormented myself much. I also carried the mysterious letter into the appearance and pursuits of the deceased; wondering whether he dressed in Blue, wore Boots (he couldn't have been Bald), was a boy of Brains, liked Books, was good at Bowling, had any skill as a Boxer, even in his Buoyant Boyhood Bathed from a Bathing-machine at Bognor, Bangor, Bournemouth, Brighton, or Broadstairs, like a Bounding Billiard Ball?

So, from the first, I was haunted by the letter B.

It was not long before I remarked that I never by any hazard had a dream of Master B., or of anything belonging to him. But, the instant I awoke from sleep, at whatever hour of the night, my thoughts took him up, and roamed away, trying to attach his initial letter to something that would fit it and keep it quiet.

For six nights, I had been worried thus in Master B.'s room, when I began to perceive that things were going wrong.

The first appearance that presented itself was early in the morning when it was but just daylight and no more. I was standing shaving at my glass, when I suddenly discovered, to my consternation and amazement, that I was shaving—not myself—I am fifty—but a boy. Apparently Master B.!

I trembled and looked over my shoulder; nothing there. I looked again in the glass, and distinctly saw the features and expression of a boy, who was shaving, not to get rid of a beard, but to get one. Extremely troubled in my mind, I took a few turns in the room, and went back to the looking-glass, resolved to steady my hand and complete the operation in which I had been disturbed. Opening my eyes, which I had shut while recovering my firmness, I now met in the glass, looking straight at me, the eyes of a young man of four or five and twenty. Terrified by this new ghost, I closed my eyes, and made a strong effort to recover myself. Opening them again, I saw, shaving his cheek in the glass, my father, who has long been dead. Nay, I even saw my grandfather too, whom I never did see in my life.

Although naturally much affected by these remarkable visitations, I determined to keep my secret, until the time agreed upon for the present general disclosure. Agitated by a multitude of curious thoughts, I retired to my room, that night, prepared to encounter some new experience of a spectral character. Nor was my preparation needless, for, waking from an uneasy sleep at exactly two o'clock in the morning, what were my feelings to find that I was sharing my bed with the skeleton of Master B.!

I sprang up, and the skeleton sprang up also. I then heard a plaintive voice saying, 'Where am I! What is become of me?' and, looking hard in that direction, perceived the ghost of Master B.

The young spectre was dressed in an obsolete fashion: or rather, was not so much dressed as put into a case of inferior pepper-and-salt cloth, made horrible by means of shining buttons. I observed that these buttons went, in a double row, over each shoulder of the young ghost, and appeared to descend his back. He wore a frill round his neck. His right hand (which I distinctly noticed to be inky) was laid upon his stomach; connecting this action with some feeble pimples on his countenance, and his general air of nausea, I concluded this ghost to be the ghost of a boy who had habitually taken a great deal too much medicine.

'Where am I?' said the little spectre, in a pathetic voice. 'And why was I born in the Calomel days, and why did I have all that Calomel given me?'

I replied, with sincere earnestness, that upon my soul I couldn't tell him.

'Where is my little sister,' said the ghost, 'and where my angelic little wife, and where is the boy I went to school with?'

I entreated the phantom to be comforted, and above all things to take heart respecting the loss of the boy he went to school with. I represented to him that probably that boy never did, within human experience, come out well, when discovered. I urged that I myself had, in later life, turned up several boys whom I went to school with, and none of them had at all answered. I expressed my humble belief that the boy never did answer. I represented that he was a mythic character, a delusion, and a snare. I recounted how, the last time I found him, I found him at a dinner party behind a wall of white cravat, with an inconclusive opinion on every possible subject, and a power of silent boredom absolutely Titanic. I related how, on the strength of our having been together at 'Old Doylance's', he had asked himself to breakfast with me (a social offence of the largest magnitude); how, fanning my weak embers of belief in Doylance's boys, I had let him in; and how he had proved to be a fearful wanderer about the earth, pursuing the race of Adam with inexplicable notions concerning the currency, and with a proposition that the Bank of England should, on pain of being abolished, instantly strike off and circulate, God knows how many thousand millions of ten-and-sixpenny notes.

The ghost heard me in silence, and with a fixed stare. 'Barber!' it apostrophized me when I had finished.

'Barber?' I repeated—for I am not of that profession.

'Condemned,' said the ghost, 'to shave a constant change of customers—now, me—now, a young man—now, thyself as thou art—now, thy father—now, thy grandfather; condemned, too, to lie down with a skeleton every night, and to rise with it every morning—'

(I shuddered on hearing this dismal announcement.)

'Barber! Pursue me!'

I had felt, even before the words were uttered, that I was under a spell to pursue the phantom. I immediately did so, and was in Master B.'s room no longer.

Most people know what long and fatiguing night journeys had been forced upon the witches who used to confess, and who, no doubt, told the exact truth—particularly as they were always assisted with leading questions, and the Torture was always ready. I asseverate that, during my occupation of Master B.'s room, I was taken by the ghost that haunted it, on expeditions fully as long and wild as any of those. Assuredly, I was presented to no shabby old man with a goat's horns and tail (something between Pan and an old clothesman), holding conventional receptions, as stupid as those of real life and less decent; but, I came upon other things which appeared to me to have more meaning.

Confident that I speak the truth and shall be believed, I declare without hesitation that I followed the ghost, in the first instance on a broom-stick, and afterwards on a rocking-horse. The very smell of the animal's paint—especially when I brought it out, by making him warm—I am ready to swear to. I followed the ghost, afterwards, in a hackney coach; an institution with the peculiar smell of which, the present generation is unacquainted, but to which I am again ready to swear as a combination of stable, dog with the mange, and very old bellows. (In this, I appeal to previous generations to confirm or refute me.) I pursued the phantom, on a headless donkey: at least, upon a donkey who was so interested in the state of his stomach that his head was always down there, investigating it; on ponies, expressly born to kick up behind; on roundabouts and swings, from fairs; in the first cab—another forgotten institution where the fare regularly got into bed, and was tucked up with the driver.

Not to trouble you with a detailed account of all my travels in pursuit of the ghost of Master B., which were longer and more wonderful than those of Sinbad the Sailor, I will confine myself to one experience from which you may judge of many.

I was marvellously changed. I was myself, yet not myself. I was conscious of something within me, which has been the same all through my life, and which I have always recognized under all its phases and varieties as never altering, and yet I was not the I who had gone to bed in Master B.'s room. I had the smoothest of faces and the shortest of legs, and I had taken another creature like myself, also with the smoothest of faces and the shortest of legs, behind a door, and was confiding to him a proposition of the most astounding nature.

This proposition was, that we should have a Seraglio.

The other creature assented warmly. He had no notion of respectability, neither had I. It was the custom of the East, it was the way of the good Caliph Haroun Alraschid (let me have the corrupted name again for once, it is so scented with sweet memories!), the usage was highly laudable, and most worthy of imitation. 'O, yes! Let us,' said the other creature with a jump, 'have a Seraglio.'

It was not because we entertained the faintest doubts of the meritorious character of the Oriental establishment we proposed to import, that we perceived it must be kept a secret from Miss Griffin. It was because we knew Miss Griffin to be bereft of human sympathies, and incapable of appreciating the greatness of the great Haroun. Mystery impenetrably shrouded from Miss Griffin then, let us entrust it to Miss Bule.

We were ten in Miss Griffin's establishment by Hampstead Ponds; eight ladies and two gentlemen. Miss Bule, whom I judged to have attained the ripe age of eight or nine, took the lead in society. I opened the subject to her in the course of the day, and proposed that she should become the Favourite.

Miss Bule, after struggling with the diffidence so natural to, and charming in, her adorable sex, expressed herself as flattered by the idea, but wished to know how it was proposed to provide for Miss Pipson? Miss Bule—who was understood to have vowed towards that young lady, a friendship, halves, and no secrets, until death, on the Church Service and Lessons complete in two volumes with case and lock—Miss Bule said she could not, as the friend of Pipson, disguise from herself, or me, that Pipson was not one of the common.

Now, Miss Pipson, having curly light hair and blue eyes (which was my idea of anything mortal and feminine that was called Fair), I promptly replied that I regarded Miss Pipson in the light of a Fair Circassian.

'And what then?' Miss Bule pensively asked.

I replied that she must be inveigled by a Merchant, brought to me veiled, and purchased as a slave.

(The other creature had already fallen into the second male place in the State, and was set apart for Grand Vizier. He afterwards resisted this disposal of events, but had his hair pulled until he yielded.)

'Shall I not be jealous?' Miss Bule enquired, casting down her eyes.

'Zobeide, no,' I replied; 'you will ever be the favourite Sultana; the first place in my heart, and on my throne, will be ever yours.'

Miss Bule, upon that assurance, consented to propound the idea to her seven beautiful companions. It occurring to me, in the course of the same day, that we knew we could trust a grinning and good-natured soul called Tabby, who was the serving drudge of the house, and had no more figure than one of the beds, and upon whose face there was always more or less black-lead, I slipped into Miss Bule's hand after supper, a little note to that effect: dwelling on the black-lead as being in a manner deposited by the finger of Providence, pointing Tabby out for Mesrour, the celebrated chief of the Blacks of the Hareem.

There were difficulties in the formation of the desired institution, as there are in all combinations. The other creature showed himself of a low character, and, when defeated in aspiring to the throne, pretended to have conscientious scruples about prostrating himself before the Caliph; wouldn't call him Commander of the Faithful; spoke of him slightingly and inconsistently as a mere 'chap'; said he, the other creature, 'wouldn't play'—Play! and was otherwise coarse and offensive. This meanness of disposition was, however, put down by the general indignation of an united Seraglio, and I became blessed in the smiles of eight of the fairest of the daughters of men.

The smiles could only be bestowed when Miss Griffin was looking another way, and only then in very wary manner, for there was a legend among the followers of the Prophet that she saw with a little round ornament in the middle of the pattern on the back of her shawl. But every day after dinner, for an hour, we were all together, and then the Favourite and the rest of the Royal Hareem competed who should most beguile the leisure of the Serene Haroun reposing from the cares of

State—which were generally, as in most affairs of State, of an arithmetical character, the Commander of the Faithful being a fearful boggler at a sum.

On these occasions, the devoted Mesrour, chief of the Blacks of the Hareem, was always in attendance (Miss Griffin usually ringing for that officer, at the same time, with great vehemence), but never acquitted himself in a manner worthy of his historical reputation. In the first place, his bringing a broom into the Divan of the Caliph, even when Haroun wore on his shoulders the red robe of anger (Miss Pipson's pelisse), though it might be got over for the moment, was never to be quite satisfactorily accounted for. In the second place, his breaking out into grinning exclamations of 'Lork you pretties!' was neither Eastern nor respectful. In the third place, when specially instructed to say 'Bismillah!' he always said 'Hallelujah!' This officer, unlike his class, was too good-humoured altogether, kept his mouth open far too wide, expressed approbation to an incongruous extent, and even once—it was on the occasion of the purchase of the Fair Circassian for five hundred thousand purses of gold, and cheap, too—embraced the Slave, the Favourite, and the Caliph, all round. (Parenthetically let me say God bless Mesrour, and may there have been sons and daughters on that tender bosom, softening many a hard day since!)

Miss Griffin was a model of propriety, and I am at a loss to imagine what the feelings of the virtuous woman would have been, if she had known, when she paraded us down the Hampstead-road two and two, that she was walking with a stately step at the head of Polygamy and Mahomedanism. I believe that a mysterious and terrible joy with which the contemplation of Miss Griffin, in this unconscious state, inspired us, and a grim sense prevalent among us that there was a dreadful power in our knowledge of what Miss Griffin (who knew all things that could be learnt out of book) didn't know, were the mainspring of the preservation of our secret. It was wonderfully kept, but was once upon the verge of self-betrayal. The danger and escape occurred upon a Sunday. We were all ten ranged in a conspicuous part of the gallery at church, with Miss Griffin at our head—as we were every Sunday—advertising the establishment in an unsecular sort of way—when the description of Solomon in his domestic glory happened to be read. The moment that monarch was thus referred to, conscience whispered me, 'Thou, too, Haroun!' The officiating minister had a cast in his eye, and it assisted conscience by giving him the appearance of reading personally at me.

A crimson blush, attended by a fearful perspiration, suffused my features. The Grand Vizier become more dead than alive, and the whole Seraglio reddened as if the sunset of Bagdad shone direct upon their lovely faces. At this portentous time the awful Griffin rose, and balefully surveyed the children of Islam. My own impression was, that Church and State had entered into a conspiracy with Miss Griffin to expose us, and that we should all be put into white sheets, and exhibited in the centre aisle. But, so Westerly—if I may be allowed the expression as opposite to Eastern associations—was Miss Griffin's sense of rectitude, that she merely suspected Apples, and we were saved.

I have called the Seraglio, united. Upon the question, solely, whether the Commander of the Faithful durst exercise a right of kissing in that sanctuary of the palace, were its peerless inmates divided. Zobeide asserted a counter-right in the Favourite to scratch, the fair Circassian put her face, for refuge, into a green baize bag, originally designed for books. On the other hand, a young antelope of transcendent beauty from the fruitful plains of Camdentown (whence she had been brought, by traders, in the half-yearly caravan that crossed the inter-mediate desert after the holidays), held more liberal opinions, but stipu-lated for limiting the benefit of them to that dog, and son of a dog, the Grand Vizier—who had no rights, and was not in question. At length, the difficulty was compromised by the installation of a very youthful slave as Deputy. She, raised upon a stool, officially received upon her cheeks the salutes intended by the gracious Haroun for other Sultanas, and was privately rewarded from the coffers of the Ladies of the Hareem.

And now it was, at the full height of enjoyment of my bliss, that I became heavily troubled. I began to think of my mother, and what she would say to my taking home at midsummer eight of the most beauti-ful of the daughers of men, but all unexpected. I thought of the number of beds we made up at our house, of my father's income, and of the baker, and my despondency redoubled. The Seraglio and malicious Vizier, divining the cause of their Lord's unhappiness, did their utmost to augment it. They professed unbounded fidelity, and declared that they would live and die with him. Reduced to the utmost wretchedness by these protestations of attachment, I lay awake, for hours at a time, ruminating on my frightful lot. In my despair, I think I might have taken an early opportunity of falling on my knees before Miss Griffin, avow-ing my resemblance to Solomon, and praying to be dealt with according to the outraged laws of my country, if an unthought-of means of escape had not opened before me.

One day, we were out walking, two and two—on which occasion the Vizier had his usual instructions to take note of the boy at the turnpike, and if he profanely gazed (which he always did) at the beauties of the Hareem, to have him bow-strung in the course of the night—and it happened that our hearts were veiled in gloom. An unaccountable action on the part of the antelope had plunged the State into disgrace. That charmer, on the representation that the previous day was her birthday, and that vast treasures had been sent in a hamper for its cele-bration (both baseless assertions), had secretly but most pressingly invited thirty-five neighbouring princes and princesses to a ball and supper: with a special stipulation that they were 'not to be fetched till twelve'. This wandering of the antelope's fancy, led to the surprising arrival at Miss Griffin's door, in divers equipages and under various escorts, of a great company in full dress, who were deposited on the top step in a flush of high expectancy, and who were dismissed in tears. At the beginning of the double knocks attendant on these ceremonies, the antelope had retired to a back attic, and bolted herself in; and at every new arrival Miss Griffin had gone so much more and more distracted, that at last she had been seen to tear her front. Ultimate capitulation on the part of the offender, had been followed by solitude in the linen-closet, bread and water and a lecture to all, of vindictive length, in which Miss Griffin had used expressions: firstly, 'I believe you all of you knew of it'; secondly, 'Every one of you is as wicked as another'; thirdly, 'A pack of little wretches'.

Under these circumstances, we were walking drearily along; and I especially, with my Moosulmaun responsibilities heavy on me, was in a very low state of mind; when a strange man accosted Miss Griffin, and, after walking on at her side for a little while and talking with her, looked at me. Supposing him to be a minion of the law, and that my hour was come, I instantly ran away, with the general purpose of making for Egypt.

The whole Seraglio cried out, when they saw me making off as fast as my legs would carry me (I had an impression that the first turning on the left, and round by the public-house, would be the shortest way to the Pyramids), Miss Griffin screamed after me, the faithless Vizier ran after me, and the boy at the turnpike dodged me into a corner, like a sheep, and cut me off. Nobody scolded me when I was taken and brought back;

Miss Griffin only said, with a stunning gentleness, This was very curious! Why had I run away when the gentleman looked at me?

If I had had any breath to answer with, I dare say I should have made no answer; having no breath, I certainly made none. Miss Griffin and the strange man took me between them, and walked me back to the palace in a sort of state; but not at all (as I couldn't help feeling, with astonishment), in culprit state.

When we got there, we went into a room by ourselves, and Miss Griffin called in to her assistance, Mesrour, chief of the dusky guards of the Hareem. Mesrour, on being whispered to, began to shed tears.

'Bless you, my precious!' said that officer, turning to me; 'your pa's took bitter bad!'

I asked, with a fluttered heart, 'Is he very ill?'

'Lord temper the wind to you, my lamb!' said the good Mesrour, kneeling down, that I might have a comforting shoulder for my head to rest on, 'your pa's dead!'

Haroun Alraschid took to flight at the words; the Seraglio vanished; from that moment, I never again saw one of the eight of the fairest of the daughters of men.

I was taken home, and there was Debt at home as well as Death, and we had a sale there. My own little bed was so superciliously looked upon by a Power unknown to me, hazily called 'The Trade', that a brass coal-scuttle, a roasting-jack, and a birdcage, were obliged to be put into it to make a Lot of it, and then it went for a song. So I heard mentioned and I wondered what song, and thought what a dismal song it must have been to sing!

Then, I was sent to a great, cold, bare, school of big boys; where everything to eat and wear was thick and clumpy, without being enough; where everybody, large and small, was cruel; where the boys knew all about the sale, before I got there, and asked me what I had fetched, and who had bought me, and hooted at me. 'Going, going, gone!' I never whispered in that wretched place that I had been Haroun or had had a Seraglio: for, I knew that if I mentioned my reverses, I should be so worried, that I should have to drown myself in the muddy pond near the playground, which looked like the beer.

Ah me, ah me! no other ghost has haunted the boy's room, my friends, since I have occupied it, than the ghost of my own childhood, the ghost of my own innocence, the ghost of my own airy belief. Many a time have I pursued the phantom: never with this man's stride of mine to come up with it, never with these man's hands of mine to touch it, never more to this man's heart of mine to hold it in its purity. And here you see me working out, as cheerfully and thankfully as I may, my doom of shaking in the glass a constant change of customers, and of lying down and rising up with the skeleton allotted to me for my mortal companion.

ANTHONY TROLLOPE

Relics of General Chassé: A Tale of Antwerp

THAT Belgium is now one of the European kingdoms, living by its own laws, resting on its own bottom, with a king and court, palaces and parliament of its own, is known to all the world. And a very nice little kingdom it is; full of old towns, fine Flemish pictures, and interesting Gothic churches. But in the memory of very many of us who do not think ourselves old men, Belgium, as it is now called—in those days it used to be Flanders and Brabant—was a part of Holland; and it obtained its own independence by a revolution. In that revolution the most important military step was the siege of Antwerp, which was defended on the part of the Dutch by General Chassé, with the utmost gallantry, but nevertheless ineffectually.

After the siege Antwerp became quite a show place; and among the visitors who flocked there to talk of the gallant general, and to see what remained of the great effort which he had made to defend the place, were two Englishmen. One was the hero of this little history; and the other was a young man of considerably less weight in the world. The less I say of the latter the better; but it is necessary that I should give some description of the former.

The Revd Augustus Horne was, at the time of my narrative, a beneficed clergyman of the Church of England. The profession which he had graced sat easily on him. Its external marks and signs were as pleasing to his friends as were its internal comforts to himself. He was a man of much quiet mirth, full of polished wit, and on some rare occasions he could descend to the more noisy hilarity of a joke. Loved by his friends he loved all the world. He had known no care and seen no sorrow. Always intended for holy orders he had entered them without a scruple, and remained within their pale without a regret. At twenty-four he had been a deacon, at twenty-seven a priest, at thirty a rector, and at thirty-five a prebendary; and as his rectory was rich and his prebendal stall well paid, the Revd Augustus Horne was called by all, and called himself, a happy man. His stature was about six feet two, and his corpulence exceeded even those bounds which symmetry would have preferred as being most perfectly compatible even with such a height. But nevertheless Mr Horne was a well-made man; his hands and feet were small; his face was handsome, frank, and full of expression; his bright eyes twinkled with humour; his finely-cut mouth disclosed two marvellous rows of well-preserved ivory; and his slightly aquiline nose was just such a projection as one would wish to see on the face of a well-fed, good-natured dignitary of the Church of England. When I add to all this that the reverend gentleman was as generous as he was rich—and the kind mother in whose arms he had been nurtured had taken care that he should never want—I need hardly say that I was blessed with a very pleasant travelling companion.

I must mention one more interesting particular. Mr Horne was rather inclined to dandyism, in an innocent way. His clerical starched neckcloth was always of the whitest, his cambric handkerchief of the finest, his bands adorned with the broadest border; his sable suit never degenerated to a rusty brown; it not only gave on all occasions glossy evidence of freshness, but also of the talent which the artisan had displayed in turning out a well-dressed clergyman of the Church of England. His hair was ever brushed with scrupulous attention, and showed in its regular waves the guardian care of each separate bristle. And all this was done with that ease and grace which should be the characteristics of a dignitary of the established English Church.

I had accompanied Mr Horne to the Rhine; and we had reached Brussels on our return, just at the close of that revolution which ended in affording a throne to the son-in-law of George the Fourth. At that moment General Chassé's name and fame were in every man's mouth, and, like other curious admirers of the brave, Mr Horne determined to devote two days to the scene of the late events at Antwerp. Antwerp, moreover, possesses perhaps the finest spire, and certainly one of the three or four finest pictures, in the world. Of General Chassé, of the cathedral, and of the Rubens, I had heard much, and was therefore well pleased that such should be his resolution. This accomplished we were to return to Brussels; and thence, *via* Ghent, Ostend, and Dover, I to complete my legal studies in London, and Mr Horne to enjoy once more the peaceful retirement of Ollerton rectory. As we were to be absent from Brussels but one night we were enabled to indulge in the gratification of travelling without our luggage. A small *sac-de-nuit* was prepared; brushes, combs, razors, strops, a change of linen, etc., etc., were carefully put up; but our heavy baggage, our coats, waistcoats, and other wearing apparel were unnecessary. It was delightful to feel oneself so light-handed. The reverend gentleman, with my humble self by his side, left the portal of the Hôtel de Belle Vue at 7 a.m., in good humour with all the world. There were no railroads in those days; but a cabriolet, big enough to hold six persons, with rope traces and corresponding appendages, deposited us at the Golden Fleece in something less than six hours. The inward man was duly fortified, and we started for the castle.

It boots not here to describe the effects which gunpowder and grapeshot had had on the walls of Antwerp. Let the curious in these matters read the horrors of the siege of Troy, or the history of Jerusalem taken by Titus. The one may be found in Homer, and the other in Josephus. Or if they prefer doings of a later date there is the taking of Sebastopol, as narrated in the columns of the *Times* newspaper. The accounts are equally true, instructive, and intelligible. In the mean time allow the Revd Augustus Horne and myself to enter the private chambers of the renowned though defeated general.

We rambled for a while through the covered way, over the glacis and along the counterscarp, and listened to the guide as he detailed to us, in already accustomed words, how the siege had gone. Then we got into the private apartments of the general, and, having dexterously shaken off our attendant, wandered at large among the deserted rooms.

'It is clear that no one ever comes here,' said I.

'No,' said the Revd Augustus; 'it seems not: and to tell the truth, I don't know why any one should come. The chambers in themselves are not attractive.'

What he said was true. They were plain, ugly, square, unfurnished rooms, here a big one and there a little one, as is usual in most houses;— unfurnished, that is, for the most part. In one place we did find a table and a few chairs, in another a bedstead, and so on. But to me it was pleasant to indulge in those ruminations which any traces of the great or unfortunate create in softly sympathizing minds. For a time we communicated our thoughts to each other as we roamed free as air through the apartments; and then I lingered for a few moments behind, while Mr Horne moved on with a quicker step.

At last I entered the bedchamber of the general, and there I overtook my friend. He was inspecting, with much attention, an article of the great man's wardrobe which he held in his hand. It was precisely that virile habiliment to which a well-known gallant captain alludes in his conversation with the posthumous appearance of Miss Bailey, as containing a Bank of England 5*l.* note.

'The general must have been a large man, George, or he would hardly have filled these,' said Mr Horne, holding up to the light the respectable leathern articles in question. 'He must have been a very large man,—the largest man in Antwerp, I should think; or else his tailor has done him more than justice.'

They were certainly large, and had about them a charming regimental military appearance. They were made of white leather, with bright metal buttons at the knees and bright metal buttons at the top. They owned no pockets, and were, with the exception of the legitimate outlet, continuous in the circumference of the waistband. No dangling strings gave them an appearance of senile imbecility. Were it not for a certain rigidity, sternness, and mental inflexibility,—we will call it military ardour,—with which they were imbued, they would have created envy in the bosom of a fox-hunter.

Mr Horne was no fox-hunter, but still he seemed to be irresistibly taken with the lady-like propensity of wishing to wear them. 'Surely, George,' he said, 'the general must have been a stouter man than I am'— and he contemplated his own proportions with complacency—'these what's-the-names are quite big enough for me.'

I differed in opinion, and was obliged to explain that I thought he did the good living of Ollerton insufficient justice.

'I am sure they are large enough for me,' he repeated, with considerable obstinacy. I smiled incredulously; and then to settle the matter he resolved that he would try them on. Nobody had been in these rooms for the last hour, and it appeared as though they were never visited. Even the guide had not come on with us, but was employed in showing other parties about the fortifications. It was clear that this portion of the building was left desolate, and that the experiment might be safely made. So the sportive rector declared that he would for a short time wear the regimentals which had once contained the valorous heart of General Chassé.

With all decorum the Revd Mr Horne divested himself of the work of the London artist's needle, and, carefully placing his own garments beyond the reach of dust, essayed to fit himself in military garb.

At that important moment—at the critical instant of the attempt— the clatter of female voices was heard approaching the chamber. They must have suddenly come round some passage corner, for it was evident by the sound that they were close upon us before we had any warning of their advent. At this very minute Mr Horne was somewhat embarrassed in his attempts, and was not fully in possession of his usual active powers of movement, nor of his usual presence of mind. He only looked for escape; and seeing a door partly open he with difficulty retreated through it, and I followed him. We found that we were in a small dressing-room; and as by good luck the door was defended by an inner bolt, my friend was able to protect himself.

'There shall be another siege, at any rate as stout as the last, before I surrender,' said he.

As the ladies seemed inclined to linger in the room it became a matter of importance that the above-named articles should fit, not only for ornament but for use. It was very cold, and Mr Horne was altogether unused to move in a Highland sphere of life. But alas, alas! General Chassé had not been nurtured in the classical retirement of Ollerton. The ungiving leather would stretch no point to accommodate the divine, though it had been willing to minister to the convenience of the soldier. Mr Horne was vexed and chilled; and throwing the now hateful garments into a corner, and protecting himself from the cold as best he might by standing with his knees together and his body somewhat bent so as to give the skirts of his coat an opportunity of doing extra duty, he begged me to see if those jabbering females were not going to leave him in peace to recover his own property. I accordingly went to the door, and opening it to a small extent I peeped through.

Who shall describe my horror at the sight which I then saw? The scene, which had hitherto been tinted with comic effect, was now becoming so decidedly tragic that I did not dare at once to acquaint my worthy pastor with that which was occurring,—and, alas! had already occurred.

Five country-women of our own—it was easy to know them by their dress and general aspect—were standing in the middle of the room; and one of them, the centre of the group, the senior harpy of the lot, a maiden lady—I could have sworn to that—with a red nose, held in one hand a huge pair of scissors and in the other—the already devoted goods of my most unfortunate companion! Down from the waistband, through that goodly expanse, a fell gash had already gone through and through; and in useless, unbecoming disorder the broadcloth fell pendant from her arm on this side and on that. At that moment I confess that I had not the courage to speak to Mr Horne,—not even to look at him.

I must describe that group. Of the figure next to me I could only see the back. It was a broad back done up in black silk not of the newest. The whole figure, one may say, was dumpy. The black silk was not long, as dresses now are worn, nor wide in its skirts. In every way it was skimpy, considering the breadth it had to cover; and below the silk I saw the heels of two thick shoes, and enough to swear by of two woollen stockings. Above the silk was a red-and-blue shawl; and above that a ponderous, elaborate brown bonnet, as to the materials of which I should not wish to undergo an examination. Over and beyond this I could only see the backs of her two hands. They were held up as though in wonder at that which the red-nosed holder of the scissors had dared to do.

Opposite to this lady, and with her face fully turned to me, was a kindly-looking, fat motherly woman, with light-coloured hair, not in the best order. She was hot and scarlet with exercise, being perhaps too stout for the steep steps of the fortress; and in one hand she held a hand-kerchief, with which from time to time she wiped her brow. In the other hand she held one of the extremities of my friend's property, feel-ing—good, careful soul!—what was the texture of the cloth. As she did so, I could see a glance of approbation pass across her warm features. I liked that lady's face, in spite of her untidy hair, and felt that had she been alone my friend would not have been injured.

On either side of her there stood a flaxen-haired maiden, with long curls, large blue eyes, fresh red cheeks, an undefined lumpy nose, and large good-humoured mouth. They were as like as two peas, only that one was half an inch taller than the other; and there was no difficulty in discovering, at a moment's glance, that they were the children of that overheated matron who was feeling the web of my friend's cloth.

But the principal figure was she who held the centre place in the group. She was tall and thin, with fierce-looking eyes, rendered more fierce by the spectacles which she wore; with a red nose as I said before; and about her an undescribable something which quite convinced me that she had never known—could never know—aught of the comforts of married life. It was she who held the scissors and the black garments. It was she who had given that unkind cut. As I looked at her she whisked herself quickly round from one companion to the other, triumphing in what she had done, and ready to triumph further in what she was about to do. I immediately conceived a deep hatred for that Queen of the Harpies.

'Well, I suppose they can't be wanted again,' said the mother, rubbing her forehead.

'Oh dear no!' said she of the red nose. 'They are relics!'

I thought to leap forth; but for what purpose should I have leaped? The accursed scissors had already done their work; and the symmetry, nay, even the utility of the vestment was destroyed.

'General Chassé wore a very good article;—I will say that for him,' continued the mother.

'Of course he did!' said the Queen Harpy. 'Why should he not, seeing that the country paid for it for him? Well, ladies, who's for having a bit?'

'Oh my! you won't go for to cut them up,' said the stout back.

'Won't I?' said the scissors; and she immediately made another incision. 'Who's for having a bit? Don't all speak at once.'

'I should like a morsel for a pincushion,' said flaxen-haired Miss No. 1, a young lady about nineteen, actuated by a general affection for all sword-bearing, fire-eating heroes. 'I should like to have something to make me think of the poor general!'

Snip, snip went the scissors with professional rapidity, and a round piece was extracted from the back of the calf of the left leg. I shuddered with horror; and so did the Revd Augustus Horne with cold.

'I hardly think it's proper to cut them up,' said Miss No. 2.

'Oh isn't it?' said the harpy. 'Then I'll do what's improper!' And she got her finger and thumb well through the holes in the scissors' handles. As she spoke resolution was plainly marked on her brow.

'Well; if they are to be cut up, I should certainly like a bit for a pen-wiper,' said No. 2. No. 2 was a literary young lady with a periodical correspondence, a journal, and an album. Snip, snip went the scissors again, and the broad part of the upper right division afforded ample materials for a pen-wiper.

Then the lady with the back, seeing that the desecration of the article had been completed, plucked up heart of courage and put in her little request: 'I think I might have a needle-case out of it,' said she, 'just as a *suvneer* of the poor general'—and a long fragment cut rapidly out of the waistband afforded her unqualified delight.

Mamma, with the hot face and untidy hair, came next. 'Well, girls,' she said, 'as you are all served, I don't see why I'm to be left out. Perhaps,

Miss Grogram'—she was an old maid, you see—'perhaps, Miss Grogram, you could get me as much as would make a decent-sized reticule.'

There was not the slightest difficulty in doing this. The harpy in the centre again went to work, snip, snip, and extracting from that portion of the affairs which usually sustained the greater portion of Mr Horne's weight two large round pieces of cloth, presented them to the well-pleased matron. 'The general knew well where to get a bit of good broadcloth, certainly,' said she, again feeling the pieces.

'And now for No. 1,' said she whom I so absolutely hated; 'I think there is still enough for a pair of slippers. There's nothing so nice for the house as good black cloth slippers that are warm to the feet and don't show the dirt.' And so saying, she spread out on the floor the lacerated remainders.

'There's a nice bit there,' said young lady No. 2, poking at one of the pockets with the end of her parasol.

'Yes,' said the harpy, contemplating her plunder. 'But I'm thinking whether I couldn't get leggings as well. I always wear leggings in the thick of the winter.' And so she concluded her operations, and there was nothing left but a melancholy skeleton of seams and buttons.

All this having been achieved, they pocketed their plunder and prepared to depart. There are people who have a wonderful appetite for relics. A stone with which Washington had broken a window when a boy—with which he had done so or had not, for there is little difference; a button that was on a coat of Napoleon's, or on that of one of his lackeys; a bullet said to have been picked up at Waterloo or Bunker's Hill; these, and suchlike things are great treasures. And their most desirable characteristic is the ease with which they are attained. Any bullet or any button does the work. Faith alone is necessary. And now these ladies had made themselves happy and glorious with 'Relics' of General Chassé cut from the ill-used habiliments of an elderly English gentleman!

They departed at last, and Mr Horne, for once in an ill humour, followed me into the bedroom. Here I must be excused if I draw a veil over his manly sorrow at discovering what fate had done for him. Remember what was his position, unclothed in the castle of Antwerp! The nearest suitable change for those which had been destroyed was locked up in his portmanteau at the Hôtel de Belle Vue in Brussels! He had nothing left to him—literally nothing, in that Antwerp world. There was no other wretched being wandering then in that Dutch town so utterly

denuded of the goods of life. For what is a man fit,—for what can he be
fit,—when left in such a position? There are some evils which seem
utterly to crush a man; and if there be any misfortune to which a man
may be allowed to succumb without imputation on his manliness, surely
it is such as this. How was Mr Horne to return to his hotel without
incurring the displeasure of the municipality? That was my first thought.

He had a cloak, but it was at the inn; and I found that my friend was
oppressed with a great horror at the idea of being left alone; so that I
could not go in search of it. There is an old saying, that no man is a hero
to his *valet de chambre*,—the reason doubtless being this, that it is customary for his valet to see the hero divested of those trappings in which
so much of the heroic consists. Who reverences a clergyman without his
gown, or a warrior without his sword and sabre-tasche? What would
even Minerva be without her helmet?

I do not wish it to be understood that I no longer reverenced
Mr Horne because he was in an undress; but he himself certainly lost
much of his composed, well-sustained dignity of demeanour. He was
fearful and querulous, cold, and rather cross. When, forgetting his size,
I offered him my own he thought that I was laughing at him. He began
to be afraid that the story would get abroad, and he then and there
exacted a promise that I would never tell it during his lifetime. I have
kept my word; but now my old friend has been gathered to his fathers,
full of years.

At last I got him to the hotel. It was long before he would leave the
castle, cloaked though he was;—not, indeed, till the shades of evening
had dimmed the outlines of men and things, and made indistinct the
outward garniture of those who passed to and fro in the streets. Then,
wrapped in his cloak, Mr Horne followed me along the quays and
through the narrowest of the streets; and at length, without venturing
to return the gaze of any one in the hotel court, he made his way up to
his own bedroom.

Dinnerless and supperless he went to his couch. But when there he
did consent to receive some consolation in the shape of mutton cutlets
and fried potatoes, a savoury omelet, and a bottle of claret. The mutton
cutlets and fried potatoes at the Golden Fleece at Antwerp are—or were
then, for I am speaking now of wellnigh thirty years since—remarkably
good; the claret, also, was of the best; and so, by degrees, the look of
despairing dismay passed from his face, and some scintillations of the old
fire returned to his eyes.

'I wonder whether they find themselves much happier for what they have got?' said he.

'A great deal happier,' said I. 'They'll boast of those things to all their friends at home, and we shall doubtless see some account of their success in the newspapers.'

'It would be delightful to expose their blunder,—to show them up. Would it not, George? To turn the tables on them?'

'Yes,' said I, 'I should like to have the laugh against them.'

'So would I, only that I should compromise myself by telling the story. It wouldn't do at all to have it told at Oxford with my name attached to it.'

To this also I assented. To what would I not have assented in my anxiety to make him happy after his misery?

But all was not over yet. He was in bed now, but it was necessary that he should rise again on the morrow. At home, in England, what was required might perhaps have been made during the night; but here, among the slow Flemings, any such exertion would have been impossible. Mr Horne, moreover, had no desire to be troubled in his retirement by a tailor.

Now the landlord of the Golden Fleece was a very stout man,—a very stout man indeed. Looking at him as he stood with his hands in his pockets at the portal of his own establishment, I could not but think that he was stouter even than Mr Horne. But then he was certainly much shorter, and the want of due proportion probably added to his unwieldy appearance. I walked round him once or twice wishfully, measuring him in my eye, and thinking of what texture might be the Sunday best of such a man. The clothes which he then had on were certainly not exactly suited to Mr Horne's tastes.

He saw that I was observing him, and appeared uneasy and offended. I had already ascertained that he spoke a little English. Of Flemish I knew literally nothing, and in French, with which probably he was also acquainted, I was by no means voluble. The business which I had to transact was intricate, and I required the use of my mother-tongue.

It was intricate and delicate, and difficult withal. I began by remarking on the weather, but he did not take my remarks kindly. I am inclined to fancy that he thought I was desirous of borrowing money from him. At any rate he gave me no encouragement in my first advances.

'Vat misfortune?' at last he asked, when I had succeeded in making him understand that a gentleman upstairs required his assistance.

'He has lost these things,' and I took hold of my own garments. 'It's a long story, or I'd tell you how; but he has not a pair in the world till he gets back to Brussels,—unless you can lend him one.'

'Lost hees br—?' and he opened his eyes wide, and looked at me with astonishment.

'Yes, yes, exactly so,' said I, interrupting him. 'Most astonishing thing, isn't it? But it's quite true.'

'Vas hees money in de pocket?' asked my suspicious landlord.

'No, no, no. It's not so bad as that. His money is all right. I had the money, luckily.'

'Ah! dat is better. But he have lost hees b—?'

'Yes, yes'; I was now getting rather impatient. 'There is no mistake about it. He has lost them as sure as you stand there.' And then I proceeded to explain that as the gentleman in question was very stout, and as he, the landlord, was stout also, he might assist us in this great calamity by a loan from his own wardrobe.

When he found that the money was not in the pocket, and that his bill therefore would be paid, he was not indisposed to be gracious. He would, he said, desire his servant to take up what was required to Mr Horne's chamber. I endeavoured to make him understand that a sombre colour would be preferable; but he only answered that he would put the best that he had at the gentleman's disposal. He could not think of offering anything less than his best on such an occasion. And then he turned his back and went his way, muttering as he went something in Flemish, which I believed to be an exclamation of astonishment that any man should, under any circumstances, lose such an article.

It was now getting late; so when I had taken a short stroll by myself, I went to bed without disturbing Mr Horne again that night. On the following morning I thought it best not to go to him unless he sent for me; so I desired the boots to let him know that I had ordered breakfast in a private room, and that I would await him there unless he wished to see me. He sent me word back to say that he would be with me very shortly.

He did not keep me waiting above half an hour, but I confess that that half-hour was not pleasantly spent. I feared that his temper would be tried in dressing, and that he would not be able to eat his breakfast in a happy state of mind. So that when I heard his heavy footstep advancing along the passage my heart did misgive me, and I felt that I was trembling.

That step was certainly slower and more ponderous than usual. There was always a certain dignity in the very sound of his movements, but now this seemed to have been enhanced. To judge merely by the step one would have said that a bishop was coming that way instead of a prebendary.

And then he entered. In the upper half of his august person no alteration was perceptible. The hair was as regular and as graceful as ever, the handkerchief as white, the coat as immaculate; but below his well-filled waistcoat a pair of red plush began to shine in unmitigated splendour, and continued from thence down to within an inch above his knee; nor, as it appeared, could any pulling induce them to descend lower. Mr Horne always wore black silk stockings,—at least so the world supposed,—but it was now apparent that the world had been wrong in presuming him to be guilty of such extravagance. Those, at any rate, which he exhibited on the present occasion were more economical. They were silk to the calf, but thence upwards they continued their career in white cotton. These then followed the plush; first two snowy, full-sized pillars of white, and then two jet columns of flossy silk. Such was the appearance, on that well-remembered morning, of the Reverend Augustus Horne, as he entered the room in which his breakfast was prepared.

I could see at a glance that a dark frown contracted his eyebrows, and that the compressed muscles of his upper lip gave a strange degree of austerity to his open face. He carried his head proudly on high, determined to be dignified in spite of his misfortunes, and advanced two steps into the room without a remark, as though he were able to show that neither red plush nor black cloth could disarrange the equal poise of his mighty mind!

And after all what are a man's garments but the outward husks in which the fruit is kept, duly tempered from the wind?

> The rank is but the guinea stamp,
> The man's the gowd for a' that.

And is not the tailor's art as little worthy, as insignificant as that of the king who makes

> A marquis, duke and a' that?

Who would be content to think that his manly dignity depended on his coat and waistcoat, or his hold on the world's esteem on any other garment of usual wear? That no such weakness soiled his mind Mr Horne was determined to prove; and thus he entered the room with measured tread, and stern dignified demeanour.

Having advanced two steps his eye caught mine. I do not know whether he was moved by some unconscious smile on my part;—for in truth I endeavoured to seem as indifferent as himself to the nature of his dress;—or whether he was invincibly tickled by some inward fancy of his own, but suddenly his advancing step ceased, a broad flash of comic humour spread itself over his features, he retreated with his back against the wall, and then burst out into an immoderate roar of loud laughter.

And I—what else could I then do but laugh? He laughed, and I laughed. He roared, and I roared. He lifted up his vast legs to view till the rays of the morning sun shone through the window on the bright hues which he displayed; and he did not sit down to his breakfast till he had in every fantastic attitude shown off to the best advantage the red plush of which he had so recently become proud.

An Antwerp private cabriolet on that day reached the yard of the Hôtel de Belle Vue at about 4 p.m., and four waiters, in a frenzy of astonishment, saw the Reverend Augustus Horne descend from the vehicle and seek his chamber dressed in the garments which I have described. But I am inclined to think that he never again favoured any of his friends with such a sight.

It was on the next evening after this that I went out to drink tea with two maiden ladies, relatives of mine, who kept a seminary for English girls at Brussels. The Misses Macmanus were very worthy women, and earned their bread in an upright, painstaking manner. I would not for worlds have passed through Brussels without paying them this compliment. They were, however, perhaps a little dull, and I was aware that I should not probably meet in their drawing-room many of the fashionable inhabitants of the city. Mr Horne had declined to accompany me; but in doing so he was good enough to express a warm admiration for the character of my worthy cousins.

The elder Miss Macmanus, in her little note, had informed me that she would have the pleasure of introducing me to a few of my 'compatriots'. I presumed she meant Englishmen; and as I was in the habit of meeting such every day of my life at home, I cannot say that I was peculiarly elevated by the promise. When, however, I entered the room, there was no Englishman there;—there was no man of any kind. There were twelve ladies collected together with the view of making the evening pass agreeably to me, the single virile being among them all. I felt as though I were a sort of Mohammed in Paradise; but I certainly felt also that the Paradise was none of my own choosing.

In the centre of the amphitheatre which the ladies formed sat the two Misses Macmanus;—there, at least, they sat when they had completed the process of shaking hands with me. To the left of them, making one wing of the semicircle, were arranged the five pupils by attending to whom the Misses Macmanus earned their living; and the other wing consisted of the five ladies who had furnished themselves with relics of General Chassé. They were my 'compatriots'.

I was introduced to them all, one after the other; but their names did not abide in my memory one moment. I was thinking too much of the singularity of the adventure, and could not attend to such minutiae. That the red-nosed harpy was Miss Grogram, that I remembered;—that, I may say, I shall never forget. But whether the motherly lady with the somewhat blowsy hair was Mrs Jones or Mrs Green, or Mrs Walker, I cannot now say. The dumpy female with the broad back was always called Aunt Sally by the young ladies.

Too much sugar spoils one's tea; I think I have heard that even prosperity will cloy when it comes in overdoses; and a schoolboy has been known to be overdone with jam. I myself have always been peculiarly attached to ladies' society, and have avoided bachelor parties as things execrable in their very nature. But on this special occasion I felt myself to be that schoolboy;—I was literally overdone with jam. My tea was all sugar, so that I could not drink it. I was one among twelve. What could I do or say? The proportion of alloy was too small to have any effect in changing the nature of the virgin silver, and the conversation became absolutely feminine.

I must confess also that my previous experience as to these compatriots of mine had not prejudiced me in their favour. I regarded them with,—I am ashamed to say so, seeing that they were ladies,—but almost with loathing. When last I had seen them their occupation had reminded me of some obscene feast of harpies, or almost of ghouls. They had brought down to the verge of desperation the man whom of all men I most venerated. On these accounts I was inclined to be taciturn with reference to them;—and then what could I have to say to the Misses Macmanus's five pupils?

My cousin at first made an effort or two in my favour, but these efforts were fruitless. I soon died away into utter unrecognized insignificance, and the conversation, as I have before said, became feminine. And indeed that horrid Miss Grogram, who was, as it were, the princess of the ghouls, nearly monopolized the whole of it. Mamma Jones—we will call her Jones for the occasion—put in a word now and then, as did also the elder and more energetic Miss Macmanus. The dumpy lady with the broad back ate tea-cake incessantly; the two daughters looked scornful, as though they were above their company with reference to the five pupils; and the five pupils themselves sat in a row with the utmost propriety, each with her hands crossed on her lap before her.

Of what they were talking at last I became utterly oblivious. They had ignored me, going into realms of muslin, questions of maid-servants, female rights, and cheap under-clothing; and I therefore had ignored them. My mind had gone back to Mr Horne and his garments. While they spoke of their rights, I was thinking of his wrongs; when they mentioned the price of flannel I thought of that of broadcloth.

But of a sudden my attention was arrested. Miss Macmanus had said something of the black silks of Antwerp, when Miss Grogram replied that she had just returned from that city and had there enjoyed a great success. My cousin had again asked something about the black silks, thinking, no doubt, that Miss Grogram had achieved some bargain; but that lady had soon undeceived her.

'Oh no,' said Miss Grogram, 'it was at the castle. We got such beauti-ful relics of General Chassé! Didn't we, Mrs Jones?'

'Indeed we did,' said Mrs Jones, bringing out from beneath the skirts of her dress and ostensibly displaying a large black bag.

'And I've got such a beautiful needle-case,' said the broad-back, dis-playing her prize. 'I've been making it up all the morning.' And she handed over the article to Miss Macmanus.

'And only look at this duck of a pen-wiper,' simpered flaxen-hair No. 2. 'Only think of wiping one's pens with relics of General Chassé!' and she handed it over to the other Miss Macmanus.

'And mine's a pin-cushion,' said No. 1, exhibiting the trophy.

'But that's nothing to what I've got,' said Miss Grogram. 'In the first place, there's a pair of slippers,—a beautiful pair;—they're not made up yet, of course; and then—'

The two Misses Macmanus and their five pupils were sitting open-eared, open-eyed, and open-mouthed. How all these sombre-looking articles could be relics of General Chassé did not at first appear clear to them.

'What are they, Miss Grogram?' said the elder Miss Macmanus, hold-ing the needle-case in one hand and Mrs Jones's bag in the other. Miss Macmanus was a strong-minded female, and I reverenced my cousin when I saw the decided way in which she intended to put down the greedy arrogance of Miss Grogram.

'They are relics.'

'But where do they come from, Miss Grogram?'

'Why, from the castle, to be sure;—from General Chassé's own rooms.'

'Did anybody sell them to you?'

'No.'

'Or give them to you?'

'Why, no;—at least not exactly give.'

'There they were, and she took 'em,' said the broad-back.

Oh, what a look Miss Grogram gave her! 'Took them! of course I took them. That is, you took them as much as I did. They were things that we found lying about.'

'What things?' asked Miss Macmanus, in a peculiarly strong-minded tone.

Miss Grogram seemed to be for a moment silenced. I had been ignored, as I have said, and my existence forgotten; but now I observed that the eyes of the culprits were turned towards me,—the eyes, that is, of four of them. Mrs Jones looked at me from beneath her fan; the two girls glanced at me furtively, and then their eyes fell to the lowest flounces of their frocks. Miss Grogram turned her spectacles right upon me, and I fancied that she nodded her head at me as a sort of answer to Miss Macmanus. The five pupils opened their mouths and eyes wider; but she of the broad-back was nothing abashed. It would have been nothing to her had there been a dozen gentlemen in the room. 'We just found a pair of black—.' The whole truth was told in the plainest pos-sible language.

'Oh, Aunt Sally!' 'Aunt Sally, how can you?' 'Hold your tongue, Aunt Sally!'

'And then Miss Grogram just cut them up with her scissors,' continued Aunt Sally, not a whit abashed, 'and gave us each a bit, only she took more than half for herself.' It was clear to me that there had been some quarrel, some delicious quarrel, between Aunt Sally and Miss Grogram. Through the whole adventure I had rather respected Aunt Sally. 'She took more than half for herself,' continued Aunt Sally. 'She kept all the—.'

'Jemima,' said the elder Miss Macmanus, interrupting the speaker and addressing her sister, 'it is time, I think, for the young ladies to retire. Will you be kind enough to see them to their rooms?' The five pupils thereupon rose from their seats and courtesied. They then left the room in file, the younger Miss Macmanus showing them the way.

'But we haven't done any harm, have we?' asked Mrs Jones, with some tremulousness in her voice.

'Well, I don't know,' said Miss Macmanus. 'What I'm thinking of now is this;—to whom, I wonder, did the garments properly belong? Who had been the owner and wearer of them?'

'Why General Chassé, of course,' said Miss Grogram.

'They were the general's,' repeated the two young ladies; blushing, however, as they alluded to the subject.

'Well, we thought they were the general's, certainly; and a very excellent article they were,' said Mrs Jones.

'Perhaps they were the butler's?' said Aunt Sally. I certainly had not given her credit for so much sarcasm.

'Butler's!' exclaimed Miss Grogram, with a toss of her head.

'Oh! Aunt Sally, Aunt Sally! how can you?' shrieked the two young ladies.

'Oh laws!' ejaculated Mrs Jones.

'I don't think that they could have belonged to the butler,' said Miss Macmanus, with much authority, 'seeing that domestics in this country are never clad in garments of that description; so far my own observation enables me to speak with certainty. But it is equally sure that they were never the property of the general lately in command at Antwerp. Generals, when they are in full dress, wear ornamental lace upon their—their regimentals; and when—' So much she said, and something more, which it may be unnecessary that I should repeat; but such were her eloquence and logic that no doubt would have been left on the mind of any impartial hearer. If an argumentative speaker ever proved anything, Miss Macmanus proved that General Chassé had never been the wearer of the article in question.

'But I know very well they were his!' said Miss Grogram, who was not an impartial hearer. 'Of course they were; whose else's should they be?'

'I'm sure I hope they were his,' said one of the young ladies, almost crying.

'I wish I'd never taken it,' said the other.

'Dear, dear, dear!' said Mrs Jones.

'I'll give you my needle-case, Miss Grogram,' said Aunt Sally.

I had sat hitherto silent during the whole scene, meditating how best I might confound the red-nosed harpy. Now, I thought, was the time for me to strike in.

'I really think, ladies, that there has been some mistake,' said I.

'There has been no mistake at all, sir!' said Miss Grogram.

'Perhaps not,' I answered, very mildly; 'very likely not. But some affair of a similar nature was very much talked about in Antwerp yesterday.'

'Oh laws!' again ejaculated Mrs Jones.

'The affair I allude to has been talked about a good deal, certainly,' I continued. 'But perhaps it may be altogether a different circumstance.'

'And what may be the circumstance to which you allude?' asked Miss Macmanus, in the same authoritative tone.

'I dare say it has nothing to do with these ladies,' said I; 'but an article of dress, of the nature they have described, was cut up in the Castle of Antwerp on the day before yesterday. It belonged to a gentleman who was visiting the place; and I was given to understand that he is determined to punish the people who have wronged him.'

'It can't be the same,' said Miss Grogram; but I could see that she was trembling.

'Oh laws! what will become of us?' said Mrs Jones.

'You can all prove that I didn't touch them, and that I warned her not,' said Aunt Sally. In the mean time the two young ladies had almost fainted behind their fans.

'But how had it come to pass,' asked Miss Macmanus, 'that the gentleman had—'

'I know nothing more about it, cousin,' said I; 'only it does seem that there is an odd coincidence.'

Immediately after this I took my leave. I saw that I had avenged my friend, and spread dismay in the hearts of those who had injured him. I had learned in the course of the evening at what hotel the five ladies were staying; and in the course of the next morning I sauntered into the hall, and finding one of the porters alone, asked if they were still there. The man told me that they had started by the earliest diligence. 'And,' said he, 'if you are a friend of theirs, perhaps you will take charge of these things, which they have left behind them?' So saying, he pointed to a table at the back of the hall, on which were lying the black bag, the black needle-case, the black pin-cushion, and the black pen-wiper. There was also a heap of fragments of cloth which I well knew had been intended by Miss Grogram for the comfort of her feet and ankles.

I declined the commission, however. 'They were no special friends of mine,' I said; and I left all the relics still lying on the little table in the back hall.

'Upon the whole, I am satisfied!' said the Revd Augustus Horne, when I told him the finale of the story.

THOMAS HARDY

A Mere Interlude

I

THE traveller in school-books, who vouched in driest tones for the fidelity to fact of the following narrative, used to add a ring of truth to it by opening with a nicety of criticism on the heroine's personality. People were wrong, he declared, when they surmised that Baptista Trewthen was a young woman with scarcely emotions or character. There was nothing in her to love, and nothing to hate—so ran the general opinion. That she showed few positive qualities was true. The colours and tones which changing events paint on the faces of active womankind were looked for in vain upon hers. But still waters run deep; and no crisis had come in the years of her early maidenhood to demonstrate what lay hidden within her, like metal in a mine.

She was the daughter of a small farmer in St Maria's, one of the Isles of Lyonesse beyond Off-Wessex, who had spent a large sum, as there understood, on her education, by sending her to the mainland for two years. At nineteen she was entered at the Training College for Teachers, and at twenty-one nominated to a school in the country, near Tor-upon-Sea, whither she proceeded after the Christmas examination and holidays.

The months passed by from winter to spring and summer, and Baptista applied herself to her new duties as best she could, till an uneventful year had elapsed. Then an air of abstraction pervaded her bearing as she walked to and fro, twice a day, and she showed the traits of a person who had something on her mind. A widow, by name Mrs Wace, in whose house Baptista Trewthen had been provided with a sitting-room and bedroom till the schoolhouse should be built, noticed this change in her youthful tenant's manner, and at last ventured to press her with a few questions.

'It has nothing to do with the place, nor with you,' said Miss Trewthen.

'Then it is the salary?'

'No, nor the salary.'

'Then it is something you have heard from home, my dear.'

Baptista was silent for a few moments. 'It is Mr Heddegan,' she murmured. 'Him they used to call David Heddegan before he got his money.'

'And who is the Mr Heddegan they used to call David?'

'An old bachelor at Giant's Town, St Maria's, with no relations whatever, who lives about a stone's throw from father's. When I was a child he used to take me on his knee and say he'd marry me some day. Now I am a woman the jest has turned earnest, and he is anxious to do it. And father and mother say I can't do better than have him.'

'He's well off?'

'Yes—he's the richest man we know—as a friend and neighbour.'

'How much older did you say he was than yourself?'

'I didn't say. Twenty years at least.'

'And an unpleasant man in the bargain perhaps?'

'No—he's not unpleasant.'

'Well, child, all I can say is that I'd resist any such engagement if it's not palatable to 'ee. You are comfortable here, in my little house, I hope. All the parish like 'ee: and I've never been so cheerful, since my poor husband left me to wear his wings, as I've been with 'ee as my lodger.'

The schoolmistress assured her landlady that she could return the sentiment. 'But here comes my perplexity,' she said. 'I don't like keeping school. Ah, you are surprised—you didn't suspect it. That's because I've concealed my feeling. Well, I simply hate school. I don't care for children—they are unpleasant, troublesome little things, whom nothing would delight so much as to hear that you had fallen down dead. Yet I would even put up with them if it was not for the inspector. For three months before his visit I didn't sleep soundly. And the Committee of Council are always changing the Code, so that you don't know what to teach, and what to leave untaught. I think father and mother are right. They say I shall never excel as a schoolmistress if I dislike the work so, and that therefore I ought to get settled by marrying Mr Heddegan. Between us two, I like him better than school; but I don't like him quite so much as to wish to marry him.'

These conversations, once begun, were continued from day to day; till at length the young girl's elderly friend and landlady threw in her opinion on the side of Miss Trewthen's parents. All things considered, she declared, the uncertainty of the school, the labour, Baptista's natural dislike for teaching, it would be as well to take what fate offered, and make the best of matters by wedding her father's old neighbour and prosperous friend.

The Easter holidays came round, and Baptista went to spend them as usual in her native isle, going by train into Off-Wessex and crossing by packet from Pen-zephyr. When she returned in the middle of April her face wore a more settled aspect.

'Well?' said the expectant Mrs Wace.

'I have agreed to have him as my husband,' said Baptista, in an off-hand way. 'Heaven knows if it will be for the best or not. But I have agreed to do it, and so the matter is settled.'

Mrs Wace commended her; but Baptista did not care to dwell on the subject; so that allusion to it was very infrequent between them. Nevertheless, among other things, she repeated to the widow from time to time in monosyllabic remarks that the wedding was really impending; that it was arranged for the summer, and that she had given notice of leaving the school at the August holidays. Later on she announced more specifically that her marriage was to take place immediately after her return home at the beginning of the month aforesaid.

She now corresponded regularly with Mr Heddegan. Her letters from him were seen, at least on the outside, and in part within, by Mrs Wace. Had she read more of their interiors than the occasional sentences shown her by Baptista she would have perceived that the scratchy, rusty handwriting of Miss Trewthen's betrothed conveyed little more matter than details of their future housekeeping, and his preparations for the same, with innumerable 'my dears' sprinkled in disconnectedly, to show the depth of his affection without the inconveniences of syntax.

2

It was the end of July—dry, too dry, even for the season, the delicate green herbs and vegetables that grew in this favoured end of the kingdom tasting rather of the watering-pot than of the pure fresh moisture from the skies. Baptista's boxes were packed, and one Saturday morning she departed by a waggonette to the station, and thence by train to Pen-zephyr, from which port she was, as usual, to cross the water immediately to her home, and become Mr Heddegan's wife on the Wednesday of the week following.

She might have returned a week sooner. But though the wedding day had loomed so near, and the banns were out, she delayed her departure till this last moment, saying it was not necessary for her to be at home long beforehand. As Mr Heddegan was older than herself, she said, she was to be married in her ordinary summer bonnet and grey silk frock, and there were no preparations to make that had not been amply made by her parents and intended husband.

In due time, after a hot and tedious journey, she reached Pen-zephyr. She here obtained some refreshment, and then went towards the pier, where she learnt to her surprise that the little steamboat plying between the town and the islands had left at eleven o'clock; the usual hour of departure in the afternoon having been forestalled in consequence of the fogs which had for a few days prevailed towards evening, making twilight navigation dangerous.

This being Saturday, there was now no other boat till Tuesday, and it became obvious that here she would have to remain for the three days, unless her friends should think fit to rig out one of the island sailing-boats and come to fetch her—a not very likely contingency, the sea distance being nearly forty miles.

Baptista, however, had been detained in Pen-zephyr on more than one occasion before, either on account of bad weather or some such reason as the present, and she was therefore not in any personal alarm. But, as she was to be married on the following Wednesday, the delay was certainly inconvenient to a more than ordinary degree, since it would leave less than a day's interval between her arrival and the wedding ceremony.

Apart from this awkwardness she did not much mind the accident. It was indeed curious to see how little she minded. Perhaps it would not be too much to say that, although she was going to do the critical deed of her life quite willingly, she experienced an indefinable relief at the postponement of her meeting with Heddegan. But her manner after making discovery of the hindrance was quiet and subdued, even to passivity itself; as was instanced by her having, at the moment of receiving information that the steamer had sailed, replied 'Oh' so coolly to the porter with her luggage, that he was almost disappointed at her lack of disappointment.

The question now was, should she return again to Mrs Wace, in the village of Lower Wessex, or wait in the town at which she had arrived? She would have preferred to go back, but the distance was too great; moreover, having left the place for good, and somewhat dramatically, to become a bride, a return, even for so short a space, would have been a trifle humiliating.

Leaving, then, her boxes at the station, her next anxiety was to secure a respectable, or rather genteel, lodging in the popular seaside resort confronting her. To this end she looked about the town, in which, though she had passed through it half-a-dozen times, she was practically a stranger.

Baptista found a room to suit her over a fruiterer's shop; where she made herself at home, and set herself in order after her journey. An early cup of tea having revived her spirits she walked out to reconnoitre.

Being a schoolmistress she avoided looking at the schools, and having a sort of trade connection with books, she avoided looking at the book-sellers; but wearying of the other shops she inspected the churches; not that for her own part she cared much about ecclesiastical edifices; but tourists looked at them, and so would she—a proceeding for which no one would have credited her with any great originality, such, for instance, as that she subsequently showed herself to possess. The churches soon oppressed her. She tried the Museum, but came out because it seemed lonely and tedious.

Yet the town and the walks in this land of strawberries, these head-quarters of early English flowers and fruit, were then, as always, attract-ive. From the more picturesque streets she went to the town gardens, and the Pier, and the Harbour, and looked at the men at work there, loading and unloading as in the time of the Phoenicians.

'Not Baptista? Yes, Baptista it is!'

The words were uttered behind her. Turning round she gave a start, and became confused, even agitated, for a moment. Then she said in her usual undemonstrative manner, 'O—is it really you, Charles?'

Without speaking again at once, and with a half-smile, the new-comer glanced her over. There was much criticism, and some resent-ment—even temper—in his eye.

'I am going home,' continued she. 'But I have missed the boat.'

He scarcely seemed to take in the meaning of this explanation, in the intensity of his critical survey. 'Teaching still? What a fine schoolmistress you make, Baptista, I warrant!' he said with a slight flavour of sarcasm, which was not lost upon her.

'I know I am nothing to brag of,' she replied. 'That's why I have given up.'

'O—given up? You astonish me.'

'I hate the profession.'

'Perhaps that's because I am in it.'

'O no, it isn't. But I am going to enter on another life altogether. I am going to be married next week to Mr David Heddegan.'

The young man—fortified as he was by a natural cynical pride and passionateness—winced at this unexpected reply, notwithstanding.

'Who is Mr David Heddegan?' he asked, as indifferently as lay in his power.

She informed him the bearer of the name was a general merchant of Giant's Town, St Maria's Island—her father's nearest neighbour and oldest friend.

'Then we shan't see anything more of you on the mainland?' enquired the schoolmaster.

'O, I don't know about that,' said Miss Trewthen.

'Here endeth the career of the belle of the boarding-school your father was foolish enough to send you to. A "general merchant's" wife in the Lyonesse Isles. Will you sell pounds of soap and pennyworths of tin tacks, or whole bars of saponaceous matter, and great tenpenny nails?'

'He's not in such a small way as that!' she almost pleaded. 'He owns ships, though they are rather little ones!'

'O, well, it is much the same. Come, let us walk on; it is tedious to stand still. I thought you would be a failure in education,' he continued, when she obeyed him and strolled ahead. 'You never showed power that way. You remind me much of some of those women who think they are sure to be great actresses if they go on the stage, because they have a pretty face, and forget that what we require is acting. But you found your mistake, didn't you?'

'Don't taunt me, Charles.' It was noticeable that the young school-master's tone caused her no anger or retaliatory passion; far otherwise: there was a tear in her eye. 'How is it you are at Pen-zephyr?' she enquired.

'I don't taunt you. I speak the truth, purely in a friendly way, as I should to anyone I wished well. Though for that matter I might have some excuse even for taunting you. Such a terrible hurry as you've been in. I hate a woman who is in such a hurry.'

'How do you mean that?'

'Why—to be somebody's wife or other—anything's wife rather than nobody's. You couldn't wait for me, O, no. Well, thank God, I'm cured of all that!'

'How merciless you are!' she said bitterly. 'Wait for you? What does that mean, Charley? You never showed—anything to wait for—anything special towards me.'

'O come, Baptista dear; come!'

'What I mean is, nothing definite,' she expostulated. 'I suppose you liked me a little; but it seemed to me to be only a pastime on your part, and that you never meant to make an honourable engagement of it.'

'There, that's just it! You girls expect a man to mean business at the first look. No man when he first becomes interested in a woman has any definite scheme of engagement to marry her in his mind, unless he is meaning a vulgar mercenary marriage. However, I *did* at last mean an honourable engagement, as you call it, come to that.'

'But you never said so, and an indefinite courtship soon injures a woman's position and credit, sooner than you think.'

'Baptista, I solemnly declare that in six months I should have asked you to marry me.'

She walked along in silence, looking on the ground, and appearing very uncomfortable. Presently he said, 'Would you have waited for me if you had known?' To this she whispered in a sorrowful whisper, 'Yes!'

They went still farther in silence—passing along one of the beautiful walks on the outskirts of the town, yet not observant of scene or situation. Her shoulder and his were close together, and he clasped his fingers round the small of her arm—quite lightly, and without any attempt at impetus; yet the act seemed to say, 'Now I hold you, and my will must be yours.'

Recurring to a previous question of hers he said, 'I have merely run down here for a day or two from school near Trufal, before going off to the North for the rest of my holiday. I have seen my relations at Redrutin quite lately, so I am not going there this time. How little I thought of meeting you! How very different the circumstances would have been if, instead of parting again as we must in half-an-hour or so, possibly for ever, you had been now just going off with me, as my wife, on our honeymoon trip. Ha-ha—well—so humorous is life!'

She stopped suddenly. 'I must go back now—this is altogether too painful, Charley! It is not at all a kind mood you are in today.'

'I don't want to pain you—you know I do not,' he said more gently. 'Only it just exasperates me—this you are going to do. I wish you would not.'

'What?'

'Marry him. There, now I have showed you my true sentiments.'

'I must do it now,' said she.

'Why?' he asked, dropping the off-hand masterful tone he had hitherto spoken in, and becoming earnest; still holding her arm, however, as if she were his chattel to be taken up or put down at will. 'It is never too late to break off a marriage that's distasteful to you. Now I'll say one thing; and it is truth: I wish you would marry me instead of him, even now, at the last moment, though you have served me so badly.'

'O, it is not possible to think of that!' she answered hastily, shaking her head. 'When I get home all will be prepared—it is ready even now—the things for the party, the furniture, Mr Heddegan's new suit, and everything. I should require the courage of a tropical lion to go home there and say I wouldn't carry out my promise!'

'Then go, in Heaven's name! But there would be no necessity for you to go home and face them in that way. If we were to marry, it would have to be at once, instantly; or not at all. I should think your affection not worth the having unless you agreed to come back with me to Trufal this evening, where we could be married by licence on Monday morning. And then no Mr David Heddegan or anybody else could get you away from me.'

'I must go home by the Tuesday boat,' she faltered. 'What would they think if I did not come?'

'You could go home by that boat just the same. All the difference would be that I should go with you. You could leave me on the quay, where I'd have a smoke, while you went and saw your father and mother privately; you could then tell them what you had done, and that I was waiting not far off; that I was a schoolmaster in a fairly good position, and a young man you had known when you were at the Training College. Then I would come boldly forward; and they would see that it could not be altered, and so you wouldn't suffer a lifelong misery by being the wife of a wretched old gaffer you don't like at all. Now, honestly; you do like me best, don't you, Baptista?'

'Yes.'

'Then we will do as I say.'

She did not pronounce a clear affirmative. But that she consented to the novel proposition at some moment or other of that walk was apparent by what occurred a little later.

3

An enterprise of such pith required, indeed, less talking than consideration. The first thing they did in carrying it out was to return to the railway station, where Baptista took from her luggage a small trunk of immediate necessaries which she would in any case have required after missing the boat. That same afternoon they travelled up the line to Trufal.

Charles Stow (as his name was), despite his disdainful indifference to things, was very careful of appearances, and made the journey independently of her though in the same train. He told her where she could get board and lodgings in the city; and with merely a distant nod to her of a provisional kind, went off to his own quarters, and to see about the licence.

On Sunday she saw him in the morning across the nave of the procathedral. In the afternoon they walked together in the fields, where he told her that the licence would be ready next day, and would be available the day after, when the ceremony could be performed as early after eight o'clock as they should choose.

His courtship, thus renewed after an interval of two years, was as impetuous, violent even, as it was short. The next day came and passed, and the final arrangements were made. Their agreement was to get the ceremony over as soon as they possibly could the next morning, so as to go on to Pen-zephyr at once, and reach that place in time for the boat's departure the same day. It was in obedience to Baptista's earnest request that Stow consented thus to make the whole journey to Lyonesse by land and water at one heat, and not break it at Pen-zephyr; she seemed to be oppressed with a dread of lingering anywhere, this great first act of disobedience to her parents once accomplished, with the weight on her mind that her home had to be convulsed by the disclosure of it. To face her difficulties over the water immediately she had created them was, however, a course more desired by Baptista than by her lover; though for once he gave way.

The next morning was bright and warm as those which had preceded it. By six o'clock it seemed nearly noon, as is often the case in that part of England in the summer season. By nine they were husband and wife. They packed up and departed by the earliest train after the service; and on the way discussed at length what she should say on meeting her parents, Charley dictating the turn of each phrase. In her anxiety they had travelled so early that when they reached Pen-zephyr they found there were nearly two hours on their hands before the steamer's time of sailing.

Baptista was extremely reluctant to be seen promenading the streets of the watering-place with her husband till, as above stated, the household at Giant's Town should know the unexpected course of events from her own lips; and it was just possible, if not likely, that some Lyonessian might be prowling about there, or even have come across the sea to look for her. To meet anyone to whom she was known, and to have to reply to awkward questions about the strange young man at her side before her well-framed announcement had been delivered at proper time and place, was a thing she could not contemplate with equanimity. So, instead of looking at the shops and harbour, they went along the coast a little way.

The heat of the morning was by this time intense. They clambered up on some cliffs, and while sitting there, looking around at St Michael's Mount and other objects, Charles said to her that he thought he would run down to the beach at their feet, and take just one plunge into the sea.

Baptista did not much like the idea of being left alone; it was gloomy, she said. But he assured her he would not be gone more than a quarter of an hour at the outside, and she passively assented.

Down he went, disappeared, appeared again, and looked back. Then he again proceeded, and vanished, till, as a small waxen object, she saw him emerge from the nook that had screened him, cross the white fringe of foam, and walk into the undulating mass of blue. Once in the water he seemed less inclined to hurry than before; he remained a long time; and, unable either to appreciate his skill or criticize his want of it at that distance, she withdrew her eyes from the spot, and gazed at the still outline of St Michael's—now beautifully toned in gray.

Her anxiety for the hour of departure, and to cope at once with the approaching incidents that she would have to manipulate as best she could, sent her into a reverie. It was now Tuesday; she would reach home in the evening—a very late time they would say; but, as the delay was a pure accident, they would deem her marriage to Mr Heddegan tomorrow still practicable. Then Charles would have to be produced from the background. It was a terrible undertaking to think of, and she almost regretted her temerity in wedding so hastily that morning. The rage of her father would be so crushing; the reproaches of her mother so bitter; and perhaps Charles would answer hotly, and perhaps cause estrangement till death. There had obviously been no alarm about her at St Maria's, or somebody would have sailed across to enquire for her. She had, in a letter written at the beginning of the week, spoken of the hour at which she intended to leave her country schoolhouse; and from this her friends had probably perceived that by such timing she would run a risk of losing the Saturday boat. She had missed it, and as a consequence sat here on the shore as Mrs Charles Stow.

This brought her to the present, and she turned from the outline of St Michael's Mount to look about for her husband's form. He was, as far as she could discover, no longer in the sea. Then he was dressing. By moving a few steps she could see where his clothes lay. But Charles was not beside them.

Baptista looked back again at the water in bewilderment, as if her senses were the victim of some sleight of hand. Not a speck or spot resembling a man's head or face showed anywhere. By this time she was alarmed, and her alarm intensified when she perceived a little beyond the scene of her husband's bathing a small area of water, the quality of whose surface differed from that of the surrounding expanse as the coarse vegetation of some foul patch in a mead differs from the fine green of the remainder. Elsewhere it looked flexuous, here it looked vermiculated and lumpy, and her marine experiences suggested to her in a moment that two currents met and caused a turmoil at this place.

She descended as hastily as her trembling limbs would allow. The way down was terribly long, and before reaching the heap of clothes it occurred to her that, after all, it would be best to run first for help. Hastening along in a lateral direction she proceeded inland till she met a man, and soon afterwards two others. To them she exclaimed, 'I think a gentleman who was bathing is in some danger. I cannot see him as I could. Will you please run and help him, at once, if you will be so kind?'

She did not think of turning to show them the exact spot, indicating it vaguely by the direction of her hand, and still going on her way with the idea of gaining more assistance. When she deemed, in her faintness, that she had carried the alarm far enough, she faced about and dragged herself back again. Before reaching the now dreaded spot she met one of the men.

'We can see nothing at all, Miss,' he declared.

Having gained the beach, she found the tide in, and no sign of Charley's clothes. The other men whom she had besought to come had disappeared, it must have been in some other direction, for she had not met them going away. They, finding nothing, had probably thought her alarm a mere conjecture, and given up the quest.

Baptista sank down upon the stones near at hand. Where Charley had undressed was now sea. There could not be the least doubt that he was drowned, and his body sucked under by the current; while his clothes, lying within high-water mark, had probably been carried away by the rising tide.

She remained in a stupor for some minutes, till a strange sensation succeeded the aforesaid perceptions, mystifying her intelligence, and leaving her physically almost inert. With his personal disappearance, the last three days of her life with him seemed to be swallowed up, also his image, in her mind's eye, waned curiously, receded far away, grew stranger and stranger, less and less real. Their meeting and marriage had been so sudden, unpremeditated, adventurous, that she could hardly believe that she had played her part in such a reckless drama. Of all the few hours of her life with Charles, the portion that most insisted in coming back to memory was their fortuitous encounter on the previous Saturday, and those bitter reprimands with which he had begun the attack, as it might be called, which had piqued her to an unexpected consummation.

A sort of cruelty, an imperiousness, even in his warmth, had characterized Charles Stow. As a lover he had ever been a bit of a tyrant; and it might pretty truly have been said that he had stung her into marriage with him at last. Still more alien from her life did these reflections operate to make him; and then they would be chased away by an interval of passionate weeping and mad regret. Finally, there returned upon the confused mind of the young wife the recollection that she was on her way homeward, and that the packet would sail in three-quarters of an hour.

Except the parasol in her hand, all she possessed was at the station awaiting her onward journey.

She looked in that direction; and, entering one of those undemonstrative phases so common with her, walked quietly on.

At first she made straight for the railway; but suddenly turning she went to a shop and wrote an anonymous line announcing his death by drowning to the only person she had ever heard Charles mention as a relative. Posting this stealthily, and with a fearful look around her, she seemed to acquire a terror of the late events, pursuing her way to the station as if followed by a spectre.

When she got to the office she asked for the luggage that she had left there on the Saturday as well as the trunk left on the morning just lapsed. All were put in the boat, and she herself followed. Quickly as these things had been done, the whole proceeding, nevertheless, had been almost automatic on Baptista's part, ere she had come to any definite conclusion on her course.

Just before the bell rang she heard a conversation on the pier, which removed the last shade of doubt from her mind, if any had existed, that she was Charles Stow's widow. The sentences were but fragmentary, but she could easily piece them out.

'A man drowned—swam out too far—was a stranger to the place— people in boat—saw him go down—couldn't get there in time.'

The news was little more definite than this as yet; though it may as well be stated once for all that the statement was true. Charley, with the over-confidence of his nature, had ventured out too far for his strength, and succumbed in the absence of assistance, his lifeless body being at that moment suspended in the transparent mid-depths of the bay. His clothes, however, had merely been gently lifted by the rising tide, and floated into a nook hard by, where they lay out of sight of the passers-by till a day or two after.

4

In ten minutes they were steaming out of the harbour for their voyage of four or five hours, at whose ending she would have to tell her strange story.

As Pen-zephyr and all its environing scenes disappeared behind Mouse-hole and St Clement's Isle, Baptista's ephemeral, meteor-like husband impressed her yet more as a fantasy. She was still in such a trance-like state that she had been an hour on the little packet-boat before she became aware of the agitating fact that Mr Heddegan was on board with her. Involuntarily she slipped from her left hand the symbol of her wifehood.

'Hee-hee! Well, the truth is, I wouldn't interrupt 'ee. "I reckon she don't see me, or won't see me," I said, "and what's the hurry? She'll see enough o' me soon!" I hope ye be well, mee deer?'

He was a hale, well-conditioned man of about five-and-fifty, of the complexion common to those whose lives are passed on the bluffs and beaches of an ocean isle. He extended the four quarters of his face in a genial smile, and his hand for a grasp of the same magnitude. She gave her own in surprised docility, and he continued:

'I couldn't help coming across to meet 'ee. What an unfortunate

thing you missing the boat and not coming Saturday! They meant to
have warned 'ee that the time was changed, but forgot it at the last
moment. The truth is that I should have informed 'ee myself, but I was
that busy finishing up a job last week, so as to have this week free, that
I trusted to your father for attending to these little things. However,
so plain and quiet as it is all to be, it really do not matter so much as it
might otherwise have done, and I hope ye haven't been greatly put out.
Now, if you'd sooner that I should not be seen talking to 'ee—if 'ee feel
shy at all before strangers—just say. I'll leave 'ee to yourself till we get
home.'

'Thank you much. I am indeed a little tired, Mr Heddegan.'

He nodded urbane acquiescence, strolled away immediately, and
minutely inspected the surface of the funnel, till some female passengers
of Giant's Town tittered at what they must have thought a rebuff—for
the approaching wedding was known to many on St Maria's Island,
though to nobody elsewhere. Baptista coloured at their satire, and called
him back, and forced herself to commune with him in at least a
mechanically friendly manner.

The opening event had been thus different from her expectation, and
she had adumbrated no act to meet it. Taken aback, she passively
allowed circumstances to pilot her along; and so the voyage was made.

It was near dusk when they touched the pier of Giant's Town, where
several friends and neighbours stood awaiting them. Her father had a
lantern in his hand. Her mother, too, was there, reproachfully glad that
the delay had at last ended so simply. Mrs Trewthen and her daughter
went together along the Giant's Walk, or promenade, to the house,
rather in advance of her husband and Mr Heddegan, who talked in loud
tones which reached the women over their shoulders.

Some would have called Mrs Trewthen a good mother; but though
well-meaning she was maladroit, and her intentions missed their mark.
This might have been partly attributable to the slight deafness from
which she suffered. Now, as usual, the chief utterances came from her
lips.

'Ah, yes, I'm so glad, my child, that you've got over safe. It is all ready,
and everything so well arranged, that nothing but misfortune could
hinder you settling as, with God's grace, becomes 'ee. Close to your
mother's door a'most, 'twill be a great blessing, I'm sure; and I was very
glad to find from your letters that you'd held your word sacred. That's
right—make your word your bond always. Mrs Wace seems to be a sen-

sible woman. I hope the Lord will do for her as he's doing for you no long time hence. And how did 'ee get over the terrible journey from Tor-upon-Sea to Pen-zephyr? Once you'd done with the railway, of course, you seemed quite at home. Well, Baptista, conduct yourself seemly, and all will be well.'

Thus admonished, Baptista entered the house, her father and Mr Heddegan immediately at her back. Her mother had been so didactic that she had felt herself absolutely unable to broach the subjects in the centre of her mind.

The familiar room, with the dark ceiling, the well-spread table, the old chairs, had never before spoken so eloquently of the times ere she knew or had heard of Charley Stow. She went upstairs to take off her things, her mother remaining below to complete the disposition of the supper, and attend to the preparation of tomorrow's meal, altogether composing such an array of pies, from pies of fish to pies of turnips, as was never heard of outside the Western Duchy. Baptista, once alone, sat down and did nothing; and was called before she had taken off her bonnet.

'I'm coming,' she cried, jumping up, and speedily disapparelling herself, brushed her hair with a few touches and went down.

Two or three of Mr Heddegan's and her father's friends had dropped in, and expressed their sympathy for the delay she had been subjected to. The meal was a most merry one except to Baptista. She had desired privacy, and there was none; and to break the news was already a greater difficulty than it had been at first. Everything around her, animate and inanimate, great and small, insisted that she had come home to be married; and she could not get a chance to say nay.

One or two people sang songs, as overtures to the melody of the morrow, till at length bedtime came, and they all withdrew, her mother having retired a little earlier. When Baptista found herself again alone in her bedroom the case stood as before: she had come home with much to say, and she had said nothing.

It was now growing clear even to herself that Charles being dead, she had not determination sufficient within her to break tidings which, had he been alive, would have imperatively announced themselves. And thus with the stroke of midnight came the turning of the scale; her story should remain untold. It was not that upon the whole she thought it best not to attempt to tell it; but that she could not undertake so explosive a matter. To stop the wedding now would cause a convulsion in

Giant's Town little short of volcanic. Weakened, tired, and terrified as she had been by the day's adventures, she could not make herself the author of such a catastrophe. But how refuse Heddegan without telling? It really seemed to her as if her marriage with Mr Heddegan were about to take place as if nothing had intervened.

Morning came. The events of the previous days were cut off from her present existence by scene and sentiment more completely than ever. Charles Stow had grown to be a special being of whom, owing to his character, she entertained rather fearful than loving memory. Baptista could hear when she awoke that her parents were already moving about downstairs. But she did not rise till her mother's rather rough voice resounded up the staircase as it had done on the preceding evening.

'Baptista! Come, time to be stirring! The man will be here, by Heaven's blessing, in three-quarters of an hour. He has looked in already for a minute or two—and says he's going to the church to see if things be well forward.'

Baptista arose, looked out of the window, and took the easy course. When she emerged from the regions above she was arrayed in her new silk frock and best stockings, wearing a linen jacket over the former for breakfasting, and her common slippers over the latter, not to spoil the new ones on the rough precincts of the dwelling.

It is unnecessary to dwell at any great length on this part of the morning's proceedings. She revealed nothing; and married Heddegan, as she had given her word to do, on that appointed August day.

5

Mr Heddegan forgave the coldness of his bride's manner during and after the wedding ceremony, full well aware that there had been considerable reluctance on her part to acquiesce in this neighbourly arrangement, and, as a philosopher of long standing, holding that whatever Baptista's attitude now, the conditions would probably be much the same six months hence as those which ruled among other married couples.

An absolutely unexpected shock was given to Baptista's listless mind about an hour after the wedding service. They had nearly finished the midday dinner when the now husband said to her father, 'We think of starting about two. And the breeze being so fair we shall bring up inside Pen-zephyr new pier about six at least.'

'What—are we going to Pen-zephyr?' said Baptista. 'I don't know anything of it.'

'Didn't you tell her?' asked her father of Heddegan.

It transpired that, owing to the delay in her arrival, this proposal too, among other things, had in the hurry not been mentioned to her, except some time ago as a general suggestion that they would go somewhere. Heddegan had imagined that any trip would be pleasant, and one to the mainland the pleasantest of all.

She looked so distressed at the announcement that her husband willingly offered to give it up, though he had not had a holiday off the island for a whole year. Then she pondered on the inconvenience of staying at Giant's Town, where all the inhabitants were bonded, by the circumstances of their situation, into a sort of family party, which permitted and encouraged on such occasions as these oral criticism that was apt to disturb the equanimity of newly married girls, and would especially worry Baptista in her strange situation. Hence, unexpectedly, she agreed not to disorganize her husband's plans for the wedding jaunt, and it was settled that, as originally intended, they should proceed in a neighbour's sailing boat to the metropolis of the district.

In this way they arrived at Pen-zephyr without difficulty or mishap. Bidding adieu to Jenkin and his man, who had sailed them over, they strolled arm in arm off the pier, Baptista silent, cold, and obedient. Heddegan had arranged to take her as far as Plymouth before their return, but to go no further than where they had landed that day. Their first business was to find an inn; and in this they had unexpected difficulty, since for some reason or other—possibly the fine weather—many of the nearest at hand were full of tourists and commercial travellers. He led her on till he reached a tavern which, though comparatively unpretending, stood in as attractive a spot as any in the town; and this, somewhat to their surprise after their previous experience, they found apparently empty. The considerate old man, thinking that Baptista was educated to artistic notions, though he himself was deficient in them, had decided that it was most desirable to have, on such an occasion as the present, an apartment with 'a good view' (the expression being one he had often heard in use among tourists); and he therefore asked for a favourite room on the first floor, from which a bow-window protruded, for the express purpose of affording such an outlook.

The landlady, after some hesitation, said she was sorry that particular apartment was engaged; the next one, however, or any other in the house, was unoccupied.

'The gentleman who has the best one will give it up tomorrow, and then you can change into it,' she added, as Mr Heddegan hesitated about taking the adjoining and less commanding one.

'We shall be gone tomorrow, and shan't want it,' he said.

Wishing not to lose customers, the landlady earnestly continued that since he was bent on having the best room, perhaps the other gentleman would not object to move at once into the one they despised, since, though nothing could be seen from the window, the room was equally large.

'Well, if he doesn't care for a view,' said Mr Heddegan, with the air of a highly artistic man who did.

'O no—I am sure he doesn't,' she said. 'I can promise that you shall have the room you want. If you would not object to go for a walk for half-an-hour, I could have it ready, and your things in it, and a nice tea laid in the bow-window by the time you come back?'

This proposal was deemed satisfactory by the fussy old tradesman, and they went out. Baptista nervously conducted him in an opposite direction to her walk of the former day in other company, showing on her wan face, had he observed it, how much she was beginning to regret her sacrificial step for mending matters that morning.

She took advantage of a moment when her husband's back was turned to enquire casually in a shop if anything had been heard of the gentleman who was sucked down in the eddy while bathing.

The shopman said, 'Yes, his body has been washed ashore,' and had just handed Baptista a newspaper on which she discerned the heading, 'A Schoolmaster drowned while bathing', when her husband turned to join her. She might have pursued the subject without raising suspicion; but it was more than flesh and blood could do, and completing a small purchase she almost ran out of the shop.

'What is your terrible hurry, mee deer?' said Heddegan, hastening after.

'I don't know—I don't want to stay in shops,' she gasped.

'And we won't,' he said. 'They are suffocating this weather. Let's go back and have some tay!'

They found the much desired apartment awaiting their entry. It was a sort of combination bed- and sitting-room, and the table was prettily spread with high tea in the bow-window, a bunch of flowers in the midst, and a best-parlour chair on each side. Here they shared the meal by the ruddy light of the vanishing sun. But though the view had been engaged, regardless of expense, exclusively for Baptista's pleasure, she did not direct any keen attention out of the window. Her gaze as often fell on the floor and walls of the room as elsewhere, and on the table as much as on either, beholding nothing at all.

But there was a change. Opposite her seat was the door, upon which her eyes presently became riveted like those of a little bird upon a snake. For, on a peg at the back of the door, there hung a hat; such a hat— surely, from its peculiar make, the actual hat—that had been worn by Charles. Conviction grew to certainty when she saw a railway ticket sticking up from the band. Charles had put the ticket there—she had noticed the act.

Her teeth almost chattered; she murmured something incoherent. Her husband jumped up and said, 'You are not well! What is it? What shall I get 'ee?'

'Smelling salts!' she said, quickly and desperately; 'at that chemist's shop you were in just now.'

He jumped up like the anxious old man that he was, caught up his own hat from a back table, and without observing the other hastened out and downstairs.

Left alone she gazed and gazed at the back of the door, then spas- modically rang the bell. An honest-looking country maidservant appeared in response.

'A hat!' murmured Baptista, pointing with her finger. 'It does not belong to us.'

'O yes, I'll take it away,' said the young woman with some hurry. 'It belongs to the other gentleman.'

She spoke with a certain awkwardness, and took the hat out of the room. Baptista had recovered her outward composure. 'The other gen- tleman?' she said. 'Where is the other gentleman?'

'He's in the next room, ma'am. He removed out of this to oblige 'ee.'

'How can you say so? I should hear him if he were there,' said Bap- tista, sufficiently recovered to argue down an apparent untruth.

'He's there,' said the girl, hardily.

'Then it is strange that he makes no noise,' said Mrs Heddegan, con- victing the girl of falsity by a look.

'He makes no noise; but it is not strange,' said the servant.

All at once a dread took possession of the bride's heart, like a cold hand laid thereon; for it flashed upon her that there was a possibility of reconciling the girl's statement with her own knowledge of facts.

'Why does he make no noise?' she weakly said.

The waiting-maid was silent, and looked at her questioner. 'If I tell you, ma'am, you won't tell missis?' she whispered.

Baptista promised.

'Because he's a-lying dead!' said the girl. 'He's the schoolmaster that was drownded yesterday.'

'O!' said the bride, covering her eyes. 'Then he was in this room till just now?'

'Yes,' said the maid, thinking the young lady's agitation natural enough. 'And I told missis that I thought she oughtn't to have done it, because I don't hold it right to keep visitors so much in the dark where death's concerned; but she said the gentleman didn't die of anything infectious; she was a poor, honest, innkeeper's wife, she says, who had to get her living by making hay while the sun sheened. And owing to the drownded gentleman being brought here, she said, it kept so many people away that we were empty, though all the other houses were full. So when your good man set his mind upon the room, and she would have lost good paying folk if he'd not had it, it wasn't to be supposed, she said, that she'd let anything stand in the way. Ye won't say that I've told ye, please, m'm? All the linen has been changed, and as the inquest won't be till tomorrow, after you are gone, she thought you wouldn't know a word of it, being strangers here.'

The returning footsteps of her husband broke off further narration. Baptista waved her hand, for she could not speak. The waiting-maid quickly withdrew, and Mr Heddegan entered with the smelling salts and other nostrums.

'Any better?' he questioned.

'I don't like the hotel,' she exclaimed, almost simultaneously. 'I can't bear it—it doesn't suit me!'

'Is that all that's the matter?' he returned pettishly (this being the first time of his showing such a mood). 'Upon my heart and life such trifling is trying to any man's temper, Baptista! Sending me about from here to yond, and then when I come back saying 'ee don't like the place that I have sunk so much money and words to get for 'ee. 'Od dang it all, 'tis enough to— But I won't say any more at present, mee deer, though it is just too much to expect to turn out of the house now. We shan't get another quiet place at this time of the evening—every other inn in the town is bustling with rackety folk of one sort and t'other, while here 'tis as quiet as the grave—the country, I would say. So bide still, d'ye hear, and tomorrow we shall be out of the town altogether—as early as you like.'

The obstinacy of age had, in short, overmastered its complaisance, and the young woman said no more. The simple course of telling him that in the adjoining room lay a corpse which had lately occupied their own might, it would have seemed, have been an effectual one without further disclosure, but to allude to *that* subject, however it was disguised, was more than Heddegan's young wife had strength for. Horror broke her down. In the contingency one thing only presented itself to her paralysed regard—that here she was doomed to abide, in a hideous contiguity to the dead husband and the living, and her conjecture did, in fact, bear itself out. That night she lay between the two men she had married—Heddegan on the one hand, and on the other through the partition against which the bed stood, Charles Stow.

6

Kindly time had withdrawn the foregoing event three days from the present of Baptista Heddegan. It was ten o'clock in the morning; she had been ill, not in an ordinary or definite sense, but in a state of cold stupefaction, from which it was difficult to arouse her so much as to say a few sentences. When questioned she had replied that she was pretty well.

Their trip, as such, had been something of a failure. They had gone on as far as Falmouth, but here he had given way to her entreaties to return home. This they could not very well do without repassing through Pen-zephyr, at which place they had now again arrived.

In the train she had seen a weekly local paper, and read there a paragraph detailing the inquest on Charles. It was added that the funeral was to take place at his native town of Redrutin on Friday.

After reading this she had shown no reluctance to enter the fatal neighbourhood of the tragedy, only stipulating that they should take their rest at a different lodging from the first; and now comparatively braced up and calm—indeed a cooler creature altogether than when last in the town, she said to David that she wanted to walk out for a while, as they had plenty of time on their hands.

'To a shop as usual, I suppose, mee deer?'

'Partly for shopping,' she said. 'And it will be best for you, dear, to stay in after trotting about so much, and have a good rest while I am gone.'

He assented; and Baptista sallied forth. As she had stated, her first visit was made to a shop, a draper's. Without the exercise of much choice she purchased a black bonnet and veil, also a black stuff gown; a black mantle she already wore. These articles were made up into a parcel which, in spite of the saleswoman's offers, her customer said she would take with her. Bearing it on her arm she turned to the railway, and at the station got a ticket for Redrutin.

Thus it appeared that, on her recovery from the paralysed mood of the former day, while she had resolved not to blast utterly the happiness of her present husband by revealing the history of the departed one, she had also determined to indulge a certain odd, inconsequent, feminine sentiment of decency, to the small extent to which it could do no harm to any person. At Redrutin she emerged from the railway carriage in the black attire purchased at the shop, having during the transit made the change in the empty compartment she had chosen. The other clothes were now in the bandbox and parcel. Leaving these at the cloak-room she proceeded onward, and after a wary survey reached the side of a hill whence a view of the burial ground could be obtained.

It was now a little before two o'clock. While Baptista waited a funeral procession ascended the road. Baptista hastened across, and by the time the procession entered the cemetery gates she had unobtrusively joined it.

In addition to the schoolmaster's own relatives (not a few), the paragraph in the newspapers of his death by drowning had drawn together many neighbours, acquaintances, and onlookers. Among them she passed unnoticed, and with a quiet step pursued the winding path to the chapel, and afterwards thence to the grave. When all was over, and the relatives and idlers had withdrawn, she stepped to the edge of the chasm. From beneath her mantle she drew a little bunch of forget-me-nots, and dropped them in upon the coffin. In a few minutes she also turned and went away from the cemetery. By five o'clock she was again in Pen-zephyr.

'You have been a mortal long time!' said her husband, crossly. 'I allowed you an hour at most, mee deer.'

'It occupied me longer,' said she.

'Well—I reckon it is wasting words to complain. Hang it, ye look so tired and wisht that I can't find heart to say what I would!'

'I am—weary and wisht, David; I am. We can get home tomorrow for certain, I hope?'

'We can. And please God we will!' said Mr Heddegan heartily, as if he too were weary of his brief honeymoon. 'I must be into business again on Monday morning at latest.'

They left by the next morning steamer, and in the afternoon took up their residence in their own house at Giant's Town.

The hour that she reached the island it was as if a material weight had been removed from Baptista's shoulders. Her husband attributed the change to the influence of the local breezes after the hot-house atmosphere of the mainland. However that might be, settled here, a few doors from her mother's dwelling, she recovered in no very long time much of her customary bearing, which was never very demonstrative. She accepted her position calmly, and faintly smiled when her neighbours learned to call her Mrs Heddegan, and said she seemed likely to become the leader of fashion in Giant's Town.

Her husband was a man who had made considerably more money by trade than her father had done: and perhaps the greater profusion of surroundings at her command than she had heretofore been mistress of, was not without an effect upon her. One week, two weeks, three weeks passed; and, being pre-eminently a young woman who allowed things to drift, she did nothing whatever either to disclose or conceal traces of her first marriage; or to learn if there existed possibilities—which there undoubtedly did—by which that hasty contract might become revealed to those about her at any unexpected moment.

While yet within the first month of her marriage, and on an evening just before sunset, Baptista was standing within her garden adjoining the house, when she saw passing along the road a personage clad in a greasy black coat and battered tall hat, which, common enough in the slums of a city, had an odd appearance in St Maria's. The tramp, as he seemed to be, marked her at once—bonnetless and unwrapped as she was her features were plainly recognizable—and with an air of friendly surprise came and leant over the wall.

'What! don't you know me?' said he.

She had some dim recollection of his face, but said that she was not acquainted with him.

'Why, your witness to be sure, ma'am. Don't you mind the man that was mending the church-window when you and your intended husband walked up to be made one; and the clerk called me down from the ladder, and I came and did my part by writing my name and occupation?'

Baptista glanced quickly around; her husband was out of earshot. That would have been of less importance but for the fact that the wedding witnessed by this personage had not been the wedding with Mr Heddegan, but the one on the day previous.

'I've had a misfortune since then, that's pulled me under,' continued her friend. 'But don't let me damp yer wedded joy by naming the particulars. Yes, I've seen changes since; though 'tis but a short time ago—let me see, only a month next week, I think; for 'twere the first or second day in August.'

'Yes—that's when it was,' said another man, a sailor, who had come up with a pipe in his mouth, and felt it necessary to join in (Baptista having receded to escape further speech). 'For that was the first time I set foot in Giant's Town; and her husband took her to him the same day.'

A dialogue then proceeded between the two men outside the wall, which Baptista could not help hearing.

'Ay, I signed the book that made her one flesh,' repeated the decayed glazier. 'Where's her goodman?'

'About the premises somewhere; but you don't see 'em together much,' replied the sailor in an undertone. 'You see, he's older than she.'

'Older? I should never have thought it from my own observation,' said the glazier. 'He was a remarkably handsome man.'

'Handsome? Well, there he is—we can see for ourselves.'

David Heddegan had, indeed, just shown himself at the upper end of the garden; and the glazier, looking in bewilderment from the husband to the wife, saw the latter turn pale.

Now that decayed glazier was a far-seeing and cunning man—too far-seeing and cunning to allow himself to thrive by simple and straightforward means—and he held his peace, till he could read more plainly the meaning of this riddle, merely adding carelessly, 'Well—marriage do alter a man, 'tis true. I should never ha' knowed him!'

He then stared oddly at the disconcerted Baptista, and moving on to where he could again address her, asked her to do him a good turn, since he once had done the same for her. Understanding that he meant money, she handed him some, at which he thanked her, and instantly went away.

7

She had escaped exposure on this occasion; but the incident had been an awkward one, and should have suggested to Baptista that sooner or later the secret must leak out. As it was, she suspected that at any rate she had not heard the last of the glazier.

In a day or two, when her husband had gone to the old town on the other side of the island, there came a gentle tap at the door, and the worthy witness of her first marriage made his appearance a second time.

'It took me hours to get to the bottom of the mystery—hours!' he said with a gaze of deep confederacy which offended her pride very deeply. 'But thanks to a good intellect I've done it. Now, ma'am, I'm not a man to tell tales, even when a tale would be so good as this. But I'm going back to the mainland again, and a little assistance would be as rain on thirsty ground.'

'I helped you two days ago,' began Baptista.

'Yes—but what was that, my good lady? Not enough to pay my passage to Pen-zephyr. I came over on your account, for I thought there was a mystery somewhere. Now I must go back on my own. Mind this—'twould be very awkward for you if your old man were to know. He's a queer temper, though he may be fond.'

She knew as well as her visitor how awkward it would be; and the hush-money she paid was heavy that day. She had, however, the satisfaction of watching the man to the steamer, and seeing him diminish out of sight. But Baptista perceived that the system into which she had been led of purchasing silence thus was one fatal to her peace of mind, particularly if it had to be continued.

Hearing no more from the glazier she hoped the difficulty was past. But another week only had gone by, when, as she was pacing the Giant's Walk (the name given to the promenade), she met the same personage in the company of a fat woman carrying a bundle.

'This is the lady, my dear,' he said to his companion. 'This, ma'am, is my wife. We've come to settle in the town for a time, if so be we can find room.'

'That you won't do,' said she. 'Nobody can live here who is not privileged.'

'I am privileged,' said the glazier, 'by my trade.'

Baptista went on, but in the afternoon she received a visit from the man's wife. This honest woman began to depict, in forcible colours, the necessity for keeping up the concealment.

'I will intercede with my husband, ma'am,' she said. 'He's a true man if rightly managed; and I'll beg him to consider your position. 'Tis a very nice house you've got here,' she added, glancing round, 'and well worth a little sacrifice to keep it.'

The unlucky Baptista staved off the danger on this third occasion as she had done on the previous two. But she formed a resolve that, if the attack were once more to be repeated, she would face a revelation—worse though that must now be than before she had attempted to purchase silence by bribes. Her tormentors, never believing her capable of acting upon such an intention, came again; but she shut the door in their faces. They retreated, muttering something; but she went to the back of the house, where David Heddegan was.

She looked at him, unconscious of all. The case was serious; she knew that well; and all the more serious in that she liked him better now than she had done at first. Yet, as she herself began to see, the secret was one that was sure to disclose itself. Her name and Charles's stood indelibly written in the registers; and though a month only had passed as yet it was a wonder that his clandestine union with her had not already been discovered by his friends. Thus spurring herself to the inevitable, she spoke to Heddegan.

'David, come indoors. I have something to tell you.'

He hardly regarded her at first. She had discerned that during the last week or two he had seemed preoccupied, as if some private business harassed him. She repeated her request. He replied with a sigh, 'Yes, certainly, mee deer.'

When they had reached the sitting-room and shut the door she repeated, faintly, 'David, I have something to tell you—a sort of tragedy I have concealed. You will hate me for having so far deceived you; but perhaps my telling you voluntarily will make you think a little better of me than you would do otherwise.'

'Tragedy?' he said, awakening to interest. 'Much you can know about tragedies, mee deer, that have been in the world so short a time!'

She saw that he suspected nothing, and it made her task the harder. But on she went steadily. 'It is about something that happened before we were married,' she said.

'Indeed!'

'Not a very long time before—a short time. And it is about a lover,' she faltered.

'I don't much mind that,' he said mildly. 'In truth, I was in hopes 'twas more.'

'In hopes!'

'Well, yes.'

This screwed her up to the necessary effort. 'I met my old sweetheart. He scorned me, chid me, dared me, and I went and married him. We were coming straight here to tell you all what we had done; but he was drowned; and I thought I would say nothing about him: and I married you, David, for the sake of peace and quietness. I've tried to keep it from you, but have found I cannot. There—that's the substance of it, and you can never, never forgive me, I am sure!'

She spoke desperately. But the old man, instead of turning black or blue, or slaying her in his indignation, jumped up from his chair, and began to caper around the room in quite an ecstatic emotion.

'O, happy thing! How well it falls out!' he exclaimed, snapping his fingers over his head. 'Ha-ha—the knot is cut—I see a way out of my trouble—ha-ha!'

She looked at him without uttering a sound, till, as he still continued smiling joyfully, she said, 'O—what do you mean? Is it done to torment me?'

'No—no! O, mee deer, your story helps me out of the most heart-aching quandary a poor man ever found himself in! You see, it is this—*I've* got a tragedy, too; and unless you had had one to tell, I could never have seen my way to tell mine!'

'What is yours—what is it?' she asked, with altogether a new view of things.

'Well—it is a bouncer; mine is a bouncer!' said he, looking on the ground and wiping his eyes.

'Not worse than mine?'

'Well—that depends upon how you look at it. Yours had to do with the past alone; and I don't mind it. You see, we've been married a month, and it don't jar upon me as it would if we'd only been married a day or two. Now mine refers to past, present, and future; so that—'

'Past, present, and future!' she murmured. 'It never occurred to me that *you* had a tragedy too.'

'But I have!' he said, shaking his head. 'In fact, four.'

'Then tell 'em!' cried the young woman.

'I will—I will. But be considerate, I beg 'ee, mee deer. Well—I wasn't a bachelor when I married 'ee, any more than you were a spinster. Just as you was a widow-woman, I was a widow-man.'

'Ah!' said she, with some surprise. 'But is that all?—then we are nicely balanced,' she added, relieved.

'No—it is not all. There's the point. I am not only a widower.'

'O, David!'

'I am a widower with four tragedies—that is to say, four strapping girls—the eldest taller than you. Don't 'ee look so struck—dumb-like!

It fell out in this way. I knew the poor woman, their mother, in Pen-zephyr for some years; and—to cut a long story short—I privately mar-ried her at last, just before she died. I kept the matter secret, but it is getting known among the people here by degrees. I've long felt for the children—that it is my duty to have them here, and do something for them. I have not had courage to break it to 'ee, but I've seen lately that it would soon come to your ears, and that hev worried me.'

'Are they educated?' said the ex-schoolmistress.

'No. I am sorry to say they have been much neglected; in truth, they can hardly read. And so I thought that by marrying a young schoolmistress I should get some one in the house who could teach 'em, and bring 'em into genteel condition, all for nothing. You see, they are growed up too tall to be sent to school.'

'O, mercy!' she almost moaned. 'Four great girls to teach the rudi-ments to, and have always in the house with me spelling over their books; and I hate teaching, it kills me. I am bitterly punished—I am, I am!'

'You'll get used to 'em, mee deer, and the balance of secrets—mine against yours—will comfort your heart with a sense of justice. I could send for 'em this week very well—and I will! In faith, I could send this very day. Baptista, you have relieved me of all my difficulty!'

Thus the interview ended, so far as this matter was concerned. Bap-tista was too stupefied to say more, and when she went away to her room she wept from very mortification at Mr Heddegan's duplicity. Educa-tion, the one thing she abhorred; the shame of it to delude a young wife so!

The next meal came round. As they sat, Baptista would not suffer her eyes to turn towards him. He did not attempt to intrude upon her reserve, but every now and then looked under the table and chuckled with satisfaction at the aspect of affairs. 'How very well matched we be!' he said, comfortably.

Next day, when the steamer came in, Baptista saw her husband rush down to meet it; and soon after there appeared at her door four tall, hip-less, shoulderless girls, dwindling in height and size from the eldest to the youngest, like a row of Pan pipes; at the head of them standing Hed-degan. He smiled pleasantly through the gray fringe of his whiskers and beard, and turning to the girls said, 'Now come forrard, and shake hands properly with your stepmother.'

Thus she made their acquaintance, and he went out, leaving them together. On examination the poor girls turned out to be not only plain-looking, which she could have forgiven, but to have such a lamentably meagre intellectual equipment as to be hopelessly inadequate as companions. Even the eldest, almost her own age, could only read with difficulty words of two syllables; and taste in dress was beyond their comprehension. In the long vista of future years she saw nothing but dreary drudgery at her detested old trade without prospect of reward.

She went about quite despairing during the next few days—an unpromising, unfortunate mood for a woman who had not been married six weeks. From her parents she concealed everything. They had been amongst the few acquaintances of Heddegan who knew nothing of his secret, and were indignant enough when they saw such a ready-made household foisted upon their only child. But she would not support them in their remonstrances.

'No, you don't yet know all,' she said.

Thus Baptista had sense enough to see the retributive fairness of this issue. For some time, whenever conversation arose between her and Heddegan, which was not often, she always said, 'I am miserable, and you know it. Yet I don't wish things to be otherwise.'

But one day when he asked, 'How do you like 'em now?' her answer was unexpected. 'Much better than I did,' she said, quietly. 'I may like them very much some day.'

This was the beginning of a serener season for the chastened spirit of Baptista Heddegan. She had, in truth, discovered, underneath the crust of uncouthness and meagre articulation which was due to their Troglodytean existence, that her unwelcomed daughters had natures that were unselfish almost to sublimity. The harsh discipline accorded to their young lives before their mother's wrong had been righted, had operated less to crush them than to lift them above all personal ambition. They considered the world and its contents in a purely objective way, and their own lot seemed only to affect them as that of certain human beings among the rest, whose troubles they knew rather than suffered.

This was such an entirely new way of regarding life to a woman of Baptista's nature, that her attention, from being first arrested by it, became deeply interested. By imperceptible pulses her heart expanded in sympathy with theirs. The sentences of her tragi-comedy, her life, confused till now, became clearer daily. That in humanity, as exemplified by these girls, there was nothing to dislike, but infinitely much to pity, she learnt with the lapse of each week in their company. She grew to like the girls of unpromising exterior, and from liking she got to love them; till they formed an unexpected point of junction between her own and her husband's interests, generating a sterling friendship at least, between a pair in whose existence there had threatened to be neither friendship nor love.

MARY MANN

Little Brother

I MET the parish nurse hurrying from the cottage in which a baby had, that morning, been born, towards a cottage at the other end of the village where a baby was due to be born, that night.

'All well over!' she said. 'Mrs Hodd going on nicely as can be expected.'

'She ought to be used to it by now, Nurse! The thirteenth!'

'Well, this one is dead. Born dead.'

'What a mercy!'

But our nurse does not like a case where the baby is born dead. 'Such a beautiful child too!'

'It's more than can be said of the other twelve.'

'How can you tell?' Nurse said. 'Look at their clothes; look at their hair, standing on end; look at the scenes they live in!'

'The Hodds ought to be sent to prison for having thirteen children.'

'Go and tell Hodd himself so. You'll find him, if you go through the farm-yard. In the turnip-house. He slept there, last night; did not come home at all. He always clears out on these occasions. "A good riddance", Mrs Hodd says.'

Mr Hodd answered my greeting by a sideways chuck of his head, and went on turning the handle of the cutting-machine which a small boy, working with him, replenished with whole turnips. The father of thirteen was a wild, unkempt-looking creature, habited in an outer garment composed of a dirty sack, through the hole cut in the bottom of which his head projected; a tangle of matted red hair met a tangle of matted red beard; a small portion of white cheek beneath the angry-looking blue eyes was the only part of his face uncovered. His arms, thrust through the slits cut in the sides of the sack, were hung about with rags which might once have been sleeves of a grey flannel shirt. Not such a family as the Hodds do we often see in Dulditch, but in the present shortage of labour the farmers are glad to welcome what help they can get.

'So I hear your wife's given birth to a dead baby, Hodd.'

Swish—swish—swish went the knife through the turnips, the neat sections dropping into the basket beneath. Two revolutions of the handle, then a curt, 'So they tell me.'

'Haven't you been home to see your wife?'

'No.' Swish—swish. 'Nor ain't a-goin'.'

'I think you ought to go. Mrs Hodd will be wanting to see you.'

Two vicious turns of the handle of the machine which the boy feeds assiduously. Hodd is 'putting his back into it', this morning!

'She's borne you many children, Hodd.'

'A sight too many!' Swish—swish 'The place is chuck full of 'em. You stamp on 'em as you walk.'

'They keep you poor, I'm afraid!'

'Ah!' Swish—swish—swish.

'At any rate this poor little one won't have to be fed; you're no worse off than before it came.'

'There'll soon be another,' Hodd grunted, savagely prophetic. 'There's no stoppin' my missus, once she's got a-goin'.'

The reflection that it was hardly fair to put it all on to Mrs Hodd, this way, I kept to myself.

The little boy, pitching the turnips into the voracious maw of the machine, looked at me brightly. He also was red-headed, he also was attired for the most part in a sack. He was the eldest hope of the Hodd family, helping his father in the hour between morning and afternoon school.

'Him and me—,' a nod in the direction of his parent, 'have got to make a box tonight, when we laves off wark', he said. 'Mother, she've sent ward by Nurse we've got to make a box to put little brother in.'

'Ah, poor little one!'

'Then him and me,' a chuck of his chin at the parent Hodd 'is a-goin' to carry 'm to the corner of the chech-yard where there ain't no blessin'.'

'Now then! Git on wi' them turmits, boy.' In his pleasurable anticipation of the jaunt before him, the boy had stopped in his work. But he at once re-addressed himself to the task of throwing the turnips into the ever-open mouth of the cutter, where they bobbed about merrily for a moment or two before settling into position for the knives to slice.

'Well, good morning, Hodd,' I said. 'I shall go to see your wife and the poor baby before it is put in the box.'

Swish. Swish. Swish.

In the kitchen I passed through on my way upstairs, a pair of Hodds, of too tender an age to be at school, were seated on a sack—again a sack!—spread before the fire, and were playing with a large battered doll. Mrs Hodd, above, lay in her big squalid bed, alone.

'Have you no one to wait on you?'

'Blesh you, yes! There's the gal Maude.' Maude was the twelve years old daughter. 'Nonly she've gone on a narrand now, to let the parson's folk know as I'm brought to bed, and to ask for a drop o' soup, and a packet o' gro'ts, and a few nouraging matters o' that sort. For I've got to have life kep' in me somehow, I s'pose. And if parson's folk don't do it I don't know who should.'

'So the poor baby is dead, this time, Mrs Hodd!'

Mrs Hodd wrung her nose round to the middle of her cheek with a loud snuffle, tears streamed from her blue eyes. (All the Hodd family have red hair and blue eyes; so adorned themselves, and having started on a family thus endowed, Mr and Mrs Hodd had never paused to alter the pattern.)

'That fare hard,' she gurgled, 'to go t'rough it all, and then to lose 'em.'

'But you have so many, Mrs Hodd. This little one could well be spared. Hodd thinks as I do.'

'Ah! Hodd, he han't a mother's heart!'

'I am sure it is all you can do to feed and clothe the twelve.'

'Clothe? I don't clothe 'em. I look after their insides. No one can't say as my child'en look starved. If parson's folk want to see 'em clothed they must do it theirselves. My job's their insides, I take it.'

'I should like to see the poor baby, Mrs Hodd. I hear it was a very fine child.'

'Mine allers is!' Mrs Hodd testified. 'A crop o' heer he'd got all over his poll like golden suverins. My little uns, they're all that plased wi' their little brother! A fine hollerin' there'll be when he's took off to the buryin'.'

'Where is he? Look, I've brought a few flowers to lay upon his tiny coffin.'

Mrs Hodd, without lifting her tousled head, cast a glance of enquiry round the almost bare room. Near the door a rude bed had been made by spreading a towel over a frowsy pillow laid on two chairs.

'Ain't he theer?' the woman asked, her eyes upon the chairs.

'Nothing's there, Mrs Hodd.'

'Randolph!' Mrs Hodd screamed with startling abruptness. ' 'Vangeline! Come you here, this minute; don't I'll warm yer jackets for ye when I git yer.'

'Pray do not excite yourself,' I cried, alarmed. 'If you want the children who are in the kitchen I will fetch them for you.'

The tiny children on the filthy hearth were too much engrossed with their play to be aware of me, standing to watch. They were striving to draw over the rigid legs of the doll the grey calico nightgown of which they were stripping it when I saw them last. Their fat dirty little hands trembled with their eagerness to accomplish this feat. The mite who had the toy on her knees rocked herself maternally, and gave chirrups of encouragement as she worked.

'Theer! put ickle arms in! Put in ickle arms!'

Failing in every effort to insert the arms, she decided to dispense with that formality; pulling the awful nightgown over the shoulders she knotted it at the back of a little red head.

Then she turned the battered doll on its back and I saw that it was the dead baby.

Evangeline and Randolph pushed their grubby fingers into the open mouth, and tried to force them into the sunken eyes, in order to raise the lids.

'Wake up! Wake up, ickle brudder!' they said.

When I had rescued the desecrated body, and borne it to its poor bier in the mother's room, I spoke a word to Mrs Hodd which she resented.

'Time is long for sech little uns, when t' others 're at school and I'm laid by,' she said. 'Other folkes' child'en have a toy, now and then, to kape 'em out o' mischief. My little uns han't. He've kep' 'em quite (quiet) for hours, the po'r baby have; and I'll lay a crown they han't done no harm to their little brother.'

M. R. JAMES

Two Doctors

IT is a very common thing, in my experience, to find papers shut up in old books; but one of the rarest things to come across any such that are at all interesting. Still it does happen, and one should never destroy them unlooked at. Now it was a practice of mine before the war occasionally to buy old ledgers of which the paper was good, and which possessed a good many blank leaves, and to extract these and use them for my own notes and writings. One such I purchased for a small sum in 1911. It was tightly clasped, and its boards were warped by having for years been obliged to embrace a number of extraneous sheets. Three-quarters of this inserted matter had lost all vestige of importance for any living human being: one bundle had not. That it belonged to a lawyer is certain, for it is endorsed: *The strangest case I have yet met*, and bears initials, and an address in Gray's Inn. It is only materials for a case, and consists of statements by possible witnesses. The man who would have been the defendant or prisoner seems never to have appeared. The *dossier* is not complete, but, such as it is, it furnishes a riddle in which the supernatural appears to play a part. You must see what you can make of it.

The following is the setting and the tale as I elicit it.

The scene is Islington in 1718, and the time the month of June: a countrified place, therefore, and a pleasant season. Dr Abell was walking in his garden one afternoon waiting for his horse to be brought round that he might set out on his visits for the day. To him entered his confidential servant, Luke Jennett, who had been with him twenty years.

'I said I wished to speak to him, and what I had to say might take some quarter of an hour. He accordingly bade me go into his study, which was a room opening on the terrace path where he was walking, and came in himself and sat down. I told him that, much against my will, I must look out for another place. He enquired what was my reason, in consideration I had been so long with him. I said if he would excuse me he would do me a great kindness, because (this appears to have been common form even in 1718) I was one that always liked to have every-thing pleasant about me. As well as I can remember, he said that was his case likewise, but he would wish to know why I should change my mind after so many years, and, says he, "You know there can be no talk of a remembrance of you in my will if you leave my service now." I said I had made my reckoning of that.

' "Then," says he, "you must have some complaint to make, and if I could I would willingly set it right." And at that I told him, not seeing how I could keep it back, the matter of my former affidavit and of the bedstaff in the dispensing-room, and said that a house where such things happened was no place for me. At which he, looking very black upon me, said no more, but called me fool, and said he would pay what was owing me in the morning; and so, his horse being waiting, went out. So for that night I lodged with my sister's husband near Battle Bridge and came early next morning to my late master, who then made a great mat-ter that I had not lain in his house and stopped a crown out of my wages owing.

'After that I took service here and there, not for long at a time, and saw no more of him till I came to be Dr Quinn's man at Dodds Hall in Islington.'

There is one very obscure part in this statement—namely, the refer-ence to the former affidavit and the matter of the bedstaff. The former affidavit is not in the bundle of papers. It is to be feared that it was taken out to be read because of its special oddity, and not put back. Of what nature the story was may be guessed later, but as yet no clue has been put into our hands.

The Rector of Islington, Jonathan Pratt, is the next to step forward. He furnishes particulars of the standing and reputation of Dr Abell and Dr Quinn, both of whom lived and practised in his parish.

'It is not to be supposed,' he says, 'that a physician should be a regular attendant at morning and evening prayers, or at the Wednesday lectures, but within the measure of their ability I would say that both these persons fulfilled their obligations as loyal members of the Church of England. At the same time (as you desire my private mind) I must say, in the language of the schools, *distinguo*. Dr A. was to me a source of per-plexity, Dr Q. to my eye a plain, honest believer, not enquiring over closely into points of belief, but squaring his practice to what lights he had. The other interested himself in questions to which Providence, as I hold, designs no answer to be given us in this state: he would ask me, for example, what place I believed those beings now to hold in the scheme of creation which by some are thought neither to have stood fast when the rebel angels fell, nor to have joined with them to the full pitch of their transgression.

'As was suitable, my first answer to him was a question, What warrant he had for supposing any such beings to exist? for that there was none in Scripture I took it he was aware. It appeared—for as I am on the subject, the whole tale may be given—that he grounded himself on such passages as that of the satyr which Jerome tells us conversed with Antony; but thought too that some parts of Scripture might be cited in support. "And besides," said he, "you know 'tis the universal belief among those that spend their days and nights abroad, and I would add that if your calling took you so continuously as it does me about the country lanes by night, you might not be so surprised as I see you to be by my suggestion." "You are then of John Milton's mind," I said, "and hold that 'Millions of spiritual creatures walk the earth | Unseen, both when we wake and when we sleep.'"

' "I do not know," he said, "why Milton should take upon himself to say 'unseen'; though to be sure he was blind when he wrote that. But for the rest, why, yes, I think he was in the right." "Well," I said, "though not so often as you, I am not seldom called abroad pretty late; but I have no mind of meeting a satyr in our Islington lanes in all the years I have been here; and if you have had the better luck, I am sure the Royal Society would be glad to know of it."

'I am reminded of these trifling expressions because Dr A. took them so ill, stamping out of the room in a huff with some such word as that these high and dry parsons had no eyes but for a prayer-book or a pint of wine.

'But this was not the only time that our conversation took a remarkable turn. There was an evening when he came in, at first seeming gay and in good spirits, but afterwards as he sat and smoked by the fire falling into a musing way; out of which to rouse him I said pleasantly that I supposed he had had no meetings of late with his odd friends. A question which did effectually arouse him, for he looked most wildly, and as if scared, upon me, and said, "*You* were never there? I did not see you. Who brought you?" And then in a more collected tone, "What was this about a meeting? I believe I must have been in a doze." To which I answered that I was thinking of fauns and centaurs in the dark lane, and not of a witches' Sabbath; but it seemed he took it differently.

' "Well," said he, "I can plead guilty to neither; but I find you very much more of a sceptic than becomes your cloth. If you care to know about the dark lane you might do worse than ask my housekeeper that lived at the other end of it when she was a child." "Yes," said I, "and the old women in the almshouse and the children in the kennel. If I were you, I would send to your brother Quinn for a bolus to clear your brain." "Damn Quinn," says he; "talk no more of him: he has embezzled four of my best patients this month; I believe it is that cursed man of his, Jennett, that used to be with me, his tongue is never still; it should be nailed to the pillory if he had his deserts." This, I may say, was the only time of his showing me that he had any grudge against either Dr Quinn or Jennett, and as was my business, I did my best to persuade him he was mistaken in them. Yet it could not be denied that some respectable families in the parish had given him the cold shoulder, and for no reason that they were willing to allege. The end was that he said he had not done so ill at Islington but that he could afford to live at ease elsewhere when he chose, and anyhow he bore Dr Quinn no malice. I think I now remember what observation of mine drew him into the train of thought which he next pursued. It was, I believe, my mentioning some juggling tricks which my brother in the East Indies had seen at the court of the Rajah of Mysore. "A convenient thing enough," said Dr Abell to me, "if by some arrangement a man could get the power of communicating motion and energy to inanimate objects." "As if the axe should move itself against him that lifts it; something of that kind?" "Well, I don't know that that was in my mind so much; but if you could summon such a volume from your shelf or even order it to open at the right page."

'He was sitting by the fire—it was a cold evening—and stretched out his hand that way, and just then the fire-irons, or at least the poker, fell over towards him with a great clatter, and I did not hear what else he said. But I told him that I could not easily conceive of an arrangement, as he called it, of such a kind that would not include as one of its conditions a heavier payment than any Christian would care to make; to which he assented. "But," he said, "I have no doubt these bargains can be made very tempting, very persuasive. Still, you would not favour them, eh, Doctor? No, I suppose not."

'This is as much as I know of Dr Abell's mind, and the feeling between these men. Dr Quinn, as I said, was a plain, honest creature, and a man to whom I would have gone—indeed I have before now gone to him—for advice on matters of business. He was, however, every now and again, and particularly of late, not exempt from troublesome fancies. There was certainly a time when he was so much harassed by his dreams that he could not keep them to himself, but would tell them to his acquaintances and among them to me. I was at supper at his house, and he was not inclined to let me leave him at my usual time. "If you go," he said, "there will be nothing for it but I must go to bed and dream of the chrysalis." "You might be worse off," said I. "I do not think it," he said, and he shook himself like a man who is displeased with the complexion of his thoughts. "I only meant," said I, "that a chrysalis is an innocent thing." "This one is not," he said, "and I do not care to think of it."

'However, sooner than lose my company he was fain to tell me (for I pressed him) that this was a dream which had come to him several times of late, and even more than once in a night. It was to this effect, that he seemed to himself to wake under an extreme compulsion to rise and go out of doors. So he would dress himself and go down to his garden door. By the door there stood a spade which he must take, and go out into the garden, and at a particular place in the shrubbery, somewhat clear, and upon which the moon shone (for there was always in his dream a full moon), he would feel himself forced to dig. And after some time the spade would uncover something light-coloured, which he would perceive to be a stuff, linen or woollen, and this he must clear with his hands. It was always the same: of the size of a man and shaped like the chrysalis of a moth, with the folds showing a promise of an opening at one end.

'He could not describe how gladly he would have left all at this stage and run to the house, but he must not escape so easily. So with many groans, and knowing only too well what to expect, he parted these folds of stuff, or, as it sometimes seemed to be, membrane, and disclosed a head covered with a smooth pink skin, which breaking as the creature stirred, showed him his own face in a state of death. The telling of this so much disturbed him that I was forced out of mere compassion to sit with him the greater part of the night and talk with him upon indifferent subjects. He said that upon every recurrence of this dream he woke and found himself, as it were, fighting for his breath.'

Another extract from Luke Jennett's long continuous statement comes in at this point.

'I never told tales of my master, Dr Abell, to anybody in the neighbourhood. When I was in another service I remember to have spoken to my fellow-servants about the matter of the bedstaff, but I am sure I never said either I or he were the persons concerned, and it met with so little credit that I was affronted and thought best to keep it to myself. And when I came back to Islington and found Dr Abell still there, who I was told had left the parish, I was clear that it behoved me to use great discretion, for indeed I was afraid of the man, and it is certain I was no party to spreading any ill report of him. My master, Dr Quinn, was a very just, honest man, and no maker of mischief. I am sure he never stirred a finger nor said a word by way of inducement to a soul to make them leave going to Dr Abell and come to him; nay, he would hardly be persuaded to attend them that came, until he was convinced that if he did not they would send into the town for a physician rather than do as they had hitherto done.

'I believe it may be proved that Dr Abell came into my master's house more than once. We had a new chambermaid out of Hertfordshire, and she asked me who was the gentleman that was looking after the master, that is Dr Quinn, when he was out, and seemed so disappointed that he was out. She said whoever he was he knew the way of the house well, running at once into the study and then into the dispensing-room, and last into the bedchamber. I made her tell me what he was like, and what she said was suitable enough to Dr Abell; but besides she told me she saw the same man at church, and someone told her that was the Doctor.

'It was just after this that my master began to have his bad nights, and complained to me and other persons, and in particular what discomfort he suffered from his pillow and bedclothes. He said he must buy some to suit him, and should do his own marketing. And accordingly brought home a parcel which he said was of the right quality, but where he bought it we had then no knowledge, only they were marked in thread with a coronet and a bird. The women said they were of a sort not commonly met with and very fine, and my master said they were the comfortablest he ever used, and he slept now both soft and deep. Also the feather pillows were the best sorted and his head would sink into them as if they were a cloud: which I have myself remarked several times when I came to wake him of a morning, his face being almost hid by the pillow closing over it.

'I had never any communication with Dr Abell after I came back to Islington, but one day when he passed me in the street and asked me whether I was not looking for another service, to which I answered I was very well suited where I was, but he said I was a tickleminded fellow and he doubted not he should soon hear I was on the world again, which indeed proved true.'

Dr Pratt is next taken up where he left off.

'On the 16th I was called up out of my bed soon after it was light—that is about five—with a message that Dr Quinn was dead or dying. Making my way to his house I found there was no doubt which was the truth. All the persons in the house except the one that let me in were already in his chamber and standing about his bed, but none touching him. He was stretched in the midst of the bed, on his back, without any disorder, and indeed had the appearance of one ready laid out for burial. His hands, I think, were even crossed on his breast. The only thing not usual was that nothing was to be seen of his face, the two ends of the pillow or bolster appearing to be closed quite over it. These I immediately pulled apart, at the same time rebuking those present, and especially the man, for not at once coming to the assistance of his master. He, however, only looked at me and shook his head, having evidently no more hope than myself that there was anything but a corpse before us.

'Indeed it was plain to anyone possessed of the least experience that he was not only dead, but had died of suffocation. Nor could it be conceived that his death was accidentally caused by the mere folding of the pillow over his face. How should he not, feeling the oppression, have lifted his hands to put it away? whereas not a fold of the sheet which was closely gathered about him, as I now observed, was disordered. The next thing was to procure a physician. I had bethought me of this on leaving my house, and sent on the messenger who had come to me to Dr Abell; but I now heard that he was away from home, and the nearest surgeon was got, who, however, could tell no more, at least without opening the body, than we already knew.

'As to any person entering the room with evil purpose (which was the next point to be cleared), it was visible that the bolts of the door were burst from their stanchions, and the stanchions broken away from the door-post by main force; and there was a sufficient body of witnesses, the smith among them, to testify that this had been done but a few minutes before I came. The chamber being, moreover, at the top of the house, the window was neither easy of access nor did it show any sign of an exit made that way, either by marks upon the sill or footprints below upon soft mould.'

The surgeon's evidence forms of course part of the report of the inquest, but since it has nothing but remarks upon the healthy state of the larger organs and the coagulation of blood in various parts of the body, it need not be reproduced. The verdict was 'Death by the visitation of God'.

Annexed to the other papers is one which I was at first inclined to suppose had made its way among them by mistake. Upon further consideration I think I can divine a reason for its presence.

It relates to the rifling of a mausoleum in Middlesex which stood in a park (now broken up), the property of a noble family which I will not name. The outrage was not that of an ordinary resurrection man. The object, it seemed likely, was theft. The account is blunt and terrible. I shall not quote it. A dealer in the North of London suffered heavy penalties as a receiver of stolen goods in connexion with the affair.

ARTHUR MORRISON

Behind the Shade

THE street was the common East End street—two parallels of brick pierced with windows and doors. But at the end of one, where the builder had found a remnant of land too small for another six-roomer, there stood an odd box of a cottage, with three rooms and a wash-house. It had a green door with a well-blacked knocker round the corner; and in the lower window in front stood a 'shade of fruit'—a cone of waxen grapes and apples under a glass cover.

Although the house was smaller than the others, and was built upon a remnant, it was always a house of some consideration. In a street like this mere independence of pattern gives distinction. And a house inhabited by one sole family makes a figure among houses inhabited by two or more, even though it be the smallest of all. And here the seal of respectability was set by the shade of fruit—a sign accepted in those parts. Now, when people keep a house to themselves, and keep it clean; when they neither stand at the doors nor gossip across back-fences; when, moreover, they have a well-dusted shade of fruit in the front window; and, especially, when they are two women who tell nobody their business: they are known at once for well-to-do, and are regarded with the admixture of spite and respect that is proper to the circumstances. They are also watched.

Still, the neighbours knew the history of the Perkinses, mother and daughter, in its main features, with little disagreement: having told it to each other, filling in the details when occasion seemed to serve. Perkins, ere he died, had been a shipwright; and this was when the shipwrights were the aristocracy of the work-shops, and he that worked more than three or four days a week was counted a mean slave: it was long (in fact) before depression, strikes, iron plates, and collective blindness had driven shipbuilding to the Clyde. Perkins had laboured no harder than his fellows, had married a tradesman's daughter, and had spent his money with freedom; and some while after his death his widow and daughter came to live in the small house, and kept a school for tradesmen's little girls in a back room over the wash-house. But as the School Board waxed in power, and the tradesmen's pride in regard thereunto waned, the attendance, never large, came down to twos and threes. Then Mrs Perkins met with her accident. A dweller in Stidder's Rents overtook her one night, and, having vigorously punched her in the face and the breast, kicked her and jumped on her for five minutes as she lay on the pavement. (In the dark, it afterwards appeared, he had mistaken her for his mother.) The one distinct opinion the adventure bred in the street was Mrs Webster's, the Little Bethelite, who considered it a judgment for sinful pride—for Mrs Perkins had been a churchgoer. But the neighbours never saw Mrs Perkins again. The doctor left his patient 'as well as she ever would be', but bed-ridden and helpless. Her daughter was a scraggy, sharp-faced woman of thirty or so, whose black dress hung from her hips as from a wooden frame; and some people got into the way of calling her Mrs Perkins, seeing no other thus to honour. And meantime, the school had ceased, although Miss Perkins essayed a revival, and joined a Dissenting chapel to that end.

Then, one day, a card appeared in the window, over the shade of fruit, with the legend 'Pianoforte Lessons'. It was not approved by the street. It was a standing advertisement of the fact that the Perkinses had a piano, which others had not. It also revealed a grasping spirit on the part of people able to keep a house to themselves, with red curtains and a shade of fruit in the parlour window; who, moreover, had been able to give up keeping a school because of ill-health. The pianoforte lessons were eight-and-sixpence a quarter, two a week. Nobody was ever known to take them but the relieving officer's daughter, and she paid sixpence a lesson, to see how she got on, and left off in three weeks. The card stayed in the window a fortnight longer, and none of the neighbours saw the cart that came in the night and took away the old cabinet piano with the channelled keys, that had been fourth-hand when Perkins bought it twenty years ago. Mrs Clark, the widow who sewed far into the night, may possibly have heard a noise and looked; but she said nothing if she did. There was no card in the window next morning, but the shade of fruit stood primly respectable as ever. The curtains were drawn a little closer across, for some of the children playing in the street were used to flatten their faces against the lower panes, and to discuss the piano, the stuff-bottomed chairs, the antimacassars, the mantelpiece ornaments, and the loo table with the family Bible and the album on it.

It was soon after this that the Perkinses altogether ceased from shop-ping—ceased, at any rate, in that neighbourhood. Trade with them had already been dwindling, and it was said that Miss Perkins was getting stingier than her mother—who had been stingy enough herself. Indeed, the Perkins demeanour began to change for the worse, to be significant of a miserly retirement and an offensive alienation from the rest of the street. One day the deacon called, as was his practice now and then; but, being invited no further than the doorstep, he went away in dudgeon, and did not return. Nor, indeed, was Miss Perkins seen again at chapel.

Then there was a discovery. The spare figure of Miss Perkins was sel-dom seen in the streets, and then almost always at night; but on these occasions she was observed to carry parcels, of varying wrappings and shapes. Once, in broad daylight, with a package in newspaper, she made such haste past a shop-window where stood Mrs Webster and Mrs Jones, that she tripped on the broken sole of one shoe, and fell headlong. The newspaper broke away from its pins, and although the woman reached and recovered her parcel before she rose, it was plain to see that it was made up of cheap shirts, cut out ready for the stitching. The street had the news the same hour, and it was generally held that such a taking of the bread out of the mouths of them that wanted it by them that had plenty was a scandal and a shame, and ought to be put a stop to. And Mrs Webster, foremost in the setting right of things, undertook to find out whence the work came, and to say a few plain words in the right quarter.

All this while nobody watched closely enough to note that the parcels brought in were fewer than the parcels taken out. Even a hand-truck, late one evening, went unremarked: the door being round the corner, and most people within. One morning, though, Miss Perkins, her best foot foremost, was venturing along a near street with an out-going parcel—large and triangular and wrapped in white drugget—when the relieving officer turned the corner across the way.

The relieving officer was a man in whose system of etiquette the Perkinses had caused some little disturbance. His ordinary female acquaintances (not, of course, professional) he was in the habit of rec-ognizing by a gracious nod. When he met the minister's wife he lifted his hat, instantly assuming an intense frown, in the event of irreverent observation. Now he quite felt that the Perkinses were entitled to some advance upon the nod, although it would be absurd to raise them to a level with the minister's wife. So he had long since established a compromise: he closed his finger and thumb upon the brim of his hat, and let his hand fall forthwith. Preparing now to accomplish this salute, he was astounded to see that Miss Perkins, as soon as she was aware of his approach, turned her face, which was rather flushed, away from him, and went hurrying onward, looking at the wall on her side of the street. The relieving officer, checking his hand on its way to his hat, stopped and looked after her as she turned the corner, hugging her parcel on the side next the wall. Then he shouldered his umbrella and pursued his way, holding his head high, and staring fiercely straight before him; for a relieving officer is not used to being cut.

It was a little after this that Mr Crouch, the landlord, called. He had not been calling regularly, because of late Miss Perkins had left her five shillings of rent with Mrs Crouch every Saturday evening. He noted with satisfaction the whitened sills and the shade of fruit, behind which the curtains were now drawn close and pinned together. He turned the corner and lifted the bright knocker. Miss Perkins half opened the door, stood in the opening, and began to speak.

His jaw dropped. 'Beg pardon—forgot something. Won't wait—call next week—do just as well'; and he hurried round the corner and down the street, puffing and blowing and staring. 'Why, the woman frightened me,' he afterward explained to Mrs Crouch. 'There's something wrong with her eyes, and she looked like a corpse. The rent wasn't ready—I could see that before she spoke; so I cleared out.'

'P'r'aps something's happened to the old lady,' suggested Mrs Crouch. 'Anyhow, I should think the rent 'ud be all right.' And he thought it would.

Nobody saw the Perkinses that week. The shade of fruit stood in its old place, but was thought not to have been dusted after Tuesday. Certainly the sills and the doorstep were neglected. Friday, Saturday and Sunday were swallowed up in a choking brown fog, wherein men lost their bearings, and fell into docks, and stepped over embankment edges. It was as though a great blot had fallen, and had obliterated three days from the calendar. It cleared on Monday morning, and, just as the women in the street were sweeping their steps, Mr Crouch was seen at the green door. He lifted the knocker, dull and sticky now with the foul vapour, and knocked a gentle rat-tat. There was no answer. He knocked again, a little louder, and waited, listening. But there was neither voice nor movement within. He gave three heavy knocks, and then came round to the front window. There was the shade of fruit, the glass a little duller on the top, the curtains pinned close about it, and nothing to see beyond them. He tapped at the window with his knuckles, and backed into the roadway to look at the one above. This was a window with a striped holland blind and a short net curtain; but never a face was there.

The sweepers stopped to look, and one from opposite came and reported that she had seen nothing of Miss Perkins for a week, and that certainly nobody had left the house that morning. And Mr Crouch grew excited, and bellowed through the keyhole.

In the end they opened the sash-fastening with a knife, moved the shade of fruit, and got in. The room was bare and empty, and their steps and voices resounded as those of people in an unfurnished house. The wash-house was vacant, but it was clean, and there was a little net curtain in the window. The short passage and the stairs were bare boards. In the back room by the stair-head was a drawn window-blind, and that was all. In the front room with the striped blind and the short curtain there was a bed of rags and old newspapers; also a wooden box; and on each of these was a dead woman.

Both deaths, the doctor found, were from syncope, the result of inanition; and the better-nourished woman—she on the bed—had died the sooner; perhaps by a day or two. The other case was rather curious; it exhibited a degree of shrinkage in the digestive organs unprecedented in his experience. After the inquest the street had an evening's fame: for the papers printed coarse drawings of the house, and in leaderettes demanded the abolition of something. Then it became its wonted self. And it was doubted if the waxen apples and the curtains fetched enough to pay Mr Crouch his fortnight's rent.

RUDYARD KIPLING

'Wireless'

KASPAR'S SONG IN 'VARDA'

(From the Swedish of Stagnelius.)

Eyes aloft, over dangerous places,
  The children follow where Psyche flies,
And, in the sweat of their upturned faces,
  Slash with a net at the empty skies.

So it goes they fall amid brambles,
  And sting their toes on the nettle-tops,
Till after a thousand scratches and scrambles
  They wipe their brows, and the hunting stops.

Then to quiet them comes their father
  And stills the riot of pain and grief,
Saying, 'Little ones, go and gather
  Out of my garden a cabbage leaf.

'You will find on it whorls and clots of
  Dull grey eggs that, properly fed,
Turn, by way of the worm, to lots of
  Radiant Psyches raised from the dead.'

★   ★   ★

'Heaven is beautiful, Earth is ugly,'
  The three-dimensioned preacher saith,
So we must not look where the snail and the slug lie
  For Psyche's birth: . . . And that is our death!

'IT's a funny thing, this Marconi business, isn't it?' said Mr Shaynor, coughing heavily. 'Nothing seems to make any difference, by what they tell me—storms, hills, or anything; but if that's true we shall know before morning.'

'Of course it's true,' I answered, stepping behind the counter. 'Where's old Mr Cashell?'

'He's had to go to bed on account of his influenza. He said you'd very likely drop in.'

'Where's his nephew?'

'Inside, getting the things ready. He told me that the last time they experimented they put the pole on the roof of one of the big hotels here, and the batteries electrified all the water-supply, and'—he giggled—'the ladies got shocks when they took their baths.'

'I never heard of that.'

'The hotel wouldn't exactly advertise it, would it? Just now, by what Mr Cashell tells me, they're trying to signal from here to Poole, and they're using stronger batteries than ever. But, you see, he being the guvnor's nephew and all that (and it will be in the papers too), it doesn't matter how they electrify things in this house. Are you going to watch?'

'Very much. I've never seen this game. Aren't you going to bed?'

'We don't close till ten on Saturdays. There's a good deal of influenza in town, too, and there'll be a dozen prescriptions coming in before morning. I generally sleep in the chair here. It's warmer than jumping out of bed every time. Bitter cold, isn't it?'

'Freezing hard. I'm sorry your cough's worse.'

'Thank you. I don't mind cold so much. It's this wind that fair cuts me to pieces.' He coughed again hard and hackingly, as an old lady came in for ammoniated quinine. 'We've just run out of it in bottles, madam,' said Mr Shaynor, returning to the professional tone, 'but if you will wait two minutes, I'll make it up for you, madam.'

I had used the shop for some time, and my acquaintance with the proprietor had ripened into friendship. It was Mr Cashell who revealed to me the purpose and power of Apothecaries' Hall what time a fellow-chemist had made an error in a prescription of mine, had lied to cover his sloth, and when error and lie were brought home to him had written vain letters.

'A disgrace to our profession,' said the thin, mild-eyed man, hotly, after studying the evidence. 'You couldn't do a better service to the profession than report him to Apothecaries' Hall.'

I did so, not knowing what djinns I should evoke; and the result was such an apology as one might make who had spent a night on the rack. I conceived great respect for Apothecaries' Hall, and esteem for Mr Cashell, a zealous craftsman who magnified his calling. Until

Mr Shaynor came down from the North his assistants had by no means agreed with Mr Cashell. 'They forget,' said he, 'that, first and foremost, the compounder is a medicine-man. On him depends the physician's reputation. He holds it literally in the hollow of his hand, Sir.'

Mr Shaynor's manners had not, perhaps, the polish of the grocery and Italian warehouse next door, but he knew and loved his dispensary work in every detail. For relaxation he seemed to go no farther afield than the romance of drugs—their discovery, preparation, packing, and export—but it led him to the ends of the earth, and on this subject, and the Pharmaceutical Formulary, and Nicholas Culpepper, most confident of physicians, we met.

Little by little I grew to know something of his beginnings and his hopes—of his mother, who had been a school-teacher in one of the northern counties, and of his red-headed father, a small job-master at Kirby Moors, who died when he was a child; of the examinations he had passed and of their exceeding and increasing difficulty; of his dreams of a shop in London; of his hate for the price-cutting Co-operative stores; and, most interesting, of his mental attitude towards customers.

'There's a way you get into,' he told me, 'of serving them carefully, and I hope, politely, without stopping your own thinking. I've been reading Christy's *New Commercial Plants* all this autumn, and that needs keeping your mind on it, I can tell you. So long as it isn't a prescription, of course, I can carry as much as half a page of Christy in my head, and at the same time I could sell out all that window twice over, and not a penny wrong at the end. As to prescriptions, I think I could make up the general run of 'em in my sleep, almost.'

For reasons of my own, I was deeply interested in Marconi experiments at their outset in England; and it was of a piece with Mr Cashell's unvarying thoughtfulness that, when his nephew the electrician appropriated the house for a long-range installation, he should, as I have said, invite me to see the result.

The old lady went away with her medicine, and Mr Shaynor and I stamped on the tiled floor behind the counter to keep ourselves warm. The shop, by the light of the many electrics, looked like a Paris-diamond mine, for Mr Cashell believed in all the ritual of his craft. Three superb glass jars—red, green, and blue—of the sort that led Rosamond to parting with her shoes—blazed in the broad plate-glass windows, and there was a confused smell of orris, Kodak Wlms, vulcanite, tooth-powder, sachets, and almond-cream in the air. Mr Shaynor fed the dispensary stove, and we sucked cayenne-pepper jujubes and menthol lozenges. The brutal east wind had cleared the streets, and the few passers-by were muffled to their puckered eyes. In the Italian warehouse next door some gay feathered birds and game, hung upon hooks, sagged to the wind across the left edge of our window-frame.

'They ought to take these poultry in—all knocked about like that,' said Mr Shaynor. 'Doesn't it make you feel fair perishing? See that old hare! The wind's nearly blowing the fur off him.'

I saw the belly-fur of the dead beast blown apart in ridges and streaks as the wind caught it, showing bluish skin underneath. 'Bitter cold,' said Mr Shaynor, shuddering. 'Fancy going out on a night like this! Oh, here's young Mr Cashell.'

The door of the inner office behind the dispensary opened, and an energetic, spade-bearded man stepped forth, rubbing his hands.

'I want a bit of tin-foil, Shaynor,' he said. 'Good-evening. My uncle told me you might be coming.' This to me, as I began the first of a hundred questions.

'I've everything in order,' he replied. 'We're only waiting until Poole calls us up. Excuse me a minute. You can come in whenever you like—but I'd better be with the instruments. Give me that tin-foil. Thanks.'

While we were talking, a girl—evidently no customer—had come into the shop, and the face and bearing of Mr Shaynor changed. She leaned confidently across the counter.

'But I can't,' I heard him whisper uneasily—the flush on his cheek was dull red, and his eyes shone like a drugged moth's. 'I can't. I tell you I'm alone in the place.'

'No, you aren't. Who's *that*? Let him look after it for half an hour. A brisk walk will do you good. Ah, come now, John.'

'But he isn't—'

'I don't care. I want you to; we'll only go round by St Agnes. If you don't—'

He crossed to where I stood in the shadow of the dispensary counter, and began some sort of broken apology about a lady-friend.

'Yes,' she interrupted. 'You take the shop for half an hour—to oblige *me*, won't you?'

She had a singularly rich and promising voice that well matched her outline.

'All right,' I said. 'I'll do it—but you'd better wrap yourself up, Mr Shaynor.'

'Oh, a brisk walk ought to help me. We're only going round by the church.' I heard him cough grievously as they went out together.

I refilled the stove, and, after reckless expenditure of Mr Cashell's coal, drove some warmth into the shop. I explored many of the glass-knobbed drawers that lined the walls, tasted some disconcerting drugs, and, by the aid of a few cardamoms, ground ginger, chloric-ether, and dilute alcohol, manufactured a new and wildish drink, of which I bore a glassful to young Mr Cashell, busy in the back office. He laughed shortly when I told him that Mr Shaynor had stepped out—but a frail coil of wire held all his attention, and he had no word for me bewildered among the batteries and rods. The noise of the sea on the beach began to make itself heard as the traffic in the street ceased. Then briefly, but very lucidly, he gave me the names and uses of the mechanisms that crowded the tables and the floor.

'When do you expect to get the message from Poole?' I demanded, sipping my liquor out of a graduated glass.

'About midnight, if everything is in order. We've got our installation-pole fixed to the roof of the house. I shouldn't advise you to turn on a tap or anything tonight. We've connected up with the plumbing, and all the water will be electrified.' He repeated to me the history of the agitated ladies at the hotel at the time of the first installation.

'But what *is* it?' I asked. 'Electricity is out of my beat altogether.'

'Ah, if you knew *that* you'd know something nobody knows. It's just—It—what we call Electricity, but the magic—the manifestations—the Hertzian waves—are all revealed by *this*. The coherer, we call it.'

He picked up a glass tube not much thicker than a thermometer, in which, almost touching, were two tiny silver plugs, and between them an infinitesimal pinch of metallic dust. 'That's all,' he said, proudly, as though himself responsible for the wonder. 'That is the thing that will reveal to us the Powers—whatever the Powers may be—at work—through space—a long distance away.'

Just then Mr Shaynor returned alone and stood coughing his heart out on the mat.

'Serves you right for being such a fool,' said young Mr Cashell, as annoyed as myself at the interruption. 'Never mind—we've all the night before us to see wonders.'

Shaynor clutched the counter, his handkerchief to his lips. When he brought it away I saw two bright red stains.

'I—I've got a bit of a rasped throat from smoking cigarettes,' he panted. 'I think I'll try a cubeb.'

'Better take some of this. I've been compounding while you've been away.' I handed him the brew.

''Twon't make me drunk, will it? I'm almost a teetotaller. My word! That's grateful and comforting.'

He set down the empty glass to cough afresh.

'Brr! But it was cold out there! I shouldn't care to be lying in my grave a night like this. Don't *you* ever have a sore throat from smoking?' He pocketed the handkerchief after a furtive peep.

'Oh, yes, sometimes,' I replied, wondering, while I spoke, into what agonies of terror I should fall if ever I saw those bright-red danger-signals under my nose. Young Mr Cashell among the batteries coughed slightly to show that he was quite ready to continue his scientific explanations, but I was thinking still of the girl with the rich voice and the significantly cut mouth, at whose command I had taken charge of the shop. It flashed across me that she distantly resembled the seductive shape on a gold-framed toilet-water advertisement whose charms were unholily heightened by the glare from the red bottle in the window. Turning to make sure, I saw Mr Shaynor's eyes bent in the same direction, and by instinct recognized that the flamboyant thing was to him a shrine. 'What do you take for your—cough?' I asked.

'Well, I'm the wrong side of the counter to believe much in patent medicines. But there are asthma cigarettes and there are pastilles. To tell you the truth, if you don't object to the smell, which is very like incense, I believe, though I'm not a Roman Catholic, Blaudett's Cathedral Pastilles relieve me as much as anything.'

'Let's try.' I had never raided a chemist's shop before, so I was thorough. We unearthed the pastilles—brown, gummy cones of benzoin—and set them alight under the toilet-water advertisement, where they fumed in thin blue spirals.

'Of course,' said Mr Shaynor, to my question, 'what one uses in the shop for one's self comes out of one's pocket. Why, stock-taking in our business is nearly the same as with jewellers—and I can't say more than that. But one gets them'—he pointed to the pastille-box—'at trade prices.' Evidently the censing of the gay, seven-tinted wench with the teeth was an established ritual which cost something.

'And when do we shut up shop?'

'We stay like this all night. The guv—old Mr Cashell—doesn't believe in locks and shutters as compared with electric light. Besides, it brings trade. I'll just sit here in the chair by the stove and write a letter, if you don't mind. Electricity isn't my prescription.'

The energetic young Mr Cashell snorted within, and Shaynor settled himself up in his chair over which he had thrown a staring red, black, and yellow Austrian jute blanket, rather like a table-cover. I cast about, amid patent-medicine pamphlets, for something to read, but finding little, returned to the manufacture of the new drink. The Italian warehouse took down its game and went to bed. Across the street blank shutters flung back the gaslight in cold smears; the dried pavement seemed to rough up in goose-flesh under the scouring of the savage wind, and we could hear, long ere he passed, the policeman flapping his arms to keep himself warm. Within, the flavours of cardamoms and chloric-ether disputed those of the pastilles and a score of drugs and perfume and soap scents. Our electric lights, set low down in the windows before the tun-bellied Rosamond jars, flung inward three monstrous daubs of red, blue, and green, that broke into kaleidoscopic lights on the faceted knobs of the drug-drawers, the cut-glass scent flagons, and the bulbs of the sparklet bottles. They flushed the white-tiled floor in gorgeous patches; splashed along the nickel-silver counter-rails, and turned the polished mahogany counter-panels to the likeness of intricate grained marbles—slabs of porphyry and malachite. Mr Shaynor unlocked a drawer, and ere he began to write, took out a meagre bundle of letters. From my place by the stove, I could see the scalloped edges of the paper with a flaring monogram in the corner and could even smell the reek of chypre. At each page he turned toward the toilet-water lady of the advertisement and devoured her with over-luminous eyes. He had drawn the Austrian blanket over his shoulders, and among those warring lights he looked more than ever the incarnation of a drugged moth—a tiger-moth as I thought.

He put his letter into an envelope, stamped it with stiff mechanical movements, and dropped it in the drawer. Then I became aware of the silence of a great city asleep—the silence that underlaid the even voice of the breakers along the sea-front—a thick, tingling quiet of warm life stilled down for its appointed time, and unconsciously I moved about the glittering shop as one moves in a sick-room. Young Mr Cashell was adjusting some wire that crackled from time to time with the tense, knuckle-stretching sound of the electric spark. Upstairs, where a door shut and opened swiftly, I could hear his uncle coughing abed.

'Here,' I said, when the drink was properly warmed, 'take some of this, Mr Shaynor.'

He jerked in his chair with a start and a wrench, and held out his hand for the glass. The mixture, of a rich port-wine colour, frothed at the top.

'It looks,' he said, suddenly, 'it looks—those bubbles—like a string of pearls winking at you—rather like the pearls round that young lady's neck.' He turned again to the advertisement where the female in the dove-coloured corset had seen fit to put on all her pearls before she cleaned her teeth.

'Not bad, is it?' I said.

'Eh?'

He rolled his eyes heavily full on me, and, as I stared, I beheld all meaning and consciousness die out of the swiftly dilating pupils. His figure lost its stark rigidity, softened into the chair, and, chin on chest, hands dropped before him, he rested open-eyed, absolutely still.

'I'm afraid I've rather cooked Shaynor's goose,' I said, bearing the fresh drink to young Mr Cashell. 'Perhaps it was the chloric-ether.'

'Oh, he's all right.' The spade-bearded man glanced at him pityingly. 'Consumptives go off in those sort of dozes very often. It's exhaustion . . . I don't wonder. I daresay the liquor will do him good. It's grand stuff,' he finished his share appreciatively. 'Well, as I was saying—before he interrupted—about this little coherer. The pinch of dust, you see, is nickel-filings. The Hertzian waves, you see, come out of space from the station that despatches 'em, and all these little particles are attracted together—cohere, we call it—for just so long as the current passes through them. Now, it's important to remember that the current is an induced current. There are a good many kinds of induction—'

'Yes, but what *is* induction?'

'That's rather hard to explain untechnically. But the long and the short of it is that when a current of electricity passes through a wire there's a lot of magnetism present round that wire; and if you put another wire parallel to, and within what we call its magnetic field— why then, the second wire will also become charged with electricity.'

'On its own account?'

'On its own account.'

'Then let's see if I've got it correctly. Miles off, at Poole, or wherever it is—'

'It will be anywhere in ten years.'

'You've got a charged wire—'

'Charged with Hertzian waves which vibrate, say, two hundred and thirty million times a second.' Mr Cashell snaked his forefinger rapidly through the air.

'All right—a charged wire at Poole, giving out these waves into space. Then this wire of yours sticking out into space—on the roof of the house—in some mysterious way gets charged with those waves from Poole—'

'Or anywhere—it only happens to be Poole tonight.'

'And those waves set the coherer at work, just like an ordinary telegraph-office ticker?'

'No! That's where so many people make the mistake. The Hertzian waves wouldn't be strong enough to work a great heavy Morse instrument like ours. They can only just make that dust cohere, and while it coheres (a little while for a dot and a longer while for a dash) the current from this battery—the home battery'—he laid his hand on the thing— 'can get through to the Morse printing-machine to record the dot or dash. Let me make it clearer. Do you know anything about steam?'

'Very little. But go on.'

'Well, the coherer is like a steam-valve. Any child can open a valve and start a steamer's engines, because a turn of the hand lets in the main steam, doesn't it? Now, this home battery here ready to print is the main steam. The coherer is the valve, always ready to be turned on. The Hertzian wave is the child's hand that turns it.'

'I see. That's marvellous.'

'Marvellous, isn't it? And, remember, we're only at the beginning. There's nothing we shan't be able to do in ten years. I want to live—my God, how I want to live, and see it develop!' He looked through the door at Shaynor breathing lightly in his chair. 'Poor beast! And he wants to keep company with Fanny Brand.'

'Fanny *who*?' I said, for the name struck an obscurely familiar chord in my brain—something connected with a stained handkerchief, and the word 'arterial'.

'Fanny Brand—the girl you kept shop for.' He laughed. 'That's all I know about her, and for the life of me I can't see what Shaynor sees in her, or she in him.'

'*Can't* you see what he sees in her?' I insisted.

'Oh, yes, if *that's* what you mean. She's a great, big, fat lump of a girl, and so on. I suppose that's why he's so crazy after her. She isn't his sort. Well, it doesn't matter. My uncle says he's bound to die before the year's out. Your drink's given him a good sleep, at any rate.' Young Mr Cashell could not catch Mr Shaynor's face, which was half turned to the advertisement.

I stoked the stove anew, for the room was growing cold, and lighted another pastille. Mr Shaynor in his chair, never moving, looked through and over me with eyes as wide and lustreless as those of a dead hare.

'Poole's late,' said young Mr Cashell, when I stepped back. 'I'll just send them a call.'

He pressed a key in the semi-darkness, and with a rending crackle there leaped between two brass knobs a spark, streams of sparks, and sparks again.

'Grand, isn't it? *That's* the Power—our unknown Power—kicking and fighting to be let loose,' said young Mr Cashell. 'There she goes—kick—kick—kick into space. I never get over the strangeness of it when I work a sending-machine—waves going into space, you know. T. R. is our call. Poole ought to answer with L. L. L.'

We waited two, three, five minutes. In that silence, of which the boom of the tide was an orderly part, I caught the clear '*kiss—kiss—kiss*' of the halliards on the roof, as they were blown against the installation-pole.

'Poole is not ready. I'll stay here and call you when he is.'

I returned to the shop, and set down my glass on a marble slab with a careless clink. As I did so, Shaynor rose to his feet, his eyes fixed once more on the advertisement, where the young woman bathed in the light from the red jar simpered pinkly over her pearls. His lips moved without cessation. I stepped nearer to listen. 'And threw—and threw—and threw,' he repeated, his face all sharp with some inexplicable agony.

I moved forward astonished. But it was then he found words—delivered roundly and clearly. These:—

And threw warm gules on Madeleine's young breast.

The trouble passed off his countenance, and he returned lightly to his place, rubbing his hands.

It had never occurred to me, though we had many times discussed reading and prize-competitions as a diversion, that Mr Shaynor ever read Keats, or could quote him at all appositely. There was, after all, a certain stained-glass effect of light on the high bosom of the highly-polished picture which might, by stretch of fancy, suggest, as a vile chromo recalls some incomparable canvas, the line he had spoken.

Night, my drink, and solitude were evidently turning Mr Shaynor into a poet. He sat down again and wrote swiftly on his villainous notepaper, his lips quivering.

I shut the door into the inner office and moved up behind him. He made no sign that he saw or heard. I looked over his shoulder, and read, amid half-formed words, sentences, and wild scratches:—

> —Very cold it was. Very cold
> The hare—the hare—the hare—
> The birds—

He raised his head sharply, and frowned toward the blank shutters of the poulterer's shop where they jutted out against our window. Then one clear line came:—

> The hare, in spite of fur, was very cold.

The head, moving machine-like, turned right to the advertisement where the Blaudett's Cathedral pastille reeked abominably. He grunted, and went on:—

> Incense in a censer—
> Before her darling picture framed in gold—
> Maiden's picture—angel's portrait—

'Hsh!' said Mr Cashell guardedly from the inner office, as though in the presence of spirits. 'There's something coming through from somewhere; but it isn't Poole.' I heard the crackle of sparks as he depressed the keys of the transmitter. In my own brain, too, something crackled, or it might have been the hair on my head. Then I heard my own voice, in a harsh whisper: 'Mr Cashell, there is something coming through here, too. Leave me alone till I tell you.'

'But I thought you'd come to see this wonderful thing—Sir,' indignantly at the end.

'Leave me alone till I tell you. Be quiet.'

I watched—I waited. Under the blue-veined hand—the dry hand of the consumptive—came away clear, without erasure:—

> And my weak spirit fails
> To think how the dead must freeze—

he shivered as he wrote—

> Beneath the churchyard mould.

Then he stopped, laid the pen down, and leaned back.

For an instant, that was half an eternity, the shop spun before me in a rainbow-tinted whirl, in and through which my own soul most dispassionately considered my own soul as that fought with an over-mastering fear. Then I smelt the strong smell of cigarettes from Mr Shaynor's clothing, and heard, as though it had been the rending of trumpets, the rattle of his breathing. I was still in my place of observation, much as one would watch a rifle-shot at the butts, half-bent, hands on my knees, and head within a few inches of the black, red, and yellow blanket of his shoulder. I was whispering encouragement, evidently to my other self, sounding sentences, such as men pronounce in dreams.

'If he has read Keats, it proves nothing. If he hasn't—like causes *must* beget like effects. There is no escape from this law. *You* ought to be grateful that you know "St Agnes' Eve" without the book; because, given the circumstances, such as Fanny Brand, who is the key of the enigma, and approximately represents the latitude and longitude of Fanny Brawne; allowing also for the bright red colour of the arterial blood upon the handkerchief, which was just what you were puzzling over in the shop just now; and counting the effect of the professional environment, here almost perfectly duplicated—the result is logical and inevitable. As inevitable as induction.'

Still, the other half of my soul refused to be comforted. It was cowering in some minute and inadequate corner—at an immense distance.

Hereafter, I found myself one person again, my hands still gripping my knees, and my eyes glued on the page before Mr Shaynor. As dreamers accept and explain the upheaval of landscapes and the resurrection of the dead, with excerpts from the evening hymn or the multiplication-table, so I had accepted the facts, whatever they might be, that I should witness, and had devised a theory, sane and plausible to my mind, that explained them all. Nay, I was even in advance of my facts, walking hurriedly before them, assured that they would fit my theory. And all that I now recall of that epoch-making theory are the lofty words: 'If he has read Keats it's the chloric-ether. If he hasn't, it's the identical bacillus, or Hertzian wave of tuberculosis, *plus* Fanny Brand and the professional status which, in conjunction with the main-stream of subconscious thought common to all mankind, has thrown up temporarily an induced Keats.'

Mr Shaynor returned to his work, erasing and rewriting as before with swiftness. Two or three blank pages he tossed aside. Then he wrote, muttering:—

> The little smoke of a candle that goes out.

'No,' he muttered. 'Little smoke—little smoke—little smoke. What else?' He thrust his chin forward toward the advertisement, whereunder the last of the Blaudett's Cathedral pastilles fumed in its holder. 'Ah!' Then with relief:—

> The little smoke that dies in moonlight cold.

Evidently he was snared by the rhymes of his first verse, for he wrote and rewrote 'gold—cold—mould' many times. Again he sought inspiration from the advertisement, and set down, without erasure, the line I had overheard:—

> And threw warm gules on Madeleine's young breast.

As I remembered the original it is 'fair'—a trite word—instead of 'young', and I found myself nodding approval, though I admitted that the attempt to reproduce 'its little smoke in pallid moonlight died' was a failure.

Followed without a break ten or fifteen lines of bald prose—the naked soul's confession of its physical yearning for its beloved—unclean as we count uncleanliness; unwholesome, but human exceedingly; the raw material, so it seemed to me in that hour and in that place, whence Keats wove the twenty-sixth, seventh, and eighth stanzas of his poem. Shame I had none in overseeing this revelation; and my fear had gone with the smoke of the pastille.

'That's it,' I murmured. 'That's how it's blocked out. Go on! Ink it in, man. Ink it in!'

Mr Shaynor returned to broken verse wherein 'loveliness' was made to rhyme with a desire to look upon 'her empty dress'. He picked up a fold of the gay, soft blanket, spread it over one hand, caressed it with infinite tenderness, thought, muttered, traced some snatches which I could not decipher, shut his eyes drowsily, shook his head, and dropped the stuff. Here I found myself at fault, for I could not then see (as I do now) in what manner a red, black, and yellow Austrian blanket coloured his dreams.

In a few minutes he laid aside his pen, and, chin on hand, considered the shop with thoughtful and intelligent eyes. He threw down the blanket, rose, passed along a line of drug-drawers, and read the names on the labels aloud. Returning, he took from his desk Christy's *New Commercial Plants* and the old Culpepper that I had given him, opened and laid them side by side with a clerky air, all trace of passion gone from his face, read first in one and then in the other, and paused with pen behind his ear.

'What wonder of Heaven's coming now?' I thought.

'Manna—manna—manna,' he said at last, under wrinkled brows. 'That's what I wanted. Good! Now then! Now then! Good! Good! Oh, by God, that's good!' His voice rose and he spoke rightly and fully without a falter:—

> Candied apple, quince and plum and gourd,
> And jellies smoother than the creamy curd,
> And lucent syrups tinct with cinnamon,
> Manna and dates in Argosy transferred
> From Fez; and spiced dainties, every one
> From silken Samarcand to cedared Lebanon.

He repeated it once more, using 'blander' for 'smoother' in the second line; then wrote it down without erasure, but this time (my set eyes missed no stroke of any word) he substituted 'soother' for his atrocious second thought, so that it came away under his hand as it is written in the book—as it is written in the book.

A wind went shouting down the street, and on the heels of the wind followed a spurt and rattle of rain.

After a smiling pause—and good right had he to smile—he began anew, always tossing the last sheet over his shoulder:—

> The sharp rain falling on the window-pane,
> Rattling sleet—the wind-blown sleet.

Then prose: 'It is very cold of mornings when the wind brings rain and sleet with it. I heard the sleet on the window-pane outside, and thought of you, my darling. I am always thinking of you. I wish we could both run away like two lovers into the storm and get that little cottage by the sea which we are always thinking about, my own dear darling. We could sit and watch the sea beneath our windows. It would be a fairyland all of our own—a fairy sea—a fairy sea . . .'

He stopped, raised his head, and listened. The steady drone of the Channel along the sea-front that had borne us company so long leaped up a note to the sudden fuller surge that signals the change from ebb to flood. It beat in like the change of step throughout an army—this renewed pulse of the sea—and filled our ears till they, accepting it, marked it no longer.

> A fairyland for you and me
> Across the foam—beyond . . .
> A magic foam, a perilous sea.

He grunted again with effort and bit his underlip. My throat dried, but I dared not gulp to moisten it lest I should break the spell that was drawing him nearer and nearer to the high-water mark but two of the sons of Adam have reached. Remember that in all the millions permitted there are no more than five—five little lines—of which one can say: 'These are the pure Magic. These are the clear Vision. The rest is only poetry.' And Mr Shaynor was playing hot and cold with two of them!

I vowed no unconscious thought of mine should influence the blindfold soul, and pinned myself desperately to the other three, repeating and re-repeating:—

> A savage spot as holy and enchanted
> As e'er beneath a waning moon was haunted
> By woman wailing for her demon lover.

But though I believed my brain thus occupied, my every sense hung upon the writing under the dry, bony hand, all brown-fingered with chemicals and cigarette-smoke.

> Our windows fronting on the dangerous foam,

(he wrote, after long, irresolute snatches), and then—

> Our open casements facing desolate seas
> Forlorn—forlorn—

Here again his face grew peaked and anxious with that sense of loss I had first seen when the Power snatched him. But this time the agony was tenfold keener. As I watched it mounted like mercury in the tube. It lighted his face from within till I thought the visibly scourged soul must leap forth naked between his jaws, unable to endure. A drop of sweat trickled from my forehead down my nose and splashed on the back of my hand.

> Our windows facing on the desolate seas
> And pearly foam of magic fairyland—

'Not yet—not yet,' he muttered, 'wait a minute. *Please* wait a minute.
I shall get it then—

> Our magic windows fronting on the sea,
> The dangerous foam of desolate seas . . .
> · For aye.

Ouh, my God!'

From head to heel he shook—shook from the marrow of his bones
outwards—then leaped to his feet with raised arms, and slid the chair
screeching across the tiled floor where it struck the drawers behind and
fell with a jar. Mechanically, I stooped to recover it.

As I rose, Mr Shaynor was stretching and yawning at leisure.

'I've had a bit of a doze,' he said. 'How did I come to knock the chair
over? You look rather—'

'The chair startled me,' I answered. 'It was so sudden in this quiet.'

Young Mr Cashell behind his shut door was offendedly silent.

'I suppose I must have been dreaming,' said Mr Shaynor.

'I suppose you must,' I said. 'Talking of dreams—I—I noticed you
writing—before—'

He flushed consciously.

'I meant to ask you if you've ever read anything written by a man
called Keats.'

'Oh! I haven't much time to read poetry, and I can't say that I remember the name exactly. Is he a popular writer?'

'Middling. I thought you might know him because he's the only poet
who was ever a druggist. And he's rather what's called the lover's poet.'

'Indeed. I must dip into him. What did he write about?'

'A lot of things. Here's a sample that may interest you.'

Then and there, carefully, I repeated the verse he had twice spoken
and once written not ten minutes ago.

'Ah! Anybody could see he was a druggist from that line about the
tinctures and syrups. It's a fine tribute to our profession.'

'I don't know,' said young Mr Cashell, with icy politeness, opening
the door one half-inch, 'if you still happen to be interested in our trifling experiments. But, should such be the case—'

I drew him aside, whispering, 'Shaynor seemed going off into some
sort of fit when I spoke to you just now. I thought, even at the risk of
being rude, it wouldn't do to take you off your instruments just as the
call was coming through. Don't you see?'

'Granted—granted as soon as asked,' he said, unbending. 'I *did* think it a shade odd at the time. So that was why he knocked the chair down?'

'I hope I haven't missed anything,' I said.

'I'm afraid I can't say that, but you're just in time for the end of a rather curious performance. You can come in too, Mr Shaynor. Listen, while I read it off.'

The Morse instrument was ticking furiously. Mr Cashell interpreted: ' "*K.K.V. Can make nothing of your signals.*" ' A pause. ' "*M.M.V. M.M.V. Signals unintelligible. Purpose anchor Sandown Bay. Examine instruments tomorrow.*" Do you know what that means? It's a couple of men-o'-war working Marconi signals off the Isle of Wight. They are trying to talk to each other. Neither can read the other's messages, but all their messages are being taken in by our receiver here. They've been going on for ever so long. I wish you could have heard it.'

'How wonderful!' I said. 'Do you mean we're overhearing Portsmouth ships trying to talk to each other—that we're eavesdropping across half South England?'

'Just that. Their transmitters are all right, but their receivers are out of order, so they only get a dot here and a dash there. Nothing clear.'

'Why is that?'

'God knows—and Science will know tomorrow. Perhaps the induction is faulty; perhaps the receivers aren't tuned to receive just the number of vibrations per second that the transmitter sends. Only a word here and there. Just enough to tantalize.'

Again the Morse sprang to life.

'That's one of 'em complaining now. Listen: "*Disheartening—most disheartening.*" It's quite pathetic. Have you ever seen a spiritualistic seance? It reminds me of that sometimes—odds and ends of messages coming out of nowhere—a word here and there—no good at all.'

'But mediums are all impostors,' said Mr Shaynor, in the doorway, lighting an asthma-cigarette. 'They only do it for the money they can make. I've seen 'em.'

'Here's Poole, at last—clear as a bell. L. L. L. *Now* we shan't be long.' Mr Cashell rattled the keys merrily. 'Anything you'd like to tell 'em?'

'No, I don't think so,' I said. 'I'll go home and get to bed. I'm feeling a little tired.'

H. G. WELLS

Under the Knife

'WHAT if I die under it?' The thought recurred again and again as I walked home from Haddon's. It was a purely personal question. I was spared the deep anxieties of a married man, and I knew there were few of my intimate friends but would find my death troublesome chiefly on account of their duty of regret. I was surprised indeed and perhaps a little humiliated, as I turned the matter over, to think how few could possibly exceed the conventional requirement. Things came before me stripped of glamour, in a clear dry light, during that walk from Haddon's house over Primrose Hill. There were the friends of my youth; I perceived now that our affection was a tradition which we foregathered rather laboriously to maintain. There were the rivals and helpers of my later career: I suppose I had been cold-blooded or undemonstrative—one perhaps implies the other. It may be that even the capacity for friendship is a question of physique. There had been a time in my own life when I had grieved bitterly enough at the loss of a friend; but as I walked home that afternoon the emotional side of my imagination was dormant. I could not pity myself, nor feel sorry for my friends, nor conceive of them as grieving for me.

I was interested in this deadness of my emotional nature—no doubt a concomitant of my stagnating physiology; and my thoughts wandered off along the line it suggested. Once before, in my hot youth, I had suffered a sudden loss of blood and had been within an ace of death. I remembered now that my affections as well as my passions had drained out of me, leaving scarcely anything but a tranquil resignation, a dreg of self-pity. It had been weeks before the old ambitions, and tendernesses, and all the complex moral interplay of a man, had reasserted themselves. Now again I was bloodless; I had been feeding down for a week or more. I was not even hungry. It occurred to me that the real meaning of this numbness might be a gradual slipping away from the pleasure–pain guidance of the animal man. It has been proven, I take it, as thoroughly as anything can be proven in this world, that the higher emotions, the moral feelings, even the subtle tendernesses of love, are evolved from the elemental desires and fears of the simple animal: they are the harness in which man's mental freedom goes. And it may be that, as death overshadows us, as our possibility of acting diminishes, this complex growth of balanced impulse, propensity, and aversion whose interplay inspires our acts, goes with it. Leaving what?

I was suddenly brought back to reality by an imminent collision with a butcher-boy's tray. I found that I was crossing the bridge over the Regent's Park Canal which runs parallel with that in the Zoological Gardens. The boy in blue had been looking over his shoulder at a black barge advancing slowly, towed by a gaunt white horse. In the Gardens a nurse was leading three happy little children over the bridge. The trees were bright green; the spring hopefulness was still unstained by the dusts of summer; the sky in the water was bright and clear, but broken by long waves, by quivering bands of black, as the barge drove through. The breeze was stirring; but it did not stir me as the spring breeze used to do.

Was this dullness of feeling in itself an anticipation? It was curious that I could reason and follow out a network of suggestion as clearly as ever: so, at least, it seemed to me. It was calmness rather than dullness that was coming upon me. Was there any ground for the belief in the presentiment of death? Did a man near to death begin instinctively to withdraw himself from the meshes of matter and sense, even before the cold hand was laid upon his? I felt strangely isolated—isolated without regret—from the life and existence about me. The children playing in the sun and gathering strength and experience for the business of life, the park-keeper gossiping with a nursemaid, the nursing mother, the young couple intent upon each other as they passed me, the trees by the wayside spreading new pleading leaves to the sunlight, the stir in their branches—I had been part of it all, but I had nearly done with it now.

Some way down the Broad Walk I perceived that I was tired, and that my feet were heavy. It was hot that afternoon, and I turned aside and sat down on one of the green chairs that line the way. In a minute I had dozed into a dream, and the tide of my thoughts washed up a vision of the resurrection. I was still sitting in the chair, but I thought myself actually dead, withered, tattered, dried, one eye (I saw) pecked out by birds. 'Awake!' cried a voice; and incontinently the dust of the path and the mould under the grass became insurgent. I had never before thought of Regent's Park as a cemetery, but now through the trees, stretching as far as eye could see, I beheld a flat plain of writhing graves and heeling tombstones. There seemed to be some trouble: the rising dead appeared to stifle as they struggled upward, they bled in their struggles, the red flesh was tattered away from the white bones. 'Awake!' cried a voice: but I determined I would not rise to such horrors. 'Awake!' They would not let me alone. 'Wike up!' said an angry voice. A cockney angel! The man who sells the tickets was shaking me, demanding my penny.

I paid my penny, pocketed my ticket, yawned, stretched my legs, and, feeling now rather less torpid, got up and walked on towards Langham Place. I speedily lost myself again in a shifting maze of thoughts about death. Going across Marylebone Road into that crescent at the end of Langham Place, I had the narrowest escape from the shaft of a cab, and went on my way with a palpitating heart and a bruised shoulder. It struck me that it would have been curious if my meditations on my death on the morrow had led to my death that day.

But I will not weary you with more of my experiences that day and the next. I knew more and more certainly that I should die under the operation; at times I think I was inclined to pose to myself. At home I found everything prepared; my room cleared of needless objects and hung with white sheets; a nurse installed and already at loggerheads with my housekeeper. They wanted me to go to bed early, and after a little resistance I obeyed.

In the morning I was very indolent, and though I read my news-papers and the letters that came by the first post, I did not find them very interesting. There was a friendly note from Addison, my old school friend, calling my attention to two discrepancies and a printer's error in my new book, with one from Langridge venting some vexation over Minton. The rest were business communications. I had a cup of tea but nothing to eat. The glow of pain at my side seemed more massive. I knew it was pain, and yet, if you can understand, I did not find it very painful. I had been awake and hot and thirsty in the night, but in the morning bed felt comfortable. In the night-time I had lain thinking of things that were past; in the morning I dozed over the question of immortality. Haddon came, punctual to the minute, with a neat black bag; and Mowbray soon followed. Their arrival stirred me up a little. I began to take a more personal interest in the proceedings. Haddon moved the little octagonal table close to the bedside, and, with his broad black back to me, began taking things out of his bag. I heard the light click of steel upon steel. My imagination, I found, was not altogether stagnant. 'Will you hurt me much?' I said in an off-hand tone.

'Not a bit,' Haddon answered over his shoulder. 'We shall chloroform you. Your heart's as sound as a bell.' And as he spoke, I had a whiff of the pungent sweetness of the anaesthetic.

They stretched me out, with a convenient exposure of my side, and, almost before I realized what was happening, the chloroform was being administered. It stings the nostrils, and there is a suffocating sensation, at first. I knew I should die—that this was the end of consciousness for me. And suddenly I felt that I was not prepared for death: I had a vague sense of a duty overlooked—I knew not what. What was it I had not done? I could think of nothing more to do, nothing desirable left in life; and yet I had the strangest disinclination for death. And the physical sensation was painfully oppressive. Of course the doctors did not know they were going to kill me. Possibly I struggled. Then I fell motionless, and a great silence, a monstrous silence, and an impenetrable blackness came upon me.

There must have been an interval of absolute unconsciousness, seconds or minutes. Then, with a chilly, unemotional clearness, I perceived that I was not yet dead. I was still in my body; but all the multitudinous sensations that come sweeping from it to make up the background of consciousness had gone, leaving me free of it all. No, not free of it all; for as yet something still held me to the poor stark flesh upon the bed—held me, yet not so closely that I did not feel myself external to it, independent of it, straining away from it. I do not think I saw, I do not think I heard; but I perceived all that was going on, and it was as if I both heard and saw. Haddon was bending over me, Mowbray behind me; the scalpel—it was a large scalpel—was cutting my flesh at the side under the flying ribs. It was interesting to see myself cut like cheese, without a pang, without even a qualm. The interest was much of a quality with that one might feel in a game of chess between strangers. Haddon's face was firm and his hand steady; but I was surprised to perceive (*how* I know not) that he was feeling the gravest doubt as to his own wisdom in the conduct of the operation.

Mowbray's thoughts, too, I could see. He was thinking that Haddon's manner showed too much of the specialist. New suggestions came up like bubbles through a stream of frothing meditation, and burst one after another in the little bright spot of his consciousness. He could not help noticing and admiring Haddon's swift dexterity, in spite of his envious quality and his disposition to detract. I saw my liver exposed. I was puzzled at my own condition. I did not feel that I was dead, but I was different in some way from my living self. The grey depression that had weighed on me for a year or more and coloured all my thoughts, was gone. I perceived and thought without any emotional tint at all. I wondered if everyone perceived things in this way under chloroform, and forgot it again when he came out of it. It would be inconvenient to look into some heads, and not forget.

Although I did not think that I was dead, I still perceived quite clearly that I was soon to die. This brought me back to the consideration of Haddon's proceedings. I looked into his mind, and saw that he was afraid of cutting a branch of the portal vein. My attention was distracted from details by the curious changes going on in his mind. His consciousness was like the quivering little spot of light which is thrown by the mirror of a galvanometer. His thoughts ran under it like a stream, some through the focus bright and distinct, some shadowy in the half-light of the edge. Just now the little glow was steady; but the least movement on Mowbray's part, the slightest sound from outside, even a faint difference in the slow movement of the living flesh he was cutting, set the light-spot shivering and spinning. A new sense-impression came rushing up through the flow of thoughts, and lo! the light-spot jerked away towards it, swifter than a frightened fish. It was wonderful to think that upon that unstable, fitful thing depended all the complex motions of the man; that for the next five minutes, therefore, my life hung upon its movements. And he was growing more and more nervous in his work. It was as if a little picture of a cut vein grew brighter, and struggled to oust from his brain another picture of a cut falling short of the mark. He was afraid: his dread of cutting too little was battling with his dread of cutting too far.

Then, suddenly, like an escape of water from under a lock-gate, a great uprush of horrible realization set all his thoughts swirling, and simultaneously I perceived that the vein was cut. He started back with a hoarse exclamation, and I saw the brown-purple blood gather in a swift bead, and run trickling. He was horrified. He pitched the red-stained scalpel on to the octagonal table; and instantly both doctors flung themselves upon me, making hasty and ill-conceived efforts to remedy the disaster. 'Ice!' said Mowbray, gasping. But I knew that I was killed, though my body still clung to me.

I will not describe their belated endeavours to save me, though I perceived every detail. My perceptions were sharper and swifter than they had ever been in life; my thoughts rushed through my mind with incredible swiftness, but with perfect definition. I can only compare their crowded clarity to the effects of a reasonable dose of opium. In a moment it would all be over, and I should be free. I knew I was immortal, but what would happen I did not know. Should I drift off presently, like a puff of smoke from a gun, in some kind of half-material body, an attenuated version of my material self? Should I find myself suddenly among the innumerable hosts of the dead, and know the world about me for the phantasmagoria it had always seemed? Should I drift to some spiritualistic *séance*, and there make foolish, incomprehensible attempts to affect a purblind medium? It was a state of unemotional curiosity, of colourless expectation. And then I realized a growing stress upon me, a feeling as though some huge human magnet was drawing me upward out of my body. The stress grew and grew. I seemed an atom for which monstrous forces were fighting. For one brief, terrible moment sensation came back to me. That feeling of falling headlong which comes in nightmares, that feeling a thousand times intensified, that and a black horror swept across my thoughts in a torrent. Then the two doctors, the naked body with its cut side, the little room, swept away from under me and vanished as a speck of foam vanishes down an eddy.

I was in mid-air. Far below was the West End of London, receding rapidly,—for I seemed to be flying swiftly upward,—and, as it receded, passing westward, like a panorama. I could see, through the faint haze of smoke the innumerable roofs chimney-set, the narrow roadways stippled with people and conveyances, the little specks of squares, and the church steeples like thorns sticking out of the fabric. But it spun away as the earth rotated on its axis, and in a few seconds (as it seemed) I was over the scattered clumps of town about Ealing, the little Thames a thread of blue to the south, and the Chiltern Hills and the North Downs coming up like the rim of a basin, far away and faint with haze. Up I rushed. And at first I had not the faintest conception what this headlong rush upward could mean.

Every moment the circle of scenery beneath me grew wider and wider, and the details of town and field, of hill and valley, got more and more hazy and pale and indistinct, a luminous grey was mingled more and more with the blue of the hills and the green of the open meadows; and a little patch of cloud, low and far to the west, shone ever more dazzlingly white. Above, as the veil of atmosphere between myself and outer space grew thinner, the sky, which had been a fair springtime blue at first, grew deeper and richer in colour, passing steadily through the intervening shades until presently it was as dark as the blue sky of midnight, and presently as black as the blackness of a frosty starlight, and at last as black as no blackness I had ever beheld. And first one star and then many, and at last an innumerable host broke out upon the sky: more stars than anyone has ever seen from the face of the earth. For the blueness of the sky is the light of the sun and stars sifted and spread abroad blindingly: there is diffused light even in the darkest skies of winter, and we do not see the stars by day only because of the dazzling irradiation of the sun. But now I saw things—I know not how; assuredly with no mortal eyes—and that defect of bedazzlement blinded me no longer. The sun was incredibly strange and wonderful. The body of it was a disc of blinding white light: not yellowish as it seems to those who live upon the earth, but livid white, all streaked with scarlet streaks ánd rimmed about with a fringe of writhing tongues of red fire. And, shooting halfway across the heavens from either side of it, and brighter than the Milky Way, were two pinions of silver-white, making it look more like those winged globes I have seen in Egyptian sculpture, than anything else I can remember upon earth. These I knew for the solar corona, though I had never seen anything of it but a picture during the days of my earthly life.

When my attention came back to the earth again, I saw that it had fallen very far away from me. Field and town were long since indistinguishable, and all the varied hues of the country were merging into a uniform bright grey, broken only by the brilliant white of the clouds that lay scattered in flocculent masses over Ireland and the west of England. For now I could see the outlines of the north of France and Ireland, and all this island of Britain save where Scotland passed over the horizon to the north, or where the coast was blurred or obliterated by cloud. The sea was a dull grey, and darker than the land; and the whole panorama was rotating slowly towards the east.

All this had happened so swiftly that, until I was some thousand miles or so from the earth, I had no thought for myself. But now I perceived I had neither hands nor feet, neither parts nor organs, and that I felt neither alarm nor pain. All about me I perceived that the vacancy (for I had already left the air behind) was cold beyond the imagination of man; but it troubled me not. The sun's rays shot through the void, powerless to light or heat until they should strike on matter in their course. I saw things with a serene self-forgetfulness, even as if I were God. And down below there, rushing away from me,—countless miles in a second,—where a little dark spot on the grey marked the position of London, two doctors were struggling to restore life to the poor hacked and outworn shell I had abandoned. I felt then such release, such serenity as I can compare to no mortal delight I have ever known.

It was only after I had perceived all these things that the meaning of that headlong rush of the earth grew into comprehension. Yet it was so simple, so obvious, that I was amazed at my never anticipating the thing that was happening to me. I had suddenly been cut adrift from matter: all that was material of me was there upon earth, whirling away through space, held to the earth by gravitation, partaking of the earth's inertia, moving in its wreath of epicycles round the sun, and with the sun and the planets on their vast march through space. But the immaterial has no inertia, feels nothing of the pull of matter for matter: where it parts from its garment of flesh, there it remains (so far as space concerns it any longer) immovable in space. I was not leaving the earth: the earth was leaving *me*, and not only the earth, but the whole solar system was streaming past. And about me in space, invisible to me, scattered in the wake of the earth upon its journey, there must be an innumerable multitude of souls, stripped like myself of the material, stripped like myself of the passions of the individual and the generous emotions of the gregarious brute, naked intelligences, things of newborn wonder and thought, marvelling at the strange release that had suddenly come on them!

As I receded faster and faster from the strange white sun in the black heavens, and from the broad and shining earth upon which my being had begun, I seemed to grow, in some incredible manner, vast: vast as regards this world I had left, vast as regards the moments and periods of a human life. Very soon I saw the full circle of the earth, slightly gibbous, like the moon when she nears her full, but very large; and the silvery shape of America was now in the noonday blaze wherein (as it seemed) little England had been basking but a few minutes ago. At first the earth was large and shone in the heavens, filling a great part of them; but every moment she grew smaller and more distant. As she shrunk, the broad moon in its third quarter crept into view over the rim of her disc. I looked for the constellations. Only that part of Aries directly behind the sun, and the Lion, which the earth covered, were hidden. I recognized the tortuous, tattered band of the Milky Way, with Vega very bright between sun and earth; and Sirius and Orion shone splendid against the unfathomable blackness in the opposite quarter of the heavens. The Pole Star was overhead, and the Great Bear hung over the circle of the earth. And away beneath and beyond the shining corona of the sun were strange groupings of stars I had never seen in my life—notably, a dagger-shaped group that I knew for the Southern Cross. All these were no larger than when they had shone on earth; but the little stars that one scarcely sees shone now against the setting of black vacancy as brightly as the first-magnitudes had done, while the larger worlds were points of indescribable glory and colour. Aldebaran was a spot of blood-red fire, and Sirius condensed to one point the light of a world of sapphires. And they shone steadily: they did not scintillate, they were calmly glorious. My impressions had an adamantine hardness and brightness: there was no blurring softness, no atmosphere, nothing but infinite darkness set with the myriads of these acute and brilliant points and specks of light. Presently, when I looked again, the little earth seemed no bigger than the sun, and it dwindled and turned as I looked until, in a second's space (as it seemed to me), it was halved; and so it went on swiftly dwindling. Far away in the opposite direction, a little pinkish pin's head of light, shining steadily, was the planet Mars. I swam motionless in vacancy, and, without a trace of terror or astonishment, watched the speck of cosmic dust we call the world fall away from me.

Presently it dawned upon me that my sense of duration had changed: that my mind was moving not faster but infinitely slower, that between each separate impression there was a period of many days. The moon spun once round the earth as I noted this; and I perceived clearly the motion of Mars in his orbit. Moreover, it appeared as if the time between thought and thought grew steadily greater, until at last a thousand years was but a moment in my perception.

At first the constellations had shone motionless against the black background of infinite space; but presently it seemed as though the group of stars about Hercules and the Scorpion was contracting, while Orion and Aldebaran and their neighbours were scattering apart. Flashing suddenly out of the darkness there came a flying multitude of particles of rock, glittering like dust-specks in a sunbeam, and encompassed in a faintly luminous haze. They swirled all about me, and vanished again in a twinkling far behind. And then I saw that a bright spot of light, that shone a little to one side of my path, was growing very rapidly larger, and perceived that it was the planet Saturn rushing towards me. Larger and larger it grew, swallowing up the heavens behind it, and hiding every moment a fresh multitude of stars. I perceived its flattened, whirling body, its disc-like belt, and seven of its little satellites. It grew and grew, till it towered enormous; and then I plunged amid a streaming multitude of clashing stones and dancing dust-particles and gas-eddies, and saw for a moment the mighty triple belt like three concentric arches of moonlight above me, its shadow black on the boiling tumult below. These things happened in one-tenth of the time it takes to tell of them. The planet went by like a flash of lightning; for a few seconds it blotted out the sun, and there and then became a mere black, dwindling, winged patch against the light. The earth, the mother mote of my being, I could no longer see.

So with a stately swiftness, in the profoundest silence, the solar system fell from me, as it had been a garment, until the sun was a mere star amid the multitude of stars, with its eddy of planet-specks, lost in the confused glittering of the remoter light. I was no longer a denizen of the solar system: I had come to the Outer Universe, I seemed to grasp and comprehend the whole world of matter. Ever more swiftly the stars closed in about the spot where Antares and Vega had vanished in a luminous haze, until that part of the sky had the semblance of a whirling mass of nebulae, and ever before me yawned vaster gaps of vacant blackness and the stars shone fewer and fewer. It seemed as if I moved towards a point between Orion's belt and sword; and the void about that region opened vaster and vaster every second, an incredible gulf of nothingness, into which I was falling. Faster and ever faster the universe rushed by, a hurry of whirling motes at last, speeding silently into the void. Stars glowing brighter and brighter, with their circling planets catching the light in a ghostly fashion as I neared them, shone out and vanished again into inexistence; faint comets, clusters of meteorites, winking specks of matter, eddying light-points, whizzed past, some perhaps a hundred millions of miles or so from me at most, few nearer, travelling with unimaginable rapidity, shooting constellations, momentary darts of fire, through that black, enormous night. More than anything else it was like a dusty draught, sunbeam-lit. Broader, and wider, and deeper grew the starless space, the vacant Beyond, into which I was being drawn. At last a quarter of the heavens was black and blank, and the whole headlong rush of stellar universe closed in behind me like a veil of light that is gathered together. It drove away from me like a monstrous jack-o'-

lantern driven by the wind. I had come out into the wilderness of space. Ever the vacant blackness grew broader, until the hosts of the stars seemed only like a swarm of fiery specks hurrying away from me, inconceivably remote, and the darkness, the nothingness and emptiness, was about me on every side. Soon the little universe of matter, the cage of points in which I had begun to be, was dwindling, now to a whirling disc of luminous glittering, and now to one minute disc of hazy light. In a little while it would shrink to a point, and at last would vanish altogether.

Suddenly feeling came back to me—feeling in the shape of overwhelming terror: such a dread of those dark vastitudes as no words can describe, a passionate resurgence of sympathy and social desire. Were there other souls, invisible to me as I to them, about me in the blackness? Or was I indeed, even as I felt, alone? Had I passed out of being into something that was neither being nor not-being? The covering of the body, the covering of matter, had been torn from me, and the hallucinations of companionship and security. Everything was black and silent. I had ceased to be. I was nothing. There was nothing, save only that infinitesimal dot of light that dwindled in the gulf. I strained myself to hear and see, and for a while there was naught but infinite silence, intolerable darkness, horror, and despair.

Then I saw that about the spot of light into which the whole world of matter had shrunk there was a faint glow. And in a band on either side of that the darkness was not absolute. I watched it for ages, as it seemed to me, and through the long waiting the haze grew imperceptibly more distinct. And then about the band appeared an irregular cloud of the faintest, palest brown. I felt a passionate impatience; but the things grew brighter so slowly that they scarcely seemed to change. What was unfolding itself? What was this strange reddish dawn in the interminable night of space?

The cloud's shape was grotesque. It seemed to be looped along its lower side into four projecting masses, and, above, it ended in a straight line. What phantom was it? I felt assured I had seen that figure before; but I could not think what, nor where, nor when it was. Then the realization rushed upon me. *It was a clenched Hand.* I was alone in space, alone with his huge, shadowy Hand, upon which the whole Universe of Matter lay like an unconsidered speck of dust. It seemed as though I watched it through vast periods of time. On the forefinger glittered a ring; and the universe from which I had come was but a spot of light upon the ring's curvature. And the thing that the hand gripped had the likeness of a black rod. Through a long eternity I watched this Hand, with the ring and the rod, marvelling and fearing and waiting helplessly on what might follow. It seemed as though nothing could follow: that I should watch for ever, seeing only the Hand and the thing it held, and understanding nothing of its import. Was the whole universe but a refracting speck upon some greater Being? Were our worlds but the atoms of another universe, and those again of another, and so on through an endless progression? And what was I? Was I indeed immaterial? A vague persuasion of a body gathering about me came into my suspense. The abysmal darkness about the Hand filled with impalpable suggestion, with uncertain, fluctuating shapes.

Came a sound, like the sound of a tolling bell; faint, as if infinitely far, muffled as though heard through thick swathings of darkness: a deep, vibrating resonance, with vast gulfs of silence between each stroke. And the Hand appeared to tighten on the rod. And I saw far above the Hand, towards the apex of the darkness, a circle of dim phosphorescence, a ghostly sphere whence these sounds came throbbing; and at the last stroke the Hand vanished, for the hour had come, and I heard a noise of many waters. But the black rod remained as a great band across the sky. And then a voice, which seemed to run to the uttermost parts of space, spoke, saying, 'There will be no more pain.'

At that an almost intolerable gladness and radiance rushed upon me, and I saw the circle shining white and bright, and the rod black and shining, and many things else distinct and clear. And the circle was the face of the clock, and the rod the rail of my bed. Haddon was standing at the foot, against the rail, with a small pair of scissors on his fingers; and the hands of my clock on the mantel over his shoulder were clasped together over the hour of twelve. Mowbray was washing something in a basin at the octagonal table, and at my side I felt a subdued feeling that could scarce be spoken of as pain.

The operation had not killed me. And I perceived, suddenly, that the dull melancholy of half a year was lifted from my mind.

CHARLOTTE MEW

A White Night

'THE incident', said Cameron, 'is spoiled inevitably in the telling, by its merely accidental quality of melodrama, its sensational machinery, which, to the view of anyone who didn't witness it, is apt to blur the finer outlines of the scene. The subtlety, or call it the significance, is missed, and unavoidably, as one attempts to put the thing before you, in a certain casual crudity, and inessential violence of fact. Make it a medieval matter—put it back some centuries—and the affair takes on its proper tone immediately, is tinctured with the sinister solemnity which actually enveloped it. But as it stands, a recollection, an experience, a picture, well, it doesn't reproduce; one must have the original if one is going to hang it on one's wall.'

In spite of which I took it down the night he told it and, thanks to a trick of accuracy, I believe you have the story as I heard it, almost word for word.

It was in the spring of 1876, a rainless spring, as I remember it, of white roads and brown crops and steely skies.

Sent out the year before on mining business, I had been then some eighteen months in Spain. My job was finished; I was leaving the Black Country, planning a vague look round, perhaps a little sport among the mountains, when a letter from my sister Ella laid the dust of doubtful schemes.

She was on a discursive honeymoon. They had come on from Florence to Madrid, and disappointed with the rank modernity of their last halt, wished to explore some of the least known towns of the interior: 'Something unique, untrodden, and uncivilized', she indicated modestly. Further, if I were free and amiable, and so on, they would join me anywhere in Andalusia. I was in fact to show them round.

I did 'my possible'; we roughed it pretty thoroughly, but the young person's passion for the strange bore her robustly through the risks and discomforts of those wilder districts which at best, perhaps, are hardly woman's ground.

King, on occasion, nursed anxiety, and mourned his little luxuries; Ella accepted anything that befell, from dirt to danger, with a humorous composure dating back to nursery days—she had the instincts and the physique of a traveller, with a brilliancy of touch and a decision of attack on human instruments which told. She took our mule-drivers in hand with some success. Later, no doubt, their wretched beasts were made to smart for it, in the reaction from a lull in that habitual brutality which makes the animals of Spain a real blot upon the gay indifferentism of its people.

It pleased her to devise a lurid *Dies Irae* for these affable barbarians, a special process of reincarnation for the Spaniard generally, whereby the space of one dog's life at least should be ensured to him.

And on the day I'm coming to, a tedious, dislocating journey in a springless cart had brought her to the verge of quite unusual weariness, a weariness of spirit only, she protested, waving a hand toward our man who lashed and sang alternately, fetching at intervals a sunny smile for the poor lady's vain remonstrances before he lashed again.

The details of that day—our setting forth, our ride, and our arrival— all the minor episodes stand out with singular distinctness, forming a background in one's memory to the eventual, central scene.

We left our inn—a rough *posada*—about sunrise, and our road, washed to a track by winter rains, lay first through wide half-cultivated slopes, capped everywhere with orange trees and palm and olive patches, curiously bare of farms or villages, till one recalls the lawless state of those outlying regions and the absence of communication between them and town.

Abruptly, blotted in blue mist, vineyards and olives, with the groups of aloes marking off field boundaries, disappeared. We entered on a land of naked rock, peak after peak of it, cutting a jagged line against the clear intensity of the sky.

This passed again, with early afternoon our straight, white road grew featureless, a dusty stretch, save far ahead the sun-tipped ridge of a sierra, and the silver ribbon of the river twisting among the barren hills. Toward the end we passed one of the wooden crosses set up on these roads to mark some spot of violence or disaster. These are the only signposts one encoun- ters, and as we came up with it, our beasts were goaded for the last ascent.

Irregular grey walls came into view; we skirted them and turned in through a Roman gateway and across a bridge into a maze of narrow stone-pitched streets, spanned here and there by Moorish arches, and execrably rough to rattle over.

A strong illusion of the Orient, extreme antiquity and dreamlike stillness marked the place.

Crossing the grey arcaded Plaza, just beginning at that hour to be splashed with blots of gaudy colour moving to the tinkling of the mulebells, we were soon upon the outskirts of the town—the most untouched, remote and, I believe, the most remarkable that we had dropped upon.

In its neglect and singularity, it made a claim to something like supremacy of charm. There was the quality of diffidence belonging to unrecognized abandoned personalities in that appeal.

That's how it's docketed in memory—a city with a claim, which, as it happened, I was not to weigh.

Our inn, a long, one-storeyed building with caged windows, most of them unglazed, had been an old palacio; its broken fortunes hadn't robbed it of its character, its air.

The spacious place was practically empty, and the shuttered rooms, stone-flagged and cool, after our shadeless ride, invited one to a prolonged siesta; but Ella wasn't friendly to a pause. Her buoyancy survived our meal. She seemed even to face the morrow's repetition of that indescribable experience with serenity. We found her in the small paved garden, sipping chocolate and airing Spanish with our host, a man of some distinction, possibly of broken fortunes too.

The conversation, delicately edged with compliment on his side, was on hers a little blunted by a limited vocabulary, and left us both presumably a margin for imagination.

Si, la Señora, he explained as we came up, knew absolutely nothing of fatigue, and the impetuosity of the *Señora*, this attractive eagerness to make acquaintance with it, did great honour to his much forgotten, much neglected town. He spoke of it with rather touching ardour, as a place unvisited, but '*digno de renombre illustre*', worthy of high fame.

It has stood still, it was perhaps too stationary; innovation was repellent to the Spaniard, yet this conservatism, lack of enterprise, the virtue or the failing of his country—as we pleased—had its aesthetic value. Was there not, he would appeal to the *Señora*, '*una belleza de reposo*', a beauty of quiescence, a dignity above prosperity? '*Muy bien.*' Let the *Señora* judge, you had it there!

We struck out from the town, perhaps insensibly toward the

landmark of a Calvary, planted a mile or so beyond the walls, its three black shafts above the mass of roofs and pinnacles, in sharp relief against the sky, against which suddenly a flock of vultures threw the first white cloud. With the descending sun, the clear persistence of the blue was losing permanence, a breeze sprang up and birds began to call.

The Spanish evening has unique effects and exquisite exhilarations: this one led us on some distance past the Calvary and the last group of scattered houses—many in complete decay—which straggle, thinning outwards from the city boundaries into the *campo*.

Standing alone, after a stretch of crumbling wall, a wretched little *venta*, like a stop to some meandering sentence, closed the broken line.

The place was windowless, but through the open door an oath or two—the common blend of sacrilege and vileness—with a smell of charcoal, frying oil-cakes and an odour of the stable, drifted out into the freshness of the evening air.

Immediately before us lay a dim expanse of treeless plain: behind, clear cut against a smokeless sky, the flat roof lines and towers of the city, seeming, as we looked back on them, less distant than in fact they were.

We took a road which finally confronted us with a huge block of buildings, an old church and convent, massed in the shadow of a hill and standing at the entrance to three cross-roads.

The convent, one of the few remaining in the south, not fallen into ruin, nor yet put, as far as one could judge, to worldly uses, was exceptionally large. We counted over thirty windows in a line upon the western side below the central tower with its pointed turret; the eastern wing, an evidently older part, was cut irregularly with a few square gratings.

The big, grey structure was impressive in its loneliness, its blank negation of the outside world, its stark expressionless detachment.

The church, of darker stone, was massive too; its only noticeable feature a small cloister with Romanesque arcades joining the nave on its south-western wall.

A group of peasant women coming out from vespers passed us and went chattering up the road, the last, an aged creature shuffling painfully some yards behind the rest still muttering her

> *Madre purisima,*
> *Madre castisima,*
> *Ruega por nosostros,*

in a kind of automatic drone.

We looked in, as one does instinctively: the altar lights which hang like sickly stars in the profound obscurity of Spanish churches were being quickly blotted out.

We didn't enter then, but turned back to the convent gate, which stood half open, showing a side of the uncorniced cloisters, and a crowd of flowers, touched to an intensity of brilliance and fragrance by the twilight. Six or seven dogs, the sandy-coloured lurchers of the country, lean and wolfish-looking hounds, were sprawling round the gateway; save for this dejected crew, the place seemed resolutely lifeless; and this absence of a human note was just. One didn't want its solitude or silence touched, its really fine impersonality destroyed.

We hadn't meant—there wasn't light enough—to try the church again, but as we passed it, we turned into the small cloister. King, who had come to his last match, was seeking shelter from the breeze which had considerably freshened, and at the far end we came upon a little door, unlocked. I don't know why we tried it, but mechanically, as the conscientious tourist will, we drifted in and groped round. Only the vaguest outlines were discernible; the lancets of the lantern at the transept crossing, and a large rose window at the western end seemed, at a glance, the only means of light, and this was failing, leaving fast the fading panes.

One half-detected, almost guessed, the blind triforium, but the enormous width of the great building made immediate mark. The darkness, masking as it did distinctive features, emphasized the sense of space, which, like the spirit of a shrouded form, gained force, intensity, from its material disguise.

We stayed not more than a few minutes, but on reaching the small door again we found it fast; bolted or locked undoubtedly in the short interval. Of course we put our backs to it and made a pretty violent outcry, hoping the worthy sacristan was hanging round or somewhere within call. Of course he wasn't. We tried two other doors; both barred, and there was nothing left for it but noise. We shouted, I suppose, for half an hour, intermittently, and King persisted hoarsely after I had given out.

The echo of the vast, dark, empty place caught up our cries, seeming to hold them in suspension for a second in the void invisibility of roof and arches, then to fling them down in hollow repetition with an accent of unearthly mimicry which struck a little grimly on one's ear; and when we paused the silence seemed alert, expectant, ready to repel the first recurrence of unholy clamour. Finally, we gave it up; the hope of a release before the dawn, at earliest, was too forlorn. King, explosive and solicitous, was solemnly perturbed, but Ella faced the situation with an admirable tranquillity. Some chocolate and a muff would certainly, for her, she said, have made it more engaging, but poor dear men, the really tragic element resolved itself into—No matches, no cigar!

Unluckily we hadn't even this poor means of temporary light. Our steps and voices sounded loud, almost aggressive, as we groped about; the darkness then was shutting down and shortly it grew absolute. We camped eventually in one of the side chapels on the south side of the chancel, and kept a conversation going for a time, but gradually it dropped. The temperature, the fixed obscurity, and possibly a curious oppression in the spiritual atmosphere relaxed and forced it down.

The scent of incense clung about; a biting chillness crept up through the aisles; it got intensely cold. The stillness too became insistent; it was literally deathlike, rigid, exclusive, even awfully remote. It shut us out and held aloof; our passive presences, our mere vitality, seemed almost a disturbance of it; quiet as we were, we breathed, but it was breathless, and as time went on, one's impulse was to fight the sort of shapeless personality it presently assumed, to talk, to walk about and make a definite attack on it. Its influence on the others was presumably more soothing, obviously they weren't that way inclined.

Five or six hours must have passed. Nothing had marked them, and they hadn't seemed to move. The darkness seemed to thicken, in a way, to muddle thought and filter through into one's brain, and waiting, cramped and cold for it to lift, the soundlessness again impressed itself unpleasantly—it was intense, unnatural, acute.

And then it stirred.

The break in it was vague but positive; it might have been that, scarcely audible, the wind outside was rising, and yet not precisely that. I barely caught, and couldn't localize the sound.

Ella and King were dozing, they had had some snatches of uncomfortable sleep; I, I suppose, was preternaturally awake. I heard a key turn, and the swing back of a door, rapidly followed by a wave of voices breaking in. I put my hand out and touched King, and in a moment, both of them waked and started up.

I can't say how, but it at once occurred to us that quiet was our cue, that we were in for something singular.

The place was filling slowly with a chant, and then, emerging from the eastern end of the north aisle and travelling down just opposite, across the intervening dark, a line of light came into view, crossing the opening of the arches, cut by the massive piers, a moving, flickering line, advancing and advancing with the voices.

The outlines of the figures in the long procession weren't perceptible, the faces, palely lit and level with the tapers they were carrying, one rather felt than saw; but unmistakably the voices were men's voices, and the chant, the measured, reiterated cadences, prevailed over the wavering light.

Heavy and sombre as the stillness which it broke, vaguely akin to it, the chant swept in and gained upon the silence with a motion of the tide. It was a music neither of the senses, nor the spirit, but the mind, as set, as stately, almost as inanimate as the dark aisles through which it echoed; even, colourless and cold.

And then, quite suddenly, against its grave and passionless inflections something clashed, a piercing intermittent note, an awful discord, shrilling out and dying down and shrilling out again—a cry—a scream.

The chant went on; the light, from where we stood, was steadily retreating, and we ventured forward. Judging our whereabouts as best we could, we made towards the choir and stumbled up some steps, placing ourselves eventually behind one of the pillars of the apse. And from this point, the whole proceeding was apparent.

At the west end the line of light was turning; fifty or sixty monks (about—and at a venture) habited in brown and carrying tapers, walking two and two, were moving up the central aisle towards us, headed by three, one with the cross between two others bearing heavy silver candlesticks with tapers, larger than those carried by the rest.

Reaching the chancel steps, they paused; the three bearing the cross and candlesticks stood facing the altar, while those following diverged to right and left and lined the aisle. The first to take up this position were quite young, some almost boys; they were succeeded gradually by older men, those at the tail of the procession being obviously aged and infirm.

And then a figure, white and slight, erect—a woman's figure—struck a startling note at the far end of the brown line, a note as startling as the shrieks which jarred recurrently, were jarring still against the chant.

A pace or two behind her walked two priests in surplices, and after them another, vested in a cope. And on the whole impassive company her presence, her disturbance, made no mark. For them, in fact, she wasn't there.

Neither was she aware of them. I doubt if to her consciousness, or mine, as she approached, grew definite, there was a creature in the place besides herself.

She moved and uttered her successive cries as if both sound and motion were entirely mechanical—more like a person in some trance of terror or of anguish than a voluntary rebel; her cries bespoke a physical revulsion into which her spirit didn't enter; they were not her own— they were outside herself; there was no discomposure in her carriage, nor, when we presently saw it, in her face. Both were distinguished by a certain exquisite hauteur, and this detachment of her personality from her distress impressed one curiously. She wasn't altogether real, she didn't altogether live, and yet her presence there was the supreme reality of the unreal scene, and lent to it, at least as I was viewing it, its only element of life.

She had, one understood, her part to play: she wasn't, for the moment, quite prepared; she played it later with superb effect.

As she came up with the three priests, the monks closed in and formed a semi-circle round them, while the priests advanced and placed themselves behind the monks who bore the cross and candlesticks, immediately below the chancel steps, facing the altar. They left her standing some few paces back, in the half-ring of sickly light shed by the tapers.

Now one saw her face. It was of striking beauty, but its age? One couldn't say. It had the tints, the purity of youth—it might have been extremely young, matured merely by the moment; but for a veil of fine repression which only years, it seemed, could possibly have woven. And it was itself—this face—a mask, one of the loveliest that spirit ever wore. It kept the spirit's counsel. Though what stirred it then, in that unique emergency, one saw—to what had stirred it, or might stir it gave no clue. It threw one back on vain conjecture.

Put the match of passion to it—would it burn? Touch it with grief and would it cloud, contract? With joy—and could it find, or had it ever found, a smile? Again, one couldn't say.

Only, as she stood there, erect and motionless, it showed the faintest flicker of distaste, disgust, as if she shrank from some repellent contact. She was clad, I think I said, from head to foot in a white linen garment; head and ears were covered too, the oval of the face alone was visible, and this was slightly flushed. Her screams were changing into little cries or moans, like those of a spent animal, from whom the momentary pressure of attack has been removed. They broke from her at intervals, unnoticed, unsuppressed, and now in silence, for the monks had ceased their chanting.

As they did so one realized the presence of these men, who, up to now, had scarcely taken shape as actualities, been more than an accompaniment—a drone. They shifted from a mass of voices to a row of pallid faces, each one lit by its own taper, hung upon the dark, or thrown abruptly, as it were, upon a screen; all different; all, at first distinct, but linked together by a subtle likeness, stamped with that dye which blurs the print of individuality—the signet of the cloister.

Taking them singly, though one did it roughly, rapidly enough, it wasn't difficult at starting to detect varieties of natural and spiritual equipment. There they were, spread out for sorting, nonentities and saints and devils, side by side, and what was queerer, animated by one purpose, governed by one law.

Some of the faces touched upon divinity; some fell below humanity; some were, of course, merely a blotch of book and bell, and all were set impassively toward the woman standing there.

And then one lost the sense of their diversity in their resemblance; the similarity persisted and persisted till the row of faces seemed to merge into one face—the face of nothing human—of a system, of a rule. It framed the woman's and one felt the force of it: she wasn't in the hands of men.

There was a pause filled only by her cries, a space of silence which they hardly broke; and then one of the monks stepped forward, slid into the chancel and began to light up the high altar. The little yellow tongues of flame struggled and started up, till first one line and then another starred the gloom.

Her glance had followed him; her eyes were fixed upon that point of darkness growing to a blaze. There was for her, in that illumination, some intense significance, and as she gazed intently on the patch of brilliance, her cries were suddenly arrested—quelled. The light had lifted something, given back to her an unimpaired identity. She was at last in full possession of herself. The flicker of distaste had passed and left her face to its inflexible, inscrutable repose.

She drew herself to her full height and turned towards the men behind her with an air of proud surrender, of magnificent disdain. I think she made some sign.

Another monk stepped out, extinguished and laid down his taper, and approached her.

I was prepared for something singular, for something passably bizarre, but not for what immediately occurred. He touched her eyes and closed them; then her mouth, and made a feint of closing that, while one of the two priests threw over his short surplice a black stole and started audibly with a *Sub venite*. The monks responded. Here and there I caught the words or sense of a response. The prayers for the most part were unintelligible: it was no doubt the usual office for the dead, and if it was, no finer satire for the work in hand could well have been devised. Loudly and unexpectedly above his unctuous monotone a bell clanged out three times. An *Ave* followed, after which two bells together, this time muffled, sounded out again three times. The priest proceeded with a *Miserere*, during which they rang the bells alternately, and there was something curiously suggestive and determinate about this part of the performance. The real action had, one felt, begun.

At the first stroke of the first bell her eyelids fluttered, but she kept them down; it wasn't until later at one point in the response, '*Non intres in judicium cum ancilla tua Domine*', she yielded to an impulse of her lips, permitted them the shadow of a smile. But for this slip she looked the thing of death they reckoned to have made of her—detached herself, with an inspired touch, from all the living actors in the solemn farce, from all apparent apprehension of the scene. I, too, was quite incredibly outside it all.

I hadn't even asked myself precisely what was going to take place. Possibly I had caught the trick of her quiescence, acquiescence, and I went no further than she went; I waited—waited with her, as it were, to see it through. And I experienced a vague, almost resentful sense of interruption, incongruity, when King broke in to ask me what was up. He brought me back to Ella's presence, to the consciousness that this, so far as the spectators were concerned, was not a woman's comedy.

I made it briefly plain to them, as I knew something of the place and people, that any movement on our side would probably prove more than rash, and turned again to what was going forward.

They were clumsily transforming the white figure. Two monks had robed her in a habit of their colour of her order, I suppose, and were now putting on the scapular and girdle. Finally they flung over her the long white-hooded cloak and awkwardly arranged the veil, leaving her face uncovered; then they joined her hands and placed between them a small cross.

This change of setting emphasized my first impression of her face; the mask was lovelier now and more complete.

Two voices started sonorously, '*Libera me, Domine*', the monks took up the chant, the whole assembly now began to move, the muffled bells to ring again at intervals, while the procession formed and filed into the choir. The monks proceeded to their stalls, the younger taking places in the rear. The two who had assisted at the robing led the passive figure to the centre of the chancel, where the three who bore the cross and candlesticks turned round and stood a short way off confronting her. Two others, carrying the censer and *bénitier*, stationed themselves immediately behind her with the priests and the officiant, who now, in a loud voice, began his recitations.

They seemed, with variations, to be going through it all again. I caught the *Non intres in judicium* and the *Sub venite* recurring with the force of a refrain. It was a long elaborate affair. The grave deliberation of its detail heightened its effect. Not to be tedious, I give it you in brief. It lasted altogether possibly two hours.

The priest assisting the officiant, lifting the border of his cope, attended him when he proceeded first to sprinkle, then to incense the presumably dead figure, with the crucifix confronting it, held almost like a challenge to its sightless face. They made the usual inclinations to the image as they passed it, and repeated the performance of the incensing and sprinkling with extreme formality at intervals, in all, I think, three times.

There was no break in the continuous drone proceeding from the choir; they kept it going; none of them looked up—or none at least of whom I had a view—when four young monks slid out, and, kneeling down in the clear space between her and the crucifix, dislodged a stone which must have previously been loosened in the paving of the chancel, and disclosed a cavity, the depth of which I wasn't near enough to see.

For this I wasn't quite prepared, and yet I wasn't discomposed. I can't attempt to make it clear under what pressure I accepted this impossible *dénouement*, but I did accept it. More than that, I was exclusively absorbed in her reception of it. Though she couldn't, wouldn't see, she must have been aware of what was happening. But on the other hand, she was prepared, dispassionately ready, for the end.

All through the dragging length of the long offices, although she hadn't stirred or given any sign (except that one faint shadow of a smile) of consciousness, I felt the force of her intense vitality, the tension of its absolute impression. The life of those enclosing presences seemed to have passed into her presence, to be concentrated there. For to my view it was these men who held her in death's grip who didn't live, and she alone who was absorbently alive.

The candles, burning steadily on either side the crucifix, the soft illumination of innumerable altar lights confronting her, intensified the darkness which above her and behind her—everywhere beyond the narrow confines of the feeble light in which she stood—prevailed.

This setting lent to her the aspect of an unsubstantial, almost supernatural figure, suddenly arrested in its passage through the dark.

She stood compliantly and absolutely still. If she had swayed, or given any hint of wavering, of an appeal to God or man, I must have answered it magnetically. It was she who had the key to what I might have done but didn't do. Make what you will of it—we were inexplicably *en rapport*.

But failing failure I was backing her; it hadn't once occurred to me, without her sanction, to step in, to intervene; that I had anything to do with it beyond my recognition of her—of her part, her claim to play it as she pleased. And now it was—a thousand years too late!

They managed the illusion for themselves and me magnificently. She had come to be a thing of spirit only, not in any sort of clay. She was already in the world of shades; some power as sovereign and determinate as Death itself had lodged her there, past rescue or the profanation of recall.

King was in the act of springing forward; he had got out his revolver; meant, if possible, to shoot her before closing with the rest. It was the right and only workable idea. I held him back, using the first deterrent that occurred to me, reminding him of Ella, and the notion of her danger may have hovered on the outskirts of my mind. But it was not for her at all that I was consciously concerned. I was impelled to stand aside, to force him, too, to stand aside and see it through.

What followed, followed as such things occur in dreams; the senses seize, the mind, or what remains of it, accepts mechanically the natural or unnatural sequence of events.

I saw the grave surrounded by the priests and blessed; and then the woman and the grave repeatedly, alternately, incensed and sprinkled with deliberate solemnity; and heard, as if from a great distance, the recitations of the prayers, and chanting of interminable psalms.

At the last moment, with their hands upon her, standing for a second still erect, before she was committed to the darkness, she unclosed her eyes, sent one swift glance towards the light, a glance which caught it, flashed it back, recaptured it and kept it for the lighting of her tomb. And then her face was covered with her veil.

The final act was the supreme illusion of the whole. I watched the lowering of the passive figure as if I had been witnessing the actual entombment of the dead.

The grave was sprinkled and incensed again, the stone replaced and fastened down. A long sequence of prayers said over it succeeded, at the end of which, the monks put out their tapers, only one or two remaining lit with those beside the Crucifix.

The priests and the officiant at length approached the altar, kneeling and prostrating there some minutes and repeating *Pater Nosters*, followed by the choir.

Finally in rising, the officiant pronounced alone and loudly '*Requiescat in pace*'. The monks responded sonorously, 'Amen'.

The altar lights were one by one extinguished; at a sign, preceded by the cross, the vague, almost invisible procession formed and travelled down the aisle, reciting quietly the *De Profundis* and guided now, by only, here and there, a solitary light. The quiet recitation, growing fainter, was a new and unfamiliar impression; I felt that I was missing something—what? I missed, in fact, the chanting; then quite suddenly and certainly I missed—the scream. In place of it there was this *De Profundis* and her silence. Out of her deep I realized it, dreamily, of course she would not call.

The door swung to; the church was dark and still again—immensely dark and still.

There was a pause, in which we didn't move or speak; in which I doubted for a second the reality of the incredibly remote, yet almost present scene, trying to reconstruct it in imagination, pit the dream against the fact, the fact against the dream.

'Good God!' said King at length, 'what are we going to do?'

His voice awoke me forcibly to something nearer daylight, to the human and inhuman elements in the remarkable affair, which hitherto had missed my mind; they struck against it now with a tremendous shock, and mentally I rubbed my eyes. I saw what King had all along been looking at, the sheer, unpicturesque barbarity. What *were* we going to do?

She breathed perhaps, perhaps she heard us—something of us—we were standing not more than a yard or so away; and if she did, she waited, that was the most poignant possibility, for our decision, our attack.

Ella was naturally unstrung: we left her crouching by the pillar; later I think she partially lost consciousness. It was as well—it left us free.

Striking, as nearly as we could, the centre of the altar, working from it, we made a guess at the position of the stone, and on our hands and knees felt blindly for some indication of its loosened edge. But everywhere the paving, to our touch, presented an unevenness of surface, and we picked at random, chiefly for the sake of doing something. In that intolerable darkness there was really nothing to be done but wait for dawn or listen for some guidance from below. For that we listened breathless and alert enough, but nothing stirred. The stillness had become again intense, acute, and now a grim significance attached to it.

The minutes, hours, dragged; time wasn't as it had been, stationary, but desperately, murderously slow.

Each moment of inaction counted—counted horribly, as we stood straining ears and eyes for any hint of sound, of light.

At length the darkness lifted, almost imperceptibly at first; the big rose window to the west became a scarcely visible grey blot; the massive piers detached themselves from the dense mass of shadow and stood out, immense and vague; the windows of the lantern just above us showed a ring of slowly lightening panes; and with the dawn, we found the spot and set to work.

The implements we improvised we soon discovered to be practically useless. We loosened, but we couldn't move the stone.

At intervals we stopped and put our ears to the thin crevices. King thought, and still believes, he heard some sound or movement; but I didn't. I was somehow sure, for that, it was too late.

For everything it was too late, and we returned reluctantly to a consideration of our own predicament; we had, if possible, to get away unseen. And this time luck was on our side. The sacristan, who came in early by the cloister door which we had entered by, without perceiving us, proceeded to the sacristy.

We made a rapid and effectual escape.

We sketched out and elaborated, on our way back to the town, the little scheme of explanation to be offered to our host, which was to cover an announcement of abrupt departure. He received it with polite credulity, profound regret. He ventured to believe that the *Señora* was unfortunately missing a unique experience—cities, like men, had elements of beauty, or of greatness which escape the crowd; but the *Señora* was not of the crowd, and he had hoped she would be able to remain.

Nothing, however, would induce her to remain for more than a few hours. We must push on without delay and put the night's occurrences before the nearest British Consul. She made no comments and admitted no fatigue, but on this point she was persistent to perversity. She carried it.

The Consul proved hospitable and amiable. He heard the story and was suitably impressed. It was a truly horrible experience—remarkably dramatic—yes. He added it—we saw him doing it—to his collection of strange tales.

The country was, he said, extremely rich in tragic anecdote; and men in his position earned their reputation for romance. But as to *doing* anything in this case, as in others even more remarkable, why, there was absolutely nothing to be done!

The laws of Spain were theoretically admirable, but practically, well—the best that could be said of them was that they had their comic side.

And this was not a civil matter, where the wheels might often, certainly, be oiled. The wheel ecclesiastic was more intractable.

He asked if we were leaving Spain immediately. We said, 'Perhaps in a few days.' 'Take my advice,' said he, 'and make it a few hours.'

We did.

Ella would tell you that the horror of those hours hasn't ever altogether ceased to haunt her, that it visits her in dreams and poisons sleep.

She hasn't ever understood, or quite forgiven me my attitude of temporary detachment. She refuses to admit that, after all, what one is pleased to call reality is merely the intensity of one's illusion. My illusion was intense.

'Oh, for you,' she says, and with a touch of bitterness, 'it was a spectacle. The woman didn't really count.'

For me it was a spectacle, but more than that: it was an acquiescence in a rather splendid crime.

On looking back I see that, at the moment in my mind, the woman didn't really count. She saw herself she didn't. That's precisely what she made me see.

What counted chiefly with her, I suspect, was something infinitely greater to her vision than the terror of men's dreams.

She lies, one must remember, in the very centre of the sanctuary— has a place uniquely sacred to her order, the traditions of her kind. It was this honour, satisfying, as it did, some pride of spirit or of race, which bore her honourably through.

She had, one way or other, clogged the wheels of an inflexible machine. But for the speck of dust she knew herself to be, she was—oh horribly, I grant you!—yet not lightly, not dishonourably, swept away.

SAKI

The Toys of Peace

'HARVEY,' said Eleanor Bope, handing her brother a cutting from a London morning paper* of the 19th of March, 'just read this about children's toys, please; it exactly carries out some of our ideas about influence and upbringing.'

'In the view of the National Peace Council,' ran the extract, 'there are grave objections to presenting our boys with regiments of fighting men, batteries of guns, and squadrons of "Dreadnoughts". Boys, the Council admits, naturally love fighting and all the panoply of war . . . but that is no reason for encouraging, and perhaps giving permanent form to, their primitive instincts. At the Children's Welfare Exhibition, which opens at Olympia in three weeks' time, the Peace Council will make an alternative suggestion to parents in the shape of an exhibition of "peace toys". In front of a specially painted representation of the Peace Palace at The Hague will be grouped, not miniature soldiers but miniature civilians, not guns but ploughs and the tools of industry. . . . It is hoped that manufacturers may take a hint from the exhibit, which will bear fruit in the toy shops.'

'The idea is certainly an interesting and very well-meaning one,' said Harvey; 'whether it would succeed well in practice—'

'We must try,' interrupted his sister; 'you are coming down to us at Easter, and you always bring the boys some toys, so that will be an excellent opportunity for you to inaugurate the new experiment. Go about in the shops and buy any little toys and models that have special bearing on civilian life in its more peaceful aspects. Of course you must explain the toys to the children and interest them in the new idea. I regret to say that the "Siege of Adrianople" toy, that their Aunt Susan sent them, didn't need any explanation; they knew all the uniforms and flags, and even the names of the respective commanders, and when I heard them one day using what seemed to be the most objectionable language they said it was Bulgarian words of command; of course it *may* have been, but

* An actual extract from a London paper of March 1914.

at any rate I took the toy away from them. Now I shall expect your Easter gifts to give quite a new impulse and direction to the children's minds; Eric is not eleven yet, and Bertie is only nine-and-a-half, so they are really at a most impressionable age.'

'There is primitive instinct to be taken into consideration, you know,' said Harvey doubtfully, 'and hereditary tendencies as well. One of their great-uncles fought in the most intolerant fashion at Inkerman—he was specially mentioned in dispatches, I believe—and their great-grandfather smashed all his Whig neighbours' hothouses when the great Reform Bill was passed. Still, as you say, they are at an impressionable age. I will do my best.'

On Easter Saturday Harvey Bope unpacked a large, promising-looking red cardboard box under the expectant eyes of his nephews. 'Your uncle has brought you the newest thing in toys,' Eleanor had said impressively, and youthful anticipation had been anxiously divided between Albanian soldiery and a Somali camel-corps. Eric was hotly in favour of the latter contingency. 'There would be Arabs on horseback,' he whispered; 'the Albanians have got jolly uniforms, and they fight all day long, and all night too, when there's a moon, but the country's rocky, so they've got no cavalry.'

A quantity of crinkly paper shavings was the first thing that met the view when the lid was removed; the most exciting toys always began like that. Harvey pushed back the top layer and drew forth a square, rather featureless building.

'It's a fort!' exclaimed Bertie.

'It isn't, it's the palace of the Mpret of Albania,' said Eric, immensely proud of his knowledge of the exotic title; 'it's got no windows, you see, so that passers-by can't fire in at the Royal Family.'

'It's a municipal dust-bin,' said Harvey hurriedly; 'you see all the refuse and litter of a town is collected there, instead of lying about and injuring the health of the citizens.'

In an awful silence he disinterred a little lead figure of a man in black clothes.

'That,' he said, 'is a distinguished civilian, John Stuart Mill. He was an authority on political economy.'

'Why?' asked Bertie.

'Well, he wanted to be; he thought it was a useful thing to be.'

Bertie gave an expressive grunt, which conveyed his opinion that there was no accounting for tastes.

Another square building came out, this time with windows and chimneys.

'A model of the Manchester branch of the Young Women's Christian Association,' said Harvey.

'Are there any lions?' asked Eric hopefully. He had been reading Roman history and thought that where you found Christians you might reasonably expect to find a few lions.

'There are no lions,' said Harvey. 'Here is another civilian, Robert Raikes, the founder of Sunday schools, and here is a model of a municipal wash-house. These little round things are loaves baked in a sanitary bakehouse. That lead figure is a sanitary inspector, this one is a district councillor, and this one is an official of the Local Government Board.'

'What does he do?' asked Eric wearily.

'He sees to things connected with his Department,' said Harvey. 'This box with a slit in it is a ballot-box. Votes are put into it at election times.'

'What is put into it at other times?' asked Bertie.

'Nothing. And here are some tools of industry, a wheelbarrow and a hoe, and I think these are meant for hop-poles. This is a model beehive, and that is a ventilator, for ventilating sewers. This seems to be another municipal dust-bin—no, it is a model of a school of art and a public library. This little lead figure is Mrs Hemans, a poetess, and this is Rowland Hill, who introduced the system of penny postage. This is Sir John Herschel, the eminent astrologer.'

'Are we to play with these civilian figures?' asked Eric.

'Of course,' said Harvey, 'these are toys; they are meant to be played with.'

'But how?'

It was rather a poser. 'You might make two of them contest a seat in Parliament,' said Harvey, 'and have an election—'

'With rotten eggs, and free fights, and ever so many broken heads!' exclaimed Eric.

'And noses all bleeding and everybody drunk as can be,' echoed Bertie, who had carefully studied one of Hogarth's pictures.

'Nothing of the kind,' said Harvey, 'nothing in the least like that. Votes will be put in the ballot-box, and the Mayor will count them— the district councillor will do for the Mayor—and he will say which has received the most votes, and then the two candidates will thank him for presiding, and each will say that the contest has been conducted throughout in the pleasantest and most straightforward fashion, and they part with expressions of mutual esteem. There's a jolly game for you boys to play. I never had such toys when I was young.'

'I don't think we'll play with them just now,' said Eric, with an entire absence of the enthusiasm that his uncle had shown; 'I think perhaps we ought to do a little of our holiday task. It's history this time; we've got to learn up something about the Bourbon period in France.'

'The Bourbon period,' said Harvey, with some disapproval in his voice.

'We've got to know something about Louis the Fourteenth,' continued Eric; 'I've learnt the names of all the principal battles already.'

This would never do. 'There were, of course, some battles fought during his reign,' said Harvey, 'but I fancy the accounts of them were much exaggerated; news was very unreliable in those days, and there were practically no war correspondents, so generals and commanders could magnify every little skirmish they engaged in till they reached the proportions of decisive battles. Louis was really famous, now, as a landscape gardener; the way he laid out Versailles was so much admired that it was copied all over Europe.'

'Do you know anything about Madame Du Barry?' asked Eric; 'didn't she have her head chopped off?'

'She was another great lover of gardening,' said Harvey evasively; 'in fact, I believe the well-known rose Du Barry was named after her, and now I think you had better play for a little and leave your lessons till later.'

Harvey retreated to the library and spent some thirty or forty minutes in wondering whether it would be possible to compile a history, for use in elementary schools, in which there should be no prominent mention of battles, massacres, murderous intrigues, and violent deaths. The York and Lancaster period and the Napoleonic era would, he admitted to himself, present considerable difficulties, and the Thirty Years' War would entail something of a gap if you left it out altogether. Still, it would be something gained if, at a highly impressionable age, children could be got to fix their attention on the invention of calico printing instead of the Spanish Armada or the Battle of Waterloo.

It was time, he thought, to go back to the boys' room, and see how they were getting on with their peace toys. As he stood outside the door he could hear Eric's voice raised in command; Bertie chimed in now and again with a helpful suggestion.

'That is Louis the Fourteenth,' Eric was saying, 'that one in knee-breeches, that Uncle said invented Sunday schools. It isn't a bit like him, but it'll have to do.'

'We'll give him a purple coat from my paintbox by and by,' said Bertie.

'Yes, an' red heels. That is Madame de Maintenon, that one he called Mrs Hemans. She begs Louis not to go on this expedition, but he turns a deaf ear. He takes Marshal Saxe with him, and we must pretend that they have thousands of men with them. The watchword is *Qui vive?* and the answer is *L'état c'est moi*—that was one of his favourite remarks, you know. They land at Manchester in the dead of night, and a Jacobite conspirator gives them the keys of the fortress.'

Peeping in through the doorway Harvey observed that the municipal dust-bin had been pierced with holes to accommodate the muzzles of imaginary cannon, and now represented the principal fortified position in Manchester; John Stuart Mill had been dipped in red ink, and apparently stood for Marshal Saxe.

'Louis orders his troops to surround the Young Women's Christian Association and seize the lot of them. "Once back at the Louvre and the girls are mine," he exclaims. We must use Mrs Hemans again for one of the girls; she says "Never," and stabs Marshal Saxe to the heart.'

'He bleeds dreadfully,' exclaimed Bertie, splashing red ink liberally over the façade of the Association building.

'The soldiers rush in and avenge his death with the utmost savagery. A hundred girls are killed'—here Bertie emptied the remainder of the red ink over the devoted building—'and the surviving five hundred are dragged off to the French ships. "I have lost a Marshal," says Louis, "but I do not go back empty-handed." '

Harvey stole away from the room, and sought out his sister.

'Eleanor,' he said, 'the experiment—'

'Yes?'

'Has failed. We have begun too late.'

G. K. CHESTERTON

The Tremendous Adventures
of Major Brown

RABELAIS, or his wild illustrator Gustave Doré, must have had something to do with the designing of the things called flats in England and America. There is something entirely Gargantuan in the idea of economizing space by piling houses on top of each other, front doors and all. And in the chaos and complexity of those perpendicular streets anything may dwell or happen, and it is in one of them, I believe, that the enquirer may find the offices of the Club of Queer Trades. It may be thought at the first glance that the name would attract and startle the passer-by, but nothing attracts or startles in these dim immense hives. The passer-by is only looking for his own melancholy destination, the Montenegro Shipping Agency or the London office of the *Rutland Sentinel*, and passes through the twilight passages as one passes through the twilight corridors of a dream. If the Thugs set up a Strangers' Assassination Company in one of the great buildings in Norfolk Street, and sent in a mild man in spectacles to answer enquiries, no enquiries would be made. And the Club of Queer Trades reigns in a great edifice hidden like a fossil in a mighty cliff of fossils.

The nature of this society, such as we afterwards discovered it to be, is soon and simply told. It is an eccentric and Bohemian Club, of which the absolute condition of membership lies in this, that the candidate must have invented the method by which he earns his living. It must be an entirely new trade. The exact definition of this requirement is given in the two principal rules. First, it must not be a mere application or variation of an existing trade. Thus, for instance, the Club would not admit an insurance agent simply because instead of insuring men's furniture against being burnt in a fire, he insured, let us say, their trousers against being torn by a mad dog. The principle (as Sir Bradcock Burnaby-Bradcock, in the extraordinarily eloquent and soaring speech to the club on the occasion of the question being raised in the Stormby

Smith affair, said wittily and keenly) is the same. Secondly, the trade must be a genuine commercial source of income, the support of its inventor. Thus the Club would not receive a man simply because he chose to pass his days collecting broken sardine tins, unless he could drive a roaring trade in them. Professor Chick made that quite clear. And when one remembers what Professor Chick's own new trade was, one doesn't know whether to laugh or cry.

The discovery of this strange society was a curiously refreshing thing; to realize that there were ten new trades in the world was like looking at the first ship or the first plough. It made a man feel what he should feel, that he was still in the childhood of the world. That I should have come at last upon so singular a body was, I may say without vanity, not altogether singular, for I have a mania for belonging to as many societies as possible: I may be said to collect clubs, and I have accumulated a vast and fantastic variety of specimens ever since, in my audacious youth, I collected the Athenaeum. At some future day, perhaps, I may tell tales of some of the other bodies to which I have belonged. I will recount the doings of the Dead Man's Shoes Society (that superficially immoral, but darkly justifiable communion); I will explain the curious origin of the Cat and Christian, the name of which has been so shamefully misinterpreted; and the world shall know at last why the Institute of Typewriters coalesced with the Red Tulip League. Of the Ten Teacups, of course I dare not say a word. The first of my revelations, at any rate, shall be concerned with the Club of Queer Trades, which, as I have said, was one of this class, one which I was almost bound to come across sooner or later, because of my singular hobby. The wild youth of the metropolis call me facetiously 'The King of Clubs'. They also call me 'The Cherub', in allusion to the roseate and youthful appearance I have presented in my declining years. I only hope the spirits in the better world have as good dinners as I have. But the finding of the Club of Queer Trades has one very curious thing about it. The most curious thing about it is that it was not discovered by me; it was discovered by my friend Basil Grant, a star-gazer, a mystic, and a man who scarcely stirred out of his attic.

Very few people knew anything of Basil; not because he was in the least unsociable, for if a man out of the street had walked into his rooms he would have kept him talking till morning. Few people knew him, because, like all poets, he could do without them; he welcomed a human face as he might welcome a sudden blend of colour in a sunset;

but he no more felt the need of going out to parties than he felt the need of altering the sunset clouds. He lived in a queer and comfortable garret in the roofs of Lambeth. He was surrounded by a chaos of things that were in odd contrast to the slums around him; old fantastic books, swords, armour—the whole dust-hole of romanticism. But his face, amid all these quixotic relics, appeared curiously keen and modern—a powerful, legal face. And no one but I knew who he was.

Long ago as it is, everyone remembers the terrible and grotesque scene that occurred in ——, when one of the most acute and forcible of the English judges suddenly went mad on the bench. I had my own view of that occurrence; but about the facts themselves there is no question at all. For some months, indeed for some years, people had detected something curious in the judge's conduct. He seemed to have lost interest in the law, in which he had been beyond expression brilliant and terrible as a KC, and to be occupied in giving personal and moral advice to the people concerned. He talked more like a priest or a doctor, and a very outspoken one at that. The first thrill was probably given when he said to a man who had attempted a crime of passion: 'I sentence you to three years' imprisonment, under the firm, and solemn, and God-given conviction, that what you require is three months at the seaside.' He accused criminals from the bench, not so much of their obvious legal crimes, but of things that had never been heard of in a court of justice, monstrous egoism, lack of humour, and morbidity deliberately encouraged. Things came to a head in that celebrated diamond case in which the Prime Minister himself, that brilliant patrician, had to come forward, gracefully and reluctantly, to give evidence against his valet. After the detailed life of the household had been thoroughly exhibited, the judge requested the Premier again to step forward, which he did with quiet dignity. The judge then said, in a sudden, grating voice: 'Get a new soul. That thing's not fit for a dog. Get a new soul.' All this, of course, in the eyes of the sagacious, was premonitory of that melancholy and farcical day when his wits actually deserted him in ·open court. It was a libel case between two very eminent and powerful financiers, against both of whom charges of considerable defalcation were brought. The case was long and complex; the advocates were long and eloquent; but at last, after weeks of work and rhetoric, the time came for the great judge to give a summing-up; and one of his celebrated masterpieces of lucidity and pulverizing logic was eagerly looked for. He had spoken very little during the prolonged affair, and he looked sad and lowering at the end of it. He was silent for a few moments, and then burst into a stentorian song. His remarks (as reported) were as follows:

> O Rowty-owty tiddly-owty
> Tiddly-owty tiddly-owty
> Highty-ighty tiddly-ighty
> Tiddly-ighty ow.

He then retired from public life and took the garret in Lambeth.

I was sitting there one evening, about six o'clock, over a glass of that gorgeous Burgundy which he kept behind a pile of black-letter folios; he was striding about the room, fingering, after a habit of his, one of the great swords in his collection; the red glare of the strong fire struck his square features and his fierce grey hair; his blue eyes were even unusually full of dreams, and he had opened his mouth to speak dreamily, when the door was flung open, and a pale, fiery man, with red hair and a huge furred overcoat, swung himself panting into the room.

'Sorry to bother you, Basil,' he gasped. 'I took a liberty—made an appointment here with a man—a client—in five minutes—I beg your pardon, sir,' and he gave me a bow of apology.

Basil smiled at me. 'You didn't know,' he said, 'that I had a practical brother. This is Rupert Grant, Esquire, who can and does all there is to be done. Just as I was a failure at one thing, he is a success at everything. I remember him as a journalist, a house-agent, a naturalist, an inventor, a publisher, a schoolmaster, a—what are you now, Rupert?'

'I am and have been for some time,' said Rupert, with some dignity, 'a private detective, and there's my client.'

A loud rap at the door had cut him short, and, on permission being given, the door was thrown sharply open and a stout, dapper man walked swiftly into the room, set his silk hat with a clap on the table, and said, 'Good evening, gentle*men*,' with a stress on the last syllable that somehow marked him out as a martinet, military, literary and social. He had a large head streaked with black and grey, and an abrupt black moustache, which gave him a look of fierceness which was contradicted by his sad sea-blue eyes.

Basil immediately said to me, 'Let us come into the next room, Gully,' and was moving towards the door, but the stranger said:

'Not at all. Friends remain. Assistance possibly.'

The moment I heard him speak I remembered who he was, a certain

Major Brown I had met years before in Basil's society. I had forgotten altogether the black dandified figure and the large solemn head, but I remembered the peculiar speech, which consisted of only saying about a quarter of each sentence, and that sharply, like the crack of a gun. I do not know, it may have come from giving orders to troops.

Major Brown was a VC, and an able and distinguished soldier, but he was anything but a warlike person. Like many among the iron men who recovered British India, he was a man with the natural beliefs and tastes of an old maid. In his dress he was dapper and yet demure; in his habits he was precise to the point of the exact adjustment of a tea-cup. One enthusiasm he had, which was of the nature of a religion—the cultivation of pansies. And when he talked about his collection, his blue eyes glittered like a child's at a new toy, the eyes that had remained untroubled when the troops were roaring victory round Roberts at Candahar.

'Well, Major,' said Rupert Grant, with a lordly heartiness, flinging himself into a chair, 'what is the matter with you?'

'Yellow pansies. Coal-cellar. P. G. Northover,' said the Major, with righteous indignation.

We glanced at each other with inquisitiveness. Basil, who had his eyes shut in his abstracted way, said simply:

'I beg your pardon.'

'Fact is. Street, you know, man, pansies. On wall. Death to me. Something. Preposterous.'

We shook our heads gently. Bit by bit, and mainly by the seemingly sleepy assistance of Basil Grant, we pieced together the Major's fragmentary, but excited narration. It would be infamous to submit the reader to what we endured; therefore I will tell the story of Major Brown in my own words. But the reader must imagine the scene. The eyes of Basil closed as in a trance, after his habit, and the eyes of Rupert and myself getting rounder and rounder as we listened to one of the most astounding stories in the world, from the lips of the little man in black, sitting bolt upright in his chair and talking like a telegram.

Major Brown was, I have said, a successful soldier, but by no means an enthusiastic one. So far from regretting his retirement on half-pay, it was with delight that he took a small neat villa, very like a doll's house, and devoted the rest of his life to pansies and weak tea. The thought that battles were over when he had once hung up his sword in the little front hall (along with two patent stew-pots and a bad water-colour), and betaken himself instead to wielding the rake in his little sunlit garden, was to him like having come into a harbour in heaven. He was Dutch-like and precise in his taste in gardening, and had, perhaps, some tendency to drill his flowers like soldiers. He was one of those men who are capable of putting four umbrellas in the stand rather than three, so that two may lean one way and two another; he saw life like a pattern in a freehand drawing-book. And assuredly he would not have believed, or even understood, any one who had told him that within a few yards of his brick paradise he was destined to be caught in a whirlpool of incredible adventure, such as he had never seen or dreamed of in the horrible jungle, or the heat of battle.

One certain bright and windy afternoon, the Major, attired in his usual faultless manner, had set out for his usual constitutional. In crossing from one great residential thoroughfare to another, he happened to pass along one of those aimless-looking lanes which lie along the back-garden walls of a row of mansions, and which in their empty and discoloured appearance give one an odd sensation as of being behind the scenes of a theatre. But mean and sulky as the scene might be in the eyes of most of us, it was not altogether so in the Major's, for along the coarse gravel footway was coming a thing which was to him what the passing of a religious procession is to a devout person. A large, heavy man, with fish-blue eyes and a ring of irradiating red beard, was pushing before him a barrow, which was ablaze with incomparable flowers. There were splendid specimens of almost every order, but the Major's own favourite pansies predominated. The Major stopped and fell into conversation, and then into bargaining. He treated the man after the manner of collectors and other mad men, that is to say, he carefully and with a sort of anguish selected the best roots from the less excellent, praised some, disparaged others, made a subtle scale ranging from a thrilling worth and rarity to a degraded insignificance, and then bought them all. The man was just pushing off his barrow when he stopped and came close to the Major.

'I'll tell you what, sir,' he said. 'If you're interested in them things, you just get on to that wall.'

'On the wall!' cried the scandalized Major, whose conventional soul quailed within him at the thought of such fantastic trespass.

'Finest show of yellow pansies in England in that there garden, sir,' hissed the tempter. 'I'll help you up, sir.'

How it happened no one will ever know, but that positive enthusiasm of the Major's life triumphed over all its negative traditions, and with an easy leap and swing that showed that he was in no need of physical assistance, he stood on the wall at the end of the strange garden. The second after, the flapping of the frock-coat at his knees made him feel inexpressibly a fool. But the next instant all such trifling sentiments were swallowed up by the most appalling shock of surprise the old soldier had ever felt in all his bold and wandering existence. His eyes fell upon the garden, and there across a large bed in the centre of the lawn was a vast pattern of pansies; they were splendid flowers, but for once it was not their horticultural aspects that Major Brown beheld, for the pansies were arranged in gigantic capital letters so as to form the sentence:

DEATH TO MAJOR BROWN

A kindly-looking old man, with white whiskers, was watering them.

Brown looked sharply back at the road behind him; the man with the barrow had suddenly vanished. Then he looked again at the lawn with its incredible inscription. Another man might have thought he had gone mad, but Brown did not. When romantic ladies gushed over his VC and his military exploits, he sometimes felt himself to be a painfully prosaic person, but by the same token he knew he was incurably sane. Another man, again, might have thought himself a victim of a passing practical joke, but Brown could not easily believe this. He knew from his own quaint learning that the garden arrangement was an elaborate and expensive one; he thought it extravagantly improbable that any one would pour out money like water for a joke against him. Having no explanation whatever to offer, he admitted the fact to himself, like a clear-headed man, and waited as he would have done in the presence of a man with six legs.

At this moment the stout old man with white whiskers looked up, and the watering can fell from his hand, shooting a swirl of water down the gravel path.

'Who on earth are you?' he gasped, trembling violently.

'I am Major Brown,' said that individual, who was always cool in the hour of action.

The old man gaped helplessly like some monstrous fish. At last he stammered wildly, 'Come down—come down here!'

'At your service,' said the Major, and alighted at a bound on the grass beside him, without disarranging his silk hat.

The old man turned his broad back and set off at a sort of waddling run towards the house, followed with swift steps by the Major. His guide led him through the back passages of a gloomy, but gorgeously appointed house, until they reached the door of the front room. Then the old man turned with a face of apoplectic terror dimly showing in the twilight.

'For heaven's sake,' he said, 'don't mention jackals.'

Then he threw open the door, releasing a burst of red lamplight, and ran downstairs with a clatter.

The Major stepped into a rich, glowing room, full of red copper, and peacock and purple hangings, hat in hand. He had the finest manners in the world, and, though mystified, was not in the least embarrassed to see that the only occupant was a lady, sitting by the window, looking out.

'Madam,' he said, bowing simply, 'I am Major Brown.'

'Sit down,' said the lady; but she did not turn her head.

She was a graceful, green-clad figure, with fiery red hair and a flavour of Bedford Park. 'You have come, I suppose,' she said mournfully, 'to tax me about the hateful title-deeds.'

'I have come, madam,' he said, 'to know what is the matter. To know why my name is written across your garden. Not amicably either.'

He spoke grimly, for the thing had hit him. It is impossible to describe the effect produced on the mind by that quiet and sunny garden scene, the frame for a stunning and brutal personality. The evening air was still, and the grass was golden in the place where the little flowers he studied cried to heaven for his blood.

'You know I must not turn round,' said the lady; 'every afternoon till the stroke of six I must keep my face turned to the street.'

Some queer and unusual inspiration made the prosaic soldier resolute to accept these outrageous riddles without surprise.

'It is almost six,' he said; and even as he spoke the barbaric copper clock upon the wall clanged the first stroke of the hour. At the sixth the lady sprang up and turned on the Major one of the queerest and yet most attractive faces he had ever seen in his life; open, and yet tantalizing, the face of an elf.

'That makes the third year I have waited,' she cried. 'This is an anniversary. The waiting almost makes one wish the frightful thing would happen once and for all.'

And even as she spoke, a sudden rending cry broke the stillness. From low down on the pavement of the dim street (it was already twilight) a voice cried out with a raucous and merciless distinctness:

'Major Brown, Major Brown, where does the jackal dwell?'

Brown was decisive and silent in action. He strode to the front door and looked out. There was no sign of life in the blue gloaming of the street, where one or two lamps were beginning to light their lemon sparks. On returning, he found the lady in green trembling.

'It is the end,' she cried, with shaking lips; 'it may be death for both of us. Whenever—'

But even as she spoke her speech was cloven by another hoarse proclamation from the dark street, again horribly articulate.

'Major Brown, Major Brown, how did the jackal die?'

Brown dashed out of the door and down the steps, but again he was frustrated; there was no figure in sight, and the street was far too long and empty for the shouter to have run away. Even the rational Major was a little shaken as he returned in a certain time to the drawing-room. Scarcely had he done so than the terrific voice came:

'Major Brown, Major Brown, where did—'

Brown was in the street almost at a bound, and he was in time—in time to see something which at first glance froze the blood. The cries appeared to come from a decapitated head resting on the pavement.

The next moment the pale Major understood. It was the head of a man thrust through the coal-hole in the street. The next moment, again, it had vanished, and Major Brown turned to the lady. 'Where's your coal-cellar?' he said, and stepped out into the passage.

She looked at him with wild grey eyes. 'You will not go down,' she cried, 'alone, into the dark hole, with that beast?'

'Is this the way?' replied Brown, and descended the kitchen stairs three at a time. He flung open the door of a black cavity and stepped in, feeling in his pocket for matches. As his right hand was thus occupied, a pair of great slimy hands came out of the darkness, hands clearly belonging to a man of gigantic stature, and seized him by the back of the head. They forced him down, down in the suffocating darkness, a brutal image of destiny. But the Major's head, though upside down, was perfectly clear and intellectual. He gave quietly under the pressure until he had slid down almost to his hands and knees. Then finding the knees of the invisible monster within a foot of him, he simply put out one of his long, bony, and skilful hands, and gripping the leg by a muscle pulled it off the ground and laid the huge living man, with a crash, along the floor. He strove to rise, but Brown was on top like a cat. They rolled over and over. Big as the man was, he had evidently now no desire but to escape; he made sprawls hither and thither to get past the Major to the door, but that tenacious person had him hard by the coat collar and hung with the other hand to a beam. At length there came a strain in holding back this human bull, a strain under which Brown expected his hand to rend and part from the arm. But something else rent and parted; and the dim fat figure of the giant vanished out of the cellar, leaving the torn coat in the Major's hand; the only fruit of his adventure and the only clue to the mystery. For when he went up and out at the front door, the lady, the rich hangings, and the whole equipment of the house had disappeared. It had only bare boards and whitewashed walls.

'The lady was in the conspiracy, of course,' said Rupert, nodding. Major Brown turned brick red. 'I beg your pardon,' he said, 'I think not.'

Rupert raised his eyebrows and looked at him for a moment, but said nothing. When next he spoke he asked:

'Was there anything in the pockets of the coat?'

'There was sevenpence halfpenny in coppers and a threepenny-bit,' said the Major carefully; 'there was a cigarette-holder, a piece of string, and this letter,' and he laid it on the table. It ran as follows:

Dear Mr Plover,

I am annoyed to hear that some delay has occurred in the arrangements *re* Major Brown. Please see that he is attacked as per arrangement tomorrow. The coal-cellar, of course.

Yours faithfully,
P. G. Northover.

Rupert Grant was leaning forward listening with hawk-like eyes. He cut in:

'Is it dated from anywhere?'

'No—oh, yes!' replied Brown, glancing upon the paper; '14 Tanner's Court, North—'

Rupert sprang up and struck his hands together.

'Then why are we hanging here? Let's get along. Basil, lend me your revolver.'

Basil was staring into the embers like a man in a trance; and it was some time before he answered:

'I don't think you'll need it.'

'Perhaps not,' said Rupert, getting into his fur coat. 'One never knows. But going down a dark court to see criminals—'

'Do you think they are criminals?' asked his brother.

Rupert laughed stoutly. 'Giving orders to a subordinate to strangle a harmless stranger in a coal-cellar may strike you as a very blameless experiment, but—'

'Do you think they wanted to strangle the Major?' asked Basil, in the same distant and monotonous voice.

'My dear fellow, you've been asleep. Look at the letter.'

'I am looking at the letter,' said the mad judge calmly; though, as a matter of fact, he was looking at the fire. 'I don't think it's the sort of letter one criminal would write to another.'

'My dear boy, you are glorious,' cried Rupert, turning round, with laughter in his blue bright eyes. 'Your methods amaze me. Why, there *is* the letter. It *is* written, and it does give orders for a crime. You might as well say that the Nelson Column was not at all the sort of thing that was likely to be set up in Trafalgar Square.'

Basil Grant shook all over with a sort of silent laughter, but did not otherwise move.

'That's rather good,' he said; 'but, of course, logic like that's not what is really wanted. It's a question of spiritual atmosphere. It's not a criminal letter.'

'It is. It's a matter of fact,' cried the other in an agony of reasonableness.

'Facts,' murmured Basil, like one mentioning some strange, far-off animals, 'how facts obscure the truth. I may be silly—in fact, I'm off my head—but I never could believe in that man—what's his name, in those capital stories?—Sherlock Holmes. Every detail points to something, certainly; but generally to the wrong thing. Facts point in all directions, it seems to me, like the thousands of twigs on a tree. It's only the life of the tree that has unity and goes up—only the green blood that springs, like a fountain, at the stars.'

'But what the deuce else can the letter be but criminal?'

'We have eternity to stretch our legs in,' replied the mystic. 'It can be an infinity of things. I haven't seen any of them—I've only seen the letter. I look at that, and say it's not criminal.'

'Then what's the origin of it?'

'I haven't the vaguest idea.'

'Then why don't you accept the ordinary explanation?'

Basil continued for a little to glare at the coals, and seemed collecting his thoughts in a humble and even painful way. Then he said:

'Suppose you went out into the moonlight. Suppose you passed through silent, silvery streets and squares until you came into an open and deserted space, set with a few monuments, and you beheld one dressed as a ballet girl dancing in the argent glimmer. And suppose you looked, and saw it was a man disguised. And suppose you looked again, and saw it was Lord Kitchener. What would you think?'

He paused a moment, and went on:

'You could not adopt the ordinary explanation. The ordinary explanation of putting on singular clothes is that you look nice in them; you would not think that Lord Kitchener dressed up like a ballet girl out of ordinary personal vanity. You would think it much more likely that he inherited a dancing madness from a great grandmother; or had been hypnotized at a séance; or threatened by a secret society with death if he refused the ordeal. With Baden-Powell, say, it might be a bet—but not with Kitchener. I should know all that, because in my public days I knew him quite well. So I know that letter quite well, and criminals quite well. It's not a criminal's letter. It's all atmospheres.' And he closed his eyes and passed his hand over his forehead.

Rupert and the Major were regarding him with a mixture of respect and pity. The former said:

'Well, I'm going, anyhow, and shall continue to think—until your spiritual mystery turns up—that a man who sends a note recommending a crime, that is, actually a crime that is actually carried out, at least tentatively, is, in all probability, a little casual in his moral tastes. Can I have that revolver?'

'Certainly,' said Basil, getting up. 'But I am coming with you.' And he flung an old cape or cloak round him, and took a sword-stick from the corner.

'You!' said Rupert, with some surprise, 'you scarcely ever leave your hole to look at anything on the face of the earth.'

Basil fitted on a formidable old white hat.

'I scarcely ever,' he said, with an unconscious and colossal arrogance, 'hear of anything on the face of the earth that I do not understand at once, without going to see it.'

And he led the way out into the purple night.

We four swung along the flaring Lambeth streets, across Westminster Bridge, and along the Embankment in the direction of that part of Fleet Street which contained Tanner's Court. The erect, black figure of Major Brown, seen from behind, was a quaint contrast to the hound-like stoop and flapping mantle of young Rupert Grant, who adopted, with childlike delight, all the dramatic poses of the detective of fiction. The finest among his many fine qualities was his boyish appetite for the colour and poetry of London. Basil, who walked behind, with his face turned blindly to the stars, had the look of a somnambulist.

Rupert paused at the corner of Tanner's Court, with a quiver of delight at danger, and gripped Basil's revolver in his great-coat pocket.

'Shall we go in now?' he asked.

'Not get police?' asked Major Brown, glancing sharply up and down the street.

'I am not sure,' answered Rupert, knitting his brows. 'Of course, it's quite clear, the thing's all crooked. But there are three of us, and—'

'I shouldn't get the police,' said Basil in a queer voice. Rupert glanced at him and stared hard.

'Basil,' he cried, 'you're trembling. What's the matter—are you afraid?'

'Cold, perhaps,' said the Major, eyeing him. There was no doubt that he was shaking.

At last, after a few moments' scrutiny, Rupert broke into a curse.

'You're laughing,' he cried. 'I know that confounded, silent, shaky laugh of yours. What the deuce is the amusement, Basil? Here we are, all three of us, within a yard of a den of ruffians—'

'But I shouldn't call the police,' said Basil. 'We four heroes are quite equal to a host', and he continued to quake with his mysterious mirth.

Rupert turned with impatience and strode swiftly down the court, the rest of us following. When he reached the door of No. 14 he turned abruptly, the revolver glittering in his hand.

'Stand close,' he said in the voice of a commander. 'The scoundrel may be attempting an escape at this moment. We must fling open the door and rush in.'

The four of us cowered instantly under the archway, rigid, except for the old judge and his convulsion of merriment.

'Now,' hissed Rupert Grant, turning his pale face and burning eyes suddenly over his shoulder, 'when I say "Four", follow me with a rush. If I say "Hold him", pin the fellows down, whoever they are. If I say "Stop", stop. I shall say that if there are more than three. If they attack us I shall empty my revolver on them. Basil, have your sword-stick ready. Now—one, two three, four!'

With the sound of the word the door burst open, and we fell into the room like an invasion, only to stop dead.

The room, which was an ordinary and neatly appointed office, appeared, at the first glance, to be empty. But on a second and more careful glance, we saw seated behind a very large desk with pigeon-holes and drawers of bewildering multiplicity, a small man with a black waxed moustache, and the air of a very average clerk, writing hard. He looked up as we came to a standstill.

'Did you knock?' he asked pleasantly. 'I am sorry if I did not hear. What can I do for you?'

There was a doubtful pause, and then, by general consent, the Major himself, the victim of the outrage, stepped forward.

The letter was in his hand, and he looked unusually grim.

'Is your name P. G. Northover?' he asked.

'That is my name,' replied the other, smiling.

'I think,' said Major Brown, with an increase in the dark glow of his face, 'that this letter was written by you.' And with a loud clap he struck open the letter on the desk with his clenched fist. The man called Northover looked at it with unaffected interest and merely nodded.

'Well, sir,' said the Major, breathing hard, 'what about that?'

'What about it, precisely,' said the man with the moustache.

'I am Major Brown,' said that gentleman sternly.

Northover bowed. 'Pleased to meet you, sir. What have you to say to me?'

'Say!' cried the Major, loosing a sudden tempest; 'why, I want this confounded thing settled. I want—'

'Certainly, sir,' said Northover, jumping up with a slight elevation of the eyebrows. 'Will you take a chair for a moment.' And he pressed an electric bell just above him, which thrilled and tinkled in a room beyond. The Major put his hand on the back of the chair offered him, but stood chafing and beating the floor with his polished boot.

The next moment an inner glass door was opened, and a fair, weedy, young man, in a frock-coat, entered from within.

'Mr Hopson,' said Northover, 'this is Major Brown. Will you please finish that thing for him I gave you this morning and bring it in?'

'Yes, sir,' said Mr Hopson, and vanished like lightning.

'You will excuse me, gentlemen,' said the egregious Northover, with his radiant smile, 'if I continue to work until Mr Hopson is ready. I have some books that must be cleared up before I get away on my holiday tomorrow. And we all like a whiff of the country, don't we? Ha! ha!'

The criminal took up his pen with a childlike laugh, and a silence ensued; a placid and busy silence on the part of Mr P. G. Northover; a raging silence on the part of everybody else.

At length the scratching of Northover's pen in the stillness was mingled with a knock at the door, almost simultaneous with the turning of the handle, and Mr Hopson came in again with the same silent rapidity, placed a paper before his principal, and disappeared again.

The man at the desk pulled and twisted his spiky moustache for a few moments as he ran his eye up and down the paper presented to him. He took up his pen, with a slight, instantaneous frown, and altered something, muttering—'Careless.' Then he read it again with the same impenetrable reflectiveness, and finally handed it to the frantic Brown, whose hand was beating the devil's tattoo on the back of the chair.

'I think you will find that all right, Major,' he said briefly.

The Major looked at it; whether he found it all right or not will appear later, but he found it like this:

Major Brown to P. G. Northover.

	£	s.	d.
January 1, to account rendered..................................	5	6	0
May 9, to potting and embedding of 200 pansies.........	2	0	0
To cost of trolley with flowers	0	15	0
To hiring of man with trolley	0	5	0
To hire of house and garden for one day	1	0	0
To furnishing of room in peacock curtains, copper ornaments, etc...	3	0	0
To salary of Miss Jameson...	1	0	0
To salary of Mr Plover..	1	0	0
Total........................... £14		6	0

A remittance will oblige.

'What,' said Brown, after a dead pause, and with eyes that seemed slowly rising out of his head, 'What in heaven's name is this?'

'What is it?' repeated Northover, cocking his eyebrow with amusement. 'It's your account, of course.'

'My account!' The Major's ideas appeared to be in a vague stampede. 'My account! And what have I got to do with it?'

'Well,' said Northover, laughing outright, 'naturally I prefer you to pay it.'

The Major's hand was still resting on the back of the chair as the words came. He scarcely stirred otherwise, but he lifted the chair bodily into the air with one hand and hurled it at Northover's head.

The legs crashed against the desk, so that Northover only got a blow on the elbow as he sprang up with clenched fists, only to be seized by the united rush of the rest of us. The chair had fallen clattering on the empty floor.

'Let me go, you scamps,' he shouted. 'Let me—'

'Stand still,' cried Rupert authoritatively. 'Major Brown's action is excusable. The abominable crime you have attempted—'

'A customer has a perfect right,' said Northover hotly, 'to question an alleged overcharge, but, confound it all, not to throw furniture.'

'What, in God's name, do you mean by your customers and overcharges?' shrieked Major Brown, whose keen feminine nature, steady in pain or danger, became almost hysterical in the presence of a long and exasperating mystery. 'Who are you? I've never seen you or your insolent tomfool bills. I know one of your cursed brutes tried to choke me—'

'Mad,' said Northover, gazing blankly round; 'all of them mad. I didn't know they travelled in quartettes.'

'Enough of this prevarication,' said Rupert; 'your crimes are discovered. A policeman is stationed at the corner of the court. Though only a private detective myself, I will take the responsibility of telling you that anything you say—'

'Mad,' repeated Northover, with a weary air.

And at this moment, for the first time, there struck in among them the strange, sleepy voice of Basil Grant.

'Major Brown,' he said, 'may I ask you a question?'

The Major turned his head with an increased bewilderment.

'You?' he cried; 'certainly, Mr Grant.'

'Can you tell me,' said the mystic, with sunken head and lowering brow, as he traced a pattern in the dust with his sword-stick, 'can you tell me what was the name of the man who lived in your house before you?'

The unhappy Major was only faintly more disturbed by this last and futile irrelevancy, and he answered vaguely:

'Yes, I think so; a man named Gurney something—a name with a hyphen—Gurney-Brown; that was it.'

'And when did the house change hands?' said Basil, looking up sharply. His strange eyes were burning brilliantly.

'I came in last month,' said the Major.

And at the mere word the criminal Northover suddenly fell into his great office chair and shouted with a volleying laughter.

'Oh! it's too perfect—it's too exquisite,' he gasped, beating the arms with his fists. He was laughing deafeningly; Basil Grant was laughing voicelessly; and the rest of us only felt that our heads were like weather-cocks in a whirlwind.

'Confound it, Basil,' said Rupert, stamping. 'If you don't want me to go mad and blow your metaphysical brains out, tell me what all this means.'

Northover rose.

'Permit me, sir, to explain,' he said. 'And, first of all, permit me to apologize to you, Major Brown, for a most abominable and unpardonable blunder, which has caused you menace and inconvenience, in which, if you will allow me to say so, you have behaved with astonishing courage and dignity. Of course you need not trouble about the bill. We will stand the loss.' And, tearing the paper across, he flung the halves into the waste-paper basket and bowed.

Poor Brown's face was still a picture of distraction. 'But I don't even begin to understand,' he cried. 'What bill? what blunder? what loss?'

Mr P. G. Northover advanced in the centre of the room, thoughtfully, and with a great deal of unconscious dignity. On closer consideration, there were apparent about him other things beside a screwed moustache, especially a lean, sallow face, hawk-like, and not without a careworn intelligence. Then he looked up abruptly.

'Do you know where you are, Major?' he said.

'God knows I don't,' said the warrior, with fervour.

'You are standing,' replied Northover, 'in the office of the Adventure and Romance Agency, Limited.'

'And what's that?' blankly enquired Brown.

The man of business leaned over the back of the chair, and fixed his dark eyes on the other's face.

'Major,' said he, 'did you ever, as you walked along the empty street upon some idle afternoon, feel the utter hunger for something to happen—something, in the splendid words of Walt Whitman: "Something pernicious and dread; something far removed from a puny and pious life; something unproved; something in a trance; something loosed from its anchorage, and driving free." Did you ever feel that?'

'Certainly not,' said the Major shortly.

'Then I must explain with more elaboration,' said Mr Northover, with a sigh. 'The Adventure and Romance Agency has been started to meet a great modern desire. On every side, in conversation and in literature, we hear of the desire for a larger theatre of events—for something to waylay us and lead us splendidly astray. Now the man who feels this desire for a varied life pays a yearly or a quarterly sum to the Adventure and Romance Agency; in return, the Adventure and Romance Agency undertakes to surround him with startling and weird events. As a man is leaving his front door, an excited sweep approaches him and assures him of a plot against his life; he gets into a cab, and is driven to an opium den; he receives a mysterious telegram or a dramatic visit, and is immediately in a vortex of incidents. A very picturesque and moving story is first written by one of the staff of distinguished novelists who are at present hard at work in the adjoining room. Yours, Major Brown (designed by our Mr Grigsby), I consider peculiarly forcible and pointed; it is almost a pity you did not see the end of it. I need scarcely explain further the monstrous mistake. Your predecessor in your present house, Mr Gurney-Brown, was a subscriber to our agency, and our foolish clerks, ignoring alike the dignity of the hyphen and the glory of military rank, positively imagined that Major Brown and Mr Gurney-Brown were the same person. Thus you were suddenly hurled into the middle of another man's story.'

'How on earth does the thing work?' asked Rupert Grant, with bright and fascinated eyes.

'We believe that we are doing a noble work,' said Northover warmly. 'It has continually struck us that there is no element in modern life that is more lamentable than the fact that the modern man has to seek all artistic existence in a sedentary state. If he wishes to float into fairyland, he reads a book; if he wishes to dash into the thick of battle, he reads a book; if he wishes to soar into heaven, he reads a book; if he wishes to slide down the banisters, he reads a book. We give him these visions, but we give him exercise at the same time, the necessity of leaping from wall to wall, of fighting strange gentlemen, of running down long streets from pursuers—all healthy and pleasant exercises. We give him a glimpse of that great morning world of Robin Hood or the Knights Errant, when one great game was played under the splendid sky. We give him back his childhood, that godlike time when we can act stories, be our own heroes, and at the same instant dance and dream.'

Basil gazed at him curiously. The most singular psychological discovery had been reserved to the end, for as the little business man ceased speaking he had the blazing eyes of a fanatic.

Major Brown received the explanation with complete simplicity and good humour.

'Of course; awfully dense, sir,' he said. 'No doubt at all, the scheme excellent. But I don't think—' He paused a moment, and looked dreamily out of the window. 'I don't think you will find me in it. Somehow, when one's seen—seen the thing itself, you know—blood and men screaming, one feels about having a little house and a little hobby; in the Bible, you know, "There remaineth a rest".'

Northover bowed. Then after a pause he said:

'Gentlemen, may I offer you my card. If any of the rest of you desire, at any time, to communicate with me, despite Major Brown's view of the matter—'

'I should be obliged for your card, sir,' said the Major, in his abrupt but courteous voice. 'Pay for chair.'

The agent of Romance and Adventure handed his card, laughing.

It ran, 'P. G. Northover, BA, CQT, Adventure and Romance Agency, 14 Tanner's Court, Fleet Street.'

'What on earth is "CQT"?' asked Rupert Grant, looking over the Major's shoulder.

'Don't you know?' returned Northover. 'Haven't you ever heard of the Club of Queer Trades?'

'There seems to be a confounded lot of funny things we haven't heard of,' said the little Major reflectively. 'What's this one?'

'The Club of Queer Trades is a society consisting exclusively of people who have invented some new and curious way of making money. I was one of the earliest members.'

'You deserve to be,' said Basil, taking up his great white hat, with a smile, and speaking for the last time that evening.

When they had passed out the Adventure and Romance agent wore a queer smile, as he trod down the fire and locked up his desk. 'A fine chap, that Major; when one hasn't a touch of the poet one stands some chance of being a poem. But to think of such a clockwork little creature of all people getting into the nets of one of Grigsby's tales,' and he laughed out aloud in the silence.

Just as the laugh echoed away, there came a sharp knock at the door. An owlish head, with dark moustaches, was thrust in, with deprecating and somewhat absurd enquiry.

'What! back again, Major?' cried Northover in surprise. 'What can I do for you?'

The Major shuffled feverishly into the room.

'It's horribly absurd,' he said. 'Something must have got started in me that I never knew before. But upon my soul I feel the most desperate desire to know the end of it all.'

'The end of it all?'

'Yes,' said the Major. ' "Jackals", and the title-deeds, and "Death to Major Brown".'

The agent's face grew grave, but his eyes were amused.

'I am terribly sorry, Major,' said he, 'but what you ask is impossible. I don't know any one I would sooner oblige than you; but the rules of the agency are strict. The Adventures are confidential; you are an outsider; I am not allowed to let you know an inch more than I can help. I do hope you understand—'

'There is no one,' said Brown, 'who understands discipline better than I do. Thank you very much. Good night.'

And the little man withdrew for the last time.

He married Miss Jameson, the lady with the red hair and the green garments. She was an actress, employed (with many others) by the Romance Agency; and her marriage with the prim old veteran caused some stir in her languid and intellectualized set. She always replied very quietly that she had met scores of men who acted splendidly in the charades provided for them by Northover, but that she had only met one man who went down into a coal-cellar when he really thought it contained a murderer.

The Major and she are living as happily as birds, in an absurd villa, and the former has taken to smoking. Otherwise he is unchanged—except, perhaps, there are moments when, alert and full of feminine unselfishness as the Major is by nature, he falls into a trance of abstraction. Then his wife recognizes with a concealed smile, by the blind look in his blue eyes, that he is wondering what were the title-deeds, and why he was not allowed to mention jackals. But, like so many old soldiers, Brown is religious, and believes that he will realize the rest of those purple adventures in a better world.

A. E. COPPARD

Some Talk of Alexander

WHEN ALEXANDER COLE at the age of twenty-five was frustrated in love he became so overpowered by grief that he resolved to end his sorrow by putting an end to himself. But while lamenting his romantic ill-fortune to a certain trusted friend he was unwise enough to reveal this desperate intention to him—and that was fatal. It was fatal, I say, because no deeply tragic soul in such circumstances could shrink from taking up the challenge of a sceptical grin, Mr Cole least of all, for he was a something in Marine Insurance and accustomed to taking up risks of all kinds. He had courted Martha Bott, *née* Shrimpton, for many months, all through that bitter winter when Martha had worn the beastly fur-necklet. It was wintry and snowy on the night he first met her at the dinner of the MITC. That stands for the Marine Insurance Thespians Club, of which Martha was one of those attractive members who sold programmes in appropriate costumes. She had been very beautiful—she was naturally beautiful anyhow—though when Alexander spoke to her for the first time she was eating and there was an onion impaled on her fork waiting to be attended to. Martha paused, holding up the onion, and smiled across the table at him. It was a braised onion, as large as an egg, and eventually she swallowed it, as it seemed to him, whole. But neither of them ate much at their next meeting because, of course, the next time they met he drove her in his car to dinner at 'The Prospect' inn out on the Great Coast Road, and there they just fiddled about with lobster and Chianti and discoursed for some reason of gold watches until they were both utterly run down and could neither continue nor think of anything else to talk about. That time she had worn, and afterwards often wore, the fur-necklet which he secretly disliked, its smell so reminded him of menageries whenever he kissed her cold, cold cheek, though there was very little of the jungle about Martha herself; indeed no, nor, if it came to that, about Alexander either. Cold, cold cheek, so exquisitely cold that when he pressed his own against it he experienced a sharp shock all over his person; rather sweet.

For months they went about together, were inseparable, and Alexander got to look upon Martha as quite his own special friend, although propriety rather than possessiveness was ever the high note of his quality whenever occasion offered the sweet reasonableness of gallantry, as witness that Sunday afternoon in the spring-time when they had stopped for tea in a cottager's parlour and Miss Shrimpton had been forced to exclaim most energetically against a flea. Of all things!

'Oh, this flea! Oh dear!' Martha had cried, plunging her hand into her bosom and reflectively scratching. 'Excuse me. Oh dear, bother it!' Alexander had turned his eyes modestly away as a sweet scent stole into the air of the musty parlour.

Oh, they had shared innumerable enjoyments, terrific times really, and Alexander was gradually making up his mind to do something or other about it and bring things to a head when Martha all of a sudden went off and got shatteringly married to a sort of golfing person named Bott. What made it all the more tragic was the fact that Alexander was almost an orphan as it was, his mother being already in heaven, though his father was only in Hull. A dreadful gloom overshadowed his existence and he informed a chosen few of his readiness for death.

One of the chosen few was the widow, Mrs Golanty, a relative of the fickle Martha, who lived in a large house and was the centre of a set of people who flourished on their excessive accessibility to one another. Cole rang up this Mrs Golanty late one boisterous afternoon in summer. Mrs Golanty was strenuously engaged, her drawing-room was full of card-playing people, when a maid informed her that she was wanted on the phone.

'But, Evangeline!' expostulated Mrs Golanty, 'you know quite well I am not to be disturbed when I am giving a bridge-party. Just say I am engaged. Who is it?'

'Mr Cole, madam.'

'Blow Mr Cole! Am I never to have a moment to myself! It's impossible! He must ring up later.'

The maid went away and reported to Mr Cole, but Mr Cole was insistent and Evangeline was prevailed on to approach her mistress once more.

'He says it is rather important, madam, and begs you to spare a moment.'

Mrs Golanty flounced up—'Oh, what a pig of a man!'—and went out to the telephone in a great fume with her: 'Hello! hello! Is that you? Are you there? Hello! Is that you, Alexander?'

'Yes, Alice. I . . . er . . . I just wanted to say . . . er . . .'

'Oh, what *is* it you want to say?' she broke in impatiently. 'I've a bridge-party at this very moment, you know quite well. Why didn't you come as I invited? No answer, no nothing! I'm furious with you!'

'Yes, I know,' said the sad voice of Mr Cole. 'You must really excuse me, Alice; I only wanted to say goodbye.'

'Why, what, where . . . where are you off to so suddenly?'

'Oh, well . . . the beach, I think.'

'Alexander!' Mrs Golanty coughed twice into the telephone, murmured, 'Beg pardon,' and then proceeded ominously: 'Would you mind saying what it is you want to say?'

'Well . . . it's only . . . I'm just going out to commit suicide.'

'What!'

'I'm going to drown myself.'

'Alexander, you're impossible! You're to do nothing of the kind, do you hear! What nonsense; you are so enraging at times, it's not fair.'

'Well,' the sad voice added, 'you can't say I didn't tell you.'

'Tell me!' Mrs Golanty shrieked. 'When I've got a room full of people waiting, and you go on yammering like a lunatic! Really, you make me despair of human nature. I'm in a colossal rage. Go away, you absurd creature, do, before I lose my faith in the goodness of God!' And she slammed down the instrument. Yet, for a moment or two she lingered, hesitated, took up the receiver again, listened, and then whispered: 'Alexander? Are you there? Are you there, Alexander?'

No answer came. 'Oh dear, what a bore!' She sailed away back into the drawing-room. 'My dears! What *do* you think? It was that dreadful Alexander, so pathetic, talking of suicide again—Martha, you know.' The whole party tittered. 'And he said goodbye to me!' Mrs Golanty's waggish partner, a potato-factor in turquoise plus-fours with a pink tie, flourished his handkerchief and simulated a spasm of acute mental suffering. Mrs Golanty gathered up her cards and discovered a desolating Yarborough.

'Farcical, perfectly farcical. I detest people who run about blubbering of suicide. No bid.'

'Yes,' exclaimed the gushing young girl in lilac on her left, 'you simply can't escape them, can you? One heart.'

'But do they ever do it?' Mrs Golanty asked.

'Not very often,' Potatoes said. 'One spade.'

'Often! They don't do it at all. They never do. It's farcical, perfectly farcical. There was that brute Ramshorn who wrote to Connie Frodingham, "When you receive this letter I shall be no more," and that very day he'd gone off to the races at Yarmouth and won seventy-nine pounds. Wasn't a bit in love with her, never had been, or at least only in a very ordinary kind of way.'

'I used to think Alexander was in love with you, Alice,' the third player ventured. 'Two hearts.'

And Mrs Golanty replied: 'My dear! That wouldn't be any reason for suicide, would it! Two hearts? Good heavens, no! No bid.'

Meanwhile Cole was walking down to the sea, the place of doom chosen by him, for he had neither firearms nor poison and no fancy at all for hurling himself from the top of a church tower. The town lay upon a hill on one side of a river. The river was crossed by a bridge, and then a road led you across a wide solitary heath to the next town several miles away. Alexander did not cross the bridge, he went instead to the nearer beach. It was deserted. The wind blew strongly across the fields between the town and the shore, and the sea was driven in mile-long rollers that scooped out trenches in the ridge of beach. Where that shingle all went to, Neptune only knew, but the longshoremen declared it always came back when the wind changed about. Save for the wind it would have been a genial day; a few trails of cloud were racing high over the fields, a white pony was skipping about in the highest of spirits, and a windmill steadily turned its sails, though Cole could have sworn that somehow it was turning them the wrong way round.

He stripped himself to the buff, calmly folded his clothes, the mauve socks, the collar and striped tie, piled them all neatly and placed his shoes atop. Last of all was the letter, in a plain envelope, not stuck down. For the last time he opened the letter and read it:

To all whom it may concern. I have drowned myself for private reasons. I acknowledge nothing and I declare I am not insane. I did not ask to be born and I have no wish to go on living.

ALEXANDER STOAKLEY COLE

PS—My will is deposited with my lawyers, Thurgill Cooley and Wiggs.

There was something vaguely unsatisfactory about the letter, but it was too late to amend it now, and he replaced it under the shoes; the wind chilled him, the sea was waiting. Martha, the cause of it all, was almost forgotten, and his only concern was with the job of keeping to his desperate resolve. Scurrying down over the beach-stones he splashed his way into the sea. It was only about half-tide and the water inshore not deep; as soon as the rollers struck him he plunged seawards. How warm the water was, and how nice to be out of the wind! Although not much of a swimmer he had determined to swim out to sea, there was to be no turning back, but out, out, out, until he could swim no more. So he did that and swam and swam and did not seem to tire. He swam and swam, over, under, over, and although the waves swooped with blustering rise and fall he was not bothered. Day was fading, the low sun lit vividly a leaning ship with sails far out where the sea was darkly blue. Cole did not look back, he was leaving the earth for ever. Never before had he swum so far or with such ease and zest; he thought he must surely have been going full steam ahead for at least twenty minutes without a sign of weariness, and it was quite enjoyable until the dark thought came croaking to his mind: 'Turn back now, beware!'

'Never.' He kept stoutly on. 'Never.'

Then, without any warning, his energy utterly departed and he found himself floundering at last; the waves poured blindingly over his head. Still he would not turn back, and that might have been the end of Alexander Cole had not a shoal of porpoises come tumbling around him just there and then. For a horrible moment he was in the midst of whirling leviathans; he thought of sharks and things that bit you in half, and in panic turned and threshed madly for the shore. The harmless creatures rolled on without injuring him, and then Cole saw that the shore was surprisingly close, though he could not recognize it. There was a likeness, but it was different, and it was some time before he realized that he had been borne in a current across the river-mouth and along to the other shore. The town was half a mile away by now. What a swim! He had not dreamed he could do so well. The shore was close; he was still being swept in the coastwise current, and not only along but towards the coast, for the tide was flowing and the wind was with it.

By now all desire for extinction had mysteriously gone from him; he surrendered to life, and although almost blind and utterly spent, he was only half dead when the breakers rolled him back to safety on the shore.

For a while the poor wretch huddled, like the Dying Gladiator, panting and helpless at the brink of the seas. By God, it had been a close shave with those sharks! When he was able to drag himself up over the beach he felt no better than a sailor who had been marooned, for he was confronted by the wild heath. Nothing else, not a soul, not a house, not even an animal. Some distance inland lay the road leading to the bridge. A few motor cars were streaming along it. Lamps were already lit on some of the cars, night was beginning to fall. The mouth of the river was a mile away, and somehow he would have to get over that, for his clothes were on the opposite shore. His flesh was cold and bloodless, his limbs were limp and trembling, and his teeth drumming with the burr of a dentist's drill. He crawled into the bracken to gain some shelter from the wind behind a clump of furze, squeezed the water from his hair, and swept the drops from his body. The wind travelled over the heath with long melancholy cries. What was to be done now? It was impossible for him to swim back against wind and tide. Besides, he had had enough of the sea, he no longer wanted to drown, he had tried, he had justified himself, and now he was utterly contemptuous of the perfidious Martha—she could go and hang herself in her own garters for all he cared.

Still, he would *have* to walk back along the heath as far as the river, and then he would have to swim across the river-mouth because his clothes were on the other side. Cole feared he would never be able to cross the fierce incoming tide in the darkness, yet how else was he to get back to his clothes? He couldn't walk over the bridge, and you couldn't go stalking across the heath as naked as Adam to hail a passing motorist—might be a lady, and though the plea of escape from drowning was all very well, there were limits even to that—so thought Mr Cole—and decency would not suffer it. He would have to get clothes, clothes, clothes! How otherwise could he approach his home, those bachelor rooms at the abode of the spinster Angela Jolly, a name so ironical that it was almost nefarious? She was a perfect steeple of propriety.

Well, well, when it was dark he got up and struggled wearily along to the river. He could not see across to the opposite bank, but the tide was swirling in, and he was so stiff with cold, so cramped in every limb, so exhausted, that soul and body alike recoiled from the horror of entering the dark ferocious water. Not far off was the bridge where the town lights began, but that way too was barred to him.

Some time later he came across a motor car drawn up on a corner of the heath. It had no lights on and probably belonged to some lovers. By divine favour of the gods Cole found a rug on the seat. He wrapped himself in this and half an hour later arrived at his lodgings. In the hall stood Miss Jolly, in tears. With her were a policeman and an inspector. Alexander slammed the door behind him.

'Oh, Mr Cole!' gasped the lady, as though seeing a ghost.

'Excuse me coming in like this,' he explained hurriedly. 'I lost my clothes bathing, got nearly drowned too.'

'Bathing!' she echoed. 'We all thought you were dead.'

'It's a mercy I'm not,' Alexander retorted. 'The current carried me right down the coast.'

Miss Jolly scratched her head and said: 'Of course Mrs Golanty has been here.'

'What for?'

'To find out what had happened to you. I couldn't tell her anything except that you hadn't come home, and then she was so alarmed that she went straight to the police-station.'

'Good gracious, what a lot of fuss!' As he said this, however, Alexander quite definitely sagged in the stolen rug. Miss Jolly looked queerly at the inspector, a man with the forbidding aspect of scorched face, grey hair, and unsympathetic eyes.

The inspector said: 'I received certain information from Mrs Golanty. They your clothes?' And he pointed to a bundle on the hall chair.

'My goodness, yes, that's them!' cried Alexander.

'Huh!' the inspector said. 'My men found them on the beach.'

'Ah, thanks, thanks,' Alexander murmured.

'With a letter,' continued the inspector. 'That your writing?' He held out the incriminating letter which Alexander had placed under his shoes.

'That! Oh, that's just a joke.'

Inspector took back letter. 'Joke, eh? Queer sort of joke!'

'Yes, perhaps it was,' Alexander admitted.

Inspector put the note into his wallet and said grimly: 'I'm afraid you'll find it a rather unfortunate joke, Mr Cole. This is a very serious offence.'

'I'm sorry, officer, very sorry . . .'

'You certainly will be!' the inspector snapped, and the policeman beside him grinned.

'Oh,' wailed Miss Jolly, 'how could you be so wicked, Mr Cole? Think of the disgrace.'

Alexander remained silent. He looked and felt sheepish. The inspector went on: 'You may or may not know that an attempt at suicide is an indictable offence. I've got to charge you with it, Mr Cole.'

'Oh, look here!' pleaded Alexander. 'It's all bosh. I'm half dead now and can't argue with you. We can discuss it all in the morning. I'm off to bed.'

'Oh dear no,' said the inspector; 'not here, Mr Cole. You've got to come along with me. Suicide is suicide, and it's my duty to look after you for the present. Put on your clothes quickly, if you please.'

P. G. WODEHOUSE

The Reverent Wooing of Archibald

THE conversation in the bar-parlour of the Angler's Rest, which always tends to get deepish towards closing-time, had turned to the subject of the Modern Girl; and a Gin-and-Ginger-Ale sitting in the corner by the window remarked that it was strange how types die out.

'I can remember the days,' said the Gin-and-Ginger-Ale, 'when every other girl you met stood about six feet two in her dancing-shoes, and had as many curves as a scenic railway. Now they are all five foot nothing and you can't see them sideways. Why is this?'

The Draught Stout shook his head.

'Nobody can say. It's the same with dogs. One moment the world is full of pugs as far as the eye can reach; the next, not a pug in sight, only Pekes and Alsatians. Odd!'

The Small Bass and the Double-Whisky-and-Splash admitted that these things were very mysterious, and supposed we should never know the reason for them. Probably we were not meant to know.

'I cannot agree with you, gentlemen,' said Mr Mulliner. He had been sipping his hot Scotch and lemon with a rather abstracted air: but now he sat up alertly, prepared to deliver judgment. 'The reason for the disappearance of the dignified, queenly type of girl is surely obvious. It is Nature's method of ensuring the continuance of the species. A world full of the sort of young woman that Meredith used to put into his novels and du Maurier into his pictures in *Punch* would be a world full of permanent spinsters. The modern young man would never be able to summon up the nerve to propose to them.'

'Something in that,' assented the Draught Stout.

'I speak with authority on that point,' said Mr Mulliner, 'because my nephew, Archibald, made me his confidant when he fell in love with Aurelia Cammarleigh. He worshipped that girl with a fervour which threatened to unseat his reason, such as it was: but the mere idea of asking her to be his wife gave him, he informed me, such a feeling of sick faintness that only by means of a very stiff brandy and soda, or some similar restorative, was he able to pull himself together on the occasions when he contemplated it. Had it not been for. . . . But perhaps you would care to hear the story from the beginning?'

People who enjoyed a merely superficial acquaintance with my nephew Archibald (said Mr Mulliner) were accustomed to set him down as just an ordinary pinheaded young man. It was only when they came to know him better that they discovered their mistake. Then they realized that his pinheadedness, so far from being ordinary, was exceptional. Even at the Drones Club, where the average of intellect is not high, it was often said of Archibald that, had his brain been constructed of silk, he would have been hard put to it to find sufficient material to make a canary a pair of cami-knickers. He sauntered through life with a cheerful insouciance, and up to the age of twenty-five had only once been moved by anything in the nature of a really strong emotion—on the occasion when, in the heart of Bond Street and at the height of the London season, he discovered that his man, Meadowes, had carelessly sent him out with odd spats on.

And then he met Aurelia Cammarleigh.

The first encounter between these two has always seemed to me to bear an extraordinary resemblance to the famous meeting between the poet Dante and Beatrice Fortinari. Dante, if you remember, exchanged no remarks with Beatrice on that occasion. Nor did Archibald with Aurelia. Dante just goggled at the girl. So did Archibald. Like Archibald, Dante loved at first sight: and the poet's age at the time was, we are told, nine—which was almost exactly the mental age of Archibald Mulliner when he first set eyeglass on Aurelia Cammarleigh.

Only in the actual locale of the encounter do the two cases cease to be parallel. Dante, the story relates, was walking on the Ponte Vecchio, while Archibald Mulliner was having a thoughtful cocktail in the window of the Drones Club, looking out on Dover Street.

And he had just relaxed his lower jaw in order to examine Dover Street more comfortably when there swam into his line of vision something that looked like a Greek goddess. She came out of a shop opposite the club and stood on the pavement waiting for a taxi. And, as he saw her standing there, love at first sight seemed to go all over Archibald Mulliner like nettlerash.

It was strange that this should have been so, for she was not at all the sort of girl with whom Archibald had fallen in love at first sight in the past. I chanced, while in here the other day, to pick up a copy of one of the old yellowback novels of fifty years ago—the property, I believe, of Miss Postlethwaite, our courteous and erudite barmaid. It was entitled *Sir Ralph's Secret*, and its heroine, the Lady Elaine, was described as a superbly handsome girl, divinely tall, with a noble figure, the arched Montresor nose, haughty eyes beneath delicately pencilled brows, and that indefinable air of aristocratic aloofness which marks the daughter of a hundred Earls. And Aurelia Cammarleigh might have been this formidable creature's double.

Yet Archibald, sighting her, reeled as if the cocktail he had just consumed had been his tenth instead of his first.

'Golly!' said Archibald.

To save himself from falling, he had clutched at a passing fellow-member: and now, examining his catch, he saw that it was young Algy Wymondham-Wymondham. Just the fellow-member he would have preferred to clutch at, for Algy was a man who went everywhere and knew everybody and could doubtless give him the information he desired.

'Algy, old prune,' said Archibald in a low, throaty voice, 'a moment of your valuable time, if you don't mind.'

He paused, for he had perceived the need for caution. Algy was a notorious babbler, and it would be the height of rashness to give him an inkling of the passion which blazed within his breast. With a strong effort, he donned the mask. When he spoke again, it was with a deceiving nonchalance.

'I was just wondering if you happened to know who that girl is, across the street there. I suppose you don't know what her name is in rough numbers? Seems to me I've met her somewhere or something, or seen her, or something. Or something, if you know what I mean.'

Algy followed his pointing finger and was in time to observe Aurelia as she disappeared into the cab.

'That girl?'

'Yes,' said Archibald, yawning. 'Who is she, if any?'

'Girl named Cammarleigh.'

'Ah?' said Archibald, yawning again. 'Then I haven't met her.'

'Introduce you if you like. She's sure to be at Ascot. Look out for us there.'

Archibald yawned for the third time.

'All right,' he said, 'I'll try to remember. Tell me about her. I mean, has she any fathers or mothers or any rot of that description?'

'Only an aunt. She lives with her in Park Street. She's potty.'

Archibald started, stung to the quick.

'Potty? That divine . . . I mean, that rather attractive-looking girl?'

'Not Aurelia. The aunt. She thinks Bacon wrote Shakespeare.'

'Thinks who wrote what?' asked Archibald, puzzled, for the names were strange to him.

'You must have heard of Shakespeare. He's well known. Fellow who used to write plays. Only Aurelia's aunt says he didn't. She maintains that a bloke called Bacon wrote them for him.'

'Dashed decent of him,' said Archibald, approvingly. 'Of course, he may have owed Shakespeare money.'

'There's that, of course.'

'What was the name again?'

'Bacon.'

'Bacon,' said Archibald, jotting it down on his cuff. 'Right.'

Algy moved on, and Archibald, his soul bubbling within him like a Welsh rarebit at the height of its fever, sank into a chair and stared sightlessly at the ceiling. Then, rising, he went off to the Burlington Arcade to buy socks.

The process of buying socks eased for a while the turmoil that ran riot in Archibald's veins. But even socks with lavender clocks can only alleviate: they do not cure. Returning to his rooms, he found the anguish rather more overwhelming than ever. For at last he had leisure to think: and thinking always hurt his head.

Algy's careless words had confirmed his worst suspicions. A girl with an aunt who knew all about Shakespeare and Bacon must of necessity live in a mental atmosphere into which a lame-brained bird like himself could scarcely hope to soar. Even if he did meet her—even if she asked him to call—even if in due time their relations became positively cordial, what then? How could he aspire to such a goddess? What had he to offer her?

Money?

Plenty of that, yes, but what was money?

Socks?

Of these he had the finest collection in London, but socks are not everything.

A loving heart?

A fat lot of use that was.

No, a girl like Aurelia Cammarleigh would, he felt, demand from the man who aspired to her hand something in the nature of gifts, of accomplishments. He would have to be a man who Did Things.

And what, Archibald asked himself, could he do? Absolutely nothing except give an imitation of a hen laying an egg.

That he could do. At imitating a hen laying an egg he was admittedly a master. His fame in that one respect had spread all over the West End of London. 'Others abide our question. Thou art free,' was the verdict of London's gilded youth on Archibald Mulliner when considered purely in the light of a man who could imitate a hen laying an egg. 'Mulliner,' they said to one another, 'may be a pretty minus quantity in many ways, but he can imitate a hen laying an egg.'

And, so far from helping him, this one accomplishment of his would, reason told him, be a positive handicap. A girl like Aurelia Cammarleigh would simply be sickened by such coarse buffoonery. He blushed at the very thought of her ever learning that he was capable of sinking to such depths.

And so, when some weeks later he was introduced to her in the paddock at Ascot and she, gazing at him with what seemed to his sensitive mind contemptuous loathing, said:

'They tell me you give an imitation of a hen laying an egg, Mr Mulliner.'

He replied with extraordinary vehemence.

'It is a lie—a foul and contemptible lie which I shall track to its source and nail to the counter.'

Brave words! But had they clicked? Had she believed him? He trusted so. But her haughty eyes were very penetrating. They seemed to pierce through to the depths of his soul and lay it bare for what it was—the soul of a hen-imitator.

However, she did ask him to call. With a sort of queenly, bored disdain and only after he had asked twice if he might—but she did it. And Archibald resolved that, no matter what the mental strain, he would show her that her first impression of him had been erroneous; that, trivial and vapid though he might seem, there were in his nature deeps whose existence she had not suspected.

For a young man who had been superannuated from Eton and believed everything he read in the Racing Expert's column in the morning paper,

Archibald, I am bound to admit, exhibited in this crisis a sagacity for which few of his intimates would have given him credit. It may be that love stimulates the mind, or it may be that when the moment comes Blood will tell. Archibald, you must remember, was, after all, a Mulliner: and now the old canny strain of the Mulliners came out in him.

'Meadowes, my man,' he said to Meadowes, his man.

'Sir,' said Meadowes.

'It appears,' said Archibald, 'that there is—or was—a cove of the name of Shakespeare. Also a second cove of the name of Bacon. Bacon wrote plays, it seems, and Shakespeare went and put his own name on the programme and copped the credit.'

'Indeed, sir?'

'If true, not right, Meadowes.'

'Far from it, sir.'

'Very well, then. I wish to go into this matter carefully. Kindly pop out and get me a book or two bearing on the business.'

He had planned his campaign with infinite cunning. He knew that, before anything could be done in the direction of winning the heart of Aurelia Cammarleigh, he must first establish himself solidly with the aunt. He must court the aunt, ingratiate himself with her—always, of course, making it clear from the start that she was not the one. And, if reading about Shakespeare and Bacon could do it, he would, he told himself, have her eating out of his hand in a week.

Meadowes returned with a parcel of forbidding-looking volumes, and Archibald put in a fortnight's intensive study. Then, discarding the monocle which had up till then been his constant companion, and substituting for it a pair of horn-rimmed spectacles which gave him something of the look of an earnest sheep, he set out for Park Street to pay his first call. And within five minutes of his arrival he had declined a cigarette on the plea that he was a non-smoker, and had managed to say some rather caustic things about the practice, so prevalent among his contemporaries, of drinking cocktails.

Life, said Archibald, toying with his teacup, was surely given to us for some better purpose than the destruction of our brains and digestions with alcohol. Bacon, for instance, never took a cocktail in his life, and look at him.

At this, the aunt, who up till now had plainly been regarding him as just another of those unfortunate incidents, sprang to life.

'You admire Bacon, Mr Mulliner?' she asked eagerly.

And, reaching out an arm like the tentacle of an octopus, she drew him into a corner and talked about Cryptograms for forty-seven minutes by the drawing-room clock. In short, to sum the thing up, my nephew Archibald, at his initial meeting with the only relative of the girl he loved, went like a sirocco. A Mulliner is always a Mulliner. Apply the acid test, and he will meet it.

It was not long after this that he informed me that he had sown the good seed to such an extent that Aurelia's aunt had invited him to pay a long visit to her country house, Brawstead Towers, in Sussex.

He was seated at the Savoy bar when he told me this, rather feverishly putting himself outside a Scotch and soda: and I was perplexed to note that his face was drawn and his eyes haggard.

'But you do not seem happy, my boy,' I said.

'I'm not happy.'

'But surely this should be an occasion for rejoicing. Thrown together as you will be in the pleasant surroundings of a country house, you ought easily to find an opportunity of asking this girl to marry you.'

'And a lot of good that will be,' said Archibald moodily. 'Even if I do get a chance I shan't be able to make any use of it. I wouldn't have the nerve. You don't seem to realize what it means being in love with a girl like Aurelia. When I look into those clear, soulful eyes, or see that perfect profile bobbing about on the horizon, a sense of my unworthiness seems to slosh me amidships like some blunt instrument. My tongue gets entangled with my front teeth, and all I can do is stand there feeling like a piece of Gorgonzola that has been condemned by the local sanitary inspector. I'm going to Brawstead Towers, yes, but I don't expect anything to come of it. I know exactly what's going to happen to me. I shall just buzz along through life, pining dumbly, and in the end slide into the tomb a blasted, blighted bachelor. Another whisky, please, and jolly well make it a double.'

Brawstead Towers, situated as it is in the pleasant Weald of Sussex, stands some fifty miles from London: and Archibald, taking the trip easily in his car, arrived there in time to dress comfortably for dinner. It was only when he reached the drawing-room at eight o'clock that he discovered that the younger members of the house-party had gone off in a body to dine and dance at a hospitable neighbour's, leaving him to waste the evening tie of a lifetime, to the composition of which he had devoted no less than twenty-two minutes, on Aurelia's aunt.

Dinner in these circumstances could hardly hope to be an unmixedly exhilarating function. Among the things which helped to differentiate it from a Babylonian orgy was the fact that, in deference to his known prejudices, no wine was served to Archibald. And, lacking artificial stimulus, he found the aunt even harder to endure philosophically than ever.

Archibald had long since come to a definite decision that what this woman needed was a fluid ounce of weedkiller, scientifically administered. With a good deal of adroitness he contrived to head her off from her favourite topic during the meal: but after the coffee had been disposed of she threw off all restraint. Scooping him up and bearing him off into the recesses of the west wing, she wedged him into a corner of a settee and began to tell him all about the remarkable discovery which had been made by applying the Plain Cipher to Milton's well-known Epitaph on Shakespeare.

'The one beginning "What needs my Shakespeare for his honoured bones?",' said the aunt.

'Oh, that one?' said Archibald.

' "What needs my Shakespeare for his honoured bones? The labour of an Age in piled stones? Or that his hallowed Reliques should be hid under a starry-pointing Pyramid?",' said the aunt.

Archibald, who was not good at riddles, said he didn't know.

'As in the Plays and Sonnets,' said the aunt, 'we substitute the name equivalents of the figure totals.'

'We do what?'

'Substitute the name equivalents of the figure totals.'

'The which?'

'The figure totals.'

'All right,' said Archibald. 'Let it go. I daresay you know best.'

The aunt inflated her lungs.

'These figure totals,' she said, 'are always taken out in the Plain Cipher, A equalling one to Z equals twenty-four. The names are counted in the same way. A capital letter with the figures indicates an occasional variation in the Name Count. For instance, A equals twenty-seven, B twenty-eight, until K equals ten is reached, when K, instead of ten, becomes one, and T instead of nineteen is one, and R or Reverse, and so on, until A equals twenty-four is reached. The short or single Digit is not used here. Reading the Epitaph in the light of this Cipher, it becomes: "What need Verulam for Shakespeare? Francis Bacon

England's King be hid under a W. Shakespeare? William Shakespeare. Fame, what needst Francis Tudor, King of England? Francis. Francis W. Shakespeare. For Francis thy William Shakespeare hath England's King took W. Shakespeare. Then thou our W. Shakespeare Francis Tudor bereaving Francis Bacon Francis Tudor such a tomb William Shakespeare." '

The speech to which he had been listening was unusually lucid and simple for a Baconian, yet Archibald, his eye catching a battle-axe that hung on the wall, could not but stifle a wistful sigh. How simple it would have been, had he not been a Mulliner and a gentleman, to remove the weapon from its hook, spit on his hands, and haul off and dot this doddering old ruin one just above the imitation pearl necklace. Placing his twitching hands underneath him and sitting on them, he stayed where he was until, just as the clock on the mantelpiece chimed the hour of midnight, a merciful fit of hiccoughs on the part of his hostess enabled him to retire. As she reached the twenty-seventh 'hic', his fingers found the door-handle and a moment later he was outside, streaking up the stairs.

The room they had given Archibald was at the end of a corridor, a pleasant, airy apartment with French windows opening upon a broad balcony. At any other time he would have found it agreeable to hop out on to this balcony and revel in the scents and sounds of the summer night, thinking the while long, lingering thoughts of Aurelia. But what with all that Francis Tudor Francis Bacon such a tomb William Shakespeare count seventeen drop one knit purl and set them up in the other alley stuff, not even thoughts of Aurelia could keep him from his bed.

Moodily tearing off his clothes and donning his pyjamas, Archibald Mulliner climbed in and instantaneously discovered that the bed was an apple-pie bed. When and how it had happened he did not know, but at a point during the day some loving hand had sewn up the sheets and put two hairbrushes and a branch of some prickly shrub between them.

Himself from earliest boyhood an adept at the construction of booby traps, Archibald, had his frame of mind been sunnier, would doubtless have greeted this really extremely sound effort with a cheery laugh. As it was, weighed down with Verulams and Francis Tudors, he swore for a while with considerable fervour: then, ripping off the sheets and tossing the prickly shrub wearily into a corner, crawled between the blankets and was soon asleep.

His last waking thought was that if the aunt hoped to catch him on the morrow, she would have to be considerably quicker on her pins than her physique indicated.

How long Archibald slept he could not have said. He woke some hours later with a vague feeling that a thunderstorm of unusual violence had broken out in his immediate neighbourhood. But this, he realized as the mists of slumber cleared away, was an error. The noise which had disturbed him was not thunder but the sound of someone snoring. Snoring like the dickens. The walls seemed to be vibrating like the deck of an ocean liner.

Archibald Mulliner might have had a tough evening with the aunt, but his spirit was not so completely broken as to make him lie supinely down beneath that snoring. The sound filled him, as snoring fills every right-thinking man, with a seething resentment and a passionate yearning for justice, and he climbed out of bed with the intention of taking the proper steps through the recognized channels. It is the custom nowadays to disparage the educational methods of the English public school and to maintain that they are not practical and of a kind to fit the growing boy for the problems of after-life. But you do learn one thing at a public school, and that is how to act when somebody starts snoring.

You jolly well grab a cake of soap and pop in and stuff it down the blighter's throat. And this Archibald proposed—God willing—to do. It was the work of a moment with him to dash to the washstand and arm himself. Then he moved softly out through the French windows on to the balcony.

The snoring, he had ascertained, proceeded from the next room. Presumably this room also would have French windows; and presumably, as the night was warm, these would be open. It would be a simple task to oil in, insert the soap, and buzz back undetected.

It was a lovely night, but Archibald paid no attention to it. Clasping his cake of soap, he crept on and was pleased to discover, on arriving outside the snorer's room, that his surmise had been correct. The windows were open. Beyond them, screening the interior of the room, were heavy curtains. And he had just placed his hand upon these when from inside a voice spoke. At the same moment the light was turned on.

'Who's that?' said the voice.

And it was as if Brawstead Towers with all its stabling, outhouses and messuages had fallen on Archibald's head. A mist rose before his eyes. He gasped and tottered.

The voice was that of Aurelia Cammarleigh.

For an instant, for a single long, sickening instant, I am compelled to admit that Archibald's love, deep as the sea though it was, definitely wobbled. It had received a grievous blow. It was not simply the discovery that the girl he adored was a snorer that unmanned him: it was the thought that she could snore like that. There was something about those snores that had seemed to sin against his whole conception of womanly purity.

Then he recovered. Even though this girl's slumber was not, as the poet Milton so beautifully puts it, 'airy light', but rather reminiscent of a lumber-camp when the wood-sawing is proceeding at its briskest, he loved her still.

He had just reached this conclusion when a second voice spoke inside the room.

'I say, Aurelia.'

It was the voice of another girl. He perceived now that the question 'Who's that?' had been addressed not to him but to this newcomer fumbling at the door-handle.

'I say, Aurelia,' said the girl complainingly, 'you've simply got to do something about that bally bulldog of yours. I can't possibly get to sleep with him snoring like that. He's making the plaster come down from the ceiling in my room.'

'I'm sorry,' said Aurelia. 'I've got so used to it that I don't notice.'

'Well, I do. Put a green-baize cloth over him or something.'

Out on the moonlit balcony Archibald Mulliner stood shaking like a blancmange. Although he had contrived to maintain his great love practically intact when he had supposed the snores to proceed from the girl he worshipped, it had been tough going, and for an instant, as I have said, a very near thing. The relief that swept over him at the discovery that Aurelia could still justifiably remain on her pinnacle was so profound that it made him feel filleted. He seemed for a moment in a daze. Then he was brought out of the ether by hearing his name spoken.

'Did Archie Mulliner arrive tonight?' asked Aurelia's friend.

'I suppose so,' said Aurelia. 'He wired that he was motoring down.'

'Just between us girls,' said Aurelia's friend, 'what do you think of that bird?'

To listen to a private conversation—especially a private conversation between two modern girls when you never know what may come next—is rightly considered an action incompatible with the claim to be a gentleman. I regret to say, therefore, that Archibald, ignoring the fact that he belonged to a family whose code is as high as that of any in the land, instead of creeping away to his room edged at this point a step closer to the curtains and stood there with his ears flapping. It might be an ignoble thing to eavesdrop, but it was apparent that Aurelia Cammarleigh was about to reveal her candid opinion of him: and the prospect of getting the true facts—straight, as it were, from the horse's mouth—held him so fascinated that he could not move.

'Archie Mulliner?' said Aurelia meditatively.

'Yes. The betting at the Junior Lipstick is seven to two that you'll marry him.'

'Why on earth?'

'Well, people have noticed he's always round at your place, and they seem to think it significant. Anyway, that's how the odds stood when I left London—seven to two.'

'Get in on the short end,' said Aurelia earnestly, 'and you'll make a packet.'

'Is that official?'

'Absolutely,' said Aurelia.

Out in the moonlight, Archibald Mulliner uttered a low, bleak moan rather like the last bit of wind going out of a dying duck. True, he had always told himself that he hadn't a chance, but, however much a man may say that, he never in his heart really believes it. And now from an authoritative source he had learned that his romance was definitely blue round the edges. It was a shattering blow. He wondered dully how the trains ran to the Rocky Mountains. A spot of grizzly bear shooting seemed indicated.

Inside the room, the other girl appeared perplexed.

'But you told me at Ascot,' she said, 'just after he had been introduced to you, that you rather thought you had at last met your ideal. When did the good thing begin to come unstuck?'

A silvery sigh came through the curtains.

'I did think so then,' said Aurelia wistfully. 'There was something about him. I liked the way his ears wiggled. And I had always heard he was such a perfectly genial, cheery, merry old soul. Algy Wymondham-Wymondham told me that his imitation of a hen laying an egg was alone enough to keep any reasonable girl happy through a long married life.'

'Can he imitate a hen?'

'No. It was nothing but an idle rumour. I asked him, and he stoutly denied that he had ever done such a thing in his life. He was quite stuffy about it. I felt a little uneasy then, and the moment he started calling and hanging about the house I knew that my fears had been well-founded. The man is beyond question a flat tyre and a wet smack.'

'As bad as that?'

'I'm not exaggerating a bit. Where people ever got the idea that Archie Mulliner is a bonhomous old bean beats me. He is the world's worst monkey-wrench. He doesn't drink cocktails, he doesn't smoke cigarettes, and the thing he seems to enjoy most in the world is to sit for hours listening to the conversation of my aunt, who, as you know, is pure goof from the soles of the feet to the tortoiseshell comb and should long ago have been renting a padded cell in Earlswood. Believe me, Muriel, if you can really get seven to two, you are on to the best thing since Buttercup won the Lincolnshire.'

'You don't say!'

'I do say. Apart from anything else, he's got a beastly habit of looking at me reverently. And if you knew how sick I am of being looked at reverently! They will do it, these lads. I suppose it's because I'm rather an out-size and modelled on the lines of Cleopatra.'

'Tough!'

'You bet it's tough. A girl can't help her appearance. I may look as if my ideal man was the hero of a Viennese operetta, but I don't feel that way. What I want is some good sprightly sportsman who sets a neat booby trap, and who'll rush up and grab me in his arms and say to me, "Aurelia, old girl, you're the bee's roller-skates"!'

And Aurelia Cammarleigh emitted another sigh.

'Talking of booby traps,' said the other girl, 'if Archie Mulliner has arrived he's in the next room, isn't he?'

'I suppose so. That's where he was to be. Why?'

'Because I made him an apple-pie bed.'

'It was the right spirit,' said Aurelia warmly. 'I wish I'd thought of it myself.'

'Too late now.'

'Yes,' said Aurelia. 'But I'll tell you what I can and will do. You say you object to Lysander's snoring. Well, I'll go and pop him in at Archie Mulliner's window. That'll give him pause for thought.'

'Splendid,' agreed the girl Muriel. 'Well, goodnight.'

'Goodnight,' said Aurelia.

There followed the sound of a door closing.

There was, as I have indicated, not much of my nephew Archibald's mind, but what there was of it was now in a whirl. He was stunned. Like every man who is abruptly called upon to revise his entire scheme of values, he felt as if he had been standing on top of the Eiffel Tower and some practical joker had suddenly drawn it away from under him. Tottering back to his room, he replaced the cake of soap in its dish and sat down on the bed to grapple with this amazing development.

Aurelia Cammarleigh had compared herself to Cleopatra. It is not too much to say that my nephew Archibald's emotions at this juncture were very similar to what Mark Antony's would have been had Egypt's queen risen from her throne at his entry and without a word of warning started to dance the Black Bottom.

He was roused from his thoughts by the sound of a light footstep on the balcony outside. At the same moment he heard a low woofly gruffle, the unmistakable note of a bulldog of regular habits who has been jerked out of his basket in the small hours and forced to take the night air.

> *She is coming, my own, my sweet!*
> *Were it never so airy a tread,*
> *My heart would hear her and beat,*
> *Were it earth in an earthly bed*

whispered Archibald's soul, or words to that effect. He rose from his seat and paused for an instant, irresolute. Then inspiration descended on him. He knew what to do, and he did it.

Yes, gentlemen, in that supreme crisis of his life, with his whole fate hanging, as you might say, in the balance, Archibald Mulliner, showing for almost the first time in his career a well-nigh human intelligence, began to give his celebrated imitation of a hen laying an egg.

Archibald's imitation of a hen laying an egg was conceived on broad and sympathetic lines. Less violent than Salvini's *Othello*, it had in it something of the poignant wistfulness of Mrs Siddons in the sleepwalking scene of *Macbeth*. The rendition started quietly, almost inaudibly, with a sort of soft, liquid crooning—the joyful yet half-incredulous murmur of a mother who can scarcely believe as yet that her union has really been blessed, and that it is indeed she who is responsible for that oval mixture of chalk and albumen which she sees lying beside her in the straw.

202 · P. G. Wodehouse

Then, gradually, conviction comes.

'It looks like an egg,' one seems to hear her say. 'It feels like an egg. It's shaped like an egg. Damme, it *is* an egg!'

And at that, all doubting resolved, the crooning changes; takes on a firmer note; soars into the upper register; and finally swells into a maternal paean of joy—a 'Charawk-chawk-chawk-chawk' of such a calibre that few had ever been able to listen to it dry-eyed. Following which, it was Archibald's custom to run round the room, flapping the sides of his coat, and then, leaping on to a sofa or some convenient chair, to stand there with his arms at right angles, crowing himself purple in the face.

All these things he had done many a time for the idle entertainment of fellow-members in the smoking room of the Drones, but never with the gusto, the *brio* with which he performed them now. Essentially a modest man, like all the Mulliners, he was compelled, nevertheless, to recognize that tonight he was surpassing himself. Every artist knows when the authentic divine fire is within him, and an inner voice told Archibald Mulliner that he was at the top of his form and giving the performance of a lifetime. Love thrilled through every 'Brt-t't-t't' that he uttered, animated each flap of his arms. Indeed, so deeply did Love drive in its spur that he tells me that, instead of the customary once, he actually made the circle of the room three times before coming to rest on top of the chest of drawers.

When at length he did so he glanced towards the window and saw that through the curtains the loveliest face in the world was peering. And in Aurelia Cammarleigh's glorious eyes there was a look he had never seen before, the sort of look Kreisler or somebody like that beholds in the eyes of the front row as he lowers his violin and brushes his forehead with the back of his hand. A look of worship.

There was a long silence. Then she spoke.

'Do it again!' she said.

And Archibald did it again. He did it four times and could, he tells me, if he had pleased, have taken a fifth encore or at any rate a couple of bows. And then, leaping lightly to the floor, he advanced towards her. He felt conquering, dominant. It was his hour. He reached out and clasped her in his arms.

'Aurelia, old girl,' said Archibald Mulliner in a clear, firm voice, 'you are the bee's roller-skates.'

And at that she seemed to melt into his embrace. Her lovely face was raised to his.

'Archibald!' she whispered.

There was another throbbing silence, broken only by the beating of two hearts and the wheezing of the bulldog, who seemed to suffer a good deal in his bronchial tubes. Then Archibald released her.

'Well, that's that,' he said. 'Glad everything's all settled and hotsytotsy. Gosh, I wish I had a cigarette. This is the sort of moment a bloke needs one.'

She looked at him, surprised.

'But I thought you didn't smoke.'

'Oh yes, I do.'

'And do you drink as well?'

'Quite as well,' said Archibald. 'In fact, rather better. Oh, by the way.'

'Yes?'

'There's just one other thing. Suppose that aunt of yours wants to come and visit us when we are settled down in our little nest, what, dearest, would be your reaction to the scheme of socking her on the base of the skull with a stuffed eelskin?'

'I should like it,' said Aurelia warmly, 'above all things.'

'Twin souls,' cried Archibald. 'That's what we are, when you come right down to it. I suspected it all along, and now I know. Two jolly old twin souls.' He embraced her ardently. 'And now,' he said, 'let us pop downstairs and put this bulldog in the butler's pantry, where he will come upon him unexpectedly in the morning and doubtless get a shock which will do him as much good as a week at the seaside. Are you on?'

'I am,' whispered Aurelia. 'Oh, I am.'

And hand in hand they wandered out together on to the broad staircase.

VIRGINIA WOOLF

Solid Objects

THE only thing that moved upon the vast semicircle of the beach was one small black spot. As it came nearer to the ribs and spine of the stranded pilchard boat, it became apparent from a certain tenuity in its blackness that this spot possessed four legs; and moment by moment it became more unmistakable that it was composed of the persons of two young men. Even thus in outline against the sand there was an unmistakable vitality in them; an indescribable vigour in the approach and withdrawal of the bodies, slight though it was, which proclaimed some violent argument issuing from the tiny mouths of the little round heads. This was corroborated on closer view by the repeated lunging of a walking-stick on the right-hand side. 'You mean to tell me . . . You actually believe . . .' thus the walking-stick on the right-hand side next the waves seemed to be asserting as it cut long straight stripes upon the sand.

'Politics be damned!' issued clearly from the body on the left-hand side, and, as these words were uttered, the mouths, noses, chins, little moustaches, tweed caps, rough boots, shooting coats, and check stockings of the two speakers became clearer and clearer; the smoke of their pipes went up into the air; nothing was so solid, so living, so hard, red, hirsute, and virile as these two bodies for miles and miles of sea and sandhill.

They flung themselves down by the six ribs and spine of the black pilchard boat. You know how the body seems to shake itself free from an argument, and to apologize for a mood of exaltation; flinging itself down and expressing in the looseness of its attitude a readiness to take up with something new—whatever it may be that comes next to hand. So Charles, whose stick had been slashing the beach for half a mile or so, began skimming flat pieces of slate over the water; and John, who had exclaimed 'Politics be damned!' began burrowing his fingers down, down, into the sand. As his hand went further and further beyond the wrist, so that he had to hitch his sleeve a little higher, his eyes lost their intensity, or rather the background of thought and experience which gives an inscrutable depth to the eyes of grown people disappeared, leaving only the clear transparent surface, expressing nothing but won-der, which the eyes of young children display. No doubt the act of bur-rowing in the sand had something to do with it. He remembered that, after digging for a little, the water oozes round your finger-tips; the hole then becomes a moat; a well; a spring; a secret channel to the sea. As he was choosing which of these things to make it, still working his fingers in the water, they curled round something hard—a full drop of solid matter—and gradually dislodged a large irregular lump, and brought it to the surface. When the sand coating was wiped off, a green tint appeared. It was a lump of glass, so thick as to be almost opaque; the smoothing of the sea had completely worn off any edge or shape, so that it was impossible to say whether it had been bottle, tumbler or window-pane; it was nothing but glass; it was almost a precious stone. You had only to enclose it in a rim of gold, or pierce it with a wire, and it became a jewel; part of a necklace, or a dull, green light upon a finger. Perhaps after all it was really a gem; something worn by a dark Princess trailing her finger in the water as she sat in the stern of the boat and listened to the slaves singing as they rowed her across the Bay. Or the oak sides of a sunk Elizabethan treasure-chest had split apart, and, rolled over and over, over and over, its emeralds had come at last to shore. John turned it in his hands; he held it to the light; he held it so that its irregular mass blotted out the body and extended right arm of his friend. The green thinned and thickened slightly as it was held against the sky or against the body. It pleased him; it puzzled him; it was so hard, so concentrated, so definite an object compared with the vague sea and the hazy shore.

Now a sigh disturbed him—profound, final, making him aware that his friend Charles had thrown all the flat stones within reach, or had come to the conclusion that it was not worth while to throw them. They ate their sandwiches side by side. When they had done, and were shaking themselves and rising to their feet, John took the lump of glass and looked at it in silence. Charles looked at it too. But he saw immedi-ately that it was not flat, and filling his pipe he said with the energy that dismisses a foolish strain of thought:

'To return to what I was saying—'

He did not see, or if he had seen would hardly have noticed, that John, after looking at the lump for a moment, as if in hesitation, slipped it inside his pocket. That impulse, too, may have been the impulse which leads a child to pick up one pebble on a path strewn with them, promising it a life of warmth and security upon the nursery mantelpiece, delighting in the sense of power and benignity which such an action confers, and believing that the heart of the stone leaps with joy when it sees itself chosen from a million like it, to enjoy this bliss instead of a life of cold and wet upon the high road. 'It might so easily have been any other of the millions of stones, but it was I, I, I!'

Whether this thought or not was in John's mind, the lump of glass had its place upon the mantelpiece, where it stood heavy upon a little pile of bills and letters and served not only as an excellent paper-weight, but also as a natural stopping place for the young man's eyes when they wandered from his book. Looked at again and again half consciously by a mind thinking of something else, any object mixes itself so profoundly with the stuff of thought that it loses its actual form and recomposes itself a little differently in an ideal shape which haunts the brain when we least expect it. So John found himself attracted to the windows of curiosity shops when he was out walking, merely because he saw something which reminded him of the lump of glass. Anything, so long as it was an object of some kind, more or less round, perhaps with a dying flame deep sunk in its mass, anything—china, glass, amber, rock, marble—even the smooth oval egg of a prehistoric bird would do. He took, also, to keeping his eyes upon the ground, especially in the neighbourhood of waste land where the household refuse is thrown away. Such objects often occurred there—thrown away, of no use to anybody, shapeless, discarded. In a few months he had collected four or five specimens that took their place upon the mantelpiece. They were useful, too, for a man who is standing for Parliament upon the brink of a brilliant career has any number of papers to keep in order—addresses to constituents, declarations of policy, appeals for subscriptions, invitations to dinner, and so on.

One day, starting from his rooms in the Temple to catch a train in order to address his constituents, his eyes rested upon a remarkable object lying half-hidden in one of those little borders of grass which edge the bases of vast legal buildings. He could only touch it with the point of his stick through the railings; but he could see that it was a piece of china of the most remarkable shape, as nearly resembling a starfish as anything—shaped, or broken accidentally, into five irregular but unmistakable points. The colouring was mainly blue, but green stripes or spots of some kind overlaid the blue, and lines of crimson gave it a richness and lustre of the most attractive kind. John was determined to possess it; but the more he pushed, the further it receded. At length he was forced to go back to his rooms and improvise a wire ring attached to the end of a stick, with which, by dint of great care and skill, he finally drew the piece of china within reach of his hands. As he seized hold of it he exclaimed in triumph. At that moment the clock struck. It was out of the question that he should keep his appointment. The meeting was held without him. But how had the piece of china been broken into this remarkable shape? A careful examination put it beyond doubt that the star shape was accidental, which made it all the more strange, and it seemed unlikely that there should be another such in existence. Set at the opposite end of the mantelpiece from the lump of glass that had been dug from the sand, it looked like a creature from another world— freakish and fantastic as a harlequin. It seemed to be pirouetting through space, winking light like a fitful star. The contrast between the china so vivid and alert, and the glass so mute and contemplative, fascinated him, and wondering and amazed he asked himself how the two came to exist in the same world, let alone to stand upon the same narrow strip of marble in the same room. The question remained unanswered.

He now began to haunt the places which are most prolific of broken china, such as pieces of waste land between railway lines, sites of demolished houses, and commons in the neighbourhood of London. But china is seldom thrown from a great height; it is one of the rarest of human actions. You have to find in conjunction a very high house, and a woman of such reckless impulse and passionate prejudice that she flings her jar or pot straight from the window without thought of who is below. Broken china was to be found in plenty, but broken in some trifling domestic accident, without purpose or character. Nevertheless, he was often astonished, as he came to go into the question more deeply, by the immense variety of shapes to be found in London alone, and there was still more cause for wonder and speculation in the differences of qualities and designs. The finest specimens he would bring home and place upon his mantelpiece, where, however, their duty was more and more of an ornamental nature, since papers needing a weight to keep them down became scarcer and scarcer.

He neglected his duties, perhaps, or discharged them absent-mindedly, or his constituents when they visited him were unfavourably impressed by the appearance of his mantelpiece. At any rate he was not elected to represent them in Parliament, and his friend Charles, taking it much to heart and hurrying to condole with him, found him so little cast down by the disaster that he could only suppose that it was too serious a matter for him to realize all at once.

In truth, John had been that day to Barnes Common, and there under a furze bush had found a very remarkable piece of iron. It was almost identical with the glass in shape, massy and globular, but so cold and heavy, so black and metallic, that it was evidently alien to the earth and had its origin in one of the dead stars or was itself the cinder of a moon. It weighed his pocket down; it weighed the mantelpiece down; it radiated cold. And yet the meteorite stood upon the same ledge with the lump of glass and the star-shaped china.

As his eyes passed from one to another, the determination to possess objects that even surpassed these tormented the young man. He devoted himself more and more resolutely to the search. If he had not been consumed by ambition and convinced that one day some newly-discovered rubbish heap would reward him, the disappointments he had suffered, let alone the fatigue and derision, would have made him give up the pursuit. Provided with a bag and a long stick fitted with an adaptable hook, he ransacked all deposits of earth; raked beneath matted tangles of scrub; searched all alleys and spaces between walls where he had learned to expect to find objects of this kind thrown away. As his standard became higher and his taste more severe the disappointments were innumerable, but always some gleam of hope, some piece of china or glass curiously marked or broken lured him on. Day after day passed. He was no longer young. His career—that is his political career—was a thing of the past. People gave up visiting him. He was too silent to be worth asking to dinner. He never talked to anyone about his serious ambitions; their lack of understanding was apparent in their behaviour.

He leaned back in his chair now and watched Charles lift the stones on the mantelpiece a dozen times and put them down emphatically to mark what he was saying about the conduct of the Government, without once noticing their existence.

'What was the truth of it, John?' asked Charles suddenly, turning and facing him. 'What made you give it up like that all in a second?'

'I've not given it up,' John replied.

'But you've not the ghost of a chance now,' said Charles roughly.

'I don't agree with you there,' said John with conviction. Charles looked at him and was profoundly uneasy; the most extraordinary doubts possessed him; he had a queer sense that they were talking about different things. He looked round to find some relief for his horrible depression, but the disorderly appearance of the room depressed him still further. What was that stick, and the old carpet bag hanging against the wall? And then those stones? Looking at John, something fixed and distant in his expression alarmed him. He knew only too well that his mere appearance upon a platform was out of the question.

'Pretty stones,' he said as cheerfully as he could; and saying that he had an appointment to keep, he left John—for ever.

D. H. LAWRENCE

The Man who Loved Islands

I

THERE was a man who loved islands. He was born on one, but it didn't suit him, as there were too many other people on it, besides himself. He wanted an island all of his own: not necessarily to be alone on it, but to make it a world of his own.

An island, if it is big enough, is no better than a continent. It has to be really quite small, before it *feels* like an island; and this story will show how tiny it has to be, before you can presume to fill it with your own personality.

Now circumstances so worked out that this lover of islands, by the time he was thirty-five, actually acquired an island of his own. He didn't own it as freehold property, but he had a ninety-nine years' lease of it, which, as far as a man and an island are concerned, is as good as ever-lasting. Since, if you are like Abraham, and want your offspring to be numberless as the sands of the sea-shore, you don't choose an island to start breeding on. Too soon there would be over-population, over-crowding, and slum conditions. Which is a horrid thought, for one who loves an island for its insulation. No, an island is a nest which holds one egg, and one only. This egg is the islander himself.

The island acquired by our potential islander was not in the remote oceans. It was quite near at home, no palm trees nor boom of surf on the reef, nor any of that kind of thing; but a good solid dwelling-house, rather gloomy, above the landing-place, and beyond, a small farmhouse with sheds, and a few outlying fields. Down on the little landing-bay were three cottages in a row, like coastguards' cottages, all neat and whitewashed.

What could be more cosy and home-like? It was four miles if you walked all round your island, through the gorse and the blackthorn bushes, above the steep rocks of the sea and down in the little glades where the primroses grew. If you walked straight over the two humps of hills, the length of it, through the rocky fields where the cows lay chewing, and through the rather sparse oats, on into the gorse again, and so to the low cliffs' edge, it took you only twenty minutes. And when you came to the edge, you could see another, bigger island lying beyond. But the sea was between you and it. And as you returned over the turf where the short, downland cowslips nodded, you saw to the east still another island, a tiny one this time, like the calf of the cow. This tiny island also belonged to the islander.

Thus it seems that even islands like to keep each other company.

Our islander loved his island very much. In early spring, the little ways and glades were a snow of blackthorn, a vivid white among the Celtic stillness of close green and grey rock, blackbirds calling out in the whiteness their first long, triumphant calls. After the blackthorn and the nestling primroses came the blue apparition of hyacinths, like elfin lakes and slipping sheets of blue, among the bushes and under the glade of trees. And many birds with nests you could peep into, on the island all your own. Wonderful what a great world it was!

Followed summer, and the cowslips gone, the wild roses faintly fragrant through the haze. There was a field of hay, the foxgloves stood looking down. In a little cove, the sun was on the pale granite where you bathed, and the shadow was in the rocks. Before the mist came stealing, you went home through the ripening oats, the glare of the sea fading from the high air as the fog-horn started to moo on the other island. And then the sea-fog went, it was autumn, the oat-sheaves lying prone, the great moon, another island, rose golden out of the sea, and rising higher, the world of the sea was white.

So autumn ended with rain, and winter came, dark skies and dampness and rain, but rarely frost. The island, your island, cowered dark, holding away from you. You could feel, down in the wet, sombre hollows, the resentful spirit coiled upon itself, like a wet dog coiled in gloom, or a snake that is neither asleep nor awake. Then in the night, when the wind left off blowing in great gusts and volleys, as at sea, you felt that your island was a universe, infinite and old as the darkness; not an island at all, but an infinite dark world where all the souls from all the other bygone nights lived on, and the infinite distance was near.

Strangely, from your little island in space, you were gone forth into the dark, great realms of time, where all the souls that never die veer and swoop on their vast, strange errands. The little earthly island has dwindled, like a jumping-off place, into nothingness, for you have jumped off, you know not how, into the dark wide mystery of time, where the past is vastly alive, and the future is not separated off.

This is the danger of becoming an islander. When, in the city, you wear your white spats and dodge the traffic with the fear of death down your spine, then you are quite safe from the terrors of infinite time. The moment is your little islet in time, it is the spatial universe that careers round you.

But once isolate yourself on a little island in the sea of space, and the moment begins to heave and expand in great circles, the solid earth is gone, and your slippery, naked dark soul finds herself out in the timeless world, where the chariots of the so-called dead dash down the old streets of centuries, and souls crowd on the footways that we, in the moment, call bygone years. The souls of all the dead are alive again, and pulsating actively around you. You are out in the other infinity.

Something of this happened to our islander. Mysterious 'feelings' came upon him that he wasn't used to; strange awarenesses of old, far-gone men, and other influences; men of Gaul, with big moustaches, who had been on his island, and had vanished from the face of it, but not out of the air of night. They were there still, hurtling their big, violent, unseen bodies through the night. And there were priests, with golden knives and mistletoe; then other priests with a crucifix; then pirates with murder on the sea.

Our islander was uneasy. He didn't believe, in the day-time, in any of this nonsense. But at night it just was so. He had reduced himself to a single point in space, and, a point being that which has neither length nor breadth, he had to step off it into somewhere else. Just as you must step into the sea, if the waters wash your foothold away, so he had, at night, to step off into the other worlds of undying time.

He was uncannily aware, as he lay in the dark, that the blackthorn grove that seemed a bit uncanny even in the realm of space and day, at night was crying with old men of an invisible race, around the altar stone. What was a ruin under the hornbeam trees by day, was a moaning of blood-stained priests with crucifixes, on the ineffable night. What was a cave and a hidden beach between coarse rocks, became in the invisible dark the purple-lipped imprecation of pirates.

To escape any more of this sort of awareness, our islander daily concentrated upon his material island. Why should it not be the Happy Isle at last? Why not the last small isle of the Hesperides, the perfect place, all filled with his own gracious, blossom-like spirit? A minute world of pure perfection, made by man himself.

He began, as we begin all our attempts to regain Paradise, by spending money. The old, semi-feudal dwelling-house he restored, let in more light, put clear lovely carpets on the floor, clear, flower-petal curtains at the sullen windows, and wines in the cellars of rock. He brought over a buxom housekeeper from the world, and a soft-spoken, much-experienced butler. These two were to be islanders.

In the farmhouse he put a bailiff, with two farm-hands. There were Jersey cows, tinkling a slow bell, among the gorse. There was a call to meals at midday, and the peaceful smoking of chimneys at evening, when rest descended.

A jaunty sailing-boat with a motor accessory rode in the shelter in the bay, just below the row of three white cottages. There was also a little yawl, and two row-boats drawn up on the sand. A fishing-net was drying on its supports, a boatload of new white planks stood criss-cross, a woman was going to the well with a bucket.

In the end cottage lived the skipper of the yacht, and his wife and son. He was a man from the other, large island, at home on this sea. Every fine day he went out fishing, with his son, every fair day there was fresh fish in the island.

In the middle cottage lived an old man and wife, a very faithful couple. The old man was a carpenter, and man of many jobs. He was always working, always the sound of his plane or his saw; lost in his work, he was another kind of islander.

In the third cottage was a mason, a widower with a son and two daughters. With the help of his boy, this man dug ditches and built fences, raised buttresses and erected a new outbuilding, and hewed stone from the little quarry. One daughter worked at the big house.

It was a quiet, busy little world. When the islander brought you over as his guest, you met first the dark-bearded, thin, smiling skipper, Arnold, then his boy Charles. At the house, the smooth-lipped butler who had lived all over the world valeted you, and created that curious creamy-smooth, disarming sense of luxury around you which only a perfect and rather untrustworthy servant can create. He disarmed you and had you at his mercy. The buxom housekeeper smiled and treated you with the subtly respectful familiarity that is only dealt out to the true gentry. And the rosy maid threw a glance at you, as if you were very wonderful, coming from the greater outer world. Then you met the smiling but watchful bailiff, who came from Cornwall, and the shy farm-hand from Berkshire, with his clean wife and two little children: then the rather sulky farm-hand from Suffolk. The mason, a Kent man, would talk to you by the yard if you let him. Only the old carpenter was gruff and elsewhere absorbed.

Well then, it was a little world to itself, and everybody feeling very safe, and being very nice to you, as if you were really something special. But it was the islander's world, not yours. He was the Master. The special smile, the special attention was to the Master. They all knew how well off they were. So the islander was no longer Mr So-and-So. To everyone on the island, even to you yourself, he was 'the Master'.

Well, it was ideal. The Master was no tyrant. Ah, no! He was a delicate, sensitive, handsome Master, who wanted everything perfect and everybody happy. Himself, of course, to be the fount of this happiness and perfection.

But in his way, he was a poet. He treated his guests royally, his servants liberally. Yet he was shrewd, and very wise. He never came the boss over his people. Yet he kept his eye on everything, like a shrewd, blue-eyed young Hermes. And it was amazing what a lot of knowledge he had at hand. Amazing what he knew about Jersey cows, and cheese-making, ditching and fencing, flowers and gardening, ships and the sailing of ships. He was a fount of knowledge about everything, and this knowledge he imparted to his people in an odd, half-ironical, half-portentous fashion, as if he really belonged to the quaint, half-real world of the gods.

They listened to him with their hats in their hands. He loved white clothes; or creamy white; and cloaks, and broad hats. So, in fine weather, the bailiff would see the elegant tall figure in creamy-white serge coming like some bird over the fallow, to look at the weeding of the turnips. Then there would be a doffing of hats, and a few minutes of whimsical, shrewd, wise talk, to which the bailiff answered admiringly, and the farm-hands listened in silent wonder, leaning on their hoes. The bailiff was almost tender, to the Master.

Or, on a windy morning, he would stand with his cloak blowing in the sticky sea-wind, on the edge of the ditch that was being dug to drain a little swamp, talking in the teeth of the wind to the man below, who looked up at him with steady and inscrutable eyes.

Or at evening in the rain he would be seen hurrying across the yard, the broad hat turned against the rain. And the farm-wife would hurriedly exclaim: 'The Master! Get up, John, and clear him a place on the sofa.' And then the door opened, and it was a cry of: 'Why, of all things, if it isn't the Master! Why, have ye turned out then, of a night like this, to come across to the like of we?' And the bailiff took his cloak, and the farm-wife his hat, the two farm-hands drew their chairs to the back, he sat on the sofa and took a child up near him. He was wonderful with children, talked to them simply wonderful, made you think of Our Saviour Himself, said the woman.

He was always greeted with smiles, and the same peculiar deference, as if he were a higher, but also frailer being. They handled him almost tenderly, and almost with adulation. But when he left, or when they spoke of him, they had often a subtle, mocking smile on their faces. There was no need to be afraid of 'the Master'. Just let him have his own way. Only the old carpenter was sometimes sincerely rude to him; so he didn't care for the old man.

It is doubtful whether any of them really liked him, man to man, or even woman to man. But then it is doubtful if he really liked any of them, as man to man, or man to woman. He wanted them to be happy, and the little world to be perfect. But anyone who wants the world to be perfect must be careful not to have real likes or dislikes. A general goodwill is all you can afford.

The sad fact is, alas, that general goodwill is always felt as something of an insult, by the mere object of it; and so it breeds a quite special brand of malice. Surely general goodwill is a form of egoism, that it should have such a result!

Our islander, however, had his own resources. He spent long hours in his library, for he was compiling a book of references to all the flowers mentioned in the Greek and Latin authors. He was not a great classical scholar; the usual public-school equipment. But there are such excellent translations nowadays. And it was so lovely, tracing flower after flower as it blossomed in the ancient world.

So the first year on the island passed by. A great deal had been done. Now the bills flooded in, and the Master, conscientious in all things, began to study them. The study left him pale and breathless. He was not a rich man. He knew he had been making a hole in his capital to get the island into running order. When he came to look, however, there was hardly anything left but hole. Thousands and thousands of pounds had the island swallowed into nothingness.

But surely the bulk of the spending was over! Surely the island would now begin to be self-supporting, even if it made no profit! Surely he was safe. He paid a good many of the bills, and took a little heart. But he had had a shock, and the next year, the coming year, there must be economy, frugality. He told his people so in simple and touching language. And they said: 'Why, surely! Surely!'

So, while the wind blew and the rain lashed outside, he would sit in his library with the bailiff over a pipe and pot of beer, discussing farm projects. He lifted his narrow, handsome face, and his blue eyes became dreamy. '*What* a wind!' It blew like cannon-shots. He thought of his island, lashed with foam, and inaccessible, and he exulted . . . No, he must not lose it. He turned back to the farm projects with the zest of genius, and his hands flicked white emphasis, while the bailiff intoned: 'Yes, sir! Yes, sir! You're right, Master!'

But the man was hardly listening. He was looking at the Master's blue lawn shirt and curious pink tie with the fiery red stone, at the enamel sleeve-links, and at the ring with the peculiar scarab. The brown searching eyes of the man of the soil glanced repeatedly over the fine, immaculate figure of the Master, with a sort of slow, calculating wonder. But if he happened to catch the Master's bright, exalted glance, his own eye lit up with a careful cordiality and deference, as he bowed his head slightly.

Thus between them they decided what crops should be sown, what fertilizers should be used in different places, which breed of pigs should be imported, and which line of turkeys. That is to say, the bailiff, by continually cautiously agreeing with the Master, kept out of it, and let the young man have his own way.

The Master knew what he was talking about. He was brilliant at grasping the gist of a book, and knowing how to apply his knowledge. On the whole, his ideas were sound. The bailiff even knew it. But in the man of the soil there was no answering enthusiasm. The brown eyes smiled their cordial deference, but the thin lips never changed. The Master pursed his own flexible mouth in a boyish versatility, as he cleverly sketched in his ideas to the other man, and the bailiff made eyes of admiration, but in his heart he was not attending, he was only watching the Master as he would have watched a queer, caged animal, quite without sympathy, not implicated.

So, it was settled, and the Master rang for Elvery, the butler, to bring a sandwich. He, the Master, was pleased. The butler saw it, and came back with anchovy and ham sandwiches, and a newly opened bottle of vermouth. There was always a newly opened bottle of something.

It was the same with the mason. The Master and he discussed the drainage of a bit of land, and more pipes were ordered, more special bricks, more this, more that.

Fine weather came at last; there was a little lull in the hard work on the island. The Master went for a short cruise in his yacht. It was not really a yacht, just a little bit of a thing. They sailed along the coast of the mainland, and put in at the ports. At every port some friend turned up, the butler made elegant little meals in the cabin. Then the Master was invited to villas and hotels, his people disembarked him as if he were a prince.

And oh, how expensive it turned out! He had to telegraph to the bank for money. And he went home again to economize.

The marsh-marigolds were blazing in the little swamp where the ditches were being dug for drainage. He almost regretted, now, the work in hand. The yellow beauties would not blaze again.

Harvest came, and a bumper crop. There must be a harvest-home supper. The long barn was now completely restored and added to. The carpenter had made long tables. Lanterns hung from the beams of the high-pitched roof. All the people of the island were assembled. The bailiff presided. It was a gay scene.

Towards the end of the supper the Master, in a velvet jacket, appeared with his guests. Then the bailiff rose and proposed 'The Master! Long life and health to the Master!' All the people drank the health with great enthusiasm and cheering. The Master replied with a little speech: They were on an island in a little world of their own. It depended on them all to make this world a world of true happiness and content. Each must do his part. He hoped he himself did what he could, for his heart was in his island, and with the people of his island.

The butler responded: As long as the island had such a Master, it could not help but be a little heaven for all the people on it. This was seconded with virile warmth by the bailiff and the mason, the skipper was beside himself. Then there was dancing, the old carpenter was fiddler.

But under all this, things were not well. The very next morning came the farm-boy to say that a cow had fallen over the cliff. The Master went to look. He peered over the not very high declivity, and saw her lying dead on a green ledge under a bit of late-flowering broom. A beautiful, expensive creature, already looking swollen. But what a fool, to fall so unnecessarily!

It was a question of getting several men to haul her up the bank, and then of skinning and burying her. No one would eat the meat. How repulsive it all was!

This was symbolic of the island. As sure as the spirits rose in the human breast, with a movement of joy, an invisible hand struck malevolently out of the silence. There must not be any joy, nor even any quiet peace. A man broke a leg, another was crippled with rheumatic fever. The pigs had some strange disease. A storm drove the yacht on a rock. The mason hated the butler, and refused to let his daughter serve at the house.

Out of the very air came a stony, heavy malevolence. The island itself seemed malicious. It would go on being hurtful and evil for weeks at a time. Then suddenly again one morning it would be fair, lovely as a morning in Paradise, everything beautiful and flowing. And everybody would begin to feel a great relief, and a hope for happiness.

Then as soon as the Master was opened out in spirit like an open flower, some ugly blow would fall. Somebody would send him an anonymous note, accusing some other person on the island. Somebody else would come hinting things against one of his servants.

'Some folks think they've got an easy job out here, with all the pickings they make!' the mason's daughter screamed at the suave butler, in the Master's hearing. He pretended not to hear.

'My man says this island is surely one of the lean kine of Egypt, it would swallow a sight of money, and you'd never get anything back out of it,' confided the farm-hand's wife to one of the Master's visitors.

The people were not contented. They were not islanders. 'We feel we're not doing right by the children,' said those who had children. 'We feel we're not doing right by ourselves,' said those who had no children. And the various families fairly came to hate one another.

Yet the island was so lovely. When there was a scent of honeysuckle and the moon brightly flickering down on the sea, then even the grumblers felt a strange nostalgia for it. It set you yearning, with a wild yearning; perhaps for the past, to be far back in the mysterious past of the island, when the blood had a different throb. Strange floods of passion came over you, strange violent lusts and imaginations of cruelty. The blood and the passion and the lust which the island had known. Uncanny dreams, half-dreams, half-evocated yearnings.

The Master himself began to be a little afraid of his island. He felt here strange, violent feelings he had never felt before, and lustful desires that he had been quite free from. He knew quite well now that his people didn't love him at all. He knew that their spirits were secretly against him, malicious, jeering, envious, and lurking to down him. He became just as wary and secretive with regard to them.

But it was too much. At the end of the second year, several departures took place. The housekeeper went. The Master always blamed self-important women most. The mason said he wasn't going to be monkeyed about any more, so he took his departure, with his family. The rheumatic farm-hand left.

And then the year's bills came in, the Master made up his accounts. In spite of good crops, the assets were ridiculous, against the spending. The island had again lost, not hundreds but thousands of pounds. It was incredible. But you simply couldn't believe it! Where had it all gone?

The Master spent gloomy nights and days going through accounts in the library. He was thorough. It became evident, now the housekeeper had gone, that she had swindled him. Probably everybody was swindling him. But he hated to think it, so he put the thought away.

He emerged, however, pale and hollow-eyed from his balancing of unbalanceable accounts, looking as if something had kicked him in the stomach. It was pitiable. But the money had gone, and there was an end of it. Another great hole in his capital. How could people be so heartless?

It couldn't go on, that was evident. He would soon be bankrupt. He had to give regretful notice to his butler. He was afraid to find out how much his butler had swindled him. Because the man was such a wonderful butler, after all. And the farm bailiff had to go. The Master had no regrets in that quarter. The losses on the farm had almost embittered him.

The third year was spent in rigid cutting down of expenses. The island was still mysterious and fascinating. But it was also treacherous and cruel, secretly, fathomlessly malevolent. In spite of all its fair show of white blossom and bluebells, and the lovely dignity of foxgloves bending their rose-red bells, it was your implacable enemy.

With reduced staff, reduced wages, reduced splendour, the third year went by. But it was fighting against hope. The farm still lost a good deal. And once more there was a hole in that remnant of capital. Another hole in that which was already a mere remnant round the old holes. The island was mysterious in this also: it seemed to pick the very money out of your pocket, as if it were an octopus with invisible arms stealing from you in every direction.

Yet the Master still loved it. But with a touch of rancour now.

He spent, however, the second half of the fourth year intensely work-ing on the mainland, to be rid of it. And it was amazing how difficult he found it, to dispose of an island. He had thought that everybody was pining for such an island as his; but not at all. Nobody would pay any price for it. And he wanted now to get rid of it, as a man who wants a divorce at any cost.

It was not till the middle of the fifth year that he transferred it, at a considerable loss to himself, to an hotel company who were willing to speculate in it. They were to turn it into a handy honeymoon-and-golf island.

There, take that, island which didn't know when it was well off. Now be a honeymoon-and-golf island!

2

THE SECOND ISLAND

The islander had to move. But he was not going to the mainland. Oh, no! He moved to the smaller island, which still belonged to him. And he took with him the faithful old carpenter and wife, the couple he never really cared for; also a widow and daughter, who had kept house for him the last year; also an orphan lad, to help the old man.

The small island was very small; but being a hump of rock in the sea, it was bigger than it looked. There was a little track among the rocks and bushes, winding and scrambling up and down around the islet, so that it took you twenty minutes to do the circuit. It was more than you would have expected.

Still, it was an island. The islander moved himself, with all his books, into the commonplace six-roomed house up to which you had to scramble from the rocky landing-place. There were also two joined-together cottages. The old carpenter lived in one, with his wife and the lad, the widow and daughter lived in the other.

At last all was in order. The Master's books filled two rooms. It was already autumn, Orion lifting out of the sea. And in the dark nights, the Master could see the lights on his late island, where the hotel company were entertaining guests who would advertise the new resort for honeymoon-golfers.

On his lump of rock, however, the Master was still master. He explored the crannies, the odd hand-breadths of grassy level, the steep little cliffs where the last harebells hung and the seeds of summer were brown above the sea, lonely and untouched. He peered down the old well. He examined the stone pen where the pig had been kept. Himself, he had a goat.

Yes, it was an island. Always, always underneath among the rocks the Celtic sea sucked and washed and smote its feathery greyness. How many different noises of the sea! Deep explosions, rumblings, strange long sighs and whistling noises; then voices, real voices of people clamouring as if they were in a market, under the waters: and again, the far-off ringing of a bell, surely an actual bell! Then a tremendous trilling noise, very long and alarming, and an undertone of hoarse gasping.

On this island there were no human ghosts, no ghosts of any ancient race. The sea, and the spume and the weather, had washed them all out, washed them out so there was only the sound of the sea itself, its own ghost, myriad-voiced, communing and plotting and shouting all winter long. And only the smell of the sea, with a few bristly bushes of gorse and coarse tufts of heather, among the grey, pellucid rocks, in the grey, more-pellucid air. The coldness, the greyness, even the soft, creeping fog of the sea, and the islet of rock humped up in it all, like the last point in space.

Green star Sirius stood over the sea's rim. The island was a shadow. Out at sea a ship showed small lights. Below, in the rocky cove, the row-boat and the motor-boat were safe. A light shone in the carpenter's kitchen. That was all.

Save, of course, that the lamp was lit in the house, where the widow was preparing supper, her daughter helping. The islander went in to his meal. Here he was no longer the Master, he was an islander again and he had peace. The old carpenter, the widow and daughter were all faithfulness itself. The old man worked while ever there was light to see, because he had a passion for work. The widow and her quiet, rather delicate daughter of thirty-three worked for the Master, because they loved looking after him, and they were infinitely grateful for the haven he provided them. But they didn't call him 'the Master'. They gave him his name: 'Mr Cathcart, sir!' softly and reverently. And he spoke back to them also softly, gently, like people far from the world, afraid to make a noise.

The island was no longer a 'world'. It was a sort of refuge. The islander no longer struggled for anything. He had no need. It was as if he and his few dependents were a small flock of sea-birds alighted on this rock, as they travelled through space, and keeping together without a word. The silent mystery of travelling birds.

He spent most of his day in his study. His book was coming along. The widow's daughter could type out his manuscript for him, she was not uneducated. It was the one strange sound on the island, the type-writer. But soon even its spattering fitted in with the sea's noises, and the wind's.

The months went by. The islander worked away in his study, the people of the island went quietly about their concerns. The goat had a little black kid with yellow eyes. There were mackerel in the sea. The old man went fishing in the row-boat with the lad, when the weather was calm enough; they went off in the motor-boat to the biggest island for the post. And they brought supplies, never a penny wasted. And the days went by, and the nights, without desire, without ennui.

The strange stillness from all desire was a kind of wonder to the islander. He didn't want anything. His soul at last was still in him, his spirit was like a dim-lit cave under water, where strange sea-foliage expands upon the watery atmosphere, and scarcely sways, and a mute fish shadowily slips in and slips away again. All still and soft and uncry-ing, yet alive as rooted seaweed is alive.

The islander said to himself: 'Is this happiness?' He said to himself: 'I am turned into a dream. I feel nothing, or I don't know what I feel. Yet it seems to me I am happy.'

Only he had to have something upon which his mental activity could work. So he spent long, silent hours in his study, working not very fast, nor very importantly, letting the writing spin softly from him as if it were drowsy gossamer. He no longer fretted whether it were good or not, what he produced. He slowly, softly spun it like gossamer, and if it were to melt away as gossamer in autumn melts, he would not mind. It was only the soft evanescence of gossamy things which now seemed to him permanent. The very mist of eternity was in them. Whereas stone buildings, cathedrals for example, seemed to him to howl with tempor-ary resistance, knowing they must fall at last; the tension of their long endurance seemed to howl forth from them all the time.

Sometimes he went to the mainland and to the city. Then he went elegantly, dressed in the latest style, to his club. He sat in a stall at the theatre, he shopped in Bond Street. He discussed terms for publishing his book. But over his face was that gossamy look of having dropped out of the race of progress, which made the vulgar city people feel they had won it over him, and made him glad to go back to his island.

He didn't mind if he never published his book. The years were blending into a soft mist, from which nothing obtruded. Spring came. There was never a primrose on his island, but he found a winter-aconite. There were two little sprayed bushes of blackthorn, and some wind-flowers. He began to make a list of the flowers of his islet, and that was absorbing. He noted a wild currant bush and watched for the elder flowers on a stunted little tree, then for the first yellow rags of the broom, and wild roses. Bladder campion, orchids, stitchwort, celandine, he was prouder of them than if they had been people on his island. When he came across the golden saxifrage, so inconspicuous in a damp corner, he crouched over it in a trance, he knew not for how long, looking at it. Yet it was nothing to look at. As the widow's daughter found, when he showed it her.

He had said to her in real triumph:

'I found the golden saxifrage this morning.'

The name sounded splendid. She looked at him with fascinated brown eyes, in which was a hollow ache that frightened him a little.

'Did you, sir? Is it a nice flower?'

He pursed his lips and tilted his brows.

'Well—not showy exactly. I'll show it you if you like.'

'I should like to see it.'

She was so quiet, so wistful. But he sensed in her a persistency which made him uneasy. She said she was so happy: really happy. She followed him quietly, like a shadow, on the rocky track where there was never room for two people to walk side by side. He went first, and could feel her there, immediately behind him, following so submissively, gloating on him from behind.

It was a kind of pity for her which made him become her lover: though he never realized the extent of the power she had gained over him, and how *she* willed it. But the moment he had fallen, a jangling feeling came upon him, that it was all wrong. He felt a nervous dislike of her. He had not wanted it. And it seemed to him, as far as her physical self went, she had not wanted it either. It was just her will. He went away, and climbed at the risk of his neck down to a ledge near the sea. There he sat for hours, gazing all jangled at the sea, and saying miserably to himself: 'We didn't want it. We didn't really want it.'

It was the automatism of sex that had caught him again. Not that he hated sex. He deemed it, as the Chinese do, one of the great life-mysteries. But it had become mechanical, automatic, and he wanted to escape that. Automatic sex shattered him, and filled him with a sort of death. He thought he had come through, to a new stillness of desire-lessness. Perhaps beyond that there was a new fresh delicacy of desire, an unentered frail communion of two people meeting on untrodden ground.

Be that as it might, this was not it. This was nothing new or fresh. It was automatic, and driven from the will. Even she, in her true self, hadn't wanted it. It was automatic in her.

When he came home, very late, and saw her face white with fear and apprehension of his feeling against her, he pitied her, and spoke to her delicately, reassuringly. But he kept himself remote from her.

She gave no sign. She served him with the same silence, the same hidden hunger to serve him, to be near where he was. He felt her love following him with strange, awful persistency. She claimed nothing. Yet now, when he met her bright, brown, curiously vacant eyes, he saw in them the mute question. The question came direct at him, with a force and a power of will he never realized.

So he succumbed, and asked her again.

'Not,' she said, 'if it will make you hate me.'

'Why should it?' he replied, nettled. 'Of course not.'

'You know I would do anything on earth for you.'

It was only afterwards, in his exasperation, he remembered what she said, and was more exasperated. Why should she pretend to do this *for him*? Why not herself? But in his exasperation, he drove himself deeper in. In order to achieve some sort of satisfaction, which he never did achieve, he abandoned himself to her. Everybody on the island knew. But he did not care.

Then even what desire he had left him, and he felt only shattered. He felt that only with her will had she wanted him. Now he was shattered and full of self-contempt. His island was smirched and spoiled. He had lost his place in the rare, desireless levels of Time to which he had at last arrived, and he had fallen right back. If only it had been true, delicate desire between them, and a delicate meeting on the third rare place where a man might meet a woman, when they were both true to the frail, sensitive, crocus-flame of desire in them. But it had been no such thing: automatic, an act of will, not of true desire, it left him feeling humiliated.

He went away from the islet, in spite of her mute reproach. And he wandered about the continent, vainly seeking a place where he could stay. He was out of key; he did not fit in the world any more.

There came a letter from Flora—her name was Flora—to say she was afraid she was going to have a child. He sat down as if he were shot, and he remained sitting. But he replied to her: 'Why be afraid? If it is so, it is so, and we should rather be pleased than afraid.'

At this very moment, it happened there was an auction of islands. He got the maps, and studied them. And at the auction he bought, for very little money, another island. It was just a few acres of rock away in the north, on the outer fringe of the isles. It was low, it rose low out of the great ocean. There was not a building, not even a tree on it. Only northern sea-turf, a pool of rain-water, a bit of sedge, rock, and sea-birds. Nothing else. Under the weeping wet western sky.

He made a trip to visit his new possession. For several days, owing to the seas, he could not approach it. Then, in a light sea-mist, he landed, and saw it hazy, low, stretching apparently a long way. But it was illusion. He walked over the wet, springy turf, and dark-grey sheep tossed away from him, spectral, bleating hoarsely. And he came to the dark pool, with the sedge. Then on in the dampness, to the grey sea sucking angrily among the rocks.

This was indeed an island.

So he went home to Flora. She looked at him with guilty fear, but also with a triumphant brightness in her uncanny eyes. And again he was gentle, he reassured her, even he wanted her again, with that curious desire that was almost like toothache. So he took her to the mainland, and they were married, since she was going to have his child.

They returned to the island. She still brought in his meals, her own along with them. She sat and ate with him. He would have it so. The widowed mother preferred to stay in the kitchen. And Flora slept in the guest-room of his house, mistress of his house.

His desire, whatever it was, died in him with nauseous finality. The child would still be months coming. His island was hateful to him, vulgar, a suburb. He himself had lost all his finer distinction. The weeks passed in a sort of prison, in humiliation. Yet he stuck it out, till the child was born. But he was meditating escape. Flora did not even know.

A nurse appeared, and ate at table with them. The doctor came sometimes, and, if the sea were rough, he too had to stay. He was cheery over his whisky.

They might have been a young couple in Golders Green.

The daughter was born at last. The father looked at the baby, and felt depressed, almost more than he could bear. The millstone was tied round his neck. But he tried not to show what he felt. And Flora did not know. She still smiled with a kind of half-witted triumph in her joy, as she got well again. Then she began again to look at him with those aching, suggestive, somehow impudent eyes. She adored him so.

This he could not stand. He told her that he had to go away for a time. She wept, but she thought she had got him. He told her he had settled the best part of his property on her, and wrote down for her what income it would produce. She hardly listened, only looked at him with those heavy, adoring, impudent eyes. He gave her a cheque-book, with the amount of her credit duly entered. This did arouse her interest. And he told her, if she got tired of the island, she could choose her home wherever she wished.

She followed him with those aching, persistent brown eyes, when he left, and he never even saw her weep.

He went straight north, to prepare his third island.

3
THE THIRD ISLAND

The third island was soon made habitable. With cement and the big pebbles from the shingle beach, two men built him a hut, and roofed it with corrugated iron. A boat brought over a bed and table, and three chairs, with a good cupboard, and a few books. He laid in a supply of coal and paraffin and food—he wanted so little.

The house stood near the flat shingle bay where he landed, and where he pulled up his light boat. On a sunny day in August the men sailed away and left him. The sea was still and pale blue. On the horizon he saw the small mail-steamer slowly passing northwards, as if she were walking. She served the outer isles twice a week. He could row out to her if need be, in calm weather, and he could signal her from a flagstaff behind his cottage.

Half a dozen sheep still remained on the island, as company; and he had a cat to rub against his legs. While the sweet, sunny days of the northern autumn lasted, he would walk among the rocks, and over the springy turf of his small domain, always coming to the ceaseless, restless sea. He looked at every leaf, that might be different from another, and he watched the endless expansion and contraction of the water-tossed seaweed. He had never a tree, not even a bit of heather to guard. Only the turf, and tiny turf-plants, and the sedge by the pool, the seaweed in the ocean. He was glad. He didn't want trees or bushes. They stood up like people, too assertive. His bare, low-pitched island in the pale blue sea was all he wanted.

He no longer worked at his book. The interest had gone. He liked to sit on the low elevation of his island, and see the sea; nothing but the pale, quiet sea. And to feel his mind turn soft and hazy, like the hazy ocean. Sometimes, like a mirage, he would see the shadow of land rise hovering to northwards. It was a big island beyond. But quite without substance.

He was soon almost startled when he perceived the steamer on the near horizon, and his heart contracted with fear, lest it were going to pause and molest him. Anxiously he watched it go, and not till it was out of sight did he feel truly relieved, himself again. The tension of waiting for human approach was cruel. He did not want to be approached. He did not want to hear voices. He was shocked by the sound of his own voice, if he inadvertently spoke to his cat. He rebuked himself for having broken the great silence. And he was irritated when his cat would look up at him and mew faintly, plaintively. He frowned at her. And she knew. She was becoming wild, lurking in the rocks, perhaps fishing.

But what he disliked most was when one of the lumps of sheep opened its mouth and baa-ed its hoarse, raucous baa. He watched it, and it looked to him hideous and gross. He came to dislike the sheep very much.

He wanted only to hear the whispering sound of the sea, and the sharp cries of the gulls, cries that came out of another world to him. And best of all, the great silence.

He decided to get rid of the sheep when the boat came. They were accustomed to him now, and stood and stared at him with yellow or colourless eyes, in an insolence that was almost cold ridicule. There was a suggestion of cold indecency about them. He disliked them very much. And when they jumped with staccato jumps off the rocks, and their hoofs made the dry, sharp hit, and the fleece flopped on their square backs, he found them repulsive, degrading.

The fine weather passed, and it rained all day. He lay a great deal on his bed, listening to the water trickling from his roof into the zinc water-butt, looking through the open door at the rain, the dark rocks, the hidden sea. Many gulls were on the island now: many sea-birds of all sorts. It was another world of life. Many of the birds he had never seen before. His old impulse came over him, to send for a book, to know their names. In a flicker of the old passion, to know the name of everything he saw, he even decided to row out to the steamer. The names of these birds! He must know their names, otherwise he had not got them, they were not quite alive to him.

But the desire left him, and he merely watched the birds as they wheeled or walked around him, watched them vaguely, without discrimination. All interest had left him. Only there was one gull, a big, handsome fellow, who would walk back and forth, back and forth in front of the open door of the cabin, as if he had some mission there. He was big, and pearl-grey, and his roundnesses were as smooth and lovely as a pearl. Only the folded wings had shut black pinions, and on the closed black feathers were three distinct white dots, making a pattern. The islander wondered very much, why this bit of trimming on the bird out of the far, cold seas. And as the gull walked back and forth, back and forth in front of the cabin, strutting on pale-dusky gold feet, holding up his pale yellow beak, that was curved at the tip, with curious alien importance, the man wondered over him. He was portentous, he had a meaning.

Then the bird came no more. The island, which had been full of sea-birds, the flash of wings, the sound and cut of wings and sharp eerie cries in the air, began to be deserted again. No longer they sat like living eggs on the rocks and turf, moving their heads, but scarcely rising into flight round his feet. No longer they ran across the turf among the sheep, and lifted themselves upon low wings. The host had gone. But some remained, always.

The days shortened, and the world grew eerie. One day the boat came: as if suddenly, swooping down. The islander found it a violation. It was torture to talk to those two men, in their homely clumsy clothes. The air of familiarity around them was very repugnant to him. Himself, he was neatly dressed, his cabin was neat and tidy. He resented any intrusion, the clumsy homeliness, the heavy-footedness of the two fishermen was really repulsive to him.

The letters they had brought he left lying unopened in a little box. In one of them was his money. But he could not bear to open even that one. Any kind of contact was repulsive to him. Even to read his name on an envelope. He hid the letters away.

And the hustle and horror of getting the sheep caught and tied and put in the ship made him loathe with profound repulsion the whole of the animal creation. What repulsive god invented animals and evil-smelling men? To his nostrils, the fishermen and the sheep alike smelled foul: an uncleanness on the fresh earth.

He was still nerve-racked and tortured when the ship at last lifted sail and was drawing away, over the still sea. And sometimes, days after, he would start with repulsion, thinking he heard the munching of sheep.

The dark days of winter drew on. Sometimes there was no real day at all. He felt ill, as if he were dissolving, as if dissolution had already set in inside him. Everything was twilight, outside, and in his mind and soul. Once, when he went to the door, he saw black heads of men swimming in his bay. For some moments he swooned unconscious. It was the shock, the horror of unexpected human approach. The horror in the twilight! And not till the shock had undermined him and left him dis-embodied, did he realize that the black heads were the heads of seals swimming in. A sick relief came over him. But he was barely conscious, after the shock. Later on, he sat and wept with gratitude, because they were not men. But he never realized that he wept. He was too dim. Like some strange, ethereal animal, he no longer realized what he was doing.

Only he still derived his single satisfaction from being alone, absolutely alone, with the space soaking into him. The grey sea alone, and the footing of his sea-washed island. No other contact. Nothing human to bring its horror into contact with him. Only space, damp, twilit, sea-washed space! This was the bread of his soul.

For this reason, he was most glad when there was a storm, or when the sea was high. Then nothing could get at him. Nothing could come through to him from the outer world. True, the terrific violence of the wind made him suffer badly. At the same time, it swept the world utterly out of existence for him. He always liked the sea to be heavily rolling and tearing. Then no boat could get at him. It was like eternal ramparts round his island.

He kept no track of time, and no longer thought of opening a book. The print, the printed letters, so like the depravity of speech, looked obscene. He tore the brass label from his paraffin stove. He obliterated any bit of lettering in his cabin.

His cat had disappeared. He was rather glad. He shivered at her thin, obtrusive call. She had lived in the coal-shed. And each morning he had put her a dish of porridge, the same as he ate. He washed her saucer with repulsion. He did not like her writhing about. But he fed her scrupu-lously. Then one day she did not come for her porridge; she always mewed for it. She did not come again.

He prowled about his island in the rain, in a big oilskin coat, not knowing what he was looking at, nor what he went out to see. Time had ceased to pass. He stood for long spaces, gazing from a white, sharp face, with those keen, far-off blue eyes of his, gazing fiercely and almost cruelly at the dark sea under the dark sky. And if he saw the labouring sail of a fishing-boat away on the cold waters, a strange malevolent anger passed over his features.

Sometimes he was ill. He knew he was ill, because he staggered as he walked, and easily fell down. Then he paused to think what it was. And he went to his stores and took out dried milk and malt, and ate that. Then he forgot again. He ceased to register his own feelings.

The days were beginning to lengthen. All winter the weather had been comparatively mild, but with much rain, much rain. He had forgotten the sun. Suddenly, however, the air was very cold, and he began to shiver. A fear came over him. The sky was level and grey, and never a star appeared at night. It was very cold. More birds began to arrive. The island was freezing. With trembling hands he made a fire in his grate. The cold frightened him.

And now it continued, day after day, a dull, deathly cold. Occasional crumblings of snow were in the air. The days were greyly longer, but no change in the cold. Frozen grey daylight. The birds passed away, flying away. Some he saw lying frozen. It was as if all life were drawing away, contracting away from the north, contracting southwards. 'Soon,' he said to himself, 'it will all be gone, and in all these regions nothing will be alive.' He felt a cruel satisfaction in the thought.

Then one night there seemed to be a relief; he slept better, did not tremble half-awake, and writhe so much, half-conscious. He had become so used to the quaking and writhing of his body, he hardly noticed it. But when for once it slept deep, he noticed that.

He woke in the morning to a curious whiteness. His window was muffled. It had snowed. He got up and opened his door, and shuddered. Ugh! How cold! All white, with a dark leaden sea, and black rocks curiously speckled with white. The foam was no longer pure. It seemed dirty. And the sea ate at the whiteness of the corpse-like land. Crumbles of snow were silting down the dead air.

On the ground the snow was a foot deep, white and smooth and soft, windless. He took a shovel to clear round his house and shed. The pallor of morning darkened. There was a strange rumbling of far-off thunder in the frozen air, and through the newly-falling snow, a dim flash of lightning. Snow now fell steadily down in the motionless obscurity.

He went out for a few minutes. But it was difficult. He stumbled and fell in the snow, which burned his face. Weak, faint, he toiled home. And when he recovered, took the trouble to make hot milk.

It snowed all the time. In the afternoon again there was a muffled rumbling of thunder, and flashes of lightning blinking reddish through the falling snow. Uneasy, he went to bed and lay staring fixedly at nothingness.

Morning seemed never to come. An eternity long he lay and waited for one alleviating pallor on the night. And at last it seemed the air was paler. His house was a cell faintly illuminated with white light. He realized the snow was walled outside his window. He got up, in the dead cold. When he opened his door, the motionless snow stopped him in a wall as high as his breast. Looking over the top of it, he felt the dead wind slowly driving, saw the snow-powder lift and travel like a funeral train. The blackish sea churned and champed, seeming to bite at the snow, impotent. The sky was grey, but luminous.

He began to work in a frenzy, to get at his boat. If he was to be shut in, it must be by his own choice, not by the mechanical power of the elements. He must get to the sea. He must be able to get at his boat.

But he was weak, and at times the snow overcame him. It fell on him, and he lay buried and lifeless. Yet every time he struggled alive before it was too late, and fell upon the snow with the energy of fever. Exhausted, he would not give in. He crept indoors and made coffee and bacon. Long since he had cooked so much. Then he went at the snow once more. He must conquer the snow, this new, white brute force which had accumulated against him.

He worked in the awful, dead wind, pushing the snow aside, pressing it with his shovel. It was cold, freezing hard in the wind, even when the sun came out for a while, and showed him his white, lifeless surroundings, the black sea rolling sullen, flecked with dull spume, away to the horizons. Yet the sun had power on his face. It was March.

He reached the boat. He pushed the snow away, then sat down under the lee of the boat, looking at the sea, which swirled nearly to his feet, in the high tide. Curiously natural the pebbles looked, in a world gone all uncanny. The sun shone no more. Snow was falling in hard crumbs, that vanished as if by a miracle as they touched the hard blackness of the sea. Hoarse waves rang in the shingle, rushing up at the snow. The wet rocks were brutally black. And all the time the myriad swooping crumbs of snow, demonish, touched the dark sea and disappeared.

During the night there was a great storm. It seemed to him he could hear the vast mass of snow striking all the world with a ceaseless thud; and over it all, the wind roared in strange hollow volleys, in between which came a jump of blindfold lightning, then the low roll of thunder heavier than the wind. When at last the dawn faintly discoloured the dark, the storm had more or less subsided, but a steady wind drove on. The snow was up to the top of his door.

Sullenly, he worked to dig himself out. And he managed through sheer persistency to get out. He was in the tail of a great drift, many feet high. When he got through, the frozen snow was not more than two feet deep. But his island was gone. Its shape was all changed, great heaping white hills rose where no hills had been, inaccessible, and they fumed like volcanoes, but with snow powder. He was sickened and overcome.

His boat was in another, smaller drift. But he had not the strength to clear it. He looked at it helplessly. The shovel slipped from his hands, and he sank in the snow, to forget. In the snow itself, the sea resounded.

Something brought him to. He crept to his house. He was almost without feeling. Yet he managed to warm himself, just that part of him which leaned in snow-sleep over the coal fire. Then again he made hot milk. After which, carefully, he built up the fire.

The wind dropped. Was it night again? In the silence, it seemed he could hear the panther-like dropping of infinite snow. Thunder rumbled nearer, crackled quick after the bleared reddened lightning. He lay in bed in a kind of stupor. The elements! The elements! His mind repeated the word dumbly. You can't win against the elements.

How long it went on, he never knew. Once, like a wraith, he got out and climbed to the top of a white hill on his unrecognizable island. The sun was hot. 'It is summer,' he said to himself, 'and the time of leaves.' He looked stupidly over the whiteness of his foreign island, over the waste of the lifeless sea. He pretended to imagine he saw the wink of a sail. Because he knew too well there would never again be a sail on that stark sea.

As he looked, the sky mysteriously darkened and chilled. From far off came the mutter of the unsatisfied thunder, and he knew it was the signal of the snow rolling over the sea. He turned, and felt its breath on him.

RONALD FIRBANK

A Tragedy in Green

TO
THE INSPIRER OF THE TRAGEDY,
SIR COLERIDGE KENNARD

Pierrot: Pierrette, you are looking so serious today, I am going to invent
you a story; a perfectly heartless story.

Pierrette (her hands clasped): Oh! Dearest Pierrot, I love stories, especially the kind that make one cry! I enjoy to cry, besides I have the
sweetest pocket-handkerchiefs—real Venetian Point . . .

Pierrot: My incomprehensible Pierrette, there will be no need for that;
it's a Funny Story.

Pierrette (bursting into tears): A Funny Story! How vulgar!

Pierrot (kissing her): Rose of my life! you already weep?

IN her bedroom at Seven Stones Castle, Lady Georgia Blueharnis
awaited the dinner gong. She had arrived only that evening, leaving her
husband unavoidably detained at the Foreign Office; and this was the
second halting place on her Autumn round of visits.

'My dress is far too beautiful to be down first,' she murmured to herself, 'and it was foolish of me to have dressed so soon.'

She was wearing a gown in three shades of green, with profusions of
falling crystals, her dull red hair shrouded in a silver net. As she moved,
a diamond crucifix swung lightly from an almost imperceptible chain.

'I am a work of art,' she sighed, 'and this evening I feel nearly as
wicked as Herodias.'

It was one of Lady Georgia's habits to find equivalents for all her
worser feelings in the Bible.

Smiling with the candour of a Mona Lisa she looked about her. In the
penumbra from the mullioned windows the tapestried walls looked dim
and aërie. Here, and there, a unicorn fed unconcernedly in a flowery
field, or sometimes a virgin passed, with neck bowed, absorbed in the

perusal of an austere Missal, her threadbare feet very pale on the ice-blue grass. On a bracket, above the bed, stood a little boxwood image of a saint, with a very long neck, holding a sheaf of lilies, and behind the dressing table, white as an altar, steps rose to a platform in the bay window, where a luxurious sofa, piled with many cushions, stood solitary, offering rest and a view of the stars.

Lady Georgia sighed again. 'If only,' she said, addressing herself to the nearest, and most sympathetic unicorn, 'if only something would happen! Why did I marry a man who is forever busy compiling his *Memoirs*, or doing nothing at the Foreign Office all day, ah! why? To live solely for dress, or for what people so curiously misname "pleasure", to be spoken of invariably as "the aesthetic Lady Georgia", even when one is only wearing a muslin blouse, and a bunch of primroses, is surely not to exhaust all the possible emotions of life?' and piqued by the unicorn's unintelligent silence, she added sadly: 'Silly beast, graze on!'

Far away, over the gardens, from the village of Seven Stones the church clock struck eight. Eight silver notes like the petals falling from a rose. On the terrace below she could see the upturned face of a statue smiling at her through the dusk. Above, the sky was thick with stars, little fragments of the moon, blown away by the wind; and through the open windows came a scent of flowers—a subtle mingling of wallflower and stock—wafted in upon the night air in overpowering persistence.

Lady Georgia's irritation against life increased.

The scent of certain flowers often made her unhappy, and an alliance of stock and wallflowers was more than she could bear.

'Why is that horrid Mrs Gaveston staying here?' she complained, 'the sort of woman who will play Debussy before lunch when every village child knows that he should be only listened to by electric light, and why did Genevieve pack my Vauvenargues—the only man that has ever really understood me—in my riding skirt at the bottom of my box? Still perhaps a little poetry will compose me almost as well, something about daffodils, I think, and tired, tired shepherds, asleep under great big trees, with a glimpse of Mount Etna through the branches.'

And she crossed over to the bookcase, moving slowly, her hands clasped above her head, carefully, to avoid crushing her Greek coiffure.

There were a great many books, and the choice was embarrassing.

Lady Georgia read the titles over, murmuring them to herself: *Fabulous Histories of Maids of Honour, The Home Life of Lucrezia Borgia, Mrs Turrit's Adventures in the Harz Mountains, The Cult of Osiris, Prayers for*

Pierrot, and then suddenly her eyes fell on a curious-looking book, bound in ivory-coloured parchment.

At the sight of the book—she could scarcely explain it—her heart stood still. Trembling, she stretched out a hand towards it, setting as she did so, a-shiver, like breaking icicles, the crystals on her gown. Something warned her not to touch it, she felt the book would wield a fatal influence over her life, over the lives perhaps of others . . .

For a moment her hands fluttered like two lost doves towards the motherly linen back of *Mrs Turrit*; she would find safety there. But no! the very shape of the little parchment-bound volume fascinated her, and realizing the futility of resistance, with trembling fingers she untied the strings.

The book seemed of great age, it felt damp to the touch, and as Lady Georgia opened the cover she expectantly shuddered.

At first, one might have supposed it to be an unused diary: it seemed to contain only a number of blank pages, stained at the edges to the faint gold of autumn leaves, but in the centre, a small red blot, dusky, and not unlike a drop of blood, made Lady Georgia scream beneath her breath. Above the blot, in a sinister and quivering hand, was written in Gothic characters: *Spells and Incantations*.

Starting exquisitely, Lady Georgia glanced fearfully over her shoulder.

In the long mirror behind her, she could see her willowy form, misty as a painting by Carrière, and even at such a moment, she could not help admiring the sheen of her dressing-gold gown as it caught the light or the ravishing angle of her arm. 'It's no use . . .'

In the dim flare of candles, the tapestried walls lurked with shadows. Here, and there, the white form of a unicorn feeding unconcernedly in a flowery field, made startling the summer twilight, and walking demurely through the tall grasses strange virgins passed in never ceasing chain, with necks bowed, absorbed in the perusal of austere Missals, their threadbare feet very pale on the ice-blue grass. While, through the open windows, over the still branches of the trees, the full moon rose languidly, like a heavy flower, tired with the little moon, still unborn, she carried with her.

Her nerves delicately vibrating with a fear of the Unknown, withal pleasurable, Lady Georgia sank down amidst the piled-up cushions, determined to read everything, missing not even the preface should there so happen to be one. Her attention was arrested from the very first. With breathless interest she read the opening chapter, written in the same wizardlike hand, and entitled: 'On the Invocation of Devils'.

Enthralled, she passed on to the second which dealt minutely with 'The Conjuring up of Spooks and of Divers Furious Beasts', but it was the third chapter with the simple heading: 'On the Overthrowing and Upsetting of Public Buildings, and the Houses of Private Individuals', which made her pause and look up. After a brief interval in which it would be difficult to follow her dazzling train of thought Lady Georgia continued to read: 'It is better,' began the chapter, 'and in order to ensure complete success, that the building selected be situated within a short distance of lake, river, or sea.' Here followed an amiable dissertation on fifteenth-century architecture, in which the author spoke in glowing terms of Cathedrals, Mosques, and Venetian palaces, mentioning casually, that he himself had, after an unsettled boyhood, lived for many years in Paris, in the belfry of the Church of Saint Julian des Pauvres. The chapter, after pleasant gossip, went on to say that: 'A firm faith in, and a proper conviction of the uselessness, architecturally or otherwise, of the said building, was essential in bringing about its irrevocable doom.'

Then followed a number of mystic words, and the directions for the casting of the spell. The book came impressively to an abrupt end with the words, 'Amen Selah!'

The sound of the dinner gong at that moment brought Lady Georgia to reality.

Radiant with happy purpose, she rose from her depth of cushions, shaking out, as she did so, her green skirts as might a bird its wings. Her plans were made . . . she had only to write them down in her engagement book. Proceeding mechanically to the dressing table, with the aid of Poudre Rachel, and spirits of roses, she obliterated with expert fingers all traces of her recent emotion.

'I want to be beautiful tonight', she murmured, 'and just a trifle abandoned-looking for I think I caught sight of Captain Dimsdale in the hall, as I came upstairs. I do hope so, superb pet!' An entrancing vision stretched before her. At last her prayer was granted, she was to be a *force* in the world. Emperors should quail before her. With the edge of her handkerchief she waved aside the last trace of powder from her nose. But before turning her attention to various little places abroad—Mrs Gaveston's villa at Cannes for instance—she decided there was work for her to do nearer home. A few of her friends' town houses must be seen

to first, and hurriedly, she made the following little list on the fly leaf of
a *Life of St Rose de Lima*.

> Madame Lemoine
> The Dowager Lady Hoop
> Jane Seafairer
> Lady Lydia Lamp
> Mr Pecklesnaff
> Miss Venetia Yorking
> Princess Doria Grimaldi
> Rachel and Emily Blueharnis.

'Nobody could possibly know what the list means,' she said to herself
as she went downstairs, 'anybody would think it a dinner list, if (which
is not very probable) they had the curiosity to peep into St Rose's *Life*;
although poor little Mr Pecklesnaff amongst eight women . . .!' and she
laughed. But her initial experiment? Who could for a moment doubt
it? She would overturn the Foreign Office into the lake in St James's
Park, and at the same time debarrass herself of her husband.

2

It was a Tuesday afternoon, a Tuesday more drowsy than any Tuesday he
could remember, in all his long reign at the Foreign Office, and Lord
Blueharnis nodded in his efforts to keep awake. He was writing to his
old friend General Lovelock to thank him for a rare cactus that had
arrived that morning from the East. 'The flower is most exceptional,' he
wrote, 'It is a most exceptional flower.'

Decidedly there was something peculiar in the atmosphere that day,
the air was so still, it seemed bewitched.

In St James's Park, the swans brooded motionless under the shadow
of the trees, and a woman, hidden behind a green parasol, had sat by the
water's edge since early morning, as though too indolent to walk away.

There was something sinister Lord Blueharnis thought in that
motionless green parasol; the very shape of it troubled him. From the
adjoining room the faint sound of 'presses' opening and shutting broke
the drowsy stillness. For twenty years he had been familiar with the
sound, and just now it soothed him.

'It is a most exceptional flower', and again his eyes strayed towards the
park.

'Monstrous,' he thought, 'to be detained in London at this time of year; there was Georgia gadding about in Scotland and enjoying her-self . . . but was she in Scotland? She had not written for over a week; it was most extraordinary.'

A young man entered the room with a sheaf of papers.

'Any news?' asked Lord Blueharnis.

'They have caught King Bomba at last,' murmured the young man vaguely, 'but excuse me, Sir, have you noticed the colour of the sky?'

'Is it not the colour of the seventh veil of that remarkable Greek dancer, whom I once had the pleasure of seeing perform at "Tea" in your mother's drawing room? To be more precise, is the sky not blue?'

It was one of Lord Blueharnis's idiosyncrasies to address those younger than himself in the tones of a duke in a Jacobean melodrama.

'The sky is *not* blue,' answered the young man in a strange voice, 'it is vert de paon', and with that he withdrew as quietly as he came. The sky had in truth undergone a sudden metamorphosis.

A gold and peacock-green cloud, like an Eastern prayer carpet, was advancing leisurely towards St James's Park; it seemed for a moment as though it would shatter itself against the tower of Westminster Cath-edral, but swooping cautiously aside avoided the contact. Following at a short distance behind, two small clouds in close conspiracy threaded their way; and these two small clouds were the most beautiful Lord Blueharnis had ever seen. They were of all the colours of an Indian twi-light, fringed at the edges with a deep rim of silver fire.

'If a painter were to paint such a sky,' reflected Lord Blueharnis, 'everybody would say it was quite incredible.'

A golden gloom sweeping up from the direction of the Embankment added to the strange feeling of unreality, but what astonished Lord Blue-harnis most, was the extraordinary steely glint on the lake in St James's Park. He noticed also that the green parasol was no longer there. The wind, suddenly rising, began to sway the yielding trees in a riotous valse, and bore off triumphantly the last loose petals of the summer roses, scat-tering them like a handful of gems through the park. An ilex tree, unas-sailable, one would have supposed, by the virtue of size, and age, became infected by the mad music of the storm, and lifting up a pon-derous branch, proceeded to perform a pas de seul; her myriad leaves, fluttering about her in the wind, like the ribbons on a monster crino-line, oblivious both of her dignity as the oldest tree in the park, and of the little white hands of the Queen who had planted her there, two hundred years ago.

'Can it be a portent of war?' asked Lord Blueharnis anxiously. 'It would be too tiresome if it were, for I have not had a change since Easter.'

It was now no longer possible to see and turning on the electric light, his Lordship sat down to complete his letter. Outside, the wind and lightning were terrific, and a gentle swaying of the floor gave him the impression of being in a train de luxe; and this reminded him of a curious incident that had once befallen him in a train de luxe, between Seville and Madrid, and with a sigh he took down a sumptuous folio, in which for some time, he had been writing his reminiscences.

Whenever Lord Blueharnis took down his reminiscences he sighed, for what were reminiscences but a vain crying after a youth that had slipped beyond recall?

After a few moments he began to write.

'It was a gorgeous evening, I remember,' he began, 'I was second attaché in Madrid in those days, and . . . it was a corridor train. Sh! but I anticipate. I had noticed on the platform at Seville, a lady—deeply veiled. Distinguished? She was the most distinguished creature I had ever seen; even under her heavy veil and long dust-cloak. I think she first attracted my attention as she stooped to buy some violets, and wild cyclamen, from a little barefooted child. There was something regal about her as she stooped, and irresistibly she suggested to me Alcestis. But her nationality was what puzzled me, and hoping to gain a clue I followed her to the bookstall. Evidently, she, on her side, had been studying me through her veil, and not impossibly suspecting my motive, made her choice of papers expressly for my benefit; for it was decidedly complex.

'*Gil Blas, The Morning Post, Der Vaterland, Osservatore Romano, Los Madrileños*, a Russian novel by Maxim Gorki, and a Turkish periodical, with a gorgeous supplement of a massacre, printed in two colours—red and blue. As she turned away from the bookstall laden, I saw the gleam of her eyes beneath her veil, and . . . they were the most magnetic eyes; eyes once seen never forgotten. By the time the train arrived—which was quite an hour late—I was enormously intrigued to find out who my Alcestis could be. To my delight she installed herself in the next compartment to mine, and through the thin partition I could hear her directing the porter where to place her luggage in a voice of quite exceptional beauty. It was a gorgeous evening, and after a while, we both watched the sun dip below the mountains from the corridor;

when it had quite disappeared, she sighed a long fluttering sigh—and returned to her seat to watch the moon rise from the other side. Alas, the pity of it! the opportunity to ingratiate myself seemed to have forever gone. Soon afterwards, I am ashamed to say I fell asleep. My dreams took me to the Opéra Comique and as I slept I seemed to hear Gluck's music, and the voice of Alcestis chanting at the cavern's mouth, "Divinité du Styx". I awoke suddenly; surely there could be no mistaking it . . . the low penetrating voice of a woman, and the soft thrum-thrum of a guitar. *She* was evidently singing. Tiptoe I stole out into the corridor, and as I stood there spellbound, watching her, I think I may have experienced some of the emotion the Magi felt, when they first saw the Madonna's face. Seated in the full light of the Spanish moon, the intensely white moonlight of Spain, her veil raised, a guitar pressed against her breast, her eyes drinking in as she sang, the shadowy mountains, the orange-clad hills, sat the Empress of——.'

3

It was Easter. Six months had gone by since the 'sad affair of the Foreign Office'; and in the solitude of a landaulette Lady Georgia sat turning over the leaves of her husband's newly published *Memoirs*, the only thing saved out of the débris with the exception of an agate tie-pin which nobody had yet claimed. Instinctively she glanced at the last page. 'Tiptoe I stole out into the corridor,' she read, 'and as I stood there spellbound, watching her, I think I may have experienced some of the emotion the Magi felt, when they first saw the Madonna's face. Seated in the full light of the Spanish moon, the intensely white moonlight of Spain, her veil raised, a guitar pressed against her breast, her eyes drinking in as she sang, the shadowy mountains, the orange-clad hills, sat the Empress of——.'

'Poor man!' murmured Lady Georgia, 'he was evidently writing when the blow came, but how like him to leave off where he did!'

She was looking her very best, in an immense mourning hat, turned up behind, and caught together by a bunch of black violets almost as large as pansies; a penitent-looking feather waved about her left ear, whilst an audacious veil, thickly speckled with velvet, was thrown over all. This veil, which scarcely suggested widowhood, was the only little licence she allowed herself; the rest of her gown was of the strictest rigour; 'decorous' her maid had described it as she put it on.

She closed the book impatiently. 'I am miserable, utterly, utterly miserable,' she complained. 'How Blueharnis has made me suffer . . . how much renounce! Oh! the weariness of a long mourning! but I suppose I should feel thankful that Rachel and Emily went about the same time, it will save beginning all over again. And to think I may not wear green without making everyone look shocked or surprised for at least another six months. Green!' she cried lyrically, 'colour—mine! I do not care about you in trees, nor do I like you in vineyards, or meadows, and least of all at sea! But in *rooms*, in *carpets*, in *brocades*, and oh! in *gowns*, you are the only colour that brings to me content. When I remember that green négligé at Clotilde's, the tears start to my eyes. Consider! a négligé is as short-lived as a flower, shorter sometimes, for sleeves will alter in a night! and this particular négligé was so perishable, a puff of air would have destroyed it. The subtlest thing! I see it now . . . neither blue nor green, like the eggshell of a thrush, with frail clusters of Hops, falling from the arms, and the model that wore it—an ugly plain little thing— had silver vine leaves in her hair. Oh! if I have committed any sin (and my conscience does not tell me that I have), I have been cruelly and bitterly punished.' She leaned back, tired a little, with the excess of her emotion. After a moment, she picked up one of two unopened letters that lay beside her. Of one she knew the writing, it was from Captain Dimsdale, the other looked dull and official.

Breaking the seal she read.

Dearest Queen,

Your handwriting is beautiful. It is both mystical, and emotional, but like all really beautiful things, it does not reveal itself at once. I gather you ask me to dine with you tonight at a quarter to eight? Nothing could give me greater pleasure.

Guy Dimsdale

'Enchanting being! how he understands me!' Lady Georgia sighed.

At the second letter she smiled; the exquisitely candid smile of the Gioconda . . . The letter was to ask her whether she would lay the foundation stone of the new Foreign Office.

'I think I must!' she exclaimed, 'it will be a delightful situation, and I shall enjoy it immensely. There will be solemn speeches, and I shall be presented with a trowel and a bouquet of flowers. I suppose I must be in half-mourning—violet chiffon, and emeralds, and an elaborate sunshade; it will be the greatest fun!'

At Stanhope Gate, Lady Georgia leaned forward with languid

interest. Men were removing the last stones that were left standing of the Princess Doria Grimaldi's house.

'It was the least successful of all my attempts, but certainly it made the most perfect ruin,' she mused, 'and now I have an uninterrupted view of the Park.'

'Where next your ladyship?' asked her chauffeur.

'Back to Clotilde's.'

But at the corner of Dover Street she changed her mind.

After all one must pay the price of one's actions—that was life, as a widow 'green' would be a scandal, the négligé must be renounced. The punishment seemed out of all proportion to the offence.

'Clotilde's, your ladyship?'

'No, to the Oratory,' she called faintly.

SYLVIA TOWNSEND WARNER

A Widow's Quilt

'EMMA loves museums,' said Helena, 'and I think it's good for her to look at things being still, for a change, instead of that incessant jiggety-jog of television. Not like us when we were young, Charlotte—though you were never so tied to the box as I was.'

'I hated watching people breathe.'

The sisters were visiting the American Museum at Claverton, in Somerset. It was Charlotte's first visit.

'Do you come here often?'

'Yes. It's an easy run from Bristol, and I enjoy buying fancy jams from their shop. Expensive. But traditional things are always expensive. And Henry likes them. You should take something back to Everard.'

'Remind me to.'

Emma was staring into a quiescent period parlour. 'That clock doesn't strike,' she said. 'Why doesn't it strike, Mummy? Hasn't it got an inside? Is it too old to be wound up?' Other visitors smiled, murmured, seemed inclined to enter into conversation. 'Now I want to see the blue dogs.'

They moved on into the quilt room. It was hung with pieced and appliqué quilts, brilliant as an assembly of macaws. Emma ran from one to another, identifying the blue dogs in an appliqué miscellany of rose-buds, hatchets, stars, kites, apples, horsemen, and shawled ladies en-circling Abraham Lincoln in a stovepipe hat, quitting them for a geometrical pieced design of lilac and drab.

'Queen Charlotte's Crown—that's for you, Aunt Charlotte. And here's Fox and Geese.'

'Darling! Don't touch.'

One would always have to be being patient, thought Charlotte. On the whole she was glad she did not have a child. Her attention was caught by a quilt that stood out from the others, dominating their rich vivacity with a statement of dulled black on white. She moved towards it.

'That's a widow's quilt,' said Helena. 'Narrow, you see, for a single bed. I suppose you made one for yourself, when your husband died. Or your friends made it for you. Rather grisly.'

'I think it's a hideous quilt,' Emma said.

They descended to the shop, where Charlotte was reminded of the something she must take back to Everard, and chose horehound candies. Then Helena drove her to the station, and she made her platform thanks and farewells. 'I particularly enjoyed the quilts,' she said. 'One doesn't see enough blue dogs.'

But between Bath and London Charlotte sat in a dreamlike frenzy, planning the construction of her own black-and-white quilt. Built up from hexagons, and narrow, it would not be more than a winter's work, once she had assembled its materials: half a dozen exact geometrical hexagons; heavy paper, over which she would tack her patches; fine needles for the small stitches; a couple of sheets. The black would not be so easily found—that lustreless soot-black, dead-rook black. Perhaps she might find some second-hand weeds in the Chelsea fantasy boutiques. Or should she qualify the white unanimity of the sheets by using a variety of blacks already available? There were remains of the official blacking-out curtains drawn over the windows at home during the war, kept to come in useful, her mother had said, and still kept in the inherited piece box from which she had pulled fragments of chintz for the patchwork cushion cover started for Great-Aunt Emma but never completed. There was the black shawl bought at Avignon; some black taffeta; some sateen; quantities of black velvet. As she recalled these varieties of black, the design of her widow's quilt shaped itself to her mind's eye. In the centre, a doubled, even a trebled ring of black velvet hexagons massively enclosing the primal hexagon of white wedding-dress brocade. Extending to the four corners of the quilt, long black diagonals, the spaces between interspersed with star-spangled black hexagons not too close together, and for a border a funeral wreath of black hexagons conjoined.

Dizzied, she got out of the terminus because everyone else was doing so, and took a wasteful taxi to the usual address without realizing she was going home.

Next morning, as soon as Everard had tapped the barometer, put on the indicated topcoat, and left for his office (he was a partner in a firm that sold rare postage stamps), she chose the pair of sheets and went out to buy the fine needles, going on to F. Wilkens, Electrician and Household Repairs—for during the night it had occurred to her that the basic

hexagons would be much more satisfactory if they were exact to measure and cut out of tin. F. Wilkens, oddly calling them templates, knew
exactly what she meant, and would have them ready in half an hour. She
spent the interval in the Health Food Shop, buying Everard's muesli,
then collected the templates and went back to the flat in Perivale Mansions. By the time he returned she had assembled most of the double
garland of black velvet round the wedding-dress brocade, folded it away
in a pillowcase, and prepared supper.

That night her pleasure in the progress of the black velvet garland was
soured by seeing it as so much done already. At this rate, the quilt would
be snatched from her hands, no more to the purpose than a daisy chain.
Patch after patch would lessen her private entertainment; the last patch
in the border of black hexagons would topple her over the edge to
drown in the familiar tedium. She did not want to make another quilt,
or any other kind of quilt. This was her only, her nonpareil, her one
assertion of a life of her own. When Everard left for his office, she hardly
dared take out the pillowcase. While stitching in the first white hexagons, she realized the extent of even a single-bed quilt. She need not
despair for some time yet.

By midday it was raining steadily. The barometer's counsel of an
umbrella was, as usual, justified. The sound of rain was agreeable to
work to. It rained. She worked. Between two and three in the afternoon, finding herself extremely hungry, she ravaged the larder for an
impromptu meal—unwontedly delicious, since she fed on the tinned
delicacies.

The weekend jolted her out of her contentment. Two days of Everard at home she was inured to, but to waste two days without setting a
stitch in the quilt was torment. She festered in idleness; she had never
hated his company more. And it increased her exasperation that he
should be unaware of it.

Yet as time went on, and the quilt enlarged, and weekends fell into
the pattern of her existence as though they were recurring hexagons of
an unassimilable material which she would presently unpick, her disposition changed; she was complacent, she was even benign. Strange, to
think that Everard, whose demands and inroads had compelled her to
such an abiding rancour that seeing the widow's quilt had given her a
purpose in life, should have supplied this soothing influence. Meanwhile she went on with the quilt, never losing sight of its intimations
and in the main preserving her original scheme—though the diagonal

had to be revised: the single black line lacked emphasis, and had to be changed to a couple of lines hedging a band of white. This, in turn, involved a reconsideration of the corners. The solution had been found (there was exactly the right amount of the black shawl to supply its hexagons) when Christmas stared her in the face—and Everard. She could not securely hope that his seasonal influenza would keep him coughing in bed and out of her way; but she was on fire to get at the revised corners, and told herself that a little publicity would be the surest safeguard of the secrecy which was an essential ingredient in her pleasure. On Christmas Eve Everard came home to find her with the quilt on her knee. He glanced at it warily, as though it were something that might disagree with him. When it was there next day and the day after, he mentioned its presence.

'What's that, Charlotte—all those bits you're sewing together?'

She displayed it.

'How nicely you've done it. What's it for?'

'In time it will be a quilt.'

'Oh. So it's not finished yet.'

'No. Not yet.'

She stitched in another hexagon.

'Do you make it up as you go along?'

'I saw one like it in the American Museum.'

'In a museum. How interesting. Was that black and white too?'

'Yes. It's a traditional pattern. It's called a magpie quilt.'

'Magpie? Magpie? Oh, because it's black and white, I suppose. Quite imaginative.'

She stitched, Everard pondered.

'I wonder the United States Post Office doesn't use these old designs—now that they go in for so many commemorative stamps.'

She thought of the blue dogs, but refrained.

By the New Year Everard's cough was so insistent that he had to give up taking his temperature. She foresaw herself stitching her widow's quilt at his bedside. Instead, his partner brought a Puerto Rican violet for his opinion. Finding it spurious, Everard felt equal to going back to his office.

With the enlarging days the quilt gathered momentum. It outgrew the pillowcase and had to be folded away in a bedspread. Each morning it seemed to have grown in the night; each day it was more responsive, more compliant. The hexagons fitted into place as if drawn by a magnet. It had a rationality now, a character; the differing blacks superimposed a pattern of their own, as well-kept fields do with the various tints of their crops. She was so much at ease with it that she could let her thoughts stray as she worked—not so far as to make a mistake, though. She hated mistakes, even those she could unpick. But looking forward to the time when she would rightfully sleep under it, her mind made excursions to places where she might go as a quiet travelling widow. To Lincolnshire, perhaps, with its 'fields of barley and of rye' bordering the river—a sinuous, slow-flowing river with no conversation, effortlessly engulfing the chatter of Tennysonian brooks. Then, on the one hand, a quiet cross-country bus would show her Boston Stump outlined against the pale eastern sky, or, catching a train at Dukeries Junction Station, she would survey the Vale of Beauvoir.

Not since her marriage had she gone beyond the Home Counties, and these had only been visited at licensed holiday seasons: a dab of green at Easter, in August a smear of summer with Everard's cousins in Surrey. Meanwhile, she had travelled a great deal in theory, studying guidebooks and ordnance maps and railway guides, even a list of bus routes in East Anglia which had chanced her way. The row of Methuen's Little Guides in the bookcase on her side of the bed had assured her in detail of the existence of what imagination left visionary: churches (E. E., Perp., restored in 1870), the number of different species of bat in Essex, an almshouse or a gasworks, a disused bridge, a local industry, an extensive prospect of rolling country, a forgotten battlefield, a clay soil, a sandy loam, floodmarks, plantations of conifer, a canal. On the whole, it was the dullish Midlands she preferred; romantic extremities, like Cornwall, could come later.

She was stitching away at Everard's demise—every hexagon brought it a step nearer—when Helena, who was in London to visit her dressmaker, came on to Perivale Mansions. After a momentary gasp, Helena admired the quilt, now three-quarters done.

'And what are you going to stuff it with?'

'Stuff it?'

'It would have to be interlined and stitched through to the backing, you know. Otherwise it wouldn't be a quilt. The one you admired in the museum has harps outlined in stitching—I suppose she felt strongly about Ireland.' She talked on about New England quilting bees, and left before Everard was due to return.

There was nothing for it but to swallow the shock, be glad that the quilt could continue into summer, and decide on the stitched design which should complete it. Not harps, anyhow. A speedy crisscross would be about as much as she could manage. For with the added weight of the backing and the interlined padding, the quilt would be too heavy to handle comfortably, could become a drudgery—another marital obligation, almost another Everard.

She began to make mistakes, straying from the order of her design, choosing the black sateen when it should have been the fustier black of the curtain material. Twice she sewed in a hexagon back side uppermost. The thread tangled, slid out of the needle's eye. When she came to re-thread a needle, she had to make shot after shot at it, holding the needle with a grip of iron, poking the thread at it with a shaking hand. Her heart thumped. Her fingers swelled.

If I were sensible, she thought, I would take to my bed. But the voice of reason reminded her of Everard's disconsolate fidgeting, his dependence on her (Where do I find the toaster? Oh dear, the milk has boiled over again! What am I to mop it up with?) when she had rheumatic fever. She was not in a fit state to be an invalid. The widow's quilt, even if at the moment it was thwarting her intentions, was the more enlivening companion.

She was in the last corner now. It was mid-March, and the east wind was howling down the street like the harlot's curse, when the last of her misfortunes, the silliest and most derisive, tripped her: she had no more thread. She shook some of the ache out of her back, put on her thickest coat, eased her swollen hands into gloves, grimaced at the barometer, and went downstairs and out. It was as though the wind had whirled her out of herself. She was loose again, the solitary traveller, and back in Lincolnshire. She took the narrow road across the saltmarsh flats between her and the sea. They stretched on either hand, featureless, limitless. Nothing would gainsay their level till the enormous breakers reared up, one driven forward on another, and fell with a crash and a flump on the beach. The wind streamed through her; she fought it with every step, and was one with it. At the corner of Perivale Street and Sebastopol Terrace a burly holidaymaker off an advertisement was blown overhead, exclaiming 'Skegness Is So Bracing!'

She had to struggle for breath before she could ask for thread and civilly agree with the shopwoman that the wind was quite savage, wasn't it. And, indeed, as she walked back she could hardly walk straight. The wind was still roaring in her ears when she stood in the hallway of Perivale Mansions, with the stairs in front of her—three flights, each of seventeen steps. She paused on the first landing. The roaring in her ears had changed and was now loud beats on a gong. Twice seventeen was twice seventeen. She mounted the second flight. The gong beat on, but irregularly—thunder to the flashes of lightning across her eyes. At the foot of the third flight she stumbled and fell. She saw her gloved hands clutch the air. A little paper bag fell from one of them. Two reels of thread escaped from it, rolled along the landing, and went tap-tapping down the stairs. Another of her misfortunes. Her lips tried to grin but had turned to lead. The wind had blown out all the lights, and down in the hallway the sea rose higher and higher. A seventh wave, a master wave, would surge up the stairs she had climbed so painfully, thrust its strength beneath her, carry her away like a wisp of seaweed. She was still vaguely alive when Everard almost tripped over her. He called 'Help! Help!' and blew the police whistle he always carried on his key ring.

'There was something wrong with her heart,' he said to Helena, who came next morning. 'It might have happened at any moment. You can imagine what a shock it was to me. I think I must move.' He had not much to say, but he talked incessantly. 'At first I thought she had been killed. You can imagine what I felt. There is so much violence about nowadays—no post office is safe. I never felt easy leaving her. But it was something wrong with her heart. She was everything to me, every-thing, my poor Charlotte. Where do you think I should go?'

Helena had picked up the quilt and began folding it.

'And there's that quilt. What should we do about it? It's not finished, you see. Poor Charlotte, so unfortunate! It's a magpie quilt.'

'Magpie?'

'Yes, because it's all black and white—like the birds, she said.'

'I see.'

'I can't very well take it with me. Yet it would be a pity to throw it away. Could you take charge of it, Helena? It would be a weight off my mind if you would. You'd know how to finish it, and I don't suppose it would take you very long. Not that there's any hurry now. And then you could keep it, to remember her by. I'm sure she'd like you to have it. It meant a great deal to her.'

ALDOUS HUXLEY

Nuns at Luncheon

'WHAT have I been doing since you saw me last?' Miss Penny repeated my question in her loud, emphatic voice. 'Well, when did you see me last?'

'It must have been June,' I computed.

'Was that after I'd been proposed to by the Russian General?'

'Yes; I remember hearing about the Russian General.'

Miss Penny threw back her head and laughed. Her long earrings swung and rattled—corpses hanging in chains: an agreeably literary simile. And her laughter was like brass, but that had been said before.

'That was an uproarious incident. It's sad you should have heard of it. I love my Russian General story. "*Vos yeux me rendent fou.*" ' She laughed again.

Vos yeux—she had eyes like a hare's, flush with her head and very bright with a superficial and expressionless brightness. What a formidable woman. I felt sorry for the Russian General.

' "*Sans cœur et sans entrailles*," ' she went on, quoting the poor devil's words. 'Such a delightful motto, don't you think? Like "*Sans peur et sans reproche*". But let me think; what have I been doing since then?' Thoughtfully she bit into the crust of her bread with long, sharp, white teeth.

'Two mixed grills,' I said parenthetically to the waiter.

'But of course,' exclaimed Miss Penny suddenly. 'I haven't seen you since my German trip. All sorts of adventures. My appendicitis; my nun.'

'Your nun?'

'My marvellous nun. I must tell you all about her.'

'Do.' Miss Penny's anecdotes were always curious. I looked forward to an entertaining luncheon.

'You knew I'd been in Germany this autumn?'

'Well, I didn't, as a matter of fact. But still—'

'I was just wandering round.' Miss Penny described a circle in the air with her gaudily jewelled hand. She always twinkled with massive and improbable jewellery. 'Wandering round, living on three pounds a week, partly amusing myself, partly collecting materials for a few little articles. "What it Feels Like to be a Conquered Nation"—sob-stuff for the Liberal press, you know—and "How the Hun is Trying to Wriggle out of the Indemnity", for the other fellows. One has to make the best of all possible worlds, don't you find? But we mustn't talk shop. Well, I was wandering round, and very pleasant I found it. Berlin, Dresden, Leipzig. Then down to Munich and all over the place. One fine day I got to Grauburg. You know Grauburg? It's one of those picture-book German towns with a castle on a hill, hanging beer-gardens, a Gothic church, an old university, a river, a pretty bridge, and forests all round. Charming. But I hadn't much opportunity to appreciate the beauties of the place. The day after I arrived there—bang!—I went down with appendicitis—screaming, I may add.'

'But how appalling!'

'They whisked me off to hospital, and cut me open before you could say knife. Excellent surgeon, highly efficient Sisters of Charity to nurse me—I couldn't have been in better hands. But it was a bore being tied there by the leg for four weeks—a great bore. Still, the thing had its compensations. There was my nun, for example. Ah, here's the food, thank Heaven!'

The mixed grill proved to be excellent. Miss Penny's description of the nun came to me in scraps and snatches. A round, pink, pretty face in a winged coif; blue eyes and regular features; teeth altogether too perfect—false, in fact; but the general effect extremely pleasing. A youthful Teutonic twenty-eight.

'She wasn't my nurse,' Miss Penny explained. 'But I used to see her quite often when she came in to have a look at the *tolle Engländerin*. Her name was Sister Agatha. During the war, they told me, she had converted any number of wounded soldiers to the true faith—which wasn't surprising, considering how pretty she was.'

'Did she try and convert you?' I asked.

'She wasn't such a fool.' Miss Penny laughed, and rattled the miniature gallows of her ears.

I amused myself for a moment with the thought of Miss Penny's conversion—Miss Penny confronting a vast assembly of Fathers of the Church, rattling her ear-rings at their discourses on the Trinity, laughing her appalling laugh at the doctrine of the Immaculate Conception, meeting the stern look of the Grand Inquisitor with a flash of her bright, emotionless hare's eyes. What was the secret of the woman's formidableness?

But I was missing the story. What had happened? Ah yes, the gist of it was that Sister Agatha had appeared one morning, after two or three days' absence, dressed, not as a nun, but in the overalls of a hospital charwoman, with a handkerchief instead of a winged coif on her shaven head.

'Dead,' said Miss Penny; 'she looked as though she were dead. A walking corpse, that's what she was. It was a shocking sight. I shouldn't have thought it possible for anyone to change so much in so short a time. She walked painfully, as though she had been ill for months, and she had great burnt rings round her eyes and deep lines in her face. And the general expression of unhappiness—that was something quite appalling.'

She leaned out into the gangway between the two rows of tables, and caught the passing waiter by the end of one of his coat-tails. The little Italian looked round with an expression of surprise that deepened into terror on his face.

'Half a pint of Guinness,' ordered Miss Penny. 'And, after this, bring me some jam roll.'

'No jam roll today, madam.'

'Damn!' said Miss Penny. 'Bring me what you like, then.'

She let go of the waiter's tail, and resumed her narrative.

'Where was I? Yes, I remember. She came into my room, I was telling you, with a bucket of water and a brush, dressed like a charwoman. Naturally I was rather surprised. "What on earth are you doing, Sister Agatha?" I asked. No answer. She just shook her head, and began to scrub the floor. When she'd finished, she left the room without so much as looking at me again. "What's happened to Sister Agatha?" I asked my nurse when she next came in. "Can't say."—"Won't say," I said. No answer. It took me nearly a week to find out what really had happened. Nobody dared tell me; it was *strengst verboten*, as they used to say in the good old days. But I wormed it out in the long run. My nurse, the doctor, the charwomen—I got something out of all of them. I always get what I want in the end.' Miss Penny laughed like a horse.

'I'm sure you do,' I said politely.

'Much obliged,' acknowledged Miss Penny. 'But to proceed. My information came to me in fragmentary whispers. "Sister Agatha ran away with a man."—Dear me!—"One of the patients."—You don't say so.—"A criminal out of the jail."—The plot thickens.—"He ran away from her."—It seems to grow thinner again.—"They brought her back here; she's been disgraced. There's been a funeral service for her in the chapel—coffin and all. She had to be present at it—her own funeral. She isn't a nun any more. She has to do charwoman's work now, the roughest in the hospital. She's not allowed to speak to anybody, and nobody's allowed to speak to her. She's regarded as dead." ' Miss Penny paused to signal to the harassed little Italian. 'My small "Guinness",' she called out.

'Coming, coming,' and the foreign voice cried 'Guinness' down the lift, and from below another voice echoed, 'Guinness'.

'I filled in the details bit by bit. There was our hero, to begin with; I had to bring him into the picture, which was rather difficult, as I had never seen him. But I got a photograph of him. The police circulated one when he got away; I don't suppose they ever caught him.' Miss Penny opened her bag. 'Here it is,' she said. 'I always carry it about with me; it's become a superstition. For years, I remember, I used to carry a little bit of heather tied up with string. Beautiful, isn't it? There's a sort of Renaissance look about it, don't you think? He was half-Italian, you know.'

Italian. Ah, that explained it. I had been wondering how Bavaria could have produced this thin-faced creature with the big dark eyes, the finely modelled nose and chin, and the fleshy lips so royally and sensually curved.

'He's certainly very superb,' I said, handing back the picture.

Miss Penny put it carefully away in her bag. 'Isn't he?' she said. 'Quite marvellous. But his character and his mind were even better. I see him as one of those innocent, childlike monsters of iniquity who are simply unaware of the existence of right and wrong. And he had genius—the real Italian genius for engineering, for dominating and exploiting nature. A true son of the Roman aqueduct builders he was, and a brother of the electrical engineers. Only Kuno—that was his name—didn't work in water; he worked in women. He knew how to harness the natural energy of passion; he made devotion drive his mills. The commercial exploitation of love-power, that was his speciality. I sometimes wonder,' Miss Penny added in a different tone, 'whether I shall ever be exploited, when I get a little more middle-aged and celibate, by one of these young engineers of the passions. It would be humiliating, particularly as I've done so little exploiting from my side.'

She frowned and was silent for a moment. No, decidedly, Miss Penny was not beautiful; you could not even honestly say that she had charm or was attractive. That high Scotch colouring, those hare's eyes, the voice, the terrifying laugh, and the size of her, the general formidableness of the woman. No, no, no.

'You said he had been in prison,' I said. The silence, with all its implications, was becoming embarrassing.

Miss Penny sighed, looked up, and nodded. 'He was fool enough,' she said, 'to leave the straight and certain road of female exploitation for the dangerous courses of burglary. We all have our occasional accesses of folly. They gave him a heavy sentence, but he succeeded in getting pneumonia, I think it was, a week after entering jail. He was transferred to the hospital. Sister Agatha, with her known talent for saving souls, was given him as his particular attendant. But it was he, I'm afraid, who did the converting.'

Miss Penny finished off the last mouthful of the ginger pudding which the waiter had brought in lieu of jam roll.

'I suppose you don't smoke cheroots,' I said, as I opened my cigar-case.

'Well, as a matter of fact, I do,' Miss Penny replied. She looked sharply round the restaurant. 'I must just see if there are any of those horrible little gossip paragraphers here today. One doesn't want to figure in the social and personal column tomorrow morning: "A fact which is not so generally known as it ought to be, is that Miss Penny, the well-known woman journalist, always ends her luncheon with a six-inch Burma cheroot. I saw her yesterday in a restaurant—not a hundred miles from Carmelite Street—smoking like a house on fire." You know the touch. But the coast seems to be clear, thank goodness.'

She took a cheroot from the case, lit it at my proffered match, and went on talking.

'Yes, it was young Kuno who did the converting. Sister Agatha was converted back into the worldly Melpomene Fugger she had been before she became the bride of holiness.'

'Melpomene Fugger?'

'That was her name. I had her history from my old doctor. He had seen all Grauburg, living and dying and propagating, for generations. Melpomene Fugger—why, he had brought little Melpel into the world, little Melpchen. Her father was Professor Fugger, the great Professor Fugger, the *berühmter Geolog*. Oh yes, of course, I know the name. So

well . . . He was the man who wrote the standard work on Lemuria—
you know, the hypothetical continent where the lemurs come from. I
showed due respect. Liberal-minded he was, a disciple of Herder, a
world-burgher, as they beautifully call it over there. Anglophile, too,
and always ate porridge for breakfast—up till August 1914. Then, on the
radiant morning of the fifth, he renounced it for ever, solemnly and
with tears in his eyes. The national food of a people who had betrayed
culture and civilization—how could he go on eating it? It would stick
in his throat. In future he would have a lightly boiled egg. He sounded,
I thought, altogether charming. And his daughter, Melpomene—she
sounded charming, too; and such thick, yellow pigtails when she was
young! Her mother was dead, and a sister of the great Professor's ruled
the house with an iron rod. Aunt Bertha was her name. Well,
Melpomene grew up, very plump and appetizing. When she was seventeen, something very odious and disagreeable happened to her. Even
the doctor didn't know exactly what it was; but he wouldn't have been
surprised if it had had something to do with the then Professor of Latin,
an old friend of the family's, who combined, it seems, great erudition
with a horrid fondness for very young ladies.'

Miss Penny knocked half an inch of cigar ash into her empty glass.

'If I wrote short stories,' she went on reflectively '(but it's too much
bother), I should make this anecdote into a sort of potted life history,
beginning with a scene immediately after this disagreeable event in
Melpomene's life. I see the scene so clearly. Poor little Melpel is leaning
over the bastions of Grauburg Castle, weeping into the June night and
the mulberry trees in the gardens thirty feet below. She is besieged by
the memory of what happened this dreadful afternoon. Professor
Engelmann, her father's old friend, with the magnificent red Assyrian
beard . . . Too awful—too awful! But then, as I was saying, short stories
are really too much bother; or perhaps I'm too stupid to write them. I
bequeath it to you. You know how to tick these things off.'

'You're generous.'

'Not at all,' said Miss Penny. 'My terms are a ten per cent commission
on the American sale. Incidentally there won't be an American sale.
Poor Melpchen's history is not for the chaste public of Those States.
But let me hear what you propose to do with Melpomene now you've
got her on the castle bastions.'

'That's simple,' I said. 'I know all about German university towns and
castles on hills. I shall make her look into the June night, as you suggest;

into the violet night with its points of golden flame. There will be the black silhouette of the castle, with its sharp roofs and hooded turrets, behind her. From the hanging beer-gardens in the town below the voices of the students, singing in perfect four-part harmony, will float up through the dark-blue spaces. "*Röslein, Röslein, Röslein rot*" and "*Das Ringlein sprang in zwei*"—the heart-rendingly sweet old songs will make her cry all the more. Her tears will patter like rain among the leaves of the mulberry trees in the garden below. Does that seem to you adequate?'

'Very nice,' said Miss Penny. 'But how are you going to bring the sex problem and all its horrors into your landscape?'

'Well, let me think.' I called to memory those distant foreign summers when I was completing my education. 'I know. I shall suddenly bring a swarm of moving candles and Chinese lanterns under the mulberry trees. You imagine the rich lights and shadows, the jewel-bright leafage, the faces and moving limbs of men and women, seen for an instant and gone again. They are students and girls of the town come out to dance, this windless, blue June night, under the mulberry trees. And now they begin, thumping round and round in a ring, to the music of their own singing:

> *Wir können spielen*
> *Vio-vio-vio-lin,*
> *Wir können spielen*
> *Vi-o-lin.*

Now the rhythm changes, quickens:

> *Und wir können tanzen Bumstarara,*
> *Bumstarara, Bumstarara,*
> *Und wir können tanzen Bumstarara,*
> *Bumstarara-rara.*

The dance becomes a rush, an elephantine prancing on the dry lawn under the mulberry trees. And from the bastion Melpomene looks down and perceives, suddenly and apocalyptically, that everything in the world is sex, sex, sex. Men and women, male and female—always the same, and all, in the light of the horror of the afternoon, disgusting. That's how I should do it, Miss Penny.'

'And very nice, too. But I wish you could find a place to bring in my conversation with the doctor. I shall never forget the way he cleared his throat and coughed before embarking on the delicate subject. "You may know, ahem, gracious Miss," he began—"you may know that religious phenomena are often, ahem, closely connected with sexual causes." I replied that I had heard rumours which might justify me in believing this to be true among Roman Catholics, but that in the Church of England—and I for one was a practitioner of Anglicanismus—it was very different. That might be, said the doctor; he had had no opportunity in the course of his long medical career of personally studying Anglicanismus. But he could vouch for the fact that among his patients, here in Grauburg, mysticismus was very often mixed up with the *Geschlechtsleben*. Melpomene was a case in point. After that hateful afternoon she had become extremely religious; the Professor of Latin had diverted her emotions out of their normal channels. She rebelled against the placid Agnosticismus of her father, and at night, in secret, when Aunt Bertha's dragon eyes were closed, she would read such forbidden books as *The Life of St Theresa*, *The Little Flowers of St Francis*, *The Imitation of Christ*, and the horribly enthralling *Book of Martyrs*. Aunt Bertha confiscated these works whenever she came upon them; she considered them more pernicious than the novels of Marcel Prévost. The character of a good potential housewife might be completely undermined by reading of this kind. It was rather a relief for Melpomene when Aunt Bertha shuffled off, in the summer of 1911, this mortal coil. She was one of those indispensables of whom one makes the discovery, when they are gone, that one can get on quite as well without them. Poor Aunt Bertha!'

'One can imagine Melpomene trying to believe she was sorry, and horribly ashamed to find that she was really, in secret, almost glad.' The suggestion seemed to me ingenious, but Miss Penny accepted it as obvious.

'Precisely,' she said; 'and the emotion would only further confirm and give new force to the tendencies which her aunt's death left her free to indulge as much as she liked. Remorse, contrition—they would lead to the idea of doing penance. And for one who was now wallowing in the martyrology, penance was the mortification of the flesh. She used to kneel for hours, at night, in the cold; she ate too little, and when her teeth ached, which they often did,—for she had a set, the doctor told me, which had given trouble from the very first,—she would not go and see the dentist, but lay awake at night, savouring to the full her excruciations, and feeling triumphantly that they must, in some strange way, be pleasing to the Mysterious Powers. She went on like that for two or three years, till she was poisoned through and through. In the end she went down with gastric ulcer. It was three months before she came out of hospital, well for the first time in a long space of years, and with a brand new set of imperishable teeth, all gold and ivory. And in mind, too, she was changed—for the better, I suppose. The nuns who nursed her had made her see that in mortifying herself she had acted supererogatively and through spiritual pride; instead of doing right, she had sinned. The only road to salvation, they told her, lay in discipline, in the orderliness of established religion, in obedience to authority. Secretly, so as not to distress her poor father, whose Agnosticismus was extremely dogmatic, for all its unobtrusiveness, Melpomene became a Roman Catholic. She was twenty-two. Only a few months later came the war and Professor Fugger's eternal renunciation of porridge. He did not long survive the making of that patriotic gesture. In the autumn of 1914 he caught a fatal influenza. Melpomene was alone in the world. In the spring of 1915 there was a new and very conscientious Sister of Charity at work among the wounded in the hospital of Grauburg. Here,' explained Miss Penny, jabbing the air with her forefinger, 'you put a line of asterisks or dots to signify a six years' gulf in the narrative. And you begin again right in the middle of a dialogue between Sister Agatha and the newly convalescent Kuno.'

'What's their dialogue to be about?' I asked.

'Oh, that's easy enough,' said Miss Penny. 'Almost anything would do. What about this, for example? You explain that the fever has just abated; for the first time for days the young man is fully conscious. He feels himself to be well, reborn, as it were, in a new world—a world so bright and novel and jolly that he can't help laughing at the sight of it. He looks about him; the flies on the ceiling strike him as being extremely comic. How do they manage to walk upside down? They have suckers on their feet, says Sister Agatha, and wonders if her natural history is quite sound. Suckers on their feet—ha, ha! What an uproarious notion! Suckers on their feet—that's good that's damned good! You can say charming, pathetic, positively tender things about the irrelevant mirth of convalescents—the more so in this particular case, where the mirth is expressed by a young man who is to be taken back to jail as soon as he can stand firmly on his legs. Ha, ha! Laugh on, unhappy boy! It is the quacking of the Fates, the Parcae, the Norns!'

Miss Penny gave an exaggerated imitation of her own brassy laughter. At the sound of it the few lunchers who still lingered at the other tables looked up, startled.

'You can write pages about Destiny and its ironic quacking. It's tremendously impressive, and there's money in every line.'

'You may be sure I shall.'

'Good! Then I can get on with my story. The days pass and the first hilarity of convalescence fades away. The young man remembers and grows sullen; his strength comes back to him, and with it a sense of despair. His mind broods incessantly on the hateful future. As for the consolations of religion, he won't listen to them. Sister Agatha perseveres—oh, with what anxious solicitude!—in the attempt to make him understand and believe and be comforted. It is all so tremendously important, and in this case, somehow, more important than in any other. And now you see the *Geschlechtsleben* working yeastily and obscurely, and once again the quacking of the Norns is audible. By the way,' said Miss Penny, changing her tone and leaning confidentially across the table, 'I wish you'd tell me something. Do you really—honestly, I mean—do you seriously believe in literature?'

'Believe in literature?'

'I was thinking,' Miss Penny explained, 'of Ironic Fate and the quacking of the Norns and all that.'

' 'M yes.'

'And then there's this psychology and introspection business; and construction and good narrative and word pictures and *le mot juste* and verbal magic and striking metaphors.'

I remembered that I had compared Miss Penny's tinkling ear-rings to skeletons hanging in chains.

'And then, finally, and to begin with—Alpha and Omega—there's ourselves: two professionals gloating, with an absolute lack of sympathy, over a seduced nun, and speculating on the best method of turning her misfortunes into cash. It's all very curious, isn't it?—when one begins to think about it dispassionately.'

'Very curious,' I agreed. 'But, then, so is everything else if you look at it like that.'

'No, no,' said Miss Penny. 'Nothing's so curious as our business. But I shall never get to the end of my story if I get started on first principles.'

Miss Penny continued her narrative. I was still thinking of literature. Do you believe in it? Seriously? Ah! Luckily the question was quite meaningless. The story came to me rather vaguely, but it seemed that the young man was getting better; in a few more days, the doctor had said, he would be well—well enough to go back to jail. No, no. The question was meaningless. I would think about it no more. I concentrated my attention again.

'Sister Agatha,' I heard Miss Penny saying, 'prayed, exhorted, indoctrinated. Whenever she had half a minute to spare from her other duties she would come running into the young man's room. "I wonder if you fully realize the importance of prayer?" she would ask, and, before he had time to answer, she would give him a breathless account of the uses and virtues of regular and patient supplication. Or else it was: "May I tell you about St Theresa?" or "St Stephen, the first martyr—you know about him, don't you?" Kuno simply wouldn't listen at first. It seemed so fantastically irrelevant, such an absurd interruption to his thoughts, his serious, despairing thoughts about the future. Prison was real, imminent, and this woman buzzed about him with her ridiculous fairy-tales. Then, suddenly, one day he began to listen, he showed signs of contrition and conversion. Sister Agatha announced her triumph to the other nuns, and there was rejoicing over the one lost sheep. Melpomene had never felt so happy in her life, and Kuno, looking at her radiant face, must have wondered how he could have been such a fool as not to see from the first what was now so obvious. The woman had lost her head about him. And he had only four days now—four days in which to tap the tumultuous love power, to canalize it, to set it working for his escape. Why hadn't he started a week ago? He could have made certain of it then. But now? There was no knowing. Four days was a horribly short time.'

'How did he do it?' I asked, for Miss Penny had paused.

'That's for you to say,' she replied, and shook her earrings at me. 'I don't know. Nobody knows, I imagine, except the two parties concerned and perhaps Sister Agatha's confessor. But one can reconstruct the crime, as they say. How would you have done it? You're a man, you ought to be familiar with the processes of amorous engineering.'

'You flatter me,' I answered. 'Do you seriously suppose—' I extended my arms. Miss Penny laughed like a horse. 'No. But, seriously, it's a problem. The case is a very special one. The person, a nun; the place, a hospital; the opportunities, few. There could be no favourable circumstances—no moonlight, no distant music; and any form of direct attack would be sure to fail. That audacious confidence which is your amorist's best weapon would be useless here.'

'Obviously,' said Miss Penny. 'But there are surely other methods. There is the approach through pity and the maternal instincts. And there's the approach through Higher Things, through the soul. Kuno must have worked on those lines, don't you think? One can imagine him letting himself be converted, praying with her, and at the same time appealing for her sympathy and even threatening—with a great air of seriousness—to kill himself rather than go back to jail. You can write that up easily and convincingly enough. But it's the sort of thing that bores me so frightfully to do. That's why I can never bring myself to write fiction. What is the point of it all? And the way you literary men think yourselves so important—particularly if you write tragedies. It's all very queer, very queer indeed.'

I made no comment. Miss Penny changed her tone and went on with the narrative.

'Well,' she said, 'whatever the means employed, the engineering process was perfectly successful. Love was made to find out a way. On the afternoon before Kuno was to go back to prison, two Sisters of Charity walked out of the hospital gates, crossed the square in front of it, glided down the narrow streets towards the river, boarded a tram at the bridge, and did not descend till the car had reached its terminus in the farther suburbs. They began to walk briskly along the high road out into the country. "Look!" said one of them, when they were clear of the houses; and with the gesture of a conjurer produced from nowhere a red leather purse. "Where did it come from?" asked the other, opening her eyes. Memories of Elisha and the ravens, of the widow's cruse, of the loaves and fishes, must have floated through the radiant fog in poor Melpomene's mind. "The old lady I was sitting next to in the tram left her bag open. Nothing could have been simpler." "Kuno! You don't mean to say you stole it?" Kuno swore horribly. He had opened the purse. "Only sixty marks. Who'd have thought that an old camel, all dressed up in silk and furs, would only have sixty marks in her purse? And I must have a thousand at least to get away." It's easy to reconstruct the rest of the conversation down to the inevitable, "For God's sake, shut up," with which Kuno put an end to Melpomene's dismayed moralizing. They trudge on in silence. Kuno thinks desperately. Only sixty marks; he can do nothing with that. If only he had something to sell, a piece of jewellery, some gold or silver—anything, anything. He knows such a good place for selling things. Is he to be caught again for lack of a few marks? Melpomene is also thinking. Evil must often be done that good may follow. After all, had not she herself stolen Sister Mary of the Purification's clothes when she was asleep after night duty? Had not she run away from the convent, broken her vows? And yet how convinced she was that she was doing rightly! The mysterious Powers emphatically approved; she felt sure of it. And now there was the red purse. But what was a red purse in comparison with a saved soul—and, after all, what was she doing but saving Kuno's soul?' Miss Penny, who had adopted the voice and gestures of a debater asking rhetorical questions, brought her hand with a slap on to the table. 'Lord, what a bore this sort of stuff is!' she exclaimed. 'Let's get to the end of this dingy anecdote as quickly as possible. By this time, you must imagine, the shades of night were falling fast—the chill November twilight, and so on; but I leave the natural descriptions to you. Kuno gets into the ditch at the roadside and takes off his robes. One imagines that he would feel himself safer in trousers, more capable of acting with decision in a crisis. They tramp on for miles. Late in the evening they leave the high road and strike up through the fields towards the forest. At the fringe of the wood they find one of those wheeled huts where the shepherds sleep in the lambing season.'

'The real "Maison du Berger".'

'Precisely,' said Miss Penny, and she began to recite:

> *Si ton cœur gémissant du poids de notre vie*
> *Se traîne et se débat comme un aigle blessé. . . .*

'How does it go on? I used to adore it all so much when I was a girl:

> *Le seuil est parfumé, l'alcôve est large et sombre,*
> *Et là parmi les fleurs, nous trouverons dans l'ombre,*
> *Pour nos cheveux unis un lit silencieux.*

I could go on like this indefinitely.'

'Do,' I said.

'No, no. No, no. I'm determined to finish this wretched story. Kuno broke the padlock of the door. They entered. What happened in that little hut?' Miss Penny leaned forward at me. Her large hare's eyes glittered, the long earrings swung and faintly tinkled. 'Imagine the emotions of a virgin of thirty, and a nun at that, in the terrifying presence of desire. Imagine the easy, familiar brutalities of the young man. Oh, there's pages to be made out of this—the absolutely impenetrable darkness, the smell of straw, the voices, the strangled crying, the movements!

And one likes to fancy that the emotions pulsing about in that confined space made palpable vibrations like a deep sound that shakes the air. Why, it's ready-made literature, this scene. In the morning,' Miss Penny went on, after a pause, 'two woodcutters on their way to work noticed that the door of the hut was ajar. They approached the hut cautiously, their axes raised and ready for a blow if there should be need of it. Peeping in, they saw a woman in a black dress lying face downwards in the straw. Dead? No; she moved, she moaned. "What's the matter?" A blubbered face, smeared with streaks of tear-clotted grey dust, is lifted towards them. "What's the matter?"—"He's gone!" What a queer, indistinct utterance. The woodcutters regard one another. What does she say? She's a foreigner, perhaps. "What's the matter?" they repeat once more. The woman bursts out violently crying. "Gone, gone! He's gone," she sobs out in her vague, inarticulate way. "Oh, gone. That's what she says. Who's gone?"—"He's left me."—"What?"—"Left me . . ."—"What the devil . . .? Speak a little more distinctly."—"I can't," she wails; "he's taken my teeth."—"Your what?"—"My teeth!"—and the shrill voice breaks into a scream, and she falls back sobbing into the straw. The woodcutters look significantly at one another. They nod. One of them applies a thick yellow-nailed forefinger to his forehead.'

Miss Penny looked at her watch.

'Good heavens!' she said, 'it's nearly half-past three. I must fly. Don't forget about the funeral service,' she added, as she put on her coat. 'The tapers, the black coffin in the middle of the aisle, the nuns in their white-winged coifs, the gloomy chanting, and the poor cowering creature without any teeth, her face all caved in like an old woman's, wondering whether she wasn't really and in fact dead—wondering whether she wasn't already in hell. Goodbye.'

MALACHI WHITAKER

Landlord of the Crystal Fountain

A TALL, good-looking, red-haired school teacher of about thirty stood in King's Cross Station one Friday afternoon trying to find enough change for her ticket. She had a violent headache, and frowned as she fumbled in her brown leather bag.

Her name was Brenda Millgate, and she was going north for the week-end to see her sister. It was purely a visit of duty; she had nothing whatever in common with Doris, and she looked upon the week-end as wasted already.

Nothing would go right for her. A few coppers rolled from her fingers, and she felt embarrassed as obsequious strangers handed pennies back to her. But at length the ticket was bought, and she picked up her week-end case and walked resolutely on to Platform Ten. The bookstall was further down on her left, but she felt too tired to go down and buy any of the alluring-looking magazines offered for sale. There was not much time. She had had to hurry as it was. And now she found the train was crowded.

She was dressed very neatly in brown, and had on a cream-coloured blouse with buttons that very nearly matched the colour of her hair. She had also a brown silk umbrella with a shining orange knob on it, and there was an orange leather band across her brown handbag.

In spite of her knowledge that she looked both well and intelligent, there seemed to be no room for her. There was a place or two in the non-smoking carriages, but she did not like the stink that came out of them. 'You can get the smell of smoke out of your clothes,' she thought, 'but not that—that other.' She did not know what to call it. But though she walked quickly up and down the platform in her brown shoes, she could find nowhere suitable, and had to jump up and stand in the corridor at last. Just behind her, she heard a loud, hearty voice saying something that was followed by a burst of laughter. She put down her case, and watched the bookstall glide smoothly past the window. Then she turned her head to see how many people were in the carriage behind her.

Why, there was a seat! In fact, only five men were sitting down, but five such big men she had never before seen together. They seemed to fill the place to overflowing. Probably there were lots more seats on the train, but her head was so bad that she could hardly see them. The door of the carriage opened, and a friendly voice said, 'Do come in here, miss. There's plenty of room.'

'Thank you,' she said gratefully. She felt tired enough to faint or to fall asleep.

The five big men rearranged themselves and let her sit in a corner seat near the window. For a few minutes they gave her all their attention until they had her settled and comfortable. One put her case on the rack, another even helped her off with her hat, the one opposite moved so that she could put her feet up on the seat, the fourth asked her if she would like a paper to read, and the fifth one stood up laughing and said, 'Now we're all comfortable, aren't we?'

She sank back with a sigh of relief. 'I've got such an awful headache. This is lovely, lovely.'

One of them made a joke about her red hair, and she laughed softly. 'You're all together, aren't you?' she asked. 'Friends?'

'Yes, friends,' they answered, and one of them said 'All together.'

She sank almost immediately into a kind of stupor, in which she could hear the dulled rattle of the train wheels and the quiet hum of voices. 'Why are these men so pleasant?' she wondered. 'So steeped in comfortableness?' It felt nice to be with them.

After a short while she woke, feeling much better, and began to study her fellow-travellers. 'What great hulking men,' she thought, 'and yet how considerate they are.' Not one of them had started to smoke.

'Smoke if you like,' she said. 'I like the smell. But first of all, do tell me what you are. What do you do? I've been wondering ever since I saw you.'

The man in the far corner leaned forward. He had thinning black hair brushed as far as it would go round a dome-like forehead.

'We're landlords, my girl,' he said. 'Landlords, all of us. We've every one got licensed houses.'

'Pubs,' her mind flashed.

'You're all very big landlords,' she said.

He wagged his finger at her, 'Ah, it's the life.' He took out a pipe and filled it, and began to smoke.

'Tell me the names of your—your houses,' she said.

'The Golden Lion at Firley Green; The White Horse at Itterington; The Case is Altered (that's a puzzler, isn't it, miss?) just at the entrance to Hay Park; The Crown, Bridge Road.'

They were all busy, but one, pulling card-cases out of their pockets. 'We've been up to a convention; a spree, by God. Hush, we've had the time of our lives!'

Then she looked across at the man who sat opposite, the one who had moved so that she might put her feet up. He was, she thought, the tallest of them all. He had a red face and tight, straw-coloured curls thick over his head. His eyes were blue-grey. He wore a dark suit and a black tie. He had not yet spoken. 'What's the name of yours?'

'I'm proud of the name of mine,' he said, 'but I haven't any cards on me.'

The others all handed their cards to her, and she took them impatiently, leaning forward, looking at the straw-haired giant, whose deep voice had at the same time pleased and startled her. 'What is it? What's the name of yours?'

'All in good time,' he said, smiling slowly. 'It's called the Crystal Fountain.'

Then the others began to talk about their homes and their lives. They discussed their wives, and announced themselves as henpecked men, all but the landlord of the Crystal Fountain, who kept silent. He and Brenda sat looking at each other in perfect contentment, listening to the talk around them.

Casually they brought out stacks of sandwiches, and made her share them. At first, she was full of dismay. Sandwiches—dry sandwiches in a train! Yet presently she was eating one of salmon and cucumber.

'But this is real salmon,' she cried in astonishment, 'and the cucumber's as fresh as a drink of water.'

'Of course it is,' one shouted. 'We know what to buy and where to buy it.'

'You didn't get them near here, I'll bet.'

'But we did. And within a stone's throw of King's Cross, too.'

The sandwiches melted away like snow in a thaw. There was enough for everybody. Brenda got plenty of compliments—on her height, on her appetite, on her red hair. She blushed with pleasure.

After the meal, they all relaxed, leaning back and unfastening buttons that had become too tight. One or two smoked. The dome-headed one offered her cigarettes, and when she refused one, he was glad.

'Not speaking in a business way, of course,' he said. 'I've nothing against it. We see it, practically speaking, every evening of our lives. It wouldn't do for us to be prejudiced. But I'm glad.'

Brenda slipped her feet down from the opposite seat, sighing with joy. She had not the least idea why she now felt so happy.

'I've never met any landlords socially,' she thought. 'No, I've never met a landlord before in my life. Publicans. Publicans and sinners. Perhaps they were like this when Jesus was alive. No wonder He . . .' She dozed again.

She thought of her life, of her mother's ambition that she should be a teacher. She thought with astonishment of the examinations she had passed, the years of pleasant training. She was not in the least clever. She had no retentive memory. But somehow everything had come to her. Flukes, flukes. And she *was* good with children—just plain good at getting on with people, with the heads, with her fellow teachers.

And because she had liked the children who flowed under, rather than passed through her hands, and had spent her time hoping that here and there a silk purse dwelt among the pigs' ears, she had not thought a great deal about men.

There was one who thought of her, and she knew it. But she was not in any way satisfied with him. He was shorter than she was—small, dark, dry and meticulous. He liked her to be a kind of imitation of himself. He had the power of making her feel that she would eventually marry him; that one day, when she was tired and sick of school and all that it meant, she would turn to him. So he simply waited.

She did not dislike him physically. She was tolerant, and adaptable, ready to make the best of anything. His name was Claud Foden.

She opened her eyes and looked across at the landlord of the Crystal Fountain. He was studying her gravely. He leaned forward and spoke quietly. 'My God,' he said, 'but you're a nice woman. I suppose you're more a lady, though.'

'No,' she answered him just as quietly, 'woman's the word,' and soon she was telling him about herself.

'My father kept a shop. Well, my stepfather, and Doris—that's my sister—and I went to school on his money. He was a butcher, a big fine man with curly hair like yours, only white. I don't remember my own father. My mother always used to tell us that she had married again so that we could have a good education. She didn't know much, but she was ambitious. I'm supposed to know a lot, but I'm not ambitious that way, at all. I'm a teacher, but I've just begun to wonder why I'm a teacher, for my heart isn't in it. It's with the children, all right, but not with what I'm supposed to be teaching them.'

She felt astonished to hear these words coming from her mouth. She did not usually talk like that. No, she used a sort of jargon, a 'we're all girls together' kind of language. Anything to crush down her height and healthiness, her over-exuberance. She really envied the dim creatures who tripped about like neat mice, knowing she could never grow like them. Her red hair was thick and curly, and it shone; when she saw it in a mirror, she knew that it was beautiful, but always thought disparagingly of people who liked that kind of thing.

The two sat looking at each other, admiring each other. The other four men were talking among themselves. They leaned back, stretching out their legs. Their firm calves touched each other, so that their blood seemed to flow through one body rather than two. They kept on looking at each other with absorbed pleasure as the train rushed through the gathering darkness.

Brenda began to think dreamily that she would like to have a dressing-gown of orange and green, and a link of great amber beads like lumps of sucked toffee. And imitation pearls—only they must be great big ones, too. She would like to have rings on her fingers, 'and bells on my toes' she murmured, and dangling gold earrings.

'And now listen to me,' the man opposite said, in his voice that could be deep and quiet at the same time, 'for I've got a lot to say to you. I don't know much about you—you're not married, by any chance, are you?'

'No.'

'Well, I have been, to a fine girl, none better. For five years. But she's dead now. She's gone and can't be brought back. I'm wanting another wife. I'm wanting her quick, and I think you'll do. What do you say?'

'You'll have to let me think.'

'Well, don't take long, then, for we haven't far to go. I want you to come with me to see the place, but you'll like it. I've no fear of that. I like it. It's out at Ella Syke, on the moor edge. You might find it a bit quiet, but I don't. What do you say, lass?'

She was thinking, 'This can't often happen to people. It's never happened to anyone I know. But I'm going to do it.'

A silence had fallen over the carriage. She said, 'All right, then, as soon as you like.'

'That's good.'

'I'll have to send a telegram to Doris. She's expecting me. But do you think I'd make you a good wife—in a business way, I mean?' She had no other qualms.

'I'll soon teach you. But you might have been born to it.' He stood up and presented her gravely to his four friends. 'Any one of them'll vouch for me,' he said. 'There's no underhand business here. And I expect to call and see your sister in a day or so. We'll make a special day of the wedding.'

The five big men took everything for granted, and fell to talking again, while the girl leaned back and thought. There would certainly be a lot of fuss about her job. Doris would be astounded. It would mean a fresh start in life. She would never see Claud Foden again as long as she lived.

On the other hand, this new bliss that had grown up in her would never leave her. She was ready to go on. 'It'll be hard work, and different work, but I'll do it.' There must be some of her mother's ambition in her, she thought. Here it was. Her eyes blazed with a new light.

She carried her own case, because he had one of his own. They walked across the grey northern station to find a telegraph office behind the closed Post Office. But he took hold of her arm with his free hand, and she liked the firm way it held her. Yet she could think of nothing to put in the telegram except: 'Don't worry about me. I am going to the Crystal Fountain.'

V. S. PRITCHETT

On the Edge of the Cliff

THE sea fog began to lift towards noon. It had been blowing in, thin and loose for two days, smudging the tops of the trees up the ravine where the house stood. 'Like the cold breath of old men,' Rowena wrote in an attempt at a poem, but changed the line, out of kindness, to 'the breath of ghosts', because Harry might take it personally. The truth was that his breath was not foggy at all, but smelt of the dozens of cigarettes he smoked all day. He would walk about, taking little steps, with his hand outstretched, tapping the ash off as he talked. This gave an abstracted searching elegance which his heavy face and long sentences needed. In her dressing gown Rowena went to his room. His glasses were off and he had finished shaving and he turned a face savaged to the point of saintliness by age, but with a heavy underlip that made him look help-lessly brutal. She laughed at the soap in his ears.

'The ghosts have gone,' she said poetically. 'We can go to Withy Hole! I'll drive by the Guilleth road, there's a fair there. They'll tell our fortunes.'

'Dull place,' he said. 'It used to be full of witches in the sixteenth century.'

'I'm a witch,' she said. 'I want to go to the fair. I saw the poster. It starts today.'

'We'll go,' he said, suspicious, but giving in.

He was seventyish, and with a young girl of twenty-five one had, of course, to pretend to be suspicious. There are rules for old men who are in love with young girls, all the stricter when the young girls are in love with them. It has to be played as a game.

'The sea pinks will be out on the cliffs,' he said.

'You old botanist!' she said.

He was about to say 'I know that' and go on to say that girls were like flowers with voices and that he had spent a lot of his life collecting both, but he had said these things to her often before and at his age one had to avoid repeating oneself, if possible. Anyway, it was more effective as a compliment when other people were there and they would turn to look at her. When young girls turned into women they lost his interest: he had always lived for reverie.

'So it's settled,' she said.

Now he looked tragic as he gazed at her. Waving his razor, he began his nervous trick of taking a few dance-like steps and she gave him one of her light hugs and ran out of the room.

What with his organizing fusses and her habit of vanishing to do something to a drawing she was working on, the start was late.

'We'll have to eat something,' she said, giving an order.

But it was his house, not hers. He'd lived alone long enough not to be able to stand a woman in his kitchen, could not bear to see her cut a loaf or muddle the knives and forks or choke the sink with tea leaves.

'Rowena and I,' he said to people who came to see them, in his military voice, 'eat very little. We see no one.'

This was not true, but like a general with a literary turn, he organized his imagination. He was much guided by literature. His wife had gone mad and had killed herself. So in the house he saw himself as a Mr Rochester, or in the car as Count Mosca with the young duchess in *La Chartreuse de Parme*; if they met people, as Tolstoy's worldly aunt. This was another game: it educated the girl.

While he fussed between the kitchen and the room they ate in, she came down late and idled, throwing back her long black hair, lassoing him with smiles and side glances thrown out and rushed at him while he had a butter plate in his hand and gave him another of her light engulfing hugs and laughed at the plate he waved in the air.

'Rowena!' he shouted, for she had gone off again. 'Get the car out.'

The house was halfway up the long ravine, backed and faced by an army of ash trees and beeches. There was the terrace and the ingenious steep garden and the plants that occupied him most of the day, and down from the terrace he had had to cut the twenty or thirty steps himself, heaving his pickaxe. Rowena had watched his thick stack of coarse grey hair and his really rather brutal face and his pushed-out lips, as he hacked and the pick hit the stones. He worked with such anger and pride, but he looked up at her sometimes with appealing, brilliant eyes. His furious ancient's face contained pain naturally.

She knew he hated to be told to be careful when he came down the steps. She knew the ceremony of getting him into the car, for he was a tall, angular man and had to fold himself in, his knees nearly touching his chin, to which the long deep despondent lines of his face ran heavily down. It was exciting for her to drive the old man dangerously fast down the long circling lane through the trees, to show how dangerous she could be, while he talked. He would talk nonstop for the next hour, beginning, of course, with the country fair.

'It's no good. Plastic, like cheap food. Not worth seeing. The twentieth century has packaged everything.'

And he was on to the pre-Roman times, the ancient spirit of carnival, Celtic gods and devils, as they drove out of the ravine into deep lanes, where he could name the ferns in the stone walls, and the twisting hills and corners that shook the teeth and the spine. Historical instances poured out of him. He was, she said, Old Father Time himself, but he did not take that as a joke, though he humoured her with a small laugh. It was part of the game. He was not Father Time, for in one's seventies, one is a miser of time, putting it by, hiding the minutes, while she spent fast, not knowing she was living in time at all.

Guilleth was a dull, dusty, Methodistical little town with geraniums in the windows of the houses. Sammy's Fair was in a rough field just outside it, where dogs and children ran about. There was only one shooting gallery; they were still putting up the back canvas of the coconut shy. There were hoopla stalls, a lot of shouting and few customers. But the small roundabout gave out its engine whistle and the children packed the vulgar circle of spotted cows with huge pink udders, the rocking horses, the pigs, the tigers and a pair of giraffes.

The professor regarded it as a cultural pathos. He feared Rowena. She was quite childishly cruel to him. With a beautiful arrogance that mocked him, she got out of the car and headed for ice cream. He had to head her off the goldfish in their bowls. She'd probably want to bring one home.

'Give me some money,' she said, going to the roundabout. There was a small crowd near that. 'I'm going on the giraffe. Come on.'

'I'll watch you,' he complained and cleaned his glasses.

There she was, riding a giraffe already, tall and like a schoolmistress among the town children, with her long hair, which she kept on throwing back as she whirled round, a young miracle, getting younger and younger. There were other girls. There were town youths and there was an idiotic young man riding backwards on a cow, kicking out his legs and every now and then waving to the crowd. Rowena on her giraffe did not smile, but as she came round sedately, waved to the old man as she sailed by.

He looked at his watch. How much longer?

'I'm going on again,' she called, and did not get off.

He found himself absurdly among the other patient watchers, older than all, better dressed too, on his dignity, all curiosity gone. He moved away to separate himself from his bunch of them, but he had the impression they all moved with him. There was a young woman in a bright-red coat who always seemed to be in the next bunch he joined. Round came the giraffe: round came the young man on the cow. The young woman in red waved. Seeing that to wave was the correct thing, the old man too waved at the giraffe. The woman waved again a moment later and stared at him as if annoyed. He moved a yard from her, then five yards, then to the other side of the roundabout. Here he could wave without being conspicuous, yet the woman was standing close to him once more. She was small with reddish hair, her chin up, looking at him.

'You don't remember me,' she accused him in a high voice. Her small eyes were impudent. He stepped back, gaping.

'Daisy Pyke,' she said.

Pyke? Pyke? He gaped at her briefly, his mind was sailing round with Rowena.

'George's wife,' she said, challenging his stupidity.

'George . . .' But he stopped. George Pyke's wife must be fifty by now. This woman could not be more than thirty. Her daughter—had they had a daughter?

'Have I changed as much as that?' she said. Her manner was urchin-like and she grinned with pleasure at his confusion and then her mouth drooped at the corners plaintively, begging. Nowadays he thought only of Rowena's wide mouth, which made all other women vague to him. And then the hard little begging, pushing mouth and its high voice broke into his memory. He stepped back with embarrassment and a short stare of horror which he covered quickly, his feet dancing a few steps, and saying with foolish smiles, 'Daisy! I thought . . . I was watching that thing. What are you doing here?'

Now that he remembered, he could not conceal a note of indignation and he stood still, his eyes peered coldly. He could see this had its effect on her.

'The same as you,' she said in that curt off-hand voice. 'Waiting. Waiting for them to come off.' And she turned away from him, offended, waved wildly at the roundabout and shouted, 'Stephen, you fool!' The young man riding backwards on the cow waved back and shouted to her.

What an appalling thing! But there it is—one must expect it when one is old: the map in one's head, indeed the literal map of the country empties and loses its contours, towns and villages, and people sink out of sight. The protective faces of friends vanish and one is suddenly alone, naked and exposed. The population ranked between oneself and old enemies suddenly dissolves and the enemy stands before one. Daisy Pyke!

The old man could not get away. He said as politely as he could manage, 'I thought you went abroad. How is George?'

'We did. George,' she said, 'died in Spain.' And added briskly, 'On a golf course.'

'I'm sorry. I didn't know.'

She looked back at the roundabout and turned again to say to him, 'I know all about you. You've got a new house at Colfe. I've still got the old house, though actually it's let.'

Forty miles lay between Colfe and Daisy Pyke—but no people in between! Now the roundabout stopped. There was a scramble of children getting on and getting off, and the local watchers moved forward too.

'I must get Rowena,' he said ruthlessly and he hurried off, calling out in his peremptory voice, 'Rowena!'

He knew that Daisy Pyke was watching him as he held out a hand to help Rowena off, but Rowena ignored it and jumped off herself.

'Rowena. We must go.'

'Why? It was lovely. Did you see that ridiculous young man?'

'No, Rowena,' he said. 'Where?'

'Over there,' she said, 'with the girl in red, the one you were chatting up, you old rip. I saw you!' She laughed and took his arm. 'You're blushing.'

'She's not a girl,' he said. 'She's a woman I used to know in London twenty years ago. It was rather awful! I didn't recognize her. I used to know her husband. She used to be a friend of Violet's.'

'Violet's!' said Rowena. 'But you *must* introduce me.' She was always eager to know, as if to possess, everyone he had ever known, to have all of him, even the dead. Above all Violet, his wife. Rowena longed to be as old as that dead woman.

'Really, Harry, you are frightful with people.'

'Oh, well . . . But she's appalling. We had a terrible row.'

'One of your old loves,' she teased.

'I had to throw her out of the house,' he said. 'She's a liar.'

'Then I *must* see her,' said Rowena. 'How thrilling.'

'I think they've gone,' he said.

'No,' said Rowena. 'There they are. Take me over.'

And she pulled him towards the hoopla stall where Daisy Pyke and the young man were standing. There lay the delightfulness of Rowena: she freed him from the boredom into which his memories had set and hardened. He had known many young girls who in this situation would be eagerly storing opportunities for jealousy of his past life. Rowena was not like that.

At the stall, with its cunningly arranged bowls, jugs, and toys, the young man with the yellow curling hair was pitching rings onto the table, telling Daisy to try and altering the angle of the ring in her hand.

'Choose what you want, hold the ring level and lightly, don't skim fast. Don't bowl it like that! Like this.'

Daisy's boldness had gone. She was fond and serious, glancing at the young man before she threw.

'Daisy,' said the old man, putting on a shady and formal manner as if he were at a party, 'I have brought Rowena to meet you.'

And Rowena stepped forward gushingly. 'How d'you do! I was telling Harry about the young man on the cow.'

'Here he is,' said Daisy stiffly. 'Stephen!'

The young man turned and said 'Hello' and went on throwing rings. 'Like that,' he said.

Rowena watched him mockingly.

'We are just off,' said Harry.

'I've heard a lot about you,' said Daisy to Rowena.

'We're going to walk along the cliffs,' said Harry.

'To Withy Hole,' said Rowena.

'It was extraordinary meeting you here,' said Harry.

'Perhaps,' said Daisy, 'we'll meet again.'

'Oh, well—you know we hardly see anyone now,' said Harry.

Daisy studied Rowena impudently and she laughed at the boy, who had failed again.

'I won a goldfish once,' said Rowena, laughing. 'It died on the way home.'

'Extraordinary,' the old man said as he and Rowena walked away. 'That must be George's son, but taller. George was short.'

When she got him back into the car she saw by his leaden look that the subject was closed. She had met one more of his friends—that was the main thing.

The hills seemed to pile up and the sea to get farther and farther away and then, suddenly, as they got over the last long hill, they passed the caravan sites that were empty at this time of the year and looked like those flat white Andalusian towns he remembered, from a distance. The old man was saying, 'But we have this new rootless civilization, anarchic but standardized'—suddenly the sea appeared between the dunes below, not grey and choppy, but deep blue, all candour, like a young mouth, between the dunes and beyond it, wide and still and sleepily serene. The old man was suddenly in command, fussing about the exact place where they could leave the car, struggling over the sand dunes dotted with last year's litter, on to the huge cliffs. At the top there they could look back and see on the wide bay the shallow sea breaking idly, in changing lines of surf, like lips speaking lines that broke unfinished and could not be heard. A long way off a dozen surfers were wading out, deeper and deeper, towards the bigger waves as if they were leaving the land for good and might be trying to reach the horizon. Rowena stopped to gaze at them, waiting for one of them to come in on a long glissade, but the old man urged her on to the close turf of the cliffs. That is what he had come for: boundlessness, distance. For thirty miles on a clear day in May like this, one could walk without meeting a soul, from headland to headland, gazing through the hum of the wind and under the cries of the dashing gulls, at what seemed to be an unending procession of fading promontories, each dropping to its sandy cove, yet still riding out into the water. The wind did not move the old man's tough thatch of hair but made his big ears stick out. Rowena bound her loose hair with a scarf. From low cliff to high cliff, over the cropped turf, which was like a carpet, where the millions of sea pinks and daisies were scattered, mile after mile in their colonies, the old man led the way, digging his knees into the air, gesticulating, talking, pointing to a kestrel above or a cormorant black as soot on a rock, while she followed lazily yards behind him. He stopped impatiently to show her some small cushioned plant or stood on the cliff's edge, like a prophet, pointing down to the falls of rock, the canyons, caverns, and tunnels into which the green water poured in black and was sucked out into green again and spilled in waterfalls down the outer rocks. The old man was a strong walker, bending to it, but when he stopped he straightened, and Rowena smiled at his air of detachment as he gazed at distant things as if he knew them. To her he looked like a frightening mixture of pagan saint and toiling animal. They would rest at the crest of a black cliff for a few minutes, feel the sun burn their skin, and then on they went.

'We can't see the bay any more,' she said. She was thinking of the surf-riders.

'The cliff after the next is the Hole,' he said and pulled her to her feet.

'Yes, the Hole,' she said.

He had a kind of mania about the Hole. This was the walk he liked best and so did she, except for that ugly final horror. The sea had tunnelled under the rock in several places along this wild coast and had sucked out enormous slaty craters fifty yards across and this one a hundred and eighty feet deep, so that even at the edge one could not see the water pouring in. One stood listening for the bump of hidden water on a quiet day: on wild ones it seethed in the bottom of the pot. The place terrified Rowena and she held back, but he stumbled through the rough grasses to the edge, calling back bits of geology and navigation—and to amuse her, explained how smugglers had had to wait for the low wave to take them in.

Now, once more, they were looking at the great meaningless wound. As he stood at the edge he seemed to her to be at one with it. It reminded her of his mouth when she had once seen it (with a horror she tried to wipe from her mind) before he had put his dentures in. Of her father's too.

Well, the objective was achieved. They found a bank on the seaward side out of the wind where the sun burned and they rested.

'Heaven,' she said and closed her eyes.

They sat in silence for a long time but he gazed at the rising floor of eventless water. Far out, from time to time, in some small eddy of the wind, little families of whitecaps would appear. They were like faces popping up or perhaps white hands shooting out and disappearing pointlessly. Yes, they were the pointless dead.

'What are you thinking about?' she asked without opening her eyes.

He was going to say 'At my age one is always thinking about death,' but he said 'You.'

'What about me?' she said with that shamelessness of girls.

'Your ears,' he said.

'You are a liar,' she said. 'You're thinking about Daisy Pyke.'

'Not now,' he said.

'But you must be,' she said. She pointed. 'Isn't the cove just below where you all used to bathe with nothing on? Did she come?'

'Round the corner,' he said, correcting her. 'Violet and I used to bathe there. Everyone came. Daisy came once when George was on the golf course. She swam up and down, hour after hour, as cold as a fish. Hopeless on dry land. Gordon and Vera came, but Daisy only once. She didn't fit in—very conventional—sat telling dirty stories. Then she went swimming, to clean up. George was playing golf all day and bridge all evening; that didn't go down well. They had a dartboard in their house: the target was a naked woman. A pretty awful, jokey couple. You can guess the bull's-eye.'

'What was this row?' she said.

'She told lies,' he said, turning to her. And he said this with a hiss of finality which she knew. She waited for one of his stories, but it did not come.

'I want to swim in the cove,' said Rowena.

'It's too cold this time of the year,' he said.

'I want to go,' she said.

'It's a long way down and hard coming back.'

'Yes, but I want to go—where you all used to go.'

She was obstinate about this, and of course he liked that.

'All right,' he said, getting up. Like all girls she wanted to leave her mark on places. He noticed how she was impelled to touch pictures in galleries when he had taken her to Italy. Ownership! Power! He used to dislike that but now he did not; the change was a symptom of his adoration of her. And she did want to go. She did want to assert her presence on that empty sand, to make the sand feel her mark.

They scrambled the long way down the rocks until the torn cliffs were gigantic above them. On the smooth sand she ran barefoot to the edge of the sea rippling in.

'It's ice!' she screamed.

He stood there, hunched. There was a litter of last year's rags and cartons near the rocks. Summer crowds now swarmed into the place, which had been secret. He glowered with anger at the debris.

'I'm going to pee,' he said.

She watched the sea, for he was a long time gone.

'That was a big one,' she shouted.

But he was not there. He was out on the rocks, he had pulled off his clothes. He was standing there, his body furred with grey hair, his belly wrinkled, his thighs shrunk. Up went his bony arms.

'You're not to! It will kill you! Your heart!' she shouted.

He gave a wicked laugh, she saw his yellow teeth, and in he dived and was crawling and shouting in the water as he swam out farther, defying her, threshing the water, and then as she screamed at him, really frightened, he came crawling in like some ugly hairy sea animal, his skin reddened with cold, and stood dripping with his arms wide as if he was going to give a howl. He climbed over the rocks and back to the sand and got his clothes and was drying himself with his shirt.

'You're mad,' she said. 'You're not to put that wet thing on.'

'It will dry in this sun,' he said.

'What was all that for?' she said. 'Did you find her?'

'Who?' he said, looking round in bewilderment. He had dived in boastfully and in a kind of rage, a rage against time, a rage against Daisy Pyke too. He did not answer, but looked at her with a glint of shrewdness in his eyes. She was flattered by the glitter in this look from a sometimes terrifying old man.

He was tired now and they took the short inland road to the car close to those awful caravans, and when she got him into the car again he fell asleep and snorted. He went to his room early but could not sleep; he had broken one of his rules for old men. For the first time he had let her see him naked. He was astounded when she came into his room and got into his bed: she had not done this before. 'I've come to see the Ancient Mariner,' she said.

How marvellous. She is jealous, after all. She loves me, he went about saying to himself in the next weeks. She drove to what they called 'our town' to buy cakes. 'I am so thin,' she said.

The first time she returned saying she had seen his 'dear friend Daisy'. She was in the supermarket.

'What's she doing there?' he said. 'She lives forty miles away. What did she say?'

'We did not speak. I mean, I don't think she saw me. Her son was with her. He said hello. He'd got the hood of the car up. She came out and gave me a nod—I don't think she likes me,' she said with satisfaction.

The next week she went again to get petrol. The old man stayed at the house, shook one or two mats, and swept the sitting-room floor. It was his house and Rowena was untidy. Then he sat on the terrace, listening for her car, anxiously.

Presently he picked up the sound, much earlier than her usual time, and saw the distant glint in the trees as the car wound its way up. There she was, threading her beauty through the trees. He heard with alarm the sudden silences of the car at some turn in the hill, then heard it getting louder as it turned a corner, then passing into silence again. He put his book down and went inside in a dutiful panic to put the kettle on, and while he waited for it to boil he took the cups out pedantically, one by one, to the table on the terrace and stood listening again. Now it was on the last stretch, now he heard a crackling of wheels below. He ran in to heat the teapot and ran out with his usual phrase: 'Did you get what you wanted?'

Then, puffing up the last steps, she came. But it was not she; it was a small woman, bare-legged and in sandals, with a swaggering urchin grin on her face, pulling a scarf off her head. Daisy!

'Gosh!' she said.

Harry skipped back a yard and stood, straightening and forbidding. 'Daisy!' he said, annoyed, as if waving her off.

'Those steps! Harry!' she said. 'Gosh, what a view.'

She gave a dry dismissive laugh at it. She had, he remembered, always defied what she saw. The day when he had seen her at the fair seemed to slide away under his feet and years slid by, after that, following that day.

'What—' he began. Then in his military way, he jerked out, 'Rowena's gone into town. I am waiting for her.'

'I know,' said Daisy. 'Can I sit down and get my breath? I know. I saw her.' And with a plotting satisfaction: 'Not to speak to. She passed me. Ah, that's better.'

'We never see people,' said Harry sternly. 'You see I am working. If the telephone rings, we don't answer it.'

'The same with us. I hope I'm not interrupting. I thought—I'll dash up, just for a minute.'

'And Rowena has her work . . .' he said. Daisy was always an interrupter.

'I gave you a surprise,' said Daisy comfortably. 'She is lovely. That's why I came. You're lucky—how d'you do it? Where did you find her? And what a place you've got here! I made Stephen go and see his friends. It was such a long time—years, isn't it? I had to come. You haven't changed, you know. But you didn't recognize me, did you? You were trying not to see me, weren't you?'

Her eyes and her nose were small. She is at her old game of shock tactics, he thought. He looked blankly at her.

'I explained that,' he said nervously. 'I must go and turn the kettle off,' he said. He paused to listen for Rowena's car, but there was no sound.

'Well,' she said. 'There you are. Time goes on.'

When he came back with a teapot and another cup, she said, 'I knew you wouldn't come and see me, so I came to see you. Let me see,' she said and took off the scarf from her head. 'I told you George died, didn't I? Of course I did,' she said briskly.

'Yes.'

'Well . . .' she said. 'Harry, I had to see you. You are the only wise man I know.' She looked nervously at the garden and across to the army of trees stacked on the hill and then turned to him. 'You're happy and I am happy, Harry. I didn't come to make a scene and drag it all up. I was in love with you, that was the trouble, but I'm not now. I was wrong about you, about you and Violet. I couldn't bear to see her suffer. I was out of my mind. I couldn't bear to see you grieving for her. I soon knew what it was when poor George died. Harry, I just don't want you to hate me any more. I mean, you're not still furious, are you? We do change. The past is past.'

The little liar, he thought. What has she come up here for? To cause trouble between himself and Rowena as she had tried to do with his wife and himself. He remembered Daisy's favourite word: honesty. She was trying for some reason to confuse him about things he had settled a long time ago in his mind.

He changed the subject. 'What is—' —he frowned—'I'm sorry, I can't remember names nowadays—your son doing?'

She was quick to notice the change, he saw. Nothing ever escaped Daisy.

'Oh, Tommy, the ridiculous Tommy. He's in Africa,' she said, merrily dismissing him. 'Well, it was better for him—problems. I'm a problem to him—George was so jealous too.'

'He looks exactly like George,' Harry said. 'Taller, of course, the curly hair.'

'What are you talking about? You haven't seen him since he was four.' She laughed.

'Don't be stupid, Daisy, we saw him last week at that—what is the name of the place?—at the fair.'

The blood went from Daisy's face. She raised her chin. 'That's a nasty one,' she said and gave her head a fierce shake. 'You meant it to, didn't you? That was Stephen. I thought you'd be the last to think a thing like that, with your Rowena. I expect people say it and I don't care and if anyone said it to him he wouldn't know what they were talking about. Stephen's my lover.'

The old sentimental wheedling Daisy was in the coy smile that quickly followed her sharpness. 'He's mad about me,' she said. 'I may be old enough to be his mother, but he's sick of squealing, sulky girls of seventeen. If we had met years ago, he would have hated me. Seriously, Harry, I'd go down on my knees to him.'

'I am sorry—I—that's why I didn't recognize you. You can ask Rowena. I said to her, "That's Daisy Pyke's daughter," Harry said, when I saw you.'

Daisy gaped at him and slowly her lips curled up with delight. 'Oh, good! Is that true? Is it? You always told the truth. You really thought that! Thank you, Harry, that's the nicest thing you ever said to me. I love you for it.'

She leaned forward, appealing to him quietly.

'George never slept with me for seven years before he died. Don't ask me about it, but that's the truth. I'd forgotten what it was. When Stephen asked me I thought it was an insult—you know, all this rape about. I got into the car and slammed the door in his face and left him on the road—well, not on the road, but wherever it was—and drove off. I looked back. He was still standing there. Well, I mean, at my age! That next day—*you* know what it is with women better than anyone—I was in such a mood. When I got back to the house I shouted for George, howled for him to come back and poured myself a tumblerful of whisky and wandered about the house slopping it on the carpet.' She laughed. 'George would have killed me for *that* if he had come—and I went out into the garden and there was Stephen, you won't believe it, walking bold as brass up from the gate. He came up quickly and just took the glass from me very politely—the stuff was pouring down my dress—and put it on the grass and he wiped my blouse. That's what did it.'

She paused thoughtfully and frowned. 'Not there,' she said prudishly, 'not at the house, of course. I wanted to get away from it. I can't bear it. We went to the caravan camp. That's where he was living. I don't know why I'm telling you this. I mean, there's a lot more.'

She paused. 'Love is something at our age, isn't it? I mean, when I saw you and Rowena at Guilleth—I thought I must go and talk to you. Being in the same boat.'

'We're not,' he said, annoyed. 'I am twenty years older than you.'

'Thirty, if you don't mind,' she said, opening her bag and looking into her mirror. When she had put it away with a snap she looked over the flowers in the steep garden to the woods. She was listening for the sound of a car. He realized he had stopped listening for it. He found himself enjoying this hour, despite his suspicions of her. It drove away the terrors that seemed to dissolve even the trees of the ravine. With women, nature returned to its place, the trees became real trees. One lived in a long moment in which time had stopped. He did not care for Daisy, but she had that power of enticement which lay in stirring one with the illusion that she was defying one to put her right. With Rowena he had thrown away his vanity; with Daisy it returned.

'Where did you and Rowena go the day we saw you?' she asked suddenly.

'Along the cliffs,' he said.

'You didn't go to the cove, did you? It's a long way. And you can't swim at this time of the year.'

'We went to the cove and I *did* swim,' he said. 'I wouldn't let Rowena.'

'I should hope not! You don't forget old times, do you?' She laughed coolly. 'I hope you didn't tell Rowena—young girls can be so jealous. I *was*—d'you remember? Gosh, I'm glad I'm not young still, aren't you?'

'Stop being so romantic, Daisy,' said the old man.

'Oh, I'm not romantic any more,' she said. 'It doesn't pay else one would pity *them*, Rowena and Stephen. So you did go to the cove—did you think of me?'

'I only think of death now,' he said.

'You always were an interesting man, the type that goes on to his nineties, like they do now,' she said. 'I never think about it. Stephen would have a fit. He doesn't even know what he's going to do. Last week he thought he'd be a beach guard. Or teach tennis. Or a singer! He was surfing on the beach when I first saw him. He was living at the camp.'

She paused, offended. 'Did you know they switch off the electric light at ten o'clock at the office in those places? No one protests. Like sheep. It would make me furious to be treated like that. You could hear everyone snoring at once. Not that we joined in, I must say. Actually, we're staying in his mother's house now, the bunks are too narrow in those caravans, but she's come back. So we're looking for something— I've let my house. The money is useful.'

The old man was alarmed. He was still trying to make out the real reason for her visit. He remembered the old Daisy—there was always a hidden motive, something she was trying out. And he started listening urgently again for Rowena's car. I know what it is, he thought; she wants to move in here!

'I'm afraid it would be impossible to have you here,' he said.

'Here, Harry?' she said, astonished. 'None of that! That's not what I came for. Anyway,' she said archly, 'I wouldn't trust you.'

But she considered the windows and the doors of the house and then the view. She gave a business-like sniff and said seriously, 'You can't keep her a prisoner here. It won't last.'

'Rowena is not a prisoner. She can come and go when she likes. We understand that.'

'It depends what you mean by coming and going,' said Daisy shrewdly. 'You mean you are the prisoner. That is it! So am I!'

'Oh,' said Harry. 'Love is always like that. I live only for her.'

'That is it! I will tell you why I came to see you, Harry. When I saw Rowena in town I kept out of her way. You won't believe it—I can be tactful.'

She became very serious. 'Because I don't want us to meet again.' It was an open declaration. 'I mean not see you for a long time, I mean all of us. You see, Rowena is so beautiful and Stephen—well, you've seen him. You and I would start talking about old times and people, and they'd be left out and drawn together—now, wouldn't they? I just couldn't bear to see him talking to her, looking at her. I wish we had not met down at the fair. It's all right now, he's with his surfing friends, but you understand?'

She got up and said, 'I mean it, Harry. I know what would happen and so do you and I don't want to *see* it happen.'

She went up to him because he had stood up and she tapped him hard on the chest with her firm bold finger. He could feel it on his skin, a determined blow, after she had stepped away.

'I know it can't last,' she said. 'And you know it can't. But I don't want *you* to see it happen,' she said in her old hard taunting style. 'We never really use your town anyway. I'll see *he* doesn't. Give me your word. We've got to do this for each other. We've managed quite well all these years, haven't we? And it's not saying we'll *never* meet someday, is it?'

'You're a bitch, Daisy,' he said, and he smiled.

'Yes, I'm a bitch still, Harry,' she said. 'But I'm not a fool.'

She put out her hand again and he feared she was going to dig that hard finger in his chest again, but she didn't. She tied her scarf round her hair. 'If anything happened I'd throw myself down Withy Hole.'

'Stop being so melodramatic, Daisy,' he said.

'Well, I don't want you conniving,' she said coarsely. 'I don't want any of your little arrangements.'

And she turned to the ravine and listened. 'Car coming up,' she said.

'Rowena,' he said.

'I'll be off. Remember.'

'Be careful at the turns,' he said helplessly. 'She drives fast. You'll pass her on the road.'

They did not kiss or even shake hands. He listened to her cursing the steps as she went down and calling out, 'I bet you dug out these bloody steps yourself.'

He listened to the two cars whining their way towards each other as they circled below, now Rowena's car glinted, now Daisy's. At last Rowena's slowed down at the steps, spitting stones.

Rowena came up and said, 'I've just passed Daisy on the road.'

'Yes, she's been here. What a tale!'

She looked at the empty cups. 'And you didn't give your dearest friend any tea, you wretch.'

'Oh, tea—no—er—she didn't want any,' he stammered.

'As gripping as all that, was it?' she laughed.

'Very,' he said. 'She's talking of marrying that young man. Stephen's not her son.'

'You can't mean that,' she said, putting on a very proper air. 'She's old enough—' but she stopped, and instead of giving him one of her light hugs, she rumpled his hair. 'People do confide in you, I must say,' she said. 'I don't think I like her coming up here. Tell me what she said.'

ROSAMUND LEHMANN

A Dream of Winter

IN the middle of the great frost she was in bed with influenza; and that was the time the bee man came from the next village to take the swarm that had been for years buried in the wall of her country house; deep under the leads roofing the flat platform of the balcony outside her bedroom window.

She lay staring out upon a mineral landscape: iron, ice and stone. Powdered with a wraith of spectral blue, the chalky frost-fog stood, thickened in the upper air; and behind it a glassy disc stared back, livid, drained of heat, like a gas lamp turned down, forgotten, staring down uselessly, aghast, upon the impersonal shrouded objects and dark relics in an abandoned house. The silence was so absolute that it reversed itself and became in her ears continuous reverberation. Or was it the bees, still driving their soft throbbing dynamo, as mostly they did, day in, day out, all the year round?—all winter a subdued companionship of sound, a buried murmur; fiercer, louder, daily more insistent with the coming of the warm days; materializing then into that snarling, struggling, multiple-headed organism pinned as if by centripetal force upon the outside of the wall, and seeming to strive in vain to explode away from its centre and disperse itself.

No. The bees were silent. As for the children, not one cry. They were in the garden somewhere: frost-struck perhaps like all the rest.

All at once, part of a ladder oscillated across the window space, became stationary. A pause; then a battered hat appeared, then a man's head and shoulders. Spying her among the pillows, his face creased in a wide grin. He called cheerfully: 'Good morning!'

She had lost her voice, and waved and smiled, pointing to her throat.

'Feeling a bit rough? Ah, that's a shame. There's a lot of nasty colds and that about. Bed's the best place this weather, if you ask *me*.'

He stepped up on to the little balcony, and stood framed full-length in the long sash window—a short, broad figure in a roll-collared khaki

pull-over, with a twinkling blue small peasant's eye in a thin lined face
of elliptical structure, a comedian's face, blurred in its angles and hollows by a day's growth of beard.

'Come to take that there swarm. Wrong weather to take a swarm.
I don't like the job on a day like this. Bad for 'em. Needs a mild spell.
Still, it don't look like breaking and I hadn't nothink else on and you
wanted the job done.'

His speech had a curious humming drawl, not altogether following
the pattern of the local dialect: brisker, more positive. She saw that, separated by the frosty pane, they were to be day-long companions. The
lady of the house, on her bed of sickness, presented him with no problems in etiquette. He experienced a simple pleasure in her society:
someone to chat to on a long job.

'I'll fetch my mate up.'

He disappeared, and below in the garden he called: 'George!' Then
an unintelligible burr of conversation, and up he came again, followed
by a young workman with a bag of tools. George felt the embarrassment
of the situation, and after one constricted glance through the window,
addressed himself to his task and never looked towards her again. He was
very young, and had one of those nobly modelled faces of working
men; jaw, brows profoundly carved out, lips shutting clearly, salient
cheekbone, sunk cheek, and in the deep cavities of the eye-sockets, eyes
of extreme sadness. The sorrow is fixed, impersonal, expressing nothing
but itself, like the eyes of animals or of portraits. This face was abstract,
belonging equally to youth or age, turning up here and there, with an
engine-driver's cap on, or a soldier's; topping mechanics' overalls, lifting from the roadmender's gang to gaze at her passing car. Each time she
saw it, so uncorrupted, she thought vaguely, romantically, it was enough
to believe in. She had had a lot of leisure in her life to look at faces. She
had friends with revolutionary ideas, and belonged to the Left Book
Club.

'Be a long job this,' called the bee man. 'Looks like they've got down
very deep.'

A sense of terror overcame her, as if some dreaded exploratory physical operation of doubtful issue, and which she would be forced to witness, was about to take place. This growth was deep down in the body
of the house. The waves of fever started to beat up again.

The men disappeared. She waited for the children to appear upon the
ladder; and soon, there they were. John had taken the precaution of

tucking his sister's kilt into her bloomers. In his usual manner of rather disgusted patience, he indicated her footing for her. They pranced on the balcony, tapped on the pane, peered in with faces of lunatic triumph, presenting themselves as the shock of her life.

'A man's come to do the bees!'

'It's perfectly safe,' yelled John, in scorn, forestalling her. But voiceless, she could only nod, beam, roll her eyes.

'Shall we get Jock up?'

Frantically she shook her head.

'But he's whining to come up,' objected Jane, dismayed.

The hysterical clamour of a Cairn terrier phenomenally separated from his own rose up from below.

'We'd better go down to him,' said John wearily, acknowledging one more victory for silliness. 'Here come the workmen anyway. We'd only be in their way. Here—put your foot *here*, ass.'

They vanished. Insane noises of reunion uprose; then silence. She knew that Jane had made off, her purely subjective frivolous interest exhausted; but that John had taken up his post for the day, a scientific observer with ears of deepening carmine, waiting, under the influence of an inexpressible desire for co-operation, for a chance to steady the ladder, hand up a tool, or otherwise insinuate himself within the framework of the ritual.

Up came the bee man and his mate. They set to work to lift the leads. They communicated with each other in a low drone, bee-like, rising and sinking in a minor key, punctuated by an occasional deep-throated 'Ah!' Knocking, hammering, wrenching developed. Somebody should tell them she could not stand it. Nobody would. She rang for the curtains to be drawn, and when they were, she lay down flat and turned her face to the wall and sank into burning sleep.

She woke to the sound of John shouting through her door.

'They've gone to have their lunch. He's coming back this afternoon to take the swarm. Most of the roof's off. I've seen the bees. If only you'd drawn back your curtains you could have too. I called to you but you didn't seem to hear. The cat's brought in two more birds, a pigeon and a tit, but we saved them and we're thawing them behind the boiler.'

Down the passage he went, stumping and whistling.

Three o'clock. The petrified day had hardened from hour to hour. But as light began to fail, there came a moment when the blue spirit drew closer, explored the tree-tops, bloomed against the ghostly pane; like a blue tide returning, invading the white caves, the unfructifying salt stones of the sea.

The ladder shook. He was there again, carrying a kind of lamp with a funnel from which poured black smoke.

'Take a look,' he called cheerfully. 'It's worth it. Don't suppose you ever see nothink o' the kind before.'

She rose from her bed, put on dressing-gown and shawl and stumbled to the window. With a showman's flourish he flung off the black sacking—and what a sight was revealed! Atolls of pale honeycomb ridging the length and breadth of beam and lath, thrusting down in serrated blocks into the cavity; the vast amorphous murmuring black swarm suddenly exposed, stirring resentful, helpless, transfixed in the icy air. A few of the more vigorous insects crawled out from the conglomeration, spun up into the air, fell back stupefied.

'They're more lively than you'd think for,' said the bee man, thoughtful. She pointed to his face, upon which three or four bees were languidly creeping. He brushed them off with a chuckle. 'They don't hurt me. Been stung too often. Inoculated like.'

He broke off a piece of honeycomb and held it up. She wished so much to hold it in her hand that she forced herself to push down the window, receiving the air's shock like a blow on the face; and took it from him. Frail, blond, brittle, delicate as coral in construction, weightless as a piece of dried sponge or seaweed.

'Dry, see,' said the bee man. 'You won't get much honey out of here. It's all that wet last summer. If I'd 'a' taken this swarm a year ago, you'd a' got a whole heap. You won't get anythink to speak of out of here now.'

She saw now: the papery transparent aspect of these ethereal growths meant a world extinct. She shivered violently, her spirit overwhelmed by symbols of frustration. Her dream had been rich: of honey pouring bountifully out from beneath her roof tree, to be stored up in family jars, in pots and bowls, to spread on the bread and sweeten the puddings, and save herself a little longer from having to tell the children: No more sugar.

Too late! The sweet cheat gone.

'It's no weather to take a swarm,' repeated the bee man. Dejectedly he waved the lamp over the bubbling glistening clumps, giving them a casual smoke-over. 'Still, you wanted the job done.'

She wished to justify herself, to explain the necessity of dispossessing the bees, to say that she had been waiting for him since September; but she was dumb. She pushed up the window, put the honeycomb on her dressing-table, and tumbled heavily into bed again.

Her Enemy, so attentive since the outbreak of the war, whispered in her ear:

'Just as I thought. Another sentimental illusion. Schemes to produce food by magic strokes of fortune. Life doesn't arrange stories with happy endings any more, see? *Never again.* This source of energy whose living voice comforted you at dawn, at dusk, saying: We work for you. Our surplus is yours, there for the taking—vanished! You left it to accumulate, thinking: There's time; thinking: when I will. You left it too late. What you took for the hum of growth and plenty is nothing, you see, but the buzz of an outworn machine running down. The workers have eaten up their fruits, there's nothing left for you. It's no use this time, my girl! Supplies are getting scarce for people like you. An end, soon, of getting more than their fair share for dwellers in country houses. Ripe gifts unearned out of traditional walls, no more. All the while your roof was being sealed up patiently, cunningly, with spreading plasters and waxy shrouds.'

Through half-closed eyes she watched him bending, peering here and there. Suddenly he whipped out his knife, plunging his arm forward out of sight. A pause; then up came knife, hand again, lifting a clot of thick yellow sticky stuff. Honey.

'Honey!'

There it was, the richness, the substance. The knife carried a packed edge of crusted sugar, and as he held it up, the syrup began to drip down slow, gummy, amber-dark. Isled in the full attack of total winter there it hung, inviolable, a microcosm of summer, melting in sweet oils.

'Honey!' yelled John from below.

'*Now* we're all right,' called back the bee man in a happy voice, as if released all at once from his own weight of disappointment. 'Plenty here—right in the corner. Did you ever see anythink so artful? Near shave me not spotting it. Oh, we'll get you some! Run and beg us a dish off Cook, Sonny, and I'll dish you out a nice little lot for your tea.'

She heard the urgency of the start of her son's boots. It was as if he ran away with her, ran through her, bursting all obstacles to be back with the dish before he had gone, to offer it where it was required: his part in the serious task. This pure goodwill and disinterestedness of children, this concentration of spirit so entire that they seemed to fuse with and become the object, lifted her on a cool wave above her sickness, threw her up in a moment of absolute peace, as after love or childbirth, upon a white and abstract shore.

'That's a nice boy you've got,' said the bee man, cutting, scraping busily. 'Sensible. I'm ever so glad to see this honey. There's one thing I do hate to see, and that's a swarm starved.'

The words shocked her. Crawling death by infinitesimal stages. Not a question of no surplus, but of the bare necessities of life. Not making enough to live on. A whole community entombed, like miners trapped.

A scuffle below. John's fluting voice came up:

'This do?'

'Fine. Bring it up, Sonny.'

The largest meat platter from the kitchen dresser hove in sight.

'Thanks, mate. Now we'll get you a bit o' somethink to sweeten you. Need it? What does your Mammy think, eh?' He shouted with laughter.

Unable to cope with repartee of so personal a character, John cast her a wry self-conscious grin, and rapidly vanished.

Light was rapidly failing, but the rising moon arrested the descent of darkness. In the opaque bleached twilight his silhouette persisted on the pane, bending, straightening. He hummed and whistled. Now and then he spoke softly to the bees. 'Run off, my girl, run off.' Once he held up his hands to show her the insects clustering upon them.

'They don't worry me, the jokers. Just a sore sort of a tingle, like as if I'd rapped myself over the fingers with a hammer.'

He brushed them off and they fell down like a string of beads breaking. They smiled at one another. She closed her eyes.

Roused by a rap on the pane, she lay in confused alarm. The lower window ran up with a swift screech, and, heaving towards her over the sill in the semi-darkness, she saw a phantasmagoric figure climb in and straighten itself up. A headless figure. Where the face should have been, nothing but swaying darkness. It's the fever. Wait, and it will go away.

She found courage to switch on the lamp and saw the bee man. He was wearing a round hat with a long circular veil of thick gauze that hung to his shoulders.

Fishing up a fragment of voice she croaked:

'Is that your hat for taking swarms?'

'Oh, him,' he said laughing, removing it. 'Forgot I had him on. Did I give you a scare?'

'Stylish,' she said.

'Thought you'd like to know the job's done. I've got 'em down below there. Got you a nice bit of honey, too. I'm glad of that. I hate to see a swarm starved.'

He drew her curtains together. 'Better dror 'em or you'll get into trouble with the black-out, bother it.' Then he moved over to the fireplace. 'Your fire's gorn right down. That's why I come in. Thought I'd make it up for you.' He knelt down, riddled the ashes, and with his bruised, swollen, wax-stuck fingers piled on more coal. 'That'll be more cheerful soon. Ain't you got nobody to see to you then?'

'Oh, yes,' she whispered. 'There'll be somebody coming soon. I forgot to ring.' She felt self-pity, and wanted to weep.

'You do seem poorly. You need giving your chest a good rub with camphorated. I believe in that.'

In another few moments he would be rubbing her chest.

But he remained by the fire, looking thoughtfully round the room. 'This is a nice old place. I knew it when I was a young lad, of course. The old Squire used to have us up for evening classes. Improve our minds. He was a great one for that.' He chuckled. 'Must be ten years since he died. I'm out o' touch. Went out to Canada when I was seventeen. Twenty years ago that was. Never got a wife, nor a fortune, nor nothink.' He chuckled again. 'I'm glad I got back before this war. Back where I started—that's where I am. Living with my married sister.'

She said:

'Won't you have a cup of tea?'

'No, I'll be off home, thanks all the same. I'd best get that swarm in. They're in a bad way.'

'Will they recover?'

'Ah, I couldn't say. It wasn't no weather to take a swarm. And then it demoralizes 'em like when you steals their honey. They sings a mournful song—ever so mournful.' He strode to the window. 'Still, we'll hope for the best. George'll be up in the morning to put them leads right. Well, I'll wish you goodnight. Hope you'll be more yourself tomorrow.' At the window he paused. 'Well, there's no call to go out that way, is there?' he remarked. 'Might as well go out like a Christian.'

He marched briskly across the room, opened her bedroom door, closed it quietly after him. She heard his light feet on the oak staircase, dying away.

She took her temperature and found it was lower: barely a hundred. He had done her good. Then she lay listening to the silence she had created. One performs acts of will, and in doing so one commits acts of negation and destruction. A portion of life is suppressed for ever. The image of the ruined balcony weighed upon her: torn out, exposed, violated, obscene as the photograph of a bombed house.

What an extraordinary day, what an odd meeting and parting. It seemed to her that her passive, dreaming, leisured life was nothing, in the last analysis, but a fluid element for receiving and preserving faint paradoxical images and symbols. They were all she ultimately remembered.

Somewhere in the garden a big branch snapped off and fell crackling down.

The children burst in, carrying plates of honey.

'Want some?'

'Not now, thanks. I can't really swallow anything, not even delicious honey.'

'It isn't delicious. It's beastly. It looks like seccotine and it tastes *much* too sweet. Ugh!'

It was certainly an unappetizing colour—almost brown; the texture gluey. It had been there too long. She croaked:

'You oughtn't to be in this room. Where's Mary? Don't come near me.'

'Oh, we shan't catch your old 'flu,' said John, throwing himself negligently backwards over the arm of the sofa and writhing on the floor. 'Look here, Mum, what on earth did you want to get rid of the poor blighters for? They never did any harm.'

'Think what a maddening noise they made.'

'We like the noise. If you can't stand the hum of a wretched little bee, what'll you do in an air-raid?'

'You had a lovely day watching the bee man.'

'I dare say.'

But now all was loss, satiety, disappointment.

'Think how everybody got stung last summer. Poor Robert. And Mr Fanshawe.'

'Oh, your old visitors.'

What an entertainment the bees had been, a topic, a focusing point at week-ends. But from now on, of course, there would be no more week-end parties. It was time for the bees to go.

'Remember Jane's eye, all bandaged up for days.'

'I remember that.' Jane flushed, went solemn. 'It didn't 'alf 'urt.'

'Your *English*!' cried John, revolted.

'I got not 'alf off Pippy Didcock,' said Jane, complacent. 'They all says that. It's Oxfordshire accident.'

She started to run up and down the room, kilt flying, hair bouncing, then stood still, her hand on her chest.

'What's the most important thing about a person?' she said.

'Dopey,' said her brother. 'What's biting you?'

'Don't you know?' said Jane. 'Your heart. If it stops, you die. I can hear mine after that running.'

'It won't stop,' said her mother.

'It will some day,' said John. 'It might stop tonight. Reminds me—' He fished in his pocket and drew out a dark object. 'I brought up this tit to give it a last chance by your fire. It was at the back of the boiler, but the cats would keep prowling about. They got the pigeon. It must have been stiff eating.' He examined the tit. 'It's alive!'

He rushed with it to the fire and crouched down, holding it in his palms before the now leaping flames. 'Its eyes opened. It's fluttering.'

Jane came and knelt beside him.

'Isn't it a *sweet* little tiny bird?'

Suddenly it flew straight up out of his hands, dashed against the mantelpiece, fell down again upon the hearth-rug. They were all perfectly silent.

After a moment his hand went out to pick it up again. Then it flew straight into the fire, and started to roast, to whirr and cheep over the coals.

In a split second she was there, plunged in her hand, out again. Smell of burnt feathers, charred fragments flaking down. It was on the hearth-stone. Everybody stared.

Suddenly it revived, it began to stagger about. The tenacity of life in its minute frame appalled her. Over the carpet it bounced, one wing burnt off, one leg shrivelled up under its breast, no tail; up and down, vigorously, round and about.

'Is it going to be alive?' said Jane.

'Yes,' said John coldly, heavily. 'We can't do anything about it now.'

EVELYN WAUGH

An Englishman's Home

I

MR BEVERLEY METCALFE tapped the barometer in the back hall and noted with satisfaction that it had fallen several points during the night. He was by nature a sun-loving man, but he believed it was one of the marks of a true countryman to be eternally in need of rain. He had made a study and noted the points of true countrymen. Had he been of literary habit and of an earlier generation, his observations might have formed a little book of aphorisms. The true countryman wore a dark suit on Sundays unlike the flannelled tripper from the cities; he loved a bargain and would go to any expense to do his marketing by private treaty instead of through the normal channels of retail trade; while ostensibly sceptical and conservative he was readily fascinated by mechanical gadgets; he was genial but inhospitable, willing to gossip for hours across a fence with any passing stranger, but reluctant to allow his closest friends into his house . . . These and a hundred other characteristics Mr Metcalfe noted for emulation.

'That's what we need—rain,' he said to himself, and opening the garden door stepped into the balmy morning air. There was no threat in the cloudless heavens. His gardener passed, pushing the water-barrow.

'Good morning, Boggett. The glass has dropped, I'm glad to say.'

'Ur.'

'Means rain.'

'Noa.'

'Down quite low.'

'Ah.'

'Pity to spend a lot of time watering.'

'Them'll burn up else.'

'Not if it rains.'

'Am't agoin to rain. Don't never rain around heres except you can see clear down-over.'

'See clear down-over?'

'Ur. Can always see Pilbury Steeple when rain's a-coming.'

Mr Metcalfe accepted this statement gravely. 'These old fellows know a thing or two that the scientists don't,' he would often remark, simulating an air of patronage which was far from sincere. Boggett, the gardener, was not particularly old and he knew very little; the seeds he planted seldom grew; he wrought stark havoc whenever he was allowed to use the pruning-knife; his ambition in horticulture went no further than the fattening of the largest possible pumpkin; but Mr Metcalfe regarded him with the simple reverence of peasant for priest. For Mr Metcalfe was but lately initiated into the cult of the countryside, and any features of it still claimed his devotion—its agricultural processes, its social structure, its vocabulary, its recreations; the aspect of it, glittering now under the cool May sunshine, fruit trees in flower, chestnut in full leaf, the ash budding; the sound and smell of it—Mr Westmacott calling his cows at dawn, the scent of wet earth and Boggett splashing clumsily among the wallflowers; the heart of it—or what Mr Metcalfe took to be its heart—pulsing all round him; his own heart beating time, for was he not part of it, a true countryman, a landowner?

He was, it is true, a landowner in rather a small way, but, as he stood on his terrace and surveyed the untroubled valley below him, he congratulated himself that he had not been led away by the house agents into the multitudinous cares of a wider territory. He owned seven acres, more or less, and it seemed to him exactly the right amount; they comprised the policies of the house and a paddock; sixty further acres of farmland had also been available, and for a day or two he had toyed with the rather inebriating idea of acquiring them. He could well have afforded it, of course, but to his habit of mind there was something perverse and downright wrong in an investment which showed a bare two per cent yield on his capital. He wanted a home, not a 'seat', and he reflected on the irony of that word; he thought of Lord Brakehurst, with whose property he sometimes liked to say that his own 'marched'— there was indeed a hundred yards of ha-ha between his paddock and one of Lord Brakehurst's pastures. What could be less sedentary than Lord Brakehurst's life, every day of which was agitated by the cares of his great possessions? No, seven acres, judiciously chosen, was the ideal property, and Mr Metcalfe *had* chosen judiciously. The house-agent had spoken no more than the truth when he described Much Malcock as one of the most unspoilt Cotswold villages. It was exactly such a place as Mr Metcalfe had dreamed of in the long years in the cotton trade in Alexandria. Mr Metcalfe's own residence, known for generations by the singular name of Grumps, had been rechristened by a previous owner as Much Malcock Hall. It bore the new name pretty well. It was 'a dignified Georgian house of mellowed Cotswold stone; four recep., six principal bed and dressing rooms, replete with period features'. The villagers, Mr Metcalfe observed with regret, could not be induced to speak of it as 'the Hall'. Boggett always said that he worked 'up to Grumps', but the name was not of Mr Metcalfe's choosing and it looked well on his notepaper. It suggested a primacy in the village that was not undisputed.

Lord Brakehurst, of course, was in a class apart; he was Lord Lieutenant of the County with property in fifty parishes. Lady Brakehurst had not in fact called on Mrs Metcalfe, living as she did in a world where card-leaving had lost its importance, but, of the calling, there were two other households in Much Malcock, and a border-line case—besides the vicar, who had a plebeian accent and an inclination to preach against bankers.

The rival gentry were Lady Peabury and Colonel Hodge, both, to the villagers, newcomers, but residents of some twenty years' priority to Mr Metcalfe.

Lady Peabury lived at Much Malcock House, whose chimneys, soon to be hidden in the full foliage of summer, could still be seen among its budding limes on the opposite slope of the valley. Four acres of meadow-land lay between her property and Mr Metcalfe's, where Westmacott's plump herd enriched the landscape and counterbalanced the slightly suburban splendour of her flower gardens. She was a widow and, like Mr Metcalfe, had come to Much Malcock from abroad. She was rich and kind and rather greedy, a diligent reader of fiction, mistress of many Cairn terriers and of five steady old maidservants who never broke the Crown Derby.

Colonel Hodge lived at the Manor, a fine gabled house in the village street, whose gardens, too, backed on to Westmacott's meadow. He was impecunious but active in the affairs of the British Legion and the Boy Scouts; he accepted Mr Metcalfe's invitation to dinner, but spoke of him, in his family circle, as 'the cotton wallah'.

These neighbours were of unequivocal position; the Hornbeams at the Old Mill were a childless, middle-aged couple who devoted themselves to craftsmanship. Mr Hornbeam senior was a genuine, commercial potter in Staffordshire; he supported them reluctantly and rather exiguously, but this backing of unearned quarterly cheques placed them definitely in the upper strata of local society. Mrs Hornbeam attended church and Mr Hornbeam was quite knowledgeable about vegetables. In fact, had they preferred a tennis court to their herb garden, and had Mr Hornbeam possessed an evening-suit, they might easily have mixed with their neighbours on terms of ostensible equality. At the time of the Peace Ballot, Mrs Hornbeam had canvassed every cottage in bicycling distance, but she eschewed the Women's Institute, and in Lady Peabury's opinion failed to pull her weight in the village. Mr Metcalfe thought Mr Hornbeam Bohemian, and Mr Hornbeam thought Mr Metcalfe Philistine. Colonel Hodge had fallen out with them some time back, on a question relating to his Airedale, and cut them year in, year out, three or four times a day.

Under their stone-tiled roofs the villagers derived substantial comfort from all these aliens. Foreign visitors impressed by the charges of London restaurants and the splendour of the more accessible ducal palaces often express wonder at the wealth of England. A half has not been told them. It is in remote hamlets like Much Malcock that the great reservoirs of national wealth seep back to the soil. The villagers had their Memorial Hall and their club. In the rafters of their church the death-watch beetle had been expensively exterminated for them: their scouts had a bell tent and silver bugles; the district nurse drove her own car; at Christmas their children were surfeited with trees and parties and the cottagers loaded with hampers; if one of them was indisposed port and soup and grapes and tickets for the seaside arrived in profusion; at evening their menfolk returned from work laden with perquisites, and all the year round they feasted on forced vegetables. The vicar found it impossible to interest them in the Left Book Club.

'God gave all men all earth to love,' Mr Metcalfe quoted, dimly remembering the lines from a calendar which had hung in his office in Alexandria, 'but since our hearts are small, Ordained for each one spot should prove, Beloved over all.'

He pottered round to the engine-house where his chauffeur was brooding over batteries. He popped his head into another outbuilding and saw that no harm had befallen the lawn-mower during the night. He paused in the kitchen garden to nip the blossom off some newly-planted blackcurrant which must not be allowed to fruit that summer. Then, his round finished, he pottered in to breakfast.

His wife was already there.

'I've done my round,' he said.

'Yes, dear.'

'Everything coming along very nicely.'

'Yes, dear.'

'You can't see Pilbury Steeple, though.'

'Good gracious, Beverley, why should you want to do that?'

'It's a sign of rain when you can.'

'What a lot of nonsense. You've been listening to Boggett again.'

She rose and left him with his papers. She had to see the cook. Servants seem to take up so much time in England; she thought wistfully of the white-gowned Berber boys who had pattered about the cool, tiled floors of her house in Alexandria.

Mr Metcalfe finished his breakfast and retired to his study with pipe and papers. The *Gazette* came out that morning. A true countryman always reads his 'local rag' first, so Mr Metcalfe patiently toiled through the columns of Women's Institute doings and the reports of a Council meeting on the subject of sewage, before he allowed himself to open *The Times*.

Serene opening of a day of wrath!

2

Towards eleven o'clock Mr Metcalfe put aside the crossword. In the lobby by the garden-door he kept a variety of garden implements specially designed for the use of the elderly. Selecting from among them one which had newly arrived, he sauntered out into the sunshine and addressed himself to the plantains on the lawn. The tool had a handsomely bound leather grip, a spliced cane handle and a head of stainless steel; it worked admirably, and with a minimum of effort Mr Metcalfe had soon scarred a large area with neat little pits.

He paused and called towards the house, 'Sophie, Sophie, come and see what I've done.'

His wife's head emerged from an upper window. 'Very pretty, dear,' she said.

Encouraged, he set to work again. Boggett passed.

'Useful little tool this, Boggett.'

'Ur.'

'Think we ought to sow seed in the bare patches?'

'Noa.'

'You think the grass will grow over them?'

'Noa. Plantains'll come up again.'

'You don't think I've killed the roots?'

'Noa. Makes the roots powerful strong topping 'em off same as you've done.'

'Well, what ought I to do?'

'Bain't nothing you can do with plantains. They do always come up again.'

Boggett passed. Mr Metcalfe looked at his gadget with sudden distaste, propped it petulantly against the sundial, and with his hands in his pockets stared out across the valley. Even at this distance Lady Peabury's aubretias struck a discordant note. His eyes dropped and he noticed, casually at first, then with growing curiosity, two unfamiliar figures among Westmacott's cows. They were young men in dark, urban clothes, and they were very busy about something. They had papers in their hands which they constantly consulted; they paced up and down the field as though measuring it; they squatted on their haunches as though roughly taking level; they pointed into the air, to the ground, and to the horizon.

'Boggett,' said Mr Metcalfe sharply, 'come here a minute.'

'Urr.'

'Do you see two men in Mr Westmacott's field?'

'Noa.'

'You don't?'

' 'Er bain't Mr Westmacott's field. 'E've a sold of 'er.'

'Sold it! Good heavens! Who to?'

'Couldn't rightly say who 'e've a sold 'er to. Gentleman from London staying at the Brakehurst. Paid a tidy price for 'er too I've a heard said.'

'What on earth for?'

'Couldn't rightly say, but I reckon it be to build hissel a house.'

Build. It was a word so hideous that no one in Much Malcock dared use it above a whisper. 'Housing scheme', 'Development', 'Clearance', 'Council houses', 'Planning'—these obscene words had been expunged from the polite vocabulary of the district, only to be used now and then, with the licence allowed to anthropologists, of the fierce tribes beyond the parish boundary. And now the horror was in their midst, the mark of Plague in the court of the Decameron.

After the first moment of shock, Mr Metcalfe rallied for action, hesitated for a moment whether or no to plunge down the hill and challenge the enemy on his own ground, and decided against it; this was the moment to act with circumspection. He must consult Lady Peabury.

It was three-quarters of a mile to the house; the lane ran past the gate which gave access to Westmacott's field; a crazily-hung elm gate and deep cow-trodden mud, soon in Mr Metcalfe's imagination to give place to golden privet and red gravel. Mr Metcalfe could see the heads of the intruders bobbing beyond the hedge; they bore urban, purposeful black hats. He drove on, miserably.

Lady Peabury was in the morning-room reading a novel; early training gave a guilty spice to this recreation, for she had been brought up to believe that to read a novel before luncheon was one of the gravest sins it was possible for a gentlewoman to commit. She slipped the book under a cushion and rose to greet Mr Metcalfe.

'I was just getting ready to go out,' she explained.

Mr Metcalfe had no time for politenesses.

'Lady Peabury,' he began at once, 'I have very terrible news.'

'Oh dear! Is poor Mr Cruttwell having trouble with the Wolf Cub account again?'

'No; at least, he is; there's another fourpence gone astray; on the credit side this time, which makes it more worrying. But that isn't what I came about. It is something that threatens our whole lives. They are going to build in Westmacott's field.' Briefly, but with emotion, he told Lady Peabury what he had seen.

She listened gravely. When he had finished there was silence in the morning-room; six little clocks ticked among the chintzes and the potted azaleas. At last Lady Peabury spoke:

'Westmacott has behaved very badly,' she said.

'I suppose you can't blame him.'

'I do blame him, Mr Metcalfe, very severely. I can't understand it at all. He always seemed a very decent man . . . I was thinking of making Mrs Westmacott secretary of the Women's Institute. He had no right to do a thing like that without consulting us. Why, I look right on to that field from my bedroom windows. I could never understand why you didn't buy the field yourself.'

It was let for £3. 18s.; they had asked £170 for it; there was tithe and property tax on top of that. Lady Peabury knew this.

'Any of us could have bought it at the time of sale,' said Mr Metcalfe rather sharply.

'It always went with your house.'

In another minute, Mr Metcalfe felt, she would be telling him that *he* had behaved very badly; that *he* had always seemed a very decent man.

She was, in fact, thinking on just those lines at the moment. 'I daresay it's not too late even now for you to make an offer,' she said.

'We are all equally threatened,' said Mr Metcalfe. 'I think we ought to act together. Hodge won't be any too pleased when he hears the news.'

Colonel Hodge had heard, and he was none too pleased. He was waiting at the Hall when Mr Metcalfe got back.

'Do you know what that scoundrel Westmacott has done?'

'Yes,' said Mr Metcalfe rather wearily, 'I know.' The interview with Lady Peabury had not gone off quite as he had hoped. She had shown no enthusiasm for common action.

'Sold his field to a lot of jerry builders.'

'Yes, I know.'

'Funny, I always thought it was *your* field.'

'No' said Mr Metcalfe, 'never.'

'It always used to go with this house.'

'Yes, I know, but I didn't happen to want it.'

'Well, it's put us all in a pretty nasty fix, I must say. D'you suppose they'd sell it back to you now?'

'I don't know that I want to buy it. Why, they'll probably want a building-land price—seventy or eighty pounds an acre.'

'More, I daresay. But, good heavens man, you wouldn't let that stop you. Think how it would depreciate your property having a whole town of bungalows right under your windows.'

'Come, come, Hodge. We've no reason to suppose that it will be bungalows.'

'Well, villas then. You surely aren't sticking up for the fellows?'

'Certainly not. We shall all suffer very much from any development there. My belief is that it can be stopped by law; there's the Society for the Protection of Rural England. We could interest them in it. The County Council could be approached. We could write letters to the papers and petition the Office of Works. The great thing is that we must all stand together over this.'

'Fat lot of change we shall get out of that. Think of the building that's gone on over at Metbury.'

Mr Metcalfe thought, and shuddered.

'I should say that this was one of the times when money talked loudest. Have you tried Lady Peabury?'

For the first time in their acquaintance Mr Metcalfe detected a distinctly coarse strain in Colonel Hodge. 'I have discussed it with her. She is naturally very much concerned.'

'That field has always been known as Lower Grumps,' said the Colonel, reverting to his former and doubly offensive line of thought. 'It's not really her chicken.'

'It is all our chickens,' said Mr Metcalfe, getting confused with the metaphor.

'Well, I don't know what you expect me to do about it,' said Colonel Hodge. 'You know how I'm placed. It all comes of that parson preaching Bolshevism Sunday after Sunday.'

'We ought to get together and discuss it.'

'Oh, we'll discuss it all right. I don't suppose we shall discuss anything else for the next three months.'

No one in Much Malcock took the crisis harder than the Hornbeams. News of it reached them at midday by means of the village charwoman who dropped in twice a week to despoil their larder. She told them with some pride, innocently assuming that all city gentlemen—as she continued to regard Mr Hornbeam, in spite of his homespuns and his beard—would welcome an addition to their numbers.

Nervous gloom descended on the Old Mill. There was no explosion of wrath as there had been at the Manor; no moral condemnation as at the House; no call to action as had come from the Hall. Hopeless sorrow reigned unrelieved. Mrs Hornbeam's pottery went to pieces. Mr Hornbeam sat listless at the loom. It was their working hour; they sat at opposite ends of the raftered granary. Often, on other afternoons, they sang to one another catches and refrains of folk music as their busy fingers muddled with the clay and the shuttles. Today they sat in silence each, according to a Japanese mystical practice, attempting to drive the new peril into the World of Unbeing. It had worked well enough with Colonel Hodge and the Airedale, with the Abyssinian War, and with Mr Hornbeam senior's yearly visit, but by sunset the new peril remained obstinately concrete.

Mrs Hornbeam set their simple meal of milk, raisins, and raw turnip; Mr Hornbeam turned away from his elm platter. 'There is no place for the Artist in the Modern World,' he said. 'We ask nothing of their brutish civilization except to be left alone, to be given one little corner of land, an inch or two of sky where we can live at peace and occupy ourselves with making seemly and beautiful things. You wouldn't think it was too much to ask. We give them the entire globe for their machines. But it is not enough. They have to hunt us out and harry us. They know that as long as there is one spot of loveliness and decency left it is a standing reproach to them.'

It was growing dark; Mrs Hornbeam struck a flint and lit the rush lights. She wandered to the harp and plucked a few poignant notes. 'Perhaps Mr Metcalfe will stop it,' she said.

'That we should be dependent for the essentials of life upon a vulgarian like that . . .'

It was in this mood that he received an invitation from Mr Metcalfe to confer with his neighbours at Much Malcock House on the following afternoon.

The choice of meeting place had been a delicate one, for Lady Peabury was loth to abdicate her position of general leadership or to appear as leader in this particular matter; on the other hand, it touched her too closely for her to be able to ignore it. Accordingly the invitations were issued by Mr Metcalfe, who thereby accepted responsibility for the agenda, while the presence of the meeting in her morning-room gave something of the atmosphere of a Cabinet meeting at the Palace.

Opinion had hardened during the day and there was general agreement with Colonel Hodge's judgement: 'Metcalfe has got us into this hole by not buying the field in the first place; it's up to him to get us out of it.' Though nothing as uncompromising as this was said in front of Mr Metcalfe, he could feel it in the air. He was the last to arrive. Lady Peabury's welcome to her guests had been lukewarm. 'It is very kind of you to come. I really cannot think that it is necessary, but Mr Metcalfe particularly wished it. I suppose he intends telling us what he is going to do.' To Mr Metcalfe she said, 'We are full of curiosity.'

'Sorry to be late. I've had a day of it, I can tell you. Been to all the local offices, got on to all the Societies, and I may as well tell you at once, there's nothing doing from that end. We are not even scheduled as a rural area.'

'No,' said Colonel Hodge, 'I saw to that. Halves the potential value of one's property.'

'*Schedules*,' moaned Mr Hornbeam, 'that is what we have become. We must be *scheduled* to lead a free life.'

'. . . And so,' persisted Mr Metcalfe, in his board-room manner, 'we are left to find the solution ourselves. Now this young man has no particular reason, I imagine, for preferring this district above any other in the country. The building has not yet begun; he has no commitments. I cannot help feeling that if he were tactfully approached and offered a reasonable profit on the transaction, he might be induced to re-sell.'

'I am sure,' said Lady Peabury, 'we shall all owe a deep debt of gratitude to Mr Metcalfe.'

'Very public spirited of you,' said Colonel Hodge.

'Profits, the cancer of the age . . .'

'I am perfectly willing,' said Mr Metcalfe, 'to bear my share of the burden . . .' At the word 'share' his hearers stiffened perceptibly. 'My suggestion is that we make a common fund proportionate to our present land holdings. By a rough calculation I work that out as being in the ratio of one to Mr Hornbeam, two to Colonel Hodge, two to myself, and five to our hostess here. The figures could be adjusted,' he added as he noted that his suggestion was falling a little flat.

'You can count me out,' said Colonel Hodge. 'Couldn't possibly run to it.'

'And me,' said Mr Hornbeam.

Lady Peabury was left in, with a difficult hand to stake. Delicacy forbade recognition of the vital fact that Mr Metcalfe was very much the richer—delicacy tempered with pride. The field must be saved, but there seemed no system of joint purchase by which she could honourably fail to bear the largest part. Duty called, clearly and unmistakably, to Mr Metcalfe alone. She held her cards and passed the bidding. 'Surely,' she said, 'as a business man you must see a great many objections to joint ownership. Do you propose to partition the field, or are we all to share the rent, the tithe and the tax? It would be highly inconvenient. I doubt if it is even legal.'

'Certainly, certainly. I merely wished to assure you of my readiness to cooperate. The field, as such, is of no interest to me, I can assure you. I would willingly stand down.'

There was a threat, almost a lack of politeness in his tone. Colonel Hodge scented danger.

'Wouldn't it be best,' he said, 'to find out first if this fellow is willing to re-sell. Then you can decide which of you keep it.'

'I am sure we shall be very interested to hear the results of Mr Metcalfe's negotiations,' said Lady Peabury.

She should not have said that. She would gladly have recalled the words the moment after they were uttered. She had vaguely wanted to say something disagreeable, to punish Mr Metcalfe for the discomfort in which she found herself. She had not meant to antagonize him, and this she had unmistakably done.

Mr Metcalfe left the House abruptly, almost precipitately, and all that evening he chafed. For fifteen years Mr Metcalfe had been president of the British Chamber of Commerce. He had been greatly respected by the whole business community. No one could put anything across him, and he would not touch anything that was not above-board. Egyptian and Levantine merchants who tried to interest Metcalfe in shady business went away with a flea in the ear. It was no good trying to squeeze Metcalfe. That was his reputation in the Union Club, and here, at home, in his own village, an old woman had tried to catch him napping. There was a sudden change. He was no longer the public-spirited countryman; he was cards-on-the-table-brass-tacks-and-twenty-shillings-in-the-pound-treat-him-or-mind-your-step Metcalfe, Metcalfe with his back up, fighting Metcalfe once again, Metcalfe who would cut off his nose any day to spite his face, sink any ship for a ha'p'orth of tar that was not legally due, Metcalfe the lion of the Rotarians.

'She should not have said that,' said Colonel Hodge, reporting the incident to his wife over their horrible dinner. 'Metcalfe won't do anything now.'

'Why don't *you* go and talk to the man who's bought the field?' said Mrs Hodge.

'I might . . . I think I will . . . Tell you what, I'll go now.'

He went.

He found the man without difficulty, since there was no other visitor staying at the Brakehurst Arms. An enquiry from the landlord elicited his name—Mr Hargood-Hood. He was sitting alone in the parlour, sipping whisky and soda and working at *The Times* crossword.

The Colonel said, 'Evening. My name is Hodge.'

'Yes?'

'I daresay you know who I am.'

'I'm very sorry, I'm afraid . . .'

'I own the Manor. My garden backs on to Westmacott's field—the one you've bought.'

'Oh,' said Mr Hargood-Hood, 'was he called Westmacott? I didn't know. I leave all these things to my lawyer. I simply told him to find me a suitable, secluded site for my work. He told me last week he had found one here. It seems very suitable. But he didn't tell me anyone's name.'

'You didn't pick this village for any particular reason?'

'No, no. But I think it perfectly charming,' he added politely.

There was a pause.

'I wanted to talk to you,' said Colonel Hodge superfluously. 'Have a drink.'

'Thank you.'

Another pause.

'I'm afraid you won't find it a very healthy site,' said the Colonel. 'Down in the hollow there.'

'I never mind things like that. All I need is seclusion.'

'Ah, a writer, no doubt.'

'No.'

'A painter?'

'No, no. I suppose you would call me a scientist.'

'I see. And you would be using your house for week-ends?'

'No, no, quite the reverse. I and my staff will be working here all the week. And it's not exactly a house I'm building, although, of course, there will be living quarters attached. Perhaps, since we are going to be such close neighbours, you would like to see the plans . . .'

' . . . You never saw such a thing,' said Colonel Hodge next morning to Mr Metcalfe. 'An experimental industrial laboratory he called it. Two great chimneys—have to have those, he said, by law, because of poison fumes, a water tower to get high pressures, six bungalows for his staff . . . ghastly. The odd thing was he seemed quite a decent sort of fellow. Said it hadn't occurred to him anyone would find it objectionable. Thought we should all be interested. When I brought up the subject of re-selling—tactful, you know—he just said he left all that to his lawyer . . .'

3

Much Malcock Hall.

Dear Lady Peabury,

In pursuance of our conversation of three days ago, I beg to inform you that I have been in communication with Mr Hargood-Hood, the purchaser of the field which separates our two properties, and his legal representative. As Col. Hodge has already informed you, Mr Hargood-Hood proposes to erect an experimental industrial laboratory fatal to the amenities of the village. As you are doubtless aware, work has not yet been commenced, and Mr Hargood-Hood is willing to re-sell the property if duly compensated. The price proposed is to include re-purchase of the field, legal fees and compensation for the architect's work. The young blackguard has us in a cleft stick. He wants £500. It is excessive, but I am prepared to pay half of this if you will pay the other half. Should you not accede to this generous offer I shall take steps to safeguard my own interest *at whatever cost to the neighbourhood.*

Yours sincerely,
Beverley Metcalfe

PS—I mean I shall sell the Hall and develop the property as *building lots.*

Much Malcock House.

Lady Peabury begs to inform Mr Metcalfe that she has received his note of this morning, the tone of which I am unable to account for. She further begs to inform you that she has no wish to increase my already extensive responsibilities in the district. She cannot accept the principle of equal obligation with Mr Metcalfe as he has far less land to look after, and the field in question should rightly form part of your property. She does not think that the scheme for developing his garden as a housing estate is likely to be a success if Mr Hargood-Hood's laboratory is as unsightly as is represented, which I rather doubt.

'All right,' said Mr Metcalfe. 'That's that and be damned to her.'

4

It was ten days later. The lovely valley, so soon to be defiled, lay resplendent in the sunset. Another year, thought Mr Metcalfe, and this fresh green foliage would be choked with soot, withered with fumes; these mellow roofs and chimneys which for two hundred years or more had enriched the landscape below the terrace, would be hidden by functional monstrosities in steel and glass and concrete. In the doomed field Mr Westmacott, almost for the last time, was calling his cattle; next week building was to begin and they must seek other pastures. So, in a manner of speaking, must Mr Metcalfe. Already his desk was littered with house agents' notices. All for £500, he told himself. There would be redecorations; the cost and loss of moving. The speculative builders to whom he had viciously appealed showed no interest in the site. He was going to lose much more than £500 on the move. But so, he grimly assured himself, was Lady Peabury. She would learn that no one could put a fast one over on Beverley Metcalfe.

And she, on the opposing slope, surveyed the scene with corresponding melancholy. The great shadows of the cedars lay across the lawn; they had scarcely altered during her long tenancy, but the box hedge had been of her planting; it was she who had planned the lily pond and glorified it with lead flamingoes; she had reared the irregular heap of stones under the west wall and stocked it with Alpines; the flowering shrubs were hers; she could not take them with her where she was going. Where? She was too old now to begin another garden, to make other friends. She would move, like so many of her contemporaries, from hotel to hotel, at home and abroad, cruise a little, settle for prolonged rather unwelcome visits on her relatives. All this for £250, for £12. 10s. a year, for less than she gave to charity. It was not the money; it was Principle. She would not compromise with Wrong; with that ill-bred fellow on the hill opposite.

Despite the splendour of the evening, an unhappy spirit obsessed Much Malcock. The Hornbeams moped and drooped; Colonel Hodge fretted. He paced the threadbare carpet of his smoking-room. 'It's enough to make a fellow turn Bolshie, like that parson,' he said. 'What does Metcalfe care? He's rich. He can move anywhere. What does Lady Peabury care? It's the small man, trying to make ends meet, who suffers.'

Even Mr Hargood-Hood seemed affected by the general gloom. His lawyer was visiting him at the Brakehurst. All day they had been in intermittent, rather anxious, consultation. 'I think I might go and talk to that Colonel again,' he said, and set off up the village street, under the deepening shadows, for the Manor House. And from this dramatic last-minute move for conciliation sprang the great Hodge Plan for appeasement and peace-in-our-time.

5

' . . . the Scouts are badly in need of a new hut,' said Colonel Hodge.

'No use coming to me,' said Mr Metcalfe. 'I'm leaving the neighbourhood.'

'I was thinking,' said Colonel Hodge, 'that Westmacott's field would be just the place for it . . .'

And so it was arranged. Mr Hornbeam gave a pound, Colonel Hodge a guinea, Lady Peabury £250. A jumble sale, a white-elephant tea, a raffle, a pageant, and a house-to-house collection, produced a further 30s. Mr Metcalfe found the rest. It cost him, all told, a little over £500. He gave with a good heart. There was no question now of jockeying him into a raw deal. In the role of public benefactor he gave with positive relish, and when Lady Peabury suggested that the field should be reserved for a camping site and the building of the hut postponed, it was Mr Metcalfe who pressed on with the building and secured the old stone tiles from the roof of a dismantled barn. In the circumstances, Lady Peabury could not protest when the building was named the Metcalfe–Peabury Hall. Mr Metcalfe found the title invigorating and was soon in negotiation with the brewery for a change of name at the Brakehurst Arms. It is true that Boggett still speaks of it as 'the Brakehurst', but the new name is plainly lettered for all to read: The Metcalfe Arms.

And so Mr Hargood-Hood passed out of the history of Much Malcock. He and his lawyer drove away to their home beyond the hills. The lawyer was Mr Hargood-Hood's brother.

'We cut that pretty fine, Jock. I thought, for once, we were going to be left with the baby.'

They drove to Mr Hargood-Hood's home, a double quadrangle of mellow brick that was famous far beyond the county. On the days when the gardens were open to the public, record crowds came to admire the topiary work, yews and boxes of prodigious size and fantastic shape which gave perpetual employment to three gardeners. Mr Hargood-Hood's ancestors had built the house and planted the gardens in a happier time, before the days of property tax and imported grain. A sterner age demanded more strenuous efforts for their preservation.

'Well, that has settled Schedule A for another year and left something over for cleaning the fish-ponds. But it was an anxious month. I shouldn't care to go through it again. We must be more careful next time, Jock. How about moving east?'

Together the two brothers unfolded the inch ordnance map of Norfolk, spread it on the table of the Great Hall and began their preliminary, expert search for a likely, unspoilt, well-loved village.

GRAHAM GREENE

The Destructors

I

IT was on the eve of August Bank Holiday that the latest recruit became the leader of the Wormsley Common Gang. No one was surprised except Mike, but Mike at the age of nine was surprised by everything. 'If you don't shut your mouth,' somebody once said to him, 'you'll get a frog down it.' After that Mike kept his teeth tightly clamped except when the surprise was too great.

The new recruit had been with the gang since the beginning of the summer holidays, and there were possibilities about his brooding silence that all recognized. He never wasted a word even to tell his name until that was required of him by the rules. When he said 'Trevor' it was a statement of fact, not as it would have been with the others a statement of shame or defiance. Nor did anyone laugh except Mike, who finding himself without support and meeting the dark gaze of the newcomer opened his mouth and was quiet again. There was every reason why T., as he was afterwards referred to, should have been an object of mockery—there was his name (and they substituted the initial because otherwise they had no excuse not to laugh at it), the fact that his father, a former architect and present clerk, had 'come down in the world' and that his mother considered herself better than the neighbours. What but an odd quality of danger, of the unpredictable, established him in the gang without any ignoble ceremony of initiation?

The gang met every morning in an impromptu car-park, the site of the last bomb of the first blitz. The leader, who was known as Blackie, claimed to have heard it fall, and no one was precise enough in his dates to point out that he would have been one year old and fast asleep on the down platform of Wormsley Common Underground Station. On one side of the car-park leant the first occupied house, No. 3, of the shattered Northwood Terrace—literally leant, for it had suffered from the blast of the bomb and the side walls were supported on wooden struts.

A smaller bomb and incendiaries had fallen beyond, so that the house stuck up like a jagged tooth and carried on the further wall relics of its neighbour, a dado, the remains of a fireplace. T., whose words were almost confined to voting 'Yes' or 'No' to the plan of operations proposed each day by Blackie, once startled the whole gang by saying broodingly, 'Wren built that house, father says.'

'Who's Wren?'

'The man who built St Paul's.'

'Who cares?' Blackie said. 'It's only Old Misery's.'

Old Misery—whose real name was Thomas—had once been a builder and decorator. He lived alone in the crippled house, doing for himself: once a week you could see him coming back across the common with bread and vegetables, and once as the boys played in the car-park he put his head over the smashed wall of his garden and looked at them.

'Been to the lav,' one of the boys said, for it was common knowledge that since the bombs fell something had gone wrong with the pipes of the house and Old Misery was too mean to spend money on the property. He could do the redecorating himself at cost price, but he had never learnt plumbing. The lav was a wooden shed at the bottom of the narrow garden with a star-shaped hole in the door: it had escaped the blast which had smashed the house next door and sucked out the window-frames of No. 3.

The next time the gang became aware of Mr Thomas was more surprising. Blackie, Mike and a thin yellow boy, who for some reason was called by his surname Summers, met him on the common coming back from the market. Mr Thomas stopped them. He said glumly, 'You belong to the lot that play in the car-park?'

Mike was about to answer when Blackie stopped him. As the leader he had responsibilities. 'Suppose we are?' he said ambiguously.

'I got some chocolates,' Mr Thomas said. 'Don't like 'em myself. Here you are. Not enough to go round, I don't suppose. There never is,' he added with sombre conviction. He handed over three packets of Smarties.

The gang was puzzled and perturbed by this action and tried to explain it away. 'Bet someone dropped them and he picked 'em up,' somebody suggested.

'Pinched 'em and then got in a bleeding funk,' another thought aloud.

'It's a bribe,' Summers said. 'He wants us to stop bouncing balls on his wall.'

'We'll show him we don't take bribes,' Blackie said, and they sacrificed the whole morning to the game of bouncing that only Mike was young enough to enjoy. There was no sign from Mr Thomas.

Next day T. astonished them all. He was late at the rendezvous, and the voting for that day's exploit took place without him. At Blackie's suggestion the gang was to disperse in pairs, take buses at random and see how many free rides could be snatched from unwary conductors (the operation was to be carried out in pairs to avoid cheating). They were drawing lots for their companions when T. arrived.

'Where you been, T.?' Blackie asked. 'You can't vote now. You know the rules.'

'I've been *there*,' T. said. He looked at the ground, as though he had thoughts to hide.

'Where?'

'At Old Misery's.' Mike's mouth opened and then hurriedly closed again with a click. He had remembered the frog.

'At Old Misery's?' Blackie said. There was nothing in the rules against it, but he had a sensation that T. was treading on dangerous ground. He asked hopefully, 'Did you break in?'

'No. I rang the bell.'

'And what did you say?'

'I said I wanted to see his house.'

'What did he do?'

'He showed it me.'

'Pinch anything?'

'No.'

'What did you do it for then?'

The gang had gathered round: it was as though an impromptu court were about to form and try some case of deviation. T. said, 'It's a beautiful house,' and still watching the ground, meeting no one's eyes, he licked his lips first one way, then the other.

'What do you mean, a beautiful house?' Blackie asked with scorn.

'It's got a staircase two hundred years old like a corkscrew. Nothing holds it up.'

'What do you mean, nothing holds it up. Does it float?'

'It's to do with opposite forces, Old Misery said.'

'What else?'

'There's panelling.'

'Like in the Blue Boar?'

'Two hundred years old.'

'Is Old Misery two hundred years old?'

Mike laughed suddenly and then was quiet again. The meeting was in a serious mood. For the first time since T. had strolled into the car-park on the first day of the holidays his position was in danger. It only needed a single use of his real name and the gang would be at his heels.

'What did you do it for?' Blackie asked. He was just, he had no jealousy, he was anxious to retain T. in the gang if he could. It was the word 'beautiful' that worried him—that belonged to a class world that you could still see parodied at the Wormsley Common Empire by a man wearing a top hat and a monocle, with a haw-haw accent. He was tempted to say, 'My dear Trevor, old chap,' and unleash his hell hounds. 'If you'd broken in,' he said sadly—that indeed would have been an exploit worthy of the gang.

'This was better,' T. said. 'I found out things.' He continued to stare at his feet, not meeting anybody's eye, as though he were absorbed in some dream he was unwilling—or ashamed—to share.

'What things?'

'Old Misery's going to be away all tomorrow and Bank Holiday.'

Blackie said with relief, 'You mean we could break in?'

'And pinch things?' somebody asked.

Blackie said, 'Nobody's going to pinch things. Breaking in—that's good enough, isn't it? We don't want any court stuff.'

'I don't want to pinch anything,' T. said. 'I've got a better idea.'

'What is it?'

T. raised eyes, as grey and disturbed as the drab August day. 'We'll pull it down,' he said. 'We'll destroy it.'

Blackie gave a single hoot of laughter and then, like Mike, fell quiet, daunted by the serious implacable gaze. 'What'd the police be doing all the time?' he said.

'They'd never know. We'd do it from inside. I've found a way in.' He said with a sort of intensity, 'We'd be like worms, don't you see, in an apple. When we came out again there'd be nothing there, no staircase, no panels, nothing but just walls, and then we'd make the walls fall down—somehow.'

'We'd go to jug,' Blackie said.

'Who's to prove? and anyway we wouldn't have pinched anything.'

He added without the smallest flicker of glee, 'There wouldn't be anything to pinch after we'd finished.'

'I've never heard of going to prison for breaking things,' Summers
said.

'There wouldn't be time,' Blackie said. 'I've seen house-breakers at
work.'

'There are twelve of us,' T. said. 'We'd organize.'

'None of us know how . . .'

'I know,' T. said. He looked across at Blackie. 'Have you got a better
plan?'

'Today,' Mike said tactlessly, 'we're pinching free rides . . .'

'Free rides,' T. said. 'Kid stuff. You can stand down, Blackie, if you'd
rather . . .'

'The gang's got to vote.'

'Put it up then.'

Blackie said uneasily, 'It's proposed that tomorrow and Monday we
destroy Old Misery's house.'

'Here, here,' said a fat boy called Joe.

'Who's in favour?'

T. said, 'It's carried.'

'How do we start?' Summers asked.

'He'll tell you,' Blackie said. It was the end of his leadership. He went
away to the back of the car-park and began to kick a stone, dribbling it
this way and that. There was only one old Morris in the park, for few
cars were left there except lorries: without an attendant there was no
safety. He took a flying kick at the car and scraped a little paint off the
rear mudguard. Beyond, paying no more attention to him than to a
stranger, the gang had gathered round T.; Blackie was dimly aware of
the fickleness of favour. He thought of going home, of never returning,
of letting them all discover the hollowness of T.'s leadership, but suppose
after all what T. proposed was possible—nothing like it had ever been
done before. The fame of the Wormsley Common car-park gang
would surely reach around London. There would be headlines in the
papers. Even the grown-up gangs who ran the betting at the all-in
wrestling and the barrow-boys would hear with respect of how Old
Misery's house had been destroyed. Driven by the pure, simple and
altruistic ambition of fame for the gang, Blackie came back to where
T. stood in the shadow of Old Misery's wall.

T. was giving his orders with decision: it was as though this plan had been with him all his life, pondered through the seasons, now in his fifteenth year crystallized with the pain of puberty. 'You,' he said to Mike, 'bring some big nails, the biggest you can find, and a hammer. Anybody who can, better bring a hammer and a screwdriver. We'll need plenty of them. Chisels too. We can't have too many chisels. Can anybody bring a saw?'

'I can,' Mike said.

'Not a child's saw,' T. said. 'A real saw.'

Blackie realized he had raised his hand like any ordinary member of the gang.

'Right, you bring one, Blackie. But now there's a difficulty. We want a hacksaw.'

'What's a hacksaw?' someone asked.

'You can get 'em at Woolworth's,' Summers said.

The fat boy called Joe said gloomily, 'I knew it would end in a collection.'

'I'll get one myself,' T. said. 'I don't want your money. But I can't buy a sledge-hammer.'

Blackie said, 'They are working on No. 15. I know where they'll leave their stuff for Bank Holiday.'

'Then that's all,' T. said. 'We meet here at nine sharp.'

'I've got to go to church,' Mike said.

'Come over the wall and whistle. We'll let you in.'

2

On Sunday morning all were punctual except Blackie, even Mike. Mike had a stroke of luck. His mother felt ill, his father was tired after Saturday night, and he was told to go to church alone with many warnings of what would happen if he strayed. Blackie had difficulty in smuggling out the saw, and then in finding the sledge-hammer at the back of No. 15. He approached the house from a lane at the rear of the garden, for fear of the policeman's beat along the main road. The tired evergreens kept off a stormy sun: another wet Bank Holiday was being prepared over the Atlantic, beginning in swirls of dust under the trees. Blackie climbed the wall into Misery's garden.

There was no sign of anybody anywhere. The lav stood like a tomb in a neglected graveyard. The curtains were drawn. The house slept. Blackie lumbered nearer with the saw and the sledge-hammer. Perhaps after all nobody had turned up: the plan had been a wild invention: they had woken wiser. But when he came close to the back door he could hear a confusion of sound hardly louder than a hive in swarm: a clickety-clack, a bang bang, a scraping, a creaking, a sudden painful crack. He thought: it's true, and whistled.

They opened the back door to him and he came in. He had at once the impression of organization, very different from the old happy-go-lucky ways under his leadership. For a while he wandered up and down stairs looking for T. Nobody addressed him: he had a sense of great urgency, and already he could begin to see the plan. The interior of the house was being carefully demolished without touching the walls. Summers with hammer and chisel was ripping out the skirting-boards in the ground floor dining-room: he had already smashed the panels of the door. In the same room Joe was heaving up the parquet blocks, exposing the soft wood floorboards over the cellar. Coils of wire came out of the damaged skirting and Mike sat happily on the floor clipping the wires.

On the curved stairs two of the gang were working hard with an inadequate child's saw on the banisters—when they saw Blackie's big saw they signalled for it wordlessly. When he next saw them a quarter of the banisters had been dropped into the hall. He found T. at last in the bathroom—he sat moodily in the least cared-for room in the house, listening to the sounds coming up from below.

'You've really done it,' Blackie said with awe. 'What's going to happen?'

'We've only just begun,' T. said. He looked at the sledge-hammer and gave his instructions. 'You stay here and break the bath and the wash-basin. Don't bother about the pipes. They come later.'

Mike appeared at the door. 'I've finished the wires, T.,' he said.

'Good. You've just got to go wandering round now. The kitchen's in the basement. Smash all the china and glass and bottles you can lay hold of. Don't turn on the taps—we don't want a flood—yet. Then go into all the rooms and turn out the drawers. If they are locked get one of the others to break them open. Tear up any papers you find and smash all the ornaments. Better take a carving knife with you from the kitchen. The bedroom's opposite here. Open the pillows and tear up the sheets. That's enough for the moment. And you, Blackie, when you've finished in here crack the plaster in the passage up with your sledge-hammer.'

'What are you going to do?' Blackie asked.

'I'm looking for something special,' T. said.

It was nearly lunch-time before Blackie had finished and went in search of T. Chaos had advanced. The kitchen was a shambles of broken glass and china. The dining-room was stripped of parquet, the skirting was up, the door had been taken off its hinges, and the destroyers had moved up a floor. Streaks of light came in through the closed shutters where they worked with the seriousness of creators—and destruction after all is a form of creation. A kind of imagination had seen this house as it had now become.

Mike said, 'I've got to go home for dinner.'

'Who else?' T. asked, but all the others on one excuse or another had brought provisions with them.

They squatted in the ruins of the room and swapped unwanted sandwiches. Half an hour for lunch and they were at work again. By the time Mike returned they were on the top floor, and by six the superficial damage was completed. The doors were all off, all the skirtings raised, the furniture pillaged and ripped and smashed—no one could have slept in the house except on a bed of broken plaster. T. gave his orders—eight o'clock next morning, and to escape notice they climbed singly over the garden wall, into the car-park. Only Blackie and T. were left: the light had nearly gone, and when they touched a switch, nothing worked—Mike had done his job thoroughly.

'Did you find anything special?' Blackie asked.

T. nodded. 'Come over here,' he said, 'and look.' Out of both pockets he drew bundles of pound notes. 'Old Misery's savings,' he said. 'Mike ripped out the mattress, but he missed them.'

'What are you going to do? Share them?'

'We aren't thieves,' T. said. 'Nobody's going to steal anything from this house. I kept these for you and me—a celebration.' He knelt down on the floor and counted them out—there were seventy in all. 'We'll burn them,' he said, 'one by one,' and taking it in turns they held a note upwards and lit the top corner, so that the flame burnt slowly towards their fingers. The grey ash floated above them and fell on their heads like age. 'I'd like to see Old Misery's face when we are through,' T. said.

'You hate him a lot?' Blackie asked.

'Of course I don't hate him,' T. said. 'There'd be no fun if I hated him.' The last burning note illuminated his brooding face. 'All this hate and love,' he said, 'it's soft, it's hooey. There's only things, Blackie,' and he looked round the room crowded with the unfamiliar shadows of half things, broken things, former things. 'I'll race you home, Blackie,' he said.

3

Next morning the serious destruction started. Two were missing—Mike and another boy whose parents were off to Southend and Brighton in spite of the slow warm drops that had begun to fall and the rumble of thunder in the estuary like the first guns of the old blitz. 'We've got to hurry,' T. said.

Summers was restive. 'Haven't we done enough?' he asked. 'I've been given a bob for slot machines. This is like work.'

'We've hardly started,' T. said. 'Why, there's all the floors left, and the stairs. We haven't taken out a single window. You voted like the others. We are going to *destroy* this house. There won't be anything left when we've finished.'

They began again on the first floor picking up the top floor-boards next the outer wall, leaving the joists exposed. Then they sawed through the joists and retreated into the hall, as what was left of the floor heeled and sank. They had learnt with practice, and the second floor collapsed more easily. By the evening an odd exhilaration seized them as they looked down the great hollow of the house. They ran risks and made mistakes: when they thought of the windows it was too late to reach them. 'Cor,' Joe said, and dropped a penny down into the dry rubble-filled well. It cracked and span amongst the broken glass.

'Why did we start this?' Summers asked with astonishment; T. was already on the ground, digging at the rubble, clearing a space along the outer wall. 'Turn on the taps,' he said. 'It's too dark for anyone to see now, and in the morning it won't matter.' The water overtook them on the stairs and fell through the floorless rooms.

It was then they heard Mike's whistle at the back. 'Something's wrong,' Blackie said. They could hear his urgent breathing as they unlocked the door.

'The bogies?' Summers asked.

'Old Misery,' Mike said. 'He's on his way,' he said with pride.

'But why?' T. said. 'He told me . . .' He protested with the fury of the child he had never been, 'It isn't fair.'

'He was down at Southend,' Mike said, 'and he was on the train coming back. Said it was too cold and wet.' He paused and gazed at the water. 'My, you've had a storm here. Is the roof leaking?'

'How long will he be?'

'Five minutes. I gave Ma the slip and ran.'

'We better clear,' Summers said. 'We've done enough, anyway.'

'Oh no, we haven't. Anybody could do this—' 'this' was the shattered hollowed house with nothing left but the walls. Yet walls could be preserved. Façades were valuable. They could build inside again more beautifully than before. This could again be a home. He said angrily, 'We've got to finish. Don't move. Let me think.'

'There's no time,' a boy said.

'There's got to be a way,' T. said. 'We couldn't have got this far . . .'

'We've done a lot,' Blackie said.

'No. No, we haven't. Somebody watch the front.'

'We can't do any more.'

'He may come in at the back.'

'Watch the back too.' T. began to plead. 'Just give me a minute and I'll fix it. I swear I'll fix it.' But his authority had gone with his ambiguity. He was only one of the gang. 'Please,' he said.

'Please,' Summers mimicked him, and then suddenly struck home with the fatal name. 'Run along home, Trevor.'

T. stood with his back to the rubble like a boxer knocked groggy against the ropes. He had no words as his dreams shook and slid. Then Blackie acted before the gang had time to laugh, pushing Summers backward. 'I'll watch the front, T.,' he said, and cautiously he opened the shutters of the hall. The grey wet common stretched ahead, and the lamps gleamed in the puddles. 'Someone's coming, T. No, it's not him. What's your plan, T.?'

'Tell Mike to go out to the lav and hide close beside it. When he hears me whistle he's got to count ten and start to shout.'

'Shout what?'

'Oh, "Help", anything.'

'You hear, Mike,' Blackie said. He was the leader again. He took a quick look between the shutters. 'He's coming, T.'

'Quick, Mike. The lav. Stay here, Blackie, all of you, till I yell.'

'Where are you going, T.?'

'Don't worry. I'll see to this. I said I would, didn't I?'

Old Misery came limping off the common. He had mud on his shoes and he stopped to scrape them on the pavement's edge. He didn't want to soil his house, which stood jagged and dark between the bomb-sites, saved so narrowly, as he believed, from destruction. Even the fan-light had been left unbroken by the bomb's blast. Somewhere somebody whistled. Old Misery looked sharply round. He didn't trust whistles. A child was shouting: it seemed to come from his own garden. Then a boy ran into the road from the car-park. 'Mr Thomas,' he called, 'Mr Thomas.'

'What is it?'

'I'm terribly sorry, Mr Thomas. One of us got taken short, and we thought you wouldn't mind, and now he can't get out.'

'What do you mean, boy?'

'He's got stuck in your lav.'

'He'd no business . . . Haven't I seen you before?'

'You showed me your house.'

'So I did. So I did. That doesn't give you the right to . . .'

'Do hurry, Mr Thomas. He'll suffocate.'

'Nonsense. He can't suffocate. Wait till I put my bag in.'

'I'll carry your bag.'

'Oh no, you don't. I carry my own.'

'This way, Mr Thomas.'

'I can't get in the garden that way. I've got to go through the house.'

'But you *can* get in the garden this way, Mr Thomas. We often do.'

'You often do?' He followed the boy with a scandalized fascination. 'When? What right . . .?'

'Do you see . . .? the wall's low.'

'I'm not going to climb walls into my own garden. It's absurd.'

'This is how we do it. One foot here, one foot there, and over.' The boy's face peered down, an arm shot out, and Mr Thomas found his bag taken and deposited on the other side of the wall.

'Give me back my bag,' Mr Thomas said. From the loo a boy yelled and yelled. 'I'll call the police.'

'Your bag's all right, Mr Thomas. Look. One foot there. On your right. Now just above. To your left.' Mr Thomas climbed over his own garden wall. 'Here's your bag, Mr Thomas.'

'I'll have the wall built up,' Mr Thomas said, 'I'll not have you boys coming over here, using my loo.' He stumbled on the path, but the boy caught his elbow and supported him. 'Thank you, thank you, my boy,' he murmured automatically. Somebody shouted again through the dark. 'I'm coming, I'm coming,' Mr Thomas called. He said to the boy beside him, 'I'm not unreasonable. Been a boy myself. As long as things are done regular. I don't mind you playing round the place Saturday mornings. Sometimes I like company. Only it's got to be regular. One of you asks leave and I say Yes. Sometimes I'll say No. Won't feel like it. And you come in at the front door and out at the back. No garden walls.'

'Do get him out, Mr Thomas.'

'He won't come to any harm in my loo,' Mr Thomas said, stumbling slowly down the garden. 'Oh, my rheumatics,' he said. 'Always get 'em on Bank Holiday. I've got to be careful. There's loose stones here. Give me your hand. Do you know what my horoscope said yesterday? "Abstain from any dealings in first half of week. Danger of serious crash." That might be on this path,' Mr Thomas said. 'They speak in parables and double meanings.' He paused at the door of the loo. 'What's the matter in there?' he called. There was no reply.

'Perhaps he's fainted,' the boy said.

'Not in my loo. Here, you, come out,' Mr Thomas said, and giving a great jerk at the door he nearly fell on his back when it swung easily open. A hand first supported him and then pushed him hard. His head hit the opposite wall and he sat heavily down. His bag hit his feet. A hand whipped the key out of the lock and the door slammed. 'Let me out,' he called, and heard the key turn in the lock. 'A serious crash,' he thought, and felt dithery and confused and old.

A voice spoke to him softly through the star-shaped hole in the door. 'Don't worry, Mr Thomas,' it said, 'we won't hurt you, not if you stay quiet.'

Mr Thomas put his head between his hands and pondered. He had noticed that there was only one lorry in the car-park, and he felt certain that the driver would not come for it before the morning. Nobody could hear him from the road in front, and the lane at the back was seldom used. Anyone who passed there would be hurrying home and would not pause for what they would certainly take to be drunken cries. And if he did call 'Help', who, on a lonely Bank Holiday evening, would have the courage to investigate? Mr Thomas sat on the loo and pondered with the wisdom of age.

After a while it seemed to him that there were sounds in the silence—they were faint and came from the direction of his house. He stood up and peered through the ventilation-hole—between the cracks in one of the shutters he saw a light, not the light of a lamp, but the wavering light that a candle might give. Then he thought he heard the sound of hammering and scraping and chipping. He thought of burglars—perhaps they had employed the boy as a scout, but why should burglars engage in what sounded more and more like a stealthy form of carpentry?

Mr Thomas let out an experimental yell, but nobody answered. The noise could not even have reached his enemies.

4

Mike had gone home to bed, but the rest stayed. The question of leadership no longer concerned the gang. With nails, chisels, screwdrivers, anything that was sharp and penetrating, they moved around the inner walls worrying at the mortar between the bricks. They started too high, and it was Blackie who hit on the damp course and realized the work could be halved if they weakened the joints immediately above. It was a long, tiring, unamusing job, but at last it was finished. The gutted house stood there balanced on a few inches of mortar between the damp course and the bricks.

There remained the most dangerous task of all, out in the open at the edge of the bomb-site. Summers was sent to watch the road for passersby, and Mr Thomas, sitting on the loo, heard clearly now the sound of sawing. It no longer came from the house, and that a little reassured him. He felt less concerned. Perhaps the other noises too had no significance.

A voice spoke to him through the hole. 'Mr Thomas.'

'Let me out,' Mr Thomas said sternly.

'Here's a blanket,' the voice said, and a long grey sausage was worked through the hole and fell in swathes over Mr Thomas's head.

'There's nothing personal,' the voice said. 'We want you to be comfortable tonight.'

'Tonight,' Mr Thomas repeated incredulously.

'Catch,' the voice said. 'Penny buns—we've buttered them, and sausage-rolls. We don't want you to starve, Mr Thomas.'

Mr Thomas pleaded desperately. 'A joke's a joke, boy. Let me out and I won't say a thing. I've got rheumatics. I got to sleep comfortable.'

'You wouldn't be comfortable, not in your house, you wouldn't. Not now.'

'What do you mean, boy?' But the footsteps receded. There was only the silence of night: no sound of sawing. Mr Thomas tried one more yell, but he was daunted and rebuked by the silence—a long way off an owl hooted and made away again on its muffled flight through the soundless world.

At seven next morning the driver came to fetch his lorry. He climbed into the seat and tried to start the engine. He was vaguely aware of a voice shouting, but it didn't concern him. At last the engine responded and he backed the lorry until it touched the great wooden shore that supported Mr Thomas's house. That way he could drive right out and down the street without reversing. The lorry moved forward, was momentarily checked as though something were pulling it from behind, and then went on to the sound of a long rumbling crash. The driver was astonished to see bricks bouncing ahead of him, while stones hit the roof of his cab. He put on his brakes. When he climbed out the whole landscape had suddenly altered. There was no house beside the car-park, only a hill of rubble. He went round and examined the back of his lorry for damage, and found a rope tied there that was still twisted at the other end round part of a wooden strut.

The driver again became aware of somebody shouting. It came from the wooden erection which was the nearest thing to a house in that desolation of broken brick. The driver climbed the smashed wall and unlocked the door. Mr Thomas came out of the loo. He was wearing a grey blanket to which flakes of pastry adhered. He gave a sobbing cry. 'My house,' he said. 'Where's my house?'

'Search me,' the driver said. His eye lit on the remains of a bath and what had once been a dresser and he began to laugh. There wasn't anything left anywhere.

'How dare you laugh,' Mr Thomas said. 'It was my house. My house.'

'I'm sorry,' the driver said, making heroic efforts, but when he remembered the sudden check of his lorry, the crash of bricks falling, he became convulsed again. One moment the house had stood there with such dignity between the bomb-sites like a man in a top hat, and then, bang, crash, there wasn't anything left—not anything. He said, 'I'm sorry. I can't help it, Mr Thomas. There's nothing personal, but you got to admit it's funny.'

H. E. BATES

The Waterfall

I

THE only sound in the air as Rose Vaughan hurried across the park was the thin glassy sound of the waterfall emptying itself into the half-frozen lake. The snow that had fallen a few days after Christmas had thawed and half vanished already, leaving little snow islands dotted about the sere flattened grass among the wintry elms. It was freezing hard, the air silently brittle and bitter, the goose-grey sky threatening and even dropping at intervals new falls of snow, little handfuls of pure white dust that never settled. Now and then the black trees and the tall yellow reed-feathers and the dead plumes of pampas grass fringing the lake would stir and quiver, but with hardly a sound. The winter afternoon darkness gave the new skin of ice across the lake a leaden polish in which the shadows of a few wild duck were reflected dimly. The duck, silent and dark, stood motionless on the ice as though frozen there, but as the woman came down the path and crossed the wooden bridge over the lake-stream they rose up frightened, soaring swiftly and with wild quackings flying round and round, their outstretched necks dark against the wintry sky.

The woman, hurrying over the bridge and up the path under the trees, hardly noticed them. She walked with strange, long half-running strides, as though walking were not quick enough for her and running too undignified. As the path ascended sharply from the lake she began to pant a little, breathing the icy air in gasps through her mouth. There was the desperation of fear in her haste. Her father, the Reverend Ezekiel Vaughan, lay very ill at the rectory, which stood at the far end of the park, where she herself had been born and had lived for forty years and where she expected to go on living until she died; and she was hurrying to get across the park to the big house in order to telephone from there for the doctor. Her father was a man who had grown old before his time, and she had lived alone with him for so long that as she panted up the path, with her mouth a little open and her feet slipping backwards on the half-frozen path, she also looked prematurely middle-aged, her face joyless and negative, her pale grey eyes devoid of alertness and light.

She met no one coming down the path, and in her desperate hurry might not have seen them if she had. Until lately the path had been public, a right of way going far back in time, but at Christmas some deer in the park had been molested and the path closed. She and her father alone had been granted the special privilege of it. There had been a putting up and a breaking down of fences which had distressed her. She was distressed also because her father had said nothing, not a word, on the side of the people. 'My silence,' he said, 'will be ample evidence of my impartiality.' But it was clear enough, and to her painfully clear, that his sympathies were with Abrahams, the owner, whom he could not afford to offend. She had found herself despising for the first time the old liaison of church and property. It had struck her so forcibly that she had been angry, her anger breeding a kind of timid horror at the mere realization of that emotion. Alone, as she hurried up the path, it was difficult to realize that she had ever cherished emotions, sinful emotions, like hatred and anger. And she felt ashamed, the pain of her conscience mingling with the pain of her fears.

Where the path divided into two she took the left-hand turn to the house. The right-hand path, formerly a way to the vicarage, had been cut off by a new snake-fence. She saw that the fence had been smashed down again. It had happened since the snow. She could see the scars and fractures made by the axes on the new skinned chestnut stakes and the black footprints in the islands of snow.

She felt at once distressed again and as she hurried on she half resolved to speak to Abrahams. She would reason with him; she would make him see the pettiness of it all. He must see it. And she would make him see it, not for her own sake nor for her own satisfaction, but for his own sake and the sake of his fellow men. Words of entreaty and reason came easily to her mind: 'What you give comes back to you. It comes back a thousand fold. Surely you don't need me to tell you?' softened and quickened by her fears and agitations about her father.

But suddenly the house appeared from behind its dark barricade of yew and pine. The sight of it, huge and red, with its weather-green cupola high on the grey roof, made her suddenly and inexplicably nervous, and her footsteps on the gravel drive and their echo among the trees seemed painfully loud to her in the frost-silent air.

She hurried up the steps leading to the terrace and the house. Along the terrace formal rows of flower-beds lay bleak and empty, the earth snow-flattened and lifeless. She rang the big brass door-bell and waited, apprehensive. A servant came, she murmured a request about the telephone, and a moment later she was in the entrance-hall, the door shut behind her.

The telephone stood on a large mahogany table in the hall. She sat down in a chair by the table, picked up the receiver and gave her number. She spoke very low, so that Abrahams, if he were about, should not hear her; but the operator could not catch what she said and asked her once, twice and then even a third time, to repeat the number. She repeated it, her face growing hot and scarlet, her voice in her own ears so loud that she felt she was shouting and that Abrahams would hear and come into the hall. Her fears were multiplied into panic, all her resolutions to speak to Abrahams driven away. She gave her message for the doctor quickly, too quickly, so that again she had to repeat the words, and again louder.

In the middle of this confusion she became conscious of another voice. It was Abrahams, saying:

'Let me see what I can do, Miss Vaughan.'

In another moment he was standing by her, had the telephone from her hands and was half-shouting: 'A message for the doctor. Yes, yes. Put a jerk in it, do. Ask him to come at once, for the Reverend. Yes, he's very bad. It's urgent. For the Reverend at once, please.'

She stood apart half-nervous, half-affronted, until he had finished speaking. His way of speaking about her father, off-handedly as it were, as the Reverend, offended her. Yet when he put down the receiver she was bound to murmur her thanks.

'And now I must go,' she added quickly.

'Oh, stop an' have a cup o' tea,' he began.

'Oh no, I must get back,' she said. 'I'm urgently needed. I must get back.'

'Ah, you can swallow a cup o' tea in a jiff,' he insisted. 'It'll help to keep the cold out.'

But she was at the door, rigid, drawing on her thin kid gloves. Against her prim nervous voice Abrahams' seemed aggressively loud, almost coarsely self-confident. He himself was big-framed, getting to stoutness, his hair very grey above the red temples. He cultivated the prosperous country air, with loose check tweeds, a gold watch chain, and brown boots as polished as a chestnut. But his butterfly-collar, stiff and white, and his black necktie upset the effect. He had made his money quickly, out of boots and shoes, during the war period, rising from nothing. The tightness, the struggle of the early years had left its mark ineffaceably on his features, his lips compressing narrowly and his eyes hardening, at unexpected moments, with unconscious avarice. Coming out into the country, to enjoy his money, he had lost his wife within a year, and had presented the church with a window of stained glass in her memory. He had still about him the hardness, the bluster and the coarseness of the factory. And it was this about him which intimidated her and made her draw on her gloves, more rigidly and hastily, by the door.

Seeing that she would not stay he stood with his hand on the big iron door latch.

'And how is the Reverend?' he asked.

'He's very ill,' she said, 'very ill.'

'I'm sorry to hear it, I am that, very sorry.'

It seemed an unconscionable time before he began to lift the door latch. In the interval, remembering her resolution to speak about the fence, she half-reproached herself: it was her duty, now that her father could no longer speak, to say something. It was clearly her duty. But still she said nothing. The words she had formed so clearly and easily in her mind had been driven away by her foolish panic and fear.

'Ah, well, if you must go,' said Abrahams, lifting the door latch.

'I *must* go,' she said. Her voice was strangely distant with its prim, polite emphasis.

'Anything I can do? Can I have anything sent down?' he said.

'Nothing,' she said. 'Thank you. Nothing at all.'

She fled, buttoning her coat collar against the freezing air, not glancing back, knowing by the long interval before the sound of the door clanging, that he was watching her.

Down by the lake the waterfall fell with an even sharper, thinner sound in the ice-covered lake. The duck had not returned and the ice was empty of all life, growing darker every moment. Little patches of new black ice and frozen snow cracked under her feet as she panted up the path, beyond the lake, towards the rectory. The house, its grey stone drabbened but unsoftened by time and rain, stood half-hidden by a line of elms, a gaunt solitary place, walled in, with half its windows plastered over long ago, a squat stone belfry in the roof of the disused stables, a light burning in a single upstairs window. She hurried on, apprehensive, fearing the worst intuitively, falling into the old half-running, half-walking pace, hardly pausing to shut the gate in the stone wall of the garden.

Before she could reach the house the front door opened and the white figure of the servant-girl appeared and stood there ready to meet her. With tears in her voice she began to tell Rose Vaughan what she already half knew, that her father was dead.

2

She spent the first days of the New Year putting things in order, on wet days indoors, arranging her father's papers, packing his sermons into neat piles, which she tied together with tape, rejecting old letters, reading through them and sometimes weeping a little and then reproaching herself both for reading and weeping. On fine days she and the servant-girl carried the rejected papers out to the garden, in clothes-baskets, and set fire to them under the elms, but the earth and the dead elm leaves were never dry and the papers burnt sluggishly, with thick harsh smoke that hung under the wet trees and stung the women's eyes. At last rain set in, dismally and as though it would last the year, and a south-west wind that cried in the house and howled in the black dripping elms. The burnt and half-burnt scraps of paper were blown about the garden like black and white leaves until the rain soddened them at last and the wind hurled them into corners and under the clumps of dead chrysanthemum stalks that had never been cut down. Driven indoors again with no papers to arrange, the women scrubbed and polished the floors and furniture and washed the pictures and the windows. In that large house, built more than a hundred years before for a more spacious family than had ever lived in it, there were rooms which had never been used and some which had never been opened for twenty years. The women flung open their windows and the rain blew in on the mice-chimbled floor-boards, the old travelling-trunks, the piles of faded and forgotten church magazines, the rotting sunshades, the disused croquet sets, the piles of half-rotten apples laid out on sheets of *The Times* to dry for that winter and even the winter before. The women worked with a great show of noise and hustle, tiring themselves out in an unconscious effort to efface the effect and the memory of death.

Finally it was done: all the rooms had been cleaned and aired, the last of the big heavy foot-worn carpets had been turned and re-laid, the clumsy mahogany furniture had been polished and set back in its original places, as though it had never been moved. And suddenly there was nothing to do. The wet January days, which had seemed so short, began to seem very long, and the house, which had seemed so bustling and alive, began to recapture the air of silence and death.

Like a veneer, the lively effect of clearing up the house began to wear off, leaving a drab under-surface of realities, a troublesome sense of loss, a dread of loneliness and bills and formalities. There was a will. The rector had left a little over a hundred and fifty pounds. With the books and the furniture, it was to come to Rose; so that there would, perhaps, after the sale, be two hundred and fifty pounds.

She realized that it was nothing. It might last her, with care, with extreme, bitter care, for five years—no more than a day out of the life which lay before her. To supplement it she might do a little private teaching. She would see: she would have to see. The house would no longer be hers; there would, of course, be another rector. These things seemed to her a cruel complication of realities, a kind of equation she had never been brought up to solve.

But one thing she saw, instantly. The servant must go. And having sacked her she felt at once an insufferable loneliness. Parishioners called in the afternoons and she called in return on them, but after darkness she sat there, in the vast house, absolutely alone, with nothing to think of except herself and her dead father, her mind fretted by its own fears and its half-imagined fears. She was driven to bed at nine o'clock and then eight and even earlier, with the Bible from which her father had taught her to read a passage every night since childhood. Upset one evening and going up to bed early to cry herself to sleep she woke, half through the night, to remember that she had forgotten, for the first time, for as long as she could remember, to read that passage. She went downstairs with a candle to find her Bible. As she came back the candle-light fell on something white lying in the passage, by the front door. She picked it up, a letter.

It was a note from Abrahams, asking her if she could not go up to tea on the following day. Inexplicably she felt offended. The very tone and language of the letter seemed offensive: 'What about coming to tea one day, say tomorrow (Thursday). Should like to discuss question of memorial to Reverend. Need not reply. Will send car.' It was so common, so detestable that she felt quite suddenly enraged.

In the morning, trying to forget the letter, she succeeded only in recalling its words and renewing her own annoyance. She went about in a state of prim, rigid vexation, the very attitude she would adopt if she were to meet Abrahams. But beneath it all she was inexplicably afraid of seeing him.

And quite suddenly she saw it differently. She would go: of course she would go. Not to go would seem childish, so discourteous. She was not sure that it was not even her duty to go.

So in the afternoon she was ready, in black except for the thin stitched lines of white on the back of her tight black gloves, when the car arrived. No sooner was she sitting silent, behind the chauffeur, than she wished she had not come.

As the car drove down the hill from the rectory, towards the village, and then up by the private road through the park, she stared out of the windows at the wet January landscape, noticing for the first time the red misty flush of elm and beech buds, and then, in the park, the first flicker of aconites, coldest yellow, uncurling in the winter grass. Farther up, under the shelter of the house and its yews, a few odd half-opened snowdrops, like frailest white toadstools, bloomed about the grass. The flowers, so early, filled her with a sense of comfort shot with flashes of envy.

In the house it was so warm that she could have fallen asleep. She and Abrahams sat by a huge fire of wood in the drawing-room, she with her hat and gloves still on, parochial fashion, the words 'I mustn't stay' rising from long foolish habit to her prim lips.

'Ah, make yourself at home,' said Abrahams, genially.

Dotted about the room, on tables and in the deep window sills, were bowls of blue and white hyacinths, whose fragrance she breathed with an unconscious show of deep pleasure, longingly.

Abrahams seemed pleased and was telling her how he had planted the bulbs himself and how much he had given for them when tea arrived, the pot and jugs and tray of silver.

'After tea I'll show you round the conservatory,' said Abrahams. 'Interested in flowers, I know?'

'I am indeed,' she said.

She had withdrawn herself again, sitting stiff, straight up, on the edge of the chair.

'Take your things off,' Abrahams insisted, 'while I pour out. You'll be cold when you go out again.'

'Oh! I mustn't stay.'

'Be blowed. What's your hurry? Not such a lot to get back for, have you?'

She could have wept. There was a kind of forced geniality about his words which seemed to her brutal. They were full, too, of unconscious truth. She knew so very well that there was no hurry, that she had nothing to get back for. And she could have wept at her own hypocrisy and from the pain of his unconscious truth and brutality. But she removed her gloves instead, finger by finger, aloof and meticulous, folding and pressing them on her lap and then gently rubbing the blood back into her starved white fingers.

'You're cold,' said Abrahams. 'Why don't you come nearer the fire?'

'My hands are just a little chilled,' she told him. 'That's all.'

'Know what they say!' he laughed. 'Cold hands—warm heart.'

She was frigid. She tried to put into her silence an austere disapproval of that familiarity. It did not succeed. He had poured out tea and was handing the cup to her, not noticing either the austerity of her silence or her sudden confusion as she took the cup.

'You drink that—you'll feel a little warmer about the gills.'

'Thank you,' she said.

With the cup in her hands she tried to renew the old austere silence. But she needed the tea and she began to drink with tiny sips, cautiously, the thin scraggy guides of her neck tautening as she tried to swallow noiselessly. Abrahams drank also, stirring his tea briskly and then drinking with quick guzzling sips. Watching him, she forgot her resolution to be silent in her revulsion at the sound of his loud sipping and the sight of the tea-drips shining like spittle on the bristles of his greyish moustache.

She watched him, fascinated, until he put down his cup and wiped his tea-wet moustache with the back of his hand.

'Well now,' he said, 'about the Reverend.'

She wanted to protest, as always, against the use of that word. It was the very emblem of his familiar vulgarity. But it was useless. He went on quickly, before she could speak:

'I like to see a man have his due and—well, no use beating about the bush, Miss Vaughan. I should like to see a memorial put up to the Reverend. That's what. A stone or a window—anything, I don't care as long as it's for the church and is worthy of your father.'

He stopped abruptly. With her cup still in her hands, Miss Vaughan was crying, the thin half-checked tears falling soundlessly on her black dress and into her tea-cup.

He let her go on, without a word or a gesture. And vaguely she was aware of his silence as being a comfort to her, and her tears began to come more easily, without pain, giving her relief.

At last she could blow her nose and lift her head and glance sideways through the window, in the pretence that nothing had happened and in the hope also that he would act as though nothing had happened.

But he took her cup, and emptying the slops into the basin, said:

'Nothing like a good cry. I know what it is to lose someone.'

The words brought the tears stinging up to her eyes again, but she twisted her lips and kept silent. She felt sorry, then, not for herself but for him.

'I should—' she began, but she could go no further.

'Don't worry,' he said. 'Drink your tea.'

She found herself obeying, drinking with confusion but with a strange and inexplicable sense of comfort.

'We can talk about it later,' he said.

She only nodded. Her eyes were red from crying and her voice hardly audible, and in her black clothes and black hat she looked old and pale, tired out.

He suddenly jumped up. 'I was going to show you the conservatory, wasn't I?'

The old prim austerity of manner came back to her as his voice resumed its turn of familiarity.

'Oh! no, I think I must go.'

But he took no notice and before she could protest they were through the hall, where she had once used the telephone, and through the glass doors leading to the conservatory, the damp warmth of the place and the breath of its flowers and ferns meeting them heavily and sweetly as they entered.

He was very proud of the place. He had fitted up electric lamps in the roof along the stages where the flowers stood and he began to switch the lights on and then off and then on again so that she could see the difference between the flower-colours and greenness in the raw January light and in the white lamp-brilliance. The scents of hyacinth and freesia were exotic, the colours of the waxy petals very pure and delicate. And unconsciously, for the first time, she lived for a few moments outside herself, delighting in the flowers, forgetting that attitude of parochial stiffness which she had worn for so long that it was almost like second nature. Abrahams, delighted also, gave one or two of his sudden heavy laughs and she laughed also almost without realizing it. Between the laughter she touched and breathed the flowers, all except the frail powdery pink and yellow primulas, cowslip-scented, which he would not let her touch.

'You don't want to be infected, do you?' he asked.

'With what?'

He told of the skin disease which the touch of the primula could give.

'Oh! that's just a story,' she cried.

'No, it's right.'

'Well! I don't care!' she cried. She buried her face in the pink candelabra of blossoms with a sensation of doing something very delicious and abandoned.

It was not until she was back, alone, in the silence of the rectory that the significance of her behaviour struck her fully, and at the thought of it she broke out in a perspiration of shame, her prim soul curling up within her with horror. Oh! she had been very stupid. It had all been very silly, very thoughtless. And memory only made it more vivid and painful.

She went to bed early, trying to forget it. But in the morning a messenger and a message arrived from Abrahams, the messenger with pots of pink hyacinth and primula, the message asking her if she would go to tea, and again discuss the memorial, on Sunday.

As she read the note and saw the flowers she went very weak.

'There is no answer,' she said.

She went about for the rest of the week in an agony of shame and indecision. Yet the answer had to be written. There was no help for it. It was her duty to write.

She delayed answering till Saturday and then wrote, fearfully, to say that she would endeavour to look in, if she might, after Sunday school. The word endeavour she felt, kept her at an austere distance. It made her answer negative of all emotion, saved her from new embarrassments.

In the park the aconites had opened back flat, vivid lemon, in the watery January sun, and higher up, under the yews there were myriad snowdrops among the stiff dark crocus leaves. And again, in spite of herself, she was envious.

She put on the old prim parochial attitude, sitting with her gloves on, as Abrahams talked of the memorial to her in the warm drawing-room. 'Yes, I see,' she would say, in agreement; or, 'I am not prepared to say,' in disagreement. It was as if she were stiffly resolved not to commit herself, again, either to tears or laughter.

'Well then,' said Abrahams, as she rose to go, 'you'll decide between the broken column and the stained window.'

'It is very kind of you.'

'The sooner we know the better. What if you come up again on Sunday?'

'Oh! I really don't know.'

She spoke as though terrified, as though to say 'Yes' and to come again were against all her most cherished principles of duty and propriety.

'You can send a note and tell me,' said Abrahams, 'when I send some more flowers.'

She fled, half-glad to be back in the rectory with its silence and damp book-odours and solitude.

But on the following Sunday she was half-glad to leave it again. The agony of the silence and solitude had begun to wear her thin and white, thinner and whiter even than before. To see the aconites, to sit in the warm drawing-room, to talk with a fellow-creature again—it was all a little intoxicating to her.

Then, quite suddenly without preparation, as they were having tea and talking of the memorial, deciding on the stained glass, Abrahams asked if she would marry him.

She sat silent, staring, her face absolutely blank in pained astonishment. Suddenly, as if to reassure her, Abrahams smiled. She turned upon him instantly with a voice of half-weeping protest:

'You're joking! You're joking.'

He rose and put his arm on her shoulder. 'No, no. I'm serious, I mean it.'

'I—I—I . . .' But she could not speak and he sat for a long time with his arm on her shoulder while she sat struggling with her tears and astonishment.

'Don't cry,' he said. 'Don't cry. All in good time.'

She wept openly. He reasoned with her a little afterwards, but it was that unexpected tenderness in his voice which finally decided her. She tried to reason against it all, but the recollection of that emotion always triumphed.

A week later she accepted. The question of love never touched her. She had long ago begun to teach herself that marriage and love were words which did not interest her. She reasoned that it was not a question of love, but of duty, and she was secure in that.

They were married in the spring.

3

The rains of late winter continued desolately into spring, drenching the crocuses until they bent over like limp spent candles of orange and purple and white, weighing down the first greenish canary buds of the daffodils by the lake, along the low-lying land by the stream, the park was flooded, the young leaves of celandine struggling up, yellow-tipped, through the water, and Abrahams was worried because even when the rain ceased and the sun had attained its first spring-power, the water did not drain away. In his concern he would walk down to the stream every morning, testing the height of the water by the wooden stakes he had had driven in and marked, pacing up and down the grass, pausing often, to consider what might be done. He would come back to lunch with a frown on his face, impatient: he wanted the place right, and he must have it right, he would have it right. Rose would say nothing but 'Yes' or 'No' as his tone demanded, obedient to a half-conscious resolution never to assert herself, never to disagree, never to do anything which might bring them into a state of intimacy. She often committed a kind of sin against herself in order to keep up that negative serenity. If Abrahams suggested deepening the stream she too would say, 'I was thinking so myself', or if he changed his mind abruptly, thinking that he might raise the banks of the stream, she would change her mind also, saying, 'I feel sure it would be better'. But it was a sin of duty, the sin that she had practised so long with her father that it was already both a habit and a virtue. She was scarcely conscious of it. And if Abrahams asked, as he did very rarely, for her opinion, she would manage, by some remark like, 'Oh! it's quite beyond my poor brain', to excuse herself and at the same time flatter him. Whatever he did must be right.

So when the question of the floods and the stream worried Abrahams she was worried also, and going down to the stream with him one afternoon she stood or paced about the grass in a pretence of harassed thought, just as he did. At last, when Abrahams had walked far up the brook to survey from a fresh point, she sat down for a moment on the deer-smoothed bole of an elm and watched the flood water and the yellow hosts of celandine in the damp places beyond. The stream itself came down quietly and the spring air was so still that she could hear every drop of its gentle fall into the lake below. Then, quite suddenly, as she sat watching and listening, the whole problem of the flood seemed clear to her. Surely all that they had to do was to widen the stream and deepen its fall and make a new weir into the lake, so that the stream could take more water and take it faster.

She got up and called Abrahams, timidly, and when he came back to her she told him, repeating often 'I know it's quite silly and impossible'. He listened and walked down to the waterfall and then, looking upstream, considered it all. Standing still, she watched the sunlight on the flowers and the water again in a state of timid apprehension until he disturbed her with a shout of excitement:

'You've got it!' He was already hurrying upstream to her. 'Can't think why it didn't come to me before. Can't imagine for the life of me why I didn't think of it.' He was very excited.

'Oh! You would have thought of it,' she said.

'I don't know so much, I don't know so much,' he kept saying, as they hurried back to the house. 'You must have been thinking it all out on the quiet.'

'Oh! no, oh no,' she said. 'Only sometimes I used to notice that even when there was water still standing about there was only a trickle at the waterfall.'

'And I never noticed it,' he marvelled. 'And I never noticed it. You're a bit of a marvel.'

'Oh! no,' she deprecated. 'It's nothing, really it's nothing.'

Back at the house he telephoned to the drainage engineers; they would send over a man in the morning, early.

In the morning, soon after breakfast, a little flaphooded car, mud-flecked and ramshackle, chattered up the drive, swishing the gravel recklessly. A young man alighted and rang the front door bell six times, with comic effect, and Abrahams, in his enthusiasm, answered the door himself, and a moment or two later the car started again and chattered away into the park. When it returned again to the house, just before one o'clock, Abrahams and the young man seemed to be hilarious.

'Rose,' said Abrahams as they came in to lunch. 'This is the engineer, Mr Phillips.'

Hearing their laughter, she had put on something of the old prim austerity of manner, in unconscious disapprobation.

'How d'ye do, Mrs Abrahams?' said Phillips, shaking hands; and catching in a flash the feeling of cool distance in her outstretched hand: 'I'll bet you wondered what the tide had washed up, didn't you, Mrs Abrahams?'

'I did wonder,' she said, 'what all the laughter was about.'

'Oh! Mr Phillips is a case,' said Abrahams. 'He's a fair caution. I haven't laughed so much for years.'

'Ah! but be careful,' said Phillips. He advanced, and tapping Abrahams' waistcoat, said with a mock seriousness that set Abrahams tittering again: 'Do you know, sir, that the valves of your heart are worn out? Yes sir, worn out. Absolutely finished. You may go pop any minute. Punctured.'

And as Abrahams wiped the tears of laughter from his eyes Rose smiled a small, half-stiff, half-indulgent smile with unparted lips.

At the lunch table Phillips was irrepressible. He was a rather small, fleshy man, with a cherubic face and little vivid eyes that shone and quivered like blue glass marbles, with ecstatic joviality. His face was the face of a true comedian. He was never still, never silent. His eyes travelled electrically everywhere, untiringly, in search of fresh jokes, jokes which, when they came, might have been in bad taste, but for some reason never were. Rose sat at first aloof and frigid, as though ready to freeze the first germ of indelicacy or blasphemy, but it never came. 'The wages of gin', said Phillips once, taking up his water to drink, 'is breath.' Her face stiffened, then, with its first and only sign of offence, a sign that was lost on both Phillips and Abrahams, laughing into their serviettes. After that she sat a little less strained and less upright, though still with a shadow of severity in her face, her smiles mere polite motions of her thin lips. Phillips saw this, and as though it were all a game in which she must keep her lips set and smiling while he tried to make her smile in spite of it, he began to direct his jokes at her. It flattered her subtly and gradually, in spite of herself, she felt warmer and more tolerant of him, and at last she broke out softly, 'Oh, Mr Phillips, you're too bad!'

'You'll laugh, Mrs Abrahams, you'll laugh if you're *not* careful,' cried Phillips. 'You'll laugh, as sure as my name's Napoleon. You will—I warn you. You'll laugh. Now, now! Smile, but don't laugh. Smile—' he threw his serviette over his head, like a photographer, his voice comically muffled—'*smile*, please. That's it—now hold it—the left hand clasped on the right—splendid—exquisite—how delighted *he* will be—enchanting! Hold it—one—moment—tchtk!'

He threw the serviette off his head, making gestures of mock despair. 'But you *laughed*—you *laughed*,' he cried.

'Oh dear,' she said, her face flushed and her eyes moist with confusion and laughter. 'And no wonder.'

'Ah! didn't I tell you he was a case!' cried Abrahams.

'Oh! how silly of me,' said Rose, wiping her eyes.

Phillips was still making them laugh, Rose still half against herself, when they went down to the lake in the afternoon. Rose was unprepared to go, but first Abrahams and then Phillips insisted, Abrahams saying:

'It's really my wife's idea—she first saw how it could be done.'

'Oh, no, really,' said Rose.

'Now, now, Mrs Abrahams,' Phillips joked. 'Come, come. Don't be afraid. The big man will pull out the nasty tooth and then it will be all over.'

'Really you could do much better without me,' she said.

But she went with them, protesting a little out of politeness and biting her lips or twisting them in order to keep her laughter quite circumspect. By the lake the kingcups had opened wide, their yellow petals glistening as though varnished, and further up the slopes of grass, in the damp places, the first lady smocks trembled, tenderest mauve, still half shut, on fragile stems. In the hollow by the flood water the sun was quite hot, and Rose, sitting down on an elm-bole again, could hear spring in the silence, a silence broken only by the singing of larks, far up, and the trickling of the waterfall, both very sweet and soft, the water faintest, like an echo of the birds.

While she sat there, Abrahams and the engineer surveyed the stream, made notes, took measurements, and at intervals laughed a great deal. When they returned to her Abrahams was simmering with enthusiasm, like a boy—it could be done, the thing could be done, easily, just as she said it could!

'Not easily,' cried Phillips, serious for once. 'It will take time—all summer.'

'Time's nothing,' said Abrahams. 'Nor money. I want the thing done, that's all.'

Phillips returned to the house for tea. Abrahams had taken a fancy to him, there was more laughter, and at last Abrahams suggested that Phillips, instead of driving backwards and forwards from the town each day, should come and spend the summer at the house with them. It would be so much easier, so much more convenient. Phillips seemed to hesitate and then said:

'Could I fish in the lake?'

'Fish? You're not joking? You can fish, swim, row—do anything.'

'I should like to come then,' said Phillips.

Before the week was out he had brought over his belongings, and before the end of another week the work by the lake was in progress, a band of workmen arriving each morning in a lorry and Phillips driving down in his dilapidated car soon afterwards, to superintend. He rushed hither and thither all morning, electric, untiring, coming back to the house at noon to eat a hasty meal, flying off a joke or two, and then returning. Dumps of yellow clay and piles of pink brick and wooden shacks for the workmen appeared by the lake and became visible from the house through the half-leafed trees.

Every afternoon, if it were fine, Rose and Abrahams walked down to watch the work. She, while Abrahams talked with Phillips, sat on the elm-bole and watched the workmen digging out the pure yellow clay, like stiff cheese, as they deepened and widened the trench which later would be the new water-course. Farther up they had dammed the stream and only a thin trickle of water came down the trench, so that the waterfall was soundless and dry.

On the first evenings, when the dusk still fell early and a little cold, Abrahams and Phillips would go into the billiard room and the click of the billiard balls would be drowned by their boisterous laughter until Rose at last would join them, ostensibly to see if they needed anything but in reality to share that laughter.

And gradually it became an unconscious habit to go down to the lake each afternoon and into the billiard room each evening. It was not until the evenings became longer and warmer and the two men began to play a game of bowls on the lawn that it became a conscious thing, something to which she looked forward. Realizing it, she reproved herself at once, and she did not go down to watch the work for two afternoons. But first Phillips and then Abrahams noticed it and Phillips made gentle banter about it, half teasing. Strangely, she felt hurt, and the next afternoon she went down to watch the work again. But Phillips was not there. When Abrahams explained that he had gone off on business for the afternoon she felt a spasm of unexpected disappointment that was almost a shock.

It was already early June, and Phillips had gone into town, not on business, but to fetch his fishing-tackle. In the evening and again the next evening he was at the lake and she did not see him until late. Coming back on the second evening he carried an immense basket, covered with green reeds, staggering along with it like a man with a load of lead. The basket was for her—an offering. He went through mock solemnities. At last, when she removed the reeds it was to reveal a roach, pink and silver, no bigger than a sardine. It was all that the basket contained. At the joke Abrahams and Phillips went off into explosive laughter.

It was a laughter in which, inexplicably, she could not join. She felt hurt again, and again without knowing why. It was as if they were laughing at her, and she could not bear it. She reproached herself; it was so silly, such a trivial thing. What was she thinking about? What was coming over her? Yet the sense of injury remained.

For a day or two she felt a strange resentment against Phillips. She went down to the lake, but she hardly spoke to him, and in the evenings his laughter irritated her. And suddenly she closed up, as into a shell again, with all the old primness and straight-lipped austerity.

Phillips, as before, noticed it.

'Have I done anything to offend you?' he said, one afternoon by the stream.

'To offend me?' she said. 'Why should I be offended?'

But the very tone of her voice was offended. As soon as he had walked away she hurried over the bridge, past the lake, and took the old path up to the rectory. At the top of the slope she sat down, in the sunshine, to regain her breath and think and come to a decision about it all. When she got up again she had solved the problem with the old formula and was half-content. It was her duty to behave differently to him. She would make amends. She would apologize. It was her duty to apologize.

Yet the days went past and she never apologized. She began to avoid Phillips and then, having avoided him, would feel wretched. He, absorbed in his fishing, seemed to take not the faintest notice of her.

She half made up her mind that if he spoke to her again she would make the fishing an excuse for her behaviour. He had begun to fish on Sundays. She objected to that. Yet, when he asked if she objected she said 'No', as if she had not the heart to rob him of that pleasure. And so he fished all day on Sundays, taking food with him, sitting lost in the reeds that grew taller and ranker as the summer richened to midsummer, and to the first arid days of July. Coming back in the evening there would be the same jocularity as ever, the same mocking play on something, the same roars of laughter from Abrahams. She sat aloof, as though it did not interest her. Then, after one intense cloudless blazing Sunday by the lake, Phillips returned in the evening without a single fish, not even a stickleback, not so much as an undergrown roach with which to play another joke on her.

For the first time since she had known him Phillips was silent, in absolute dejection. She could not resist the opportunity.

'Well,' she said, 'perhaps it will be a lesson to you.'

'A lesson?—What in?'

'A lesson not to abuse the sabbath.'

He burst into roars of laughter. 'So you think the fish know Sunday when it comes!' he said.

There was no derision either in his words or his laughter. But she was bitterly hurt again. Yet it comforted her to go about nursing that sense of injury secretly.

Then also she hoped that he would, perhaps, take notice of what she had said and not go to the lake on the following Sunday. It would mean that he had, once at least, taken her seriously.

But the next Sunday, when she came down to breakfast, he had already gone. Hard and aloof, she put on her white gloves and went to church with Abrahams. It was nothing, she must forget it, it meant nothing to her. But she was troubled and would not acknowledge it and by noon she had fretted herself into a strange state of misery which her denials only increased.

In the afternoon she could endure it no longer. She left Abrahams asleep and went out into the hot Sunday stillness, across the Terrace and down into the park. She had made up her mind: she would walk by the lake, he would see her, she would speak to him, there would be an end of it all.

As she walked along, in and out of the great tree shadows, she reasoned out what she would say. It seemed very simple: she would say that his violation of her dearest principles had hurt her. That was all. Not those very words, perhaps, but she would convey that. She would make him understand.

Before she was aware of it she was by the lake. Panic-stricken, she hurried along, looking straight ahead along the reed-fringed bank, never pausing once until she caught sight, on the opposite bank, of Phillips, in his shirt-sleeves, watching over his rod, the wet float flashing scarlet in the white sunlight. But she hurried along, terrified that he might see her or shout, never pausing even when she was out of sight.

Back at the house she was angry that he had not noticed her. She felt that he had seen her and then, purposely, with deliberate indifference, had ignored her. And then, illogically, she felt a moment of acute tenderness for him. Perhaps, after all, he had not seen her, had been too absorbed even to look up. She must not misjudge him. It was her duty not to misjudge him.

For some weeks she went about half-comforted and half-troubled by the renewal of that anger and tenderness, not understanding either. Then one morning, at breakfast, Phillips declared:

'Well, another week and you can turn on the new tap.'

She sat very straight in her chair, prim but intense.

'Then you will be leaving us?' she said.

'Yes—no more fishing on Sundays.'

She could not speak.

A week later the work of the lake was finished.

'Mrs Abrahams ought to pull the lever,' suggested Phillips.

'Oh! no!' she said. 'Really no.'

'But that's only proper,' said Abrahams. 'It was your idea. Yes, you pull the lever. We must do it properly.'

'But I shouldn't be strong enough,' she protested desperately.

'You don't need to be,' said Phillips. 'I'll work it so that just a touch will be enough.'

'It's easy,' said Abrahams. 'Phillips will make it easy.'

She gave in. On the afternoon itself she walked down to the lake with Abrahams and Phillips. The first trees were turning yellow, a few leaves floated about the still lake, and the air was very quiet. An odd workman or two stood about and she felt very nervous. Phillips had arranged it so that she should raise a lever and that the old dam should collapse and release the water. It was very simple.

Everything was ready. Phillips and Abrahams and the workmen stood waiting. She lifted her hand to the lever and then, at the last moment, hesitated. Her hands were trembling.

'All you have to do is pull the lever,' said Phillips quietly. 'It's easy.'

The next moment she made an immense effort. She clenched the lever desperately and pulled it.

There was a sudden crash as the dam itself collapsed and then a roar, increasing rapidly, as the water tore down through the new channel, with Phillips and Abrahams running excitedly along the banks, to see the first leap of water into the lake, and then at last there was a sound of thunder as the water fell. The sound for a moment was terrific. She stood in suspense, startled. At her feet the water tore down the channel furiously, so that she went giddy from looking at it, and there was a shower of soft white spray as the torrent thundered into the lake. She had never believed that there could be so much water. She stood pale and motionless, with tears in her eyes, not knowing what to do.

The tears began to run down her cheeks. Afraid that the men might see her she suddenly turned away and began to walk away up the slope under the trees. She heard the voices of the men call after her but she did not turn. Her tears kept on and behind her the torrent of water roared with soft thunder. She began to hurry, trying to dry her tears as she did so, but fresh tears filled her eyes as fast as she wiped them away and the sound of the waterfall followed her persistently. She hurried on as though afraid of it and long after she could hear it no more, the echo of it, like a remembered emotion, thundered through her mind.

The next morning Phillips went away.

T. H. WHITE

The Troll

'M Y father,' said Mr Marx, 'used to say that an experience like the one I am about to relate was apt to shake one's interest in mundane matters. Naturally he did not expect to be believed, and he did not mind whether he was or not. He did not himself believe in the supernatural, but the thing happened, and he proposed to tell it as simply as possible. It was stupid of him to say that it shook his faith in mundane affairs, for it was just as mundane as anything else. Indeed the really frightening part about it was the horribly tangible atmosphere in which it took place. None of the outlines wavered in the least. The creature would have been less remarkable if it had been less natural. It seemed to over-come the usual laws without being immune to them.

'My father was a keen fisherman, and used to go to all sorts of places for his fish. On one occasion he made Abisko his Lapland base, a com-fortable railway hotel, one hundred and fifty miles within the Arctic circle. He travelled the prodigious length of Sweden (I believe it is as far from the South of Sweden to the North, as it is from the South of Sweden to the South of Italy) in the electric railway, and arrived tired out. He went to bed early, sleeping almost immediately, although it was bright daylight outside; as it is in those parts through the night at that time of the year. Not the least shaking part of his experience was that it should all have happened under the sun.

'He went to bed early, and slept, and dreamt. I may as well make it clear at once, as clear as the outlines of that creature in the northern sun, that his story did not turn out to be a dream in the last paragraph. The division between sleeping and waking was abrupt, although the feeling of both was the same. They were both in the same sphere of horrible absurdity though in the former he was asleep and in the latter almost terribly awake. He tried to be asleep several times.

'My father always used to tell one of his dreams, because it somehow seemed of a piece with what was to follow. He believed that it was a consequence of the thing's presence in the next room. My father dreamed of blood.

'It was the vividness of the dreams that was impressive, their minute detail and horrible reality. The blood came through the keyhole of a locked door which communicated with the next room. I suppose the two rooms had originally been designed *ensuite*. It ran down the door panel with a viscous ripple, like the artificial one created in the conduit of Trumpingdon Street. But it was heavy, and smelt. The slow welling of it sopped the carpet and reached the bed. It was warm and sticky. My father woke up with the impression that it was all over his hands. He was rubbing his first two fingers together, trying to rid them of the greasy adhesion where the fingers joined.

'My father knew what he had got to do. Let me make it clear that he was now perfectly wide awake, but he knew what he had got to do. He got out of bed, under this irresistible knowledge, and looked through the keyhole into the next room.

'I suppose the best way to tell the story is simply to narrate it, without an effort to carry belief. The thing did not require belief. It was not a feeling of horror in one's bones, or a misty outline, or anything that needed to be given actuality by an act of faith. It was as solid as a wardrobe. You don't have to believe in wardrobes. They are there, with corners.

'What my father saw through the keyhole in the next room was a Troll. It was eminently solid, about eight feet high, and dressed in brightly ornamented skins. It had a blue face, with yellow eyes, and on its head there was a woolly sort of nightcap with a red bobble on top. The features were Mongolian. Its body was long and sturdy, like the trunk of a tree. Its legs were short and thick like the elephant's feet that used to be cut off for umbrella stands, and its arms were wasted: little rudimentary members like the forelegs of a kangaroo. Its head and neck were very thick and massive. On the whole, it looked like a grotesque doll.

'That was the horror of it. Imagine a perfectly normal golliwog (but without the association of a Christie minstrel) standing in the corner of a room, eight feet high. The creature was as ordinary as that, as tangible, as stuffed, and as ungainly at the joints: but it could move itself about.

'The Troll was eating a lady. Poor girl, she was tightly clutched to its breast by those rudimentary arms, with her head on a level with its mouth. She was dressed in a night-dress which had crumpled up under her armpits, so that she was a pitiful naked offering, like a classical picture of Andromeda. Mercifully, she appeared to have fainted.

'Just as my father applied his eye to the keyhole, the Troll opened its mouth and bit off her head. Then, holding the neck between the bright blue lips, he sucked the bare meat dry. She shrivelled, like a squeezed orange, and her heels kicked. The creature had a look of thoughtful ecstasy. When the girl seemed to have lost succulence as an orange she was lifted into the air. She vanished in two bites. The Troll remained leaning against the wall, munching patiently and casting its eyes about with a vague benevolence. Then it leant forward from the low hips, like a jack-knife folding in half, and opened its mouth to lick the blood up from the carpet. The mouth was incandescent inside, like a gas fire, and the blood evaporated before its tongue, like dust before a vacuum cleaner. It straightened itself, the arms dangling before it in patient uselessness, and fixed its eyes upon the keyhole.

'My father crawled back to bed, like a hunted fox after fifteen miles. At first it was because he was afraid that the creature had seen him through the hole, but afterwards it was because of his reason. A man can attribute many night-time appearances to the imagination, and can ultimately persuade himself that creatures of the dark did not exist. But this was an appearance in a sunlit room, with all the solidity of a wardrobe and unfortunately almost none of its possibility. He spent the first ten minutes making sure that he was awake, and the rest of the night trying to hope that he was asleep. It was either that, or else he was mad.

'It is not pleasant to doubt one's sanity. There are no satisfactory tests. One can pinch oneself to see if one is asleep, but there are no means of determining the other problem. He spent some time opening and shutting his eyes, but the room seemed normal and remained unaltered. He also soused his head in a basin of cold water, without result. Then he lay on his back, for hours, watching the mosquitoes on the ceiling.

'He was tired when he was called. A bright Scandinavian maid admitted the full sunlight for him and told him that it was a fine day. He spoke to her several times, and watched her carefully, but she seemed to have no doubts about his behaviour. Evidently, then, he was not badly mad; and by now he had been thinking about the matter for so many hours that it had begun to get obscure. The outlines were blurring again, and he determined that the whole thing must have been a dream or a temporary delusion, something temporary, anyway, and finished with; so that there was no good in thinking about it longer. He got up, dressed himself fairly cheerfully, and went down to breakfast.

'These hotels used to run extraordinarily well. There was a hostess always handy in a little office off the hall, who was delighted to answer any questions, spoke every conceivable language, and generally made it her business to make the guests feel at home. The particular hostess at Abisko was a lovely creature into the bargain. My father used to speak to her a good deal. He had an idea that when you had a bath in Sweden one of the maids was sent to wash you. As a matter of fact this sometimes used to be the case, but it was always an old maid and highly trusted. You had to keep yourself under water and this was supposed to confer a cloak of invisibility. If you popped your knee out she was shocked. My father had a dim sort of hope that the hostess would be sent to bath him one day: and I daresay he would have shocked her a good deal. However, this is beside the point. As he passed through the hall something prompted him to ask about the room next to his. Had anybody, he enquired, taken number twenty-three?

' "But, yes," said the lady manager with a bright smile, "twenty-three is taken by a doctor professor from Uppsala and his wife, such a charming couple!"

'My father wondered what the charming couple had been doing, whilst the Troll was eating the lady in the night-dress. However, he decided to think no more about it. He pulled himself together, and went in to breakfast. The professor was sitting in an opposite corner (the manageress had kindly pointed him out), looking mild and short-sighted, by himself. My father thought he would go out for a long climb on the mountains, since exercise was evidently what his constitution needed.

'He had a lovely day. Lake Torne blazed a deep blue below him, for all its thirty miles, and the melting snow made a lacework of filigree round the tops of the surrounding mountain basin. He got away from the stunted birch trees, and the mossy bogs with the reindeer in them, and the mosquitoes, too. He forded something that might have been a temporary tributary of the Abiskojokk, having to take off his trousers to do so and tucking his shirt up round his neck. He wanted to shout, bracing himself against the glorious tug of the snow water, with his legs crossing each other involuntarily as they passed, and the boulders turning under his feet. His body made a bow wave in the water, which climbed and feathered on his stomach, on the upstream side. When he

was under the opposite bank a stone turned in earnest, and he went in.
He came up, shouting with laughter, and made a loud remark which has
since become a classic in my family, "Thank God," he said, "I rolled up
my sleeves." He wrung out everything as best he could, and dressed
again in the wet clothes, and set off for the shoulder of Niakatjavelk. He
was dry and warm again in half a mile. Less than a thousand feet took
him over the snow line, and there, crawling on hands and knees, he
came face to face with what seemed to be the summit of ambition. He
met an ermine. They were both on all fours, so that there was a sort of
equality about the encounter, especially as the ermine was higher up
than he was. They looked at each other for a fifth of a second, without
saying anything, and then the ermine vanished. He searched for it
everywhere in vain, for the snow was only patchy. My father sat down
on a dry rock, to eat his well-soaked luncheon of chocolate and rye
bread.

'Life is such unutterable hell, solely because it is sometimes beautiful.
If we could only be miserable all the time, if there could be no such
things as love or beauty or faith or hope, if I could be absolutely certain
that my love would never be returned: how much more simple life
would be. One could plod through the Siberian salt mines of existence
without being bothered about happiness. Unfortunately the happiness
is there. There is always the chance (about eight hundred and fifty to
one) that another heart will come to mine. I can't help hoping, and
keeping faith, and loving beauty. Quite frequently I am not so miserable
as it would be wise to be. And there, for my poor father sitting on his
boulder above the snow, was stark happiness beating at the gates.

'The boulder on which he was sitting had probably never been sat
upon before. It was 150 miles within the Arctic circle, on a mountain
5,000 feet high, looking down on a blue lake. The lake was so long that
he could have sworn it sloped away at the ends, proving to the naked eye
that the sweet earth was round. The railway line and the half-dozen
houses of Abisko were hidden in the trees. The sun was warm on the
boulder, blue on the snow, and his body tingled smooth from the spate
water. His mouth watered for the chocolate, just behind the tip of his
tongue.

'And yet, when he had eaten the chocolate—perhaps it was heavy on
his stomach—there was the memory of the Troll. My father fell suddenly into a black mood, and began to think about the supernatural.
Lapland was beautiful in the summer, with the sun sweeping round the

horizon day and night, and the small tree leaves twinkling. It was not the sort of place for wicked things. But what about the winter? A picture of the Arctic night came before him, with the silence and the snow. Then the legendary wolves and bears snuffled at the far encampments, and the nameless winter spirits moved on their darkling courses. Lapland had always been associated with sorcery, even by Shakespeare. It was at the outskirts of the world that the Old Things accumulated, like driftwood round the edges of the sea. If one wanted to find a wise woman, one went to the rims of the Hebrides; on the coast of Brittany one sought the mass of St Secaire. And what an outskirt Lapland was! It was an outskirt not only of Europe, but of civilization. It had no boundaries. The Lapps went with the reindeer, and where the reindeer were was Lapland. Curiously indefinite region, suitable to the indefinite things. The Lapps were not Christians. What a fund of power they must have had behind them, a power against Christ. My father realized with a shock that he was living in the age of the reindeer, a period contiguous to the mammoth and the fossil.

'Well, this was not what he had come out to do. He dismissed the nightmares with an effort, got up from his boulder, and began the scramble back to his hotel. It was impossible that a professor from Abisko could become a Troll.

'As my father was going in to dinner that evening the manageress stopped him in the hall.

' "We have had a day so sad," she said. "The poor Dr Professor has disappeared his wife. She has been missing since last night. The Dr Professor is inconsolable."

'My father then knew for certain that he had lost his reason.

'He went blindly to dinner, without making any answer, and began to eat a thick sour-cream soup that was taken cold with pepper and sugar. The professor was still sitting in his corner, a sandy-headed man with thick spectacles and a desolate expression. He was looking at my father, and my father, with the soup spoon halfway to his mouth, looked at him. You know that eye-to-eye recognition, when two people look deeply into each other's pupils, and burrow to the soul? It usually comes before love. I mean the clear, deep, milk-eyed recognition expressed by the poet Donne. Their eyebeams twisted and did thread their eyes upon a double string. My father recognized that the professor was a Troll, and the professor recognized my father's recognition. Both of them knew that the professor had eaten his wife.

'My father put down his soup spoon, and the professor began to grow. The top of his head lifted and expanded, like a great loaf rising in an oven; his face went red and purple, and finally blue; the whole ungainly upper-works began to sway and topple towards the ceiling. My father looked about him. The other diners were eating unconcernedly. Nobody else could see it, and he was definitely mad at last. When he looked at the Troll again, the creature bowed. The enormous superstructure inclined itself towards him from the hips, and grinned seductively.

'My father got up from his table experimentally, and advanced towards the Troll, arranging his feet on the carpet with excessive care. He did not find it easy to walk, or to approach the monster, but it was a question of his reason. If he was mad, he was mad; and it was essential that he should come to grips with the thing, in order to make certain.

'He stood before it like a small boy, and held out his hand, saying, "Good evening."

' "Ho! Ho!" said the Troll, "little mannikin. And what shall I have for my supper tonight?"

'Then it held out its wizened furry paw and took my father by the hand.

'My father went straight out of the dining-room, walking on air. He found the manageress in the passage and held out his hand to her.

' "I'm afraid I have burnt my hand," he said. "Do you think you could tie it up?"

'The manageress said, "But it is a very bad burn. There are blisters all over the back. Of course, I will bind it up at once."

'He explained that he had burnt it on one of the spirit lamps at the sideboard. He could scarcely conceal his delight. One cannot burn one-self by being insane.

' "I saw you talking to the Dr Professor," said the manageress, as she was putting on the bandage. "He is a sympathetic gentleman, is he not?"

'The relief about his sanity soon gave place to other troubles. The Troll had eaten its wife and given him a blister, but it had also made an unpleasant remark about its supper that evening. It proposed to eat my father. Now very few people can have been in a position to decide what to do when a Troll earmarks them for its next meal. To begin with, although it was a tangible Troll in two ways, it had been invisible to the other diners. This put my father in a difficult position. He could not, for instance, ask for protection. He could scarcely go to the manageress and say, "Professor Skal is an odd kind of werewolf, ate his wife last night, and proposes to eat me this evening." He would have found himself in a loony-bin at once. Besides, he was too proud to do this, and still too confused. Whatever the proofs and blisters, he did not find it easy to believe in professors that turned into Trolls. He had lived in the normal world all his life, and at his age, it was difficult to start learning afresh. It would have been quite easy for a baby, who was still co-ordinating the world, to cope with the Troll situation: for my father, not. He kept trying to fit in somewhere, without disturbing the universe. He kept telling himself that it was nonsense: one did not get eaten by professors. It was like having a fever, and telling oneself that it was all right, really, only a delirium, only something that would pass.

'There was that feeling on the one side, the desperate assertion of all the truths that he had learned so far, the tussle to keep the world from drifting, the brave but intimidated refusal to give in or to make a fool of himself.

'On the other side there was stark terror. However much one struggled to be merely deluded, or hitched up momentarily in an odd pocket of space-time, there was panic. There was the urge to go away as quickly as possible, to flee the dreadful Troll. Unfortunately the last train had left Abisko, and there was nowhere else to go.

'My father was not able to distinguish these trends of thought. For him they were at the time intricately muddled together. He was in a whirl. A proud man, and an agnostic, he stuck to his muddled guns alone. He was terribly afraid of the Troll, but he could not afford to admit its existence. All his mental processes remained hung up, whilst he talked on the terrace, in a state of suspended animation, with an American tourist who had come to Abisko to photograph the midnight sun.

'The American told my father that the Abisko railway was the northernmost electric railway in the world, that twelve trains passed through it every day travelling between Uppsala and Narvik, that the population of Abo was 12,000 in 1862, and that Gustavus Adolphus ascended the throne of Sweden in 1611. He also gave some facts about Greta Garbo.

'My father told the American that a dead baby was required for the mass of St Secaire, that an elemental was a kind of mouth in space that sucked at you and tried to gulp you down, that homeopathic magic was practised by the Aborigines of Australia, and that a Lapland woman was careful at her confinement to have no knots or loops about her person, lest these should make the delivery difficult.

'The American, who had been looking at my father in a strange way for some time, took offence at this and walked away; so that there was nothing for it but to go to bed.

'My father walked upstairs on will-power alone. His faculties seemed to have shrunk and confused themselves. He had to help himself with the banister. He seemed to be navigating himself by wireless, from the spot about a foot above his forehead. The issues that were involved had ceased to have any meaning, but he went on doggedly up the stairs, moved forward by pride and contrariety. It was physical fear that alienated him from his body, the same fear that he had felt as a boy, walking down the long corridors to be beaten. He walked firmly up the stairs.

'Oddly enough, he went to sleep at once. He had climbed all day and been awake all night and suffered emotional extremes. Like a condemned man, who was to be hanged in the morning, my father gave the whole business up and went to sleep.

'He was woken at midnight exactly. He heard the American on the terrace below his window, explaining excitedly that there had been a cloud on the last two nights at 11:58, thus making it impossible to photograph the midnight sun. He heard the camera click.

'There seemed to be a sudden storm of hail and wind. It roared at his window-sill, and the window curtains lifted themselves taut, pointing horizontally into the room. The shriek and rattle of the tempest framed the window in a crescendo of growing sound, an increasing blizzard directed towards himself. A blue paw came over the sill.

'My father turned over and hid his head in the pillow. He could feel the domed head dawning at the window and the eyes fixing themselves upon the small of his back. He could feel the places physically, about four inches apart. They itched. Or else the rest of his body itched, except those places. He could feel the creature growing into the room, glowing like ice, and giving off a storm. His mosquito curtains rose in its afflatus, uncovering him, leaving him defenceless. He was in such an ecstasy of terror that he almost enjoyed it. He was like a bather plunging for the first time into freezing water and unable to articulate. He was trying to yell, but all he could do was to throw a series of hooting noises from his paralysed lungs. He became a part of the blizzard. The bedclothes were gone. He felt the Troll put out his hands.

'My father was an agnostic, but, like most idle men, he was not above having a bee in his bonnet. His favourite bee was the psychology of the Catholic Church. He was ready to talk for hours about psychoanalysis and the confession. His greatest discovery had been the rosary.

'The rosary, my father used to say, was intended solely as a factual occupation which calmed the lower centres of the mind. The automatic telling of the beads liberated the higher centres to meditate upon the mysteries. They were a sedative, like knitting or counting sheep. There was no better cure for insomnia than a rosary. For several years he had given up deep breathing or regular counting. When he was sleepless he lay on his back and told his beads, and there was a small rosary in the pocket of his pyjama coat.

'The Troll put out its hands, to take him round the waist. He became completely paralysed, as if he had been winded. The Troll put its hand upon the beads.

'They met, the occult forces, in a clash above my father's heart. There was an explosion, he said, a quick creation of power. Positive and negative. A flash, a beam. Something like the splutter with which the antenna of a tram meets its overhead wires again, when it is being changed about.

'The Troll made a high squealing noise, like a crab being boiled, and began rapidly to dwindle in size. It dropped my father and turned about, and ran wailing, as if it had been terribly burnt, for the window. Its colour waned as its size decreased. It was one of those air-toys now, that expire with a piercing whistle. It scrambled over the window-sill, scarcely larger than a little child, and sagging visibly.

'My father leaped out of bed and followed it to the window. He saw it drop on the terrace like a toad, gather itself together, stumble off, staggering and whistling like a bat, down the valley of the Abiskojokk.

'My father fainted.

'In the morning the manageress said, "There has been such a terrible tragedy. The poor Dr Professor was found this morning in the lake. The story about his wife had certainly unhinged his mind."

'A subscription for a wreath was started by the American, to which my father subscribed five shillings; and the body was shipped off next morning, on one of the twelve trains that travel between Uppsala and Narvik every day.'

ELIZABETH TAYLOR

The Blush

THEY were the same age—Mrs Allen and the woman who came every day to do the housework. 'I shall never have children now,' Mrs Allen had begun to tell herself. Something had not come true; the essential part of her life. She had always imagined her children in fleeting scenes and intimations; that was how they had come to her, like snatches of a film. She had seen them plainly, their chins tilted up as she tied on their bibs at meal-times; their naked bodies had darted in and out of the water-sprinkler on the lawn; and she had listened to their voices in the garden and in the mornings from their beds. She had even cried a little dreaming of the day when the eldest boy would go off to boarding-school; she pictured the train going out of the station; she raised her hand and her throat contracted and her lips trembled as she smiled. The years passing by had slowly filched from her the reality of these scenes—the gay sounds; the grave peace she had longed for; even the pride of grief.

She listened—as they worked together in the kitchen—to Mrs Lacey's troubles with her family, her grumblings about her grown-up son who would not get up till dinner-time on Sundays and then expected his mother to have cleaned his shoes for him; about the girl of eighteen who was a hairdresser and too full of dainty ways which she picked up from the women's magazines, and the adolescent girl who moped and glowered and answered back.

My children wouldn't have turned out like that, Mrs Allen thought, as she made her murmured replies. 'The more you do for some, the more you may,' said Mrs Lacey. But from gossip in the village which Mrs Allen heard, she had done all too little. The children, one night after another, for years and years, had had to run out for parcels of fish and chips while their mother sat in The Horse & Jockey drinking brown ale. On summer evenings, when they were younger, they had hung about outside the pub: when they were bored they pressed their foreheads to the window and looked in at the dark little bar, hearing the jolly laughter, their mother's the loudest of all. Seeing their faces, she would swing at once from the violence of hilarity to that of extreme annoyance and, although ginger-beer and packets of potato crisps would be handed out through the window, her anger went out with them and threatened the children as they ate and drank.

'And she doesn't always care who she goes there *with*,' Mrs Allen's gardener told her.

'She works hard and deserves a little pleasure—she has her anxieties,' said Mrs Allen, who, alas, had none.

She had never been inside The Horse & Jockey, although it was nearer to her house than The Chequers at the other end of the village where she and her husband went sometimes for a glass of sherry on Sunday mornings. The Horse & Jockey attracted a different set of customers—for instance, people who sat down and drank, at tables all round the wall. At The Chequers no one ever sat down, but stood and sipped and chatted as at a cocktail-party, and luncheons and dinners were served, which made it so much more respectable: no children hung about outside, because they were all at home with their Nannies.

Sometimes in the evenings—so many of them—when her husband was kept late in London, Mrs Allen wished that she could go down to The Chequers and drink a glass of sherry and exchange a little conversation with someone; but she was too shy to open the door and go in alone: she imagined heads turning, a surprised welcome from her friends, who would all be safely in married pairs; and then, when she left, eyes meeting with unspoken messages and conjecture in the air.

Mrs Lacey left her at midday and then there was gardening to do and the dog to be taken for a walk. After six o'clock, she began to pace restlessly about the house, glancing at the clocks in one room after another, listening for her husband's car—the sound she knew so well because she had awaited it for such a large part of her married life. She would hear, at last, the tyres turning on the soft gravel, the door being slammed, then his footsteps hurrying towards the porch. She knew that it was a wasteful way of spending her years—and, looking back, she was unable to tell one of them from another—but she could not think what else she might do. Humphrey went on earning more and more money and there was no stopping him now. Her acquaintances, in wretched quandaries about where the next term's school-fees were to come from, would turn to her and say cruelly: 'Oh, *you're* all right, Ruth. You've no idea what you are spared.'

And Mrs Lacey would be glad when Maureen could leave school and 'get out earning'. 'I've got my geometry to do,' she says, when it's time to wash-up the tea-things. 'I'll geometry you, my girl,' I said. 'When I was your age, I was out earning.'

Mrs Allen was fascinated by the life going on in that house and the children seemed real to her, although she had never seen them. Only Mr Lacey remained blurred and unimaginable. No one knew him. He worked in the town in the valley, six miles away and he kept himself to himself; had never been known to show his face in The Horse & Jockey. 'I've got my own set,' Mrs Lacey said airily.

'After all, he's nearly twenty years older than me. I'll make sure neither of my girls follow my mistake. "I'd rather see you dead at my feet," I said to Vera.' Ron's young lady was lucky; having Ron, she added. Mrs Allen found this strange, for Ron had always been painted so black; was, she had been led to believe, oafish, ungrateful, greedy and slow to put his hands in his pockets if there was any paying out to do. There was also the matter of his shoe-cleaning, for no young woman would do what his mother did for him—or said she did. Always, Mrs Lacey would sigh and say: 'Goodness me, if only I was their age and knew what I know now.'

She was an envious woman: she envied Mrs Allen her pretty house and her clothes and she envied her own daughters their youth. 'If I had your figure,' she would say to Mrs Allen. Her own had gone: what else could be expected, she asked, when she had had three children? Mrs Allen thought, too, of all the brown ale she drank at The Horse & Jockey and of the reminiscences of meals past which came so much into her conversations. Whatever the cause was, her flesh, slackly corseted, shook as she trod heavily about the kitchen. In summer, with bare arms and legs she looked larger than ever. Although her skin was very white, the impression she gave was at once colourful—from her orange hair and bright lips and the floral patterns that she always wore. Her red-painted toe-nails poked through the straps of her fancy sandals; turquoise-blue beads were wound round her throat.

Humphrey Allen had never seen her; he had always left for the station before she arrived, and that was a good thing, his wife thought. When she spoke of Mrs Lacey, she wondered if he visualized a neat, homely woman in a clean white overall. She did not deliberately mislead him, but she took advantage of his indifference. Her relationship with Mrs Lacey and the intimacy of their conversations in the kitchen he would not have approved, and the sight of those calloused feet with their chipped nail-varnish and yellowing heels would have sickened him.

One Monday morning, Mrs Lacey was later than usual. She was never very punctual and had many excuses about flat bicycle-tyres or Maureen being poorly. Mrs Allen, waiting for her, sorted out all the washing. When she took another look at the clock, she decided that it was far too late for her to be expected at all. For some time lately Mrs Lacey had seemed ill and depressed; her eyelids, which were chronically rather inflamed, had been more angrily red than ever and, at the sink or ironing-board, she would fall into unusual silences, was absent-minded and full of sighs. She had always liked to talk about the 'change' and did so more than ever as if with a desperate hopefulness.

'I'm sorry, but I was ever so sick,' she told Mrs Allen, when she arrived the next morning. 'I still feel queerish. Such heartburn. I don't like the signs, I can tell you. All I crave is pickled walnuts, just the same as I did with Maureen. I don't like the signs one bit. I feel I'll throw myself into the river if I'm taken that way again.'

Mrs Allen felt stunned and antagonistic. 'Surely not at your age,' she said crossly.

'You can't be more astonished than me,' Mrs Lacey said, belching loudly. 'Oh, pardon. I'm afraid I can't help myself.'

Not being able to help herself, she continued to belch and hiccough as she turned on taps and shook soap-powder into the washing-up bowl. It was because of this that Mrs Allen decided to take the dog for a walk. Feeling consciously fastidious and aloof she made her way across the fields, trying to disengage her thoughts from Mrs Lacey and her troubles; but unable to. 'Poor woman,' she thought again and again with bitter animosity.

She turned back when she noticed how the sky had darkened with racing, sharp-edged clouds. Before she could reach home, the rain began. Her hair, soaking wet, shrank into tight curls against her head; her woollen suit smelt like a damp animal. 'Oh, I am drenched,' she called out, as she threw open the kitchen door.

She knew at once that Mrs Lacey had gone, that she must have put on her coat and left almost as soon as Mrs Allen had started out on her walk, for nothing was done; the washing-up was hardly started and the floor was unswept. Among the stacked-up crockery a note was propped; she had come over funny, felt dizzy and, leaving her apologies and respects, had gone.

Angrily, but methodically, Mrs Allen set about making good the wasted morning. By afternoon, the grim look was fixed upon her face. 'How dare she?' she found herself whispering, without allowing herself to wonder what it was the woman had dared.

She had her own little ways of cosseting herself through the lonely hours, comforts which were growing more important to her as she grew older, so that the time would come when not to have her cup of tea at four-thirty would seem a prelude to disaster. This afternoon, disorganized as it already was, she fell out of her usual habit and instead of carrying the tray to the low table by the fire, she poured out her tea in the kitchen and drank it there, leaning tiredly against the dresser. Then she went upstairs to make herself tidy. She was trying to brush her frizzed hair smooth again when she heard the door-bell ringing.

When she opened the door, she saw quite plainly a look of astonishment take the place of anxiety on the man's face. Something about herself surprised him, was not what he had expected. 'Mrs Allen?' he asked uncertainly and the astonishment remained when she had answered him.

'Well, I'm calling about the wife,' he said. 'Mrs Lacey that works here.'

'I was worried about her,' said Mrs Allen.

She knew that she must face the embarrassment of hearing about Mrs Lacey's condition and invited the man into her husband's study, where she thought he might look less out of place than in her brocade-smothered drawing-room. He looked about him resentfully and glared down at the floor which his wife had polished. With this thought in his mind, he said abruptly: 'It's all taken its toll.'

He sat down on a leather couch with his cap and his bicycle-clips beside him.

'I came home to my tea and found her in bed, crying,' he said. This was true. Mrs Lacey had succumbed to despair and gone to lie down. Feeling better at four o'clock, she went downstairs to find some food to comfort herself with; but the slice of dough-cake was ill-chosen and brought on more heartburn and floods of bitter tears.

'If she carries on here for a while, it's all got to be very different,' Mr Lacey said threateningly. He was nervous at saying what he must and could only bring out the words with the impetus of anger. 'You may or may not know that she's expecting.'

'Yes,' said Mrs Allen humbly. 'This morning she told me that she thought . . .'

'There's no "thought" about it. It's as plain as a pikestaff.' Yet in his eyes she could see disbelief and bafflement and he frowned and looked down again at the polished floor.

Twenty years older than his wife—or so his wife had said—he really, to Mrs Allen, looked quite ageless, a crooked, bow-legged little man who might have been a jockey once. The expression about his blue eyes was like a child's: he was both stubborn and pathetic.

Mrs Allen's fat spaniel came into the room and went straight to the stranger's chair and began to sniff at his corduroy trousers.

'It's too much for her,' Mr Lacey said. 'It's too much to expect.'

To Mrs Allen's horror she saw the blue eyes filling with tears. Hoping to hide his emotion, he bent down and fondled the dog, making playful thrusts at it with his fist closed.

He was a man utterly, bewilderedly at sea. His married life had been too much for him, with so much in it that he could not understand.

'Now I know, I will do what I can,' Mrs Allen told him. 'I will try to get someone else in to do the rough.'

'It's the late nights that are the trouble,' he said. 'She comes in dog-tired. Night after night. It's not good enough. "Let them stay at home and mind their own children once in a while," I told her. "We don't need the money." '

'I can't understand,' Mrs Allen began. She was at sea herself now, but felt perilously near a barbarous, unknown shore and was afraid to make any movement towards it.

'I earn good money. For her to come out at all was only for extras. She likes new clothes. In the daytimes I never had any objection. Then all these cocktail-parties begin. It beats me how people can drink like it night after night and pay out for someone else to mind their kids. Perhaps you're thinking that it's not my business, but I'm the one who has to sit at home alone till all hours and get my own supper and see next to nothing of my wife. I'm boiling over some nights. Once I nearly rushed out when I heard the car stop down the road. I wanted to tell your husband what I thought of you both.'

'My husband?' murmured Mrs Allen.

'What am I supposed to have, I would have asked him? Is she my wife or your sitter-in? Bringing her back at this time of night. And it's no use saying she could have refused. She never would.'

Mrs Allen's quietness at last defeated him and dispelled the anger he had tried to rouse in himself. The look of her, too, filled him with doubts, her grave, uncertain demeanour and the shock her age had been to him. He had imagined someone so much younger and—because of the cocktail-parties—flighty. Instead, he recognized something of himself in her, a yearning disappointment. He picked up his cap and his bicycle-clips and sat looking down at them, turning them round in his hands. 'I had to come,' he said.

'Yes,' said Mrs Allen.

'So you won't ask her again?' he pleaded. 'It isn't right for her. Not now.'

'No, I won't,' Mrs Allen promised and she stood up as he did and walked over to the door. He stooped and gave the spaniel a final pat. 'You'll excuse my coming, I hope.'

'Of course.'

'It was no use saying any more to her. Whatever she's asked, she won't refuse. It's her way.'

Mrs Allen shut the front door after him and stood in the hall, listening to him wheeling his bicycle across the gravel. Then she felt herself beginning to blush. She was glad that she was alone, for she could feel her face, her throat, even the tops of her arms burning, and she went over to a looking-glass and studied with great interest this strange phenomenon.

PENELOPE FITZGERALD

At Hiruharama

MR TANNER was anxious to explain how it was that he had a lawyer in
the family, so that when they all decided to sell up and quit New
Zealand there had been someone they could absolutely trust with the
legal business. That meant that he had to say something about his grandfather, who had been an orphan from Stamford in Lincolnshire and was
sent out to a well-to-do family north of Auckland, supposedly as an
apprentice, but it turned out that he was to be more or less of a servant.
He cleaned the knives, saw to the horses, waited at table and chopped
the wood. On an errand to a dry goods store in Auckland he met Kitty,
Mr Tanner's grandmother. She had come out from England as a gov-
erness, and she too found she was really wanted as a servant. She was sixteen, and Tanner asked her to wait for three years while he saved his
wages, and then to marry him. All this was at a Methodist social, say a
couple of weeks later. 'What family have you got back home?' Kitty
asked him. Tanner replied just the one sister. Younger or older? Older.
She probably thinks I'm a skilled craftsman by now. She probably reck-
ons I'm made.—Haven't you sent word to her lately?—Not lately.—
Best write to her now, anyway, said Kitty, and tell her how it is between
us. I should be glad to have a new relation, I haven't many—I'll think
it over, he said. Kitty realized then that he could neither read nor
write.

They had to start in a remote country place. The land round Auckland at that time was ten shillings an acre, a third of the price going to
build the new churches and schools, but where Tanner and Kitty went,
north of Awanui, there weren't any churches and schools, and it was
considerably cheaper. They didn't have to buy their place, it had been
left deserted, and yet it had something you could give a thousand
pounds for and not get, and that was a standpipe giving constant clear
water from an underground well. But whoever lived there had given up,
because of the loneliness and because it was such poor country. Don't

picture a shack, though. There were two rooms, one with a stove and one with a bedstead, and a third one at the back for a vegetable store. Tanner grew root vegetables and went into Awanui twice a week with the horse and dray. Kitty stayed behind, because they'd taken on two hundred chickens and a good few pigs.

Tanner turned over in his mind what he'd say to his wife when she told him she was going to have a child. When she did tell him, which wasn't for another two years or so, by the way, he didn't hear her at first, because a northerly was blowing and neither of them could expect to hear each other. When he did catch what she was saying, he hitched up and drove into Awanui. The doctor was at his midday dinner, which he took at a boarding-house higher up the main street. When he got back and into his consulting-room Tanner asked him what were the life statistics of the North Island.

'Do you mean the death statistics?' the doctor asked.

'They'll do just as well,' said Tanner.

'No one dies here except from drink or drowning. Out of three thousand people in Taranaki Province there hasn't been a single funeral in the last sixteen months and only twenty-four sick and infirm. You may look upon me as a poor man.'

'What about women in childbirth?' asked Tanner.

The doctor didn't have any figures for women dying in childbirth, but he looked sharply at Tanner and asked him when his child was due.

'You don't know, of course. Well, don't ask me if it's going to be twins. Nature didn't intend us to know that.' He began to write in his notebook. 'Where are you living?'

'It's off the road to Houhora, you turn off to the right after twelve miles.'

'What's it called?'

'Hiruharama.'

'Don't know it. That's not a Maori name.'

'I think it means Jerusalem,' said Tanner.

'Are there any other women about the place?'

'No.'

'I mean someone who could come in and look after things while your wife's laid up. Who's your nearest neighbour?' Tanner told him there was no one except a man called Brinkman, who came over sometimes. He was about nine or ten miles off at Stony Loaf.

'And he has a wife?'

'No, he hasn't, that's what he complains about. You couldn't ask a woman to live out there.'

'You can ask a woman to live anywhere,' said the doctor. 'He's a crank, I dare say.'

'He's a dreamer,' Tanner replied. 'I should term Brinkman a dreamer.'

'I was thinking in terms of washing the sheets, that sort of thing. If there's no one else, can you manage about the house yourself for a few days?'

'I can do anything about the house,' said Tanner.

'You don't drink?'

Tanner shook his head, wondering if the doctor did. He asked if he shouldn't bring his wife with him for a consultation next time he drove over to Awanui. The doctor looked out of his window at the bone-shaking old dray with its iron-rimmed wheels. ' Don't.'

He tore the prescription out of his notebook. 'Get this for your wife. It's calcium water. When you want me to come, you'll have to send for me. But don't let that worry you. Often by the time I arrive I'm not needed.'

Other patients had arrived and were sitting on the wooden benches on the verandah. Some had empty medicine bottles for a refill. There was a man with his right arm strapped up, several kids with their mothers, and a woman who looked well enough but seemed to be in tears for some reason or other.—Well, you see life in the townships.

Tanner went over to the post office, where there was free pen and ink if you wanted it, and wrote a letter to his sister.—But wait a minute, surely he couldn't read or write? Evidently by that time he could. Mr Tanner's guess was that although Kitty was a quiet girl, very quiet, she'd refused to marry him until he'd got the hang of it.—Tanner wrote: My darling old sister. Well, it's come to pass and either a girl or a boy will be added unto us. It would be a help if you could send us a book on the subject. We have now a hundred full-grown hens and a further hundred at point of lay, and a good stand of potatoes.—After mailing the letter he bought soap, thread, needles, canned fish, tea and sugar. When he drove out of Awanui he stopped at the last homestead, where he knew a man called Parrish who kept racing-pigeons. Some of them, in fact were just arriving back at their loft. Parrish had cut the entrances to the nests down very small, and every time a bird got home it had to squeeze past a bell on a string so that the tinkling sound gave warning. They were all Blue Chequers, the only kind, Parrish declared, that a sane man would want to keep. Tanner explained his predicament and asked for the loan of two birds. Parrish didn't mind, because Hiruharama, Tanner's place, was on a more or less direct line from Awanui to Te Paki station, and that was the line his pigeons flew.

'If you'd have lived over the other way I couldn't have helped you,' Parrish said.

A Maori boy took the young birds out as soon as they were four months old and tossed them at three miles, ten miles, twenty miles, always in the same direction, north-north-west of Awanui.

'As long as they can do fifteen miles,' said Tanner.

'They can do two hundred and fifty.'

'How long will it take them to do fifteen miles?'

'Twenty minutes in clear weather,' said Parrish.

The Maori boy chose out two birds and packed them into a wicker hamper, which Tanner wedged into the driver's seat of the dray.

'Have you got them numbered in some way?' Tanner asked.

'I don't need to. I know them all,' said Parrish.

He added that they would need rock salt, so Tanner drove back into the town once more to buy the rock salt and a sack of millet. By the time he got to Hiruharama the dark clear night sky was pressing in on every side. I ought to have taken you with me, he told Kitty. She said she had been all right. He hadn't, though, he'd been worried. You mean you've forgotten something at the stores, said Kitty. Tanner went out to the dray and fetched the pigeons, still shifting about and conferring quietly in their wicker basket.

'Here's one thing more than you asked for,' he said. They found room for them in the loft above the vegetable store. The Blue Chequers were the prettiest things about the place.

The sister in England did send a book, although it didn't arrive for almost a year. In any case, it only had one chapter of a practical nature. Otherwise, it was religious in tone. But meanwhile Kitty's calculations couldn't have been far out, because more or less when they expected it the pains came on strong enough for Tanner to send for the doctor.

He had made the pigeons' nests out of packing-cases. They ought to have flown out daily for exercise, but he hadn't been able to manage that. Still, they looked fair enough, a bit dishevelled, but not so that you'd notice. It was four o'clock, breezy, but not windy. He took them out into the bright air which, even that far from the coast, was full of the salt of the ocean. How to toss a pigeon he had no idea. He opened the basket, and before he could think what to do next they were out and up into the blue. He watched in terror as after reaching a certain height they began turning round in tight circles as though puzzled or lost. Then, apparently sighting something on the horizon that they knew, they set off strongly towards Awanui.—Say twenty minutes for them to get to Parrish's loft. Ten minutes for Parrish or the Maori boy to walk up the street to the doctor's. Two and a half hours for the doctor to drive over, even allowing for his losing the way once. Thirty seconds for him to get down from his trap and open his bag.—

At five o'clock Tanner went out to see to the pigs and hens. At six Kitty was no better and no worse. She lay there quietly, sweating from head to foot. 'I can hear someone coming,' she said, not from Awanui, though, it was along the top road. Tanner thought it must be Brinkman. 'Why, yes, it must be six months since he came,' said Kitty, as though she was making conversation. Who else, after all, could it have been on the top road? The track up there had a deep rounded gutter each side which made it awkward to drive along. They could hear the screeching and rattling of his old buggy, two wheels in the gutter, two out. 'He's stopped at the gully now to let his horse drink,' said Kitty. 'He'll have to let it walk the rest of the way.'—'He'll have to turn round when he gets here and start right back,' said Tanner.

There used to be a photograph of Brinkman somewhere, but Mr Tanner didn't know what had become of it, and he believed it hadn't been a good likeness in any case.—Of course, in the circumstances, as he'd come eight miles over a rough road, he had to be asked to put up his horse for a while, and come in.

Like most people who live on their own Brinkman continued with the course of his thoughts, which were more real to him than the outside world's commotion. Walking straight into the front room he stopped in front of the piece of mirror-glass tacked over the sink and looked fixedly into it.

'I'll tell you something, Tanner, I thought I caught sight of my first grey hairs this morning.'

'I'm sorry to hear that.'

Brinkman looked round. 'I see the table isn't set.'

'I don't want you to feel that you're not welcome,' said Tanner, 'but Kitty's not well. She told me to be sure that you came in and rested a while, but she's not well. Truth is, she's in labour.'

'Then she won't be cooking dinner this evening, then?'

'You mean you were counting on having it here?'

'My half-yearly dinner with you and Mrs Tanner, yis, that's about it.'

'What day is it, then?' asked Tanner, somewhat at random. It was almost too much for him at that moment to realize that Brinkman existed. He seemed like a stranger, perhaps from a foreign country, not understanding how ordinary things were done or said.

Brinkman made no attempt to leave, but said; 'Last time I came here we started with canned toheroas. Your wife set them in front of me. I'm not sure that they had an entirely good effect on the intestines. Then we had fried eggs and excellent jellied beetroot, a choice between tea or Bovo, bread and butter and unlimited quantities of treacle. I have a note of all this in my daily journal. That's not to say, however, that I came over here simply to take dinner with you. It wasn't for the drive, either, although I'm always glad to have the opportunity of a change of scene and to read a little in Nature's book. No, I've come today, as I came formerly, for the sake of hearing a woman's voice.'

Had Tanner noticed, he went on, that there were no native songbirds in the territory? At that moment there was a crying, or a calling, from the next room such as Tanner had never heard before, not in a ship-wreck—and he had been in a wreck—not in a slaughterhouse.

'Don't put yourself out on my account,' said Brinkman. 'I'm going to sit here until you come back and have a quiet smoko.'

The doctor drove up bringing with him his wife's widowed sister, who lived with them and was a nurse, or had been a nurse. Tanner came out of the bedroom covered with blood, something like a butcher. He told the doctor he'd managed to deliver the child, a girl, in fact he'd wrapped it in a towel and tucked it up in the washbasket. The doctor took him back into the bedroom and made him sit down. The nurse put down the things she'd brought with her and looked round for the tea-tin. Brinkman sat there, as solid as his chair. 'You may be wondering who I am,' he said. 'I'm a neighbour, come over for dinner. I think of myself as one of the perpetually welcome.' 'Suit yourself,' said the sister-in-law. The doctor emerged, moving rather faster than he usually did. 'Please to go in there and wash the patient. I'm going to take a look at the after-birth. The father put it out with the waste.'

There Tanner had made his one oversight. It wasn't the afterbirth, it was a second daughter, smaller, but a twin.—But how come, if both of them were girls, that Mr Tanner himself still had the name of Tanner?

Well, the Tanners went on to have nine more children, some of them boys, and one of those boys was Mr Tanner's father. That evening, when the doctor came in from the yard with the messy scrap, he squeezed it as though he was wringing it out to dry, and it opened its mouth and the colder air of the kitchen rushed in and she'd got her start in life. After that the Tanners always had one of those tinplate mottoes hung up on the wall—Throw Nothing Away. You could get them then at the hardware store.—And this was the point that Mr Tanner had been wanting to make all along—whereas the first daughter never got to be anything in particular, this second little girl grew up to be a lawyer with a firm in Wellington, and she did very well.

All the time Brinkman continued to sit there by the table and smoke his pipe. Two more women born into the world! It must have seemed to him that if this sort of thing went on there should be a good chance, in the end, for him to acquire one for himself. Meanwhile, they would have to serve dinner sometime.

LEONORA CARRINGTON

My Flannel Knickers

THOUSANDS of people know my flannel knickers, and though I know this may seem flirtatious, it is not. I am a saint.

The 'Sainthood', I may say, was actually forced upon me. If anyone would like to avoid becoming holy, they should immediately read this entire story.

I live on an island. This island was bestowed upon me by the government when I left prison. It is not a desert island, it is a traffic island in the middle of a busy boulevard, and motors thunder past on all sides day and night.

So . . .

The flannel knickers are well known. They are hung at midday on a wire from the red green and yellow automatic lights. I wash them every day, and they have to dry in the sun.

Apart from the flannel knickers, I wear a gentleman's tweed jacket for golfing. It was given to me, and the gym shoes. No socks. Many people recoil from my undistinguished appearance, but if they have been told about me (mainly in the Tourist's Guide), they make a pilgrimage, which is quite easy.

Now I must trace the peculiar events that brought me to this condition. Once I was a great beauty and attended all sorts of cocktail-drinking, prize-giving-and-taking, artistic demonstrations and other casually hazardous gatherings organized for the purpose of people wasting other people's time. I was always in demand and my beautiful face would hang suspended over fashionable garments, smiling continually. An ardent heart, however, beat under the fashionable costumes, and this very ardent heart was like an open tap pouring quantities of hot water over anybody who asked. This wasteful process soon took its toll on my beautiful smiling face. My teeth fell out. The original structure of the face became blurred, and then began to fall away from the bones in small, ever-increasing folds. I sat and watched the process with a mixture of slighted vanity and acute depression. I was, I thought, solidly installed in my lunar plexus, within clouds of sensitive vapour.

If I happened to smile at my face in the mirror, I could objectively observe the fact that I had only three teeth left and these were beginning to decay.

Consequently

I went to the dentist. Not only did he cure the three remaining teeth but he also presented me with a set of false teeth, cunningly mounted on a pink plastic chassis. When I had paid a sufficiently large quantity of my diminishing wealth, the teeth were mine and I took them home and put them into my mouth.

The Face seemed to regain some of its absolutely-irresistible-attraction, although the folds were of course still there. From the lunar plexus I arose like a hungry trout and was caught fast on the sharp barbed hook that hangs inside all once-very-beautiful faces.

A thin magnetic mist formed between myself, the face, and clear perception. This is what I saw in the mist. 'Well, well. I really was beginning to petrify in that old lunar plexus. This must be me, this beautiful, smiling fully toothed creature. There I was, sitting in the dark bloodstream like a mummified foetus with no love at all. Here I am, back in the rich world, where I can palpitate again, jump up and down in the nice warm swimming pool of outflowing emotion, the more bathers the merrier. I Shall Be Enriched.'

All these disastrous thoughts were multiplied and reflected in the magnetic mist. I stepped in, wearing my face, now back in the old enigmatic smile which had always turned sour in the past.

No sooner trapped than done.

Smiling horribly, I returned to the jungle of faces, each ravenously trying to eat each other.

Here I might explain the process that actually takes place in this sort of jungle. Each face is provided with greater or smaller mouths, armed with different kinds of sometimes natural teeth. (Anybody over forty and toothless should be sensible enough to be quietly knitting an original new body, instead of wasting the cosmic wool.) These teeth bar the way to a gaping throat, which disgorges whatever it swallows back into the foetid atmosphere.

The bodies over which these faces are suspended serve as ballast to the faces. As a rule they are carefully covered with colours and shapes in current 'Fashion'. This 'fashion' is a devouring idea launched by another face snapping with insatiable hunger for money and notoriety. The bodies, in constant misery and supplication, are generally ignored and only used for ambulation of the face. As I said, for ballast.

Once, however, that I bared my new teeth I realized that something had gone wrong. For after a very short period of enigmatic smiling, the smile became quite stiff and fixed, while the face slipped away from its bonish mooring, leaving me clutching desperately to a soft grey mask over a barely animated body.

The strange part of the affair now reveals itself. The jungle faces, instead of recoiling in horror from what I already knew to be a sad sight, approached me and started to beg me for something which I thought I had not got.

Puzzled, I consulted my Friend, a Greek.

He said: 'They think you have woven a complete face and body and are in constant possession of excess amounts of cosmic wool. Even if this is not so, the very fact that you know about the wool makes them determined to steal it.'

'I have wasted practically the entire fleece,' I told him. 'And if anybody steals from me now I shall die and disintegrate totally.'

'Three-dimensional life,' said the Greek, 'is formed by attitude. Since by their attitude they expect you to have quantities of wool, you are three-dimensionally forced to "Sainthood", which means you must spin your body and teach the faces how to spin theirs.'

The compassionate words of the Greek filled me with fear. I am a face myself. The quickest way of retiring from social Face-eating competition occurred to me when I attacked a policeman with my strong steel umbrella. I was quickly put into prison, where I spent months of health-giving meditation and compulsive exercise.

My exemplary conduct in prison moved the Head Wardress to an excess of bounty, and that is how the Government presented me with the island, after a small and distinguished ceremony in a remote corner of the Protestant Cemetery.

So here I am on the island with all sizes of mechanical artifacts whizzing by in every conceivable direction, even overhead.

Here I sit.

ALAN SILLITOE

Enoch's Two Letters

ENOCH's parents parted in a singular way. He was eight years of age at the time.

It happened one morning after he had gone to school, so that he didn't know anything about it till coming home in the evening.

Jack Boden got up as usual at seven o'clock, and his wife, who was Enoch's mother, set a breakfast of bacon and egg before him. They never said much, and spoke even less on this particular morning, because both were solidly locked in their separate thoughts which, unknown to each other, they were at last intending to act on.

Instead of getting a bus to his foundry, Jack boarded one for the city centre. He sought out a public lavatory where, for the price of a penny, he was able to draw off his overalls, and emerge with them under his arm. They were wrapped in the brown paper which he had put into his pocket before leaving the house, a sly and unobtrusive movement as he called from the scullery: 'So long, love. See you this afternoon.'

Now wearing a reasonable suit, he walked to the railway station. There he met René, who had in her two suitcases a few of his possessions that he had fed to her during clandestine meetings over the past fortnight. Having worked in the same factory, they had, as many others who were employed there saw, 'fallen for each other'. René wasn't married, so there seemed nothing to stop her going away with him. And Jack's dull toothache of a conscience had, in the six months since knowing her, cured itself at last.

Yet they got on the train to London feeling somewhat alarmed at the step they had taken, though neither liked to say anything in case the other should think they wanted to back out. Hardly a word was spoken the whole way. René wondered what her parents would say when they saw she'd gone. Jack thought mostly about Enoch, but he knew he'd be safe enough with his mother, and that she'd bring him up right. He would send her a letter from London to explain that he had gone—in case she hadn't noticed it.

No sooner had Jack left for his normal daylight stint at the foundry than his wife, Edna, attended to Enoch. She watched him eat, standing by the mantelshelf for a good view of him during her stare. He looked up, half out of his sleep, and didn't smile back at her.

She kissed him, pushed sixpence into his pocket, and sent him up the street to school, then went upstairs to decide what things to take with her. It wasn't a hard choice, for though they had plenty of possessions, little of it was movable. So it turned out that two suitcases and a hand-bag held all she wanted.

There was ample time, and she went downstairs to more tea and a proper breakfast. They'd been married ten years, and for seven at least she'd had enough. The trouble with Jack was that he'd let nothing worry him. He was so trustworthy and easy-going he got on her nerves. He didn't even seem interested in other women, and the worse thing about such a man was that he hardly ever noticed when you were upset. When he did, he accused you of upsetting him.

There were so many things wrong, that now she was about to leave she couldn't bring them to mind, and this irritated her, and made her think that it had been even worse than it was, rather than the other way round. As a couple they had given up tackling any differences between them by the human method of talking. It was as if the sight of each other struck them dumb. On first meeting, a dozen years ago, they had been unable to say much—which, in their mutual attraction, they had con-fused with love at first sight. And nowadays they didn't try to talk to each other about the way they felt any more because neither of them thought it would do any good. Having come this far, the only thing left was to act. It wasn't that life was dull exactly, but they had nothing in common. If they had, maybe she could have put up with him, no matter how bad he was.

For a week she'd been trying to write a letter, to be posted from where she was going, but she couldn't get beyond: 'I'm leaving you for good, so stop bothering about me any more. Just look after Enoch, because I've had my bellyful and I'm off.' After re-reading it she put it back and clipped her handbag shut.

Having decided to act after years of thinking about it, she was now uncertain as to what she would do. A sister lived in Hull, so her first plan was to stay there till she found a job and a room. This was something to hang on to, and beyond it she didn't think. She'd just have to act again, and that was that. Once you started there was probably no stopping, she thought, not feeling too good about it now that the time had come.

An hour later she turned the clock to the wall, and walked out of the house for good, safe in knowing that shortly after Enoch came in from school his father would be home to feed him. They had lavished a lot of love on Enoch—she knew that—maybe too much, some of which they should have given to each other but had grown too mean and shy to.

She left the door unlocked so that he could just walk in. He was an intelligent lad, who'd be able to turn on the gas fire if he felt cold. When Mrs Mackley called from her back door to ask if she was going on her holidays, Edna laughed and said she was only off to see Jack's mother at Netherfield, to take some old rags that she needed to cut up and use for rug-clippings.

'Mam,' Enoch cried, going in by the back door. 'Mam, where's my tea?'

He'd come running down the road with a pocketful of marbles. His head in fact looked like one of the more psychedelic ones, with a pale round face, a lick of brilliant ginger hair down over his forehead, and a streak of red toffee-stain across his mouth.

Gossiping again, he thought scornfully, seeing the kitchen empty. He threw his coat, still with the sleeves twisted, over to the settee. The house did have more quiet than usual, he didn't know why. He turned the clock to face the right way, then went into the scullery and put the kettle on.

The tea wasn't like his mother made it. It was too weak. But it was hot, so he put a lot of sugar in to make up for it, then sat at the table to read a comic.

It was early spring, and as soon as it began to get dark he switched the light on and went to draw the curtains. One half came over easily, but the other only part of the way, leaving a foot-wide gap of dusk, like a long, open mouth going up instead of across. This bothered him for a while, until it got dark, when he decided to ignore it and switch the television on.

From hoping to see his mother, he began to wonder where his father was. If his mother had gone to Aunt Jenny's and missed the bus home, maybe his father at the foundry had had an accident and fallen into one of the moulds—from which it was impossible to get out alive, except as a skeleton.

Jam pot, butter dish, knife, and crumbs were spread over the kitchen table when he got himself something to eat. Not that it bothered him, that his father might have been killed, because when they had left him for an hour on his own a few months ago he had wondered what he would do if they never came back. Before he'd had time to decide, though, they had opened the door to tell him to get a sandwich and be off to bed sharp, otherwise he'd be too tired to get up for school in the morning. So he knew they'd be back sooner than he expected. When Johnny Bootle's father had been killed in a lorry last year he'd envied him, but Johnny Bootle himself hadn't liked it very much.

Whether they came back or not, it was nice being in the house on his own. He was boss of it, could mash another pot of tea if he felt like it, and keep the gas fire burning as long as he liked. The telly was flickering but he didn't want to switch it off, even though heads kept rolling up and up, so that when he looked at it continually for half a minute it seemed as if they were going round in a circle. He turned to scoop a spoonful of raspberry jam from the pot, and swallow some more cold tea.

He sat in his father's chair by the fire, legs stretched across the rug, but ready to jump at the click of the outdoor latch, and be back at the table before they could get into the room. His father wouldn't like him being in his chair, unless he were sitting on his knee. All he needed was a cigarette, and though he looked on the sideboard and along the shelf there were none in sight. He had to content himself with trying to whistle in a thick manly style. Johnny Bootle had been lucky in his loss, because he'd had a sister.

If they didn't come back tonight he wouldn't go to school in the morning. They'd shout at him when they found out, but that didn't matter if they were dead. It was eight o'clock, and he wondered where they were. They ought to be back by now, and he began to regret that he'd hoped they never would be, as if God's punishment for thinking this might be that He'd never let them.

He yawned, and picked up the clock to wind it. That was what you did when you yawned after eight in the evening. If they didn't come soon he would have to go upstairs to bed, but he thought he would get some coats and sleep on the sofa down here, with the gas fire shining bright, rather than venture to his bedroom alone. They'd really gone for a night out, and that was a fact. Maybe they were late coming back because they'd gone for a divorce. When the same thing had happened to Tom Brunt it was because his mam had gone to fetch a baby, though he was taken into a neighbour's house next door before he'd been alone as long as this.

He looked along the shelf to see if he had missed a cigarette that he could put into his mouth and play at smoking with. He had good eyes and no need of glasses, that was true, because he'd been right first time. In spite of the bread and jam he still felt hungry, and went into the scullery for some cheese.

When the light went, taking the flickering telly with it, he found a torch at the back of the dresser drawer, then looked for a shilling to put in the meter. Fortunately the gas fire gave off enough pink glow for him to see the borders of the room, especially when he shone the torch beam continually around the walls as if it were a searchlight looking for enemy planes.

'It was a long wait to Tipperary'—as he had sometimes heard his father sing while drunk, but his eyes closed, with the piece of cheese still in his hands, and he hoped he would drop off before they came in so that they'd be sorry for staying out so late, and wouldn't be able to be mad at him for not having gone to bed.

He walked across the room to the coat hooks in the recess, but his mother's and father's coats had gone, as he should have known they would be, since neither of them was in. There was nothing to put over himself when he went to sleep, but he still wouldn't go upstairs for a blanket. It would be as bad as going into a wood at night. He had run across the road when a bus was coming, and seen Frankenstein once on the telly, but he wouldn't go into a wood at night, even though lying Jimmy Kemp claimed to have done so.

Pushing one corner at a time, he got the table back against the side-board. There was an oval mirror above the mantelshelf, and he leaned both elbows on it to get as good a look at himself as he could in the wavering pink light—his round face and small ears, chin in shadow, and eyes popping forward. He distorted his mouth with two fingers, and curled a tongue hideously up to his nose to try and frighten himself away from the bigger fear of the house that was threatening him with tears.

It was hard to remember what they'd done at school today, and when he tried to imagine his father walking into the house and switching on the light it was difficult to make out his face very clearly. He hated him for that, and hoped one day to kill him with an axe. Even his mother's face wasn't easy to bring back, but he didn't want to kill her. He felt his knee caps burning, being too close to the gas bars, so he stood away to let them go cool.

When he was busy rolling up the carpet in front of the fire, and being away from the mirror, his parents suddenly appeared to him properly, their faces side by side with absolute clarity, and he wished they'd come back. If they did, and asked what the bloody hell he thought he was doing rolling up the carpet, he'd say well what else do you expect me to do? I've got to use something for a blanket when I go to sleep on the settee, haven't I?

If there was one skill he was glad of, it was that he could tell the time. He'd only learned it properly six months ago, so it had come just right. You didn't have to put a shilling in the clock, so that was still ticking at least, except that it made him feel tired.

He heaved at the settee, to swivel it round in front of the fire, a feat which convinced him that one day he'd be as strong as his father— wherever he was. There was certainly no hope of the gas keeping on till the morning, so he turned it down to number two. Then he lay on the settee and pulled the carpet over him. It smelled of stone and pumice, and of soap that had gone bad.

He sniffed the cold air, and sensed there was daylight in it, though he couldn't open his eyes. Weaving his hand as far as it would go, he felt that the gas fire had gone out, meaning that the cooking stove wouldn't work. He wondered why his eyelids were stuck together, then thought of chopping up a chair to make a blaze, but the grate was blocked by the gas fire. This disappointed him, because it would have been nice to lean over it, warming himself as the bottom of the kettle got blacker and blacker till it boiled at the top.

When his eyes mysteriously opened, old Tinface the clock said it was half past seven. In any case there were no matches left to light anything. He went into the scullery to wash his face.

He had to be content with a cup of milk, and a spoon of sugar in it, with more bread and cheese. People were walking along the backyards on their way to work. If they've gone for good, he thought, I shall go to my grandma's, and I'll have to change schools because she lives at Netherfield, miles away.

His mother had given him sixpence for sweets the morning before, and he already had twopence, so he knew that this was enough to get him half fare to Netherfield.

That's all I can do, he thought, turning the clock to the wall, and wondering whether he ought to put the furniture right in case his parents came in and got mad that it was all over the place, though he hoped they wouldn't care, since they'd left him all night on his own.

Apart from not wanting to spend the sixpence his mother had given him till she came back, he was sorry at having to go to his grandma's because now he wouldn't be able to go to school and tell his mates that he'd been all night in a house on his own.

He pushed a way to the upper deck of the bus, from which height he could look down on the roofs of cars, and see level into the top seats of other buses passing them through the town. You never know, he thought, I might see 'em—going home to put a shilling each in the light and gas for me. He gave his money to the conductor.

It took a long time to get clear of traffic at Canning Circus, and he wished he'd packed up some bread and cheese before leaving the house. Men were smoking foul fags all around, and a gang of boys going to Peoples' College made a big noise until the conductor told them to stop it or he'd put them off.

He knew the name of his grandmother's street, but not how to get there from the bus stop. A postman pointed the direction for him. Netherfield was on the edge of Nottingham, and huge black cauliflower clouds with the sun locked inside came over on the wind from Colwick Woods.

When his grandmother opened the back door he was turning the handle of the old mangle outside. She told him to stop it, and then asked in a tone of surprise what had brought him there at that time of the morning.

'Dad and mam have gone,' he said.

'Gone?' she cried, pulling him into the scullery. 'What do you mean?' He saw the big coal fire, and smelled the remains of bacon that she must have done for Tom's breakfast—the last of her sons living there. His face was distorted with pain. 'No,' she said, 'nay, you mustn't cry. Whatever's the matter for you to cry like that?'

The tea she poured was hot, strong, and sweet, and he was sorry at having cried in front of her. 'All right, now?' she said, drawing back to watch him and see if it was.

He nodded. 'I slept on the couch.'

'The whole night! And where can they be?'

He saw she was worried. 'They had an accident,' he told her, pouring his tea into the saucer to cool it. She fried him an egg, and gave him some bread and butter.

'Our Jack's never had an accident,' she said grimly.

'If they're dead, grandma, can I live with you?'

'Aye, you can. But they're not, so you needn't worry your little eyes.'

'They must be,' he told her, feeling certain about it.

'We'll see,' she said. 'When I've cleaned up a bit, we'll go and find out what got into 'em.' He watched her sweeping the room, then stood in the doorway as she knelt down to scrub the scullery floor, a smell of cold water and pumice when she reached the doorstep. 'I've got to keep the place spotless,' she said with a laugh, standing up, 'or your Uncle Tom would leave home. He's bound to get married one day though, and that's a fact. His three brothers did, one of 'em being your daft father.'

She held his hand back to the bus stop. If Uncle Tom does clear off it looks like she'll have me to look after. It seemed years already since he'd last seen his mother and father, and he was growing to like the adventure of it, provided they didn't stay away too long. It was rare going twice across town in one day.

It started to rain, so they stood in a shop doorway to wait for the bus. There wasn't so many people on it this time, and they sat on the bottom deck because his grandma didn't feel like climbing all them steps. 'Did you lock the door behind you?'

'I forgot.'

'Let's hope nobody goes in.'

'There was no light left,' he said. 'Nor any gas, I was cold when I woke up.'

'I'm sure you was,' she said. 'But you're a big lad now. You should have gone to a neighbour's house. They'd have given you some tea. Mrs Upton would, I'm sure. Or Mrs Mackley.'

'I kept thinking *they'd* be back any minute.'

'You always have to go to the neighbours,' she told him, when they got off the bus and walked across Ilkeston Road. Her hand had warmed up now from the pumice and cold water. 'Don't kick your feet like that.'

If it happened again, he would take her advice. He hoped it wouldn't, though next time he'd sleep in his bed and not be frightened.

They walked down the yard, and in by the back door. Nothing was missing, he could have told anybody that, though he didn't speak. The empty house seemed dead, and he didn't like that. He couldn't stay on his own, so followed his grandmother upstairs and into every room, half expecting her to find them in some secret place he'd never known of.

The beds were made, and wardrobe doors closed. One of the windows was open a few inches, so she slammed it shut and locked it. 'Come on down. There's nowt up here.'

She put a shilling in the gas meter, and set a kettle on the stove. 'Might as well have a cup of tea while I think this one out. A bloody big one it is, as well.'

It was the first time he'd heard her swear, but then, he'd never seen her worried, either. It made him feel better. She thought about the front room, and he followed her.

'They kept the house clean, any road up,' she said, touching the curtains and chair covers. 'That's summat to be said for 'em. But it ain't everything.'

'It ain't,' he agreed, and saw two letters lying on the mat just inside the front door. He watched her broad back as she bent to pick them up, thinking now that they were both dead for sure.

J. G. BALLARD

Dream Cargoes

ACROSS the lagoon an eager new life was forming, drawing its spectrum of colours from a palette more vivid than the sun's. Soon after dawn, when Johnson woke in Captain Galloway's cabin behind the bridge of the *Prospero*, he watched the lurid hues, cyanic blues and crimsons, playing against the ceiling above his bunk. Reflected in the metallic surface of the lagoon, the tropical foliage seemed to concentrate the Caribbean sunlight, painting on the warm air a screen of electric tones that Johnson had only seen on the nightclub façades of Miami and Vera Cruz.

He stepped onto the tilting bridge of the stranded freighter, aware that the island's vegetation had again surged forward during the night, as if it had miraculously found a means of converting darkness into these brilliant leaves and blossoms. Shielding his eyes from the glare, he searched the 600 yards of empty beach that encircled the *Prospero*, disappointed that there was no sign of Dr Chambers' rubber inflatable. For the past three mornings, when he woke after an uneasy night, he had seen the craft beached by the inlet of the lagoon. Shaking off the overlit dreams that rose from the contaminated waters, he would gulp down a cup of cold coffee, jump from the stern rail and set off between the pools of leaking chemicals in search of the American biologist.

It pleased Johnson that she was so openly impressed by this once barren island, a left-over of nature seven miles from the north-east coast of Puerto Rico. In his modest way he knew that he was responsible for the transformation of the nondescript atoll, scarcely more than a forgotten garbage dump left behind by the American army after World War 2. No one, in Johnson's short life, had ever been impressed by him, and the biologist's silent wonder gave him the first sense of achievement he had ever known.

Johnson had learned her name from the labels on the scientific stores in the inflatable. However, he had not yet approached or even spoken to her, embarrassed by his rough manners and shabby seaman's clothes, and the ingrained chemical stench that banned him from sailors' bars all over the Caribbean. Now, when she failed to appear on the fourth morning, he regretted all the more that he had never worked up the courage to introduce himself.

Through the acid-streaked windows of the bridge-house he stared at the terraces of flowers that hung from the forest wall. A month earlier, when he first arrived at the island, struggling with the locked helm of the listing freighter, there had been no more than a few stunted palms growing among the collapsed army huts and water-tanks buried in the dunes.

But already, for reasons that Johnson preferred not to consider, a wholly new vegetation had sprung to life. The palms rose like flagpoles into the vivid Caribbean air, pennants painted with a fresh green sap. Around them the sandy floor was thick with flowering vines and ground ivy, blue leaves like dappled metal foil, as if some midnight gardener had watered them with a secret plant elixir as Johnson lay asleep in his bunk.

He put on Galloway's peaked cap and examined himself in the greasy mirror. Stepping onto the open deck behind the wheel-house, he inhaled the acrid chemical air of the lagoon. At least it masked the odours of the captain's cabin, a rancid bouquet of ancient sweat, cheap rum and diesel oil. He had thought seriously of abandoning Galloway's cabin and returning to his hammock in the forecastle, but despite the stench he felt that he owed it to himself to remain in the cabin. The moment that Galloway, with a last disgusted curse, had stepped into the freighter's single lifeboat he, Johnson, had become the captain of this doomed vessel.

He had watched Galloway, the four Mexican crewmen and the weary Portuguese engineer row off into the dusk, promising himself that he would sleep in the captain's cabin and take his meals at the captain's table. After five years at sea, working as cabin boy and deck hand on the lowest grade of chemical waste carrier, he had a command of his own, this antique freighter, even if the *Prospero*'s course was the vertical one to the sea-bed of the Caribbean.

Behind the funnel the Liberian flag of convenience hung in tatters, its fabric rotted by the acid air. Johnson stepped onto the stern ladder, steadying himself against the sweating hull-plates, and jumped into the shallow water. Careful to find his feet, he waded through the bilious green foam that leaked from the steel drums he had jettisoned from the freighter's deck.

When he reached the clear sand above the tide-line he wiped the emerald dye from his jeans and sneakers. Leaning to starboard in the lagoon, the *Prospero* resembled an exploded paint-box. The drums of chemical waste on the foredeck still dripped their effluent through the scuppers. The more sinister below-decks cargo—nameless organic by-products that Captain Galloway had been bribed to carry and never entered into his manifest—had dissolved the rusty plates and spilled an eerie spectrum of phosphorescent blues and indigos into the lagoon below.

Frightened of these chemicals, which every port in the Caribbean had rejected, Johnson had begun to jettison the cargo after running the freighter aground. But the elderly diesels had seized and the winch had jarred to a halt, leaving only a few of the drums on the nearby sand with their death's head warnings and eroded seams.

Johnson set off along the shore, searching the sea beyond the inlet of the lagoon for any sign of Dr Chambers. Everywhere a deranged horticulture was running riot. Vivid new shoots pushed past the metal debris of old ammunition boxes, filing cabinets and truck tyres. Strange grasping vines clambered over the scarlet caps of giant fungi, their white stems as thick as sailors' bones. Avoiding them, Johnson walked towards an old staff car that sat in an open glade between the palms. Wheel-less, its military markings obliterated by the rain of decades, it had settled into the sand, vines encircling its roof and windshield.

Deciding to rest in the car, which once perhaps had driven an American general around the training camps of Puerto Rico, he tore away the vines that had wreathed themselves around the driver's door pillar. As he sat behind the steering wheel it occurred to Johnson that he might leave the freighter and set up camp on the island. Nearby lay the galvanized iron roof of a barrack hut, enough material to build a beach house on the safer, seaward side of the island.

But Johnson was aware of an unstated bond between himself and the derelict freighter. He remembered the last desperate voyage of the *Prospero*, which he had joined in Vera Cruz, after being duped by Captain Galloway. The short voyage to Galveston, the debarkation port, would pay him enough to ship as a deck passenger on an inter-island boat heading for the Bahamas. It had been three years since he had seen his widowed mother in Nassau, living in a plywood bungalow by the airport with her invalid boyfriend.

Needless to say, they had never berthed at Galveston, Miami or any other of the ports where they had tried to unload their cargo. The crudely sealed cylinders of chemical waste-products, supposedly en route to a reprocessing plant in southern Texas, had begun to leak before they left Vera Cruz. Captain Galloway's temper, like his erratic seamanship and consumption of rum and tequila, increased steadily as he realized that the Mexican shipping agent had abandoned them to the seas. Almost certainly the agent had pocketed the monies allocated for reprocessing and found it more profitable to let the ancient freighter, now refused entry to Vera Cruz, sail up and down the Gulf of Mexico until her corroded keel sent her conveniently to the bottom.

For two months they had cruised forlornly from one port to another, boarded by hostile maritime police and customs officers, public health officials and journalists alerted to the possibility of a major ecological disaster. At Kingston, Jamaica, a television launch trailed them to the ten-mile limit, at Santo Domingo a spotter plane of the Dominican navy was waiting for them when they tried to slip into harbour under the cover of darkness. Greenpeace power-boats intercepted them outside Tampa, Florida, when Captain Galloway tried to dump part of his cargo. Firing flares across the bridge of the freighter, the US Coast Guard dispatched them into the Gulf of Mexico in time to meet the tail of Hurricane Clara.

When at last they recovered from the storm the cargo had shifted, and the *Prospero* listed ten degrees to starboard. Fuming chemicals leaked across the decks from the fractured seams of the waste drums, boiled on the surface of the sea and sent up a cloud of acrid vapour that left Johnson and the Mexican crewmen coughing through makeshift face-masks, and Captain Galloway barricading himself into his cabin with his tequila bottle.

First Officer Pereira had saved the day, rigging up a hose-pipe that sprayed the leaking drums with a torrent of water, but by then the *Prospero* was taking in the sea through its strained plates. When they sighted Puerto Rico the captain had not even bothered to set a course for port. Propping himself against the helm, a bottle in each hand, he signalled Pereira to cut the engines. In a self-pitying monologue, he cursed the Mexican shipping agent, the US Coast Guard, the world's agrochemists and their despicable science that had deprived him of his command. Lastly he cursed Johnson for being so foolish ever to step aboard this ill-fated ship. As the *Prospero* lay doomed in the water, Pereira appeared with his already packed suitcase, and the captain ordered the Mexicans to lower the life-boat.

It was then that Johnson made his decision to remain on board. All his life he had failed to impose himself on anything—running errands as a six-year-old for the Nassau airport shoe-blacks, cadging pennies for his mother from the irritated tourists, enduring the years of school where he had scarcely learned to read and write, working as a dishwasher at the beach restaurants, forever conned out of his wages by the thieving managers. He had always reacted to events, never initiated anything on his own. Now, for the first time, he could become the captain of the *Prospero* and master of his own fate. Long before Galloway's curses faded into the dusk Johnson had leapt down the companionway ladder into the engine room.

As the elderly diesels rallied themselves for the last time Johnson returned to the bridge. He listened to the propeller's tired but steady beat against the dark ocean, and slowly turned the *Prospero* towards the north-west. Five hundred miles away were the Bahamas, and an endless archipelago of secret harbours. Somehow he would get rid of the leaking drums and even, perhaps, ply for hire between the islands, renaming the old tub after his mother, Velvet Mae. Meanwhile Captain Johnson stood proudly on the bridge, oversize cap on his head, 300 tons of steel deck obedient beneath his feet.

By dawn the next day he was completely lost on an open sea. During the night the freighter's list had increased. Below decks the leaking chemicals had etched their way through the hull plates, and a phosphorescent steam enveloped the bridge. The engine room was a knee-deep vat of acid brine, a poisonous vapour rising through the ventilators and coating every rail and deck-plate with a lurid slime.

Then, as Johnson searched desperately for enough timber to build a raft, he saw the old World War 2 garbage island seven miles from the Puerto Rican coast. The lagoon inlet was unguarded by the US Navy or Greenpeace speedboats. He steered the *Prospero* across the calm surface and let the freighter settle into the shallows. The inrush of water smothered the cargo in the hold. Able to breathe again, Johnson rolled into Captain Galloway's bunk, made a space for himself among the empty bottles and slept his first dreamless sleep.

'Hey, you! Are you all right?' A woman's hand pounded on the roof of the staff car. 'What *are* you doing in there?'

Johnson woke with a start, lifting his head from the steering wheel. While he slept the lianas had enveloped the car, climbing up the roof and windshield pillars. Vivid green tendrils looped themselves around his left hand, tying his wrist to the rim of the wheel.

Wiping his face, he saw the American biologist peering at him through the leaves, as if he were the inmate of some bizarre zoo whose cages were the bodies of abandoned motor-cars. He tried to free himself, and pushed against the driver's door.

'Sit back! I'll cut you loose.'

She slashed at the vines with her clasp knife, revealing her fierce and determined wrist. When Johnson stepped onto the ground she held his shoulders, looking him up and down with a thorough eye. She was no more than thirty, three years older than himself, but to Johnson she seemed as self-possessed and remote as the Nassau school-teachers. Yet her mouth was more relaxed than those pursed lips of his childhood, as if she were genuinely concerned for Johnson.

'You're all right,' she informed him. 'But I wouldn't go for too many rides in that car.'

She strolled away from Johnson, her hands pressing the burnished copper trunks of the palms, feeling the urgent pulse of awakening life. Around her shoulders was slung a canvas bag holding a clip-board, sample jars, a camera and reels of film.

'My name's Christine Chambers,' she called out to Johnson. 'I'm carrying out a botanical project on this island. Have you come from the stranded ship?'

'I'm the captain,' Johnson told her without deceit. He reached into the car and retrieved his peaked cap from the eager embrace of the vines, dusted it off and placed it on his head at what he hoped was a rakish angle. 'She's not a wreck—I beached her here for repairs.'

'Really? For repairs?' Christine Chambers watched him archly, finding him at least as intriguing as the giant scarlet-capped fungi. 'So you're the captain. But where's the crew?'

'They abandoned ship.' Johnson was glad that he could speak so honestly. He liked this attractive biologist and the way she took a close interest in the island. 'There were certain problems with the cargo.'

'I bet there were. You were lucky to get here in one piece.' She took out a notebook and jotted down some observation on Johnson, glancing at his pupils and lips. 'Captain, would you like a sandwich? I've brought a picnic lunch—you look as if you could use a square meal.'

'Well . . .' Pleased by her use of his title, Johnson followed her to the beach, where the inflatable sat on the sand. Clearly she had been delayed by the weight of stores: a bell tent, plastic coolers, cartons of canned food, and a small office cabinet. Johnson had survived on a diet of salt beef, cola and oatmeal biscuits he cooked on the galley stove.

For all the equipment, she was in no hurry to unload the stores, as if unsure of sharing the island with Johnson, or perhaps pondering a different approach to her project, one that involved the participation of the human population of the island.

Trying to reassure her, as they divided the sandwiches, he described the last voyage of the *Prospero*, and the disaster of the leaking chemicals. She nodded while he spoke, as if she already knew something of the story.

'It sounds to me like a great feat of seamanship,' she complimented him. 'The crew who abandoned ship—as it happens, they reported that she went down near Barbados. One of them, Galloway I think he was called, claimed they'd spent a month in an open boat.'

'Galloway?' Johnson assumed the pursed lips of the Nassau school-marms. 'One of my less reliable men. So no one is looking for the ship?'

'No. Absolutely no one.'

'And they think she's gone down?'

'Right to the bottom. Everyone in Barbados is relieved there's no pollution. Those tourist beaches, you know.'

'They're important. And no one in Puerto Rico thinks she's here?'

'No one except me. This island is my research project,' she explained. 'I teach biology at San Juan University, but I really want to work at Harvard. I can tell you, lectureships are hard to come by. Something very interesting is happening here, with a little luck . . .'

'It is interesting,' Johnson agreed. There was a conspiratorial note to Dr Christine's voice that made him uneasy. 'A lot of old army equipment is buried here—I'm thinking of building a house on the beach.'

'A good idea . . . even if it takes you four or five months. I'll help you out with any food you need. But be careful.' Dr Christine pointed to the weal on his arm, a temporary reaction against some invading toxin in the vine sap. 'There's something else that's interesting about this island, isn't there?'

'Well . . .' Johnson stared at the acid stains etching through the *Prospero*'s hull and spreading across the lagoon. He had tried not to think of his responsibility for these dangerous and unstable chemicals. 'There are a few other things going on here.'

'A few other things?' Dr Christine lowered her voice. 'Look, Johnson, you're sitting in the middle of an amazing biological experiment. No one would allow it to happen anywhere in the world—if they knew, the US Navy would move in this afternoon.'

'Would they take away the ship?'

'They'd take it away and sink it in the nearest ocean trench, then scorch the island with flame-throwers.'

'And what about me?'

'I wouldn't like to say. It might depend on how advanced . . .' She held his shoulder reassuringly, aware that her vehemence had shocked him. 'But there's no reason why they should find out. Not for a while, and by then it won't matter. I'm not exaggerating when I say that you've probably created a new kind of life.'

As they unloaded the stores Johnson reflected on her words. He had guessed that the chemicals leaking from the *Prospero* had set off the accelerated growth, and that the toxic reagents might equally be affecting himself. In Galloway's cabin mirror he inspected the hairs on his chin and any suspicious moles. The weeks at sea, inhaling the acrid fumes, had left him with raw lungs and throat, and an erratic appetite, but he had felt better since coming ashore.

He watched Christine step into a pair of thigh-length rubber boots and move into the shallow water, ladle in hand, looking at the plant and animal life of the lagoon. She filled several specimen jars with the phosphorescent water, and locked them into the cabinet inside the tent.

'Johnson—you couldn't let me see the cargo manifest?'

'Captain . . . Galloway took it with him. He didn't list the real cargo.'

'I bet he didn't.' Christine pointed to the vermilion-shelled crabs that scuttled through the vivid filaments of kelp, floating like threads of blue electric cable. 'Have you noticed? There are no dead fish or crabs—and you'd expect to see hundreds. That was the first thing I spotted. And it isn't just the crabs—you look pretty healthy . . .'

'Maybe I'll be stronger?' Johnson flexed his sturdy shoulders.

' . . . in a complete daze, mentally, but I imagine that will change. Meanwhile, can you take me on board? I'd like to visit the *Prospero*.'

'Dr Christine . . .' Johnson held her arm, trying to restrain this determined woman. He looked at her clear skin and strong legs. 'It's too dangerous, you might fall through the deck.'

'Fair enough. Are the containers identified?'

'Yes, there's no secret.' Johnson did his best to remember. 'Organo . . .'

'Organo-phosphates? Right—what I need to know is which containers are leaking and roughly how much. We might be able to work out the exact chemical reactions—you may not realize it, Johnson, but you've mixed a remarkably potent cocktail. A lot of people will want to learn the recipe, for all kinds of reasons . . .'

Sitting in the colonel's chair on the porch of the beach-house, Johnson gazed contentedly at the luminous world around him, a fever-realm of light and life that seemed to have sprung from his own mind. The jungle wall of cycads, giant tamarinds and tropical creepers crowded the beach to the waterline, and the reflected colours drowned in swathes of phosphoresence that made the lagoon resemble a cauldron of electric dyes.

So dense was the vegetation that almost the only free sand lay below Johnson's feet. Every morning he would spend an hour cutting back the flowering vines and wild magnolia that inundated the metal shack. Already the foliage was crushing the galvanized iron roof. However hard he worked—and he found himself too easily distracted—he had been unable to keep clear the inspection pathways which Christine patrolled on her weekend visits, camera and specimen jars at the ready.

Hearing the sound of her inflatable as she neared the inlet of the lagoon, Johnson surveyed his domain with pride. He had found a metal card-table buried in the sand, and laid it with a selection of fruits he had picked for Christine that morning. To Johnson's untrained eye they seemed to be strange hybrids of pomegranate and pawpaw, cantaloupe and pineapple. There were giant tomato-like berries and clusters of purple grapes each the size of a baseball. Together they glowed through the overheated light like jewels set in the face of the sun.

By now, four months after his arrival on the *Prospero*, the one-time garbage island had become a unique botanical garden, generating new species of trees, vines and flowering plants every day. A powerful life-engine was driving the island. As she crossed the lagoon in her inflatable Christine stared at the aerial terraces of vines and blossoms that had sprung up since the previous weekend.

The dead hulk of the *Prospero*, daylight visible through its acid-etched plates, sat in the shallow water, the last of its chemical wastes leaking into the lagoon. But Johnson had forgotten the ship and the voyage that had brought him here, just as he had forgotten his past life and unhappy childhood under the screaming engines of Nassau airport. Lolling back in his canvas chair, on which was stencilled 'Colonel Pottle, US Army Engineer Corps', he felt like a plantation owner who had successfully subcontracted a corner of the original Eden. As he stood up to greet Christine he thought only of the future, of his pregnant bride and the son who would soon share the island with him.

'Johnson! My God, what have you been doing?' Christine ran the inflatable onto the beach and sat back, exhausted by the buffeting waves. 'It's a botanical mad-house!'

Johnson was so pleased to see her that he forgot his regret over their weekly separations. As she explained, she had her student classes to teach, her project notes and research samples to record and catalogue.

'Dr Christine . . .! I waited all day!' He stepped into the shallow water, a carmine surf filled with glowing animalcula, and pulled the inflatable onto the sand. He helped her from the craft, his eyes avoiding her curving abdomen under the smock.

'Go on, you can stare . . .' Christine pressed his hand to her stomach. 'How do I look, Johnson?'

'Too beautiful for me, and the island. We've all gone quiet.'

'That is gallant—you've become a poet, Johnson.'

Johnson never thought of other women, and knew that none could be so beautiful as this lady biologist bearing his child. He spotted a plastic cooler among the scientific equipment.

'Christine—you've brought me ice-cream . . .'

'Of course I have. But don't eat it yet. We've a lot to do, Johnson.'

He unloaded the stores, leaving to the last the nylon nets and spring-mounted steel frames in the bottom of the boat. These bird-traps were the one cargo he hated to unload. Nesting in the highest branches above the island was a flock of extravagant aerial creatures, sometime swallows and finches whose jewelled plumage and tail-fans transformed them into gaudy peacocks. He had set the traps reluctantly at Christine's insistence. He never objected to catching the phosphorescent fish with their enlarged fins and ruffs of external gills, which seemed to prepare them for life on the land, or the crabs and snails in their baroque armour. But the thought of Christine taking these rare and beautiful birds back to her laboratory made him uneasy—he guessed that they would soon end their days under the dissection knife.

'Did you set the traps for me, Johnson?'

'I set all of them and put in the bait.'

'Good.' Christine heaped the nets onto the sand. More and more she seemed to hurry these days, as if she feared that the experiment might end. 'I can't understand why we haven't caught one of them.'

Johnson gave an eloquent shrug. In fact he had eaten the canned sardines, and released the one bird that had strayed into the trap below the parasol of a giant cycad. The nervous creature with its silken scarlet wings and kite-like tail feathers had been a dream of flight. 'Nothing yet—they're clever, those birds.'

'Of course they are—they're a new species.' She sat in Colonel Pottle's chair, photographing the table of fruit with her small camera. 'Those grapes are huge—I wonder what sort of wine they'd make. Champagne of the gods, grand cru . . .'

Warily, Johnson eyed the purple and yellow globes. He had eaten the fish and crabs from the lagoon, when asked by Christine, with no ill effects, but he was certain that these fruits were intended for the birds. He knew that Christine was using him, like everything else on the island, as part of her experiment. Even the child she had conceived after their one brief act of love, over so quickly that he was scarcely sure it had ever occurred, was part of the experiment. Perhaps the child would be the first of a new breed of man and he, Johnson, errand runner for airport shoe-shine boys, would be the father of an advanced race that would one day repopulate the planet.

As if aware of his impressive physique, she said: 'You look wonderfully well, Johnson. If this experiment ever needs to be justified . . .'

'I'm very strong now—I'll be able to look after you and the boy.'

'It might be a girl—or something in between.' She spoke in a matter-of-fact way that always surprised him. 'Tell me, Johnson, what do you do while I'm away?' ·

'I think about you, Dr Christine.'

'And I certainly think about you. But do you sleep a lot?'

'No. I'm busy with my thoughts. The time goes very quickly.'

Christine casually opened her note-pad. 'You mean the hours go by without you noticing?'

'Yes. After breakfast I fill the oil-lamp and suddenly it's time for lunch. But it can go more slowly, too. If I look at a falling leaf in a certain way it seems to stand still.'

'Good. You're learning to control time. Your mind is enlarging, Johnson.'

'Maybe I'll be as clever as you, Dr Christine.'

'Ah, I think you're moving in a much more interesting direction. In fact, Johnson, I'd like you to eat some of the fruit. Don't worry, I've already analysed it, and I'll have some myself.' She was cutting slices of the melon-sized apple. 'I want the baby to try some.'

Johnson hesitated, but as Christine always reminded him, none of the new species had revealed a single deformity.

The fruit was pale and sweet, with a pulpy texture and a tang like alcoholic mango. It slightly numbed Johnson's mouth and left a pleasant coolness in the stomach.

A diet for those with wings.

'Johnson! Are you sick?'

He woke with a start, not from sleep but from an almost too-clear examination of the colour patterns of a giant butterfly that had settled on his hand. He looked up from his chair at Christine's concerned eyes, and at the dense vines and flowering creepers that crowded the porch, pressing against his shoulders. The amber of her eyes was touched by the same overlit spectrum that shone through the trees and blossoms. Everything on the island was becoming a prism of itself.

'Johnson, wake up!'

'I am awake. Christine . . . I didn't hear you come.'

'I've been here for an hour.' She touched his cheeks, searching for any sign of fever and puzzled by Johnson's distracted manner. Behind her, the inflatable was beached on the few feet of sand not smothered by the vegetation. The dense wall of palms, lianas and flowering plants had collapsed onto the shore. Engorged on the sun, the giant fruits had begun to split under their own weight, and streams of vivid juice ran across the sand, as if the forest was bleeding.

'Christine? You came back so soon . . .?' It seemed to Johnson that she had left only a few minutes earlier. He remembered waving goodbye to her and sitting down to finish his fruit and admire the giant butterfly, its wings like the painted hands of a circus clown.

'Johnson—I've been away for a week.' She held his shoulder, frowning at the unstable wall of rotting vegetation that towered a hundred feet into the air. Cathedrals of flower-decked foliage were falling into the waters of the lagoon.

'Johnson, help me to unload the stores. You don't look as if you've eaten for days. Did you trap the birds?'

'Birds? No, nothing yet.' Vaguely Johnson remembered setting the traps, but he had been too distracted by the wonder of everything to pursue the birds. Graceful, feather-tipped wraiths like gaudy angels, their crimson plumage leaked its ravishing hues onto the air. When he fixed his eyes onto them they seemed suspended against the sky, wings fanning slowly as if shaking the time from themselves.

He stared at Christine, aware that the colours were separating themselves from her skin and hair. Superimposed images of herself, each divided from the others by a fraction of a second, blurred the air around her, an exotic plumage that sprang from her arms and shoulders. The staid reality that had trapped them all was beginning to dissolve. Time had stopped and Christine was ready to rise into the air . . .

He would teach Christine and the child to fly.

'Christine, we can all learn.'

'What, Johnson?'

'We can learn to fly. There's no time any more—everything's too beautiful for time.'

'Johnson, look at my watch.'

'We'll go and live in the trees, Christine. We'll live with the high flowers . . .'

He took her arm, eager to show her the mystery and beauty of the sky people they would become. She tried to protest, but gave in, humouring Johnson as he led her gently from the beach house to the wall of inflamed flowers. Her hand on the radio-transmitter in the inflatable, she sat beside the crimson lagoon as Johnson tried to climb the flowers towards the sun. Steadying the child within her, she wept for Johnson, only calming herself two hours later when the siren of a naval cutter crossed the inlet.

'I'm glad you radioed in,' the US Navy lieutenant told Christine. 'One of the birds reached the base at San Juan. We tried to keep it alive but it was crushed by the weight of its own wings. Like everything else on this island.'

He pointed from the bridge to the jungle wall. Almost all the over-crowded canopy had collapsed into the lagoon, leaving behind only a few of the original palms with their bird traps. The blossoms glowed through the water like thousands of drowned lanterns.

'How long has the freighter been here?' An older civilian, a government scientist holding a pair of binoculars, peered at the riddled hull of the *Prospero*. Below the beach house two sailors were loading the last of

Christine's stores into the inflatable. 'It looks as if it's been stranded there for years.'

'Six months,' Christine told him. She sat beside Johnson, smiling at him encouragingly. 'When Captain Johnson realized what was going on he asked me to call you.'

'Only six? That must be roughly the life-cycle of these new species. Their cellular clocks seem to have stopped—instead of reproducing, they force-feed their own tissues, like those giant fruit that contain no seeds. The life of the individual becomes the entire life of the species.' He gestured towards the impassive Johnson. 'That probably explains our friend's altered time sense—great blocks of memory were coalescing in his mind, so that a ball thrown into the air would never appear to land . . .'

A tide of dead fish floated past the cutter's bow, the gleaming bodies like discarded costume jewellery.

'You weren't contaminated in any way?' the lieutenant asked Christine. 'I'm thinking of the baby.'

'No, I didn't eat any of the fruit,' Christine said firmly. 'I've been here only twice, for a few hours.'

'Good. Of course, the medical people will do all the tests.'

'And the island?'

'We've been ordered to torch the whole place. The demolition charges are timed to go off in just under two hours, but we'll be well out of range. It's a pity, in a way.'

'The birds are still here,' Christine said, aware of Johnson staring at the trees.

'Luckily, you've trapped them all.' The scientist offered her the binoculars. 'Those organic wastes are hazardous things—God knows what might happen if human beings were exposed to long-term contact. All sorts of sinister alterations to the nervous system—people might be happy to stare at a stone all day.'

Johnson listened to them talking, glad to feel Christine's hand in his own. She was watching him with a quiet smile, aware that they shared the conspiracy. She would try to save the child, the last fragment of the experiment, and he knew that if it survived it would face a fierce challenge from those who feared it might replace them.

But the birds endured. His head had cleared, and he remembered the visions that had given him a brief glimpse of another, more advanced world. High above the collapsed canopy of the forest he could see the traps he had set, and the great crimson birds sitting on their wings. At least they could carry the dream forward.

Ten minutes later, when the inflatable had been winched onto the deck, the cutter set off through the inlet. As it passed the western head-land the lieutenant helped Christine towards the cabin. Johnson fol-lowed them, then pushed aside the government scientist and leapt from the rail, diving cleanly into the water. He struck out for the shore a hun-dred feet away, knowing that he was strong enough to climb the trees and release the birds, with luck a mating pair who would take him with them in their escape from time.

JOHN FULLER

Telephone

I T' s six o'clock precisely and the telephone's just started to ring. Should I answer it? It might be the polite thing to do. Dickie said I should make myself at home, and said it in the nicest way: 'The key's the key of the whole flat, remember, not just the front door.' Well, I've taken him at his word. I'm lying on the sofa reading his letters and I've made myself a socking great vodka tonic. This afternoon was a shambles. I've never heard such a set of meaningless presentations in my life. I feel more exhausted than if I'd delivered one myself. I'm going to cut the dinner and give myself a night on the town.

I ought to answer the phone, take a message. It might be something important. But it can't be for me because no one knows I'm here. Except Dickie, and he's expecting me to be at the conference till late tonight. So it's for him, and he won't be back till tomorrow. If I answer it I shall have to explain all that, and say who I am. Boring, boring.

I thought all yuppies had answering machines these days. You could leave it on even when you were at home, so that you could decide whether to talk to the person or not. Perhaps it's become smart not to have one.

It's very persistent. You'd have thought it would have rung off by now, because clearly no one's answering it. They can't know Dickie very well. It's a tiny flat. You can practically see the phone from any part of it. You could make a dive for it if you were very eager, if you were actually waiting for a call, and catch it on the first ring like the father of a kidnap victim. If they're bothering to let it ring like this they must imagine the place is enormous, with a butler walking gravely across miles and miles of parquet. How ridiculous.

They must realize that no one's here. What would be the point of letting it ring so long? I mean, it's been ringing now for an absurdly long time. I should have been counting. I'll start counting now and call it ten rings so far. Eleven. Twelve.

Of course, it's quite wrong to say that they must realize that no one's here. After all, I'm here. But if they did know that I was here they'd surely expect me to have answered it by now. Fifteen. And it's far too late to do so. What would I say? How could I explain why I hadn't answered it earlier? So if they do suspect that I'm here, and there's no real reason why I haven't answered it (and there isn't) why are they letting it ring? Nineteen. Twenty.

And of course it wouldn't *be* me they'd think of lying here and not answering it. It would be Dickie.

So perhaps there is some point to it after all. It could be a code, a cunning way of getting relatively complicated information via British Telecom at no charge. Twenty-five. Suppose it was this Sue, for example, who's sent Dickie this really rather louche postcard with the naked bottoms on it. She could arrange to ring at six o'clock every day and he would know it was her and no one else. He'd let the phone ring for as long as she wanted, and the number of rings would correspond to a message. The more rings, the more exciting the message. Twenty-nine, thirty. It's stopped. It stopped at thirty.

Thirty possible messages! The mind boggles. The first ones could be quite routine and practical. One to seven rings: 'Jim has to be away Monday night (Tuesday night, Wednesday night, etc.).' Eight to fourteen rings: 'Ditto, but I'll come to *you*.' Fifteen rings: 'Cancel previous plans. I'll be in touch.' Sixteen rings: 'Come immediately!' What would thirty rings be? 'I'm just about to take a long soapy bath with that rubber cast you let me make of you and I'm really going to get it right this time.'

Dickie, Dickie, you sly dog. I can't bear it. I'll have to pour myself another vodka.

JOHN FULLER

My Story

Now that I'm slowing up a bit, somebody really ought to come
along and take down my story. There's time yet, but they won't have for
ever.

What would I tell them? Well now, it's a question of what's important, isn't it? There's a whole load of stuff that they wouldn't want to
hear. I roasted the very onions that Cyrus ate on the day that Babylon
fell. It was my twin sister who was chosen to be sealed into the Pyramid.
She gave me a letter which I was never to open. I broached the Great
Wall of China from the north. When my pony collapsed beneath me I
lived for forty days in the ice on its raw flesh. I returned with the first
gunpowder that the West had ever seen or heard, wrapped in pieces of
silk taken from the Porcelain Tower of Nankin. I bought my freedom
from the Turks with it and saw them topple the straddling lighthouse
giant into the bay at Rhodes, capsizing eighteen galleys. I was the first
worshipper at the Temple of Diana at Epheseus and the first Christian
to outstare the lions at the Coliseum. With my freedom and noted speed
of riding I carried greetings to the seven churches of Asia: in Epheseus
I saw a woman branded for consorting with an elkhound; in Smyrna I
stayed for the drying of the grape harvest; in Pergamos I ate the raw liv-
ers of goats, a delicacy, and contracted a tapeworm; in Thyatira I coaxed
it out, sitting for ten days over a chamber of warm milk; in Sardis I gave
my last piece of gold for a timber of the Ark, which crumbled to dust in
my saddlebag; in Philadelphia I lay with three sisters in one night,
daughters of a blind scrivener who beat me at chess; in Laodicea I saw a
mountain lion with two heads, stuffed. All these churches are now
Muslim, though I had no personal responsibility for that.

Nobody can think of themselves as a character in their own story.
Nobody in fact sees their own life *as* a story. You never get outside it to
see its shape. If anyone's going to record my story they're going to have
to make their own sense of it. Hasn't it been a restless search for some-

thing? Or simply a series of distractions and mistakes? One damned thing after another?

Another reason for not believing in your own story is not being able to see how the world can go on without you. But it has to go on without you in order to understand your story and its significance.

Perhaps obscurity would be the better destiny. Stories need resolution, but we have only the desire for achieving a state of things, a stasis, a being, suspended, quite unresolved. We don't want it to stop, whatever the glory.

There is only one story, after all: the story of our bodies telling us that we exist.

ANGELA CARTER

The Kiss

THE winters in Central Asia are piercing and bleak, while the sweating, foetid summers bring cholera, dysentery and mosquitoes, but, in April, the air caresses like the touch of the inner skin of the thigh and the scent of all the flowering trees douses this city's throat-catching whiff of cesspits.

Every city has its own internal logic. Imagine a city drawn in straightforward, geometric shapes with crayons from a child's colouring box, in ochre, in white, in pale terracotta. Low, blonde terraces of houses seem to rise out of the whitish, pinkish earth as if born from it, not built out of it. There is a faint, gritty dust over everything, like the dust those pastel crayons leave on your fingers.

Against these bleached pallors, the iridescent crusts of ceramic tiles that cover the ancient mausoleums ensorcellate the eye. The throbbing blue of Islam transforms itself to green while you look at it. Beneath a bulbous dome alternately lapis lazuli and veridian, the bones of Tamburlaine, the scourge of Asia, lie in a jade tomb. We are visiting an authentically fabulous city. We are in Samarkand.

The Revolution promised the Uzbek peasant women clothes of silk and on this promise, at least, did not welch. They wear tunics of flimsy satin, pink and yellow, red and white, black and white, red, green and white, in blotched stripes of brilliant colours that dazzle like an optical illusion, and they bedeck themselves with much jewellery made of red glass.

They always seem to be frowning because they paint a thick, black line straight across their foreheads that takes their eyebrows from one side of their faces to the other without a break. They rim their eyes with kohl. They look startling. They fasten their long hair in two or three dozen whirling plaits. Young girls wear little velvet caps embroidered with metallic thread and beadwork. Older women cover their heads with a couple of scarves of flower-printed wool, one bound tight over the forehead, the other hanging loosely on to the shoulders. Nobody has worn a veil for sixty years.

They walk as purposefully as if they did not live in an imaginary city. They do not know that they themselves and their turbaned, sheepskin jacketed, booted menfolk are creatures as extraordinary to the foreign eye as a unicorn. They exist, in all their glittering and innocent exoticism, in direct contradiction to history. They do not know what I know about them. They do not know that this city is not the entire world. All they know of the world is this city, beautiful as an illusion, where irises grow in the gutters. In the tea-house a green parrot nudges the bars of its wicker cage.

The market has a sharp, green smell. A girl with black-barred brows sprinkles water from a glass over radishes. In this early part of the year, you can buy only last summer's dried fruit—apricots, peaches, raisins—except for a few, precious, wrinkled pomegranates, stored in sawdust through the winter and now split open on the stall to show how a wet nest of garnets remains within. A local speciality of Samarkand is salted apricot kernels, more delicious, even, than pistachios.

An old woman sells arum lilies. This morning, she came from the mountains, where wild tulips have put out flowers like blown bubbles of blood, and the wheedling turtle-doves are nesting among the rocks. This old woman dips bread into a cup of buttermilk for her lunch and eats slowly. When she has sold her lilies, she will go back to the place where they are growing.

She scarcely seems to inhabit time. Or, it is as if she were waiting for Scheherazade to perceive a final dawn had come and, the last tale of all concluded, fall silent. Then, the lily-seller might vanish.

A goat is nibbling wild jasmine among the ruins of the mosque that was built by the beautiful wife of Tamburlaine.

Tamburlaine's wife started to build this mosque for him as a surprise, while he was away at the wars, but when she got word of his imminent return, one arch still remained unfinished. She went directly to the architect and begged him to hurry but the architect told her that he would complete the work in time only if she gave him a kiss. One kiss, one single kiss.

Tamburlaine's wife was not only very beautiful and very virtuous but also very clever. She went to the market, bought a basket of eggs, boiled them hard and stained them a dozen different colours. She called the architect to the palace, showed him the basket and told him to choose any egg he liked and eat it. He took a red egg. What does it taste like? Like an egg. Eat another.

He took a green egg.

What does *that* taste like? Like the red egg. Try again.

He ate a purple egg.

One egg tastes just the same as any other egg, if they are fresh, he said.

There you are! she said. Each of these eggs looks different to the rest but they all taste the same. So you may kiss any one of my serving women that you like but you must leave me alone.

Very well, said the architect. But soon he came back to her and this time he was carrying a tray with three bowls on it, and you would have thought the bowls were all full of water.

Drink from each of these bowls, he said.

She took a drink from the first bowl, then from the second; but how she coughed and spluttered when she took a mouthful from the third bowl, because it contained, not water, but vodka.

This vodka and that water both look alike but each tastes quite different, he said. And it is the same with love.

Then Tamburlaine's wife kissed the architect on the mouth. He went back to the mosque and finished the arch the same day that victorious Tamburlaine rode into Samarkand with his army and banners and his cages full of captive kings. But when Tamburlaine went to visit his wife, she turned away from him because no woman will return to the harem after she has tasted vodka. Tamburlaine beat her with a knout until she told him she had kissed the architect and then he sent his executioners hotfoot to the mosque.

The executioners saw the architect standing on top of the arch and ran up the stairs with their knives drawn but when he heard them coming he grew wings and flew away to Persia.

This is a story in simple, geometric shapes and the bold colours of a child's box of crayons. This Tamburlaine's wife of the story would have painted a black stripe laterally across her forehead and done up her hair in a dozen, dozen tiny plaits, like any other Uzbek woman. She would have bought red and white radishes from the market for her husband's dinner. After she ran away from him perhaps she made her living in the market. Perhaps she sold lilies there.

ROSE TREMAIN

The Beauty of the Dawn Shift

WHEN Hector S set out on his journey to Russia, he was wearing his uniform. It was his winter uniform, made of woollen serge, because this was December in East Berlin. While packing his knapsack, Hector S had told himself that he would have to travel in his uniform, that he had no choice; he didn't possess any other really warm clothes and where he was going, it would be as cold as death.

He was a man with a narrow frame, not tall, with pale, anxious eyes. Women thought him beautiful, but found him frigid. He was twenty-eight and he'd slept with only one girl. This one girl was his sister, Ute.

Ute kept a pet swan in a lean-to hutch on the apartment estate. She'd named it Karl and fed it on sunflower seeds. Morning and evening, she'd let it out to peck the grass and it allowed her to stroke its neck. There were no lakes or rivers in Prenzlauer Berg, the suburb of East Berlin where they lived, and when Hector informed Ute that he was leaving for Russia, she asked him to take her and Karl with him. But he told her it was impossible, that he had to go alone with almost nothing, just his bicycle and a bag of tinned food and his rifle. He told her he couldn't travel across Poland with a swan.

Ute took this badly. She clutched at Hector's arm. She was already imagining the beautiful Russian lake where Karl would remember the lost art of swimming.

'Hecti,' she said, 'don't leave us behind!'

Hector S disliked emotional scenes. When their mother, Elvira, had died in 1980 Hector had basked in the wonderful quiet that descended suddenly upon the apartment. He told Ute that it was different for her, that she would be able to fit in to the New Germany and that she had nothing to be afraid of. She began to cry in exactly the same way Elvira used to cry, grabbing two hunks of her hair and saying she hated being alive. Hector walked away from her. One part of him wanted to say: 'When I get there, Ute, I promise I will send for you,' but another part of him wanted to remain as silent as the tomb, and on this occasion it was the tomb that prevailed.

Hector's father, Erich, on the other hand, didn't try to persuade his son to take him with him; neither did he try to persuade him not to leave. All he said was: 'A frog in a well says that the sky is no bigger than the mouth of the well, but now you have to become something else, Hector, and see the whole fucking sky. In the old imperial fairy-tales, frogs turn into princes, eh?' And he slapped his knee.

Hector replied that he had no intention whatsoever of turning into a prince.

'So,' said Erich, 'what are you going to become?'

'I don't know,' said Hector. 'Don't ask me yet.'

'All right,' said Erich, 'but remember, when you walk away from one place, you are inevitably walking towards another.'

'I know that,' said Hector. 'That's why I'm going east.'

What should Hector take with him? This question troubled him more than many others. His knapsack wasn't large. It was the bag in which he carried his lunch or his supper, depending on which shift he was working. He would make more room in it by attaching his water bottle to the outside of it. Then there were the two saddle bags on his bicycle, but this was all. He decided, eventually, to line the saddle bags with underwear and socks. Then he put in jars of dill pickles and some plastic cutlery. He tucked these in with maps of Poland and the Brandenburg Marshes. He added a compass made in Dresden and five boxes of matches. The knapsack he filled almost entirely with tinned meat, wrapped in a woollen sweater. There was room for a torch and two spare batteries, a notebook and a pen. He put in a solitary lemon. He packed no books, only a small photograph album, filled with pictures of Ute, including one of her naked, developed privately by a colleague of Hector's who had dreams of becoming a professional photographer. In the naked photograph, Ute was leaning on a stool with her back to the camera and her bottom was very pale in the bleached light of early morning. Her legs looked skinny and her soft blonde hair parted at the back and hung forward, revealing her narrow white shoulders.

Hector didn't tell Ute or Erich when he was going to leave, because he thought farewells were futile and also because he didn't really know. He had to set off before the lemon in his knapsack went rotten, that was all. He knew he would recognize the moment when it came—and he did. It was the morning of 9 December 1989, one month exactly after the Wall had started to come down. He was alone in the apartment. He had exchanged all the money he possessed for D-Marks at the humiliating rate of 10 : 1. It amounted to DM143 and he laid it out on the kitchen table and looked at the blue and pink notes, then gathered them up, stuffed them into his wallet and put on his greatcoat and his hat. It was a fine morning, cold and clear. He walked to the window and looked out at the blocks of flats and the scuffed grass in between them where a few children played. He remembered being told: 'At the time of Tsar Nicolas II in Russia, the children of the poor had no toys of any kind. They invented games with knuckle bones.' And now, thought Hector, the parents of these children will save on food and light to buy their kids sophisticated toys from the West. He felt glad he had no children, nor would ever have any because his sperm count was too low. At least he wouldn't have to choose between absolute needs and infantile ones. He was a man who had always known what was important in life and what was not.

He turned away from the window and picked up his knapsack. He looked at the room he was in, the room where the family ate and played cards and watched TV, and wondered if, when he arrived at his destination, he would think about this room and feel homesick for the black plastic chairs and the painted sideboard and the wall-mounted electric fire. He knew that memory was as uncertain in its behaviour as the sea; it could wash you ashore on any old forgotten beach; it could try to drown you in remorse. But he decided, no, it wouldn't be the apartment he would miss, only certain moments in it, certain moments at dawn, just after Erich had left for work at the cement works on the Landwehr Kanal, when he walked from his own room into Ute's and got into her bed.

It is best to leave now, Hector told himself. Don't dwell on Ute.

So he walked out of the apartment without looking at anything more and went down the six flights of concrete stairs to the lobby where the post boxes had been installed. These he stared at. Neighbours passed him and said, 'Good morning, Hector,' and still he contemplated the metal post boxes, imagining news of his future life arriving one day inside them.

He took small roads out of Prenzlauer Berg and the streets were mainly deserted. These days, East Berliners trekked into the West to see what their few D-Marks would buy. He saw what they came back with: coloured shoelaces and luminous condoms. A lot of what they chose seemed to be a bright fearful pink or a harsh lime green, and these objects reminded Hector of the day when he'd been stopped by a group of Wessies, dressed in pink and green shell suits, who had asked him the way to Alexanderplatz. 'What have you come to see?' he'd asked them, more out of habit than out of interest, and they had laughed and swigged expensive beer and said: 'Oh, we've come to the East German closing-down sale! Many bargains. Everything must go.' And it had been at this moment and not at any other that Hector S had decided to leave his country and leave Ute and cycle to Russia. He said to himself, I'm not going because I'm afraid. I'm going because these people make me feel sick.

He joined the Leninallee and pedalled towards Lichtenberg. His back ached with the heaviness of the knapsack and the awkwardness of his rifle. Elvira was buried in the Socialists' Cemetery at Lichtenberg and it now occurred to Hector to make a small detour to look one last time at his mother's grave. He thought that he would confide to her his passion for Ute and in this way try to leave it behind. In her life, Elvira had relished confidences, licking her sensual lips . . . 'oh so delicious, Hecti! Tell me more!'

When he reached the cemetery, he couldn't remember where Elvira's grave was. There were so many hundreds of people buried here and he hadn't visited the place in five years. He knew he could spend hours looking for Elvira and then it would get dark and he'd still only be on the outskirts of Berlin. This would be a stupid way to waste the first day of his long journey.

Then he found her: *Elvira S 1931–1980.* A small polished stone. Hector parked his bicycle and took off his knapsack and rifle, flexing his shoulders. He removed his hat and stood, measuring the stone in his mind. The stone looked smaller than she had been. Did the state stone-cutters cheat on everyone by a few centimetres? And if they did, was this a thing of importance? Probably not. There were so many hundreds of millions of dead under the earth, it was amazing there was any earth left on which to grow cabbages or build kindergarten schools.

Before he could form any thoughts or words on the subject of Ute, Hector was disturbed by movement quite near him. He turned and looked and saw that a young man, poorly dressed, was going from grave to grave with a trowel, brazenly digging up the bulbs planted on them and putting them into a plastic carrier bag. The youth didn't seem to have noticed Hector—a figure of authority in a winter uniform—or else he *had* noticed him and was now deliberately taunting him with his distasteful little crime.

'Hey!' called Hector. 'Don't do that!'

The youth looked up. A white face, blank, without expression. No fear in the eyes.

'Who are you?' he said.

'Border Police,' announced Hector.

'*Border* Police?'

'Yes.'

The youth stood up straight and laughed. 'Border Police! The border is down, or didn't anyone tell you? You mean they didn't tell you?'

'Please leave,' said Hector, 'before I have you arrested.'

The youth didn't move. He made an obscene gesture with his hand. '*You* leave!' he said. 'You fuck off out of my world!'

Hector was used to insults. Insults had been part of his life for six years and now they troubled him no more than a few flakes of snow, say, or a shower of leaves blown across his path by the wind. Except that, under normal circumstances, he had his rifle with him and at this moment his rifle was a few feet away, leaning against a tree.

'You are stealing flowers from the dead,' said Hector.

The youth had a high-pitched laugh, the laugh of a girl. 'Ah, you think the dead planted them, do you, Border Guard? You think they stuck their bones up into the soil to make little holes for these bulbs?'

'This is a graveyard . . .' began Hector.

'Is it?' said the youth. 'Oh, I thought it was a communist rubbish dump. It contains the scum who made our lives a misery and a farce for forty years. But it's changing now, right? Every fucker in here was *wrong*! And I tell you what they're going to do with this place. They're going to bring in the bulldozers and dig up these stiffs and use them to put out Russian reactor fires and then when they've vacated it, they're going to—'

Hector walked three paces to his right and picked up his rifle. The click the youth heard was the release of the safety catch. The click stopped the flow of words and the pale face looked blank once again.

'Leave,' said Hector. 'Leave now.'

'OK, OK,' said the youth and put up his hands, one of which still held the bulb bag. The putting up of hands was a gesture which Hector had been trained to ignore when necessary. He aimed the rifle at the youth's groin.

'Hey,' said the youth, 'don't kill me! I know you bastards. Don't kill me!'

'Go, then,' said Hector. 'Go.'

The youth tried to walk away backwards, keeping his eyes on Hector's gun. He stumbled over a grave and fell down and the bag of bulbs dropped out of the hand with which he tried to save himself. Then he got to his feet and ran.

So there were no confidences shared with Elvira, nothing to make her lick her lips, or bring on one of her storms of weeping. And Ute wasn't left behind, but was carried onwards in Hector's heart.

Hector was sitting now in a café in Marzahn, the last housing estate in East Berlin, built to accommodate 160,000 people in 60,000 apartments, 2.6 humans to a unit. Beyond Marzahn were the Brandenburg Marshes and the wide open sky.

Hector had come to the café because after what happened at the cemetery, he'd started to feel chilly. He sat at a plastic table with his hands round a cup of coffee and the life of the café went on as if he wasn't there. He hoped that, in Russia, people would talk to him more, in whatever language they could muster. He really didn't want these familiar small sufferings—feeling cold inside, being ignored by people in public—to go on for the rest of his life. But nor would he ever pretend to be something other than what he was. It wasn't his fault if ideologies had a finite life span, if his world was falling away like flesh from bone, a little more each day. He'd been a communist and a patriot. He wanted to stand up in this cheap Marzahn café and say: 'My name is Hector S and, to me, the word "patriot" is not a dirty one.'

He sat in the café for a long time. He smoked four Karos. He went to the toilet and pissed and washed his face and hands in warm water. He stole a wedge of paper towels and put them into his overcoat pocket. He'd been told by a colleague that one of the marvels coming to East Germany in the near future would be toilet rolls printed with crossword puzzles.

Then he went out into the early afternoon and saw that it was later than he'd imagined and that a few lights were coming on in the tower blocks. Brought up to abhor waste, Hector admired the way East Germans used electricity. Light looked normal here. Across the Wall, he'd seen it become more and more startling and chaotic. On the long night shifts, he used to stare at all the rippling and blinking neon and wonder if it could, in the end, by reason of its absolute pointlessness, create blank spots in the human brain.

Now, he was leaving all the city light behind. It would hang in the sky at his back for a while and he'd be able to turn round and see its faint glow and say, 'That's Berlin.' And then it wouldn't even be a glow and the flicker of his cycle lamp would be all that he had to see by.

He pedalled hard. The only weapon he would have against the cold was his own blood. He grew more and more hungry and, on any ordinary trip, he would have stopped after two hours or so and opened one of the tins of Spam. But he'd set a rule for this journey—one meal a day and only one—and he was determined not to break it. So he just cycled on and the moon came up and then the stars, and he began to hear herons calling and see a second moon fallen into a wide and beautiful lake. To banish thoughts about Ute and her swan, he started to whistle some old tunes he'd picked up from Elvira who liked to sing to herself while she did the ironing.

Before night, Hector stopped at a village and bought bread. By torchlight, by the side of the road, he made a meal of tinned meat, bread and pickles. He wished he'd remembered to bring a plate to eat off as well as the plastic cutlery. Certain things, he thought, we take for granted so absolutely that they become invisible to us—and a dinner plate is one such thing.

He smoked a Karo and lay back on the frosty grass and looked at the stars. The exhaustion he now felt was suddenly intense. He knew he should repack the opened food, wrapping the bread carefully in its paper to keep it fresh for tomorrow. He knew also that he should search for some shelter, a shack or barn in which to sleep. But he couldn't move. He could barely lift his arm to stub out his cigarette.

So he closed his eyes. Some voice in him said, sleep, Hector. Sleep itself has warming properties. You'll be safe and everything will be safe till morning.

Hector was woken when the cold air of the night turned to mild but steady rain. There was enough light in the sky for him to see that a black slug was hanging off his tin of meat. He knew he ought to remove the slug and return what was left of the meat to his knapsack and that his ability to survive this journey depended upon such small acts of determination, but he felt incapable of eating meat that had been sucked at by a slug.

He saw now that he'd been lying by the side of a road and that at his back was a wood. Going into the wood to piss, he noticed that a narrow path ran between the trees, more or less parallel with the road. A red and yellow sign, nailed to an oak tree, said *Fitness path* and depicted a man in the attitude of a runner. Hector decided to follow the Fitness Path. Here, he would be protected from the rain and, for as long as the track ran roughly level with the road, he wouldn't get lost. Also, he liked the idea of coming across athletes. They were a category of people he admired, patriotic, stoical and sane. He couldn't imagine an athlete stealing bulbs from graves or doing crossword puzzles on toilet paper.

By his calculations, he had about a hundred kilometres to cycle before he reached the Polish border, and if his pace was steady, he expected to do this in three days. He hoped the beautiful forest would go on and on, right to the edge of his country. He took a long drink of water. Despite his short sleep, he felt revived, almost happy. Why, he thought, was I the only one of all my friends in the Border Police to go east? He imagined his old colleagues now, trying to sleep through this wet dawn, but most of them awake in fact, listening to the traffic beginning, listening to their blood beating, and none of them knowing which to worry about more—the past or the future.

Hector met no athletes, not even any amateur ones. And, to his disappointment, the Fitness Path quite soon veered north and he was forced to rejoin the road or risk becoming lost. But by this time, the sun was starting to glimmer through the rain clouds, making the road shine, and Hector's contentment didn't really diminish. It stemmed, he decided, from an acknowledgement of his own bravery. Bravery was the word. Most people in East Germany had their eyes turned towards the West, as if they were kids in a cinema queue and the West were the last show on earth. Only he, Hector S, had the courage and the vision to ride east towards the Russian winter, towards the wilderness.

He stopped at a public wash-house to shave and shower. Keeping clean was something he intended to do. He loved showers. He habitually masturbated under the shower, as did his father since the death of Elvira, and didn't care if anyone saw him do it. But here, the streams of hot water only soothed the ache in his back and in his calves and he had no erection. The most significant thing that he had to deny himself on this journey was Ute. He knew that his sanity and his ability to keep to his resolve depended upon this. Only when he arrived at his destination, wherever that turned out to be, would he get out the photograph of Ute leaning on the stool and take her from behind, as often as he felt inclined. And if his yearning for her then—for the real Ute, with her soft hair and her cunt that tasted of the sea—became serious like an illness, he would send for her.

He left the wash house with bright pink skin and wearing clean underwear. He went to a village café for coffee and a sweet cake and, although it was still early in the morning, there were old people dancing here, on the wooden café floor. The band consisted of an accordionist and a double bass player and these two were also old. Hector stared round him. On they danced, partner with partner, men with women, women whose men had died or been mislaid dancing together, all smiling and proud of the way they could still move their feet. Hector now realized that he was the only young person in the café and he wondered whether he was in some old persons' club and had only been served out of deference to his uniform. He closed his eyes. The music was jaunty and light. A country where old people can dance in the morning must be a good country. And Hector imagined how this music could beckon people from their beds and that instead of lying under their feather quilts waiting to die, they would examine their dancing shoes for signs of wear, comb what remained of their hair, put on a shawl or a coat and walk down to the café, humming or whistling. Yet soon this scene would be annihilated by history. Hector opened his eyes and said quite loudly to an old woman who had sat down at the next table: 'This dance café will be closed.'

She hesitated. Had Hector just uttered an order? You could never predict what extraordinary orders were going to come out of the mouths of uniformed men. Once, she had been stopped on her way to the butcher's and told to remove her wig.

'I beg your pardon?' she said.

'Yes,' said Hector. 'It will be closed. In less than a year. This place will become a discotheque. They will play Western music here, pop and rock and rap, and nobody in this village will sleep, ever again. And nor will you old people dance.'

Hector had finished his coffee and cake. He didn't want or expect a reply. He'd said what he wanted to say and now he would just leave. The old woman stared at him as he got up and shouldered his knapsack and his rifle. The musicians watched him and the dancing couples watched him, but nobody spoke out. When Hector emerged into the street, it was raining again, a light but steady rain.

Living in this way, off his meat and dill pickles, spending a little money on hot coffee and bread and sleeping on the good German earth, Hector S reached the Polish border.

He was perhaps forty kilometres inside Poland when he fell ill.

He fell ill from cold and exhaustion and from something else he couldn't name. The illness came over him just outside the town of G, when he found himself in a landscape of striped hills, strip-farmed plough and fescue grass. And coming towards him on the quaint ribbon of road was a funeral procession, led by a priest holding a mighty cross. And it was as if he—with his bicycle and his rifle—was the only living thing in a terrible old painting and the low sunlight was the varnish on that painting, yellow and sickly. His legs, so strong when his journey had begun, felt suddenly hollow, the weight of the knapsack and rifle on his back unbearable.

And he could hear singing. It was the priest and all the mourners wailing in Polish for the dead person, and to Hector this human music was more disagreeable, even, than one of Elvira's attacks of weeping in the apartment in Prenzlauer Berg. It made his stomach heave.

He got off his bicycle and leaned his weight over the handlebars and the saddle. He wanted to get right away from the road, so that he wouldn't have to come near the mourners or smell their fusty clothes or hear them breathing as they sang, but the striped hills on either side of the road were quite steep—too steep in fact for a man who has been stricken with sickness.

It occurred to Hector in the next second that he would have to shoot the mourners down. He would start with the priest. But he felt a little confused by numbers: how many mourners and how many bullets? And confused by distance: optimum range for this calibre of rifle was . . . what? He once knew it by heart, just as a man knows his own name by heart. And then, he was confused by currencies and their terminology. Was 'dollar' a universal word, or was there a Polish word for 'dollar' that was not 'dollar' differently pronounced? Was a zloty a coin or was it a note? Was it a letterbox? How many zlotys in a golden cross? How many letterboxes in a striped field . . .?

Of course, Hector felt himself begin to fall, but a person falling may not reach the ground to his certain knowledge, but instead arrive somewhere else. Hector fell on to the grey tarmac of the ribbon road and the priest and the mourners, seeing a man in a foreign uniform lying in their pathway, came on steadfastly towards him. Hector, however, is entering a different moment of time. He is reporting for duty. It is summer, perfect summer. It is dawn in East Berlin. Hector is entering the door at the base of a watchtower and he begins to climb up the concrete steps. Above him is the perfect octagonal of the tower itself, with its eight viewing windows. And through these windows will be falling . . . at the very moment Hector enters the octagon . . . at this very moment of short duration but of long residence in the mind of Hector S . . . will be falling the extraordinary beauty of the dawn light, arriving from the East.

When Hector woke, it was dark. He was lying in bed in a small room, painted brown and lit by an oil lamp. The flicker and fumes from the oil lamp eddied round on the brown ceiling. He could remember nothing.

Something cold touched his face. A dampness lay on his forehead. There was the smell of roses.

Then a voice, very near, said in broken German: 'Are you waking, Sir?'

Hector didn't recall making any reply, but the same voice decided to say next: 'I am a train driver.'

Then the lamplit room and the train driver and the smell of roses are removed from Hector's consciousness and he is submerged again in sleep, while the man who was a driver of freight trains between Poznan and Warsaw got up quietly and went to talk to his wife, Katarzyna, telling her reassuringly that the German soldier had woken up and that his fever was passing.

'Good,' said Katarzyna, 'so I hope he can leave tomorrow.'

'Well,' said the train driver, 'we shall see.'

'I don't want to "see",' said Katarzyna, who was old and afraid and had a long memory. 'I want him out of our house tomorrow. I don't know why I had to marry a man with such a stupidly kind heart.'

'He was lying in the road, Katarzyna.'

'I don't care where he was lying.'

He is lying in Ute's bed. He knows he shouldn't be here, not yet. He'd forbidden himself to come here, but here he is all the same. Outside the apartment building, in the first light of morning, Ute's swan, Karl, is screeching in his cage. Ute is lying on top of Hector, kissing his eyes. He isn't inside her, but he can feel his erection begin against her flat stomach, and with his encircling arms he presses her closer to him, moving her body so that her breasts rub against his chest. He whispers to her that he wants her, that he will want her for ever, that he can't help himself, that his passion for her will have no end, and she says to him sweetly, giggling, licking his ear: 'Hecti, it will end when you die . . .'

The dark room returned. A nightlight on a saucer had replaced the oil lamp and Hector could just make out the shape of a small window, shuttered with louvres, beyond which it was possible to imagine an icy, moonlit sky. Hector turned his head, looking for the train driver sitting beside him, but no one was there.

He lay very still. There was a wet patch in the bed and Hector supposed that he had pissed in it in his sleep, but wasn't very disconcerted because this was a thing that had gone on happening to him long after boyhood and two doctors had told him that there was nothing to be done about it.

Then, hearing a train's mournful whistle, Hector remembered that he was in Poland. He remembered the striped fields and the procession of mourners. He sat up and looked around the room for his knapsack and rifle and, not finding them, was overcome with anguish. Weeping was for the weak, for people like Elvira, not for him. But in this Polish night, Hector wept and he didn't seem able to stop, however hard he tried.

After a while, he heard someone get up in the room next door and an old woman came and stood by him, wrapped in a shawl, with her hair in a grey plait. She stared at him for a few moments, then shook his shoulder quite roughly. 'German soldier,' she said, 'stop crying, please.'

★

Hector S lay in the little room for another day and a night. Katarzyna swore at her husband and prayed on her Bible. The train driver changed Hector's sheets and fed him beetroot soup.

Katarzyna went through Hector's knapsack and removed the lemon and made herself a beautiful jug of lemon tea. She said to the train driver: 'This is the first gift I've ever had from a German. And the last.'

Then Hector and his bicycle and his knapsack were helped into a truck and driven to Poznan station and put into a freight car full of cauliflowers. 'I am sorry,' said the train driver, 'to put you with vegetables, Sir.'

After this, there was just the dark of the freight car and the sound of all the miles and miles of the Polish heartland moving under the train. Hector lay down and covered himself with his overcoat and was as still as a man can be on a bed of cauliflowers. His head and body ached and it seemed to him that this ache was right in the substance of his skull and in the marrow of his bones.

His future was going wrong. Every thought that came to him, instead of being clear and precise, was clouded and difficult. It was as though thoughts were harmful chemicals, setting off explosions in his brain. The train was taking him nearer to his destination, but he began to see, with embarrassment, that it was towards the old eternal Russia of his imagination that he was travelling and that although he'd prepared quite well for his journey, he hadn't prepared at all for his arrival. When his D-Marks ran out, where and how was he to live? For a start, he spoke only a few words of the language. He knew the Russian word for 'tomorrow', but not the Russian word for 'now'. What kind of work could he find which allowed him to be totally silent?

Then a new thought came. The colour of its chemical felt white. It was a thought about silence and the new world, the world of the West, creeping east. Westerners were thieves of silence. They stole the quiet in a place and in the mind of a man and replaced it with longing, just as they stole the mystery from a city by lighting it orange. Darkness and quiet were leaving the world. It was only a matter of time before the dawn wouldn't be the dawn any more, but some other computer-adjusted piece of time, with colours other than its own.

Hector felt pleased with this thought, not because it was an optimistic one, but because it seemed rational and not blighted by confusion, and so he said to himself that perhaps he was going all this way in search of the perfect silence. He'd imagined a wilderness, a birch grove, a lake, or at least, he'd imagined cycling or walking through this kind of landscape on his way to his future in Russia. But the truth was that the future had no location. He'd never got further with his own story than the lake. Now, he understood that he might never get further—ever. In all probability, the lake was his destination.

Hector sat up and tried to eat a pickled cucumber. He had no appetite for what remained of the tinned meat. He lay down again, liking the train now, soothed a bit by the train, as if the train were Elvira and Hector a child falling asleep on her lap, wrapped in her apron.

He didn't want to show his face in Warsaw. He knew he would be stared at and he couldn't abide the thought of meeting the stare of Polish women and girls.

He dreamed the place smelled of spun sugar, that there was dry rot in the old houses, that church bells kept ringing and ringing the hours, that pigeons continuously ruffled the air. He would fall ill again in such a place.

So he resorted to bribery. He offered DM10 to the train driver and asked him to put him in another freight going east to the border with Belorus or beyond.

The train driver took the money and looked at it and shook his head. 'Now from here in a freight going east, you will die of cold, Sir.'

'I'm used to the cold' said Hector.

'Not this one. This is more cold.'

'Please,' said Hector.

So the money was paid and a second driver was found who agreed to take him in a night train carrying medical supplies to Minsk. Katarzyna's husband then performed his last act of generosity: he gave Hector the blanket he kept in his cab. 'In the cold night,' he said, 'cover your body, German man.'

Hector missed the cauliflowers. In this second freight car, piled with boxes, every surface was hard and in whatever way he lay down, Hector's bones hurt. He tried folding the blanket in three and lying on top of it. This was more comfortable and Hector was beginning to drift towards sleep when he opened his eyes and saw in the darkness the freezing cloud of his own breath lying over him like a ghost. In time, he would have breathed all the air in the box car and the ghost would be very large and attempt to make more room for itself by entering the cavities of his body and taking away his life.

The blanket smelled of oil and it was old and worn, but there was still a little warmth in it. Hector stood up and wrapped himself round and round in it and lay down again on the boxes of pharmaceuticals. He imagined he was lying on glass syringes, as clear as ice.

The night would be so long. Poland, thought Hector, is a place where the nights have subdued the days and stolen half their territory. The bit of space left to the light is so pitiful, you just have time to cycle a few kilometres, buy some hard bread, pass a church where women kneel at open-air confessionals, hear a village band wearing hats with emperor's plumes play an ancient march, and then the dusk comes down, and it's futile to look forward to morning, because morning is so far away. It wasn't so mad, so completely foolish to imagine that here, on certain days, you could go into a post office, say, to buy a stamp, and that when you came out again with the stamp in your wallet, the day had given up hope and the words 'post office' had faded into the wall.

These thoughts made Hector remember the line of post boxes in the lobby of the apartment building in Prenzlauer Berg and how he'd imagined letters from Russia arriving here, letters which described an epic journey, an honourable arrival, a life built in a place where the structures of the old familiar world were still standing.

Now, in his freight car, wrapped in the train driver's blanket, as heavy snow starts to fall, Hector begins to compose in his mind a letter to Ute, to the sister he's desired since the day, at the age of five, when she licked his penis in the bath. It may be, he thinks, the only letter he will have time to think up and so he wants it to describe a place that will seduce Ute, a place in which she will recognize that she could be happy, a place he has made safe for her in advance:

Dear Ute,

I have arrived at the loneliest, most beautiful place in the world. Let me describe it to you. It is a great forest that has been growing silently for more time than anything else on this part of the earth. Bears inhabit it. And reindeer and wolves. Snow lies over it for seven months of the year. Sometimes, I fall into conversation with a solitary hunter and we discuss weapons and the individual characteristics of flight of certain difficult targets and how, in one's aim, one may compensate for these and so kill after all and not starve. Bears are protected and may not be shot.

And this brings me to swans. At the feet of the forest is a lake. The north side of it is frozen, but a little water still laps the snow on this southern side and here I have discovered a fine family of your favourite birds. They whoop like cranes in the early morning. They're plump and sleek from the quantity of fish they find in the lake. They are as tame as Karl and will come if I call them and feed from my hand. When you join me here, this is the first thing we will do: go down to the lake and visit the swans.

I expect you're wondering where we're going to live and how we're to find shelter. 'Hecti,' I hear you say, 'are you asking me to make love to you in the snow?' No, Ute. No, I'm not. Unless you want to do that.

I have found, at the lakeside, an old grey dacha, built of wood, with a stone chimney and a steep shingled roof. I walked into it like that girl in the fairy story and sat down in the largest of the chairs. I found a smoked ham hanging inside the chimney. I found a larder full of apples. I found folded sheets for the bed.

It's as if this dacha was designed with me in mind, with everything necessary for my survival: an axe to chop wood, a fire to cook on, even a featherbed quilt for the nights, which are as cold as nights on the moon. So now, I'm able to say to you, don't waste any more time, sell whatever you have to sell—Elvira's hairbrushes, Father's cache of cigarettes—and take the next train out of Berlin going east . . .

It was at this point in his imaginary letter that Hector was jolted forwards and almost fell off the ledge of boxes on which he was lying. The train had stopped.

Hector listened. He hadn't seen the thick snow falling, but by the temperature in the car and by the absence of any sound, he was able to judge that it was the deep middle of the night. The train would still be a long way from Minsk, a long way even from the border, so he supposed that it must have stopped at a signal and that in a few minutes it would get going again.

Somehow, the immobilization of the train made the cold inside the freight car more intense and the ghost of breath that filled the space around and above Hector became agitated and began a strange kind of wailing.

The train moved. But it was going backwards, Hector could tell by the way his body rolled. And then it stopped again. Hector raised his head off his knapsack, to hear better, to see better, but he could hear and see nothing except the ghost in the air.

What Hector couldn't know was that the train had been re-routed into a siding because the line further east was temporarily closed by snow. What he couldn't know either was that the driver of the second freight had forgotten all about him and, once the train was safe in its siding, got down from his cab and walked away across the white fields towards a village, in search of a warm fire and a bed for the rest of the night. So Hector lay there, waiting for the train to resume its journey, while the soft snow piled up on the roof of the box car.

After an hour had passed, he tried to move himself towards the edge of the car, so that he could bang on the doors with his feet, but he found that his body was unwilling to move. It asked him to let it rest. He attempted, then, to call out. He knew that a human voice inside a freight car would probably make the kind of sound that disturbed no one's peace and altered nothing in the world, but he tried to call nevertheless. 'Train driver!' he said. 'Help me!' It was a whisper, not a shout. Hector believed that he was shouting, but he was only murmuring. And anyway, the driver of the second freight was a mile away. He was sitting by a fire with a schoolteacher and his wife, drinking vodka and eating poppyseed cakes.

After his efforts at calling, Hector's throat felt sore and he was afflicted suddenly by a desperate thirst. He had no memory of where his water bottle was or when he had last seen it, but what he did remember was the solitary lemon he had put into his knapsack on the morning of his departure. And his longing, now, to suck the juice from this lemon became so great that he succeeded in extracting one hand from the blanket and with this one hand reached behind his head to try to undo the fastenings of his knapsack.

He could picture with absolute precision the colour, shape and texture of the lemon as it had been when he packed it and his mind refused to imagine it any other way.

It is difficult to say how long Hector S struggled to locate this perfect yellow fruit, but into his search for it he put every last ounce of his strength.

The snow stopped falling an hour before sunrise and the sky cleared and the dawn was bright.

Woken by the winter sunlight, the driver of the freight to Minsk remembered at this instant the German soldier he'd agreed to hide in one of his box cars in return for DM5.

He dressed hurriedly, tugging on his overcoat and his hat, and let himself out of the schoolteacher's house.

The snow was thick on the fields. The man wasn't young. Trying to make his way through this deep snow was exhausting for him and it took him the best part of half an hour to reach the train.

He opened the door of Hector's box car and stared in. The light on the snow had blinded him and, for a moment, he could see nothing. 'Hello!' he called. 'Hello! It is morning.'

Hector was lying face up, one arm behind his head that rested on his knapsack. His face had the pallor of bone, but there was a smile on it, as if, in his last moments, Hector had glimpsed something of great beauty.

The train driver walked a few paces from the car and fumbled to light a cigarette.

He stood in the snow, thinking.

It didn't take him long to decide what he was going to do. He was going to leave Hector exactly where he was. He wasn't even going to touch him or cover his face. Even if the day remained fine, the cold in the box car would preserve the body and, with a bit of luck, the train would get to Minsk before nightfall.

At the depot, the freight would be unloaded by rail workers from Belorus, and so it would be they who would find the stowaway. In this way, provided he remembered to get rid of the DM5, the driver would have shifted the burden of responsibility. The dead German, wearing some kind of military uniform, would become a Russian problem.

IAN McEWAN

Solid Geometry

IN Melton Mowbray in 1875 at an auction of articles of 'curiosity and worth', my great-grandfather, in the company of M his friend, bid for the penis of Captain Nicholls who died in Horsemonger jail in 1873. It was bottled in a glass twelve inches long, and, noted my great-grandfather in his diary that night, 'in a beautiful state of preservation'. Also for auction was 'the unnamed portion of the late Lady Barrymore. It went to Sam Israels for fifty guineas.' My great-grandfather was keen on the idea of having the two items as a pair, and M dissuaded him. This illustrates perfectly their friendship. My great-grandfather the excitable theorist, M the man of action who knew when to bid at auctions. My great-grandfather lived for sixty-nine years. For forty-five of them, at the end of every day, he sat down before going to bed and wrote his thoughts in a diary. These diaries are on my table now, forty-five volumes bound in calf leather, and to the left sits Capt. Nicholls in the glass jar. My great-grandfather lived on the income derived from the patent of an invention of his father, a handy fastener used by corset-makers right up till the outbreak of the First World War. My great-grandfather liked gossip, numbers and theories. He also liked tobacco, good port, jugged hare and, very occasionally, opium. He liked to think of himself as a mathematician, though he never had a job, and never published a book. Nor did he ever travel or get his name in *The Times*, even when he died. In 1869 he married Alice, only daughter of the Revd Toby Shadwell, co-author of a not highly regarded book on English wild flowers. I believe my great-grandfather to have been a very fine diarist, and when I have finished editing the diaries and they are published I am certain he will receive the recognition due to him. When my work is over I will take a long holiday, travel somewhere cold and clean and treeless, Iceland or the Russian Steppes. I used to think that at the end of it all I would try, if it was possible, to divorce my wife Maisie, but now there is no need at all.

Often Maisie would shout in her sleep and I would have to wake her. 'Put your arm around me,' she would say. 'It was a horrible dream. I had it once before. I was in a plane flying over a desert. But it wasn't really a desert. I took the plane lower and I could see there were thousands of babies heaped up, stretching away into the horizon, all of them naked and climbing over each other. I was running out of fuel and I had to land the plane. I tried to find a space, I flew on and on looking for a space . . .'

'Go to sleep now,' I said through a yawn. 'It was only a dream.'

'No,' she cried. 'I mustn't go to sleep, not just yet.'

'Well, *I* have to sleep now,' I told her. 'I have to be up early in the morning.'

She shook my shoulder. 'Please don't go to sleep yet, don't leave me here.'

'I'm in the same bed,' I said. 'I won't leave you.'

'It makes no difference, don't leave me awake . . .' But my eyes were already closing.

Lately I have taken up my great-grandfather's habit. Before going to bed I sit down for half an hour and think over the day. I have no mathematical whimsies or sexual theories to note down. Mostly I write out what Maisie has said to me and what I have said to Maisie. Sometimes, for complete privacy, I lock myself in the bathroom, sit on the toilet seat and balance the writing-pad on my knees. Apart from me there is occasionally a spider or two in the bathroom. They climb up the waste pipe and crouch perfectly still on the glaring white enamel. They must wonder where they have come to. After hours of crouching they turn back, puzzled, or perhaps disappointed they could not learn more. As far as I can tell, my great-grandfather made only one reference to spiders. On May 8th, 1906, he wrote, 'Bismarck is a spider.'

In the afternoons Maisie used to bring me tea and tell me her nightmares. Usually I was going through old newspapers, compiling indexes, cataloguing items, putting down this volume, picking up another. Maisie said she was in a bad way. Recently she had been sitting around the house all day glancing at books on psychology and the occult, and almost every night she had bad dreams. Since the time we exchanged physical blows, lying in wait to hit each other with the same shoe outside the bathroom, I had had little sympathy for her. Part of her problem was jealousy. She was very jealous . . . of my great-grandfather's forty-five-volume diary, and of my purpose and energy in editing it.

She was doing nothing. I was putting down one volume and picking up another when Maisie came in with the tea.

'Can I tell you my dream?' she asked. 'I was flying this plane over a kind of desert . . .'

'Tell me later, Maisie,' I said. 'I'm in the middle of something here.' After she had gone I stared at the wall in front of my desk and thought about M, who came to talk and dine with my great-grandfather regularly over a period of fifteen years up until his sudden and unexplained departure one evening in 1898. M, whoever he might have been, was something of an academic, as well as a man of action. For example, on the evening of August 9th, 1870, the two of them are talking about positions for lovemaking and M tells my great-grandfather that copulation *a posteriori* is the most natural way owing to the position of the clitoris and because other anthropoids favour this method. My great-grandfather, who copulated about half-a-dozen times in his entire life, and that with Alice during the first year of their marriage, wondered out loud what the Church's view was and straight away M is able to tell him that the seventh-century theologian Theodore considered copulation *a posteriori* a sin ranking with masturbation and therefore worthy of forty penances. Later in the same evening my great-grandfather produced mathematical evidence that the maximum number of positions cannot exceed the prime number seventeen. M scoffed at this and told him he had seen a collection of drawings by Romano, a pupil of Raphael's, in which twenty-four positions were shown. And, he said, he had heard of a Mr F. K. Forberg who had accounted for ninety. By the time I remembered the tea Maisie had left by my elbow it was cold.

An important stage in the deterioration of our marriage was reached as follows. I was sitting in the bathroom one evening writing out a conversation Maisie and I had had about the Tarot pack when suddenly she was outside, rapping on the door and rattling the door-handle.

'Open the door,' she called out. 'I want to come in.'

I said to her, 'You'll have to wait a few minutes more. I've almost finished.'

'Let me in now,' she shouted. 'You're not using the toilet.'

'Wait,' I replied, and wrote another line or two. Now Maisie was kicking the door.

'My period has started and I need to get something.' I ignored her yells and finished my piece, which I considered to be particularly important. If I left it till later certain details would be lost. There was no sound from Maisie now and I assumed she was in the bedroom. But when I opened the door she was standing right in my way with a shoe in her hand. She brought the heel of it sharply down on my head, and I only had time to move slightly to one side. The heel caught the top of my ear and cut it badly.

'There,' said Maisie, stepping round me to get to the bathroom, 'now we are both bleeding,' and she banged the door shut. I picked up the shoe and stood quietly and patiently outside the bathroom holding a handkerchief to my bleeding ear. Maisie was in the bathroom about ten minutes and as she came out I caught her neatly and squarely on the top of her head. I did not give her time to move. She stood perfectly still for a moment looking straight into my eyes.

'You worm,' she breathed, and went down to the kitchen to nurse her head out of my sight.

During supper yesterday Maisie claimed that a man locked in a cell with only the Tarot cards would have access to all knowledge. She had been doing a reading that afternoon and the cards were still spread about the floor.

'Could he work out the street plan of Valparaiso from the cards?' I asked.

'You're being stupid,' she replied.

'Could it tell him the best way to start a laundry business, the best way to make an omelette or a kidney machine?'

'Your mind is so narrow,' she complained. 'You're so narrow, so predictable.'

'Could he,' I insisted, 'tell me who M is, or why . . .'

'Those things don't matter,' she cried. 'They're not necessary.'

'They are still knowledge. Could he find them out?'

She hesitated. 'Yes, he could.'

I smiled, and said nothing.

'What's so funny?' she said. I shrugged, and she began to get angry. She wanted to be disproved. 'Why did you ask all those pointless questions?'

I shrugged again. 'I just wanted to know if you really meant *everything*.'

Maisie banged the table and screamed, 'Damn you! Why are you always trying me out? Why don't you say something real?' And with that we both recognized we had reached the point where all our discussions led and we became bitterly silent.

Work on the diaries cannot proceed until I have cleared up the mystery surrounding M. After coming to dinner on and off for fifteen years and supplying my great-grandfather with a mass of material for his theories, M simply disappears from the pages of the diary. On Tuesday, December 6th, my great-grandfather invited M to dine on the following Saturday, and although M came, my great-grandfather in the entry for that day simply writes, 'M to dinner.' On any other day the conversation at these meals is recorded at great length. M had been to dinner on Monday, December 5th, and the conversation had been about geometry, and the entries for the rest of that week are entirely given over to the same subject. There is absolutely no hint of antagonism. Besides, my great-grandfather *needed* M. M provided his material, M knew what was going on, he was familiar with London and he had been on the Continent a number of times. He knew all about socialism and Darwin, he had an acquaintance in the free love movement, a friend of James Hinton. M was *in* the world in a way which my great-grandfather, who left Melton Mowbray only once in his lifetime, to visit Nottingham, was not. Even as a young man my great-grandfather preferred to theorize by the fireside; all he needed were the materials M supplied. For example, one evening in June 1884 M, who was just back from London, gave my great-grandfather an account of how the streets of the town were fouled and clogged by horse dung. Now in that same week my great-grandfather had been reading the essay by Malthus called 'On the Principle of Population'. That night he made an excited entry in the diary about a pamphlet he wanted to write and have published. It was to be called 'De Stercore Equorum'. The pamphlet was never published and probably never written, but there are detailed notes in the diary entries for the two weeks following that evening. In 'De Stercore Equorum' ('Concerning Horseshit') he assumes geometric growth in the horse population, and working from detailed street plans he predicted that the metropolis would be impassable by 1935. By impassable he took to mean an average thickness of one foot (compressed) in every major street. He described involved experiments outside his own stables to determine the compressibility of horse dung, which he managed to express mathematically. It was all pure theory, of course. His results rested on the assumption that no dung would be shovelled aside in the fifty years to come. Very likely it was M who talked my great-grandfather out of the project.

One morning, after a long dark night of Maisie's nightmares, we were lying side by side in bed and I said,

'What is it you really want? Why don't you go back to your job? These long walks, all this analysis, sitting around the house, lying in bed all morning, the Tarot pack, the nightmares . . . what is it you want?'

And she said, 'I want to get my head straight,' which she had said many times before.

I said, 'Your head, your mind, it's not like a hotel kitchen, you know, you can't throw stuff out like old tin cans. It's more like a river than a place, moving and changing all the time. You can't make rivers flow straight.'

'Don't go through all that again,' she said. 'I'm not trying to make rivers flow straight, I'm trying to get my head straight.'

'You've got to *do* something,' I told her. 'You can't do nothing. Why not go back to your job? You didn't have nightmares when you were working. You were never so unhappy when you were working.'

'I've got to stand back from all that,' she said. 'I'm not sure what any of it means.'

'Fashion,' I said, 'it's all fashion. Fashionable metaphors, fashionable reading, fashionable malaise. What do you care about Jung, for example? You've read twelve pages in a month.'

'Don't go on,' she pleaded, 'you know it leads nowhere.'

But I went on.

'You've never been anywhere,' I told her, 'you've never done anything. You're a nice girl without even the blessing of an unhappy childhood. Your sentimental Buddhism, this junk-shop mysticism, joss-stick therapy, magazine astrology . . . none of it is yours, you've worked none of it out for yourself. You fell into it, you fell into a swamp of respectable intuitions. You haven't the originality or passion to intuit anything yourself beyond your own unhappiness. Why are you filling your mind with other people's mystic banalities and giving yourself nightmares?' I got out of bed, opened the curtains and began to get dressed.

'You talk like this was a fiction seminar,' Maisie said. 'Why are you trying to make things worse for me?' Self-pity began to well up from inside her, but she fought it down. 'When you are talking,' she went on, 'I can feel myself, you know, being screwed up like a piece of paper.'

'Perhaps we *are* in a fiction seminar,' I said grimly. Maisie sat up in bed staring at her lap. Suddenly her tone changed. She patted the pillow beside her and said softly,

'Come over here. Come and sit here. I want to touch you, I want you to touch me . . .' But I was sighing, and already on my way to the kitchen.

In the kitchen I made myself some coffee and took it through to my study. It had occurred to me in my night of broken sleep that a possible clue to the disappearance of M might be found in the pages of geometry. I had always skipped through them before because mathematics does not interest me. On the Monday, December 5th, 1898, M and my great-grandfather discussed the *vescia piscis*, which apparently is the subject of Euclid's first proposition and a profound influence on the ground plans of many ancient religious buildings. I read through the account of the conversation carefully, trying to understand as best I could the geometry of it. Then, turning the page, I found a lengthy anecdote which M told my great-grandfather that same evening when the coffee had been brought in and the cigars were lit. Just as I was beginning to read Maisie came in.

'And what about you,' she said, as if there had not been an hour break in our exchange, 'all you have is books. Crawling over the past like a fly on a turd.'

I was angry, of course, but I smiled and said cheerfully, 'Crawling? Well, at least I'm moving.'

'You don't speak to me any more,' she said, 'you play me like a pinball machine, for points.'

'Good morning, Hamlet,' I replied, and sat in my chair waiting patiently for what she had to say next. But she did not speak, she left, closing the study door softly behind her.

'In September 1870,' M began to tell my great-grandfather,

I came into the possession of certain documents which not only invalidate everything fundamental to our science of solid geometry but also undermine the whole canon of our physical laws and force one to redefine one's place in Nature's scheme. These papers outweigh in importance the combined work of Marx and Darwin. They were entrusted to me by a young American mathematician, and they are the work of David Hunter, a mathematician too and a Scotsman. The American's name was Goodman. I had corresponded with his father over a number of years in connection with his work on the cyclical theory of menstruation which, incredibly enough, is still widely discredited in this country. I met the young Goodman in Vienna where, along with Hunter and mathematicians from a dozen countries, he had been attending an international conference on mathematics. Goodman was pale and greatly disturbed when I met him, and planned to return to America the following day even though the conference was not yet half complete. He gave the papers into my care with instructions that I was to deliver them to David Hunter if I was ever to learn of his whereabouts. And then, only after much persuasion and insistence on my part, he told me what he had witnessed on the third day of the conference. The conference met every morning at nine thirty when a paper was read and a general discussion ensued. At eleven o'clock refreshments were brought in and many of the mathematicians would get up from the long, highly polished table round which they were all gathered and stroll about the large, elegant room and engage in informal discussions with their colleagues. Now, the conference lasted two weeks, and by a long-standing arrangement the most eminent of the mathematicians read their papers first, followed by the slightly less eminent, and so on, in a descending hierarchy throughout the two weeks, which caused, as it is wont to do among highly intelligent men, occasional but intense jealousies. Hunter, though a brilliant mathematician, was young and virtually unknown outside his university, which was Edinburgh. He had applied to deliver what he described as a very important paper on solid geometry, and since he was of little account in this pantheon he was assigned to read to the conference on the last day but one, by which time many of the most important figures would have returned to their respective countries. And so on the third morning, as the servants were bringing in the refreshments, Hunter stood up suddenly and addressed his colleagues just as they were rising from their seats. He was a large, shaggy man and, though young, he had about him a certain presence which reduced the hum of conversation to a complete silence.

'Gentlemen,' said Hunter, 'I must ask you to forgive this improper form of address, but I have something to tell you of the utmost importance. I have discovered the plane without a surface.' Amid derisive smiles and gentle bemused laughter, Hunter picked up from the table a large white sheet of paper. With a pocket-knife he made an incision along its surface about three inches long and slightly to one side of its centre. Then he made some rapid, complicated folds and, holding the paper aloft so all could see, he appeared to draw one corner of it through the incision, and as he did so it disappeared.

'Behold, gentlemen,' said Hunter, holding out his empty hands towards the company, 'the plane without a surface.'

Maisie came into my room, washed now and smelling faintly of perfumed soap. She came and stood behind my chair and placed her hands on my shoulders.

'What are you reading?' she said.

'Just bits of the diary which I haven't looked at before.' She began to massage me gently at the base of my neck. I would have found it soothing if it had still been the first year of our marriage. But it was the sixth year and it generated a kind of tension which communicated itself the length of my spine. Maisie wanted something. To restrain her I placed my right hand on her left, and, mistaking this for affection, she leaned forward and kissed under my ear. Her breath smelled of toothpaste and toast. She tugged at my shoulder.

'Let's go in the bedroom,' she whispered. 'We haven't made love for nearly two weeks now.'

'I know,' I replied. 'You know how it is . . . with my work.' I felt no desire for Maisie or any other woman. All I wanted to do was turn the next page of my great-grandfather's diary. Maisie took her hands off my shoulders and stood by my side. There was such a sudden ferocity in her silence that I found myself tensing like a sprinter on the starting line. She stretched forward and picked up the sealed jar containing Capt. Nicholls. As she lifted it his penis drifted dreamily from one end of the glass to the other.

'You're so COMPLACENT,' Maisie shrieked, just before she hurled the glass bottle at the wall in front of my table. Instinctively I covered my face with my hands to shield off the shattering glass. As I opened my eyes I heard myself saying,

'Why did you do that? That belonged to my great-grandfather.' Amid the broken glass and the rising stench of formaldehyde lay Capt. Nicholls, slouched across the leather covers of a volume of the diary, grey, limp and menacing, transformed from a treasured curiosity into a horrible obscenity.

'That was a terrible thing to do. Why did you do that?' I said again.

'I'm going for a walk,' Maisie replied, and slammed the door this time as she left the room.

I did not move from my chair for a long time. Maisie had destroyed an object of great value to me. It had stood in his study while he lived, and then it had stood in mine, linking my life with his. I picked a few splinters of glass from my lap and stared at the 160-year-old piece of another human on my table. I looked at it and thought of all the homunculi which had swarmed down its length. I thought of all the places it had been, Cape Town, Boston, Jerusalem, travelling in the dark, fetid inside of Capt. Nicholls's leather breeches, emerging occasionally into the dazzling sunlight to discharge urine in some jostling public place. I thought also of all the things it had touched, all the molecules, of Captain Nicholls's exploring hands on lonely unrequited nights at sea, the sweating walls of cunts of young girls and old whores, their molecules must still exist today, a fine dust blowing from Cheapside to Leicestershire. Who knows how long it might have lasted in its glass jar. I began to clear up the mess. I brought the rubbish bucket in from the kitchen. I swept and picked up all the glass I could find and swabbed up the formaldehyde. Then, holding him by just one end, I tried to ease Capt. Nicholls on to a sheet of newspaper. My stomach heaved as the foreskin began to come away in my fingers. Finally, with my eyes closed, I succeeded, and wrapping him carefully in the newspaper, I carried him into the garden and buried him under the geraniums. All this time I tried to prevent my resentment towards Maisie filling my mind. I wanted to continue with M's story. Back in my chair I dabbed at a few spots of formaldehyde which had blotted the ink, and read on.

For as long as a minute the room was frozen, and with each successive second it appeared to freeze harder. The first to speak was Dr Stanley Rose of Cambridge University, who had much to lose by Hunter's plane without a surface. His reputation, which was very considerable indeed, rested upon his 'Principles of Solid Geometry'.

'How dare you, sir. How dare you insult the dignity of this assembly with a worthless conjuror's trick.' And bolstered by the rising murmur of concurrence behind him, he added, 'You should be ashamed, young man, thoroughly ashamed.' With that, the room erupted like a volcano. With the exception of young Goodman, and of the servants who still stood by with the refreshments, the whole room turned on Hunter and directed at him a senseless babble of denunciation, invective and threat. Some thumped on the table in their fury, others waved their clenched fists. One very frail German gentleman fell to the floor in an apoplexy and had to be helped to a chair. And there stood Hunter, firm and outwardly unmoved, his head inclined slightly to one side, his fingers resting lightly on the surface of the long polished table. That such an uproar should follow a worthless conjuror's trick clearly demonstrated the extent of the underlying unease, and Hunter surely appreciated this. Raising his hand, and the company falling suddenly silent once more, he said,

'Gentlemen, your concern is understandable and I will effect another proof, the ultimate proof.' This said, he sat down and removed his shoes, stood up and removed his jacket, and then called for a volunteer to assist him, at which Goodman came forward. Hunter strode through the crowd to a couch which stood along one of the walls, and while he settled himself upon it he told the mystified Goodman that when he returned to England he should take with him Hunter's papers and keep them there until he came to collect them. When the mathematicians had gathered round the couch Hunter rolled on to his stomach and clasped his hands behind his back in a strange posture to fashion a hoop with his arms. He asked Goodman to hold his arms in that position for him, and rolled on his side where he began a number of strenuous jerking movements which enabled him to pass one of his feet through the hoop. He asked his assistant to turn him on his other side, where he performed the same movements again and succeeded in passing his other foot between his arms, and at the same time bent his trunk in such a way that his head was able to pass through the hoop in the opposite direction to his feet. With the help of his assistant he began to pass his leg and head past each other through the hoop made by his arms. It was then that the distinguished assembly vented, as one man, a single yelp of utter incredulity. Hunter was beginning to disappear, and now, as his legs and head passed through his arms with greater facility, seemed even to be drawn through by some invisible power, he was almost gone. And now . . . he was gone, quite gone, and nothing remained.

M's story put my great-grandfather in a frenzy of excitement. In his diary that night he recorded how he tried 'to prevail upon my guest to send for the papers upon the instant' even though it was by now two o'clock in the morning. M, however, was more sceptical about the whole thing. 'Americans,' he told my great-grandfather, 'often indulge in fantastic tales.' But he agreed to bring along the papers the following day. As it turned out M did not dine with my great-grandfather that night because of another engagement, but he called round in the late afternoon with the papers. Before he left he told my great-grandfather he had been through them a number of times and 'there was no sense to be had out of them'. He did not realize then how much he was underestimating my great-grandfather as an amateur mathematician. Over a glass of sherry in front of the drawing-room fire the two men arranged to dine together again at the end of the week, on Saturday. For the next three days my great-grandfather hardly paused from his reading of Hunter's theorems to eat or sleep. The diary is full of nothing else. The pages are covered with scribbles, diagrams and symbols. It seems that Hunter had to devise a new set of symbols, virtually a whole new language, to express his ideas. By the end of the second day my great-grandfather had made his first breakthrough. At the bottom of a page of mathematical scribble he wrote, 'Dimensionality is a function of consciousness'. Turning to the entry for the next day I read the words, 'It disappeared in my hands'. He had re-established the plane without a surface. And there, spread out in front of me, were step by step instructions on how to fold the piece of paper. Turning the next page I suddenly understood the mystery of M's disappearance. Undoubtedly encouraged by my great-grandfather, he had taken part that evening in a scientific experiment, probably in a spirit of great scepticism. For here my great-grandfather had drawn a series of small sketches illustrating what at first glance looked like yoga positions. Clearly they were the secret of Hunter's disappearing act.

My hands were trembling as I cleared a space on my desk. I selected a clean sheet of typing paper and laid it in front of me. I fetched a razor blade from the bathroom. I rummaged in a drawer and found an old pair of compasses, sharpened a pencil and fitted it in. I searched through the house till I found an accurate steel ruler I had once used for fitting window panes, and then I was ready. First I had to cut the paper to size. The piece that Hunter had so casually picked up from the table had obviously been carefully prepared beforehand. The length of the sides had to express a specific ratio. Using the compasses I found the centre of the paper and through this point I drew a line parallel to one of the sides and continued it right to the edge. Then I had to construct a rectangle whose measurements bore a particular relation to those of the sides of the paper. The centre of this rectangle occurred on the line in such a way as to dissect it by the Golden Mean. From the top of this rectangle I drew intersecting arcs, again of specified proportionate radii. This operation was repeated at the lower end of the rectangle, and when the two points of intersection were joined I had the line of incision. Then I started work on the folding lines. Each line seemed to express, in its length, angle of incline and point of intersection with other lines, some mysterious inner harmony of numbers. As I intersected arcs, drew lines and made folds, I felt I was blindly operating a system of the highest, most terrifying form of knowledge, the mathematics of the Absolute. By the time I had made the final fold the piece of paper was the shape of a geometric flower with three concentric rings arranged round the incision at the centre. There was something so tranquil and perfect about this design, something so remote and compelling, that as I stared into it I felt myself going into a light trance and my mind becoming clear and inactive. I shook my head and glanced away. It was time now to turn the flower in on itself and pull it through the incision. This was a delicate operation and now my hands were trembling again. Only by staring into the centre of the design could I calm myself. With my thumbs I began to push the sides of the paper flower towards the centre, and as I did so I felt a numbness settle over the back of my skull. I pushed a little further, the paper glowed whiter for an instant and then it *seemed* to disappear. I say 'seemed' because at first I could not be sure whether I could feel it still in my hands and not see it, or see it but not feel it, or whether I could sense it had disappeared while its external properties remained. The numbness had spread right across my head and shoulders. My senses seemed inadequate to grasp what was happening. 'Dimensionality is a function of consciousness,' I thought. I brought my hands together and there was nothing between them, but even when I opened them again and saw nothing I could not be sure the paper flower had completely gone. An impression remained, an after-image not on the retina but on the mind itself. Just then the door opened behind me, and Maisie said,

'What are you doing?'

I returned as if from a dream to the room and to the faint smell of formaldehyde. It was a long, long time ago now, the destruction of Capt. Nicholls, but the smell revived my resentment, which spread through me like the numbness. Maisie slouched in the doorway, muffled in a thick coat and woollen scarf. She seemed a long way off, and as I looked at her my resentment merged into a familiar weariness of our marriage. I thought, why did she break the glass? Because she wanted to make love? Because she wanted a penis? Because she was jealous of my work, and wanted to smash the connection it had with my great-grandfather's life?

'Why did you do it?' I said out loud, involuntarily. Maisie snorted. She had opened the door and found me hunched over my table staring at my hands.

'Have you been sitting there all afternoon,' she asked, 'thinking about *that*?' She giggled. 'What happened to it, anyway? Did you suck it off?'

'I buried it,' I said, 'under the geraniums.'

She came into the room a little way and said in a serious tone, 'I'm sorry about that, I really am. I just did it before I knew what was happening. Do you forgive me?' I hesitated, and then, because my weariness had blossomed into a sudden resolution, I said,

'Yes, of course I forgive you. It was only a prick in pickle,' and we both laughed. Maisie came over to me and kissed me, and I returned the kiss, prising open her lips with my tongue.

'Are you hungry?' she said, when we were done with kissing. 'Shall I make some supper?'

'Yes,' I said. 'I would love that.' Maisie kissed me on the top of my head and left the room, while I turned back to my studies, resolving to be as kind as I possibly could to Maisie that evening.

Later we sat in the kitchen eating the meal Maisie had cooked and getting mildly drunk on a bottle of wine. We smoked a joint, the first one we had had together in a very long time. Maisie told me how she was going to get a job with the Forestry Commission planting trees in Scotland next summer. And I told Maisie about the conversation M and my great-grandfather had had about *a posteriori*, and about my great-grandfather's theory that there could not be more than the prime number seventeen positions for making love. We both laughed, and Maisie squeezed my hand, and lovemaking hung in the air between us, in the warm fug of the kitchen. Then we put our coats on and went for a walk. It was almost a full moon. We walked along the main road which runs outside our house and then turned down a narrow street of tightly packed houses with immaculate and minute front gardens. We did not talk much, but our arms were linked and Maisie told me how very stoned and happy she was. We came to a small park which was locked and we stood outside the gates looking up at the moon through the almost leafless branches. When we came home Maisie took a leisurely hot bath while I browsed in my study, checking on a few details. Our bathroom is a warm, comfortable room, luxurious in its way. The bed is seven foot by eight, and I made it myself in the first year of our marriage. Maisie made the sheets, dyed them a deep, rich blue and embroidered the pillow cases. The only light in the room shone through a rough old goat-skin lampshade Maisie bought from a man who came to the door. It was a long time since I had taken an interest in the bedroom. We lay side by side in the tangle of sheets and rugs, Maisie voluptuous and drowsy after her bath and stretched full out, and I propped up on my elbow. Maisie said sleepily,

'I was walking along the river this afternoon. The trees are beautiful now, the oaks, the elms . . . there are two copper beeches about a mile past the footbridge, you should see them now . . . ahh, that feels good.' I had eased her on to her belly and was caressing her back as she spoke. 'There are blackberries, the biggest ones I've ever seen, growing all along the path, and elderberries, too. I'm going to make some wine this autumn . . .' I leaned over her and kissed the nape of her neck and brought her arms behind her back. She liked to be manipulated in this way and she submitted warmly. 'And the river is really still,' she was saying. 'You know, reflecting the trees, and the leaves are dropping into the river. Before the winter comes we should go there together, by the river, in the leaves. I found this little place. No one goes there . . .' Holding Maisie's arms in position with one hand, I worked her legs towards the 'hoop' with the other. '. . . I sat in this place for half an hour without moving, like a tree. I saw a water-rat running along the opposite bank, and different kinds of ducks landing on the river and taking off. I heard these plopping noises in the river but I didn't know what they were and I saw two orange butterflies, they almost came on my hand.' When I had her legs in place Maisie said, 'Position number eighteen,' and we both laughed softly. 'Let's go there tomorrow, to the river,' said Maisie as I carefully eased her head towards her arms. 'Careful, careful, that hurts,' she suddenly shouted, and tried to struggle. But it was too late now, her head and legs were in place in the hoop of her arms, and I was beginning to push them through, past each other. 'What's happening?' cried Maisie. Now the positioning of her limbs expressed the breathtaking beauty, the nobility of the human form, and, as in the paper flower, there was a fascinating power in its symmetry. I felt the trance coming on again and the numbness settling over the back of my head. As I drew her arms and legs through, Maisie appeared to turn in on herself like a sock. 'Oh God,' she sighed, 'what's happening?' and her voice sounded very far away. Then she was gone . . . and not gone. Her voice was quite tiny. 'What's happening?' and all that remained was the echo of her question above the deep-blue sheets.

PHILIP HENSHER

Dead Languages

I DID not know when I was a boy that most people in the world went away to school. I only knew that no one from my family had ever left the stilted house in the forest river, to travel fifteen miles in two days to arrive, with the mud dry on my bare feet, at the big white school where they laughed at the way my family had always spoken.

They kitted me out with clothes which scratched and made you sweat; clothes which either gripped you like ropes and made you want to pluck and itch, or hung loosely over your hands and feet and got in the way of running. And a pair of brown shoes which, eight months later, my father would take from around my neck, where they had been hanging during the journey back home, and sit with them for an entire week, looking at them and thinking his thoughts no one ever asked about.

The mister of the school was a Christian and had a wife. They lived in the school, in a separate wing, which the boys called the House. It was the way of the school, and the mister, for one of the younger boys, or one of those less accustomed to shoes and stuffed square beds, to be taken into the House to learn its clean domestic ways, the ways of what I learnt to call civilization. I was the youngest boy, at least at first, and unused to the life of the school, and of schools like it. So, like boys before me, I was taken into the House to work.

When I first went to see the mister to be told of this, I shook in my shoes. I stood at the end of the long dark wood room and waited to be shouted at. But the mister did not shout; he said good morning and, with his way of pausing before speaking, asked me to come closer. He asked about the place I came from, and he asked how old I was, and my family, how was it. And then he stopped asking, and in the room there was silence for so long that I raised my head, and I looked at what he looked like. He was just looking at me, in silence, without talking. And his big black eyes were sad in the way the eyes of animals are sad. Or look sad, when you know that in fact they are really nothing of the kind.

There were few duties for me, and they did not interfere with what I had to learn. I learnt that I lived on an island, too big to walk around. I learnt not only what I knew, that you could add things and take things away, but that things could be multiplied and, more often, because it was harder, divided. I learnt that there were languages which were dead, and civilizations which were gone, and I chanted the words which humans once spoke freely and in feeling, to say *I love* and *you love*, and I felt nothing except what I happened to be feeling at the time. And I learnt other things, in the mister's House.

Every day, at four, I would walk around the trim square of grass to the House. For two hours, I was supposed to do the housework. At first I dreaded going round there, because the boys of my age told me stories about the mister and the mister's wife. They said they would fight in front of you. They said he would punish you. They said the mister was afraid of his wife, and he took it out on you. I was afraid that these things would come to pass, and then quickly I saw that they would not. It did not occur to me to tell the boys who said these things about my meeting with the mister; it seemed to me then that nothing happened, when he said nothing and gazed at me.

I was intended to dust, to tidy, and to iron clothes; to make certain preparations for food. But in fact, I did not do these things. After some time, each afternoon, perhaps no more than half an hour, the mister's wife would call to me. 'Come and sit,' she said. And I went and sat, and drank *totosa* with her in the heat of the late afternoon, and we talked. I liked to listen to her.

The mister was immensely tall and his limbs were immensely long. They were insect-like, or lizardy, his limbs, in the way they gave the sense that through sheer length they would easily break, or easily turn themselves backwards. When I think of him, I think first of his loping vaguely across the thin lawn of the school; but then I think of his wife. Because the mister's wife was round and sweet and idle like a sweet yellow bun, and reminded you of the mister because she was so unlike him.

'Come here, Bobo,' she would say. A silly name she had for me. Her voice comes to me, it still comes to me; her husk and hint of a rattle which made your own throat ache with the urge to cough, and clear it. And her conversation, the silliness we let ourselves jabber about. She would ask me things which I was certain, once I knew enough, I would be able to answer. 'Why is the sea sometimes blue, and sometimes not at all?' Or she would ask me about my family, and I would tell her about my tiny mother, no taller than I, and my little brothers, and my new sister or brother who now must be born, whom I knew nothing about, and the long stilted house no more than fifteen miles, and no less than half a world away, which my father and his father together built. I did not talk too much about my family; I had a constant fear that one of them might have died, and I would know nothing about it. It would be bad to sit and talk fondly about my father and laugh about what now seemed to me the funny way he had of putting a little yaw in the middle of words. A bad thing, if he was dead and I did not know it.

We talked once about death, the mister's wife and me, and it was like another fancy of hers. 'If there was a day,' she said once, 'when nobody in the world died, nobody anywhere died, who would notice?' I sat and thought about that world without death, for one day; how it would be happy and untouched by suffering, and yet no one would know until long afterwards, when suffering and death and pain had returned. Enchanting, these conversations, and a secret they were, from the mister.

I came to understand that he slept upstairs after he had finished teaching, while his wife talked to me in the dark cool rooms with their resiny smell of teak. The creak and lollop of his coming downstairs was, for me, a sign to rise and be busy with the furniture and a rag; and, for her, a sign to sigh and stretch and smile for her husband.

'Who built the school?' I said once.

'Long long ago,' she said. 'It belongs to me now.'

I digested this.

'It was the mister's,' she said. 'But he thought he would lose it, so he gave it to me.'

'How could he lose it?' I said.

'It could be taken away from him,' she said. 'He was afraid it would be, so he gave it to me.'

I thought about it. It made no sense, to give something away because somebody would otherwise take it from you.

'And now he'd like to be off, to be rid of his old baggage, but he can't,' she said. 'He's stuck with me, and I'm stuck with him, because the school is mine.'

I thought.

'If you gave it back to him,' I began.

'They would take it away from him,' she said.

It made no sense. In the dark corner of the sitting-room, I heard the quick creak of the ceiling which meant he was getting up, and I reached for the duster.

The boys in the long room where I slept laughed at me at first, and soon I learnt to speak as they spoke, and to wear my shoes always, and not to scratch myself, under their laughter. And soon I joined in with their fanciful night talk about the mister and his wife. The tales of shouting, tales of hurled insults, the names of vegetables and beasts they yelled at each other, the throwing of objects in their epic rows; I listened, and soon I too found I could tell of arguments I had not heard. I joined in when the boys said that they knew of a machine for punishment the mister kept in his upper rooms, and they knew of a boy who, five years before, had died of fright when he had merely seen the terrible machine. I thought that there was probably no such machine, but in my duties I did not go upstairs. I did not know what punishment and secrets and humiliations lay in the bedroom of the mister, and the bedroom of the mister's wife, and I kept quiet.

'Does the mister ever speak to you?' she said to me once, one afternoon, as we sat with our cooling *totosa*.

Her conversation was like that, simple questions you could not understand.

'Yes he does,' I said.

'Does he speak to you when you're on your own?' she said.

'I don't know,' I said, after a while.

'If he asks you to come to the House when I'm not here,' she said.

There seemed to be nothing more. She was looking at something, with sudden fierceness. She was looking at a big fly, making a noise like thick paper tearing at the far wall. I sat and waited for the next thing she would say. But she said nothing more. And in six months, I was no longer the youngest boy when I came back from my six weeks with my family in the quiet stilted house in the mud by the river. Before long, the fat progress of the creamy yellow flesh of the mister's wife through the shady cloisters was as comic to me as to every other boy. For years behind and years to come.

That was the way to talk about her, in a funny story. Because I told the stories to the dormitory, the stories of how she talked to me. But it was no story, and the boys in the long room after dark laughed at me for thinking it was something to be told. And yet it was.

Years passed; they always do. And the time came to go; and I was exactly the same. Except that I knew more, and I talked differently, louder, I suppose. And I knew my father, when I jumped out of the boat back from school, would, as he had every year, seem smaller. I knew his way of talking would have suddenly developed a funny, unexpected yaw I would want to correct. The dead languages we learnt at school, we guessed at their pronunciation, I knew, and guessed wrongly; and I knew that if a speaker of those dead languages was to leap out of a boat and talk to us, his way of saying even *I love* and *you love* would seem strange to us. But it would be a way of speaking we had once known, and had forgotten; a way newly unfamiliar to us, because we have so changed.

The time came to go, and not to return, and I did not know whether I was supposed to go. The mister asked me to go to his room, once more, and I went. He was sitting behind his desk, as he had before. This time I looked at him, but his eyes were dark and sad as they always had been; and we looked at each other.

'Here,' he said eventually to me. 'You've been good. We ought to be proud of you.'

'Thank you, sir,' I said.

'I'd like to give you a leaving present,' he said. 'Something you will always keep.'

'No need, sir,' I said.

'No need to call me sir now,' he said.

'I would like to say goodbye to your wife,' I said after a time.

'My wife is out for the afternoon,' he said. I did not understand the mister and his wife. I did not know what contracts passed between them in the dark. And, in fact, I still do not. He reached for his wrist, and unhitched his watch. He glanced at it, as if checking it still told him what Now it was, and offered it to me, across the broad expanse of his desk. I shook my hands at him. His smile insisted, and I carried on shaking my hands at him. And I did not know whether my refusals were the sort of polite refusals which always intend to finish in acceptance, or if I did not want the watch. I did not know, and on either side of the desk, I shook my hands at him, and he smiled at me, and proffered.

The mister's tiny wrist-machine was what I once called *tiktik*. Knowing no better. And with every *tik* another second gone, and another moment, and a chance lost, and, perhaps, no new chances to take their place. Once I wanted to learn and learn, until I knew enough. But now I know that I will never know enough; that the exams in that unmastered subject, Enough, have never yet been set; that they have never been passed, and never will be.